Carla,

Thank you so much for all you have done for this luncheon. May the Lord you've always be shadowed by the hand of God.

The Author pulled me into this story and made me feel like I was a part of this adventure from the very beginning. They were my family, my friends, and my neighbors. It truly touched my heart in many ways.

Pam Branson
Medical Management
Largo, Florida

Libby Nance's debut novel is a wonderful adventure made up of rich, meaningful characters wrapped in an epic story of love, loss, pain, and ultimately, spiritual awakening. She can be compared to the likes of Jane Hamilton's riveting prose as well as Ann Beatie's spot on dialogue and human portrayal. Libby is truly an American Spiritual treasure.

Martín McClellan
Vice President of Publishing
Newport Communications
Irvine, CA.

Love, joy, tears, even goose bumps with anticipation of what's to come are just a few of the emotions I experienced while reading this novel. I was drawn into the lives of the characters as they opened my eyes and touched my heart.

Gina Garrett
Educational Nurse
South Carolina

An inspiring book! In a world where there is so much hatred the main character, Lacey, brings a refreshing attitude to all those around her. Because the word of God has been instilled in Lacey's upbringing, Her Faith in Him guides her as she searches for answers along *The Road* of life.

Lora Sindell Horton
Christian/Freelance Writer Photographer
Tampa Bay Newspapers - Clearwater, Florida

the road

the road

libby t. nance

Tate Publishing & *Enterprises*

TATE PUBLISHING
& *Enterprises*

Tate Publishing is committed to excellence in the publishing industry. Our staff of highly trained professionals, including editors, graphic designers, and marketing personnel, work together to produce the very finest books available. The company reflects the philosophy established by the founders, based on Psalms 68:11,

> "THE LORD GAVE THE WORD AND GREAT WAS THE COMPANY OF
> THOSE WHO PUBLISHED IT."

If you would like further information, please contact us:
1.888.361.9473 | www.tatepublishing.com
TATE PUBLISHING & *Enterprises*, LLC | 127 E. Trade Center Terrace
Mustang, Oklahoma 73064 USA

The Road
Copyright © 2007 by Libby T. Nance. All rights reserved.

No part of this publication may be reproduced, stored in a retrieval system or transmitted in any way by any means, electronic, mechanical, photocopy, recording or otherwise without the prior permission of the author except as provided by USA copyright law.

Scripture quotations are taken from the *Holy Bible, King James Version*, Cambridge, 1769. Used by permission. All rights reserved.

This novel is a work of fiction. Names, descriptions, entities and incidents included in the story are products of the author's imagination. Any resemblance to actual persons, events and entities is entirely coincidental.

Book design copyright © 2007 by Tate Publishing, LLC. All rights reserved.
Cover design by Melanie Harr-Hughes
Interior design by Leah LeFlore

Published in the United States of America

ISBN: 978-1-5988678-8-6
07.07.12

acknowledgments

I could never finish writing down all the names of people who crossed my path through the years and shared their stories with me. Without them I would not have been able to give life to the characters in this book. Pieces of their lives are woven throughout *The Road*.

My first devotion is to God for believing in me to tell His story. I pray that His will is accomplished through this work.

There are no words to express my love and devotion to my husband, Steve. I thank you from the depth of my soul. You are why I care. If you hadn't been so willing to take my chores around the farm, after working all day, this would never have seen a press. Each day with you is a great adventure. Thanks for choosing me to make the journey with you. I love you always.

Most people don't get the chance to have one true friend in a lifetime, but God has seen to send me two. Special gratification goes to Gina Ross Garrett for being my reader and editor-in-progress and spurring me on to believe that this story could touch someone else and bring them to a hunger for God's love. Thank you, Gina, for sharing yourself and your family with us. I couldn't love you more if you were our own daughter.

To my other best friend, Pam Pirone Branson, who shared those most precious years growing up through the tough years of peer pressure and comparisons. You loved me through the awkward years and still wanted to be my friend. That love reminds me that we can overcome anything and be better for it. I wouldn't have recognized unconditional love without knowing yours in those early years.

Thank you, Marty McClellan and Lori Sindell, for taking time away from family and your busy work load to spend time reading my book. What and honor to have your encouragement and willingness. Publishing is foreign to me, but knowing that you both have been successful in the publishing world has given me hope! How God has knitted us together through the years is very special to me.

To the two people, Lib and Buck Thomas, who made this life possible. I have loved and respected you from my birth, but did not know to cherish your character or spirits till I was much older. The dedication to your marriage and giving hearts to others has directed me to understanding what growing older through adversities with grace truly means. I love you Mom and Dad. Even if it's true that you found me in a ditch on the side of the road, thanks for keeping me.

That brings me to my sister, Denise Pettibone, who told me I owed her my life because she could have told Mom and Dad to leave me in the ditch! What a life we've had. It would have been lonely in the ditch! Thanks for encouraging me to come into the twenty-first century and invest in a laptop, but mostly thanks for holding off the troops so I could focus. You're a true friend and I love you very much.

A huge thank you to Anna Bush Waters for her dedication and determination to do a complete editing job for me. She's the best at all she does and having her on this team helped me finally get some rest! I love you, cuz!

My greatest thanks goes to Dr. John C. Bird, my English professor at Converse College. I had been in many English classes before his and failed because I couldn't spell or place the commas in the right place. No one else took the time to read the content and look for substance. I was judged on structure and suffered frustration. Dr. Bird, you gave my desire new life and helped me grow in so many ways. There are no words to thank you enough. You have given me the tools to open doors I never thought were possible for me. I feel as though I have no gift to give you in return so my prayer is, if it's at all possible, may God bless you even more than you have blessed me.

Few people are blessed to have their grandparents live way into their eighty and nineties and I was blessed to have all four of them live long enough to share their stories with me. So many stories I wish I had written down, but the ones that changed my life I remember well. Though they are not the grandparents in this book, they are an influence on understanding the relationship between the main character and her grandparents. Their stories of a time where hardships bonded families, and a thankfulness to have what little they did, is what made me want to write this book. Being a family was the most valued possession of my grandparents and they lived simply even though they had obtained great wealth. I write this book in memory of Nettie Williams and Lawton "Tommy" Thomas and Charlotte Bush and Bernard Hall Sr., four loving and gracious grandparents who inspired me to make the best out of every opportunity. Thank you Grandmother, Granddaddy, Mother Charlotte and Dad Nard for being great people. I'm having a hard time waiting to meet again at the feast prepared for us all. No doubt Jesus will pick Grandmother to make the biscuits.

To my great aunt Edna Bush Clarke, in the beginning she was the one who took the role of editor and chief when I first started writing this book. She helped me to understand the lifestyles of those living at the turn of the century and made sure I had described things as they were. As I reached the end of the tenth chapter she past this life and began her journey in eternity. She was a teacher all of her life and right up to a few weeks before her death she was teaching me. I put the book down for several years feeling lost without her. When Mother Charlotte, Edna's sister died, at a wonderful age of ninety-nine, she had been the last one living in a generation of ten siblings. I heard the Lord say that it was time to complete the book in memory of them all. I pray that with the book complete God has approved and told them it is finished. I love and miss you all daily.

Thanks to all those at Tate Publishing who held my book in their hands, or computer, at some point during the process. Your patience with me has been appreciated. Offering me this opportunity has blessed me in more ways than words can express.

chapter one

A bright blue sky was my surrounding as I listened to the radio announcement of the pending hurricane and the evacuation plan for those on the coast of Florida. A tragedy for those already affected by this storm, but their demise was not on my mind at that time. For I was sure I had lived through much worst than a hurricane that came in with a warning, stayed around a day or so, left a mess to clean up, and then, hopefully with all your family safe and sound, was gone. It's the tragedies that last a lifetime that challenge the soul, so the main thing was having the family safe and sound. At that time in my life I would have never entertained the thought of losing even one member of my family. I lived life believing that tomorrow would be just a wee bit more wonderful than the day before and family was what made it so.

The housework that day was routine except for that perfect peace that passes all understanding that entered me and rested there. On that morning I was fully aware of Him, yet there were numerous times in my younger life when His presence settled in, but I was insensitive to His warnings and wisdom. But, life is built on misunderstandings; nothing is gained living in ignorance. I have misunderstood Him many times, but He has never allowed me to ignore Him for long.

As I am brought back to what is real, what is now, I realize I have started telling my story in the early years of my life as my wandering thoughts always take me back to those days. I'm sure it's mentally self-preserving to wander back, grasping for an era when everything around was soothing and complete, whenever a mind lives in overwhelming unpredictability. But, I woke up this morning with that same perfect peace that I felt come over me so many years ago. On that day, because of His presence, I was not horrified for the people in the path of a storm who were in the hearts and minds of our nation. However, I have been reminded today of the lessons learned about the importance of love and prayer for strangers and I wondered if there was a stranger out there praying for me. Nevertheless, God is on my side. What more could I want? Even though today all is not right with my world, I am at peace.

I don't know where to begin and I would not be able to look back if I had not truly forgiven and understood the battle of life and love. Yet, it seems so useless to have that knowledge now that I'm nearing the end. And it must be the end, though God has never let me control anything such as someone's life before and I doubt He will allow me to do it at this time. But, He has to know my pain. He has to know the only thing that will keep me from losing my mind is if He takes me in His arms now that there are no other arms left. This kind of loneliness was not meant for mankind. And in my own strength I cannot live another day with hunger, fear and silence. Perhaps that is why He has been so gracious to visit me today.

Silence is a noise so deafening that after a while you are sure you will go mad. Most assuredly, if the silence is not of your own choosing. He was never silent; never without something to say, even when we didn't understand him. He was completely absorbed in his thoughts and willing to share every part of the workings of his thoughts with anyone. No one could have ever been him, though some did try. He was my world, my life; all my waking thoughts included him. I never asked for him or prayed to find someone like him. He was a gift I never deserved. Like a stray dog he just walked into my life and fit right in as if he had always been there.

And when he vanished, well, again I'm getting ahead of myself. I never thought that I, personally, would ever have anything of value to say, but just as this peace that floated in this morning, totally without warning, I've found that I do after all have something of great value to share. The odd thing about it is God has brought me to a place where there are no ears to hear it, but I praise Him that in the few belongings that I have there is a journal in which to write them in. I guess I'm searching for a place to begin. So I shall go to the beginning. The real beginning. To my first memory.

It was shortly before my second birthday. I recall standing in my crib crying out to my mother, because of the hunger cramps in my stomach, when I heard a familiar sound, though it didn't mean much to me until that day. The man I called "Pa" was coming in the front door in the usual stumble and then crash of the door as he flung it against the wall as an announcement of his return. However, this day was different. Mother was not happy to hear his arrival, and my hunger cries turned to tears of fear. Pa never seemed to care why I was crying; he just wanted me to stop and I knew this day would be no different. Most of the time Mother would hold me and soothe me, but not this night. This night she left me alone in my crib. Alone in the room I shared with my parents, in the dark, alone. I was afraid and I needed my mother and from the sounds on the other side of that door, she needed me, too.

There were loud voices and bumps and a crash or two that seemed to go on into the night, but I'm sure, was only for a short time. When my mother reappeared in the doorway holding a large paper sack with corded handles, she started filling the bag with things from her dresser top and chest of drawers. She wrapped me in my blanket, picked up the warn teddy bear from my crib and lifted me into her arms as she whispered in my ear, "We will *never* go hungry again. I will take care of you. I will take care of *both* of us." There was such comfort being wrapped in a blanket then wrapped in my mother's arms as if nothing could break the barrier.

The day of my second birthday, May 12, 1937, I was absorbed in my surroundings. I knew this was a special day and that this day was all about me. I was sitting at the end of a long table in the back yard of my grandparent's home with a cake in front of me, two candles burning. I heard voices shouting and screaming mixed with laughter while those closest to me clapped their hands with excitement. Children, lots of children, were running around in circles in the yard, with pointed hats on, falling down and getting up again and falling down. One boy ran into a tray table and the dishes crashed to the ground and the sound of it all was too familiar, and way too close. Suddenly, it wasn't such a nice day and fear gripped me and I began to cry for Mother to wrap me in her arms.

Everyone got quiet. Nanny and Pappy came running to me. I was pulling the bib from around my neck, as it seemed to be choking me while Mother tried to remove the tray from the high chair. Once in my mother's arms with hugs from Nanny and kisses from Pappy, I sensed that as of this day my needs would be met and I would not be left alone to face my fears. Somehow I knew my whole world had changed that night I feared so much, and the reason to be afraid was gone.

Everything was different. Even Pa, he was different. He looked different, smelled different, he dressed different and he looked at Mother, well, I don't know how to describe it. He never exhaled around her. When Mother caught his eyes looking at her she would smile a shy awkward grin and then straightened her chin with determination. At times she seemed to ignore him and focus on my needs and her busy work. He just held his hat in his hands and watched her every move.

We lived with my grandparents, my mother's parents. Pa didn't stay with us. He visited from time to time and seemed to enjoy sharing supper with us. He and Pappy were great friends. They laughed a lot when they were alone together after supper sitting by the fire while Mother and Nanny cleaned up the dishes. I would crawl up in Pappy's lap as he sat in his wooden, ladder-back rocking chair. I sucked my thumb, because Pappy would let me. The rocking chair cushions were tied with ribbon around the chair spindles and I would wrap the ties around and around my fingers remembering the day Nanny and Mother made the cushions to match the draperies in the living and dining rooms. Sucking my thumb, wrapping the ribbon around and around my finger with the rhythm of the rocking chair, all wrapped up in my grandfather's arms was just the thing to soothe a young child to sleep. And there was no greater place to be. When I was forced to go to my own bed in my own room to sleep, I would wind my hair around my fingers pushing with my feet on the footboard rocking the crib simulating Pappy's chair. I would beg Mother to wrap my blanket around me tight and pretend it was my Pappy's arms.

Life was glorious. I had no need to cry over hunger or fear. All was wonderful and I had total peace. It was just me in a world made for all my needs with people who loved me and seemingly lived to comfort me. But something wasn't right. And as early as Kindergarten I felt a gnawing, but I had no idea what it was.

My Pa moved Mother and I out of my grandparents' house and to the other side of town. It wasn't far away, though as a young girl my legs thought it was, but Mother and I walked to Nanny and Pappy's everyday after school was out. She wanted to loose the weight she had gained before the birth of my brother and I loved stopping by the bank to see Pappy as we would walk through town. Every visit was the same. Pappy would lift me into his arms and squeeze me tight. Then he would stand me on the floor and with proper etiquette he would introduce himself to me and I would introduce myself to him. We would shake hands and he would leave a bright shiny new penny in my hand. I would squeal with delight as if it was the first time I had laid eyes on such a treasure. He would pick me up, turn me around through the air, and take me to the closest bank teller so I could get a cherry red sucker after depositing my penny. He always bragged about his "beautiful little Punkin" and pointed to the stroller where my new brother was sleeping and we would snicker at his nickname "Trouble." Mother didn't think it was funny to call a baby "Trouble," but I thought it was funny and it was Pappy's way of letting me know that William Robert Rutledge Jr. was not going to get any of my Pappy's love and attention. Pappy was mine, all mine, except for Nanny. And I didn't mind sharing with her. After all, she had him first.

My baby brother arrived the same day I started five-year-old pre-school. There was really nothing good about that day except that I got to stay at Pappy's house while mother had time to recover and spend some time alone with Willie. I didn't dislike Willie; I just didn't know what I would do with him or where he would fit in. One thing I did know, my mother would take care of it. She could organize anything, even a crying baby. After all, she had completely organized my first day of school around the birth of Willie.

Before Mother walked me to One Faith Baptist Church where

Mrs. Winters taught a half-day preschool for four and five year olds, she packed my favorite lunch. Two chocolate chip cookies sandwiched with peanut butter between them and a peanut butter and honey biscuit. She placed the biscuit, cookies, and a glass bottle of milk into the empty Pennant Crystal White Syrup can. I was looking forward to lunch, even though I felt like the Loan Ranger venturing out into the wild frontier. I liked being the only child, but as with the Ranger, I was soon to have my own Tonto. I often wondered if the Ranger could have handled it all alone? Was Tonto only created to teach us that in this world we would need others and sometimes they would be different from us? Well, on this day I could have used a sidekick, too, but mine wasn't born till shortly after Mother returned to our house. After what I had anticipated to be the worst day of my life had already begun.

Mother often praised God for her new friend and neighbor, Sally, who was a nurse at the local hospital until her twins were born. That made three children so she gave up nursing, at a time when our country needed nurses, to be a full time mother. Our neighborhood was full of young couples starting out in family making, but you have to understand that neighborhoods in the thirties were not what neighborhoods are today. Our homes were separated by, sometimes, miles of pasture and farm land, but Sally's house was right across the road. I guess that a neighborhood back then was more like a county. However far she had to travel, Sally stayed busy using her skills as neighborhood midwife. Mother was thankful that Sally lived across the road and thankful that they had become such great friends.

She was older than Mother and had learned to handle three children and a household alone. She taught Mother how to manage ours. Nanny had things easier with maids and cooks when she was raising Mother. Learning how to actually do the work instead of governing others was not taught to the Hawthorne children. Because Sally knew the importance of keeping things simple in a home, with three children of her own and being a sibling of seven, she suggested naming Willie after Pa. "If you chose to have lots of kids, naming them after members of the family makes it easier to remember. Just run through every bodies name and sooner or later you're bound to hit the right one."

As for me, I had never been aware of my name until our teacher Mrs. Winters welcomed each one of us that first day of preschool by writing our names on a chalkboard. As far as I knew my name didn't come from anyone in our family. She spoke our names, and then she wrote them and slowly went over each letter.

ELIZABETH KALE RUTLEDGE

Mrs. Winters introduced me to the class as Elizabeth. I had never heard anyone call me Elizabeth before, so I raised my hand and told her my name. She erased Elizabeth and re-introduced me as Lacey. Lacey Kale. I only heard that name when I was in trouble. Most of the family called me "Punkin." It may have been because of my orange hair, though no one ever said so. Suddenly, having a name like other people made me feel grown-up, but a little unsure about what growing-up was all about.

Mrs. Winters told us that it was a privilege to get to come to this school. She was retired from teaching, lost her husband a year earlier and volunteered to start a school for four and five year olds to help the mothers in our town with childcare while they worked in the fields or other jobs to help with the family income. To her it was a blessing that the church was willing to open their doors and let her offer a pre-school to the community. I was never convinced it was a blessing; however, I adjusted easily to school.

"A born leader" was what Mrs. Settles, my first grade teacher, called me. She said I obviously took after my grandfather. "No one runs a more efficient bank than Alvin Jeremiah Hawthorne. He has been credited to building this town and keeping it alive when life was hard on all of us. As the depression hit, most of us would have lost everything without his wisdom and leadership in preparing us for the crash. Without him we wouldn't have this very school. You, Lacey Rutledge, should be very proud of your grandfather."

"Yes Ma'am. He is my best friend."

I sat at my new desk in my new space in my classroom as proud as anyone could be at six years old. Proud that I had been able to recognize a great man and name him my best friend. I had not thought of that before then, but that was exactly what he was to me. Therefore,

I would use my influence to talk to him about his part in this school thing. What on earth was he thinking?

There is a vicious cycle that begins in a person's life when they enter in the world of education. I had fallen for it completely without recognizing the trap. However large our family was in aunts, uncles, cousins, and friends, as far as I knew everyone loved each other completely. An occasional marital dispute over punishment of their children, but for the most part even those went without too much conflict. Mother backed down and father took control.

Not in my family though. My father was loving and patient with all that I got into and Mother disciplined me when Pappy wasn't around to coddle me. Pappy was my hero in every way, but I wasn't sure about Pa. He wasn't the man I remembered. He was never loud or pushy. He never screamed in a rage when I cried or cause my mother to cry. He seemed to just sit and wait for Mother to need him and be delighted when she did. He hung on every word she spoke with a look of devotion forever on his face. Mother was totally devoted to his happiness as well. I was proud of my family, but didn't know this man and couldn't seem to get close to him. This new father was gentle, but I think I feared the old father's return.

So maybe I had fallen into the trap before I entered school, but this process of comparison in my home life was something very subtle. However, I began to notice how beautiful some of the children were and how each of us differed. Our teacher would praise us for doing well and scold us for our shortcomings. Mine was my lack of interest in math, though it wasn't called math, adding or subtracting. It was referred to as "problem solving."

Well, I had no problems to solve so to me we were wasting time. The only problem that seemed to be creeping my way was my second grade teacher, Mrs. Byam, and her desire to point out my shortcomings in front of my classmates. Over time I heard them repeat what Mrs. Byam had said about my head being in the clouds, and a need to face reality that this world was changing and changing fast and I would be left behind. I might be able to float around on my grandfather's coattail for a while, but one day I would need to be able to make it on my own. Some of the children whispered in small groups that I didn't think I needed school because I was rich like my grandfather. I didn't know what rich was, but I was determined to find out. I decided to ask my Pappy. After all he was the same thing.

When I asked Pappy, he calmly answered in the simplest way. "We all are rich if we know Jesus. Don't worry your sweet head about anything someone says about you. All that matters is what God thinks, and I know first hand that He thinks you're perfect."

If I took time to think about Pappy's answer I would have realized that I now didn't know two things. What it meant to be rich in the eyes of my classmates and what it is to be rich because you know Jesus. I couldn't worry myself about it 'cause Pappy said not to. And besides all that, God said I was perfect and Pappy had talked to Him personally.

Occasionally Pappy would let me sit in his lap while he talked to God. I never heard God speak back, but Pappy always had an answer and he always knew just what to do when their conversation was over. Pappy told me all about how God created the world and all that is in it. Even me.

Something happened to me when my teacher and classmates began to recognize and compare our differences. I decided to do the problem solving as the teacher taught us and go with the flow on things that seemed to matter to our leader. It might not take much to please God, but Mrs. Byam and some of the children were another matter. As for the others who didn't measure up I made it my personal quest to befriend them in anyway. I encouraged those who were slower at catching on than the really smart kids and I praised those who got everything right. The children who wore torn dresses or trousers too short I found something else to focus on them about; their pretty curls, facial features, or strong arms and fast legs. There was something nice to say about everyone if you really looked. My mother was always quoting to me in regards to Willie, "If you can't say something nice, don't say anything at all." It was obvious that most of the children in my class had never heard *that* saying before, however, they had heard others and used them often.

Willie. I had learned to love him with a special love I had for no one else. It took me by surprise one day while I was watching him for Mother. I wanted to go to the creek and look for crawdads, but Mother wanted to mop the kitchen and Willie was in the way. We sat in the sand box, Willie propped up in his stroller seat and I built roads for my Buddy L trucks to be able to maneuver through the sand built town. Before I knew it, I was telling Willie who lived where and all about using the dump truck. He started blowing bubbles with his lips pressed hard together and he found that trick so exciting that he clapped his hands in delight.

This was the first time that calm peaceful stillness came over me and I stopped my playing, dropped the shovel and sat in awe of this little person God had placed in my life. I felt responsible for him. Kind of all grown up. I sat with my legs on either side of the wheels, wrapped my arms around the stroller looking directly into his eyes, and we laughed blowing bubbles into each other's faces as he slapped the wooden beads strung on the wire placed across the stroller bracing. That was the first time I had ever looked at Willie. He took my breath, so I kissed him right on those wet lips.

"That's it, Willie. You're my brother in every way so I promise to take care of you whenever Mother needs me to. And when you get older you can promise me that you'll always be good for me. Crying babies are no fun, and you and me's gonna have fun."

Willie started spitting and laughing again so I buried my head in his stomach. As he pulled my hair, trying to eat it, I vowed to always love him even if he hurt me, 'cause he would never mean it if he did.

When there was free time in school, I would spend it looking people over trying to find their most wonderful quality. I saw early in life what I found attractive in boys. They should all be as slow to anger as Pappy and quiet as Pa. None of the boys in my classes were able to represent those qualities for long. Cute and cuddly like Willie they had out-grown. Eager to listen like Willie and Pa would be a great asset, but most of them wouldn't even let a girl near them, much less, let them share a conversation.

There was one. As I've learned, down every road of life, there is one. Sometimes there are more, but always one. I was in the third grade and his name was Tylar Lane. No other word could describe him, just Tylar Lane. When ever I heard his name spoken feelings and emotions would swell in my lungs. It was as if his name alone represented completeness. All any one would ever need or want.

He caught my eye one day in the lunchroom when the whole

room burst into applause because someone's tray hit the floor. I never understood if we were applauding their ability to be a klutz or if it was pure encouragement that we understood their embarrassment and wanted to ease their pain.

Tylar was in the line behind Rachel when she dropped her tray. I wasn't sure if he almost fell over her and that is why he was down on the floor helping her pick up the mess, or if he genuinely felt for her and wanted to be her knight in shining armor. Either way, he caught my attention. No one would have ever known if he had simply walked away. Would I have recognized his qualities and wanted to be his friend if he had never done anything so wonderful? I don't know, but I know God would have made another way, because his life was meant to touch mine.

I helped Tylar and Rachel pick up the big stuff just as the lady with the hairnet arrived with a mop. I spotted the milk bottle near a row of folded chairs. It seemed Tylar and I had seen it at the same time, because his hand was on the bottle just seconds before mine. He had recovered it, turned to me holding out the bottle and said, "You can have it if you want." Then he smiled at me.

I was a little tongue-tied and totally frustrated by the feeling, when I said, "You got it first. You can have it."

He just laughed and asked, "What's your name?"

"Lacey Kale Rutledge."

"Nice to meet you, Lacey Kale Rutledge. Tylar Lane. You new at this school?"

"No."

He waited looking at me as if I had more to say, but if I did I didn't know it. So he said, "See ya around, Lacey Kale Rutledge," tossed the milk bottle into the air and caught it as he walked to a near by table where he had put his tray earlier.

I couldn't stop looking at him, until his eyes started in my direction, and then I pulled mine away. Walking back to the table where my lunch was waiting I began to hate myself for using my full name; it sounded so childish. Then I thought about hating my name. Who was this boy who made me notice something as simple as my name and made me feel ashamed of it? Juliet or Cleopatra would be so much better than Lacey Kale. I decided I would never use the Kale part again. But, that wouldn't work because I had been at this school for three years and every one who knew me knew me as Lacey Kale. Where had he been for the past three years? He had to be older than me, because none of the boys my age spoke to girls. And he was using complete sentences. And he was not bothered about helping Rachel out in her moment of need. And he was cute. Maybe if he wasn't so cute he would have done this deed to make the girls like him, but he didn't need to do things to make the girls like him. He was to me, what I was to God, perfect. And I sat a little uneasy with that thought.

The school year was over, summer awaiting me, and even though "problem solving" was still a problem for me, I was promoted to the fourth grade. Willie should have started Mrs. Winters' preschool in the fall. The younger of our two sisters, Retta, named Margaret after Nanny, would soon turn three and Abbie Lou, named Abigail after Mother, had just had her fourth birthday. Sally must have known that Pa and Mother were family people when she met them. I don't know what took them so long between Willie and me, but since we moved out of Pappy and Nanny's Mother was with a baby in her arms until last year. She lost that baby in her forth month and she cried for days till Pa said they would try again.

"If God wants us to have a fifth child we won't stand in His way."

Mother would deliver baby five shortly before I started the fifth grade; just three months after my tenth birthday. Pa wanted another boy, but sisters were so easy to love. Women just seemed to survive without a lot of extra attention. How I felt about Nanny, Mother, and my sisters was understood and didn't seem to take a lot of energy to re-enforce my feelings. Men for some reason need to be told daily, as well as shown, and brothers take all you will give. Pappy had my heart, and by now Pa had my love and respect, and Willie drained me of anything left.

Willie was special. He was three when Mother finally conceded to the truth of Willie's problem. He spent a lot of time watching his own fingers moving in different directions, but in sequence. A sequence of his own. He didn't speak clearly. Mostly groans and hand gestures explained his needs. He spoke *my name* clearly and loudly, especially when I was leaving the house to go to school or play down by the creek.

We lived on twenty acres of land on the edge of town where the French Broad River made a wide bend. Pappy said that God knew I would love it and respect its greatness so He directed it right to me. Our land bordered the river at its widest and deepest spot. It was great for fishing and swimming and I spent every free moment basking in the euphony of the river and its surroundings.

I think that's why Willie hollered every time I walked out of the house. The river was soothing to him as well, but I went to the river after school, not after breakfast! He couldn't differentiate between morning and afternoon yet. The doctors Sally had recommended to Mother said he would be able to one day with lots of reinforcement, but not soon.

My parents waited for the day Willie would be normal and ready to take his place in our family. I was frustrated by their remarks about Willie 'cause to me he was right where he was supposed to be. He was different, but he was mine and that's all that mattered. I'm sure that Mother prayed extra hard for baby five to be a boy, a boy Pa could teach how to build houses and work with wood as Pa did. But, she would have to wait and pray. It seemed like babies took forever to get here and with Abbie Lou, Retta and Willie to look after, this particular summer was a long one.

I kept Willie out of the house and down by the river most of the day. It seemed to relax Mother not having to watch Willie constantly. He was different with me. I guess it had to do with the promise I held him to years earlier in the sand box, because Willie was always good for me.

The spring at the end of forth grade had started out hot and humid. Perfect for fishing and swimming. The forecasters predicted a wetter summer than any other which seemed to please the farmers. There was more planting this year than any year I could remember. Every farmer was increasing the size of their fields by half if not double. Through the years Pappy invested his money in land and had several thousand acres, most of it mountains. He leased the land that was prime farming land and this year he was able to lease some of the land considered flood land. It was going to be a prosperous harvest, so everyone was convinced.

Our neighbor on the other side of Miss Sally had taken a job in New Mexico. He had left town a few months earlier to find a home for his family. His wife and all of his children, each in high school, had stayed behind to finish out the school year. Their house had been bought and the new family was waiting for them to vacate the property. Mother said the new couple's name was Collier. They were newlyweds, but the woman had children from her first marriage. She had lost her husband four years earlier in a car accident along with her oldest son. Sally knew all about Margery Collier and her family, because Margery worked in the hospital with admittance when Sally was still nursing. When her husband was killed, Sally was there for her with spiritual guidance and some childcare when it was all too much for her to bear. There had been great celebration in Sally's heart when she heard her friend had found love again and was moving in the house next door. She was sad when the Neeley's moved so far away, but a replacement that she knew so well with children who already knew hers, was a blessing. Marge Collier would complete the three musketeers of child rearing for our neighborhood.

All the other mothers worked in the different factories helping out with the war effort in the big city south of us. Marge worked there, too, till she married Bob. Now Mother and Sally would have help keeping all of us out of trouble during the summer and after school till the other mothers got home in the late afternoon. I was especially pleased because Mrs. Collier had a son who was twelve and he would be able to watch after his own brother and sister. With the Neeley's leaving there wouldn't be a lot of children older than me to help watch the smaller ones.

Mother and Sally paid the Neeley girls to help them out when there was shopping to do and other errands. Willie was enough for me, but Mother needed just as much help with the girls now that she was so late into her pregnancy. We were all looking forward to the arrival of the Colliers and Sally and Mother had planed a cookout in our backyard. We had the biggest yard and a large gazebo near the path that led through the woods to the river. The woods weren't dense with underbrush like the woods across the river, so you could see and hear the river from the gazebo, even though there was a small bank dropping down to the water. Pappy and Pa had built a dock extending over the river just big enough for the four of us to sit and fish with a little wiggle room for Willie. Pappy said we would be wasting our time building anything bigger, "'Cause one day that river's gonna come out of those banks and take whatever's in its path."

I had heard the old farmers talk about that happening years ago to my Nanny's mom and dad's peach and apple orchards. They said, "The river took them by the roots and washed them clean to the ocean." That was years ago when my Nanny was my age. Nothing like that had happened since, but Pappy said it was just a matter of timing.

Sally had her hands full with her own children, but she handled them with greater ease than Mother. I never understood how she was so strong at a time when most women were living with fear of the possibility of being alone permanently. I supposed it was her medical training that taught her to have a cool head in all adversities. Sally studied nursing at Duke Medical University and did her internship in an army hospital near Raleigh. There she met Dr. Simon Jude Foresight, "The man of her dreams." He was a colonel in the army and joined the British Army to help with the war efforts in France. They fell in love quickly, as some say, and married before he left for France. She finished her internship and came back home to wait the arrival of her first child, Jake. She had been alone for most of the twelve years that her husband, Jude, had been in France except for three years ago when he came home for a long leave. He was still in the states when she gave birth to the twins. I guess God blessed him with two babies at one time sense he missed out on the birth of his first.

Somehow, Sally was always at peace with every situation. She talked to me like I was grown. She encouraged me to pray for Willie everyday and for Mother and Pa to find peace in what seemed madness to them. I felt like we were friends. It was nice knowing that a grown woman with a family could find my company enjoyable.

She spent her days reading on the porch while her children and neighboring children played, and from time to time she would wade along the river shore with them. She never dove into the river with all her clothes on or even with a swimsuit, but neither did Mother. I never knew if they couldn't swim or if it was their hair that held them back. Pappy said that a woman's hair was their glory and their glory was always perfectly in place. Mine was wherever it landed when I got out of bed. Sometimes mother pulled it out of my eyes, but mostly I was too far away for her reach.

On the day of the party for our new neighbors I overslept. It was Saturday and we had spent all of Thursday and Friday packing up the Neeley's belongings and carrying the boxes to the truck so the men could place them in the most perfect place for each valuable to travel. Mr. Neeley was back to get his family and help with the packing. I could see in my Pa's eyes that he would miss Mr. Neeley. He had been an employee of Pa's and it was Pa who had offered the job to Mr. Neeley in New Mexico. There was a town that was being started in a valley along the Rio Grande. A very wealthy man had purchased the valley and the adjoining mountains just after the depression began. The land extended east of the continental divide then from the Rio Chama bordering the Rio Grande all the way to the Rio San Juan River. Pa said the land belonged to the Indians, but the government was in the process of buying, or as some said taking, the land when the depression hit. The government could no longer afford the land and thought no one else could either so they turned their attention elsewhere. The cost of the property greatly decreased. Just as Pappy, this wealthy man must have heard from God about the pending doom and kept his money out of the banks and in another secure place. Or maybe he just didn't trust banks. In any case, he was in the position to purchase the land. When he bought the land it was his desire to see the land stay with the Indians, as they were a people he lived with during the last twenty-five years of his life. But, he had four children who were all entrepreneurs with desires to see the valley become a thriving metropolis. He had not seen to it that the land was secure for the Indians, because he died suddenly, shortly after he purchased it.

After their father's death the children didn't have enough money between them to begin a project so costly. Some eleven years after the depression started, with wise investments, they felt like they had enough money to begin their dream. I was sad for the man who had no one to carry out his dream of leaving the land as it was with the Indians occupying the land after his death, but I was thankful that Mr. Neeley and Pa would see some of their life's work come off the drafting table and into people's lives. The man's children had made an investment in a company located in Seattle, Washington, in a building Pa had designed. They love his design and the sturdy construction so they contacted Pa about coming to New Mexico for the job. Pa said Mr. Neeley knew more about using concrete on the facing of structures than he did so he was the best person for this job. It would take years to build this town from dirt to a metropolis, but the opportunity to build a vast array of architecture was just the challenge Pa would have loved. Some of his designs would be built of course, but to be the man in charge, working directly with the carpenters was where Pa's heart was. He had a way of getting people to work together no matter where they came from, where they lived or what nationality they were.

That's why Mr. Neeley came to work for Pa. They had met in Chicago when they were studying architecture at The Art Institute of Illinois and admired each other's work. Living in the same boarding house in Chicago gave them plenty of time to become friends as well as critics. Working together was something they already did well, so when Pa told Mr. Neeley he had opened his own architecture firm and offered a place for him to work, Mr. Neeley was thrilled to pick up his family and move from Chicago to North Carolina.

I often wondered what it would have been like to move to New Mexico or any other place in America for that matter. The way Pa described it, and the pictures I saw, it looked a lot different from home. The land was flat with sudden mountains without anything growing on them much. Pa said the buildings were a lot different from our buildings, too. I thought that was why Pa didn't move us to New Mexico, but I found out later that the real reason we didn't move was because of Willie. Pa and Mother had found a special school for him to start in the fall and because there was no town in New Mexico all of us would have been home schooled, something Mother could not do with Willie.

chapter two

When I finally woke up the day of the party for the Collier family, Mother was in my room talking away at me and laying out a list for me to do as soon as I knocked the cobwebs out of my head. I heard something about a bath and my best dress and the bow on my dresser pulling the curls out of my eyes. A bath? First thing in the morning? I must be dreaming. So I pulled the covers over my head and tried to go back to sleep. Then I heard Pappy in the hall calling me and saying something about Katie's Kafe and biscuits for breakfast. I sprang to my feet only to run into Mother who had beat me to the doorway telling Pappy that I wouldn't be able to go with him because I had fallen asleep after supper and missed my bath. She looked down at me and said, "And a hair washing young lady! You could grow tomatoes on that head."

Pappy said, "Well, no tomato has ever had a prettier head to grow on. You get your bath and I'll bring breakfast to you. Meet you on the dock in twenty minutes."

"You'll meet her on the back porch, no fishing today in your dress. Make it thirty minutes, Pappy, this head will take a while." And she swept me into the bathroom with the curve of her arm and with her round belly pushed into my back.

I was always thrilled when a good scrubbing was over with because I could slide around mother for a week or so until the next big event came along. Most kids had to get a scrubbing every Saturday so they would be unrecognizable come Sunday morning. I think the mothers were hoping God wouldn't recognize their children more than pleasing those in the congregation. Mother was a strong believer that God had to look at you all week long so you better be at your best every day not just on Sundays. Pappy said God thought I was perfect so I rarely went to much trouble on Sundays. I always wanted to wear my overalls, but I wore a dress to church because that's what girls my age did, but never one with all the lace and frills that the others had to have.

Today's dress was what was called a jumper. It was teal green and it made my orange hair stand out like the sun. "A sore thumb" is what Jake Foresight called it as he yanked at my curls. "God never intended anyone to make such a display."

His mother, Sally, told him to apologize for his rudeness and ask God in his prayers to give him half as much grace as God had given to me. I didn't know exactly what grace was, but I knew it was something good so I offered him a biscuit to let him know he was forgiven and hoped the gesture would slightly pinch him. He didn't mean anything harmful in his teasing; it was just something he did. No one ever stayed mad at Jake for long.

Mother let me wear my white P. F. Flyer tennis shoes since this was a cook out in the back yard and not in someone's home. The shoes sort of matched the beige tee shirt I had on under the jumper, but when you looked closer at my shoes, you could see they were a slight reddish-orange permanently stained from the muddy banks of the river. Everything around here had that color on it sooner or later; even our toilet, tub, and sinks were stained. That color was one thing that we had in common with New Mexico, and I bet the Indian children had P. F. Flyers that looked just like mine. In any case, these were not the kind of shoes you wear to a party, but they were perfect for my backyard.

Of course the Colliers had not moved into the Neeley's old house yet seeing how the Neeley's just left early on that morning before any of us got up. The party wasn't so much of a welcome to the neighborhood party for someone who had just moved in. Instead, Mother and Sally were having the party for all the neighbors to meet the Colliers so they would hopefully be more willing to pitch in and help move them. It's easier reaching out to people you've been introduced to and feel some freedom with. Everyone likes being needed, but no one likes to feel like they are intruding. The Colliers wanted the help because of the amount of furniture they needed to get moved. Mr. Collier had a home completely furnished and so did Mrs. Collier. They didn't want to get rid of things until they had a chance to see what would fit in where. It would be next weekend before they would start moving their things and this week would be used to paint or do any repairs needed.

Our backyard was beginning to fill with family, neighbors, friends and employees that worked for Pappy and Pa. Whenever there was a party or a cookout, everyone was invited and most of the time everyone attended. The yard had been freshly mowed while I slept, and Sally had brought baskets of flowers out of her green house to brighten up the shrubbery. Because Pa had an interest in houses and their appearance, we had planted fescue in our yard around the house. Most people still had dirt yards that were kept neat by sweeping the dirt down to the hard clay. Fescue was only used to feed the cattle and horses. It was considered a bit extravagant, but Pa paid Pappy's lessee to plant the yard when they plowed and planted the land beside ours that Pappy owned. Pa had bought a hand-propelled lawn mower out of the Sears' catalogue. It took a little while to get the job done and Pa surely could have paid someone else to do the job, but he loved getting out from under his desk and working outside. Mother said the lawnmower was a lifesaver because we didn't have to have a goat tied in the yard and a goat in the yard today would have ruined everything.

Sally had garnished the gazebo with crepe paper and balloons. Willie wanted to hold every balloon in his hand calling out a color then releasing the balloon. He really wanted me to take him to the river, but mother gave me that look that said, "No matter what it takes change his mind and don't let him make a scene."

That was easier said than done when Willie had his mind set on something, but once you got his mind on something else he was content doing it till he fell asleep. At that moment no one was sitting at the gazebo. Mother had moved the record player out in the yard near the gazebo as far as the drop cord would reach. Willie loved music. His favorite was the Tommy Dorsey band with their newest singer Frank

Sinatra singing, "I'll Never Smile Again." But Willie smiled through the whole song. When nothing else entertained him, he could sit for hours clapping his hands and singing something that made sense to him. I was hoping if someone came to the gazebo and interrupted Willie's balloon game we would be able to sit by the record player and Willie would focus on the music. We would be out of the way there, but able to see the hub of the party.

Our house looked a lot like Pappy's. We had a porch that wrapped all the way around the three-story dwelling. The porch around to the back had been screened in a couple years before because of the mosquitoes in the spring. With Willie's inability to feel some things, Mother had found him on the back porch one rainy spring day eaten up by mosquitoes. For weeks he was pinkish-purple from the calamine lotion mother rubbed on him two or three times a day. We covered some of the bites with band-aids where Willie had been drawn like a magnet to their stinging and scratched until they bled. Most of our rain was in the spring and fall so the mosquitoes were not so much of a problem for our party. We usually went into a drought through the summer, but so far the farmers said we had just the right amount of rain and sunshine to bless us all. This day I was blessed, because the sky was cloudless and bright blue, and the yard was full of happy people enjoying my blessing.

I tried to teach Willie the different colors of the balloons, but once he fixated on a color word, he said it over and over for each balloon regardless of the color. Sometimes I could feel myself shut down like Willie and focus on one thing. This day I tried to get Willie to come with me to the grassy spot near the record player before anyone came to the gazebo, but he wouldn't budge. If I tried to force him he would scream with fear for ten or fifteen minutes. Mostly I let him scream, but Mother had given me that look earlier, and the yard was now full of guests. So I sat with my back to the yard, hands folded on my lap, Willie standing beside me on the gazebo bench calling out the wrong colors, and me calling out the correct colors, with balloons hitting me in the side of the head and my eyes staring down at the wooden flooring. I'm not really sure where my mind was, but it was not in my backyard. I could hear people clapping and I even sensed everyone gathering to the back porch, but I was somewhere else calling out colors that made no sense to me or Willie.

Suddenly, I heard my name being called in my Pa's voice as Pappy startled me by touched me on the shoulder. He said, "Our guests of honor are here, Punkin,' and your parents want you to meet the children." I jumped off the bench still looking into Pappy's face as he reached for my hand to guide me down the steps to where he was standing. I suddenly remembered Willie standing on the bench and ran back for him, but Pappy said, "I'll stay with Willie. You run on, they're waiting for you."

There was a crowd around the Colliers and Mother was motioning for me to come to her. My sisters were standing with her and Pa who was laughing and patting a tall slender man on the back. I was sure this was Bob Collier, though I had never met him before. My parents had played canasta with them on different occasions after they took Willie, my sisters and me to Pappy and Nanny's for the evening. I had never met any of the Colliers and Mother and Pa had not met their children until today.

My Mother was in her element when there was a party and she was hosting it. She made everyone feel welcome and like they were the reason the party was a success in her eyes. I heard my Mother calling to Mrs. Collier saying, "Marge, here comes Lacey. She's always busy with her brother Willie who is sitting in the gazebo with his Pappy."

A pretty lady, with her hair parted to the side with two combs lifting the sides up and back leading around her head down to her shoulders where the blunt cut flipped under, stepped out from behind the tall slender man. It was a hairstyle I had seen Dorothy Lamor wearing on the front of *Red Book* in the rack by the register at Woolworth's. Mrs. Collier was wearing, what I later found out was called a two-piece playsuit. Her sleeveless blouse was white with a square neck that was created by the one-inch wide straps. There were white shorts under an ankle length patterned skirt that came together in the middle and tied with a sash at the waist. Her toenails were freshly painted with the same red that contrasted with the turquoise in the patterned skirt. Strappy white sandals drew your eye to her feet and her beauty drew your eye back to her face. She was the most glamorous woman

I had ever seen. This was the latest fashion and I saw the envy on my mother's face. The Collier's had just returned from California where they honeymooned in San Francisco, then down to Los Angeles to visit in Beverly Hills and Hollywood. Mr. Collier was the nephew of the man who had started a publication in New York using the surname *Collier's*. He had spent a lot of time in California and wanted to show his new wife the glitz and glamour only found in Hollywood and the movies these days. He worked a short time with his uncle's publication, but long enough to meet some of Hollywood's stars. He had a fascination for trains so he left publishing and went to work for Chicago Great Western Railroad. Somehow he ended up in our town working down at our railroad. While they were in California, they visited some of the top designers his uncle introduced them to and Mr. Collier had bought his wife a new wardrobe for her wedding present since she hadn't been able to afford anything for herself after her husband's death.

Mrs. Collier had married into a family that was as we used to say "well to do," but she didn't seem to let it cause her to think she was better than anyone else like many of my parent's friends. She made over each of us, Abbie Lou, Retta and me, as Mother introduced us.

"Abbie Lou just had her fourth birthday. She and Willie, who will turn five in two weeks, will get along famously with your Pauley," and with Mother's cue Mrs. Collier reached around behind her pulling a small boy in view who was still trying to cling to the back of her legs. "And this is Retta; she will be three this fall."

"I'm this many," and Retta held up two fingers.

Pauley said, "That's two."

"Oh good, Pauley. You're exactly right. Tell Abbie Lou and Retta how old you are," Mrs. Collier said wrapping her arms around him as she knelt down beside him.

"I'm four," he said holding up four fingers.

"Isn't he adorable, Lacey Kale? Marge, this is my oldest daughter, Lacey Kale."

Mrs. Collier looked up at me, reached out her hand, and I took it. She gazed at my face and said, "She is just as beautiful as you said, Abigail, and all grown up. It is a pleasure to meet you and I know we will be friends. My oldest son is just two years older than you. He turns twelve in February. Your birthday's in May isn't it?"

"Yes Ma'am."

"And well mannered! Abigail, you've done a beautiful job raising three lovely young ladies. I can't wait to meet your son. Speaking of son, where is that other one of mine. I want you to meet him, Lacey... Kale? Is that right?"

"Yes Ma'am. I mostly go just by Lacey now though."

"Or Punkin,'" Abbie Lou chirped in, "that's what Pappy and me calls her."

"I think I'll call you Lacey, if that's okay with you?"

"Yes Ma'am."

Someone called from the corner of the yard where Pappy and Pa had set up an outside kitchen using the top off an old gas stove to make a portable gas cooker. It was near the fire pit where Pappy had taken the front grill off his old truck and placed it over the fire to cook the hamburgers. The burgers were done and lunch was served. There were tables and tables of other choices; fried chicken, pork hash, beef hash, chicken potpie, and ham. There were vegetables fixed any way you could want them and fresh baked bread with butter and homemade jams. And Willie's favorite; stuffed eggs. All the kids loved Nanny's stuffed eggs. She wouldn't allow us to call them Deviled Eggs. Pappy was the only one allowed to say anything about the devil. Once Jake told my cousin Theodore to go to the devil and my Nanny turned pale and I was sure she would faint.

The older boys were taking turns sitting on the ice cream churn and turning the crank. Willie was still in his own world of balloons and color only now he was sitting in the floor of the gazebo instead of standing. Pappy was talking to a friend while sitting on the steps balancing a plate on his knees pulling the meat off of a chicken bone. And Willie was missing it all. I just didn't want to miss it, too, trying to get him to be a part of something he couldn't be. With all that was in me, I forced myself to turn away from the scene and get lost in the crowd of people. Some I knew, some I did not, but it didn't matter either way right then. Something was bothering me. That same gnawing that something wasn't right, but I couldn't put my finger on it. Then I spotted them in my front yard. I suppose that's why I hadn't seen what was about to change my life.

One of my mother's brothers was stationed in Japan. There was a terrible war going on that our country was involved in, a war that some how brought us out of the depression, so people said. Others gave the credit to our president, but I really didn't know much about it. It seemed as though people had grown tired of their loved ones being away from home and they were hoping for an end. Some man had done some awful things to some Jewish people, things that made my Pappy crazy with anger anytime someone brought it up.

Pappy said, "Even if they don't believe that Jesus is their Messiah, no one deserved this! It's not about religious beliefs anyway, it's about human kindness. This man should have been stopped a long time ago, because kindness is not in him. Anytime someone thinks they are smarter than God by thinking they can choose who is worthy of life, will find out they aren't so smart after all. Apparently this man has never read The Book. The children of Israel will be here till the end of this world as we know it. Besides the Jews, he is showing hate for the people of Poland. I think he just hates everyone. Hate is not a crime, but if you act on that hate by hurting others God will make you pay. If we don't stop him we are just as guilty. I know we are doing all we can do, but sometimes you have to do more. Evil won't win this war, but it sure can make a mess till it's stopped."

My Pappy's passion was for everyone involved, but it was driven by his desire to see his oldest son home safe. Uncle Marty, Pappy's youngest son, was in the royal Air Force, Eagle Squadron, stationed in Britain. He flew Hurricanes and Spitfires for the RAF fighting the German Hunkels and Messerschmitts whenever there was a German raid on Britain. The German army and air forces were focusing on Russia now, and reports said they were losing hold, so Marty wasn't in as much danger as Uncle Alvin.

Alvin Theodore Hawthorne, Pappy's oldest son, was thirty-two years old, four years older than my mother, Abigail. Alvin's mother had died giving birth to him. Pappy gave his mother his only son to raise until Pappy could find someone willing to help him with the boy. His mother was willing to keep Alvin as long as Pappy needed her to, and Alvin seemed happy there, so Pappy's parents kept Alvin for three years. During that time the doctors recognized a speech problem with Alvin and blamed it on the trauma of not having his father permanently planted in his life. Pappy always felt guilty about leaving him so young.

Being the Vice President in a bank about fifteen miles from where his parents lived Pappy couldn't see Alvin as often as he wanted. It doesn't seem like far, but it is when you don't have a car and you start work, at sunup around your home, then from nine o'clock in the morning till five in the evenings working at the bank and then home to finish the work around your home again. There just wasn't time to drive a team of horses so far out of town. Pappy spent his Saturdays with Alvin and part of Sunday. As Alvin got older he used that excuse, being an abandoned child, for all his failures and shortcomings. When he destroyed his younger sister's porcelain dolls by strapping pillow cases to their backs and throwing them out of the upstairs bathroom window, he was patted on the head by Pappy while Nanny comforted Abigail by explaining her brother's behavior away. "He just doesn't understand love the way we do. The doctors say it's because his father wasn't there to hug him every night like he did for you, Abbie. Be thankful for what you have and forgive your brother. Families must forgive each other. Besides, maybe Alvin will grow up and be a paratrooper and his behavior will seem fully justified. We must give people room to grow."

Pappy would come home with new dolls for Abbie and some kind of treat for Alvin. There was always a treat for Alvin. As he got older he had few friends because he would get mad if someone had something that he didn't have and destroy their toy by claiming to take it apart to see how it worked. He started failing in school and blamed Pappy for not spending enough time with him helping with his studies. When Pappy hired a tutor for Alvin, he tied her to a tree down by the river and left her all night because she popped his hand with a ruler after she gave him an assignment and he shot her the bird. That's when Nanny began to recount the event of Pappy's first wife's death so it would be plain to all that she was not this child's mother.

When Pappy met Josephine Margaret Cantrell, my grandmother, two years after his wife's death, Pappy was sure she would fill that void in Alvin's life as she had filled it for him. They married a year later, reclaimed the boy, and were blessed with their own child, my mother, the next year. Alvin turned nineteen and joined the Navy placing more guilt on Pappy with his words of never really feeling like he belonged in this family. He met a girl, Penny Jackson, who lived in the town where he was stationed for basic training. Pappy said she was one of those girls who hung around at the navy base tavern looking for a husband to take them away from their mundane lives. Pappy always talked to me in secret down on the dock about the things that bothered him, his opinion of people, and what stirred his heart to get up in the morning. However, Mother and Nanny would never express their feelings about things. They said it wouldn't do any good and it would only help remind them instead of helping to forget. It was better to put on a front that all was well than to dwell on what you couldn't change and one day you might even believe it. It was just too hard for Pappy to pretend all was fine when Penny was in the picture.

According to Pappy, Penny was fifteen when she left home to get away from her mother who lived the same kind of lifestyle Penny later ended up in. She brought home a different man every other week or so and some of the men took advantage of Penny as well. She started hanging out in the navy tavern in hopes of finding someone to truly love her and take care of her when she met Uncle Alvin.

Penny recognized the Hawthorne name and saw a vulnerable young man who was missing his family, so she calculated her strategy. Three weeks later they were married. Pappy loved a romantic end as good as the next guy, but he didn't trust that Penny had been able to put the old life behind her in three short weeks.

After basic training they moved to Tokyo, Japan where their son Theodore was born. They lived there until August of 1934 when Adolph Hitler became the leader of Germany after the death of their president. It was no longer thought to be safe for his wife and son to be left alone while he was out on the ship. Alvin sent his family back to the United States, back to the place he had found Penny. After she arrived in the states, she was constantly calling and writing Pappy for money to pay the rent or food for his grandson. She always said, "It's not for me or your grandson that I ask for your help, it's for your firstborn son. He sends his check to me every month, but it's not enough. I just can't tell him that, with all that he has on him trying to keep this country out of this war. It would kill him if he thought his own family was going hungry living in the slums because he wasn't providing for us. And that's just where we will be if I can't pay the landlord." So Pappy gave in and sent her a sizable monthly check so she wouldn't have to muse over some long drawn out plea each month.

Penny was different from the others in my family. Mother said it was because she wasn't really in my family and she wasn't raised in this town or state. "People are different in other areas. It's not bad, they're just different. We've been born to privilege and lived a, somewhat, sheltered life." Well, Penny was different, and at this point in my life I couldn't give it any more thought than that.

On this day she was at her best at being different. Whenever we had a family gathering she insisted that her son had to be a part of it. They lived in a small town outside of Norfolk, Virginia. It was a six or seven hour drive to my house and Pappy had to send them bus fair to get them here and back. She told him how hard it was on little Theodore to travel on a bus that only made stops long enough to go to the bathroom every two hours. "As soon as Kimmy is out of diapers I'm going to have to have a car to bring these children back and forth to see their grandparents." Even though Kimmy was four, so far Pappy had not bought Penny a car, but I could see him starting to wear down.

It wasn't till I was older and understood the making of babies that I realized why Pappy didn't seem to make over Kimmy like he did his other grandchildren. Penny didn't push the issue with Pappy, although she did make reference to what everyone was thinking to Mother and Nanny. "I don't know why he thinks Kimmy isn't Alvin's, she has his eyes. You remember that weekend I told you about when Alvin surprised me coming home for a short leave and telling no one?"

Well, no one was buying it, not even Uncle Alvin. He had written to Uncle Marty saying he wouldn't even come home after the war if he didn't have Theodore. It seemed it was true that Alvin had come home unexpected only to find that Penny had a guest sleeping over. Alvin never told his family that he was in the states, because after looking in on Theodore, he went straight to the base and caught the next flight outbound for Japan.

Theodore was named something else on his birth certificate, but

Penny started calling him Theodore after she came back to the states. See, Theodore was Pappy's first wife's maiden name and every time Penny spoke her son's name it reminded Pappy of what he had lost and the child he had abandoned. Guilt was an awful thing to live with, but to remind someone of their guilt everyday was obscene. I didn't recognize these games until much later. As for now, I saw everyone as good; no one ever intended to hurt someone else. Just like I never intended to hurt Willie by leaving him in the gazebo while this wonderful party was going on around him. I guess I was more hurt that he didn't care and didn't even notice.

So there she was, dragging her trunk up the front yard with Theodore and Kimmy each dragging an overstuffed suitcase. I had no idea they were coming. Although all our parties included family, it was family that lived in town who were invited to a party given in honor of a non-member. Did Pappy know they would be here? He never mentioned it to me and this was something he definitely would have told me.

Theodore and I were not friends. I tried to be a friend to everyone, but I could not find one of those good qualities to focus on when I was around him. We were forced together when they came to visit, because of my age being closer to his than any of the other cousins, but I did not like it. It was obvious that he was jealous of my relationship with Pappy, something I could not do anything about, nor would I. He had another grandfather who he lived very close to. He didn't need mine. My Pa's parents had left, before my parents got married, to live in Maine with my grandmother's aging father who was widowed with no other family. Pappy was all I had and I felt very protective of him. I didn't like it when Theodore took advantage of Pappy and I hated it worse when he did bad things and blamed them on me. No one ever believed him except his mother, but I stayed clear of him just the same whenever they were staying with Nanny and Pappy. That made me wonder why were they bringing their luggage to *my* house?

One thing that made Penny noticeable to everyone, and anyone who had eyes, was her flamboyant costumes. They were nowhere near being a wardrobe like Mrs. Collier's. There was no other way to describe her. She was a sight. She always had these elaborate stories about finding her clothes in a second hand store or from the tailors down the road from her house. Whenever someone brought something in, and didn't return to claim it, the tailor would let Penny know and she would try the clothes on. All she had to do was pay the tailor charges and it was hers. Somehow she told the story about each piece of clothing she was wearing as if it was the envy of all who were blessed to see her in it. And what a bargain she had gotten for such a treasure, "So you see I'm spending Pappy Hawthorne's money wisely. Money he'll never run out of if he lived to be a hundred and threw fifty dollars a day in the wishing pond downtown."

I've always wondered how Penny knew how much money Pappy had. This outfit that Pappy had bought was one I understood why someone left at the tailors, though I know no one ever wore these pieces together. I was horrified to think how mother was going to feel not being able to prepare her new friend; however, Mrs. Collier had struck me as the kind of woman who could handle Penny Jackson Hawthorne just fine.

That's why I missed it. I never saw them coming. Without warning Marge Collier was standing beside me with her oldest son. I turned my head to see them looking at what I had been looking at, and what I saw then was even more unbelievable.

"Who's that?" Mrs. Collier asked. Then she looked at me, looking at him, when I didn't answer her.

"Oh! This is my son Tylar Lane. Tylar this is . . . "

"Lacey Kale Rutledge," Tylar interrupted, "I know her from school."

"Oh, you do? This is so much fun. Every one is having a great time, we're meeting new friends and you and Lacey," placing her hands on his shoulders and getting her mouth closer to his ear, "that's what she likes to be called," then she said with girlish giddy, " and ya'll already know each other. And now we're going to be neighbors. Come on Lacey, eat with us. I've already gotten napkins and silverware and put them on the table over there." She pointed to one of the tables in the yard on the side of the house near the porch. "Tylar, take Lacey with you and you kids get your plates. The blessing has already been said. I'm going to see if I can help your mother, Lacey, with her other guests. Maybe she will come and eat with us. Bet she hasn't had a thing all day."

"Mrs. Collier, my mother is probably in the living room right now. She might be able to use your help there if Miss Sally's not with her."

She stopped in her tracks, looked back at me, then at the front yard where Penny and her ensemble had been earlier, and said, "I like Miss Marge or Margie, Mrs. Collier is still too new for me to be used to. I'm afraid I still don't know that people are talking to me."

She seemed to get lost in herself looking at the vacant yard and then she nodded at me and sighed, "Okay," she said in her perky voice. Then she turned and walked towards the house. She somehow knew what I was talking about, I was sure of it. Well, after all, they had seen the same thing going in my front door as I had. My mother didn't need this kind of stress at this time of her pregnancy and stress was what Aunt Penny brought to everyone. Now that Tylar Lane had just walked into my yard she was causing me a little stress, too. Until he knew she was related to me I had nothing to be ashamed of, but he would find out. Right now I was going to enjoy having lunch with the boy I had met months ago, but hadn't seen since that day.

chapter three

Tylar Lane talked and talked all through lunch about school, his real father and the railroad. He wanted to be the engineer of his own train one day and travel all across the country. I told him what I knew about New Mexico and the town Mr. Neeley and Pa were working on. We talked about the day in the lunchroom where we met and why I had never seen him before or after that day. He had gone to the doctor's for a physical to play football and gotten back to school after his class had eaten lunch, so they let him eat with our grade. He remembered my name because it was so much like his new friend, the man Mr. Collier worked for at the railroad. His name was Johnny Kale Butler and he owned the loading yard in town. Johnny Kale's grandfather had been one of the men building the railroad all over this country. This was his favorite town that the railroad went through, so he settled here after the rail was complete.

Tylar admired Johnny Kale, and he loved his stepfather, but he wasn't ready to call him "Dad" yet. He missed his older brother, Garry, who was twelve when he was killed with Tylar's father in that car accident. A cow had gotten out of a fence and was standing in the curve of the road. It was dark and difficult to see around the turn. When his father saw the cow it was too late. He swerved to miss it, but ran off the road and into a tree. The cow hit on his brother's side and went through the windshield landing on his brother. His father was thrown from the car and down an embankment. I think that's why Tylar liked the railroad so much. He thought it was safer to travel in a train.

The lunch was going so great and I didn't want to leave for anything, not even Pappy, but he was calling me. He had Willie up on his shoulders and Willie was asleep. He asked me to lift him down and take him inside to bed where he could finish out his nap. Knowing that if he went inside he would find Penny and family, I thought it best not to ruin his good time. And a good time Pappy was having and I loved to see him with his friends and co-workers. He was a brilliant man and everyone loved him, because he was never rude with his knowledge or flashy with his wealth. He was a simple man with a big heart, and the last thing that heart needed today was the likes of Penny Jackson Hawthorne.

Tylar offered to help me with Willie, even though Willie was smaller than most five year olds he was beginning to get heavy to me, so I welcomed the help. Tylar took Willie under the arms and I got his feet. He didn't budge. Once Willie was asleep it took a freight train to wake him. He would sleep till supper with as much balloon tossing as he had done.

We rounded the kitchen table when I remembered Penny. I did not want Tylar to hear what was being said in the living room, but I was so shocked that I found my feet stuck to the floor unable to move. Penny was telling Nanny to get her husband used to the idea, 'cause she was moving in with somebody and it looked like they had the most room. I saw Tylar struggling to hold Willie, so I motioned for him to set him down on the floor by the foot of the stairs. I went into the washroom and got a blanket to put under Willie's head. He reached out for the blanket and snuggled up to it. Then I motioned for Tylar to come with me and we hid in the dining room near the French doors separating the two rooms. I could hear every sniffle made in that room and it was obvious that Kimmy had a cold. Penny began again with complaints of the doctor bills for Kimmy's cold and no lunch for the children at school being the very thing to keep her sick.

"It's a disgrace that anyone be in the shape that I'm in, but an even greater disgrace that a Hawthorne grandchild be poor and sick. And now homeless! It could be months, even years before Alvin comes home to take care of his family. It's your Christian duty to take care of your own when they are in need, and we are in need."

Penny didn't have a clue what a "Christian duty" was. She never darkened the door of a church after her father left her and her mother and she said it was God's fault that she had struggled all of her life. Even though she confessed to hate God she never hesitated to use Him to bring guilt to our family.

Nanny softly told Penny, "I have told you before, we have a small house by the river that no one has rented after the last family moved. You are welcome to move in there, but you are not moving into my house. As for Abigail and her family, they do not owe you a thing. You will not take advantage of her kindness.

"Abigail, I personally rescind your offer for Penny to stay here. This, my dear, is not a hotel. My daughter is too important to me, as well as Alvin and his family, but I will not allow anyone to jeopardize her pregnancy or the rest of her family. She has all she can do taking care of a child with special needs, as well as her other children. I'm sorry if you feel neglected. That house on the river is my offer, my only offer, take it or go home."

These sound like harsh words, almost fighting words, but my Nanny delivered them with all the grace and poise of the First Lady. She made it clear that no one would take advantage of her or her family and she did so with love. There was a silence that fell over the room. It stayed for a long time, too long.

I could tell people were getting uncomfortable when I heard the voice of Miss Margie saying, "Well, that settles it then. Looks like we'll be moving two families this week. The burgers have *been* done. Can I bring anyone a plate? Mrs. Jo Rett, after a deliberation of that magnitude I know you must be hungry. You sit right there while I get you some iced tea and a plate full of food fit for a queen."

I realized she was coming into the dining room to go to the kitchen, but it was too late. She came around the corner, almost tripped over my clunky shoes, saw us sitting in the floor with my hands over my mouth, Tylar's face buried on the top of his knees and never missed a beat. She turned around, stuck her head back in the door way as she indicated with the waved her hand for us to run, and said, "Don't you get up now, I'll bring you all some of the sweetest iced tea you have ever tasted and get the kids to help fix ya'll some plates."

She was still talking away, asking if there was some particular food anyone might object to while we lifted Willie up off the floor and started up the stairs with him. We put Willie in his bed and I tucked him in with his favorite rabbit and toy truck. I looked at Tylar who looked as red in the face as I felt. Then we burst out laughing at what had just happened. I had to sit down on the vanity stool to catch my breath.

"Wow, your mom is great. How did she keep from tripping over my shoes?"

"Boy, I don't know. My mom has proven that she can think on her feet even when she's about to have them flipped out from under her."

"Well, *my* mother would have scolded me for eavesdropping and embarrassed me something awful, even in front of Penny and her children."

"From what I saw of that lady she's the only one who should be embarrassed. Besides my mother may scold us yet."

"I guess we should get back down stairs and take our punishment. Your mom might be looking for us."

We started down the stairs slowly, listening for any signs of voices in the kitchen. We didn't hear any so we stepped out of the stairwell and started to run through the washroom toward the back-screened door. Somebody grabbed me and said, "Where are you going" as I screamed and Tylar laughed with hysteria. Miss Margie was in the washroom getting clean glasses for the iced tea when she heard us running through the kitchen. She laughed with Tylar and patted me on the head.

"You two were such a sight sitting there like two monkeys missing the third one with his hands over his ears! What in the world were you doing there, Miss Lacey? If it had been your Nanny Jo Rett who rounded that corner she would have fell right over you two. And your mother in her condition, well, it just wasn't smart."

I felt awful at the thought of mother losing another child.

"Well?" Miss Margie just looked deep in my eyes as they started to fill with tears. Then she tried to lighten the moment by saying,

the road

"You weren't playing hide and go seek 'cause nobodies come lookin' for you."

"No Ma'am. We were taking Willie up stairs to bed when I heard Penny say she was moving into my house. With her kids! It's too bad that "Hear No Evil" *wasn't* with us, but seeing that he wasn't, I couldn't just walk away from that."

"No, I suppose I wouldn't have walked away either. But, you don't have to worry about that now, your grandmother has seen to that."

"But where will they stay until they have beds to sleep in?"

"Nanny Jo Rett took care of that, too. Apparently she has some beds down in the barn that she said would be set up in some house by the river tonight. It has a kitchen with a wood stove and an icebox so they should be able to make it till their things get here, which should be right away by what your aunt said."

Well, it was out. My new friends and neighbors knew that Penny was my aunt and her children were my cousins and they didn't seem any more bothered by it than the rest of my friends and relatives. It was just me. Me and Pappy. We had a real problem with it and I didn't really know why.

"Pappy! Who is going to tell Pappy?"

"Your mother said she would tell him after his food digested."

"Well, that won't be for a while, Pappy eats all day long!"

We all smiled at each other and Miss Margie gave me a squeeze around my shoulders, which eased the tension, but I didn't like any of this one bit. Tylar and I helped his mother with the tea and plates. After all, she had given to us a moment of excitement and respect that I had not gotten from an adult who wasn't my Pappy. Something told me we would all be great friends until Tylar fell in love with some beautiful girl his own age who needed his strength and would appreciate his charm. But for now, we would have some great times together.

After we helped with the feeding of all those in the living room, Mother let me introduce the river to Tylar since Willie was asleep. We had to sneak out the front door and take the long way around through the apple trees so Abbie Lou and Retta wouldn't beg to come. We were told to stay out of the water in our good clothes, but we thought we were smart enough to take our shoes and sock off and wade around without ever being discovered. But there's something about the river that a simple wading just won't satisfy. Before we knew it we were in over our heads having the time of our lives. We were innocently standing on the dock looking out over the river when Tylar notice the rope hanging in the tree over our heads. He asked me what it was and I told him Pappy had put it there years ago to help me learn what flying must be like. We used it to fall out into the water doing tricks like diving and flips. He wanted to do it so badly and challenged me by saying I was a chicken. Well, that was all it took. I was never a chicken! So with my teal green jumper and cream shirt I jumped off the dock holding on to the rope and showed my new best friend how to dive into the river. It was so satisfying as I swung through the air and did a perfect dive, but when I hit that water in my good jumper I knew I was going to be grounded from the river for weeks.

"Enjoy this fun for today, Lacey Kale, 'cause this could be the last time you swim in the river this summer."

Tylar hit the water with a huge splash landing on his back after he flapped his arms wildly in the air as he fell from the rope. I couldn't help but laugh at his free fall and the way he gasped when he came up out of the water not expecting it to be so chilly. We swung on the rope swing for about an hour when I noticed it was getting late in the day and the sun was not as warm as earlier. I was sure we had no chance of getting our clothes dry before dark, but we needed to try.

We chose to take them off and ring them out to help get them to dry quicker. We twisted and twisted as tight as we could till no water dripped from them. Then we put them back on and sat on a rock in the sun rubbing and rubbing the wrinkles flat. I was sure if our clothes did dry we would still be caught because of those wrinkles. We needed an iron, but that wasn't something we could get without being seen. So we stayed on the rock rubbing our clothes and talking about the adventures we could have if we were ever allowed to play together again.

As we lay on a rock looking up at the sky laughing about the craziness of our first day as neighbors, I heard my Pappy's voice on the dock. He was talking to himself in a mumble when he spotted us on the rock below. He called out to me, "Lacey Kale, we've got an ox in the ditch and I need your help. My goodness girl, what have you done to your hair and your ribbon is all ... well, it's everywhere!"

I had forgotten to take out my bow before jumping into the water. I sat up and grabbed the hair clip with the ribbon hanging down the back of my head and tried to tie the limp ribbon without much success.

"What have you kids been doing?"

Tylar stood up and began a speech while I struggled with the bow.

"Sir, it's all my fault, Sir. I was standing on the dock talking with Lacey when I notice the rope tied to the railing. I looked up to see where the rope was coming from," then Tylar paused. I was listening to him, somewhat, but was more interested in getting this ribbon tied when he continued his explanation, "And, and I lost my footing and tumbled into Lacey and knocked her off of the dock and into the river with me falling in behind her." I was so surprised at Tylar's logical explanation that I'm sure the expression Pappy saw on my face gave us away.

He looked down on the dock and said, "It was a right smart thing planning ahead by taking your shoes and socks off when you got to the dock, you know, just incase something so unforeseen as this might happen."

There was one thing Tylar needed to know and now was as good a time as any to let him in on it. "Tylar, my Pappy never needs to hear anything but the truth." I stood to my feet and brushed the sand that came from the rock off of the back of my jumper. "Come on, Pappy needs our help and he is just the man to come to our rescue."

We climbed out of the river and up to the dock where Pappy was. "The truth is, Pappy, we let the fun of the river get the best of us and I had to show Tylar how to fly."

"Your mom would ground you for eternity if she had stumbled upon you two. He called you a chicken, didn't he? Tylar, never call her a chicken. It gets her in more trouble. She has her grandmother's determination. That's how I got the woman to marry me. One little 'bwak, bwak,' and she was mine."

"Oh Pappy, help us get out of this mess and we'll help you get that ox out of the ditch."

"Okay, here's the plan. Your mothers know I was coming after you so you go the long way around and get in the truck. I'll go in and tell them I have found you and if anyone looks out they'll see you in the truck. Somehow I'll keep them away from that old truck and we'll go to the house and iron those wrinkles out. I'm not about to ask how *those* got there, but no one will know a thing about you swimming in your good clothes or how you tried to hide it. Then we'll go to the barn and get Silas and the others to get those beds out of the barn and then we'll all go to the little house on the river and set them up. I need to talk to you about that, but we'll talk about it on the way. Now get your shoes on and get to the truck as soon as you can. Oh, and do something with your hair."

Tylar was already putting his shoes on while I hugged the greatest man in the world and watched him start walking down the path to my house. Tylar handed me my shoes and while I was putting them on he was pulling my hair out of my eyes trying to put the clip with the limp bow back in the place he remembered it being. I sat still for a moment while he locked the clip and thought how nice it was to have someone take care of me like I always did for Willie.

"Okay, that looks great," and he reached for my foot, "You tie that one and I'll tie this one. Take my hand 'cause we've got to run if we're gonna get to that truck before your Pappy tells them we're already in it!" He jerked me to my feet and we ran with the wind as fast as we could, panting like wild dogs when we reached the truck.

We didn't see anyone and we were sure no one saw us. In what seemed like seconds, we saw Pappy and Nanny standing on the front porch. Nanny was putting Pappy's hat on his head while Pappy took her into his arms to say his good-byes. Mother joined Nanny on the porch as Pappy headed down the steps toward the truck. Then Nanny and Mother walked to the porch railing to wave at Tylar and me. We were waving back feeling relieved that they were not coming off that porch when Miss Marge opened the door on the passenger side. I screamed and we both jumped at the same time. Pappy had reached the truck, too, and got in just in time to hear Miss Marge say, "What happened to you two and when will you be back. We need to get home before too late."

Pappy answered her, "Nothing happened to them. You don't see what you think you are seeing. I'm not sure when we will be back. Why don't you just leave Tylar with us tonight? We'll take him with us to church and he and Lacey can spend the day together tomorrow. Ya'll are coming back for Sunday dinner anyway."

"But he doesn't have any thing to wear except what he has on and look at those pants."

"Remember, he looks great, you don't see what you think you see. The sooner we get going the sooner he will be back to normal. Just say he can stay."

"Tylar, do you want to stay?"

"Oh, yes Mom, can I?"

"Okay. We'll be back to get you tomorrow. Please, be a good boy."

"I will. Thanks."

She reached in and gave him a hug and kiss and said, "I love you."

"Me too, *Mom*."

Pappy cranked the truck when he saw my mother coming off of the porch asking if everything was okay. He looked at Miss Marge and said, "Let them know that there's nothing wrong or different here, okay, and we'll see you tomorrow." Miss Marge started waving my mother off saying all was fine as we drove away from my house.

"I told your mother that you might get your jumper dirty so she packed you a change of clothes." He reached under his arm and laid my overalls and a shirt on my lap. "We're going to pick up Jake to help us out and Miss Sally is getting a change of clothes for Tylar. Jake's a little bit bigger than you Tylar, but Sally says she's keeping his old clothes for Lacey's brother, Willie. Surely we'll find something to fit you, Tylar. Hope you two see what trouble we're all going to to keep your mother from finding out what mischief her daughter and new neighbor can get into. After the baby is born she will be able to handle things better, maybe. That's something else we need to talk about." And we pulled into Sally's driveway.

Jake was waiting on the porch with his new puppy, Bullet. They both came out to meet us. "That's some hair-do you got there, Carrot. Mom's waiting inside with a hairbrush to fix that, if it can be fixed. Hi, Jake Foresight."

"Hi, Tylar Lane," and they shook hands as Tylar got out of the truck.

Jake looked at me and said, "Might as well bring your change of clothes in and change here while I find something for Tylar." Then he wrapped his arm around Tylar's shoulders as they walked toward the house. "And you can tell me all about how you got Lacey to go swimming in her good clothes," looking back over his shoulder at me, "after her mother told her she was not to even go near the river today." Tylar looked back at me with a questioned expression.

I jumped out of the truck with my clothes and said, "That was this morning, Jake, she said we could go while Willie was asleep."

"I want to hear Tylar's version of the story. Come on, follow me. How 'bout those wrinkles, 'ol chap? Come tell me all about how you two got those. "

I mumbled as I gathered up the overalls falling out of my arms, "Oh, for once, just shut up, Jake."

Pappy was snickering behind me as we all made our way into the house. Sally was waiting for me with a brush in her hand and she laughed hysterically when she saw me. I didn't want her to brush my hair because Tylar had fixed it, but when I suggested that it was fine she took me to her room and sat me before her mirror. All I could think to say as I looked in the mirror was, "Well, he did try." Sally just laughed.

She ironed out the ribbon while I changed my clothes. She told me to just leave them with her so she could wash them and get them back to me later. It was nice having so many motherly friends. I had always felt a gentleness and warmth in Sally's home. Even with Jake and his teasing. She was family, she and her children. My Pa and Jake were like father and son since Jake didn't have his own father at home raising him and Pa loved having a young boy to teach his passions to. Even Pappy and Nanny loved Sally and her family as if they were theirs. As I sat at her dressing table watching Sally brush my hair I noticed the picture of her and her husband on their wedding day. The silver frame had been engraved with "Dr. & Mrs. Simon Jude Foresight, March 1st 1929" along the bottom of the frame. She was beautiful and he was lovingly looking into her eyes. I picked the picture up and looked closer. "Sally, how did you know you loved him and no one else?"

"I didn't at first. One day he touched my arm in a very tender way and something inside of me just melted."

"Why was he touching your arm?"

"I burned it on the stove one morning before work and I put some butter on it, but it still hurt. We were filling out a patient's chart when he noticed the burn. He reached out and took my arm and asked me if it hurt? I was frozen and couldn't answer him. I just stared into his eyes and he into mine just like you see in that picture. Whenever he is in the room that's all I can do. Well, he bandaged my arm and I didn't even know he was doing it. I still get swimmy headed thinking about him. There will never be anyone else for me. He is my life. Sometimes I think I can't wait for him to come home, but I can't think of doing anything else."

I tried to figure out what she was talking about and how she was feeling. I shine inside when my Pappy's in the room and I can't think of doing anything other than waiting on Willie, but somehow I didn't think her feelings were anything I had ever experienced.

We found Pappy and the boys in the kitchen eating pie when Sally had me all dressed and groomed. She said she would iron Tylar's pants and shirt and we could pick them up when we brought Jake home so Tylar would have something to wear tomorrow to church. I took one of the fried apple pies with me and we headed out to the truck. Sally stopped me and whispered, "Your Pappy's going to need your help for a few weeks while he makes some adjustments in his life. He'll tell you all about it on the way to his house so don't show him you're upset when he tells you the news."

"I already know. I heard them talking in the living room. Theodore is not my favorite cousin, but he is my Pappy's grandson so I'll try to get along."

"Good girl," and she gave me a hug as she said, "be careful and have fun." Then she shouted so all could hear, "Don't let Jake give you a hard time. Take care of him, Pappy, if he doesn't behave." Those words gave me plenty of ammunition if Jake's teasing got on my nerves.

We got the beds set up in the little house and Tylar and Jake brought in wood for the stove. They also stacked some wood up on the back porch in case it got a little nippy during the night. Pappy had brought some eggs, bread, milk, butter and jam from his house for Penny and her children's breakfast. Pappy said they would not be coming to church with us in the morning so she could fix their own breakfast. That pleased me; however, they would be joining us for dinner where I would be expected to share my new friend with Theodore. Somehow, I had to keep from showing my disappointment to Pappy.

We arrived back at my house after dark. Tylar's parents and brother were already gone. His sister, Ruthy, was asleep on my bed. She, too, was going to stay the night with us and go to church in the morning. I was really excited about them spending the night, but I knew I would never sleep. I wasn't very fond of Sunday School because my teacher wasn't someone who should be working with children. I liked choir and preaching because I could sing in choir and draw during preaching. Preacher Burton was a soft-spoken man who loved children. He never fussed at us like my Sunday School teacher did, although, she always acted different when ever there was a guest in our class. There would be two guests so maybe she'd be twice as nice.

The morning came quickly after I finally fell asleep. I was tired, but excited about meeting my day. I had a hard time falling asleep, because I couldn't stop thinking about Tylar asking when we were going to see an ox. I didn't laugh when he asked the question, I simply told him he would be introduced to the ox tomorrow at dinner. He never said it, but I'm sure he thought we were all crazy once he met the ox and her family. At the least, I'm sure it crossed his mind.

Mother was dressed and in the kitchen and Pa was sitting in the library reading the paper when I made my way down the back stairs. "Oh, Lacey. You're going to have to pick out your own dress for church today. I'm way too busy with breakfast. Your Nanny and Pappy will be here soon to eat with us. Can you take the coffee server into the library for your pa? Then you need to get back up stairs and get dressed. Get your brother, Tylar and Ruthy up and find a dress for Ruthy to wear, too. Can you do all that for me? You're such a big girl and I need you so much, but sometimes I wonder if I'm not expecting too much from you."

"No Ma'am, I can do it."

I picked up the silver tray with the coffee service on it and took it in to Pa. "Good morning my Punkin.' Are you well rested? You have a big day ahead of you again."

"I think I am."

Pa held his arms out for me. "Bear hug. Um, that feels so good. You have the best hugs. Well, did you sleep well?" I jumped up on his lap and laid my head on his shoulder as he hugged me tight once again then bounced me on his knee. "You're almost too heavy for me to bounce, but you will never be too big for me to hold in my lap. How do you like our new neighbors? Kinda fun having them spend the night the first day you meet them, huh?"

"Yeah. I don't know Ruthy at all. I spent my time yesterday with Tylar. I'm looking forward to getting to know Ruthy, too. She's just a year younger than me. If her family goes to our church she will be in my Sunday School class. There are only three of us now."

"Well of course she will come to our church. What other church would they go to?"

"Pappy said there was a new church in town and a man named Johnny Kale Butler was paying for the church to be built."

Pa stiffened and sat me up off of his shoulder saying, "Your Pappy told you that?"

"Well, some of it. He told me there was a new church being built. Tylar told me that it was Mr. Butler who had the money to build the church and his best friend was in school learning how to preach so Mr. Butler had asked him to come here to preach in his church. Mr. Butler is Mr. Collier's boss and Tylar likes him a lot. That's how Tylar remembered my name when he first met me, 'cause he said it sounded like Mr. Butler's. Do you think it does, Pa?"

"No. Not really," and he laid my head back on his shoulder. "Only that you both have the same middle name, but lots of people have names the same."

"Lacey, you will never be ready for church laying in your Pa's arms all morning."

"Oh Mother, I'm so sorry. I forgot. Guess I'm not as grown up as I thought I was." I jumped out of Pa's lap and ran toward the front staircase. "Sorry Mother, really I am."

"Abigail, if you would let me hire some help for you around here you wouldn't have to employ your own children . . ."

"William, they need to grow up knowing how to do things for themselves. Just because you want to spoil me doesn't mean there is a man waiting in the wings who can afford to spoil my daughter. Just hurry up, Lacey, and get back down here before your Pappy gets here."

"Yes Ma'am," and I ran as fast as I could to Willie's room. Tylar was already up and dressed. He was coaxing Willie's socks and shoes on him having already put on his suit pants and dress shirt. "My Mother will be so impressed. I'm afraid I've already let her down this morning with my laziness. She is expecting us to be late to breakfast and church all because I spent too much time being held like a baby in my Pa's arms this morning."

"Ruthy came in, woke me up and helped get Willie dressed, all but the socks and shoes, so I'm afraid I can't take all the credit. She's looking for you now so you can tell her what dress to wear."

"Guess I better find her. It must be nice having a sister who is old enough to help you out. I can't tell you how nice it would be to have you around all the time."

"Well, it won't be long now, I'll be right down the road."

"Yeah. Well anyway, thanks," and I turned to find Ruthy when he stopped me with his words.

"Oh, by the way, good morning."

I looked back into the room and said, "And good morning to you, too, Tylar Lane."

Willie was taking to Ruthy and Tylar like a cat to milk. Tylar was able to pick Willie up and take him from one room to another without too much fuss. He said the trick was to get him to look at you and keep his attention until you got him into the room where you wanted to go. That way he didn't realize he was changing scenery.

We were all in our places at the table before Nanny and Pappy got to the house. Mother was impressed. I could tell she liked Tylar as much as I did, though not for the same reasons. He was helpful with Willie and that always won over Mother's heart. I was absorbed by Tylar's calmness. His ability to see me for me and not expect me to be like someone else just because I was a girl and they were a girl, or I was a redhead and they were a redhead, or I was a Rutledge and they were a Rutledge. Tylar was the same to everyone at all times. That's what made him very different from most people I had met. Very different from the lady I was soon going to introduce him to in my Sunday School class. As long as he was my visitor he would be able to stay in my class even though he was two years older. Whenever we turned into a teenager we were separated into an all-boy and all-girl class. I didn't like the thought of us ever being separated, though I was looking forward to moving into a different class with a different teacher.

On this day Miss Franklin was on her best behavior. She was cordial toward Ruthy and Tylar asking all kinds of questions about their family and where they were moving from. She almost didn't get to her lesson for all the questions. The rest of us very quietly colored our picture of Jesus holding the little lamb in his arms standing in a flock of sheep. We were all wishing and probably praying that she would never get to her lesson. She had a way of making us all feel worthless and guilty, though we never quite knew what we had done wrong.

However, on this day she did manage to find time to tell us, "Jesus wants to hold you in his arms like He is holding this little lamb in this picture, but most of you will never make that worthy decision to be called one of His sheep. Narrow is the way to life, wide is the road to destruction. You better get off that road of sin and get right with the Lord. All you children have lied to your parents and hidden things from them. I know you have because the Bible tells me that all have sinned and fallen short of the glory of God. And it also says that what is done in secret will be brought out in the light. You *will* be found out."

Tylar darted his eyes toward me and my heart stopped beating as Miss Franklin continued, "You better repent before you are thrown into the lake of fire. God can't love a child full of lies and secrets, so stop your lying today before it's too late."

The end of class warning bell rang and we started gathering up our crayons and scissors. Miss Franklin was telling Ruthy how much she liked having her in our class and to please come back and bring her brother. Tylar was with me over at the coat rack where I had hung my pocket book and sweater. He was getting Ruthy's sweater and whispering in my ear, "What do you think about what she said about lying and going to a fiery lake because you had secrets?"

"Is that what she was saying?"

"I'm pretty sure."

"Well, I have to talk to my Pappy. He can ask God if we're going to a fiery lake or not."

"Will he know?"

"Who? Pappy or God?"

"Either one!"

"If Pappy doesn't know he will find out for us. We'll ask him right after we get home."

Miss Franklin startled us with her words, "Lacey! Your grandfather is here to get you and your friends. Hello Mr. Hawthorne."

"We can ask him now," Tylar whispered.

"Better wait till we get home."

Miss Franklin walked over to us with a clenched smile and said, "Come on children. This is rude of you to keep your family waiting," as she grabbed the hair on the back of my head, twisted me around and leaned in close to my ear. "Go and stop being brats."

"Yes, Miss Franklin," and we ran to Pappy waiting outside the door with Ruthy.

After lunch Tylar and I begged Pappy to come fishing with us instead of taking a Sunday nap. He finally gave in and came with us to the river. We could hardly wait to get there before sharing any of the things Miss Franklin had said. After we got the bait on the hooks and the line in the water we sat down on both sides of Pappy.

"Mr. Hawthorne, Lacey and I have a question to ask you. It's real important to us and we need you to listen to all of it before you answer."

"Okay Tylar, but first you have to promise me that you will stop calling me Mr. Hawthorne and call me Pappy like my family or call me A.J. like my friends."

"What does A.J. stand for?"

"Alvin Jeremiah. Jeremiah was my father's name. Don't know where Alvin came from. Never liked it much, but let my first wife name our son Alvin. Theodore is his middle name. She named him that after her side of the family. That's why Penny named her son Theodore after his father, my son. Oh, never mind all that, you don't even know Penny."

"Well, I know who she is. Lacey told me. All that's a little bit complicated so if you don't mind someone who is a friend and not in your family calling you Pappy I would be more comfortable with that."

"Pappy it is. Now what's your question?"

"Today Miss Franklin said something that sort of shook me and Lacey up. I don't know much about the Bible so I don't know if what she said the Bible says is right or not. When we got into the preaching time I tried to remember what she said and wrote it down." Tylar reached into his pocket and pulled out a slip of paper. There was a tug at my line, but I wanted to see what Tylar had written on the paper so I wound my line in.

"She said that we had lied and had hidden stuff from our parents and we would go to a lake full of fire if we didn't bring it out in the light 'cause God would bring it up and tell everybody and Jesus couldn't hold us in His arms like the little sheep because we weren't worthy of God's glory now that we had sinned and come up short and God can't love us now that we are liars. Is all this true?"

Pappy just sat looking at his pole.

"Well Pappy, is that true?"

"Is that what she told you, Lacey?"

"I'm not sure that he has said it exactly like her, but that's real close. I don't think she said we weren't worthy, but more like we would never make a worthy decision to be one of Jesus' lambs. And she said we had to repent before we were thrown into that lake. She did say that God can't love us because we were full of lies and secrets. Pappy, I thought God loved me and said I was perfect just like I am."

Pappy rubbed his fingers over his lips and chin. "Tylar, have you and your family been in church?"

"Not really. We always moved around too much and after Dad and Garry died Mom was just too sad. My grandmother told her that's just where she needed to be, but she didn't like how people made over her and pitied us."

Pappy sat in silence and we sat with him. I put my line back in the water and watched the tip of my pole. I wasn't sure, but I felt like Pappy was praying and asking God what He thought about it all. He just didn't want to pray out loud in front of Tylar in case it might scare him. We waited for what seemed like hours then finally Pappy cleared his throat.

"I'm afraid that we both have lied to you. I knew I would have to set you straight, Lacey, once you got older and started asking questions. Funny how a little trouble in our lives makes us more anxious to get the answers. I understand where she has gotten her interpretation, but her dislike of you children has caused her to present the gospel in a way that is just short of frightening. The Gospel stands for "good news." Being thrown in a lake of fire don't sound much like good news, does it Tylar?" Pappy laughed.

"Most people don't know that Miss Franklin is a Miss by choice. She took it to heart Paul's words in the New Testament when he said it is better not to marry if you can keep from it because those who marry will have many troubles. Her long time beau got tired of chasing her and trying to convince her otherwise. He married a beautiful woman and they raised four beautiful children. Her bitterness about her choice has haunted her. Now she's convinced she's given up more than anyone else to serve God and that she has somehow earned the right to judge everyone's sin. Instead of letting that mothering instinct bring her joy when she is in the presence of children, she covers her longing by treating children with contempt.

"I, on the other hand, have not done the Word of God any justice because of my love for you. I suppose that it's time to tell you the simple facts about God and what He thinks about both of you. Let me say this first, Lacey and Tylar, until you make that decision she was talking about, the decision to ask Jesus into you heart and let Him be in control of your life, He doesn't see you as perfect. After you do ask Him into your heart, no matter what you do he will love you and see you as perfect. But see, after you let Him have control of your life, you won't be so quick to do something that isn't what He would like. Some people think you have to do stuff for God to be pleasing to Him. You know, like Miss Franklin thinks she has to teach Sunday School so God will love her. Even though her gift or talent is not teaching, and she's bitter toward children, she thinks she has to be unhappily serving the Lord to be loved by Him. That's not at all true. God isn't pleased with her sacrifice when her heart isn't in it. Do you see the love of Jesus in Miss Franklin? Of course not. No one does, because she's so unhappy serving Jesus. God is not a dictator like Hitler forcing people to do things they aren't comfortable with. No one is happy in those kind of conditions. God wants us to love Him as much as He loves us. It's a heart thing, not a bunch of works."

"How do we know how much God loves us?"

"Tylar, I can only put it simply and I hope I can help you and Lacey see how easy it is to just believe it. God is perfect. He never has done anything wrong or by mistake, but man was created to have a will. A will to do anything he wanted to do. Except God asked them not to do one thing. Don't eat the fruit of a certain tree. It was not like all the rest. He said you can have all the rest, but it's best for you if you do not eat from this tree. They listened to the devil and he tricked them into believing that God had not told them not to eat the fruit from that tree.

"Did God make that tree?"

"Of course. God made everything and He made that tree because He is not a liar."

"What do you mean?"

"God wanted man and woman to have a choice. Now, if He had never given them anything to choose about, then He would have been just like Hitler giving no choices and being a dictator. Man and woman decided to listen to the devil and chose to disobey God and eat the fruit. The Bible says that God can't look at sin, and disobedience is a sin."

"Only when you disobey God?"

"No Tylar, in the eyes of God, it's a sin to disobey your parents, too."

"So she *is* right. We're going in the lake!"

Pappy chuckled, "No. Let me tell you the rest. God had to leave the earth because man had sin in their minds now. When they ate the fruit it caused them to have the knowledge of good and evil, right and wrong. God is still telling us today not to eat that fruit. It's kind of like it represented disobedience, or even the wrong crowd. Like when Jake and Theodore get together. Jake's a pretty good boy till he gets around Theodore and then he kind of falls into doing whatever bad stuff Theodore's getting into. You two got away with yesterday's swim, even though, I know and Sally knows and even your mom knows a little bit about something going on, Tylar, but you still got away without paying the price of a good spanking or being grounded for a while. Each time you do something wrong and get away with it, it's easier to do it again. You'll try doing some other things that are wrong just because you got away with this one. I probably need to be a little stricter, but anyway. When man and woman disobeyed God the first time, God said they would now die. Well, they didn't die right then, so it was easy to forget a punishment that never came. Soon they disobeyed again and again, and God knew they would, so He had to leave their presence.

"Why did He have to leave?"

"Well, I guess He couldn't see them anyway because of their sin. One minute He knew right where they were and the next He was saying, 'Adam! Adam Where are you?' Can you two imagine God walking around with you everyday? That's what man and woman had till that first sin. As time went on, people forgot all about God. We all think death is for someone else, not us. But, it is appointed to each one of us to die an earthly death, if Jesus doesn't come get us before then. I never thought my wife would die when we were so young. She loved Jesus with all her heart and soul, but as I watched her die, I knew God wanted me to see how damaging sin is to our soul because death is an ugly thing. There is nothing graceful or honorable about it. I know she left this world and went to be with Jesus immediately after she died. Even though she died with dignity, she suffered and it was painful for her and those closest to her. Sometimes I wonder if someone received Jesus at a very young age, having done little sinning, if their death would be more peaceful and not so ugly. I don't have any reason to think that, because the Bible says we all have been born into sin. The desire to be selfish or cover up stuff we don't want someone else to know about us, you know, to pretend we are better than we really are is automatic because we are born that way. If we could just realize that the things we want to hide are the very things that would help others understand who we are and why we act like we do. Like Miss Franklin. I understand her, but most people don't know what she gave up, therefore, they see her as a hateful woman, selfish and conceited. She could be a great asset to the Kingdom of God if she would just admit her mistake, learn from it and share it with others, but that's not something that comes natural.

"Even small babies, shortly after they learn to say "Dada," learn the words "mine" and "no" as they clutch a toy that's being threatened of distribution. Sharing something so personal with another child is out of the question without a temper tantrum and then comes a crushing broken heart. As I think about it, we still react the same way. When your grandmother opens up some hidden secret emotion that's in me, telling me why I've reacted about something the way I did, she has crept into that place I thought I could hid from the world forever. First I pitch a fit in shock that she could think I would have something so awful in me. Then usually, not in her presence because I haven't quite gotten over the desire to be proud still, but alone with Jesus, I fall apart with shame and brokenness.

"That part is in God's plan, the brokenness. He's trying to get us to let Him expose those hidden lies and sins. That's how we begin the process of dying to ourselves and what *we* want. After Adam and Eve ate that fruit, all of us were given the knowledge of how to sin. It's been passed down through the generations from our parents and their parents and those who came before. Each one of us has to decide, once we understand how wrong it is to be selfish, as to whether or not we are going to continue being deceitful. Whatever we decide, and whether we decide to be like Jesus when we're young or old, we deserve no different punishment than that handed to Adam and Eve."

Tylar broke Pappy's thinking out loud with a question. "Who are Adam and Eve?"

"Those are the names of the first people God made."

"That's right, Lacey. There was a lot of meanness in the world, much like today, and God heard a few people crying out for a savior to come and walk with them, to let them know there is a God. But, God couldn't come Himself because of the sin in the hearts of the people. Remember, He can't look at sin, so He sent a part of Himself to the earth by asking a young girl to be the mother of His son. Her name was Mary and she said 'yes' to God, something we all need to be more willing to do. Because God can do all things, He sent a baby to Mary's stomach, His baby. He had a plan for His son to experience everything that Adam and Eve and all the people after them had experienced. If Jesus, His son, still wanted people to exist after living for a time with man and all our meanness, then God would carry out the plan. Even Jesus had a choice whether or not to save man. People were awful to Jesus, but there were a few who loved Him and listened to His teachings of right and wrong and who God is.

"This part gets kind of hard to explain. Whenever anyone sinned there was a death of some kind to atone that sin. That means, make it right. The way the people did this was, once a year a priest would kill an animal and pour the blood of that animal on a box where some miracles of God were kept. The top of that box was called 'the mercy seat,' because God didn't get tired of our disobedience and kill us all. Moses called the chair his brother sculpted on the top of the box 'God's mercy seat.' This box, called the 'Ark of the Covenant,' was kept in a very special place because God dwelt in and on this box. It was very holy and not just anybody could come into this room or touch this box. When an animal was killed and the blood poured on the mercy seat, if it was pleasing to God, the people were forgiven of the sins they had committed against God and man. Every year they had to kill an animal. When Jesus came to live on the earth He had a mission. He came to be tempted by the devil, just like man, but unlike man, Jesus did not fall for the temptation and sin.

"He was hated by the religious crowd who thought works were the only way to God's heart. Jesus was telling them that God wanted them to love Him because they wanted to, not work for Him because they had to. When they asked Him why he thought He knew so much He replied that He was the Son of God and He had been sent to be the Savior of the world. So they plotted to kill Him. He was offering the people a way to freedom from all these do's and don'ts that the church had put on them and the government had tried to make impossible for the people. The government wanted the people to worship them and the religious crowd wanted the people to worship them. There was a very high tax that the government got from the people, but the church could only get money from the people if they told them God was not pleased with them unless they brought their best cattle, goats or sheep to the churches. If they didn't have animals to bring, then the church would sell the people an animal and charge them way too much money. This kind of robbery makes God crazy. Taking advantage of the poor, helpless, sick and weak is something our churches are guilty of still today. As a church we should be giving to the people instead of asking them to buy a miracle. That's why I don't get involved with those bake sales and tent revivals. If I've got it and you need it, well, then I say we both have what we need. If you need a pie, I know how to cook it, and God has given me the stuff to mix it up, then why should I charge you for this blessing from God. If we need money for the church, then tell the people and let's see what we have, don't take from the poor and weak by promising them something only God can give them.

"Jesus let us and the religious crowd know what He thought about preachers robbing their congregations by turning the money changer's table over in one of the temples. Jesus had gone too far in the eyes of those who were benefiting from this scheme. The high priest went to the man in charge of the government and asked for Jesus to be killed. They never could have killed Him if He had not chosen to give up His life. Jesus knew that the only atonement for man's sin that would do away with all other sacrifices was for a sinless man to shed His blood on the mercy seat of God. People say that the Jews killed Jesus, but they didn't. Others say we all did it because of our sin, but Jesus gave up His life for all men to have eternal life. There is a place where we go when we die. One is called the lake of fire, one is called heaven. Those who believe that Jesus is the Son of God and call on His name, with their heart not their works, will be saved from the lake of fire. It's that simple. If you don't believe with your heart, and it's only with your head, you will always be doing works that mean nothing to anyone. The temptation to sin will sooner or later overcome you. Jesus said you must be born again, have a changed heart, want to stop doing things for yourself like those in the world and do things for others like Jesus did. It's about dying to what you want and wanting what God wants. It's not easy to do, but He will help you overcome those things we shouldn't do.

"To answer your question as to how much God loves us, well I don't know really, but it's a lot. Just think about this. God is so incredible, so wonderful and so loving that Jesus wanted us to be able to be a part of what He sees as the greatest thing going. He gave his life in the cruelest way to make sure we could enjoy the presence of God with Him.

"I've known Jesus as a personal friend for forty years now. I was a couple years older than you, Tylar, when I gave my life to Him. I've never regretted it. Once you and Lacey think on what I've told you and you come to that same decision, you'll never regret it either."

We sat kind of still the rest of the day watching our poles and asking a few questions when our minds came to one while we processed what Pappy had told us. One thing for sure, after Pappy told us how Jesus died, we had a greater respect for this man. I was a bit heartbroken to find out that God didn't really think I was as perfect as Pappy had always told me, but I still had a chance to make that right. I would think about it some more and even talk to Tylar about his feelings on the subject, but I would never leave my understanding of God up to Miss Franklin again. I would pray for her to do what God wanted her to do instead of doing things she hated 'cause she thought she was serving God.

I didn't understand a lot about serving God, but I did know about pretending to like doing things you don't like doing. I understood about hiding things and bad feelings so you don't have to face what makes you have them. Like Theodore. I was wondering how I was going to handle him when he got here for dinner. I wanted this time with my friend and Pappy to last as long as possible. There was a beautiful peace that had come over us on that dock. I didn't want anything to take that away and Theodore did not bring peace.

When I thought of Theodore, that uneasy feeling that something was wrong came over me again. I just couldn't figure out where it came from or what it meant. Would I be able to pull it out and face it one day? Was it even important enough to God for me to be broken over it?

I was startled by the sudden clash of the dinner bell ringing from the back porch. Pappy stretched out his legs with a long yawn. Tylar wrapped his line around his pole and I pulled the stringer of fish up from the river. Pappy had caught two, Tylar caught three and I caught one, the smallest one. I loved to sit and fish, but I wasn't one to catch a lot.

We all three hated to see this fishing trip end even with the growling in our stomachs. Now that we knew there was a meal being served we had to give it up and head back to the house. In my heart I was hoping that for some reason Penny and family would not be able to come for dinner. Surely they needed to arrange things in their new home or something. I remembered that there wasn't much food in their house. Today being Sunday there wasn't a store open to buy groceries. Even if it wasn't Sunday, I knew Penny would never walk to a store for anything. She would expect Pappy to drive her and buy what she wanted. No, there was no way that Penny and family would not be in my house for Sunday dinner.

Pappy asked Tylar to take the fish to the cool pond. That was the name we gave the spring fed shallow cement pond Pa built in the backyard with about thirty, two foot tall rocks around it to keep Willie from falling in. That's where we kept our catch so they would be fresh when Mother wanted to cook fish for super.

"I need to talk to you, Lacey, before we go in to dinner. Tylar, just turn those fish loose and we'll be up at the cool pond in a minute."

"Yes Sir, Mr. Pappy. See ya'll in a minute."

"Lacey, I know this evening is going to be difficult for you, and me, with Penny and the kids here, but we've got to find a way to overcome what is driving us to dislike them. It's all about what we were just talking about earlier. Penny and Theodore, especially, are very pushy people. They want everything their way, and when they want it. There is never any consideration of someone else. It's not that they don't like you or me or any one else. They're that same way with each other and I know they love each other. Penny has told all of us, time and time again, how she hates God for taking her father away. God didn't take her father. Her father chose to leave. She has chosen to blame God for her problems and she's become someone that is very hard to be around. Selfishness is as ugly as death, but she doesn't know any better. We are selfish, too, at times. We have to recognize it in us and say we're sorry or make up for it. She and Theodore don't know they are so undesirable when they demand us to cater to their needs. Somehow we must teach them to show respect, and teach it to them with the love that Jesus has shown us if we're ever going to help them be better people. I'm not going to let them walk all over us, or let Penny start dictating to us how things are going to be. All of my family is important to me and they will have to learn to act in a way that's best for everyone so they can be a part of this family."

"And we want that, Pappy?"

"Yes, Punkin.' We want that. We have to be willing to forgive them just like Jesus forgave us and said we were worth dying for."

"I don't think I could die for Theodore."

"Well, maybe not today, but someday you might feel different about him."

"That would be nice, 'cause I don't like what I feel now when I'm around Him."

The dinner bell rang again and I could hear Nanny calling Pappy in that voice that meant, "Come now!" Pappy smiled at me and hugged me tight and with a kiss on my forehead he said, "You are my best girl, next to Nanny Jo, and you always will be. You may have to share me with Theodore more than you want to, but remember that nothing will ever separate our love as long as I'm living."

"And that will be a long time, too, right, Pappy?"

"As long as I can."

I was seated next to my Pappy, who was at the head of the table and Tylar next to me on the other side. Ruthy was next to Tylar and Willie between Ruthy and Mother. Pa was next to Mother seated at the end of the table with Bob Collier on the other side of Pa across from Mother. Margie was next to her husband and Penny was next to her, then Theodore and then Nanny across from me. Mother set a table behind Pa for the younger children: Kimmy, Retta, Abbie Lou and Pauley. Willie had a place set to sit with them, too, but he was so happy playing with Ruthy that Mother didn't want to cause him to get upset by having him leave our table. My place was perfect. I was at the big table, so I heard all that was said, but I was far enough away that no one directed any conversation to me. I would be able to hear Pappy if he said anything under his breath. Those things he said that only I could hear were the most priceless. I wished that Mr. Bob and Miss Marge were sitting where Penny and Theodore were, but as Pappy told me, this was not a perfect world.

From time to time Theodore would look at me, when the adults were busy listening to someone's tale, and he would show me and Tylar his green beans chewed up with his potatoes and then laugh using facial expressions without making a sound. I glanced at Tylar who seemed unmoved by the whole show. His expression almost saying, "Is that the best you can do?" The entertainer was determined to find himself amusing to someone, so he tried the sweet potatoes and macaroni and cheese chewed up together. Then instead of just opening his mouth to show us his meal he hung it off the end of his tongue. That's when Pappy spotted him and in a very low voice Pappy said, "That's enough, Theodore."

Penny heard Pappy, much to my surprise, because she was in one of her long drawn out adventures in Japan when he said it.

"What are you doing, Theodore?"

"Nothing, Mother."

"He knows what he was doing, Penny, and I handled it."

"He's my son, Jeremiah, I'll discipline him without your help."

"This is my family's table. If his manors are unacceptable on this end of it, I will let him know. William will take care of things on his end. You don't need to be involved."

"What did you do, Theodore!"

"I told you, nothing. I don't know what that old man is talking about."

I glared at Theodore and said through clenched teeth, "You ungrateful . . ."

Willie finished my thought as he pointed at Theodore, "Pig, Mommy, pig," and he spit his food out on the table clapping his hands with laughter.

"No, no, Willie," Mother said as she jumped up with her napkin waving, then making it's way into her water glass, then to Willie's face and hands and last to the table. Mother always covered Willie's messes as quick as possible.

Ruthy covered her mouth and started to snicker when Penny said, "You better get your other grandchildren straightened out before you go telling mine what to do. Abigail, did you raise your daughter to be so disrespectful to her guest? She would never be asked to sit at the table with heads of states like Theodore, Kimmy and myself. And I know he's not right in the head, but you would never be able to dine in the places we've been with a child who spits their food across the table like a llama."

I had my fists in a ball wanting to take Theodore outside and show him some respect. I began to slide my chair back and rise to my feet. Tylar apparently could see the blood flushing my face. If a ten-year-old could have a stroke, I would say that I was on the verge. He stood beside me with his arm around my waist and tried to sit me back in my seat.

I stared at Theodore, who continued to shovel food into his mouth, and said, "You tell my grandfather you're sorry for calling him an old man."

"Whatcha gonna do if I don't?"

"I don't need you to fight my battles for me, Lacey. I can handle Theodore."

"But, Pappy!"

"Lacey, remember what we talked about? Now do what Tylar is trying to get you to do and sit down." I plopped down on the chair crossing my arms in disgust.

Tylar went back to his chair nodding his head toward Pappy as he prepared to sit by folding his arm across the lower part of his waist holding the end of his tie from dragging across his plate saying, "Thank you, Sir.... Pappy ... Sir."

The air of arrogance had come back around Penny as she said, "Well, my appetite is gone or maybe I'm just full. Kids, get your plates and bring them to the kitchen. This meal is over." And she got up with her plate grabbing the green beans and stomped toward the kitchen with her nose in the air.

Miss Marge stood up and chased Penny down catching her in time to intercept the green beans from Penny's hand. "I've found that I have just begun. Abbie and Jo Rett have fixed a beautiful meal and I'm planning to eat on it till it's gone. How 'bout you kids?" and she passed the retrieved green beans to Ruthy who was still quite tickled. Then Marge took hold of the mashed potatoes and passed them to Mother, who was patting her neck and forehead with the soiled wet napkin.

Miss Marge continued as she turned to Penny. "I'm sorry that you won't be able to stay, Penny. Lacey and Tylar, will you get their things while Nanny Jo and I show them to the door? Abbie, don't get up we can handle this. Penny, you can just set your plate down right there. We'll get it later."

Then Miss Margie bent over Kimmy who was still sticking jell-o in her mouth. "Oh, Kimmy. I know you look like you are still eating, but your mother is ready to go." Miss Marge picked Kimmy up from the table, jell-o clinging to her bib, and handed her to her mother. "She would be more satisfied with a little bread soaked in milk right before she goes to bed anyway. It was nice seeing you again. Too bad you're in such a hurry. Abbie's desserts look wonderful."

Tylar and I were standing at the door with their things when Marge herded them into the foyer. Nanny was standing behind Marge watching Penny take her sweater and hat from Tylar's arms. I handed Penny her purse and Kimmy's hat as Marge eased them out the door, Theodore in the lead. Penny stopped outside the door, a bit flustered, and looked back at Nanny. I was holding my breath, afraid Nanny would take pity on them and ask them to stay, but she didn't.

Miss Marge closed the door with a huge smile and said, "Let's eat." The three of us ran to the table where we were met with silence that built from a snicker to an all out horse laughing.

Pappy said he would go to Penny and make it right tomorrow. "Today I'm going to enjoy this meal with our new neighbors. And a God sent woman," and he lifted his iced tea glass up in the air and nodded at Miss Marge. "Thank you. It looks like the rest of us have grown tired of Penny and allowed her to rule us without a fight. Some times it takes some new blood to get the old bones fired up again. Here's to great friends and dear family," and with that, we all raised our glasses to each other and the God who brought us together; all but Nanny. She watched at the window as Penny and her children walked down the road leading to the river house.

chapter four

I wouldn't see Tylar and Ruthy until Friday when they moved their beds into their new house. Miss Marge was having the kitchen made larger with a pantry. That meant having the roof extended, something that would take at least a week to complete. The painters had started on Monday painting the bedrooms, living room, hallway and baths so they would be able to move into these rooms on Friday. The plan was that the roof would be on and the new walls in place by the time they moved in, even though they would eat with us till the kitchen was completed.

I had ridden my bike down to their house three times since Sunday, but Tylar and his family were not there. It was only Wednesday, but it seemed like three weeks had passed. I didn't want to do anything. I sat mostly on the porch watching the road looking for their Chevy to go by while I listened to the radio Mother had playing in the kitchen window. There were plenty of chores to do and I did them, although, I didn't remember.

Pa was working on Uncle Trell and Aunt Gail's hardware store, making it larger so they could start selling hardware again. Jeffery Cantrell Hawthorne was born a year after my mother. We called him "Trell" for short. He married Gail Satterfield in 1940. I was five and big enough to be their flower girl. They gave birth to a son named Jeffery Samuel, called Sammy, who was three. Aunt Gail was expecting another baby any day. Her due date was before Mother's, according to Sally. We hadn't seen her in a while, because she'd been so sick. She and Uncle Trell didn't make it to the cook-out for the Collier's, but Nanny sent a plate.

The hardware store was changed into a machine shop for small parts needed in a defense plant up north after the U.S. got involved in the war. Now they were making some parts for the big looms used at the mills where cloth was made for tents and canvas truck covers. When they started the loom parts the store was no longer big enough for hardware. Most people couldn't buy anything new anyway, so they sold the hardware they had for almost nothing to make room for the machine shop. However, things were better for most families, still struggling to get ahead, but at least most people were able to make a house payment and buy some groceries.

Pa was adding the hardware store to the side of Uncle Trell's old store. There was a freshly painted sign in our back yard ready to be hung reading, "J.C. Hawthorne's Hardware." The sign had been delivered, but the building wasn't anywhere near ready for a sign. However, I sure hoped the roof on the kitchen at the Collier's would be finished enough for them to move in on Friday.

I hadn't felt like leaving the porch to go to the river since the Collier's drove out of my driveway Sunday evening, but I was starting to get so bored I left the porch swing headed to the dock. It was the only place I ever felt completely content which made me wonder why I hadn't thought of it earlier. But, loneliness causes you to forget even those things that bring you pure joy, and my heart had withered from the empty time that seemed suspended out of reach.

At the dock I remembered our time with Pappy fishing on Sunday. I clung to the railing realizing that Willie, Abbie Lou and Retta had followed me off the porch and down to the river. Their bare feet slapped the water when they ran out to the big rock where Tylar and I had laid looking into the clouds waiting for our clothes to dry. I couldn't help but laugh at the thought of Tylar standing there giving Pappy his most heartfelt story of our condition. What would make someone you barely know stand and deliver such a beautiful cover for the sin of someone else? It was that same heart that Pappy said Jesus had for the world. He knew all of us, but He was a stranger to the world. A stranger still to me, I had to admit. Just like Tylar had been to me and Rachel the day he picked her tray up off the floor in the cafeteria and saved her from lots of embarrassment.

Abbie Lou shouted from the river. "Sissy, Sissy! Come down here."

"I will in a little while. I can see you from here."

"Sis-s-sy?"

"If you cry I won't come at all, Willie. Play with your baby sisters. You be the biggest right now. I need to be quiet for a little while longer."

Abbie Lou said, "Sissy's been too quiet for too long, but I won't let him cry."

"You be a good boy, Willie. We'll do something special later today."

"Us too, Lacekale?"

"Yes, you and Retta, too. We'll all do something special."

How I longed for Tylar and Ruthy to be with us when we did this special thing later. I wished Tylar was able to help me come up with a fun special thing to do. I even wished he was able to lift my spirits enough to want to do anything at all. Mother was the first to let me know that wishing never made it so, but dreams do come true, so I changed my thinking to dreams. Dreaming that the Collier's had moved into the house down the road and that Tylar was sitting with me on the dock holding his pole watching me pull in the biggest fish he had ever seen!

My dreams got even bigger as I sat looking out over my siblings enjoy the river. I thought of Jesus once enjoying the calmness of a river and then suddenly facing the hate of others. I thought of my Uncle Alvin and Uncle Marty giving up their lives for strangers in another country. What a sacrifice. A sacrifice I was sure I would never be able to share. Willie was the only sacrifice I had ever encountered. I had never thought of him once as a sacrifice, but I remembered the lady in the drug store asking about Mother and saying that she had made a great sacrifice keeping Willie at home instead of putting him in a full time asylum where someone else could be responsible. Mother had made a sacrifice if that was a choice for her, but somehow I don't think she ever considered him being a burden. Me either. He was Willie and I loved him no matter what he cost me.

I struggled most of the day with the way I felt about my family, and Willie, and my friends, and Jesus. I had a desire to talk to Pappy about the Bible, but something inside of me said to start reading it for myself and talk to Pappy if I didn't understand something. So I thanked God for Jesus and asked Him to help me read the Bible everyday; at least until I got some kind of picture in my mind of Jesus and could come to a decision for myself.

It was getting late in the afternoon. The chickens needed feeding and soon the horses would be brought in from the days plowing. I always wanted to cool the horses down and draw up their water for their night spent in the stall, even when I wasn't feeling like doing anything else.

Pa's horse slept out in the pasture under the stars with the buggy horses. Pa said a working horse needed its sleep and it would get it better in the barn than out where the wild dogs taunted in the night. If I had been a horse I would have wanted to be out in the pasture under the stars and down by the river instead of sleeping, but I was still young and Pa's plow horse was getting close to twenty-two years old. That's not young for a horse.

A large flock of geese flew over my head looking for a place to land for the night. I watched them circle overhead till they started to disappear in the tree branches. I ran off the dock and around the big oak Pappy and Pa had used to attach the dock railing to on the left side. Still looking up, I noticed a piece of paper tacked on the side of the tree. Getting to it was not easy and I almost left it believing it was put so high to keep it out of arms reach of children. But, I never saw myself as one of the children, so I took it down after standing on one of the highest roots stretching up on my tiptoes. I knew I could put it back up out of the children's reach, although it would not be up as high as it once was. I wondered why it was up there and to whom it belonged. As I got my fingertips on the corner, the tack popped out and the paper came down with my hand. I looked for the tack in the grass without quick success so I gave up to read the paper before I burst with curiosity.

It read:

> This is to Lacey Kale Rutledge from her friend Tylar Lane. Thank you for sharing your river and grandfather with me and thank you for calling me your friend. Soon we will be neighbors and fishing pals forever.
> Yours, Tylar

For the first time in my life I welcomed time standing still. Everything was perfect. I had made my first covenant with God, although at the time I didn't know that's what it was, and He seemed closer to me than ever before. I was standing in the most sacred place with the sound of joyous laughter as the water splashed it's self against the rocks in the river bed, the sun reflecting off it's churning, the sky full of the grace of birds in flight, and a friend that had touched me where no one else had was thinking of me, too.

In the distance, I heard the bell on the plow horse coming closer to the house. I turned to see Silas waving to me while he led 'O Plow down one of the furrows. I knew I had let too much time escape so I called to Willie, "Bring up the girls, Willie, and don't cry and pitch a fit, we've got work to do. If you make me come after you I won't let you be a part of our special time tonight."

Willie started to cry very softly. Abbie Lou took his hand and said, "I kin help you outa the river Willie. We's big now."

Willie followed Abbie Lou without pulling back, but the tears still rolled down his cheeks. I was so proud of him. There was no doubt that Willie was growing up and was able to reason in his mind what he had to do. This was a day the doctors had told us would come with time. I could hardly wait to tell Mother, but for now we had chores to do and Willie was going to get his first lesson in drawing up water.

When Willie got to the top of the bank I gave him and our two sisters big hugs for being so grown up. Retta spoke up to let me know that she was still Mother's baby and she didn't want to do chores, so I sent her and Abbie Lou up the back steps to pull off their wet clothes and shoes. Mother waved at me from the pantry window letting me know that she had seen the girls going up the steps. Willie and I headed to the barn to meet with Silas and get our instructions.

The chickens first, then the cats. The horse needed brushing and wood piled in the wood bin. Willie could help with that so Silas took Willie to the woodpile to load up the cart. They took the cart to the back porch and stacked the wood in the wood bin. By the time they got back I had 'O Plow brushed down. I told Silas that this was Willie's big day.

"Silas, I think Willie is ready to learn how to draw up water in a bucket down at the river. We're going to give Willie every opportunity to get this right before we take it from him. Hopefully we won't have to; he'll get it right the first time. Silas, you get a bucket, I'll get a bucket and here Willie, here is your bucket. Now follow us to the river and do everything Silas and I do."

We started walking to the river and Willie stood back at the barn. Silas asked me, "Ya want me ta gets him, Miss Lacey?"

"No Silas, keep walking, and don't look back." And in a very loud voice I said, "You know you can't learn how to draw up water standing at the barn, Silas. You gotta go to the river."

Shortly after, we heard Willie's bucket hitting his legs as he walked closer to us. When we got to the river, Silas and I knelt down on the shore at a deep spot and dropped our buckets into the water. Willie stood behind us holding his bucket.

"No Silas, you can't draw up water for that old horse standing around with the bucket in your hand instead of down in the water."

"No Miss Lacey, ya show can't. No ma'am, gots ta put it in da water."

Willie wiggled in between me and Silas, then knelt down on the shore dropping his bucket into the water. The handle slipped out of his hand, but the water filled the bucket quickly and it lodged between the rocks. Silas and I were frozen. Willie reached out for the handle and pulled with all his might trying to loosen the full bucket from the rock. We pulled our buckets up and stood to our feet. Willie pulled one more time and the bucket came loose. I closed my eyes and silently breathed a sigh of relieve. Silas said out loud, "Thank ye, Lord."

I turned my face toward Silas and just smiled when I felt water from Willie's bucket splash on my leg as he walked passed me headed back to the barn saying, "Can't draw up no water standing at the barn, Silas. Can't draw up no water standing at the barn, Silas." We grabbed our buckets and ran to catch up with Willie. After all, he was supposed to follow us. He was still chanting, "Can't draw up no water standing at the barn, Silas," so we made a song out of it to remember the day as if this day could be forgotten.

"'O Plow had three buckets of water tonight, Mother." I patted Willie on the head as Retta asked, "Won't he wet the bed with all that water to drink?"

Mother just cried while she rocked Willie in her arms and Pa pretended he was laughing with tears at Retta's joke, but I knew he was moved by what Willie had accomplished. And I was proud that Willie had finally showed us what I had always known was in him. There was no stopping him now that he had broken out of that cell his mind had been captive in.

After supper I took Abbie Lou, Retta and Willie out on the front porch for a story before we had to get ready for bed. They all loved for me to read to them and they were so excited when I told them this was their "something special" I had promised them at the river. But, the most special part was that I was not going to read them just any story, but I was going to read to them from the Bible and I would be reading it every night if they wanted to listen. They thought, as I had once, that the Bible was only for grown-ups so they were thrilled that they would get to hear a grown-up story. I didn't know where to start so I went to the beginning. That's where I always started when I read any other book.

I read the first chapter in Genesis before I lifted my eyes and saw Retta asleep in Abbie Lou's lap. "Keep reading 'bout God and the animals, Lacekale. She ain't too heavy for me."

I lifted Retta up and put her on the glider. "Come on up here with me in the swing, Abbie Lou. You want to get up here, too, Willie?" He just shook his head and stayed in his rocking chair. I picked up reading with the second chapter.

When I finished with, "And they were both naked, the man and his wife, and they were not ashamed," Abbie Lou laughed.

"Are you sure, Lacekale, they was naked like Mother says I am when I'm taking a bath? Were they taking a bath?"

"I guess they took baths, but this is saying they lived without clothes, I think. Let's keep reading, want to?"

"Yeah."

"How 'bout you, Willie?" He just nodded. I read on to the end of the third chapter. I was beginning to get tired so I told them we had to stop. I had read some words I didn't understand and I wanted to look them up in the dictionary before I went to bed.

"Lacekale, did God really run that man outta his home?"

"The Bible says He did, so I'm sure He did, Lou Lou."

Willie started chanting, "With a flaming sword. A flaming sword," and he circled his arm in the air.

Mother had been knitting and Pa was smoking his pipe listening to me read through the open window of the parlor. They both came out on to the porch to help get the children in bed. Pa picked up Retta and started up the front stairs to her room. Mother kissed Willie and Abbie Lou good night. Then she gave me a big hug and thanked me for loving my brother and sisters.

"You have really surprised me taking Willie on, teaching him things that I just can't do right now. It should be my responsibility, but you have taken this task on without so much as a grumpy word. We never knew when he would start to open up and understand what we were saying to him. I'm so glad you were with him. I'm not sure I would have noticed or stopped my chores long enough to allow him to do something on his own. I once made a promise to you that I would take care of you, but it seems like you've been taking care of me since that day. And now, you've grown into quite a young lady taking care of all of us. I love you so much and I just wanted to tell you thanks for your sacrifice and being obedient to me when I need you so much," and she hugged me again.

Willie wrapped his arms around my waist laying his head on my back. I wasn't able to speak because she had used the word "sacrifice." I wanted to ask her how she was feeling, and when she thought the baby would come, and had she ever felt like Willie was a sacrifice to her, but I couldn't. I was trying to figure out why she used the word sacrifice. Was God trying to tell me something? Why was I growing up so fast? Why was I asking all these questions? Before, I just said in my heart, "He's Willie, my brother and that's all there is to it." But, now everyone was putting a name on that feeling and I wasn't sure it was worthy of a name. Not for me anyway.

I looked up the word "sacrifice" as soon as I got to my room. I didn't see anything that sounded like anything I had ever done before. I had given up some time for the sake of helping Willie, but isn't that what every brother or sister would do? Life was starting to get good, but it was also starting to be very complicated. I wasn't sure I was grown-up enough for it all yet. I just wanted to make sure my new friend, Tylar, would be there with me. Pappy had made me aware that I needed Jesus most of all, so I spent the rest of the evening looking up those words I didn't understand.

Before I got ready for bed, I said a simple prayer asking, "Jesus, will you please help me learn to sacrifice for others, if only half as much as You, and if You want to live in me like Pappy said You did, then I'm willing to sacrifice myself and let You. I'm not sure what that means, or how You're gonna do it, but Pappy says to trust You, so I believe You can, somehow. So, now I need to get to know You if you're gonna be living here. I'm gonna keep reading the Bible every night. Help me to stick to that. Thank You. Amen."

Then I pulled the note out of my pocket that Tylar had written to me. I didn't need to read it again; it was memorized in my heart. I just needed Friday to get here and fast, before I forgot all that had happened since the last time I saw him. There was no need trying to sleep with so many thoughts swimming in my head. I knew I would never sleep if I didn't write them down. This was the first time I started keeping a journal. I got some notebook paper and wrote down the events of the day, as well as my thoughts about Tylar and his family. I used my school paste to stick Tylar's note in the pages. I cut a piece of ribbon off of one of my hair bows and looped it through the ring hole in the pages tying them all together. Because this was so personal to me and it housed my most precious possession, Tylar's note, I kept it under my pillow.

chapter five

Early Thursday morning Pappy drove into the yard in that old truck he and Silas used to bring feed from the silos to Pappy's cattle and Pa's livestock. Nanny was on the seat beside Pappy waving at me and Willie while Pappy blew the horn. Mother came running from the kitchen to the front porch waving with delight. Willie and I ran out to the truck to see what was so important that Pappy took the day off from the bank. The back of the truck was full of boxes.

"Pappy, what's with all these boxes and where are you going?"

"I'm going here! To get you, Punkin'!" and he picked me up in his arms with a big squeeze and a kiss and said, "Good morning to you. Have you had breakfast?"

"Mother was feeding the girls while Willie and I played hop scotch in the yard."

"Willie's playing hop scotch?" Nanny scooted out of the drivers side door very slowly looking directly into Willie's eyes.

"Pappy, Willie drew water out of the river for 'O Plow and he climbed out of the river when I told him to, just holding to Abbie Lou's hand."

"Well, little man, sounds like you woke up. Sissy and I always knew you would." Pappy stood me on the ground and picked up

Willie. Nanny had tears in her eyes and she wrapped her hand around the back of Willie's head while Pappy held him in his arms.

Willie said, "Pappy."

His word startled Nanny and she said, "Can you say Nanny?"

Willie just looked at her. For a moment I didn't think he would say it, but then he started laughing and said, "Nanny, Pappy, Nanny, Pappy," and everyone started laughing.

"So how is he at hop scotch?"

"Not better than me, Pappy. He's still learning the rules, but he's always been able to hop."

"Well, I wonder if he would want to hop around with me and you today?"

"We're going somewhere, Pappy?"

Then Nanny spoke up, "First we're going to get something to eat, Jeremiah. Your daughter is expecting us to eat with her and her family."

"Pa's already gone to work, Nanny, but Willie and I haven't had breakfast yet."

"Well then, let's eat."

I don't think I ever saw Pappy turn down a meal and today would be no different. It just meant that I would have to wait a little longer before finding out where we were going.

"What's in the boxes, Pappy?" Mother walked to the table with three boxes and set them down on the buffet. "Mother, you have boxes just like Pappy's. Where did you get them and what's in there?"

"Pappy brought these over last night after you had gone to bed. That's why I got up so early this morning."

"Why, Mother? Why did the boxes make you get up so early?"

"I made a few extra loaves of bread this morning to put in these boxes. There are five more in the kitchen."

"Why didn't you wake me up so I could help you?"

"Because you needed your sleep. You'll have a full day today helping your Pappy deliver all this bread."

"Where are we going, Pappy? To the bakery?"

"No, a bakery has bread, silly. Were taking them some place that has no bread. You'll see when you get there."

"When are we leaving?"

Pappy looked at his pocket watch, "In eight minutes. That gives you just enough time to wash up, grab a hat,"

"I need a hat, Pappy?"

"Yes, get a hat and one for your brother if he's going, and pick up any boxes on your way out that might still be in the house. Be sure to check the kitchen; we can't afford to forget even one loaf of bread."

"Yes sir, Pappy. If you're going with us, Willie, you better follow me." Willie put his napkin on the table and followed me to the wash basin at the back door. We washed our faces and hands, picked up our hats and found two boxes waiting for us on the dining room table. Pappy, Nanny and Mother were out at the truck watching us come out of the house and down the steps, me with one box, Willie with the other. It was a little overwhelming for the grown-ups to watch Willie function like a normal person. I guess I just expected it so I adjusted easier. Nanny and Mother, wrapped in each other's arms, were still staring at Willie as we drove off headed in the direction of town.

It was fairly quiet on the ride, just a little teasing about Tylar and questions as to when he would be a permanent resident. When we got to the other side of town we stopped at a house I had never been to, where there were ladies on the porch all holding boxes. Pappy said we could just wait in the truck 'cause there were plenty of ladies to bring the boxes out of the house and to the truck. They were very friendly with each other and spoke to Willie and me. There seemed to be more coming out of the house, some still in their housecoats and slippers. Most of them were young like Aunt Gail and all of them were beautiful. One lady, who dressed sort of like Aunt Penny, kissed Pappy on the cheek and said, "You're a fine man, Mr. Hawthorne. After what I've become, God sure can't smile on me and my little loaf of bread, but he sure will bless you for that great big heart you got."

"Sunshine, God's not mad at you. Desperate times cause us to do desperate things. I don't condemn you for what others have done and neither does God. And I won't judge you because of the darkness you're walking in. God's just gotten quiet. He's just waiting," and Pappy opened the door to the truck and got in behind the wheel.

"Pappy, what's God waiting on and aren't you going to put that box in the back?"

"Sunshine, He's waiting on Sunshine. She said the girls made some cookies for you and Willie to have later. They put them in this box. Just set them down in the floor till we break for lunch."

All the girls stood on the porch waving as we backed out of the driveway. "Can't tell your grandmother that we stopped here for bread. She'd be all upset that I didn't let her cook all the loaves instead of imposing on these ladies. I think you ought to let everybody take part of a good project like this, that way everybody gets a blessing."

"Is God going to hand out blessings to everybody today?"

"No, some blessings don't come from God, they come from people when you're doing what God asks you to do. Today, Lacey Kale, you will get a blessing from a lot of people."

We stopped at the Foster's, the Moore's, the Wheaton's and Pastor Burton's. Each one of the families had baked a little something for Willie and me. Pastor Burton had the most boxes. Pappy said it was because a lot of the church ladies brought their bread to his house so Pappy wouldn't have to make so many stops.

Pastor Burton leaned into the window on Pappy's side after they got the truck loaded and said, "You're a brave man, Jeremiah, braver than I. And it looks like everyone else in this town. You be careful. You can leave those children with me if you're having second thoughts about taking them."

"Thank you, but they're going with me. I can't get this blessing and keep it all to myself and enjoy it. I want to share it with my two best friends."

"Good luck to you."

Pappy backed the truck away from where Pastor Burton was standing. He was grumbling something about a pastor ought to know that there's no such thing as luck and that God was going with him to this camp, "Not no luck." I didn't ask him any questions because I was sure he would tell me if he wanted me to understand.

We drove for what seemed like an hour, but I later realized it was not so far away from where I lived, maybe twenty miles. We stayed on the river road most of the time unless a bridge was gone and the road had been rerouted. In the distance I could see several smoke stacks in use, but we were too far away for me to make out what the stacks were attached to. Willie started pointing at the smoke and Pappy said, "That's it. That's where were going."

"Are they baking bread, too?"

"No, I'm not sure why they keep those fires going as hot as it is and nothing to cook. I guess they want to be sure they can cook just in case they find something."

"Find something? Can't they buy something to eat or grow it?"

"There's not enough land for them to grow things and live here, too. They can't buy nothing 'cause they lost all their money in the crash."

"What crash?"

"Oh, when the depression hit. They lost their homes, their jobs and their dignity. Some of them couldn't handle it and they lost their lives."

"Mrs. Winters told us about that."

We made it to the camp Pappy called the "migrant camp" because these people migrated around like Gypsies looking for work. They had sold their last valuable thing, their automobiles, so they could no longer migrate anymore. The government set up these camps by paying the farmers for a few acres of land for them to live on during the picking season. Pappy said that once you lost it all it was almost impossible to get it back without some help, and our government couldn't do a lot with all our money going to the war right now. Most farmers couldn't pay for extra help so most of the migrants were still without a job.

That was obvious as we pulled into the camp. It looked as though most of the men were still at the camp instead of working in a field somewhere. Lots of the children were naked, and the clothing the grown-ups had on was torn, exposing their flesh if they used their hands for more than holding the pieces together. Some ladies were breast-feeding babies with older children crying at their feet. Everyone looked tired and in need of some food. There was a look of pain on my Pappy's face, but it quickly changed when he put his hand on the door handle and said, "This is the place, kids. Let's start handing out these boxes of bread."

I needed a moment longer to take in the view, so I placed my hand in the crook of Pappy's arm to stop him from getting out. The land was stripped of any grass or weed. A dessert like in New Mexico, but not a beautiful sight; I guess because it just didn't belong in this setting. There were mud caked pieces of cloth soiled by the rains splashing in the dust. The cloth was draped over tent poles to make shelters for each family. Most all of them had stove pipe sticking out of a hole cut in the side of the cloth. Every pipe had smoke coming out of the top, but I didn't see a woodpile.

Some of the men had come close to the truck not sure why we were there. Pappy pulled the door handle and loudly introduced himself and his grandchildren with an explanation as to why we were there. One man fell to his knees clasping his hands together looking up toward the sky, but not seeing what I saw when I looked up 'cause his eyes were closed. Pappy had lifted me up and into the back of the truck where I could pass him the boxes from the middle first. Pappy handed a box of bread to each person that came up to the truck with a, "Jesus loves you; God bless you," and a smile or a handshake.

Willie stood in front of the man on his knees holding out the man's box of bread, just waiting for him to notice his presence. Some people stayed at their tent homes rocking with a glazed look in their eyes. The man Willie had been holding the box out to had opened his eyes and saw Willie. He grabbed Willie in his arms and hugged him. It scared me to see this stranger grab my brother so I stood up ready to jump out of the truck and save him. Pappy said, "No Lacey, wait."

I froze waiting for Willie to let out a scream, but he didn't. The man let him go and slowly took the box Willie was holding. Through his sobs the man thanked him, but Willie did not move. Then, with the sweetest gesture I had ever seen from Willie, he bowed and turned back toward us holding his hands up to the side of the truck waiting for me to give him another box.

Willie had never been touched by a perfect stranger without screaming his head off. Now he was taking boxes from the truck to the tents of strangers where mothers would not come to us because of fear or maybe they had too many children. They were so grateful, though. I had gotten all the boxes out from the middle of the truck bed and had joined Pappy and Willie moving among the people watching the tears remove the dust from their faces.

I saw a man sitting under a makeshift tarp tied to mere sticks. He had a cot to sleep on and a bucket turned upside down for sitting, but he was sitting on the ground with a rock in his hand scratching his arm with the rock till he bled. I was slowly approaching him when I felt Pappy's hand on my shoulder.

"Let me, Lacey. He's not quite right and I don't want you to get hurt."

"He's just like your brother, Great Uncle Jeffery. He was harmless, but he wasn't right in the head like Willie and we loved him anyway."

"Jeffery's problem wasn't the same as Willie. He was fine until the war where he watched his friends be tortured at the hands of Nazis and he, himself, a victim to things we will never know. Willie was born with his problem, and this man? Well, I don't know. It could be because he lost everything in the crash and can't cope, or he may have been born like this. In either case, I don't want to take a chance by letting you get too close."

Pappy took the breadbox from my hands and walked slowly toward the man.

"Can you make him stop hurting himself, Pappy?"

"Maybe I can for a little while. Only a miracle from God can make him stop completely."

"It's too late for Great Uncle Jeffery. Maybe all those prayers that went up for him could be shifted over to this man?"

"Good idea, Lacey. I'll talk to God about that. Sir, Sir? We've brought you some bread." The man slowly lifted his eyes up to look at Pappy, but his hand with the rock kept scraping at his arm.

"Have you got an itch there, Sir? Maybe you could put that rock down and enjoy some bread?"

"No. There's no bread. No bread anywhere. I can't spare some bread."

"I'm not here to take bread; I want to give you some bread." Pappy opened the box to show the man the beautiful loaf of sourdough bread. "We have some cool water to go with that if you would like." There was silence, stares and silence.

"Give it to the children first. Give it to her," and he pointed at me.

"Oh, no Sir, I've had plenty. I'm stuffed I've had so much. Please eat it ... for me?"

He dropped the rock and took the box from Pappy's hand. "You need a doctor to look at your arm."

"Do you think he can make it stop itching? It burns and stings and itches."

"How long has it been doing that?"

"Since yesterday."

"Sure looks mighty scabbed over to have just been since yesterday."

"I don't know, maybe it was before yesterday."

"I'll come out here Saturday with my friend and let him take a look at it and see what he thinks would help you, but first I'm going to ask Jesus to heal you today. When we come back Saturday we just might see you already better."

"Is he a doctor?"

"Who?" Pappy looked behind himself.

"Jesus," the man said.

"Oh yes, Sir, the best I know."

"Bring him Saturday, I'll be waiting."

"He sent the bread. It will help in your healing, too."

"Then I will eat it," and he broke a piece off of the loaf, put it in his mouth chewing with a smile, then lifting the bread up to me nodding his head.

I heard a car pulling up to the camp and for a moment I was panic-stricken for Willie's safety. It was the sheriff's car and I spotted Willie playing with some children near Pappy's truck. Pappy looked up at the Sheriff, then back at the man.

"I'll see you Saturday."

"How many days is that from today?"

"Two. Today is Thursday."

"Thank you."

A lady with a faded pink dress on came up to the man. "Mr. Sanders? Here's some cold water the nice people brought." She handed him the cup of water.

"Thank you nice people."

"The water came from Jesus, too, Mr. Sanders."

"Send him my thanks till he can be better paid," and he raised his cup to the doctor he was expecting to meet Saturday.

the road

Pappy took my hand and we walked to the sheriff and his car.

"Jeremiah."

"Sheriff," and the two men shook hands. "What brings you all the way out here?"

"Thought I would come and make sure everything was okay. Hey Miss Lacey," and Sheriff Cromwell knelt down in front of me. "You get prettier every time I see you. I think redheads are pure glamour, don't you A.J.? Why, you would be a real looker out of those overalls and in a frilly little dress. A sweet little thing like you shouldn't have to be in boy's overalls in an unpredictable place like this."

Pappy said, "I don't know why everybody thinks these people are so dangerous. They're just trying to make it. What's so wrong with that, aren't we all?"

"People don't like people moving in and out so quickly. None of us like change and people who are not nailed down to something produce change. That's all it is, A.J.," and the sheriff pulled on the end of my braid and winked at me.

Pappy said, "If someone goes to missing something, and most of the time it wasn't missing at all, they automatically blame the migrant. That gives them a bad reputation and the next thing you know we've produced fear. Most of these people had a home and a good stable life, so they thought. They're educated people just like you and me who believed in a dream to nail down security for their families. If I hadn't heard something inside me, warning me to keep my savings out of the market, I'd be right there where they are with my family, too. Just because they've lost everything they ever worked for doesn't mean they have become thieves overnight. It's a manmade fear, that's all it is." Pappy's voice was beginning to get raised and I could tell he didn't like how this was turning out.

"Well, that's enough, A.J. Fear causes my work-load to increase. I'm just trying to head off a potential overload."

"Bob, how would you like it if people dreamed up stuff about you? Every time us men went to your house for a hand of cards, or we brought our families over for Sunday dinner, the cops showed up to make sure everything was 'okay' in such an 'unpredictable place'?" Pappy walked closer to Sheriff Cromwell, "You're presence is a threat to these people unless you've come to help feed the five thousand, 'Judas.'"

Some of the people started bringing their empty boxes back to the truck handing them to me or Pappy. They all said "thank you" as they held the boxes out to us. I was trading the empty boxes with full ones for them to have later. God was truly feeding the five thousand, cause from somewhere we just seemed to have more.

"If I didn't know you like a brother I would take that as an insult, but I know that you know," and Pappy started helping me load the empty boxes into the truck, "I'm only here as a friend making sure another friend doesn't need me. After today you can stay away from down here."

"I don't think so, Bobby. As a matter of fact, A.P. and I will be back on Saturday as soon as he closes the barber shop."

"What for?"

"We have some doctoring to do."

"My brother is a barber, not a doctor! Alvin Jeremiah, you keep my brother out of your foolishness."

"I've always said A.P. missed his calling. His hands would be better suited for surgery than shaving. But, now that I think about it, it's kind of the same thing."

"Don't make him regret ever becoming your friend. This is not where men of good stature need to be hanging out on their day off. Go to the club, play some croquet or go fox hunting, just do something else."

"Fox are out of season. Are you trying to get me arrested for hunting out of season?"

"A.J., you know what I'm trying to do. There are too many women down here, some of them half dressed. Their husbands are off in a field or walking through town hunting a job. The next thing we'll hear is that some woman got raped and our wealthy banker was seen here, alone, supposedly handing out bread and pretending to be a doctor."

"You fill your mind with too much gossip and smut, Bobby. Maybe you should stick to traffic instead of homicide; it's clouding your judgment. Why don't you get up in those hills with a pack of dog and go after those bootlegging mobsters and leave these fine people alone." Pappy put his hands on his hips and looked out across the humbled horizon. "Yea, Bobby, A.P. and I are thinking about making this our permanent mission field so get used to making a trip out this way often. If for no other reason, at least come to keep our reputations from tarnish."

"That's not going to happen, Jeremiah."

"You gonna stop us with that police force of, what ... two?" and Pappy chuckled.

"Can't stop you, A.J., but you wont need to come back here. I'm going to be forcing these people off this land at the end of next week."

Pappy stopped loading the empty boxes into the truck and walked up close to Sheriff Cromwell's face. "You wouldn't do that, Bobby."

"It's not up to me. The farmer wants to plant this field with cantaloupe. Seems were having the best weather for it. He got out of the contract with the government because we need the food more than we need the hired hands."

I couldn't keep quiet any longer. My head was spinning around the camp looking into the faces of each person we had spent time with. "Pappy, what will they do? Mr. Sanders needs some medicine and that family needs to be able to get some rest, and that little boy is laughing, Pappy. You remember him? The one playing with Willie? He was crying when we drove up, but now that his belly is full he's laughing. He's laughing, Sheriff Cromwell." I grabbed his arm and pulled with all my might and shouted, "Look! He's laughing, he's laughing, Sheriff Cromwell."

The sheriff took me by my shoulders and stared strongly into my eyes. "Miss Lacey, laughter only lasts for a moment. Reality sets in forever. They can't stay here. They have to keep moving. That's the kind of people they are now. You or your Pappy aren't big enough to change that."

I jerked my shoulders free of his grip and started running. I couldn't let him see me cry, just like I never let Theodore watch me cry after he stepped in my path and told me I couldn't do something because I was just not big enough. Sheriff Cromwell was saying the same thing Theodore had said over and over to me, "You're just not bigger than me." I wouldn't stand there and be bullied by this man either so I ran as fast as I could to the river. I could barely breath when

I got there. I was hot all over. The next thing I remembered, I was floating on my back looking up at the sun and a cloudless sky.

"Why God? Why?"

I could hardly believe I was brave enough to talk to Him, much less ask Him why He had allowed this to happen to these people.

"I know that I don't understand You or Your reasons. Okay, let's say they are just what Sheriff Cromwell says they are. Let's say they have done awful things, but don't they get a chance to do better? Don't they get a chance to say I'm sorry? Mr. Sanders doesn't even know a thing about You. If Pappy had not said Your name to him he would still not know the name Jesus. If You take them away, Pappy won't ever get to tell them about who sent the bread. They'll always think it came from an old man, a little girl and a small boy who simply bows a lot. What good will that do them, me, or You? These people have been on the road too long. They need a place to call home. You have to do something to keep them here. You have to. Not for me, 'cause I've never done anything worthy of getting my way, but do it for those tired hungry people and their children. They're the ones. Do something for them."

It was quiet, except for the water rushing by my ears, but I still heard it. "This river will come up out of its banks one day soon. Very soon."

I sat up in the water looking in all directions. "What? What did you say?"

There was no one around. I got out of the river and searched up and down the bank.

"Is that you, Pappy? Did you say something?"

I slowly sat down on the bank wondering what I heard and how I had heard it. "It said this river would come out of its bank very soon. I heard that right here." And I placed my hand on my breastbone. "Right here. I don't have ears here, but that's where I heard it, right here. This river is coming up out of its banks very soon. God's trying to help these people from having to run from the river when it floods that field. I've got to tell . . . oh my gosh, will anyone believe me?"

"Lacey! Are you alright?" I turned my head to see Pappy looking over the bank.

"Oh Pappy, have you been there all along?"

"No, I just got here. Did I miss something? What's wrong?"

"I got in the water."

"I see that."

"No Pappy, listen. I was so mad when I left Sheriff Cromwell. When I got here I just jumped in the water to cool off. I was floating out there and fussing with God."

"Fussing with God? I know who won that argument. You'll lose every time, Lacey," and he started climbing down the bank to me.

"Pappy, listen to me. I need you to listen."

"Okay. I'm right here, you have my undivided attention."

"I was fussing about the farmer making them move and asking God to fix it so they could stay when I heard a voice, not a real voice and I didn't hear it in my ears, but it was a voice and I heard it say, 'This river's gonna come up out of it's banks soon, very soon.' Pappy, God is moving these people so they don't drown in a flood."

Pappy straightened up and looked out across the river. "Where did you hear this, Lacey?"

I pointed out to the middle of the river and said, "Out there, Pappy."

"No. Where did you *hear* it?"

I placed my hand over my heart and said, "Right here. I heard it in here. Or maybe here," and I put my hand to my forehead. "Oh, I don't know exactly, but I didn't hear it here." I put my hands over my ears. "All I heard here was water and the voice was louder than the water."

Pappy was still looking out over the river. "Well my dear, we have work to do. There are more people that need to be moved besides these." Then he turned to me. "I need to talk to your father about moving those houses down by the river where your Aunt Penny lives," and he boosted me up over the bank.

"Why can't you call her your daughter-in-law instead of my aunt?"

"It's easier to say 'Aunt Penny,' silly. The government will be looking for a new sight for these folks. I think I'll try to get in touch with someone tomorrow and offer that twenty acres, up on the hill? It's mostly woods, but there is a couple acres they could plant a few vegetables and maybe the crop would make it through the rains since it's on a little bit of a slope. We'll have to warn farmers to pick early this year, not wait for stuff to be ripe. That is if we have that long."

Sheriff Cromwell was sitting with Willie when Pappy and I got back to the camp. He stood up and came over to me.

"I see you just needed to take a little swim. You got back just in time for me to take you and Willie here to the café and get some vittles. My way of apologizing," and he took his fist and touched my chin.

"Your way of getting us out of here."

"Oh, come on A.J. Let me make it up to her. I didn't mean to break her spirit."

Pappy and I just kept walking to the truck. "You didn't break my spirit, Sheriff Cromwell, you helped me find it! Come on Willie, it's time to go to work."

"See ya Saturday, Bobby. I'll be counting on you, now don't let me down." Pappy picked up Willie and put him in the truck from the driver's side. I was already sitting in my seat rolling the window down so I could stick my head out and wave to all our new friends and especially Sheriff Cromwell.

"Well Lacey, we may have to skip lunch today so how 'bout opening up those boxes in the floor and lets see what we've got."

"The Foster's baked brownies. We have two of those left."

"Left! What happened to the rest of them?"

"The same thing that happened to what the ladies from the church sent us. We gave them to the children at the camp. Didn't seem right us giving them bread and keeping the good stuff for ourselves."

"I gave brownie b-b-baby. Mommy ate."

"That was good, Willie, that baby was too little to eat a brownie. You helped that baby out even though its mother ate the brownie."

"Well, you too are getting the hang of this. I'm proud of you."

"Thanks Pappy, but I didn't give it all away. The Wheaton's sent cheese sandwiches and the Moore's sent three pieces of lemon pie. I didn't see anyone with a fork so I didn't offer them any pie. And Miss Sunshine's cookies, well, there are plenty of those left."

"And, we've got some water left so it looks like we've got the makings of lunch. We'll eat once we get to Uncle Trell's store and find your Pa."

I was looking forward to eating some of these great snacks, but I was more excited about seeing Pa and telling him about the camp, the river, and hearing God like Pappy after he prayed.

chapter six

We got to Uncle Trell's just as all the men were breaking for lunch. Pa came out to the truck on my side as we drove up to the beginnings of the new hardware store.

"You got finished a lot sooner than I expected, Jeremiah. I was thinking about driving out after lunch once I got the men back to work. I wanted to watch the children experience their first time out there. How did they do?" Pa turned his eyes toward me. "How'd you do out there? What'd you think?" Pa pulled the truck door open and kicked his leg up on the running board leaning against the inside of the door frame.

"I think it's just awful, Pa. They have no home, no food, no bath. I never thought I would ever think that was awful."

Pappy and Pa started laughing and Pa said, "Well I know what, Lacey, we'll give them ours!" Willie started clapping and laughing.

"Pa, they were so hungry and one man named Mr. Sanders is in need of a doctor."

"I'm sure they all need a doctor just to check them out. Can we get one to go out there A.J.?"

"I don't know, William. You almost have to find somebody that owes you to get them to go out there. I don't know of any doctor that wants to borrow money and I don't like cashing in favors, but I might have to. A.P. and I are going out Saturday. He knows a lot about fixing up livestock and he helps Sally bring babies into the world."

"That's it! Sally will go, Pappy. She'll do it as a favor to me. Then you won't have to worry about what Sheriff Cromwell said with another lady there."

"Sheriff Cromwell was there?"

"He helped find Sissy's spirit." Pappy and I slowly turned our heads to look at Willie.

"Yep." Pappy rubbed his knuckles on the top of Willie's head, "I knew you would wake up little man, I knew it."

I just reach my arm around Willie, snuggled him up close to me and kissed his forehead as he looked up at me.

"Amazing isn't it, Jeremiah? It's like having a new member of the family. I think I'll go with ya'll Saturday; it seems as if I missed quite a lot. I didn't think Bobby Cromwell knew a thing about someone's spirit much less care enough to help someone find it. Ya'll have to fill me in on today's events. Right now, I need to get some lunch at the café."

"You can eat with us. We're having cheese sandwiches. I need to talk to you now about the sheriff's visit and I'm pretty sure Punkin's got something to tell you."

"Okay, sounds good to me. We've got a table built out of crates inside."

We all got out of the truck and walked to the crates, each one of us carrying a box. "You can't come with us Saturday, William, you need to be doing something else much more important than going with us. Seems the good sheriff will be forcing those people to leave by the end of next week. I'm going to contact old farmer Brock and see who he talked with about contracting his land with the government. Hopefully I can get it all settled for them to move onto that twenty acres up on the hill across from where they are now. They'll still be near enough to the river to get what they need, but high enough to be safe."

"Safe from what?"

"Lacey can tell you all about that. The main thing is to have this all settled and offer it to the people before Bobby has a chance to get ugly and start pushing people around. I don't want them frightened any more than they already are."

"Will Bobby do that?"

"I would have said no this morning before I went out there, but I saw it in his eyes. He'll do anything he has to, to keep his brother's reputation and the local banker's. He's got it in his head that there will be trouble if we don't stay away from these people, because so many people in town are afraid of them."

"Well, isn't that possible?"

"Of course it is. But, I can't let what hasn't happened determine if I'm going to obey God. I'm going to believe that He will take care of any unforeseen problems."

"These cookies are incredible! Who made them?"

"Yea, Pappy, if her bread is anything as good as these cookies those people at the camp were eating like kings and queens."

"Who's bread and who's cookies?"

Willie smiled and said, "Sunny shine."

Pa dropped his chin toward the table with a look of surprise, but mischief glee and whispered, "You didn't! Jeremiah, Jo Rett finds out about this she'll—"

"She won't. God's gonna take care of that unforeseen trouble, too."

"You better hope so. You're just too soft for your own good. She's a real sweetheart, but I'm not sure you should have let her get involved in this. Talk about needing to protect your reputation, not to mention your marriage. Sheriff Cromwell doesn't have to go way out there to watch after you, he can stay right here in town!"

"William, when the lady is one of your biggest customers and she knows that the bank she keeps all her money in, or at least most of it, is sponsoring a bread drive for half of her customers, well, I couldn't tell her no. She wanted to give back to them."

My Pappy and Pa knew something I didn't; something that made them grin and shake their heads at each other while they talk about Miss Sunshine. It didn't matter to me that they knew a secret I was just thankful that my Pappy and Pa were such good friends and that they knew Miss Sunshine well enough that she had made cookies for me and Willie. I didn't mind keeping their secret, but I wasn't sure that Willie would. I was glad that Pappy didn't have parents that he was keeping this from even though God knew all about it. After all, he was the one waiting on Miss Sunshine.

"So, Lacey, tell me about these people's safety."

"Well, I ran away from Sheriff Cromwell to the river."

"Woe, woe, woe. Start at the beginning, not in the middle of running from the sheriff."

"Now William, calm down, she heard Bobby saying he was going to force these people off the land. You would have been proud of her standing up for them. Bobby just tried to humiliate her with a bunch of righteous talk about how she couldn't change these people's lives. I was proud of her for walking away from him. I would have decked him when I was her age. But, what man tries to crush, God will lift up, and He did. Tell him, Lacey."

"After I got to the river, well, I was so hot from my blood boiling, and the run, that I just jumped in the river. I was floating on my back looking up at the sky and I started talking to God. Well, fussing at Him really. See, I told Him at the dock at home yesterday that I wanted to understand more about making sacrifices for others like He did. Then last night when I went to my room I looked up the word sacrifice 'cause Mother said I had sacrificed taking care of Willie and the girls for her. I knew I hadn't sacrificed like Jesus had so I asked Him to teach me how to sacrifice for others if only half as good as He did. Then I said I would sacrifice myself and let Him live in me if He wanted to, and Pappy said He did and I believe him. So, that was really the first time I talked to God, except when I was at the river and I was just talking in my head even though I knew He was listening.

"So then I'm in the water upset about no one making a sacrifice for these people and fussing with God, begging, too, Pappy. Begging for Him to do something to help these people. And then I just got tired and lay there listening to nothing, but the water rushing by my ears when I heard it. I heard, 'This river will come up out of it's banks one day soon, very soon.' I heard it right here," and I put my fist in the middle of my chest, "not here," pointing at my ears.

"I asked if anyone was around and I looked in the bushes along the shore. I just kept going over and over in my head what I heard and then it was just like someone turned the light on. I knew that God was helping these people by having them moved away from the river to keep them from having to run when the river comes up out of its banks. Then I saw Pappy up on the bank and I told him what had happened, not all of this, but about what I had heard and he said we had to come and tell you."

"That's where you come in, William. I need you to get your workers to move my houses down on the river and anyone else that will believe this little girl and let us move their's."

"Who's gonna pay these men?"

"You know I will pay what is fair."

"For everybody?"

"I think I can swing it. The bank owns the mortgages on most of the houses that are in danger so if I want to protect my investment I better."

Pa said, "I'm sure I can get the men to work this Saturday. Maybe even employ some of the migrants?"

"Sure. We'll get done that much earlier."

"If they work out I'll let Silas be the foreman on the job and the migrants can keep working through the week. That way I can fulfill my obligation to Trell and get those houses moved as quick as possible. I don't guess you two know what is 'soon' to God, do you?"

Pappy and I shook our heads.

There was silence as we finished sharing the lemon pie slices. Willie finally spoke up to break the silence, "Soon is soon. Soon is soon. Soon is soon."

We finished our lunch and headed to the truck. We were saying our good-byes, me and Willie hugging Pa, and Pappy giving Pa last minute instructions on their new project. Pappy said he was going out to farmer Brock's to find out who he needed to talk to about the land lease. "Even if they don't want to place the contract with me, I'm still going to offer the land to the migrants. I just thought I would use the extra income to help purchase food and better shelter for them. We'll see, but no need to wait till tomorrow to get the ball rolling when I have the rest of today. See ya tonight."

I was hopping up in the truck when Pappy said, "Well, well. Will you looky there, Lacey. Tylar and his family have just driven into town."

I saw the car pulling right up beside Pappy, and, yes, Tylar was in the back seat of the car with Ruthy. Pauley was sitting in the middle between Marge and Bob in the front.

"Look Willie! It's our new friends Ruthy and Pauley and Tylar." Mr. Collier jumped out of the car first and ran to Pa shaking his hand. Pappy was opening the door for Miss Marge and Tylar was coming out of the back.

"Thought I would find you here, William, but I wasn't expecting you to be playing hooky from the bank, Jeremiah."

"I knew you were coming and there was no way I was going to miss getting a hug from your beautiful wife, Bob," and Pappy wrapped his arms around Marge's neck. Then Pa came around the car and hugged Miss Marge while Pappy hugged Pauley and Ruthy.

"Guess you're too old to hug, Tylar," and they shook hands, "Glad to see you, young man, We've missed you around here, both of us have," and Pappy put his hand on my back and directed me to Tylar.

Ruthy jumped up and down. "We've missed you, Lacey," and she threw her arms around me rocking us from side to side. Then she ran to Willie while I hugged Pauley. Tylar and I just looked at each other. With one arm lifted, Tylar placed his arm on my shoulder and around my neck pulling me closer to him and placing his other arm around my waist. He quickly asked as his mouth was near my ear, "Did you get my letter?"

Mr. Collier had come around the back of the car saying, "Boy Miss Lacey, you have been the talk of my house for a week now." Tylar and I dropped our arms to our sides and Mr. Collier scooped me up. "Something tells me that even though we are moving in today, you will still be on the hearts and minds of my children, especially this young man."

"You're moving in today?"

"Sure are. We came looking for a little help with the big stuff, and the small too, Lacey, if you and Willie have some free time."

"Sure, I think. Pappy?"

"You and I have done what we set out to do today and more. I'll go finish up my business with farmer Brock and meet ya'll at the house. Why don't you take Lacey and Willie with you? That way I can go from here and save me a little time, is that okay with you, Bob?"

"Absolutely. They can squeeze in the back with Tylar and Ruthy."

Miss Marge was standing by the car with her arms opened wide, "Lacey, you better come give me a hug now before you get in the car. We might be too busy later." She squeezed me tightly and said, "Even I have missed you and your excitement," and she winked at me. "Jeremiah, we'll stop by Abigail's and let her know we have the children. How's Mrs. Nanny Jo Rett doing?"

"Oh, she's good. You'll probably see her out at Abigail's."

"Then we'll pass along to her where you're going and when you'll be back. That way maybe she'll join us at the house if she knows your coming later."

"Hey," Pa said, "Bear hug, kids." And we ran over to Pa and hugged him goodbye. "I'll be able to leave a little early today, Bob, so I'll see you before supper. Guess we need to do that at our house? I'm sure Abbie's got that covered already."

"Thanks William, we've got a loaf of bread. We can always have cheese sandwiches if Abigail's not up to cooking."

I had started into the car behind Willie when I thought of Willie, Sunshine and cheese sandwiches so I pulled my head back out of the car and looked at Pappy just in time to see him stop his departure and say, "Ah, no Bob, think we need to have something besides cheese sandwiches."

"Yea, we had those for lunch."

"Too much of a good thing, Lacey?" and everyone snickered.

I pushed Willie into the car saying, "No, Willie just didn't seem to eat them that good. He will need something else for supper."

Willie said, "Good cheese and sunny shine cookies."

"You know we'll find something to eat and I promise it will be hot. Don't you men fret over it, us woman always make sure our men have plenty to eat. We'll see both of you later."

Then Mr. Collier opened the car door for Miss Marge while the rest of us loaded up in the car, me right next to Tylar, with Willie in my lap and Ruthy on my other side. Once back at my house, Mother and Nanny said they would walk down to the Collier's, but Tylar and I took the opportunity to have some time to catch up on the events of the week. So we volunteered to walk and let Mother and Nanny ride.

"Can I show Tylar the new kittens in the barn, Mother?"

"Yes, but don't be too long, or you'll have us out looking for you."

"We won't," and we ran in the direction of the barn. When we reached the haystack just outside the barn I fell head first right into it. Tylar flopped down beside me panting like a dog.

"Lacey Kale, I'm gonna learn one day that there's no use trying to outrun you."

"I'm not all that faster than you, I just know where I'm going."

"I thought you were really going to the barn to see those kittens."

"No, I remembered that I already showed you the kittens, I just wanted to have a little more time with you before we start working."

"Well, me too, but you know Ruthy remembers that I've seen the kittens and she's liable to tell."

"That's okay. I'm gonna believe that God will take care of that 'Unforeseen Problem'!"

"And if your mother asks you if you remembered that I had already seen the kittens, are you going to lie to her?"

"No, I'll tell her exactly why I brought you out to the barn."

"And why is that?"

"Cause we have so much to talk about and I want to know if you have thought about what Pappy talked to us about at the dock."

"You mean God and Jesus and the fiery lake?"

"Yeah."

"Well I have thought about it, but mostly I've thought about you. Did you make any kind of decision?"

"Well, yeah, I did and that's one thing I wanted to talk to you about."

"You never answered me, did you get my letter?"

The comfort of the haystack was the perfect place for us to catch up on the things we had missed by being apart. I told Tylar everything that had happened to me from the time I found his letter. He seemed pleased when I told him I had it kept under my pillow and that every night I had said goodnight to him as if he was right across the hall again.

Mostly he had spent his time packing and getting the house ready for the new family to move in. "It's surprising to find out all the things you've lived with that are just not suited for someone else. But, I guess my mother completely understood their need to change a few things and have the walls painted; after all, she insisted that we have the same done to our new home. I think Bob would have moved in like it was, and I sure didn't see anything wrong with the house we were living in, but Bob will do what ever makes my mother happy and he seems completely at rest about it. I hope I can be the same way for my wife."

"It's all about sacrifice, Tylar. I know that your wife will love whatever home you give to her."

"I guess the only homes that we need to be thinking about are those down on the river road. I love the river, but I'm going to remember not to build too close to it."

"Well, our home is close to the river, but it's fifteen or sixteen feet down to it. Counting the crawl space under the house and the knoll it's sitting on, we're close to thirty feet from the river floor. Pappy says if our house is affected then the whole town will be, cause Pa used his transit and found out that the town is only about twenty-two feet up."

"You sound like an architect. Wonder how many feet our house is from the river floor?"

"I don't know, but Pa just pulled into the yard. We'll go ask him." I stood up to walk to the house brushing the hay off my backside and pulling it out of my hair.

"Not yet, Lacey," and Tylar stopped me by grabbing my wrist. Still holding to my arm, Tylar stood up in front of me. "I'm excited about what happened to you this week and I feel very honored to be friends with someone who God has spoken to directly. I can only hope that He ever thinks of me, but I want you to know that I think of you all the time," and he put both arms around my neck and held me close.

"Tylar, God thinks of you every moment of the day, cause I'm always talking to Him about you. Now, He knows all about you and how special you are."

We stayed in each other's arms for a moment, a moment shorter than I wanted, but anything more would have kept it from being perfect.

"Tylar, can you go with us out to the camp on Saturday?"

"Just depends on how much unpacking we get done today and tomorrow."

"Guess we need to get to your house before they all come looking for us."

"Hey, there's your dad getting back in the truck. Let's catch a ride with him. Race ya!" and we ran to the side yard where Pa was driving toward the road.

It was late Friday night when I finally got in the bed after trying to get all of the Collier's belongings unpacked. There were still tools in a wagon that Mr. Collier said he needed to take his time fixing the wood shop just the way he wanted it before he unloaded that wagon. Tylar was given permission to come with us to the migrant camp. I didn't think I would be able to muster up the energy to go, but I woke before anyone else in the house. I spent the time reading my Bible, something I had not done the past two nights like I had promised Willie and the girls, but I had read to myself like I promised Jesus.

My morning prayer was focused on these people and how amazed I was that God would put them on my road of life. I prayed for Mr. Sanders' arm again and for him to be ready to meet Dr. Jesus today. Also for the lady in the pink dress, that she would continue to take care of Mr. Sanders until he was completely healed in his mind. Then I prayed for all of the men to find jobs that would help them get back on there feet and have real homes. Thinking of homes, I thought of all the people in town that just wanted the migrants to go away and prayed that they would welcome these families into our town once they were able to pay for a home or some land. Pappy didn't think anyone ever would, so I prayed that God would make a way for these people and Pappy would see God do a miracle.

There was that familiar thud of the backdoor screen downstairs. I ran to the window and looked down into the back yard to see if my mother was up gathering the wood to start our breakfast. She didn't come out to the woodpile, but Willie and Silas had filled the wood bin on the porch so I ran down the stairs expecting to find Mother in the kitchen.

She wasn't there. I stepped out on the porch just in time to see Mother bend down beside the wood bin holding her stomach with one hand and clinging to the railing with the other. I heard Pa's truck crank up as I ran to my mother.

"Mother! Are you okay? Let me go and stop Pa! Will you be all right till I get him?"

"No, Lacey. I'm fine." And she started to laugh. "I've felt this before. It feels like labor, but it's not. Your Pa has gone to get Pappy and Nanny."

"Can't we call them?"

"We tried, but the switchboard is full. Guess everyone is making their plans for this beautiful day."

"If you're okay, Mother, why did Pa go to get Nanny?"

"He wouldn't believe me. I told him your Nanny and Pappy were coming this morning, aha, and he would probably meet them in the road, but he wouldn't listen. Said they might sleep in after such a long night. Ouch! Your Pa wants to get Silas and the others started on moving those houses. Said he wouldn't go if Nanny wasn't here. Here, help me to the chair. Aha. Gees that's smart. Okay, thank you, my baby girl. I told your Pa Sally was just across the street and she would be over soon. Aha, that's better. What are you doing up so early? You must be excited about your day, too."

"Mother, Pa loves you. Don't be put out with him over his fussing about you. He really likes doing it. As for my day, I am looking forward to seeing Mr. Sanders feel better, but if you need me and Sally here, that's where we will be. Pappy and A.P. can handle the camp without us."

"I'm fine! You and Sally will go and help those poor people, something I can't do right now. So think of it as taking my place. That's the best thing you can do for me. I'll be fine here and Nanny will see to me."

"Mother, do you think the baby will be here soon?"

"Not for three or four weeks. Please believe me, I'll be just fine. We have to bring Uncle Trell and Aunt Gail's baby into the world before your new brother or sister."

"Do you know when it will get here?"

"Any day now. Your Pa said she looked like the baby had dropped some yesterday when he saw Gail at the store. That's usually a good sign that the baby will be here in a few days, maybe sooner."

"Yoo-whoo! Where is everybody?"

"Out here, Sally."

"There's not even a pot of coffee perking. What's going on here, Abigail?"

"Oh, Miss Sally, I'll get the stove going. Mother's just resting this morning."

"Out here on the porch? Why don't you get back in the bed and let us young girls wait on you?" I went into the house carrying an arm load of wood as Sally continued to scold my mother, "You did way too much last night. Having some of those pains, aren't you? Told ya you would if you didn't get off those feet."

"I'm so sorry I'm causing so much trouble to everyone, but I enjoyed every minute of it."

"Yeah, well, you'll pay for your good time today. Come on, put your arm around my shoulder. Let's get you in the house, and in the bed."

"I'm not going to bed. Sit me down at the kitchen table. I can scramble the eggs and mix up the biscuits."

"No you can't. The only thing you're going to do is have a healthy full term baby. The fifth baby never waits till the due day. Two weeks at the most and you will be holding your newest member. I'm not going to let you take a chance by forcing this baby to come before it's ready. If you tire him out in there, he'll come out here to get some rest. You can sit over on the love seat with your feet up and do nothing or you can go to bed, those are your only choices."

"The love seat, please, Doctor!"

"Miss Sally, you said 'he.' Do you know it's a 'he'?"

"No, Lacey. Just a hunch."

I heard the front door open and lots of feet coming across the floor. Nanny ran to Mother as Sally laid down the law as to how Nanny was to take full rein over Mother and make her rest. Pappy came to help me get the fire just right for baking biscuits for our breakfast and Pa went to wake up Willie and check on the girls. In no time our kitchen was filling up with family and friends once the Collier's arrived.

Miss Marge brought in some eggs she had gotten from her chickens and Tylar had milked the cow and brought a half gallon bottle full. Miss Marge went straight to work helping me with what I didn't do real well, cook. I was very thankful that she and her family were now on my road for several reasons. Before I knew it, we were finished with breakfast, the dishes were clean and Pappy, Willie, Ruthy, Tylar, Sally, Jake and I were in the truck headed out to pick up Mr. A.P. Cromwell and then head to the Brock farm where the migrants lived for two more days.

I could hardly keep from telling Tylar every feeling he would have when he saw these people and their homes, but I wanted him to tell me later. That way I would know that we were kindred spirits, like Pappy and Nanny, Mother and Pa, and the other boy and girl best friend relationships I knew.

We passed the sheriff's car parked about a mile from the camp. Mr. A.P., Sally and Pappy were sitting in the cab of the truck; us kids were in the back. We all waved as we passed the sheriff. He didn't wave back or look very pleased to see us. The families were. They were waiting for us when we drove into the camp. They had taken baths and put on better held together clothes. Mr. Sanders was one of the first to greet us with his bandage still intact. He was looking for the Doctor to show him how his arm was healing. Pappy told him that he had brought a nurse and a man who knew a lot about bad cuts and sores, but he was not the doctor who had brought him healing. While Sally took the old bandage off and Mr. A.P. looked at his scabbed scratches, Pappy told Mr. Sanders about God's only Son, Jesus, and how He had died for him and all of us. Several other people gathered around to hear the greatest story of love ever known to man.

Mr. Sanders started to cry. He, too, had lost his son. He said that even after knowing that his son would die, he didn't think he could ever have offered him to the world so that everyone in the world could live forever. "A man just loves his son too much for that," Mr. Sanders said. "He must have really loved this sick old world, or you have to be God to be able to stand the pain."

My Pappy said, "I guess that's why it's easy for me to believe that there is a heaven. No one could send their only son off to die not knowing there was something after death. God knew His Son would come to live with Him after He died. Even though Jesus went through the worst suffering ever, God knew He would have His Son with Him forever."

Tylar, Jake and Willie were walking around talking to some of the children and playing tick-tack-toe in the dirt with them. Sally asked Mr. Sanders about the itching and burning on his arm. Mr. Sanders said it had left on Thursday, after he ate the bread that Jesus sent. Mr. A.P. and Sally were ministering to some of the others that walked up looking for the doctor and stayed to hear Pappy's story when a great big shiny red car with wheel well covers over the tires that made the car look like it was dragging the ground pulled slowly into the camp. I had seen a car like this in one of the magazines Pappy and Pa liked to look at in the evenings. A few years back it was the car of the future, a Phantom Corsair, something I was sure was way too expensive for even my Pappy to own.

Two men dressed in suits, one with a patterned red tie, one without a tie, stepped out of the car. The one without a tie was wearing black shiny boots that caught my eye as soon as his foot appeared from under the passenger door as he opened it to step out. He was wearing a yellow zoot suit like the kind Cab Calloway was wearing in a picture on his record cover. He had blondish-brown hair combed straight back with some kind of tonic. It was hard to see in the sun, but there was the hint of a mustache on his face.

The one driving the car, wearing the patterned red tie, walked around the front of the car and over to his friend. He had on a gray pin-striped suit with wide lapels and top-pleated trousers. As he loosened his tie and opened the top button of his shirt I could see shiny gold cuff links sticking out from under his suit jacket sleeves. He had beautiful shiny auburn hair that looked like fire when the sun caught it just right. I thought he was every bit as handsome as Frank Sinatra.

They both put on dress hats to shade their eyes as they peered out among the people of the camp. Pappy got up and slowly walked toward them after telling me to stay where I was. The man in the red tie addressed my Pappy as Jeremiah and then he introduced Pappy to the man in the yellow suit.

"You remember Mitchell Sternfield? Mitch, this is Jeremiah Hawthorne." The two shook hands.

"Yes, Sir. I remember you from the bank. Are you still working there?"

"He owns the bank, Mitch."

"Oh, forgive me. I was only here for my high school years. I'm afraid I didn't get to know a lot about the folks here. Didn't have too much money back then either."

Pappy said, "Are you visiting or planning to stay?"

"Well, sir, I'm home for good it seems. Johnny Kale has offered me a pastoring position in his new church."

"Will it be just the two of you?"

"What do you mean, Sir?"

"Well, you called it Johnny Kale's church. Is anyone else going to be invited?"

"Oh, yeah. Of course"

"Good. It would seem fruitless to prepare a sermon just for Johnny when he spends most of his Saturday nights in the local tavern. He hasn't been able to get up on a Sunday morning and make it to a service at any of the other churches in town in what, eleven years now?"

The man in the red tie said, "I don't need to go to church, but I can support one if I want to."

"Sure you can. You can do almost anything you want to do now that your father has given you your inheritance." And Pappy leaned in to the man named Mitch, "Just try not to end up in the swine pen eating the slop, isn't that right, Pastor?"

"He's a Reverend, not like your country church preachers."

"Oh, there's a difference? You'll have to tell me sometime, Reverend Sternfield. Right now I need to get back to these people. I'm here to tell them about Jesus."

I was starting to realize who these men were. The one with the tie had to be Tylar's friend Johnny Kale Butler and this other man must be the one Tylar said was Mr. Butler's best friend who had been in school to learn how to preach. I got up from the tented area where Sally and A.P. were doctoring on folks and started to ease closer to the men. I looked around to see if I could find Tylar, but I couldn't look long, because something was drawing me to Pappy.

"You know, Jeremiah, I brought Mitch out here to see what kind of mess this town has sat back and let move in under our noses. I never expected to see our own banker just hanging out here with the likes of this."

Pappy asked, "Is it a sin to be poor, Reverend?"

"No, sir. It's not a sin. But, Jesus said 'The poor you will have with you always.' You can't do any good out here. You should spend your time raising money to support foreign missionaries so they can stay on the field teaching the Bible to lost countries. Or, send your money to help those men and woman from your own hometown who are serving in the war efforts. Those people haven't been lazy allowing poverty to take hold of them like these men and women. Or maybe you would be a better servant to God if you put your efforts into building this new church with us. I'm afraid you are wasting your time trying to undo what God has already stated would be here until His return. I'm sorry, Sir, you can't change what God has promised. I have great plans for this new church and we could sure use you to be on board with us. Are you currently an active member of a church body?"

Pappy cleared his throat. I knew he was going to make a speech that would slowly bring the whole camp in around him. "Is that how you earned your Reverend title? Going to a school that teaches such foolishness? If I remember the scripture correctly it's found in Matthew 26. Jesus is in Simon the leper's house with His disciples. You know the boys, don't you Reverend? They were in school, too.

"Anyway, a woman came into the house bringing a bottle of very expensive perfume or ointment. As Jesus was sharing, she poured the ointment all over Jesus and ministered to Him. Jesus said she was preparing His body for His burial. Well, the 'very well taken care of' disciples started complaining about her wasting the expensive ointment. That's when Jesus hit them with, 'For ye have the poor always with you; but Me ye have not always.' And some how you get the interpretation that Jesus is saying forget about the poor?

"So then, how 'bout Matthew 19:21 when the rich young man asked how to have eternal life or what good thing he could do to get into heaven? Jesus said 'give everything you have away to the poor, and you shall have treasure in heaven: and come follow me.' It doesn't sound like Jesus intended for us to forget about the poor because they would always be here. In so many words he told the rich man to become poor! Change places with them. He would have said give it to your local church or foreign mission as you have proposed if that's what He wanted. I've found that Jesus is very blunt in expressing what He wants and doesn't want. I can stand here all day and give you my opinion as to how you ought to live your life and how to spend your money, but unless I can show you that it is what God says you should do, I'm wasting my time.

"I think, Reverend, that Jesus was trying to tell His *disciple,* the one having the big problem with spending wealth on what seemed such pointless things, the one that sold Jesus out for a few silver coin, you know the one I'm talking about? Well, I believe that Jesus was saying that he, personally, would have poor people around him always, because he would never be able to stop hoarding up stuff for himself and give to someone in need because of his own greed. Just like the rich young man who wouldn't give up his wealth for the promise of heaven and eternal life, we aren't willing to give up a frivolous luxury so that someone else can have the essentials. Even the church is not willing to give up their comforts and follow Jesus' example.

"There is much poverty in Russia, in India, and South America, because of greedy leaders who won't share their wealth with the people of their country. God will tear that kingdom down and then no one will have anything. The same will happen here if we turn our backs on our own and the Word of God. He gave us a taste of that sixteen years ago when our country 'Flapped' around in her wealth liberating herself from God. Might want to get your head out of those text books you spent all that money on and get back to the scriptures.

"If we help the poor get on their feet and begin to put a stable life together, we, too, will find riches. They might be riches in heaven, or God just might send the blessing here to be used to bless someone else. We wouldn't need to send people into foreign countries where people are poor and hungry if their leadership would share their wealth with the poor. Missionaries need to go to the people who govern those countries and try to break the strong hold of greed. Just teaching them about Jesus isn't enough. You claim to know Him, but you have no passion for these people who live right here under your nose. Jesus said that even the wicked give their sons bread if the sons need bread, not a stone. So we think we are so righteous because we do as the heathen? They believe their wealth is for *their* families only, so the common people go without. But, it's a good thing *your* father believes that, isn't it Johnny, otherwise, I guess you would be out here living with these folks. Folks who aren't sons of your father's kingdom. Reverend, you'll be serving God better if you tell your new congregation what Jesus really meant instead of giving them a way out of doing the will of the Lord."

Then Pappy stepped back and looked over Johnny Kale's car. "Nice car you got there, Johnny. One day God may ask you to sell it and give the money to the poor. I hope you'll make the right choice."

The man named Johnny looked past my Pappy and around the camp. He saw Sally and took his hat off as she walked closer to the three men. A crowd had gathered around behind Pappy as he spoke just like I had thought. I was standing beside Mr. A.P. who had reached down and taken my hand.

"How are you, Sally? Nice to see you. Is Dr. Jude going to get to come home soon?"

"I hope they all will be home soon, don't you. Hi, I'm Sally Foresight."

"Mitchell Sternfield."

"Jeremiah, we need your help over here. There's a small child with a broken bone. A.P. thinks the two of you could set it. I'm just not strong enough." There was a tension between the four of them that I didn't understand, but I wanted these men to leave.

"Pappy?" Pappy never moved, but the man Johnny turned his head and looked directly at me. He started to step my direction when Sally took a hold of his arm.

"I think it's time for you boys to get back to town. It was nice seeing you again and nice to meet you Mr. Sternfield."

Pappy corrected Sally, "Reverend."

Then Johnny looked down at Sally, "I wonder if this is the kind of place to bring your granddaughter, Jeremiah."

"Don't you worry about my family, I should think that you would have learned by now that God will take care of us."

Johnny slowly straightened the rim of his hat then placed his hat on his head and gave Sally a nod. He walked to the car, opened the door, but before getting in he stopped and looked at me. Sally stepped up to his door and blocked my view of him. She said, "Goodbye, Johnny," and he, with his Reverend, drove out of the camp.

Tylar came running up behind me breathless asking, "Was that Johnny Kale Butler?"

"Tylar! You scared me. You shouldn't come up behind someone talking so loud if that person doesn't know your back there," and I walked quickly away from the crowd.

"Lacey, there were twenty people back there around you. Why are you so mad at me?"

"I'm not. I'm just confused. To answer your question, yes. That was your friend Mr. Butler."

"Why do you say it like that?"

"Because he's not my friend, because he's not my Pappy's. You should have heard them."

"Well, that's a good point. You're acting like I did hear them and that I agreed with every word they said. Maybe you could calm down and tell me what has put that bee in your bonnet."

"That's perfect! That's exactly how I would describe how I feel right now, just like there's a bee in my bonnet, if I had a bonnet." I cut my eyes toward Tylar and smiled.

"Okay, straw hat. It just doesn't sound the same saying a bee in your straw hat. Come on. Let's go over here for a minute and you can tell me how I can get rid of that bee."

"You know, Tylar, it's just possible that one day you might not be able to fix all my bees. But right now, just having you around helps to keep them tame."

I told Tylar all I could remember about the conversation between the three men. "My Pappy's right, Tylar. Poor people are poor because rich people are focused on staying rich. And I'm one of them. That's why I'm so mad, I guess."

"Who told you that you were rich? Do you have money or does your family have money?"

"Is there a difference? I am part of my family so wouldn't I be what ever they are?"

"No, not necessarily. If you wanted to buy a house today could you? You would have to wait for someone in your family to give you money. If they didn't want to, and they don't have to, you wouldn't be able to buy a house or a sandwich for that matter. If your sister stole my new book that wouldn't make you a thief."

"I was told when I was in kindergarten that I was just like my Pappy, rich. Pappy told me that everybody that knew Jesus was rich. I didn't know Him then, so I still believed that I was rich because Pappy was. They teased me about being born with a silver spoon in my mouth. I didn't know what that meant, either. I thought everyone ate with a silver spoon. But if what I saw today is what it means to be rich, born with a silver spoon in your mouth, then I can say honestly that I don't like the taste of it and I want to spit it out."

"You can, you know."

"What?"

"Spit it out. Just make up your mind that you're not going to be a part of something so ugly. It doesn't matter that you have money. It's what you do with your life that's going to count. It's all about how you treat others. Remember? It's about how you sacrifice."

"You learn quick, Mr. Lane. You could start preaching."

"Lacey, I like Johnny Kale. I think he has a great personality. You would like him too, if you wanted to get to know him, but men like your Pappy and Pa are different. Not many people are willing to be so humble and generous when they have so much. It's just not common to see a rich man give so much. I guess that's why I like being with you and your family more than anyplace else in the world."

"You know what, Tylar. I'm not stupid. I can look around this place and see that where I live is a lot different from where these people live, but when I look at Ms. Smith and her children, they look the same as my family. Mr. Sanders reminds me of my Uncle Jeffrey and even Willie a little bit. When you look at these people they aren't so different from me, so why would I think I was a better person. Why would I think they didn't matter and I did? I don't know why I'm feeling so angry and sick in side, but I know that I don't like what I'm seeing in the hearts of grown-ups and if this is growing up, I'm going to be doing it a little different from the majority in this town."

"I'm with you, Lacey. I say we make a vow to make a difference in the lives of those no one else wants, even if they throw us out of the 'elite' circles. You didn't want to be a part of them anyway, did you?

That's the group your Aunt Penny wants to be a member of!" We both chuckled at the thought of her.

"Well, she's welcome to my membership. I think God will be pleased with our hearts. If He wants us to devote our time to people hurting like these, then that's what I want. Thank you for wanting the same thing, Tylar."

chapter seven

Three weeks had passed, Tylar Lane and I were inseparable, and being ten was exciting. It was a beautiful August day in 1945 and Aunt Gail and Uncle Trell had just arrived with their family for a morning brunch with Mother, Nanny, Marge, Sally and all us children. We were welcoming their newest son, Thomas Van Hawthorne, born just four weeks earlier. This was his first outing and the first time most of us had seen him. Some of the men were down at the river moving those houses and anchoring those that had been moved. The hardware store was complete, so Pa had put all his time into moving houses. Ms. Marge's kitchen was still in need, much to my relief and mother's, so she and her family were still having their meals with us. I was starting to learn a little something about cooking. I think my Pa was thankful for that. We all knew that at any day Mother would give birth to our newest family member, so Nanny and Sally were at our house every day. I was sure that today would be the day, but Mother insisted on having the brunch for baby Thomas.

Sally, Marge, Nanny and I fixed a wonderful meal of eggs Benedict with fresh peaches and sweet iced tea. Willie and Abby Lou covered the tables on the back porch with Mother's crisp white linen tablecloths. Retta and Sally picked fresh flowers and floated the buds in Nanny's cut crystal bowls and use them as the centerpieces for the tables. There was a light breeze coming up from the river dancing in the trees and playing with the clouds. The sound of music filled the backyard from the radio playing on the kitchen windowsill.

From the back porch I called for Miss Marge to come and cook the eggs now that the clock had said that it was time. The grown-ups came up on the porch and sat at the head table. Once Mother and Aunt Gail got baby Thomas down for a nap they joined the others. Miss Marge and I went into the kitchen while Abby Lou filled the glasses with iced tea.

The water was boiling when I took the English muffins out of the oven and placed them on a serving dish. Miss Marge was ready to fix the eggs, but she was trying to hold off till the men arrived. They were late. Miss Marge had a way of organizing everything right down to the final second and I could see her grow anxious when something was not falling into place, but I never saw her sweat or lose her smile. While she tapped her foot to the music from the radio and looked several times at her watch, I walked out on the front porch to see if I could spot any sign of the men.

Tylar and Jake were riding up in the yard on their bikes and Silas was walking up the road with his wife, Tula, who was carrying a small blue package, and walking on one side of him with their granddaughter, Mayree, holding his hand on the other side. I knew the rest of our guest couldn't be far behind. I ran to the kitchen and told Miss Marge to drop the eggs into the boiling water and then I let Ms. Sally know so she could come and greet our guests and show them to their table. I wanted everything to be perfect for Aunt Gail and Uncle Trell, but mostly for Mother so she wouldn't worry. The smoother things went the sooner everyone would leave and my new brother could be born.

It was the first time I had made my mind up as to what I wanted this baby to be. I needed another brother this time and Pa needed another son. I had prayed and ask God to give us the baby that this family needed and I was sure it was a boy.

I picked up the bowls of peaches to take out to the tables. As I rounded the dish cabinet and pushed on the screen door, an interruption came on the radio. We were all programmed to stop whatever we were doing for an announcement that came over the airwaves. The last time the newsman had broken into the regular programming was when Franklin D. Roosevelt, our country's President, had died. He was in Warm Springs, Georgia vacationing when his brain started bleeding. Rumor was that he was with his girlfriend, but most people didn't like to talk about it. I tried not to think about it because I liked his wife and the work she did very much, and I hoped she hadn't had to sacrifice her marriage to be a great lady. If I remember correctly, she was out of the country helping people in need when her husband died. Pappy and I had gone to the train station to watch the train bringing the casket with our President's body in it back to Washington, D.C.

I held my breath along with everyone else waiting for the announcement to begin. Tylar and Jake had walked around to the back of the house and were headed up the back porch steps. Their bodies were frozen as we listened to the announcement. My heart was overjoyed and sorrowed at the same time. Sally was weeping openly hugging my mother and saying, "He's coming home! My Jude is coming home! They're all coming home, Abbie, all of them!"

And Nanny was being embraced by Uncle Trell, "Alvin and Marty, Momma, they're coming home."

Miss Marge came out of the kitchen bringing the eggs Benedict on the serving dish. I was still frozen in my place next to the screened door. She shoved her dish at me almost knocking the peaches to the floor and ran to Jake and Tylar. She hugged Jake, who was tearing up a bit, and she hugged Tylar and said, "This is a great day! Your Uncle, my brother, will be home. Your friend Jake's father will be coming home. Miss Sally will have her husband back. Theodore will have his father back, and Miss Nanny Jo Rett will have her sons' home, and Mr. Silas' family will be complete. You boys remember this day. The only joy war brings is when it's over, and only then is it joy for those who have someone coming home."

That was it. I couldn't feel joy because of all the people who were killed. Those who had died. For what? Why did one bomb stop the war when there had been millions of bombs dropped over these past ten or so years. What about the innocent Japanese who lost their loved ones and lost their lives and those who still might. Surely not everyone in Japan was guilty. What about this man called Hitler, where was he? Wasn't he the target?

The radio was playing "Happy Days Are Here Again" and everyone was dancing, even the children in the yard, though I doubt they knew why. I placed the bowls of peaches that now had the serving dish of eggs on top of them down on the table as the children were called to eat. The men had not yet arrived, though no one seemed to notice. Silas and Tula had found their way through the house and were celebrating the return of their two younger sons and the father of Mayree. There was such busyness around me and all I wanted was my Pappy. I had to see him. I knew that he would understand how I was feeling, better than I understood myself.

"Miz Lacey? I don't know what all this means, you?"

I turned my head to see Mayree standing beside me, a head taller than myself now, but nearly two months younger. When she was living here she was that little girl that stood out from the rest. She didn't look as much like her daddy's side of the family as she did her mother's. Her mother was a direct descendant of a Somalian King. I guess that made her a princess. The King had been killed and his family fled to the States. That's how her father met her mother. She was Silas' only granddaughter. She, her mother and father lived in one of Pappy's river houses until her father went into the army. That's when she and her mother moved to Cullowhee where her mother lived. She had been a great playmate, when she lived here, and had helped Silas and me with some of the chores. She was prettier than I expected her to grow up and be, but I don't know why I was surprised.

"Maybe this means you will be coming back to live here with all of us now that this war is over and you and I can be real good friends again."

"Is dat what's happening? Is da war over?"

"Well Mayree, that's what they all believe. That's what all this celebrating is about."

"Does yous believe it, Miz Lacey?"

I had no answer for her. I didn't know what I believed. "I believe you have the most beautiful eyes and your father is going to fall in love with you all over again." I wrapped my arms around her neck and joined the celebration by asking Mayree to sit at our table right next to me.

Pappy had come on to the porch with Aunt Penny and family. She was not enjoying the celebration like the other wives who were soon to see their husbands. I think I understood her hesitation. Kimmy and

Theodore were focusing on the food and never mentioned their father like the other boys who were making plans to take their fathers fishing and horseback riding as soon as they arrived. But, no one knew when that would be so they didn't ask for fear it would bring the atmosphere down. We all had learned one thing about war; everything took time, a long time.

Aunt Penny wasn't going to sit tight and wait for a more appropriate time to discuss with Pappy the conditions of her new home. She was demanding that Pappy, in addition to moving the house to safer ground, giving it a fresh white washing, making repairs on the kitchen and putting in a bath and water closet, that he also put on an addition of two bedrooms now that her husband would be joining her and his children.

"Theodore and Kimmy need their own rooms; they can not be in the same room with Alvin and me. It's not right. How can I welcome my husband home properly with them in our room? And Kimmy is a young lady now; she doesn't need to be sleeping with a mature young man, even if he is her brother. We see way too much of him now with the wash tub sitting in the middle of the kitchen floor. And Alvin won't be a bit comfortable hanging himself out with his daughter warming by the fire right next to him while he bathes."

"You know something, Penny, sometimes you give us more information than we really need."

"Oh, that's easy for you to say, sweet Miss Abigail. Your father has made sure that you have a bathroom in your home."

My Pa walked up on the porch just in time to hear mother and Penny's conversation and join in, "I'm the one who has made sure that my family has two baths to bathe in. We have a large family that is going to get bigger any day now," and he bent down and kissed my mother. "How is my beautiful bride today?" Mother just blushed. "Bath time is a very busy time around our house. When your husband gets home, he two can provide what your family needs. It isn't the responsibility of Jeremiah's anymore. Are you prepared to start living your life with your husband being the provider for your family only? He's going to need your support. I'd make that 'honey do list' out for Alvin so he feels like he's been missed by his wife. It sure will help him feel like he's needed and wanted, something all these men are going to need to feel once they return."

"You're absolutely correct, William. The last letter Marty wrote to Gail and I he expressed just those feelings. He wondered what he would do when the war was over. I told him I needed help with the store if he was interested. All he ever did was farm with you, Dad. He feels like you have the farming side of things covered and he doesn't want someone to lose their job because of him."

"Marty's too smart for farming, Trell. He's welcome to work with my farms or come to the bank, but he's too smart for either of those. He needs to be flying 'cause it's in his heart, but his mother doesn't sleep well thinking about that plane falling out of the sky. I just want him to be happy, same as with all my children, but he's just too smart to be saddled with farm life."

"Let's just get them home, Jeremiah. I don't care if they sit with their heads in my lap for the rest of their lives, I just want all my boys home, safe and sound."

Pappy wrapped his arm around Nanny, placing her head on his shoulder while she cried tears of joy very softly. Pappy noticed the hanging head at the end of the table. "Pass me some more peaches, Silas, I do believe these are the best crop of peaches you've ever grown."

My Pappy would never hurt another human being for all the wealth of the world, but he had seen his error in judging the occupation of farming. Though every man in my back yard was a farmer they also had other jobs, all except for Silas, and he was just as smart as any of the other men who did not farm full time. He hadn't gone to school like the rest of us, but my Pappy had taught him and Tula how to read. He helped me, on occasion, with my school work when I had a lot of home work and Pa was going to be late. He loved my family and my family loved him. His skin was different from mine, but Pappy put it like this: "It's not a man's color that matters, it's his spirit and Silas has the same colored spirit in him as we do." I know my Pappy was feeling bad right then thinking he put Silas down, but I know that the spirit in Silas told him that Pappy's heart was not seeing him any different than anyone else. Farming was hard work, from sun-up to sundown. Things were changing for our country and if a man had a little bit of smarts he could do something else to make a living that would put food on the table. My Pappy was just seeing the opportunities out there for young men and he wanted the best for his sons and daughters.

"Mr. Jeremiah, do you think there are jobs our boys will be able to get when they come home?"

"Ms. Tula, your boys are going to have every opportunity to succeed as my boys will. They've gotten training in the service to be leaders. We'll see to it that they go to college if that's what they want. Nothing will hold back a member of my family."

"Thank you, Jeremiah, but farming's a good honest living, hard work never hurt nobody. I's got plenty of good hard work ta keep them boys busy. Then maybe Tula and me can take our savings and make that trip to Asheville we's always wanted ta make and let them boys keep da farm going whiles we gone."

It seemed like everybody was having these dreams of things being different and better and happier. All kinds of plans were being made and I some how felt left out, because I didn't have someone coming home to change my life or disrupt it. I suddenly thought that I was one out of a million who had been spared the horrors of war with separation, then restoration and letting go, then rebuilding. I would simply continue to exist just as I had, normal, with a normal family, nothing changing, nothing, except maybe me.

Then I remembered my new brother. He would bring the change that would satisfy my need for a new relationship, so I began to ponder the things we would do together, the things I would show him and teach him. I was feeling very proud that I, too, had dreams to share with my friends who were talking about the return of their loved ones when my mother let out a sudden grown and then a chuckle as she looked at Ms. Sally and asked her to help her be excused. Sally jumped up and over to Mother's chair where Pa was ready to carry Mother if she needed him to.

"I can make it to my room, William, you see to our guest."

Everyone had finished eating, but no one looked like they had any plans to leave. As she was helping Mother to the screen door, Sally said to Marge, "This probably won't take long. Number five is usually pretty quick and easy. Her dress is wet and so is her chair. Can you take care of that for us?"

"I'll get it, Mother," I said as I raced to her side, "You just relax, I'll take care of everything."

Not only was my life going to change like everybody else, but it was going to change first. I couldn't remember a time when I was more excited, except when I ate my first meal with Tylar. He was standing beside me now as I watched my mother slowly walk through the pantry and into the kitchen.

"I'll help you, Lace. I know what to do. I helped bring Pauley into this world."

"He sure did, but I'll get the mop and clean up the chair if you two will take the lemonade and tea out into the yard. Maybe everyone could take their glasses out into the yard and enjoy some croquet while we wait the arrival of the newest member of the Rutledge family?"

My Pappy spoke up, "Well William, why don't you and Bob challenge Trell and Silas to some horseshoes. I'll get a game of croquet started and then slip off to the hammock in the shade."

Nanny, Gail, Marge, Tula and Penny went into the house. Everyone else went to the back yard to find entertainment, everyone except for me and Mayree. We sat very still on the porch steps hearing the laughter of the games being played, but listening to the faint cries of my mother's labor coming from the open window upstairs. Eternity passed and then it passed again before we heard the faint cry of someone other than my mother.

Jeffery Cole was born the day the war ended at 12:30 in the afternoon. Uncle Martin Cole Hawthorne would be so pleased that Mother and Pa would refer to his newest nephew as Cole. I couldn't wait to show baby Cole to the uncle I barely remembered, but loved very much.

It was November when Uncle Marty and Uncle Alvin were expected home. Most all the harvesting was finished, except for the pumpkin. Pappy and Pa had enlarged the size of our farm by three times. They wanted to be sure there was plenty of work to do if Uncle Marty or Uncle Alvin wanted to farm, but for now it was more than Willie, Silas and I could handle. Pa was busy building new houses for sons who had gone away to war and came back as men needing homes of their own with plans of getting married. Some returned already married. Pa knew that as more soldiers returned there would be even more building to be done so he hired several young men who were some of the first to be released. His crew had increased and so had mine. I was so thankful that Mayree and her mother had come back to live in one of Pappy's tenant houses that had been moved to higher ground. Mayree had become a dear friend to me and Willie as she had been before. Some people are always the same, and they are friends for life no matter what road life takes you down.

Mayree helped us with our chores every day and helped out with my sisters. It seemed that baby Cole had taken all of my mother's energy when he arrived. Most of that energy was spent crying and Mother simply didn't have the energy to do anything more than rock him and feed him.

With the increase in the farm size, my helpers and I were responsible for the chickens; all two hundred or so of them. We fed them, watered them, collected, washed and sorted the eggs everyday. Once a week the coops had to be cleaned. We did that on Saturday morning bright and early, sometimes before the chickens woke up. We were in charge of the horses, turning them out in the pasture in the day and back in the stall at night. Silas was still responsible for 'O Plow. We fed and watered the cats and Pa's coonhounds. Because Pa had several dog lots, and Pappy lived so close to town, Pappy kept his fox hounds and bird dogs at our house. They, too, were looking to me for food and water.

Once we started school we had to break down our chores into two parts. Chickens and cats were fed and watered in the morning and other than turning them out in the pasture in the morning, the horses were not fed grain until evening when the dogs were tended to. Homework and shopping were done right after school. It didn't leave much time for Tylar and me. Mayree helped Willie and the girls with their homework. She was very smart, much smarter than me. She helped Mother and Pa with the calculation of the eggs. She received a percentage of the eggs for her pay along with ten cents a day. She was worth more than that to me, but that was a fair wage at that time.

Willie and I put the eggs in baskets we had tied to our bikes and took them to the market every day. Pa had put two more wheels on Willie's bike so he didn't have to hold the bike in balance as he road. The eggs were too precious to take the chance that they might fall to the ground. We received a credit from Miller's Market to buy staples with as we needed them. If the credit became a large amount, Mr. Miller would send my Pa a check. Mayree was the one who let Pa know when the credit was large enough to request a check. Pa said Mayree was worth her weight in gold and that she was the best partner he had ever had. When Mayree heard my Pa say these things about her, she would blush for a moment beaming with love for him, then quickly find some other work that needed to be done. She never sat in praise very long. Me, I soaked in it.

There were many things to be done before my Uncles' arrival. Mother was not able to clean the spare bedroom for Uncle Marty, if he wanted to stay with us. Nanny was hoping he would stay with her and Pappy, but Pappy thought it would be better for Marty to feel useful. If he stayed with us and saw the work that needed to be done, maybe he would find a place. If he did decide to farm, he would be where most of the work was. Also, he and my mother were very close and she needed him now. Her heart would break if she couldn't see him simply because she was too weak to get to Nanny's in the evenings. So Pa was able to convince Mother to let him hire someone to come in and clean Marty's room, but she still insisted that we not be spoiled as a family hiring people to do jobs any one of us was capable of doing ourselves.

Penny, Theodore and Kimmy were still living in one of Pappy's tenant houses. Penny was constantly on to Pappy about the repairs she wanted done to the house. Pappy had agreed to another bedroom, but only one until Uncle Alvin had a chance to say what he wanted done to the house and whether or not they would stay in that house. Pa hired a lady and her husband to clean and paint Uncle Marty's room and had a crew of men working on Penny's additions that would be livable by the time Uncle Alvin arrived.

Mother had given me and Mayree a list of things needed to finish Uncle Marty's room and some things she needed from the market. She also wanted us to ask Aunt Gail to help us pick out some pants and shirts for Uncle Marty so he wouldn't have to shop the moment he got home. No one had any idea what size he was, but he had always been close to Uncle Trell's size so we were going to go with that. Nanny said she was sure he was much smaller than Trell because he hadn't had a decent meal since he left home. We decided to let him grow into the clothes; too big was better than too small.

On Saturdays Miss Sally came and sat with Mother for a few hours in the mornings. They would play a few hands of canasta if Cole would let them. Sometimes Miss Sally would just keep him quiet long enough for Mother to get some sleep. She seemed to know better than anybody what to do for a colicky baby. Sleep was far too valuable to me these days so I had learned to tune him out.

After Sally arrived, Mayree and I got our list together and walked to town to do our shopping. We hoped to find Pa or Silas and catch a ride back with them for lunch. The first store we went to was Montgomery Wards where we asked the clerk for help in finding curtains to fit the window in Uncle Marty's room. We had never hung anything bright and cheery over the blackout shades that hung in that room. The store was buzzing with ladies shopping for the men in their lives that would soon be returning. Many of the ladies I recognized from the day Pappy, Willie and I picked up bread for the migrants. Some of them recognized me and spoke as they passed us in the aisles.

Aunt Gail came hurried into the store looking in all directions for Mayree and me. "Lacey! Where are you? Hi Mrs. Waldrop. Have you seen my niece Lacey Rutledge?"

"Yes I have," and Mrs. Waldrop leaned close to my aunt Gail. "She is with that little colored girl. I sure will be glad when Abigail is feeling better. It's just not right someone of Lacey's breeding to be accompanied with . . ."

"Can you tell me in what department they were in when you last saw them?"

"Back in housewares looking at the curtains I believe. How's that beautiful boy of yours doing? Growing like a weed I'm sure."

"He is as handsome as his father and growing as you say. Thank you for asking. I must find my niece now and get back to the hardware store. Please excuse me for rushing."

"I understand. Tell the family hello for me and see you at church Sunday?"

Aunt Gail began to walk away saying, "God willing," when she spotted us standing behind the sweater table. She spun us around heading quickly away from Mrs. Waldrop. "Well, where are those curtains you've picked out?"

"I like these the best, but I can't find the size Mother wrote on the list."

"Let me see. This size will do nicely. They'll be a bit bunched up, but I like them to look full instead of skimpy don't you?"

"Guess I never thought about it, but if you think Uncle Marty will like them full then let's go with full. What do you think, Mayree?"

"I's likes'em full."

"Well then, let's see what you two think about men's clothes."

"Aunt Gail, I can honestly say I've never thought about what a man is wearing. I only know when he looks nice and when he doesn't."

"Well, today you're going to find out why you think that and what you like. You do have an opinion, you've just never thought about what it is. Have you got an opinion, Mayree?"

"Miss Gail, I likes what da GI's are wearing, dungarees and their white T-shirts. It's simple nough, it looks clean and there's not a lot ta wash. You can work in the field picking peaches or go da the drug store and get a soda pop. It's a whole lots better dan dose suits and ties. Dose shirts need too mush starch fo my liking."

"Mayree, you're a sensible girl. I can tell you've been doing the laundry in your house."

"Miss Gail, lots a times my Ma is way too tired when she gets home from dat mill ta wash and iron after she cooks our supper sos I helps. I show don't mine helping, but it be nice if I's could make it easier some how."

"Amen to that. Dungarees and T-shirts? What do you girls think about that for Uncle Marty?"

"I think I agree with Mayree. I like that style on the GIs I think Uncle Marty will look handsome and he will feel comfortable out of that uniform."

"And he wont have no excuse fo not helping us with dem chickens either, Lacey. If all he had to wear was a uniform, den I's guess heed be a bit over dressed in da chicken coop."

"Come on girls let's get him some socks too."

We got everything on Mother's list that we could buy from this store. Aunt Gail got Marty some nightclothes for a welcome home present and a bathrobe and shoes for Nanny and Pappy to give him. All the families were pitching in on the cost of the new room as Uncle Alvin's surprise. We walked down to Miller's Market to get a rump roast out of our freezer so it could thaw out in time for Uncle Alvin's welcome home party. He was expected home sometime Monday and Uncle Marty any day after that.

Aunt Gail said she would call down to my Pa's office and tell him we were almost ready if he was ready to head home for lunch. "In any case, I'll get someone to meet you two out here by the parking meter in front of the market to give you a ride back to the house. Have fun finishing up your shopping and don't forget the butter. It's not on your list." She knelt down and gave us both hugs and walked on up the street to the hardware store.

Mother had given us permission to buy some gumdrops for all of us. We couldn't resist going by the candy counter first. We just stared down into the glass cabinet at all the different kinds of chocolates and flavored gum drops. There were big glass jars with tin lids that flipped back with cookies inside made by someone named "Toms." Our mouths were watering to the point of almost drooling. I nearly choked on my own saliva when Mr. Miller asked if there was anything he could get for us.

"Yes sir. My mother would like for us to get one of the largest rump roast we have in our freezer. And then we need these things on our list."

"Okay, I can do that for you. Are you getting ready for those boys to return?"

"Oh, yes sir, Mr. Miller. We're having a party for Uncle Alvin on Monday. Mother didn't think we should wait till Monday to take the roast out of the freezer." Mrs. Waldrop walked into the store as I was telling Mr. Miller our plans. "Mayree makes the best basting for rump roast so we wanted to be sure to let it soak in that for awhile before we cook it."

"I bet that's some good eating. Mayree's mama fixed my Sarah a chicken potpie when she was feeling low, I've never tasted one better. If you learned how to cook from your mama, then you're some cook.

I'll get that roast and be right back. Pick out the candy you want and I'll bag it up when I get back with the roast. Ladies, I'll be right with you just as soon as I take care of Miss Rutledge and Miss Porter." And he disappeared behind the door leading to where the freezers were kept.

Mayree and I were planning what to buy for Willie, Abbie Lou and Retta, as well as for us. We wrote down what each of them would want and how many of each kind. I felt bad about not bringing Cole something, but he just didn't have the stomach for anything other than sugar water and a few spoons full of cereal.

I looked around the market and noticed that most of the ladies that were at Montgomery Wards had come into the market. They had their arms full of wrapped packages and overflowing corded handle paper sacks. I suddenly felt grown-up carrying my own packages and shopping for supper, as I was sure they were doing for their families.

"Here we go Miss Rutledge, your roast. Is that going to be big enough, or do you think you might need two?"

"That looks like plenty. We will have lots of side dishes to go with it after the great harvest we've had this year. I don't think the corn has ever been sweeter."

"Yes ma'am. Thanks to just the right amount of sunshine and rain. Here are the rest of your things. Shall I subtract it off your credit?"

"Yes sir, and here's a list of the candy we need. Just let Mayree know how much it all is so she can put it in the ledger."

Mr. Miller bagged up our candy in individual bags and wrote down the amount of each item on a receipt. He credited Pa's account for the eggs and handed it to Maryee. "I think you will find all of that correct."

"Yes sir, I'm show I will. Thank ye."

"Thank you, Mr. Miller," and I climbed down off the stool at his counter.

"You're welcome, girls. Tell your families hello and come back to see me. Oh, and keep up the good work. Your eggs are my best sellers."

Mayree stopped and turned back to Mr. Miller with a smile on her face, "We may need ta renegotiate our price."

Mr. Miller looked at me. "Sorry Mr. Miller, Pa and Mayree are in partnership with each other. She has all the brains, I just work for them."

"Your pa has a sharp partner. I'm sure I can work out something. I wouldn't want to lose my best account," and Mr. Miller smiled with a wink.

"Thank you. I'll tell him you'll be waiting to meet with him," and we giggled our way out of the store.

Once we got out side and heard the screened door slam behind us, we screamed and giggled some more. "Mayree, don't you ever let anybody tell you that you can't do and be what ever you want to. You have all the makings of a great businesswoman. Remind me that I would be very foolish to ever let you work for anyone else. And I must tell my father what a prize he has!"

"Somedimes dere's just dis smart thing dat happens in my head and I's just clicks in on it. It happen' when he say our eggs was selling da most. I'd noticed he was getting twenty-one cents a dozen. He's paying us ten cents a dozen. Why, he's making more dan one hundred percent on our eggs. Dat's not at all right. We's doing all da work and it cost us almost two cent an egg to gets it here, by da time you pays me, da chicken feed, my granddaddy to harvest dat corn and crush it up and ... "

"Mayree, Mayree! Tell Pa. All that stuff is way over my head. You know I don't understand a thing about business. Or even money! I only know to put it in Pappy's bank."

"Yous can know moe dan yous do, yous just havta wanna. I's didn't just wake up knowing all dis, I's wants to learn. Yous need to be wise with yos money, 'cause nobody else will be watchin' out fo ya. And whats 'bout Willie, yo needs to watch fo him, too."

"Mayree, I guess that's why God sent you in our lives."

"I mays not always be here fo you, yous neva know what God's gonna do. Everybody needs ta be able ta think on they's own."

"Oh, Mayree! We both need a little more practice with that! We forgot the butter!" And I turned to run into the store.

Mayree hollered to me, "I's wait fo whoever's gonna picks us up and tell 'em to wait fo ya. Gets me a receipt."

I reached for the door handle to pull it open when I heard preacher Burton's wife's voice, "I don't know why Jeremiah Hawthorne insists on bringing this whole town down, selling land to those beggar people in his migrant camp. Doesn't he know that trash like that will keep our town from growing with respectable folk who will join the church and bring good money in for good work into the Lord's house? Beggars don't give anything to the Lord's work, they just take. A church cannot exist giving out and never getting anything back. God helps those who help themselves. Jeremiah has slipped away from the word of the good book and he's building something that none of us understand, but you can bet he will come out on top. He always does. You know most of these people are German Jews. Maybe he thinks they will get some of their money that's back in Germany now that the war is over and they will bring that money here to put it in *his* bank. I'm sure we won't ever see any of it at the church. Jews aren't Christian, you know."

Mr. Miller spoke up. "Ladies, ladies! Jeremiah is not helping these people for his own gain. He's always looked out for this town and gave above—"

"Get your head out of the sand, Merlin Miller."

"My head isn't in the sand, but I do see a little dust on the top of your hat, Mildred." She stomped her way over to the washstand Mr. Miller had on display and peered in the mirror at the top of her hat as he continued. "Jeremiah Hawthorne has a heart as big as Texas, I'll have you to know, and I heard it from his own lips, he wanted to simply give land to the families out at the camp, and you and I both know he has enough to do that and not miss it, but God told him that he would be taking what self-worth those people have away from them. If someone gave you everything you had you would eventually feel like that person saw you as someone who couldn't provide for yourself or your family. Sure, at first it would be great having everything handed to you and doing nothing to receive it, but sooner or later you would want to do something to build your self-esteem. If Jeremiah can show those people Jesus in it all, then they will thank God for what they have and He will be glorified in it. That's truly all that Jeremiah is interested in."

"Well, if he is truly interested in God being glorified then why on earth is he letting his grandchild prance around town with a niggra as a play mate. Can't he see that niggra children and our children don't belong together? Even the scriptures teach that. I don't care how low a person is, they'll never be as low ..."

"Mrs. Waldrop, that's enough! I won't have that talk in my store! And what scriptures are you talking about? You better be careful how you distort the word of God. I would make sure what you say is in there, is really there, before you go spreading such foolishness around town. I'll serve a black man or woman same as any of you. There's not one of you that can tell me *one thing* against *one niggra* that lives within fifty miles of here, or anything wrong with those migrants that live ..."

Mrs. Burton's face was turning red. "*They're scary*, and that's enough, Merlin Miller! And they have no place being in partnership with a white man. A niggra *child* in partnership with a white man? What are they thinking? Someone must tell the Rutledges and the Hawthornes that they have to stop thinking they own this town and start acting like they're a part of it. Every niggra man around will think he has the right to own a business or be a partner if they get wind of this *child* keeping the ledger for the Rutledges, even if it seems innocent and she's only helping while Abigail recovers. It's not Christian to give these people false hope."

"Oh, it's not as innocent as you make it sound," Mrs. Waldrop said shaking her head. "Mrs. Gail Hawthorne was asking that niggra child her opinion of the curtains and the clothes they were purchasing for her brother-in-law, Martin. Why, I never once thought of asking my maid, Josephine, what she thought about any thing pertaining to my housekeeping. She can't even remember what side of the plate the forks go on, and she's worked for me for fifteen years."

Mr. Miller said "Ladies, the child's name is Mayree. She has a name you know?"

"I think I'll go to my husband and get him to talk to the deacons. They should be the ones to correct Jeremiah."

"That would be a great idea, Mrs. Burton, ever since Jeremiah started thinking his granddaughter had a special gift from God he has steered us in all kinds of mess. I worked my fingers to the bone this harvest season picking to sell and picking what I wanted to put up for my family at the same time because she *heard from God* that our river was coming out of it's banks and flood the bottoms. We moved our pasture fences, cut off timber and plowed new fields for next year's harvest, and for what? We haven't seen more than a quarter of an inch of rain at one time this whole summer. I say she's been touched all right, but not by God. I will talk to my husband who will second the decision for the deacons to go to Jeremiah and correct him."

"Mrs. Black, your husband *is* a deacon. How convenient for him to make the vote and then second the vote, and just encase he doesn't know how to vote, praise God, he has someone who can tell him! Is anyone aware that Jeremiah is a deacon, and that he is the chairman of the deacons this term, and the only one in the whole mess that I know of that meets all the criteria of a deacon according to the Bible."

"Mr. Miller, if you are trying to be funny at a time that is so desperate, you are not appreciated."

"I seldom am, Mrs. Burton. Can I get you something so that you can be on your way?"

"I simply need a pound of coffee. I want it ground fine so we can get every bit of flavor out of the bean and make sure you measure me out a full pound, Merlin Miller. Mrs. Black, do you see there being a problem with Jeremiah on the board?"

"Of course not. There are eleven more who will see exactly what we are seeing. I'm sure there will be questions as to how a man like that ever got on the deacon board, let alone the chairmanship!"

I found myself standing in a tunnel with no place to go except backward. I bumped into Mayree who was standing up close behind me. "Yo Pappy's sittin in da truck just round da corner. Yous go ahead and I's gets da butter."

Mayree grabbed the door handle and flung it open with a wild swing. I stepped back up to the door screen to watch Mayree just as big as life march right through the group of ladies and up to Mr. Miller's counter. "I's afraid I's just not so smart as I's thinks. I's plum forgots da butter my *master* needed. She'd have my head if I's got all da way out of town without dat butter. Yous be show to mark it down on dis receipt. When she goes over her books tonight I's show nough don't want her to finds even one mistake. Dat family's been ways too good ta me fo me ta be cast out now."

Mr. Miller put the butter and the receipt in Mayree's hand. "I's thanks ya, Mista. Miller, in moe ways dan yous knows. Scoos me ladies for steppin' in front of yous, but I's in a hurry. They's in the truck waitin' fo me," and she skipped down the isle and out the screened door taking some of my packages as she looped her arm through mine and drug me behind her around the corner to Pappy's truck.

"Sorry ta takes so long in dat stoe. Busy day fo shoppin' ain't it, Lacey?"

"Uhuh."

"Thinks we gots it all though, Miz Abigail will love dees curtains. My mammy would die fos curtains like dem. Perty lavender roses on a cream back ground. Not at all flashy, too flashy fo a man's room. Dey'll be just right fo Mista Marty, Don't yous thinks, Miz Lacey?"

"Uhuh."

"And we's picks him out some dungarees and white t-shirts and socks. We's boths likes 'en, don't we's, Miz Lacey?"

"Uhuh."

"Show was busy at da stoe. Show was. Dere was ladies everywhere, dere was. Ain't dat right, Miz Lacey?"

"Uhuh."

"Seen Miz Gail, too, we's did. She picks out a robe fo yous to give to Mista Marty. Real nice, real nice, ain't it, Miz Lacey?"

"Uhuh."

Other than the occasional rock in the road that flew up and hit the truck or cut a path into the weeds along the road, there was only the sound of the motor humming as we finished the ride home. When we pulled up into our drive Pappy said, "Girls, I know you're excited about your purchases, but how about giving me a little bit of your time before you jump out of the truck?"

He pushed in the clutch and the break bringing the truck to a stop. Then he turned the key in the switch cutting off the motor and slid the gear stick into first gear. "Did you see a lot of ladies in town today, a real lot?"

"Oh, yes sir, Mista Pappy. They's in every stoe today."

"What about you, Lacey? See the same thing?"

"Uhuh." I kept my eyes focused on the floor mats wanting this moment to end.

"Did you see Mrs. Burton, Mrs. Black, Mrs. Waldrop, and Miss Franklin?"

"Uhuh, show did."

"Miss Franklin? We didn't see Miss Franklin. Guess we don't know nothin' about it, Pappy, 'cause we didn't see Miss Franklin," and I reached for the door handle.

"How about you, Mayree, did you see Miss Franklin?"

"If dat's Miz. Lacey's Sunday School teacher, then I's seed her, in Montgomery Wards, not the market. Mista Miller helped us at the market. He's a fine man. He's gonna talks ta Mr. Rutledge 'bout da eggs? Think he's gonna give us moe money fo dem."

"There seems to be some talk among some of the ladies and their husband's about the way we live. Seems like some of them don't approve of us helping the migrants and they want them to leave. If they can force me to stop helping them, then they think the migrants will move on somewhere else."

"But God sent them here! Why should we tell them they can't stay?"

"Dis is dere promised land."

"Well, no it's not, but for now they are here and God has told me to help. One day He will call all His chosen people, the Israelites, back to their homeland. He may have already called them and they aren't listening. I don't know. It's not for me to judge them, He simply asked me to love them while they're here. Not everyone agrees with me and they are slandering my name. I don't care about me, but I think they are saying things about you, Lacey, to hurt me. If they want to hurt me they know they have to hurt someone I love. That's how Satan gets to Jesus by hurting the ones that He loves. Like you and Mayree. Jesus weeps when you hurt, but we have to be strong, because their words cannot really hurt us, but they can keep us from doing the will of God if we let them. Lacey, did you and Mayree hear something that hurt your feelings today?"

"Yes, Sir."

"I'm sorry. I'm not going to press you to tell me if you don't want to. Sometimes it's better to process it and make a sound judgment for yourself."

"Well, I don't have to think about it and I don't care what those ladies say, I love those migrants and Mayree will always be my friend! And that's all I'm gonna saying about it."

"When and if you want to talk, I'll be here."

"Thanks Pappy."

"Come here girls." And we both fell over into Pappy's arms. "Let's go show your mother and Nanny what you bought and get some fried chicken that Nanny has stunk up the kitchen with all morning," he said, pinching us on our noses.

I just couldn't understand why everybody didn't see what a great man my Pappy was. His heart truly was as big as Texas. We ate lunch without much small talk. Mother was tired and didn't seem to notice. Nanny and Pappy exchanged glances, but nothing was said about town or shopping or ladies. We only talked about Uncle Alvin's party and how we wish we knew exactly what day Uncle Marty would be here so we could be ready with the "fatted calf" for him.

After lunch, Mayree and I went with Nanny and Sally to Uncle Marty's room to hang the curtains. They did brighten up the room and just as Mayree had said they were not too frilly for a man. I was sure Uncle Marty would love his new room after living in barracks with a bunch of other men with no curtains and no bed spreads. "Only a cot and a blanket to call your own." That's what Uncle Trell had read to us from one of Uncle Marty's letters. Now he had a pale green bed spread on his iron bed with a lavender and cream checkered throw pillow that Mother had knitted. A cherry roll-top desk with a teak wood desk set and blotter, that Pappy used at the bank when he first opened it, was against the wall to the left of the bed. Nanny wanted Uncle Marty to have the desk so he could write to any friend he would be missing from the Air Force. As you entered the room to the right on the wall next to the door was a cherry wardrobe with an oval mirror on the closet door and five deep drawers under a small dresser top. Pappy said it was the perfect place for Marty to keep his uniform hat. On the right side of the bed, under the window, was a dark footed washstand with two kerosene lamps on either side of a rounded mirror. An electric light was hanging from the middle of the ceiling that Pa had put in after electricity had been brought down our road, although, we seldom used the lights because we were so used to the kerosene lamps. Two crisp linen hand towels that Nanny had embroidered green ivy along the hem hung on the wrought iron towel rack on the right side of the wash stand. A large porcelain pitcher and bowl that Uncle

Marty had shipped to Mother from England sat proudly in the middle. Mother had framed a picture that was taken when she and her brothers were Willie's and my age and placed it beside the bowl next to the bed. The black-out shades had been removed so there would be no evidence of a war, though we all knew it would not be something Uncle Marty would soon forget.

I went to the library to find Pappy, but he was not where I thought he would be taking his nap. I checked the living room, the parlor, the kitchen, the front porch, then the back. There was only one other place, but he seldom went to the river without me. I started walking towards the river when I heard a sound in the barn. 'O Plow was not in the field today, but this sound was not the sound a horse makes. I approached the barn with caution for fear that something was hurt and maybe it had gone mad. As I got closer I could hear the sounds of someone in great pain, groaning and weeping. I peered in from the side of the door. It was hard to see at first because my eyes were not adjusting quickly to the darkened room.

Our barn had eight stalls, four on each side of a wide hallway. It was wide enough for a team of horses to be hitched up and three rows of hay to be stacked along the stall walls on each side. Mayree, Willie and I had been stacking the hay on the right side only and then walking what hay we needed across the hall to the other stalls. We had stacked it three high and three deep, but some bails were missing. My Pappy was sitting on the side of his hip and his arms lying across the top of one of the bails with his face buried in his arms. His chest was expanding and receding with such force he looked like someone was pumping him with a bellows. Only his suspenders were keeping him together. I wanted to run to him thinking he was hurt or had fallen, but something was holding me back.

He was mumbling things I could not understand between his sobs and beating his fist on the hay bail. There was a lump that formed in my throat bringing me to nearly choking. I spun around with my back against the barn siding. I had to bend over with my bottom resting on the barn because I was sure I would throw up from the thoughts that were swimming in my head. Had he heard them? Did he lie to me when he said these words said against him couldn't hurt him? Or was it because of me? Was he so broken because of what they said about me? "Oh, Pappy, it doesn't matter what they say as long as you still love me!" My stomach was now in knots and the nausea so overwhelming that I clinched my stomach in my arms, still bent over, and walked around the barn to the stall door opening. I was where no one could see me from the house, but in better hearing range to Pappy. His cries seemed to be magnified by the walls of the barn and pumped directly out the stall door opening I was now sitting in. I listened to him cry, groan, and rant in a language I had never heard for what seemed like an hour or more. Was it something the migrants had taught him, and why would he choose to speak to God in a different language? God had always answered him before. I prayed for Pappy while he mourned, not understanding fully his pain, but dying with him inside. Suddenly there seemed to be a softening in his words, a sweetness in his weeping. I could tell that he was standing up. I could see his arms stretched over his head and he was waving them to the rhythm of a song the migrants must have taught him. He began to laugh as he sang and I guess he was dancing. I had seen him dance with Nanny in the back yard, but not this fast or like this. I walked through the stall to the inside wall where I could look through the open space between the slats. He was dancing and jumping and singing and clapping and then he went to his knees, and then fell over on his face, then he was perfectly quiet.

Tears were still streaming down my face, but nothing else in me moved, not even my lungs. He was dead. My Pappy was dead. Blood running to my face, mouth wide open, I ran to the door way leading to the hall to see him better. He was moving, ever so slightly, he was moving. As if I were a cat sneaking up on a mouse, I crept to his side. I could see him breathing faintly. With my palm stretched out ready to touch his back, I prayed he wouldn't jump or gasp his final breath. He did neither. Slowly he opened his eyes and looked at my shoes, "Hello Lacey. Been looking for me for long?"

"No Pappy, I've known where you were for a while now. I've heard you . . ." and tears broke from me like a river. He slowly stood up, lifting me into his arms. Then sitting on one of the hay bails with me in his lap, I wrapped my arms around his neck while he rocked me back and forth. For the first time in a very long time I found myself twirling my hair around my finger wishing I was that baby with my whole life ahead of me and nothing, *nothing* threatening my happiness.

"I know you have questions and this time, this is not something you need to process first, you need to ask those questions while they are fresh."

"I want to know everything, all of it. Don't leave anything out. I'm old enough to hear why this is happening." I had a flashback of two seconds ago when I wanted to be that two or three years old and wondered if what I was saying was true. I cupped my hands over my face and emerged with, "Yes Pappy, all of it. I've got to grow up sometime and now is as good a time as any. Tell me everything."

chapter eight

"I'll have to set you down to tell my story. I remember things clearer if I walk while I talk." Pappy sat me down on the hay bails and began to pace back and forth across the barn's dirt floor. Just behind him the wind began to blow in gusts as dark clouds rolled in from over the river. He staggered just a little like a drunk man, but I knew he was not.

"There are so many things to tell you and no words to help me do it quickly or simply, so I must ask you again if you want me to tell you." Pappy looked out the open barn doors and said, "I'm sure we will get rain and that means we could be stuck out here for awhile. That might be a blessing. If it rains hard enough no one will come out here and interrupt us. On the other hand we might have them all scared out of their wits wondering where we are in such a down pour."

"Pappy, you're stalling."

"And so I am. I've never been able to pull anything over on you."

I crossed my legs like an Indian waiting to smoke the peace pipe with my chin sitting on top my knuckles. "It's not getting any earlier and I'm not leaving till you tell me everything."

Pappy drew in a deep breath and began his story. His story. The story of the road less traveled that brought him to who he was today. "I was five when the doctors told my mother that she would bleed to death if a miracle did not develop on her behalf. The doctors had done all they could do for her. There were things inside of her that were torn after she gave birth to my sister. You didn't know her because she died when she was three. She was never right. My mother and sister struggled far too long during childbirth. It put way too much stress on my sister's heart and lungs. My mother was unable to heal on her own. Because there was so much bleeding the doctors could not try to do a surgery that might have helped her. No one was willing to take the chance for fear that she would die and they would be blamed. I never understood why one of them, just one, wasn't willing to be the hero if she lived. But, Lacey, sometimes that's the way God works, so remember not to judge people too quickly. In this case God had a better plan.

"My father was a very spiritual man. He trusted God to provide him anything and everything. He blamed himself for the struggle my mother suffered in delivering my sister. He said he was the head of the house, the one who was responsible for praying his family through anything we were experiencing. He was busy getting the fields prepared for the planting season and so focused on them that he didn't pray for Mother and a safe delivery. She had done this twice without a hitch and he just assumed she would have no problem with the third. He said it was a very expensive lesson to learn, losing his only daughter, but God had blessed him by saving his life mate.

"My father kept his ears open to what ever God was doing anywhere in the country. He had heard about a Holiness Revival where miraculous things were happening, where the gifts of the Spirit were being manifested."

I must have had a strange look on my face because Pappy stopped his pacing and stood before me.

"What I mean is there are gifts that the Spirit of God gives to people. When you receive one of those gifts then you can use that gift to help others. This man who was holding a revival in Cherokee County the same summer my sister was born had received numerous manifestations of spiritual gifts including healing. When my father read this in the paper he packed us up, my sister too young to go, and took us to the revival. At the time we didn't know she had problems. A.P.'s mother offered to keep my sister so A.P. went with us to the revival. Uncle Jeffery went with us, too, but he slept the whole time and missed seeing God change my mother's life and the lives of many people. I would say he changed the life of everyone that was there in some way or another, even sleeping Jeffery.

"When we arrived at the tent where the revival was held most people were kneeling at their benches praying. Some were silent, some crying softly, some speaking gibberish I didn't understand. Every now and then someone would cry out in great sobs and someone would go to them and pray with them or just hold them while they cried. I had been in a church, not the same one every Sunday, since I was born, but I had never experienced the presence of God before.

"The preacher stepped up to the podium holding a Bible. He looked down at the page he had marked and stood there for what seemed like days. Then he lifted his eyes and looked at the middle section of the congregation and those who he looked at fell back or flopped to the floor shaking and trembling.

"My father put his arms around A.P. and me and said, 'It's okay boys, don't be frightened.' Good thing he did or I may have run to the car and clung to the seat till we drove up safe in my own yard. I would have missed seeing miracles of God that night and my eyes may have never had the opportunity to be opened again.

"No one can ever convince me that these things did not happen, A.P. either. My mother and father both went to their graves praising God for what He had shown them, but living a life friendless because of their boldness in their experiences. I have never denied what has happened to me, but I have tried to be less flamboyant with the things of God so as to let everyone have their own touch from Him and not be swayed by my experience. Especially if it might influence someone in a negative way and cause them to run from God or His people.

"Those who fell to the floor experienced healings of the heart, mind and soul. They remained on the floor for most of the meeting. The pastor closed his Bible and asked for those who had come for a physical touch from Jesus to come to the front. He said, 'There is a Spirit of healing around the alter. Someone here is like the woman with the issue of blood who needs a miracle from God. No doctor can do what Jesus is going to do for you tonight.' A.P. and I froze at our bench while my father took my mother in his arms and carried her to the alter. When he reached the alter he began to sway and stagger.

Some men ran to him to hold him and take my mother, but they, too, were swaying. My father went to his knees, still holding Mother, and began to shake and tremble. The men, too, fell around my father and mother, but my mother was perfectly still as though she were dead. Others had come to the alter, some able to stand under the shaking and be prayed for by the pastor. Most of them went down. People still at their benches prayed softly. Some in the back sang hymns with their arms raised over their heads waving in the air.

"Lacey, what I'm about to tell you I didn't believe really happened for a long time, not till I was fifteen. My parents were still at the alter with their eyes closed, down on the floor. Some ladies had come around those who were at the alter and they were thanking God for the healing each one had received and for the gifts of the Spirit being given to each one who wanted to receive. Then they started asking for those who had not received the gift of Pentecost to receive now in the Name of Jesus. With those words spoken from one of the ladies' lips, the room seemed to be engulfed in flames though no one burned or ran from the flames. The ladies at the alter fell back and started talking in a language I had never heard. Those who were there already at the alter including my parents began to speak in a different language. No one sounded like the other, but each was clear and precise. There was a swelling in my throat, but I never opened my mouth. I looked at A.P. and he had his hand over his mouth looking as though he might throw up.

"But then A.P. started waving his arm in the air looking at the preacher. The preacher walked over to him and said, 'What is it son?' but A.P. could not speak. Then he said, 'Would you like to be saved young man and ask Jesus into your heart?' A.P. nodded his head. The pastor prayed for A.P. and then asked A.P. to pray with him. Tears came down his face as he tried to speak. Then he did, but not in his own language. Then the pastor began to chuckle, 'Saved and baptized with tongues of fire all at the same time. That's the way God always intended, but we've let our own traditions keep us from receiving His divine power. We need to get back to a more primitive faith and worship where God is our only tradition. Those who can, give God praise for this new believer to the faith of Jesus Christ.' And those who could, clapped their hands with me and the preacher while others got louder in their new languages.

"I was saved, as best I understood, when I was about four. I knew that I had to keep growing in my understanding of salvation and who God is, because my parents said I would always be a baby on milk if I didn't keep learning. I guess that's why I've never wanted to set my Bible down and just go on what I already know. I knew then, that something had happened to A.P., the same something that was trying to come out of me, but I was too afraid.

"During the next few years, as I studied and searched for answers to what had happened that night, A.P. offered to pray for me to receive the Pentecostal gift he had received. He and my parents told me how it had changed their prayer lives, their worship and most of all their understanding of the scriptures.

"A.P. would always say, 'You just need to receive the sealing of the Holy Spirit, as the Baptist referred to it, fire baptism, and then you will understand completely what it is you're afraid to receive. Until you do, you'll never understand it completely,' and he and my parents would chuckle.

"Looking back, they were absolutely right. I spent a lot of time listening to people tell me that I was searching for something that just didn't happen in these days, and that my family and friend had received something from the devil.

"But, when I looked at my mother I knew it didn't come from the devil. She had a peace on her face that I had never seen on my mother. She was healed completely and every doctor for miles tried to come up with a scientific reason for that, but they never did. She said she remembered being put to sleep by God, much like how Adam must have felt, and she could feel every tissue being put back in its proper place. She knew she was in the presence of God and no one could tell her different. When she told people her story they may not have believed her, but everyone knew that my mother believed it with all she had in her."

"Oh, Pappy, I want to know God like that."

"You can, Punkin,' you can."

"When did you get to know what they knew?"

"I spent several years of watching for that perfect time when God would honor my hunger. When God touched my parents they wanted everyone in this town to see the gifts of God for themselves. There wasn't a church here at that time; we met in people's homes and traveled up to Pisgan Forest and as far down as Rosman. My father liked the little church at the fork in Brevard the best, so we went there mostly, but really they were all too far to travel to with a horse and buggy. My father had a dream of starting a church here, but he was not a preacher. Different people would teach each Sunday after the building was completed and we spent many services in prayer for God to call someone to our church. A few times we experienced powerful moves of the Spirit, but nothing like the service up in Cherokee County. That congregation moved out to Cleveland Tennessee and became known as the Church Of God.

"My father and I would get every news paper we could and search it over for any writings about camp meetings or revivals where the Spirit of God had been manifested. At the turn of the century there was a great expectation as to what God was going to do. The papers were full of stories of outbreaks in congregations all over the country. There were some well known pastors whose names and ministries were in the paper a lot. They seemed to be mostly in the north and northeast like Chicago, Cincinnati, New York, and Maine. There was one in particular that my father and I looked for in the paper and that was a young man who had married into the Quaker faith. We always felt like what had happened in Cherokee County was like what the Quakers must have experienced. Anyway, this man's name was Charles Parham and he traveled to these different ministries to learn from the men who were leading these congregations. Prayer must have been the focus of these pastors where he visited, because he went back to Kansas and opened Bethel Bible College with prayer being the central focus of the school. He had a prayer tower built at the college where there was someone praying twenty-four hours a day. He also opened a short-term Bible school in Houston Texas.

"In the spring of my fifteenth year, Charles Parham wrote about a young black pastor of a Holiness congregation, William Joseph Seymour, who had attended his Bible College in Houston three months earlier. Because of the segregation laws in Texas, Seymour, being a black man, was not allowed to be in the classrooms, but Parham arranged for him to sit in the room next door with the door open so he could hear the lectures. Before the school was over Seymour was called to a Holiness congregation that had just formed in Los Angeles, California. Parham prayed with the young man about the decision and bought his train ticket when he accepted the call.

"Seymour's first sermon was on Acts 2:4 where he then stated that he was sure that speaking in tongues, or an unknown language, was the biblical evidence of Spirit baptism. He himself had not received this gift as of yet. When he returned for the evening service the elders of the church had found his message unacceptable and put a lock on the door.

"I guess he couldn't convince them of something he had not experienced. Someone in the crowd that morning must have believed something he was saying, because he was asked by the Asberry's to come and stay at their home. Mr. Asberry fell out of his chair one night while eating his supper and began to speak in tongues! Soon after that Seymour and others were baptized in the Holy Spirit and spoke in tongues, right in the Asberry's home!

"Crowds of people searching, just as I had been doing, flocked to the Asberry's house. That forced them to find another place to meet. They moved their meeting to an old Methodist Episcopal Church on Azuza Street that hadn't been used as a church in a while. It had become a warehouse and the town stables. As the people cleaned out the debris, Seymour spent his time in prayer behind the pulpit made of wooden shoe boxes. The first service held on Azuza Street was reported to have 'revival fires.'

"Well, that was it. That was what I was looking for. I hadn't spoken to my parents about the fire I had seen and A.P. never brought it up, so I wasn't sure it had really happened. I guess as time went on I started believing that I had dreamed it. You know how your mind makes things seem more dramatic as you dwell on something? Well, that's what I thought had happened to me 'cause no one else ever mentioned seeing the flames.

"Each day there were more reports about the meetings. We drove into Brevard to get the Asheville paper because they received stories from the Los Angeles press. It was reported that one evening a passerby had seen what he thought was the building on fire. Firemen had arrived to find more than a church meeting, but no building being consumed by fire.

"I had to go. I had to see for myself that what I thought was real *was* real. When I showed A.P. the articles in the paper he told me he had wished I had said something earlier about the fire. He, too, had thought it was a dream, just something in his imagination.

"Jeffery, A.P. and I left the day school was out. It seemed like the train would never get there. We rolled in about 2:00 a.m. on a Sunday. We had heard that the services sometimes went until all hours of the morning, but we checked into a room and got some sleep before the next meeting started so we wouldn't miss a minute of it, if it too, lasted till the wee hours.

"For me, it was impossible to get sleep. I tossed in my bed till I saw shadows appearing in the San Fernando Valley. I knew the sun would soon be following. I lit the lamp by my bed and began to read from the Bible. I wanted to see the words again and know that what I had seen all those years ago was in the Bible.

"*And suddenly there came a sound from heaven as a rushing mighty wind, and it filled all the house where they were sitting. And there appeared unto them tongues like as fire, and it sat upon each of them. And they were all filled with the Holy Ghost, and began to speak with other tongues, as the Spirit gave them utterance.*' I knew this scripture even then by heart. It was something I had researched and prayed about then researched some more. I had to be sure it was from heaven as the Word said. Why I couldn't believe the Word on this one thing, when I believed everything else God had to say, was beyond my understanding? But, God understood and He was very patient with me.

"I stayed in the bed praying and reading for an hour then I washed my face and got ready for breakfast; Jeffery and A.P. were still snoring away. I wrote them a note telling them I was going to breakfast down in the restaurant on the corner and then to find the meeting place. As I went to the door and looked back at Jeffery snoring I wondered if he had any idea what he was going to see that night and if he would be affected by it in the least. Jeffery was always wanting to go somewhere to watch the people have a good time, but he never seemed to take part.

"I was able to get directions to the church, but I didn't walk to it 'cause it was farther away than I had hoped. That night, after a day of sightseeing, had not come soon enough for me. I was more than ready to get to the church. We got there way early, but I didn't care. I just needed to get to where I was told God would show up.

"When we entered the vestibule we heard cries of prayer. We walked into the sanctuary to find a few men scattered around the room on there knees praying, but the loudest cries came from behind the stacked shoeboxes where a black man was calling out to God for mercy."

"Mercy for who, Pappy?"

"Mercy for everyone. He named states and cities and asked for God to send the Pentecostal Fire on each person who entered that place. He had a strong commanding voice and when he spoke you knew he was speaking truth. He knew what he was requesting from God and he expected God to just do what he was asking. He made me feel that we had indeed come to the right place. It's called faith, Lacey, and God seldom moves on anything else.

"More people started filling the room. We sat still and quiet just watching and waiting. As people came in, those who seemed to have been there before went to a bench and started praying. In the far corner some ladies whispered, then scattered around the room greeting those who were not in deep prayer. A lady in her late forties maybe, came to us and introduced herself as Mrs. Ed Burton."

"That's the name of Pastor Burton."

"She was Pastor Ed Burton Senior's wife and Pastor Eddie Burton Junior's mother. She introduced me to her son who was coming in the door looking for her as she was talking with us. He ended up sitting with us during the meeting. He asked where we were from and I told him and then he told us he had just graduated from college after the winter term and he had attended Parham's Bible school in South Texas where he had received the Holy Spirit with the evidence of speaking in tongue. He and A.P. had lots to talk about, things Jeffery and I didn't understand, but I was hoping God would show us.

"It was as if the president of the United States had suddenly popped up into the room; everyone got quiet and very still. Pastor Seymour had stood to his feet holding to the top shoe box with tears streaming down his face. He started talking in a language I didn't understand and others around the room fell to their knees weeping and crying out for forgiveness. The four of us must have sensed our need to ask God to forgive us all at the same time, because we were all on our knees with our heads buried in our arms weeping from broken hearts. I found forgiveness towards those doctors who had let my mother suffer for so long. I forgave the people in our town who made fun of my parents and called them crazies when they told them about mother's healing. Some people said she had faked the bleeding just so she could say she was healed. Then when my father built the church, they were accused of trying to take advantage of people who would believe in her healing like others who had told such lies and stolen from innocent people. I was forgiving them all.

"But something else was happening. I was seeing all the hurting, broken, rejected people who had been turned into outcasts because they were different. I could feel their pain as if it were my own. I could sense the heart of God breaking for these people, but more than that I could feel His heart pounding with anger. And I felt it too.

"Someone came to me and placed their hands on me. I found out later that it was Pastor Seymour. He started praying for me. I wanted to get up, but I was stuck to the floor. Nothing moved, not even my eyes. He prayed for me to receive what I had been praying for, but for me to receive a double portion as Elisha had received. 'God, cause him to hunger for You daily. And give him mercy, Your mercy, Lord. Let his call be mighty for you in the lives of those who need Your mercy.' Then he told me this, and I remembered it the day you came out of that river when God spoke to you, he said, 'You will have a child, though you will not raise that child directly, who will hear things from God and see visions and bring words of knowledge for mankind. This child will have many heartbreaks over the unbeliever, but there will be greater suffering and battles with those who say they are believers, but walk with the ungodly. Begin to pray now for the anointing on this child's life and when the time is right encourage the calling by nurturing their growth.' And then he asked for the Spirit of God to fill me.

"I was engulfed with a peace I had never felt. There was a desire to lay flat on my stomach, but I couldn't move. I could hear a beautiful song inside of me, but I didn't know the words, but I started to sing the same words I was hearing and then I could hear the song in my ears. I was happy, but not really. It was something so much grander than happy. I was crying with *joy* and singing a song I didn't know, but I knew it inside and inside was very pleased and familiar with the song. It sounds so confusing. I know it does, because it was every time A.P. tried to tell me what happened to him, but it is so far from confusing. When the Spirit touches you, you know for the first time what it feels like not to be confused. It's like the spirit that God placed in each one of us when He created us, is jolted with life and it is in control of us instead of our thoughts or our needs. All the troubles of the world fade, not just fade, but fades away and out of sight. And for the first time I knew what it was supposed to be like. I knew how God wanted us to feel when he made us before Adam and Eve let sin enter in to the picture. I didn't want to leave that floor. Sometimes when things get tough I think back to that day and wish I hadn't."

Pappy was sitting beside me now and he put his arm around me, "I guess I wouldn't have left except for that word I was given about a child I would be responsible to pray for," and he squeezed me.

"We went to three more meetings, God always showing up. I understood why so many had left their homes and jobs and stayed, some for months. But I had parents at home that needed me, and a church I suddenly seemed fired up about seeing come together. I told Eddie Burton about our church and the need for a pastor if he and his family ever thought of moving to the best place to live in these United States. He told me his father wanted to move closer to his family, but nothing had been decided, so he took my address and said he would be in touch. About eight months later he wrote asking if they could come by and visit on their way to Charlotte to see family and the rest, as they say, is history."

"So how did Pastor Burton become pastor if his father was the one looking for the job?"

"Eddie Burton had been his father's assistant pastor when his father became ill. The church voted for him to take over the duties until his father was well. He never got better and the church left it at that."

"But Pappy, I've never seen anything happen at the church like you just talked about. No one ever prays before we have the service or puts their hands on someone and prays. And I've never seen someone shaking, or the building on fire, or flames on someone's head."

"Yeah, I know. That's one reason I don't go as much as the rest of the family. I come to the river a lot and pray or close myself in my office and worship there. I can hear from God in a place where there is belief. When you worship with people who don't believe God for anything, it starts to rub off on you. I don't want any of that on me."

"Pastor Burton doesn't believe? Pappy, you've lost me again with whatever your saying."

"Lacey, I wish I understood it. When the three of us came back from Los Angeles we were excited about God and the things we had seen. Jeffery received what A.P. and I had received on the second night we were there. We were three fired up young men ready to take on the world and win the lost for Jesus and see them all filled with power from the Spirit. Lacey, when I was baptized by the Holy Spirit, the Word of God became alive to me. I no longer stumbled over what God was saying. I understood with newness. I wanted everyone to have this. But, we were taught no one could understand the Bible. Well, that was what everyone used as excuses for not reading it. If I could teach them about the Baptism of the Holy Ghost then the Word of God would be plain and everyone would live in peace. So I thought.

"We had great meetings and God moved on the people. The church started filling up. But, as with all wonderful things, it came to an end. At first, when men or women wanted to take control of the service by standing up to get everyone's attention, you know start to explain God and why He was doing something, well, God would just confuse them where they couldn't form their words and they would give up and sit down. Because we didn't have a pastor to see over what was going on, people found other ways to disturb God. Messages in tongue were coming all the time, but some how the messages didn't go together, but they did seem to fill the need that person who gave the interpretation needed. One day, our church was going to be a church that would send out missionaries and be able to fund them all within the year. That was a message from Freeda Black who wanted the church to pay for her daughter to go to England where she could be a missionary while she went to school. Then within the same year

Sam Waldrop heard from God that we would be a church that would build its own four-year college. A college that members would not pay tuition to, of course. Then Nellie Swan heard God rebuke all the women in the circle groups for not doing enough for the seniors in the church, something Nellie Swan had been pushing for months. It seemed everyone had a word for someone or about someone. If anyone tried to quench these outbursts they were accused of not being able to hear from God. Before long sin was rampant in the congregation. By this time Edwin Burton had come, but he was not received when he tried to bring some kind of order. He was accused of not letting the Spirit move. People were jealous of the manifestations of the Spirit in others. In other words, the gift to interpret tongues, or to give a word of knowledge, or to prophesy, or any other gift, was coveted by other members to the point of slandering that person just to see them lose confidence and stop exercising their gift. Edwin Burton fought to keep the move of God in the church. He was always fighting someone about someone or something else. But he stood faithful and God honored him, though the healings were less and less because fewer people believed or cared. He and I were great friends and he loved my mother and father as if they were his. The pressure to stop preaching and teaching about things that only caused problems and really didn't even happen so much anymore was taking a toll on his health. He had stopped sleeping, and seeking God was less exciting. He just sat down one day and refused to get up. That's when Eddie took over. He knew better, but he stopped allowing the Spirit to move, 'To stop the crazies,' he said. 'It's just for a while till things get settled down, Jeremiah. Look what has happened to my father all because he chose to fight them instead of giving them an inch to just settle down.' He was so wrong. They were given their inch and they took a mile. The next thing I knew Eddie Burton was preaching that the gifts of the Spirit were no longer needed. We had the Bible now and we didn't need anything else.

"I grieved when I heard his message that Sunday morning almost as much as I did the night I felt God's pain for the rejected. Lacey, I'm trying so hard not to put any one person down or say that all of this is one person's fault, because it's not. Satan blinds us of the work that God is doing. He causes us to believe that if it's hard, if it takes work, prayer, seeking, striving, then it's not God. But, that's the lie. God isn't easy. He said he came to cause strife between mother and son, father and daughter, neighbor against neighbor. He said He would cause man to stumble. Not make them stumble, as if He Himself pushed man down, but that man would stumble because to be obedient to Him would be too costly for most of us. And that's why when you, and you will, Lacey, because God has set your steps, when you stand on what God is telling you and you set a standard and hold to it, people will talk about you and cause a disturbance. You won't have many friends. You will be looked upon as a joke. Some kind of a freak. What happened today is nothing compared to what you will see before Jesus takes you home. He said, 'You will have many troubles and trials,' and you will."

Pappy took my shoulders in both hands and looked straight into my eyes, "I am not prophesying this to you. This is the last thing I would ever want for my best friend, but I know what it will cost you to serve God and because there is nothing greater than serving Him, I will encourage you to keep up the fight to run a great race and never, ever compromise the Word of God for personal comfort. Not for your comfort or someone else's, not even Willie. He could prove to be your greatest stumbling block or your greatest asset. You will have to make that choice. And Mayree. I know you love her as if she was your sister and Lord knows I love Silas like a brother and I will fight for him and his family same as my own. We may pay a huge price for that one day. I don't see the hate man has for people of different nationalities making a turn-a-bout any time soon, though I pray everyday that what I see coming out of the hearts of the people in this town and what I read happening in others will soon find a change."

Pappy dropped his hands and began to speak in that other language God had given to him, as he looked somewhere I couldn't see. The rain had come and gone, quite violent at times though Pappy had all my attention. He kept praying and I stared out the door watching the sun peek out from underneath the dark clouds and it's rays glistening on the freshly watered earth. I had questions for Pappy, but they just didn't seem important right then. I was thinking that I had my own set of troubles right around the corner; I didn't need to see if I could understand Pappy's.

It was probably an hour later, Pappy now worn out and sitting beside me on the hay bail, when Silas broke the silence.

"A little bit ob rain don't stop them chickens from beings hungry. Wait till tomorrow to sees to them birds and they's hate ya."

"Yes sir, Mr. Silas, I'll get right to it," and I jumped down off the bail heading to the feed bin while Silas put hay in the horses stalls.

Silas nodded, "Mr. Jeremiah."

"Good evening, Silas."

"Beens in the Holy Ghost agains, aint ya? I can smells da sweetness of His presence."

"Now, how did I miss that, Silas? And I just thought it was the rain."

chapter nine

I began this story looking back on a beautiful day listening to the radio saturated by the peace of God's presence. It was this day that I felt the depths of being a child of God and I was seeking any sign that God would give me the gift; that same fiery baptism He had given to my Pappy. I wanted to know Him as Pappy did and I was sure that He would bless me if I simply pursued Him daily.

The hurricane was hitting the southern coast of Florida, but no one was paying any attention to it because it was hundreds of miles away from us. At best we might see a little rain out of the storm. It was hard to fathom a hurricane on a beautiful day like the one we were having in late August 1949. But, slowly the skies darkened and there was a smell of rain in the air. Rain was what the town had been praying for, but not my family. Pappy and I remembered what God had promised and we hadn't let our families forget, although, those in town had long turned their backs on us, mostly me. I was the Hawthorne that was touched in the head, not my brother Willie. It only hurt my feelings because it gave people cause to draw attention to Willie, but he was doing so much better after four years in special school. Most people couldn't tell he had learning problems. It just didn't seem fair to ridicule someone for their handicaps especially when they didn't bring them on themselves. I had stayed away from town and Mayree was in full charge of our household shopping. I think that got to the likes of Ms. Franklin more than anything else they wanted to criticize us for.

I spent my days on the farm helping with the chores I could do while still watching closely after Cole. Sally and Jude had a clinic in their home so they took turns coming by once a day to spent time with Mother. My Mother had still not recovered from the birth of Cole. It was months before she was strong enough to walk. When Cole was born he brought most of where he had been living the past nine months out with him. She lost most of her blood, all but enough to stay alive, and her will to get better when she found out she would never have another child. With Pa's coaxing she finally realized that her family was complete and that we all needed her to get better.

Ms. Marge had taught me to cook, although I was nowhere near the cook she was. Abbie Lou and Retta were big enough to help me out with the house cleaning, Silas and Willie with the animals and Uncle Marty was in charge of the hands in the field. No one was more thankful for the return of my Uncle Marty than I was. He surprised us all by walking up to our front porch on the day of Uncle Alvin's welcome home party. We weren't able to find out exactly when he would be coming home because he had been wounded shortly before the war ended and was in a hospital recovering instead of being at the base with the others in his squad. That information had been kept from us at Uncle Marty's request so as to not worry Nanny Jo Rett.

Uncle Marty probably needed my Mother to get better more than any of us, but he would never tell her. He didn't say much to anyone. When he left to go into the service he had a long time crush on a girl named Joan Griffin. They were so young they had never dated, but Joan had waited for him to return. She came by to visit him often, but he didn't seem to care. I think it broke her heart, but she wasn't giving up. So many of the men who returned from this awful war were different from the boys who left. I didn't remember my Uncle Marty very well before he left, but he was not the Uncle my Mother and Pappy had told me about. I couldn't wait for that one to return.

"Lacey! Lacey! Pappy wants you out at the truck."

Uncle Marty had come in from the field and through the back door. I was in Cole's room laying in the bed beside him looking out the open window. I was hoping he would go to sleep before the rain started then I could get up and close the window on my way out. I lifted my head and saw his eyes were closed so I slowly pulled myself away from him. By now Uncle Marty was coming up the steps.

"Hey," he whispered, "Pappy wants you."

"I'll be right there as soon as I get the window shut."

"Where's your Mom?"

"Out on the porch napping on the daybed."

"Is she okay?"

"She could always use a visit from her brother."

"I'll let her nap. Pappy says you two will be gone for a while. I just want to know where everyone is if I'm going to be left in charge."

"Retta and Abbie Lou are taking in the clothes." I tiptoed across the floor from the window to the radio that was playing softly and turned it off. "Willie's with Silas in the barn. He's moving the hay up off the floor in case this is the rain that doesn't stop for a while."

"I'll check on the girls and then go help Silas. Will he be alright in here?"

"He will be if we pull the door to and you come and check on him in about thirty minutes. He might sleep an hour or longer, but if it starts to thunder he will be awake and scared. So you need to come here right away if that happens."

Uncle Marty just stared at me. I knew he didn't want to be in charge of these kids and he sure didn't want to have to comfort them. I had never seen him comfort anyone."

"Will you be alright without me?"

"Tell Pappy you can't be gone long," and he walked down the stairs.

I grabbed my raincoat and a hat and stuck some money in my pocket in case we went by the drug store. I hadn't bought any candy in a long time to spoil my sisters and brothers and I thought maybe Pappy would let me get a soda while we were in town, if we were going to town.

Pappy was in the truck parked by the front walk. It was just starting to sprinkle. When I got to the truck and pulled on the door, Pappy was already talking to me.

"We have to hurry so we can get back across that iron bridge before dark. If the water is up we won't know it till it's too late."

"Then let's not go down that road, Pappy."

"We have to, to get to where we are going."

"And where is that?"

"To see Sunshine. She's sick and she's asked to see you. You don't have to visit with her at all and I'm fine with it if you chose not to, but you have to tell her. I can't let her think I made the decision for you. She has TB. The doctors don't know if she will make it and she is going to be moved to another town where the hospital is equipped just for patients with TB. "

"What's that?"

"Tuberculosis. It's like pneumonia, but worst, I guess. It's in your lungs and it's hard to get rid of."

"Why does she want to see me?"

"She's a good friend of mine, although your grandmother doesn't need to know that, and she has a soft spot for you. She's the one who sends you and Willie cookies from time to time."

"I always knew the cookies came from her, but I just figured she brought them by the bank and you brought them to us."

"You don't have to see her if you don't want to."

"I don't mind. We're driving all that way and she did ask for me so maybe I should?"

"It's up to you. If you don't go into see her we might have time to go by the drug store and get a soda?"

"I had been hoping for that. I would like to get everyone some candy too, but I might need to make Sunshine feel better before I worry about all of us. None of us are sick enough to need a trip to a special hospital. She's gone out of her way in the past for me so I can do this for her. Is TB catchy?"

"Maybe, but the doctors will know what you have to do if it is. Remember the cookies are something between you and Sunshine. No one else needs to know."

We drove out of town about two miles and crossed that old iron bridge. The rain was coming down hard and the sun was getting low making it dark enough to need our lights even though it would be more than three hours before the sun set. We had another ten miles to go to get to the hospital where Sunshine was waiting. The slapping of the windshield wipers kept us quiet, but my mind was racing with thoughts of Sunshine and why she wanted to see me. She had never been to my house, my Mother or Nanny never spoke of her and Pa had said she was going to get Pappy in trouble one day if he didn't stay away from her. So why was he taking me to see her and why was he so set on having her as a friend? One thing for sure there was a story behind this and it would be hard for me to get to the bottom of it, but I was going to try.

We pulled into the drive for the Mountain Ridge Infirmary about 4:30. They told us we could visit till 6:00 when they brought supper to the patients. We could not stay while they ate. I was given a cloth mask to put over my nose and mouth and told not to touch anybody or anything. I could sit in a chair by her bed if wanted to sit down. Only one person could go in to talk to Sunshine at a time so I went first. I didn't think Pappy was too pleased with that, but I promised I wouldn't touch anything. He walked me to the door and said he would be right there waiting for me.

The nurse opened the door for me and reminded me again not to touch Sunshine. I stopped and looked back at Pappy and asked him, "What should I call her?"

"Sunshine. She would hate anything else."

She must have heard us talking because she was trying to sit up better in her bed when I turned to look at her.

"Come here, Lacey Kale, I've been waiting for you. Was the drive over okay? I hear it's started to rain."

"Yes, ma'am. It's raining hard, but the drive was fine."

"Lacey Kale, do you think this will be the rain God has warned us about?"

"I don't know Ma'am, but I know it's coming. If it is, the fact that we haven't had rain in weeks will make it run off quicker and cause more flooding. I'm sure glad all the migrants have been able to build themselves a house up on the hill so they will be dry."

"Your Pappy is a good man. I praise God that we have someone in our town who has a heart big enough to help people when they need it. He sure has helped me. He's helped a lot of folks. More than you will ever know about if you spent your lifetime trying. But, don't look back, Lacey Kale; you have so much ahead of you that you don't need to spend a moment looking back. A person can waste a lot of energy looking for things in the past that never meant a thing, it's just the past."

"Have you spent time looking in the past?"

"Saw right through me, didn't you? Hum. Well, I guess I did. Wishing things had been different, I had been different. Don't ever sell yourself short, Lacey Kale."

"That's what Mayree tells me all the time, 'Don't sell yourself short, just because math is not your best subject doesn't mean you can't be a great historical figure one day.' She's so funny with her dreams of greatness. But, you didn't sell yourself short. My Pappy says you are a great business lady. You have a beautiful home that he says you worked to pay for and you have taken in others who didn't have as much. That's what makes someone great, sacrificing for others. You've done that, Miss Sunshine. You even sent cookies to me and Willie!"

"Your Pappy told you about that?"

"Yes, but he just told me today. I knew about it all along, though. Remember when you sent cookie for us the day we came and got the bread for the migrant camp? Well, when he brought the first batch to us, Willie said, 'Good Sunshiny cookies,' and I knew you had made them. Willie's good at remembering things that I would have overlooked. I didn't know you sent them to us till today, I just thought Pappy was sharing, but we knew you made them. Thank you for remembering us. We have remembered you in our prayers at night."

"Thank you. Those are so much more valuable than my cookies."

"Guess the gift is all about being on the receiving end, because I know the trouble that goes into making cookies and it's a lot harder than praying. I can do that while I clean the house, work the farm, or cook. Well, maybe not cook. I really have to think when I'm doing that."

She started to laugh, but it caused her to cough. I wanted to touch her and help her stop, but she put her hand up to keep me from coming to her. Once she calmed down she said, "Your Mother never could cook with ease either," and she smiled.

"You know my Mother?"

"Vaguely."

"How?"

"My children went to school with her."

"Were they friends?"

"Not really. My daughter was a friend to someone who was a friend of your Mother's, that sort of thing. The girls that stay with me talked about her not being very good at home economics."

"What's that?"

"It's a class you will have to take in high school teaching you how to sew and cook. You sure ask a lot of questions for someone so young."

"I'm *fourteen*. My Pappy says you will never know anymore today than you did yesterday if you don't ask questions."

"I suppose he's right. So now I want to ask the questions. What do you do all day now that you are not in school?"

"Well, I don't know if you have heard, but my Mother is not well."

"Yes, your Pappy told me she has been sick since your brother Cole's birth?"

"Yes ma'am. Well, because she is sick she cannot keep up with a four-year-old so I watch him for her. I know she wishes he would be still like when he was a tiny baby. She loves cuddling a baby, but once they start to wiggle she doesn't have the strength to hold on to them."

"You had to watch over your brother Willie, too, didn't you? My goodness have you been in charge of raising that baby?"

"Well, yes. And Abbie Lou and Retta, too, if the truth was known, but I don't mind at all. I really love them and I'm thankful that I have them. I love my Mother, too. I would do anything to help her. She didn't plan it this way. If she had her wish it would be that I would never have to help her with them again. But, she would never want to cook! Mayree does most of our shopping when she goes to town. Now that Retta and Abbie Lou are older they help me with the housework and Willie is a lot of help to Silas. Do you know him?"

"Yes. I've known Silas and Tula for as long as I can remember. Fine people. Good boys, too."

"They're home now, you know? They work in our fields with my Uncle Marty."

She seemed to be getting weak and looked like she was falling asleep, "Did he ever marry that Griffin girl?"

"No Ma'am, they aren't even dating. She comes by to see him, but he doesn't show her any attention."

"That's too bad. She loves him so," and a small tear rolled down her cheek.

"Miss Sunshine, are you okay?"

"Yes, honey, I just hate to see two kids that are perfect for each other miss out on a lifetime of joy because life dealt them a bad hand and changed their destiny."

"Was your destiny changed?"

She opened her eyes looking at the ceiling. "Everyone's destiny is changed in some way or another. I'm no different than anyone else, maybe just a little more changed."

My heart was going out to her and I wanted to hold her hand so badly. I looked around the room and found a towel folded on the washstand. I picked it up and laid the towel over her hand. When she felt the towel she looked down and saw me grasping for her hand buried under the towel. She slowly turned it over and I held her hand.

"And your Uncle Alvin? I heard he was hurt in the war. Is he better?"

"He is still having to use a wheelchair to go anywhere other than just around the house. Pa and Uncle Marty put a ramp up to the front door so Aunt Penny doesn't have to help him get in and out."

"Is he happy?"

"Do you know my Aunt Penny?"

"Only what your Pappy tells me."

"Well, Uncle Alvin spends a lot of time alone. I think he likes it that way. Aunt Penny has joined a garden club out of town and a group of people who get together and play bridge. My Nanny just hates that. She says playing cards is a sin and that a wife and mother should be at home with her family."

"And what about you, Lacey? Is there someone special in your life?"

"Everyone who has ever touched my life is special to me, but I guess you could say there is someone I think about quite a lot. Well, *every day*! He not really a boyfriend if that's what you mean. I would like to be his girlfriend, but I don't think he would ever feel that way for me. He's my best friend, besides Pappy and Willie. I just think about him different than I do them. Miss Sunshine, do you have a boyfriend?"

"There you go asking the questions again. I'm too old to have one special man. I'm just thankful for the companionship of any man," and she chuckled. "Might not be around long enough to need a man full time, anyway."

"Miss Sunshine, you will get better and God will give you the destiny He has for you."

I felt the presence of God come into the room and on me. "He knows your pain and He has always been with you waiting for you to trust Him with your heart. Circumstances don't change Him or His destiny. He has brought you here to get you to need Him, and you do. You will be in a place all alone with no one to talk to, but Him. He is waiting for you. Don't let Him down. Talk to Him. He has so much to say to you. You loved Him once very much and He has been aching inside to have that love from you again. You have been trying to give it away to others to keep from bursting inside, but you can never give it away to someone else because it belongs to Him. It's a never-ending love that just keeps being filled within us. You have to talk to Him. The past is the past to Him. Don't keep going back there. Let it go."

She had a stream of tears rolling down the side of her face and she was squeezing my hand through the towel. I lifted my hand and took the towel and dabbed the tears from her face and whispered, "Thank you for asking me to come and visit. Now I know how to pray for you. I hope you will let me come and visit you when you get home."

"I would like that very much."

I laid the towel on her chest and turned to leave the room when she asked, "You didn't tell me about your Father. Is he good to you?"

"Yes ma'am, he loves me very much. He is good to my Mother and that is the best blessing in the world. Sleep well and have a safe trip to the new hospital."

"Thank you. God bless you, Lacey Kale, God bless you."

And she laid her head back on the pillow clutching the towel on her chest.

Pappy was right outside the door sitting in a chair. I told him not to be mad, but I had picked up a clean towel that was on the washstand so I might need to go wash my hands in the girl's room. He pointed in the direction and said he was going to tell Sunshine goodbye.

When I got back to Sunshine's room, Pappy was still with her. I could see him through the long narrow window in the door. He was not following the rules. He was hugging her and then he brushed her tears away. She closed her eyes while he stroked her hair from her face. In a few minutes he left her. I was sitting in the chair by the door when he came out. He didn't say a word to me he just walked straight to the men's room where I guessed he cleansed himself of any germs that he may have picked up.

When we got to the door ready to leave the hospital, a man was coming in with an umbrella. He said, "Not a night to be out. The road is flooded back to town. Hope you folks don't need to go that way."

"Well, yes we do. How bad is it flooded?"

"Flooded. You can't go that way."

"Is there another way to get back to town?"

"Yeah, about six miles out of the way, but it might be higher ground. Still got to cross that bridge."

"Did you come across the bridge?"

"Yep. Water's about two feet from the road. The way it's raining out there right now it will be just about capping the road when you get there. It will never stand the pressure of the rushing water. You don't need to try to cross that thing tonight."

"We have to get home," and Pappy pulled his hood up on his coat and pushed me towards the door.

"Don't try it, Sir, go around by South Mill Road and cross there. The bridge is shorter and newer."

"That's thirty miles from here! If this is the night God floods this town I have to be home with my family."

"Cross that bridge and your family will be out looking for you some where around Hendersonville!"

"What's the road that will take me to the iron bridge?"

"Grassy Gap."

"I know it. Thanks."

"You have to turn on to Mark's Crossing to get to the bridge. Hope you make it in time."

"Thanks."

We ran in the rain to the truck and when we got inside we were soaked as if we had jumped in the river. I was a little bit scared, but I knew Pappy would not take a chance if he didn't think we could make it all the way across the bridge. I just didn't understand why he seemed so up set. I knew he hadn't told Nanny we were coming to see Sunshine, but he had to have told her something. She would understand if we got stuck in town because the roads were flooded out.

"Did Nanny tell you she didn't want to you go anywhere after work today because of the rain coming?"

"No. She doesn't know we made this trip."

"Pappy! You didn't tell her you weren't coming straight home from work?"

"No!"

I knew it had to be close to six because I saw some supper trays in the hall while I was waiting for Pappy. He was always home by now or soon unless the money didn't add up right, but that didn't happen often and Pappy always called Nanny to let her know. She would be sick with worry.

"I don't mean to yell at you, Punkin. Why couldn't they move Sunshine in a few days? Why did she have to get sick? Why did this rain have to come now?"

"And why did she have to see *me*?"

He said nothing to that question he just stared straight ahead seeing nothing but rain. We weren't able to go fast at all and that was making him more upset so I decided to tell him what God had done while I was with Sunshine.

"Pappy, when I was in the room with Sunshine the presence of God came in the room and He spoke to Sunshine."

He turned to look at me.

"Not like came in the room and spoke to her Himself, but He spoke to her through me. I can't tell you all He said because I don't remember. It was just for her, but I do remember Him telling her that He has always been there waiting for her and that she loved Him very much once and He ached to have her love again. And He said she was where she was, because He wanted her to need Him again and so they were going to have lots of time for her to talk to Him at the TB hospital."

"Is that all you remember?"

"That's it," and he and I looked back out the window at the rain and muddy road.

He seemed to have tears rolling down his face, but it was hard to tell if they were tears or just rain. Then I remembered, "Oh yea, she will live," and then I knew they were tears.

We got to the bridge and the water was inches from the road. We sat looking at the water rushing under the bridge waiting for something. Suddenly Pappy began to pray over the drumming of the rain, "God you know why we are here. You know how badly I need to be home with Jo Rett. My life is literally on the other side of this bridge. You held back the waters for Moses and the children and I believe you will do the same for Lacey and me. If this were not a mission from You, You would not have spoke to Sunshine through Lacey. That is what brings me the faith to cross this bridge. In the mighty Name of Jesus I call this water to stand back away from this bridge and make a safe drive for us to cross to the other side. And hold back the waters from the road so we can get home quickly. Amen. Thank You Jesus, thank You Jesus!"

Pappy put the gear stick in first gear and slowly let out the clutch. I closed my eyes and prayed as we started forward. Pappy said, "Open your eyes and see the miracle of God. If you keep you eyes closed He won't know you have faith."

The water was calmer and the rain was slowing. We were able to see all the way to the end of the bridge. The water was right up to the banks and I was sure the road would be flooded as we dropped down off the other side of the bridge. There was water in the road, but we were able to drive through it with no problem. Pappy was making good time and we were in front of the drug store in no time at all. We pulled right up to the front door because no one else was out in this weather. We ran inside and Pappy went straight to the phone to call Nanny and I went to the candy counter to get surprises for the kids. I heard him tell her we had been waiting for a break in the storm and may have waited too long. It might be a while before we got home because he just didn't know what the roads would be like when we started home. "I need to take Lacey home. Do you want me to pick you up on my way out there? We'll plan to spend the night then. No need to come back into town tonight."

I paid Mr. Gregory for the candy and thought about Sunshine and if she would need some money where she was going. I wished I had given her some of mine. Pappy got two soda pops from the cooler and asked Mr. Gregory to keep this encounter under his hat.

"Now what have you two been out doing this time of evening in the pouring rain that you wouldn't want folks to know about, Jeremiah?"

"Making sure nothings floating away. Don't want the town folks to know I care that much. You got all your hay up off the floor of that barn, don't you?"

"Yeah. I just have the one horse now that I sold my fields off to the migrants. I didn't need the income anymore since the wife passed. Don't really need that horse anymore. I just like to ride her on Sunday when the store's closed. I can't sit in that empty house."

"Think I know what you mean. Jo Rett's about to go crazy right now by herself so we better get going before the roads get any worst. See ya later."

"Be safe. Thanks for coming in."

We picked up Nanny and pulled up to my house before seven o'clock. My parents were waiting for us at the front door with towels to dry our heads and the floor as we dripped all over the entryway. We had a mud room built for just this occasion, but Mother was so glad I was home and Nanny and Pappy were in our house, too, where she wouldn't have to worry about them all night, that she never gave the chore of mopping the entry a second thought. She was, however, giving Pappy a scolding about having me out in a rain like this. Somehow I knew none of us would get much sleep, but it looked like Uncle Marty was trying. He was sitting on the couch with Willie playing checkers in the living room with his eyes shut. Willie liked to stack your pieces up on his when he jumped one of yours. It was hard to understand his rules and we all took naps when we played checkers with Willie.

There were plates on the table and some dishes on the buffet. Mother had waited supper for me. I was more than hungry. We all sat down at the table, except Uncle Marty and Willie. Mother said they had eaten earlier. The rain had woken Cole from his nap and kept Uncle Marty busy so he decided to feed him and the other children. She said they were making him crazy so he wanted to get them all seated at the same time. I laughed at the insanity of that task. Abbie Lou and Retta were now playing with their dolls in the den. Cole was sitting at the table beside Mother. There wasn't much conversation about where we had been; mostly everyone was concerned about the rain. If Nanny was upset with Pappy I couldn't tell it. She always put on her best face. Pa did most of the talking. He had been down at the river just before we arrived and said that the water was definitely out of the banks up stream from us. I was seeing the day God had told me about come to pass and suddenly I didn't know where Tylar was.

"Mother! Has Tylar been by today?"

"No. I spoke to his mother earlier. Were you expecting him?"

"No and yes. I always love for him to come by in the afternoons and I thought he might check in with me on his way home from the station. He knows I want to know where everyone is especially when there is weather like this. I need to call and make sure he's home. Oh please Jesus, let him be okay." I got up from the table and made my way to the phone in the hall.

"Good thing we're having a cold supper tonight. It's hotter now than when the rain began, but I almost made soup thinking we would need something to keep us warm. I would have too if Martin hadn't had such a hard time with Cole. Even as tired as he was, he made the potato salad and the slaw for me. I can't tell you how thankful I am to have him close to home during the day, William."

"I'm thankful he's here, too, Abigail."

No one was answering at the Collier's. It was hard to imagine where they could be, but it could have been that their line was down and they couldn't get any calls. It was ringing, but the operator said she had found this problem all over town. I went back to the table and tried to eat the sandwich Mother had made.

Pappy said, "Get your coat, Lacey. We'll be back in a few minutes."

"Where are you two going now, Jeremiah? You don't need to get out in this rain again!"

"Jo Rett, this young lady will not sleep and I doubt any of us will till we know for sure that *that* young man and his family are safe. Why, they're like family to us and family takes care of family."

"But, Daddy. Leave Lacey and let William ride with you. If a tree is down or something she can't help you."

"Hey, wait a minute, Abigail. I'm eating here. I didn't have any lunch and ..."

Mother could see that I wanted to go so she said, "You're both going. Take it with you, William."

"I eat on the run all day if I eat at all." Pa took another sandwich from the serving platter as Mother draped his coat around his shoulders kissing his cheek.

Uncle Marty woke up as we made our way to the living room, "Hey, what's going on? Where's everybody going?"

"Need to check on the Collier's. Want to go or do you like watching after these kids? You can stay and help get them ready for bed if you want to do that."

"Na, Daddy, I'm going with you."

"Good. I haven't had much time to visit with you lately. We'll go in William's car."

Uncle Marty got his coat and hat and soon all of us were dressed for the walk in the rain to the car. I had on my galoshes; something I had forgotten on our first trip out, but if we needed to get out in some deep puddles, I didn't want to have wet feet again. The Collier's house was sitting up on a knoll so hopefully there wouldn't be any water standing around their home. If we checked on the Foresight's we might find a different problem. Their drive was dirt with deep ruts that had never been filled with gravel or dirt. That always made it slippery when it rained.

Pa drove into the Foresight's drive first. We didn't see any lights on in the front of the house and that alarmed Pa. He said they usually went to the living room after super and you could always expect to see a light in Jake's room upstairs. Our car slid from side to side as we turned off of the road and into the drive. The house was a great distance from the road with large oak trees in the yard. Roots from the trees gave our wheels something to grab on to, as well as make the trip quite bumpy. Dr. Jude had put down planks all the way across in front of the garage to make a pad for visitors and patients to park. He kept his truck at one end of the pad. The truck was not there. Our car bounced up onto the planks and came to a stop. Looking through the back screened porch we could see a light on in the kitchen. Pappy jumped out of the car and met Jake at the back door. They talked for a while and Jake pointed toward the Collier's barn. I could see a dim light in that direction, but we weren't close enough to make out what the light was coming from. Pappy came back to the car and told me to get out.

"Why Pappy? Are we all getting out?"

"No, Punkin. You're gonna stay with Jake. We might need the room in the car and I have to take your Pa and Marty in case we need their strong arms."

"What's happened Pappy? Who got hurt?"

"Nobody said a thing about somebody gettin' hurt. We'll be back to get you in a little while."

My eyes began to fill with tears because I knew he was not telling me everything he knew. I was afraid for Tylar and I knew Jake wouldn't tell me what was going on, but I did like Pappy said. Arguing would just keep them in the drive and away from whoever needed them. "Don't forget me, Pappy. Come get me as soon as there's room in this car for me."

"Don't cry, Punkin. It will be alright." And he hugged me out in the pouring rain.

"Can you promise me that?"

"I can promise you that no matter what has happened, it will be alright. Now get inside before you are soaked to the bone," and he jumped back into the car and closed the door. I was standing in the mud beside the car not able to move. I could hear Jake calling me from the house, but I didn't want to go in. Pa's car slid its way down the drive and out on to the road in the direction of the Collier's barn. When I could no longer see the lights on the car I turned and ran to the back porch where Jake, Molly and Millie were waiting.

I dried off on the porch not taking my eyes off of the dim light I could see through the darkness. I was sure I saw Pa's headlights arrive. I wished so badly to be there or be able to see things better, "You know what's going on out there, Jake?"

"What?"

"No, Jake. Stop it! I'm asking *you*! I knew you wouldn't tell me."

"Hold on, Carrot Head! Why are you so mad at me?"

"Because you need to be mad at. I know you know what's going on out there and you're not going to tell me just so you can make me crazy."

"First of all I don't know what's going on out there and you are crazy all by yourself."

"Stop it, Jake! I know you know! Is it Tylar? Is he hurt, or missing? Has something happened to Tylar?"

"And he's the only one that matters to you. You don't care if something has happened to his Mother or to Bob; all you ever care about is Tylar! I'm not going to tell you anything." He threw a towel at me and went back into the kitchen.

I was crying now and Mollie was drying my hair as I looked out through the screen at that dim light. I cared if anyone was hurt, but Tylar was so special to me, something Jake would never understand because he was the one who thought only about one person, himself. I got madder and madder as I watched the dim light and thought about Jake knowing what was wrong to the point that I had to leave. I pulled my hat out of my coat pocket where it had been all along and put it on my head, "I have to go Mollie. Thanks for trying to dry me, but I have to go now. Tell your brother that I said I would be back later. Not that he cares."

"Lacey! Don't go. Your Pappy will be worried about you. What if you get lost? Jake *does* care."

"I can't get lost, I have that light. Now if that light goes out I might be in trouble, but I can't worry about that now. You just make sure you keep this light on so I can find my way back to you, and help me pray," and I pushed the screened door open letting it slam behind me.

As I was running toward the field between the Foresight's and the Collier's barn, I heard the screened door slam again. I didn't look back I just ran harder. About that time I ran into the wire fence the Foresight's put up for the goats. It threw me backwards to the ground. I don't know if it was hitting the fence or hitting the ground that knocked the wind out of me, but I was slow getting up. Jake was trying to help me, and I let him, but as soon as I was standing I pulled my arm away. "Leave me alone, Jake. I don't want you out here."

"Get back in the house, Lacey. I'm not letting you go out there."

"You think you can stop me?"

"I know I can. Me and about five more fences between here and there. You won't be able to walk much less get up if you hit many more fences like you hit that one."

"And I guess you're going to make fun of me now? I just want to go over there and see what's wrong. Why is that so awful of me, Jake? Why won't you tell me." I began to sob.

Jake reached out and took me in his arms and held me so tight. I wanted to hit him, but I needed the comfort. "Tell me, Jake. Please tell me. What's wrong with Tylar."

"I can't, Lacey, I can't."

"You know? Oh God, help me. Jake, you know? You have to tell me. I have to go," and I pulled to get away from him, but he held me tighter.

"Lacey stop! Stop!" The tone of his voice was changing. "You can't go out there. You really don't want to go out there. You have to stay with me, Lacey. Please? Stay with me." and he held me so close I could hear his soft rapid sobs and feel the warmth of his breath on my neck. I felt safe in his arms, but terrified of what he knew. We stood in each other's grasp for what seemed like hours with the rain and wind beating against us. He asked me if I would promise not to run or go down to the barn if he let me go. I told him I promised.

"Now then," he said as he loosened his grip on me and looked down into my eyes.

"Will you come back to the house with me?"

Water poured off the brim of my hat as I nodded. We held on to each other as we pushed against the gusts of wind hitting us in our faces. The fight to get back to the house gave me time to finish my cry and find the strength to wait for news. I knew in my heart that Tylar was hurt and there was no reason for Jake to speculate on how bad things were. It would simply make this night unbearable.

Mollie and Millie had put the teakettle on the stove and met us at the back door with dry towels and clothes. I took my hat and coat off and hung them on the back of the kitchen chair near the stove so they could dry. The girls offered their room for me to change out of my wet clothes. Millie handed me a pair of Jake's old blue jeans. I had to roll them up and put on a belt, but it didn't matter because I was sure I wouldn't be wearing them long. Jake met me in the hallway between his room and the girls, "You okay, Lacey? Hey, those look familiar. Looks like you have plenty of growing room."

"Jake, let's say something really bad has happened out there, how long would it take for someone to get back here with some word?"

"Ah, Lacey, lets just try and be," and the phone began to ring. "Maybe we aught to get that."

"Hello," Millie had answered the phone, "No Ma'am. Yes Ma'am."

"Who is it, Millie?" Jake asked.

"It's Ms. Rutledge, she wants to talk to you," and she handed the phone to Jake.

"Hello. Yes Ms. Rutledge, they were here. They left Lacey with us. They have gone to the Collier's barn. My parents are there, too. Yes ma'am, its Tylar. There's been an accident. No ma'am, no ma'am, we haven't heard anything. Yes ma'am, just a minute. Here, Lacey, she wants to talk to you."

"Mother!"

"Lacey! Are you okay?"

"I'm not sure."

"Do you need me and Nanny to come over there?"

"The road is bad, Mother, but the drive into the Foresight's is worse. You don't need to try and make it out here. We're fine."

"Okay, call me if you need us or hear anything about Tylar. Have you had anything else to eat?"

"No ma'am, I had enough. I love you."

"I love you too, sweetie. Bye-bye."

"Bye."

"I have your tea ready for you, Lacey."

"Thanks, Mollie," and I sat at the table across from Jake. "Are you going to tell me anything?"

"Yes, I'm going to tell you that ... your hair is quite beautiful after a good soaking. Want a brush to smooth out the knots? Mollie, get Lacey a hair brush."

"Can I brush it, Lacey?"

"Yeah, sure. So you're just going to try to get my mind on something else and hope I will leave you alone?"

"I don't want you to leave me alone, I just don't want to talk about what's going on out at that barn."

"Then it's going to be awfully quiet, because that's all I can think about right now."

"I can live with quiet."

A couple hours went by and very little was talked about. Mollie and Millie had gone to bed and I had changed back into my pants after they dried. I was ready to go whenever someone came to get me. Jake and I had moved into the living room so I could see the headlights to Pa's car when they came to get me. I sat on the couch and Jake sat in a chair pulled up to a card table where he had put the checkerboard. We tried to play, but I was tired and nervous. Jake was beating me badly, but I didn't care. After three games I asked to quit. "My heart's just not in it."

Jake said he would get me and him a blanket from the hall closet. "I can't sleep, Jake."

"Well, you need to rest. Tylar might need you to be rested. I'll lay down on the floor by the couch so you won't be by yourself."

After a few minutes of pacing by the front window I sat on the couch. Jake was in the floor watching me. "Lacey, do you ever see Theodore any more?"

"Gees! You are trying to get my mind stirred up with something else. No, not much. He's been busy helping his Dad at the lumberyard.

"Does he work in the office with his Dad, or out in the yard?"

"Out in the yard," and I started yawning.

"You see your Aunt Penny?"

"No. She visits Nanny and Pappy at their house. Uncle Marty doesn't like her and he told her to stay away from him. Ahh, I'm so sleepy."

I don't remember Jake coming up on the couch and sitting with me, but I woke to find Jake sitting at the end of the couch with my head resting on his shoulder and a blanket over my legs. I sat up and looked at the clock. It was twenty minutes past six. I slowly got up and went to the kitchen and out the door onto the back porch. The light was out down at the barn. "Dear God, please tell me what's going on. I don't know what to pray!"

I didn't hear anything so I returned to the living room. Jake was still asleep. Standing at the window looking out at the road I could tell the sun was beginning to rise and the rain had lightened. Jake woke and asked, "Have you heard anything?'

"No, nothing. We should have heard something by now. Even if they had to take him to the hospital. There's no light out at the barn anymore."

Jake walked up behind me and put his arms around my neck. "If they took him to the hospital it would take a long time with as much rain as we've had. The bridge could be washed out, the road blocked with a rockslide or trees. It's no telling how far they had to drive out of the way. We'll hear something soon. Want some breakfast?"

I thought about Sunshine and wondered if Tylar would be taken to Mountain Ridge where she was. No doubt that iron bridge was gone by now so I didn't see anyway for them to take him there.

"You would think they would have brought him here to your parent's clinic, unless he's hurt really bad. But, if the roads are washed out where else could they take him. Where is the closest hospital to us?"

"I guess Mountain Ridge Infirmary, but they don't have the best equipment or faculty. Mom will know which one is the right one for Tylar."

"Jake?"

"Yeah?"

"Thanks for being my friend tonight. I'm sorry for yelling at you."

"I've always been your friend."

"I know, but I mean really caring about me."

"You didn't answer me. Are you hungry?"

"Not right now. Let's just stand right here and I'll pray while you hold me."

"Okay," and we stood there till the clock chimed seven.

Soon we heard the girls get up and start moving around in the kitchen. I didn't want to leave the window. I was sure Pappy would come for me any minute and I didn't want to start cooking something we wouldn't be able to finish or have time to eat. I needed to see Tylar and I was past being anxious. It just wasn't like Pappy to leave me in the dark so long. He had to know how upset I was. I saw a car coming down the road from the direction of my house. "Jake, look!"

"Who is it?" The car turned into the drive. "It's Mr. Bob's car."

We ran to the kitchen and out the back door. Pappy got out of the passenger side and ran to the porch door. The car pulled away. He looked tired and he was covered with mud. He stood under the roof by the door and took his work coat and overalls off. He draped them over the shrubbery. "Have you kids got breakfast ready?"

"Pappy! How long am I going to have to wait?"

"We got it started, Mr. Pappy. You want some coffee. That's ready."

"Yea, that's just what I want. Thanks, Mollie," and he walked to the back door and into the kitchen.

"Don't give him anything till he tells me where Tylar is and how he's doing."

"Come inside and sit down. I'll tell you all about it."

We went inside and sat at the table while Mollie and Millie cooked breakfast. I was hanging by a thread! Pappy looked at me with a puzzled stare. He reached out to my face and lifted my chin, "What happened to your face and chin? Looks like you got in a fight with a wet rooster."

Jake leaned across the table looking at me, "Hum. I didn't notice that last night. I'll get a wash cloth and you can wash the blood off."

"Don't worry about it, not till Pappy tells me about Tylar."

"He's going to be alright. It may be a while, but he will recover. That's what the doctor tells us, anyway."

"When can I see him, Pappy? How bad is he hurt?"

"Bad. When we got there he was fighting to keep his head above water. He lost that fight a couple times before anyone got there to help him so the doctor thinks he has mud in his lungs."

"Oh my gosh! How did this happen? Pappy I have to see him."

"He was coming in from the barn when that big oak fell over and trapped him. His leg is broken and his ribs are cracked, but the blessing is that the ground was soft so there's no sign of internal injuries. But, the down side is that the ground was soft so the tree made a deep hole in the yard and the rains began to fill it. He must have been knocked out when it first happened because when Marge got to him he was face down in the water. Thank God she knew what to do to get him to breathe again. She had to keep the water out of the hole till someone came to help her. She didn't want to pull him up too much not knowing if his back was broken, but she had to keep his face out of the water. Bob didn't get home for twenty minutes or more and it took him a while to find where they were. Ruthy was upstairs in the tub and didn't know what had happened? She ran here for help and you know the rest."

"How did you get the tree off of him and where is he now?"

"We had to saw it while Martin and Bob dug around him and helped keep the water out of the hole. That tree is huge so it took a long time. Once we made it through one side of him we had to start working on the other side. Praise God, Tylar was awake while we were doing this. That's a good sign that he's strong enough to recover. Depending on how much mud went into his lungs, he should be able to get up and try to stand in a few days."

"I have to see him. Where did you take him, Pappy?"

"He's at Mountain Ridge. They're understaffed so Sally, Jude and Marge stayed with him. Jude's his doctor, of course, so he wasn't going anywhere and he needed Sally to help. Bob brought me here and he's gone to the house to check on Ruthy and Pauley."

"How are we going to get to the hospital?"

Pappy's face changed and I knew there was more to this story.

"Pa. where's Pa?"

"He's with Martin," and he rubbed his face with his hands. "How about some more coffee, Mollie?"

"Got toast, too. Millie's almost finished with the eggs."

"Pappy," I swallowed hard, "My Pa? Is he okay?"

"Yes. Uncle Marty is not. Your Father has taken him to Western North Carolina Insane Asylum. He's not well. Thank God Jude had a sedative in his bag or we would have been waiting for someone from the hospital to drive out here to get him. Your Father could have never taken him by himself without the sedative. He will be fine. Just too much stress for him watching young Tylar in such turmoil."

We all knew what Pappy was talking about because we had seen many soldiers, who had come home from the war, snap. It seemed those who lost their loved ones during the war grieved once, and those who got their loved ones back grieved daily. This would devastate my Mother, but it might kill my Nanny.

We didn't have much to say during breakfast. I had to stop being obsessed about seeing Tylar and realize that he was getting help and would recover. My family needed me to be strong for Nanny and Mother and pray for Uncle Marty to find his mind and come home soon. My goodness, what a little rain had done to these three families in one short agonizing night. I could only imagine what had happened to the rest of the town.

chapter ten

The water had made its way to our back steps. The fish were gone from the cool pond. Our dock was gone along with the tree that held our rope swing and I knew the old iron bridge was gone because Pappy said it was not there when they went to take Tylar to the hospital. Most of their night was used finding a new route. As for the rest of our property, all was still standing. There was plenty of debris that had floated in from somewhere up stream that had to be cleared away, and we needed more help, but all the hired hands where cleaning their own property. I could only imagine what others were facing as I had not left the farm since the day after I spent the night with Jake and his sisters.

It rained another day and a half after that night. There was nothing to do, but pray and wait for it to stop. Mother was sleeping most of the day exhausted from worry. Nanny was helping Pappy at the bank because some of the tellers had to take days off in order to repair their homes. This kept Nanny busy and unable to dwell on Uncle Marty. Pa had returned late in the evening from the hospital where he had taken Uncle Marty as the rain began to clear out. He didn't speak to any of us as he came in. He went straight to Mother's room and I heard her sob as he tried to comfort her. Later that evening he went into the library alone and I saw him crying. I knew Uncle Marty was not going to be all right for some time, if ever. I was hoping Joan would go and visit him. A visit from Tylar would have brightened my day.

It was four or five days before I saw Jake. He came to the house bringing Mother a vase full of roses. He said they were from the vine that grew up on the trellis by their chimney. It was protected from the rain by the over hang of the roof so the blooms were not harmed like his other plants. I sent him up to her room and followed with a cold drink for both of them. Jake stayed with Mother for over an hour as I continued to rake debris from around our house into the huge pile Silas and I had started in the field where we could burn it later. Jake was on my mind. He had been on my mind since the night he held me so tightly not wanting me to go to the barn and help Tylar. I had felt myself blush when I saw him coming up the drive carrying roses in his arms. He was quit handsome, as all the girls had noticed, but he was Jake. The boy who teased me with no remorse! I was sure it was simply a change in the direction of our friendship. Mother said I would see my opinions of a lot of people change as I grew up. I decided that was all that was happening with Jake and me.

I had gone back into the house for a glass of water when Jake came down the stairs from Mother's room. "She's asleep now," Jake said.

"How did she seem to you? She didn't get much sleep last night." I turned from the sink and sat down at the table with my water. When I looked up Jake was holding a single rose out to me.

"Have you got a drink of water for her? I thought of you special this morning when I went out to cut some roses for your Mother and saw her. She's beautiful like you and just a hint of fire across the tips of her petals. That especially reminded me of you the other night when you were so mad at me I could see fire coming out your ears," and he slid into the chair at the end of the table, "and yet you were still so beautiful. Do you forgive me?"

"Of course I do, Jake. I told you the other night that I forgave you."

"I still want to make it up to you. Have you seen Tylar?"

"No. With all that's happened no one has time to take me and I feel selfish asking."

"Would you like to see him today?"

"Sure. But, I don't see how."

"I'll take you."

"What?"

"I have to take Mom and Dad some supplies. Mollie and Millie are staying with Ruthy today and I don't want to go alone. I asked your Mother if that would be okay with her and she said your Dad was coming back to the house this morning. He's not working in town today. He's just gone to get your Nanny to look after Cole while he and Silas cut up that big tree that fell in the river."

"Oh good; that tree is catching a lot of stuff and blocking the river. I can't keep the stuff cleared off of it. But, he will need my help, too?"

"You need to get away from here for a while. You need to see Tylar and I want a friend to keep me company. It's a long drive now that the bridge is out. Please say you will come with me. I'll know for sure that you have forgiven me if you do."

"Are you trying to bully me into going with you by making me feel guilty?'

"Guilty is not what I'm hoping you feel towards me."

I took the rose from his hand holding it close to my face looking deeper at its beauty. The fragrance was as sweet as this moment with Jake. How badly I wanted to see Tylar and I would have taken a ride with the milkman just to see him, but my desire to ride alone with Jake was equal to my desire to see Tylar. I didn't want him to know that the only thing holding me back was my fear that I wouldn't know what to talk about on the ride to the hospital now that our friendship had, somewhat, grown up. Laying the rose down, I stood from the table and went to the cupboard to find something to put it in. Mother had a small bud vase somewhere in her cabinets, but I hadn't seen it in a while. I took a large jelly glass from the cupboard, filled it with water and placed it in the center of the table. Jake picked up the rose and dropped it into the glass.

"Sorry Jake, this will have to do till I can find a vase."

Jake said, "Reminds me of us, an elegant rose and a jelly glass. I think it's perfect."

He always made me smile. "I'm not sure I'll be good company."

"Just having you ride with me is company enough. You don't have to entertain me"

"Okay then I'll get my sweater and check on Mother before we leave. I guess we'll have to wait for Nanny and Pa? Make yourself at home and I'll be right back."

"I would like to say that I'm not going anywhere, but I need to walk back over to the house and get the car."

"Okay. You can show yourself out and I'll go on up and get ready."

"Okay," and he watched me disappear up the stairs.

Mother was still sleeping and I didn't have the heart to wake her, but I wanted to ask her so many questions. She looked so peaceful finally, after a night of pacing the hall and rocking by the window in the dormer, that I just stood by her doorway quietly watching her. Even though she was the only one I had to talk to these days with Sally and Marge at the hospital and Nanny working with Pappy, she needed her sleep more than I needed answers. I didn't ask Nanny too many questions having to do with my feelings, though. She was somewhat cold about such things and saw emotions as something to just get over. "Do the right thing and never let your emotions get in the way. Everything will turn out for the best if you follow that rule." I was so different from her in that I felt everything. I seldom thought things out. It wasn't a good thing and I was trying hard to think things through now that I was faced with grown-up issues, but there was that part of me that God had been grooming that worked solely with my inter feelings and emotions. I had no communication with God at all unless my emotions were brought out into the open for Him and me to see.

As I got my sweater and good shoes from the wardrobe a thought came to me. If God could tell me about the water and rains then He could tell me what He wanted me to do next and what my heart should feel towards Jake. Would he be the tender Jake I met a few days ago or would the old Jake reappear and make me crazy right before I have a chance to see Tylar? "God, will you please give us something to talk about that will not make this ride uncomfortable for Jake or me. And please watch over us as we drive to the hospital. Don't let us get lost and please let Tylar be glad to see me? Scratch that. It's not about me; God, I pray he is feeling up to seeing me today. Amen."

I heard a car drive into the yard and pass under my bedroom window. I ran to the window and looked down to see if it was Jake. It was Pa and Nanny with Jake right behind them. Soon I heard Nanny talking to Jake in the kitchen as I took off my old work shoes. I looked in the mirror and saw the same mess I saw every morning when I sat down to brush my hair. How could anyone think that was beautiful? I had dirt on my blouse, too. I was a mess. I quickly washed my face and arms in the washbasin and changed my clothes. I had a new blouse and skirt I had not worn because there had not been an occasion, but I thought this just might be the one. After all I was dressing for two men and I shuttered at that thought. But, Jake had taken a bath and put on clean clothes and I should at least let him know I noticed by honoring him in doing the same. I brushed my hair and pulled it back with two pale pink clips on each side of my head. They matched my blouse. My shirt was a soft pink and my skirt was pink and green plaid. I was having a hard time finding bobby socks that weren't stained with red clay when I heard Nanny call softly from downstairs, "Lacey Kale, I'm here and Jake is waiting. Are you ready?"

"Almost Nanny. I'm looking for socks. I'll be right down." I found a pair of white ones with lace around the edge that covered any stains so I grabbed them and my saddle oxfords and ran bare footed down the stairs.

"You better hurry, girl. You two need to be back before dark. Now don't drive too fast and stop for lunch in town. You don't need to take the time to fix something now. Here's some money, Jake."

"Oh, no ma'am. I have some. We're fine."

"I insist, Jake. You are doing us all a big favor by taking Lacey to see Tylar. We've just not been able to stop long enough and see to her needs. I know she will *forever* be grateful to you for taking her. Besides you might need some gas. Let us treat you to lunch and buy your gas *at least,* for you trouble?"

"This is no trouble. Lacey is helping me out by keeping me company during the drive."

"I insist."

I finished tying the last shoe and said, "Take the money, Jake, so we can go. Thanks Nanny," and I kissed her cheek darting towards the door. Jake had parked close to the back steps so we left through the mud room and out the back porch. "We'll see you soon, Nanny. Don't wait supper if we aren't back. We may eat a late lunch so we can go straight to the hospital now."

"Okay, sweetie. Have fun and give our love to Tylar. Drive safe now, Jake."

We were already at the passenger side of the car. Jake reached out and opened the door for me to get in, "Yes ma'am, Ms. Nanny Jo Rett. I won't let anything happen to Lacey," and he waved at her standing on the porch.

Soon we were driving out the drive and I realized I had never seen Jake behind the wheel of an automobile before. He was growing up so fast. I guess I was too, but he was past seventeen and driving and I had just turned fourteen. Whatever feelings we might be having right now there were so many other girls his age that would better suit him than me. And besides that he knew that Tylar was the only man for me. I was sure I was reading something more into his desire to be my friend so suddenly I felt much more at ease about being with him and all I wanted to do was see Tylar.

There was plenty to talk about on our drive passing homes that had been damaged by the flood, trees that were uprooted, crops that were ruined, and so many rockslides. Men with teams of mules were out moving boulders from the roads so cars and buggies could get by. There was plenty of work to be done and I felt a bit guilty that I was not helping somewhere.

"It seems very selfish of me to be so caught up in spending the day driving to see someone who is being cared for completely when there is so much work to do for these people out here. Jake, we have to come into town tomorrow, even if we have to bring the kids with us and help in some way."

"You aren't afraid some of these people will blame you?"

"Oh my gosh! I never thought that! Do they, Jake? Do they think *I* did this?"

"I've heard some of them say that you knew more than you told us and that you could have spoke to your God and kept this from happening."

"That's crazy! That must be the Voodoo worshipers saying things like that. I can't tell the God of this universe what to do! All I can do is pray. He sent the warning and we did all we knew how to do. Now the rest is up to them ... us. Are we going to call out to Him for help? Are we going to except the help He sends? Or are we going to blame someone else for what has happened and keep living in unbelief? God is trying to teach us to rely on each other to get through this and believe Him when He speaks no matter who He speaks through. This town is so divided in what is truth and what is man made truth."

"I love it when your ears turn red and you get all passionate about what you believe."

"Are you teasing me again, Jake?"

"No. I mean that. There aren't many people who have a belief in anything anymore, much less one so passionate. I know God is trying to get us all ready for something else, something big. Maybe not big to any other town, but big to us. We better know Him so we won't be deceived when it shows up."

"Oh my gosh, Jake! That's exactly what I've been feeling. And somehow I'm going to be right in the middle of it and ... I don't know. It's like it's right here in my stomach, but I can't get it up so I can't see it. What else has God told you?"

"This flood is just a test to see if we are going to be able to pass the big exam."

"What's the exam?"

"Don't know. But, if we fail it could affect not only our town, but many. The question I always ponder is if I or you or anybody is big enough to stop a whole town if they don't see what we know?"

"No, *we* aren't, but God in us is big enough to put those rocks back on the side of that hill exactly the way they were sitting before the water pushed them down. I haven't experienced him doing that personally, but I know someone who has and I believe every word he's told me about the hand of God and how it can change people and circumstances."

There was more news on the radio of the hurricane that had come in at Palm Beach, Florida and tracked up through the state and into Georgia, South Carolina and into North Carolina with winds up to 70 miles per hour when it reached us. It went though several other states before going out to sea. I couldn't imagine things any worst than what we were facing, but those in Florida had experienced far greater destruction than we had. I felt badly for them, but all I could think about was Tylar.

We got to the hospital about eleven o'clock. Jake knew exactly where he was going and we found Sally and Jude rather quickly. "Tylar has asked about you several times this morning. He is doing much better. We took him out of his room for a short walk. He was able to walk ten steps using crutches before he got tired. His ribs are very sore so we are really proud of him for making that many steps putting the strain on those ribs," and she cupped her hands around my face, "He knows he has someone very special waiting for him to get better. I heard you ran into my goat fence the other night. Let me look at that. I see some bruising around your chin, but Tylar won't ever see it. You're beautiful," and she kissed my cheek.

I glanced at Jake, who looked down at his feet. I was blushing. "Can I see him now, Sally?"

"Sure," and we started down the hall. "He isn't expecting you, so this is going to be a nice surprise for him." She stopped for a moment and looked back, "Come on, Jake, his room is this way."

"I'm going to wait out here and give them some time together."

"Suit yourself. I'll be back in a minute," and we walked to the end of the hall and turned to the right. We weren't far at all from the room where Sunshine had been. Sally stopped outside of a door with a sign asking for "Quiet. Patient needs rest." The room number was to the right of the door's window, room 177.

"He's right through that door. I have to go and check on Mr. Green at the end of the hall. I'll be back to check on you two in a little while. Now remember, he's been in a bad accident so don't get him too riled up. If he's sleepy and falling asleep, let him. You have plenty of time today and he really needs the sleep."

"I don't care if he sleeps the whole time I'm here. I'm just so grateful to finally see him."

Sally turned and walked to the end of the hall and disappeared into a room. I was suddenly frightened of what was on the other side of that door. I slowly turned the knob and pushed the door in from my right to the left. I could see bare toes sticking out the end of a cast tied up in the air at the foot of the bed. Slowly I walked to the left where I could see the face of who was in that bed. Tylar was asleep. His face was swollen and there were cuts and stitches on his jaw and under his right eye. I suddenly felt weak so I slid into the chair against the wall. I hadn't ever seen anyone hurt this badly and I was not prepared for what I saw, but I understood how close he had come to losing his life and I was horrified to tears again at the thought. Somehow I had to pull myself together. I had come to cheer him up and be the strength he needed like he had always been for me. I couldn't let him see that I needed him to get me through this.

I took a few deep breaths and wiped the tears. Quietly I lifted the chair and walked to the side of his bed and placed it quietly down on the floor. As I turned to sit in it again I found Tylar with his eyes open and his hand stretched out. "Lacey. I've been looking for you."

I took his hand and sat in the chair, "I've missed you so much." I couldn't hold back the tears. "I'm so thankful you are going to be alright," and I pulled his hand to the side of my face. Then I placed his hand and my head down on the bed beside of him.

He stroked my hair and said, "I'm not ready to leave you, yet."

"Yet? There's coming a day when you will be ready to leave me?"

"Not till I'm old and gray and there's no fight left in me. Now come here and give me a hug."

"I won't hurt you?"

"You could never hurt me, especially when you are giving me a hug. Lacey, holding you was all I could think about when I was under that tree. I prayed, 'God! I haven't hugged Lacey in months. I promise to never get so busy that I forget to hug her again,' now come here so I can get started on my promise."

I stood up and lay across Tylar as easily as I could, but that was not necessary as Tylar wrapped his arms around me and squeezed with all his might.

"Oh my gosh, Tylar! Your ribs."

"They are fine. Everything about me is fine now that you are here."

"You haven't looked in the mirror lately, have you?"

"My symptoms are gone now; the evidence is going to take a while."

I sat up and took a long look at all of his cuts and bruises. As hard as they were to look at, seeing the eyes of my dearest friend and knowing he was still in there somewhere was so comforting.

"So what's the news from home? Did anyone else get hurt? Have all the houses stood under the flooding?"

We spent over an hour talking about the rain, the flooding, the roads, the night the tree fell and the news we had heard over the radio about the hurricane. I was never more at home or more comfortable with who I was than when I was with Tylar. Our surroundings faded away and we were anywhere, but in that hospital. Someone brought Tylar his lunch and Sally followed them into the room.

"Well Tylar, can you give her up long enough for her to go and get something to eat?"

"Do I have to?"

"Ms. Sally, I'm not hungry. I can eat anytime. I will stay and help Tylar with his lunch."

"Are you sure? Jake said he would take you into town to get something, or you two could eat something here? There's not a lot of choices if you eat here, though."

"Oh, Jake! I forgot to tell you, Tylar, that Jake has come to see you. I've been so selfish with your time and left Jake out in the hall. And he's been so wonderful to bring me to see you. I have to go and tell him that I'm sorry and ask him to join us."

"He might be hungry, Lacey. Maybe you should go with him and eat some lunch. I'll be right here when you come back."

"That's not necessary, 'O buddy."

"Jake. Come in. As you heard we are talking about you. I can't thank you enough for bringing Lacey to see me."

"I don't mind her riding with me," and Jake walked over to the other side of Tylar's bed and shook his hand, "anytime." And he looked at me. "She's a lot of company."

Jake and Tylar were both looking at me and all I could do was smile. Sally interrupted the moment, "I don't know what you two are going to do, but Tylar needs to eat so he can build his strength. He will need to rest for a little while after he eats so maybe you should go and eat your lunch now so you can stay longer this afternoon?"

"Go ahead, Lacey. I'll miss you like crazy, but Ms. Sally's right.

I can have you longer this afternoon. I will be so rested and ready to visit when you get back. Maybe we can even take a walk out side?"

"Don't push it, Tylar. You had a good walk this morning. If you are feeling up to another walk we will get you up, but don't set your goals too high. It's a long walk to the outside. Maybe a ride in a wheel chair, if I can find one big enough for you and that cast."

"I'm feeling a lot better now. I know I can do anything with Lacey here."

Sally said, "Well, right now you're gonna eat this lunch and I think you're gonna be doing it with her gone?"

"I don't have to leave, Tylar."

"I just mean now that I've seen you and I know you're okay, I can think about getting out of here and going home. You and Jake have a nice lunch in town. You deserve it after all the work you've been doing. I just wish I could be the one taking you. So be careful, Jake. Watch out for flooded roads and stuff."

"I'll take care of her, Tylar. You never have to worry about that when she's with me. I'll wait for you outside, Lacey."

"I'll be right there. I'll see you in about an hour?"

"I'll be waiting," and he lifted my hand to his lips and kissed it.

Our drive to lunch was quiet. Jake asked me what I felt like eating and if Greenway's Kitchen Café was all right with me. It didn't matter where we ate. I didn't have an appetite. I just wanted to be where Tylar was. The Café was in town and attached to Mr. and Mrs. Greenway's home. They also had a store where they sold bottled drinks, boxed candy and some hardware. The hot meal for the day was fried chicken, creamed potatoes, butter beans and corn bread. They also offered chicken or ham sandwiches with potato salad. I didn't want anything, but I ordered a chicken sandwich. Jake ordered the fried chicken. There was a green and silver jukebox sitting on our table. Jake was looking through the selection of songs. While my mind was in Tylar's room, Jake put a nickel in the slot and selected three songs just as our lunch arrived.

"Hope you haven't had to wait too long," the waitress said when she put Jake's lunch in front of him. "Do you need some more tea, sir?"

"No. This will be plenty."

"Well, just wave at me if I can get anything else for you," and she smiled flirting with Jake. He watched her as she walked away.

"Well, I bet she wouldn't mind spending time talking to me."

"Oh Jake, I don't mind spending time with you. I've just had Tylar on my mind. He's really been through a hard time. Had you seen him before today?"

"Yeah, once yesterday. He was sleeping. Why?"

"You should have told me he was going to be so swollen and that he was cut and stitched and..."

"What did you expect? He was knocked down into the mud by a tree as big around as a wagon wheel. He ought to be dead. I thought he was dead and that's why I couldn't tell you anything about what I knew that night you were at my house."

"You should have prepared me for this. I almost fell apart in front of him."

"Yeah, well, I know. But... you didn't."

"And how do you know that?"

Jake picked up his fork and started eating the butter beans. "You better get started on that sandwich so we can get back to the hospital. We wouldn't want Tylar to wake up and not find you there."

Dooley Wilson was singing *As Time Goes By* on the table jukebox. Casablanca was one of my favorite movies. Jake knew that because he and I, with our families, had gone to see it when it came to the cinema. He said we were all silly for crying. The man had no choice, but to leave and get on with his life. Why would he choose this song to play?

"I didn't think you cared much for Casablanca."

"It was okay. I just like the song."

Louis Armstrong and his band livened things up with *After You've Gone*. There was no better sound on the radio or jukebox than good swing music, even if the lyrics were sad. He slowed things down with Doris Day singing *Every Time We Say Good Bye*. I was beginning to hear a theme, but I wasn't sure what Jake was trying to say. I decided he wasn't trying to say anything and that I was just too emotional these days. I needed to get back to Tylar and spend as much time with him as I could. He was who kept me grounded.

"We have pudding or cake for desert, what will you have?"

"Cake for me," Jake said.
"Carrot, coconut or chocolate?"
"Umm, chocolate."
"And for you, miss?"
"Can I have a piece of carrot cake to take with me?"
"Sure. Would you like anything else to drink with your desert?"
"Not for me."
"Sir?"
"Yes, I'll take some more tea."
"I'll be right back with your cake and tea."

After Jake paid for lunch we drove straight to the hospital. I wanted to buy Tylar a box of chocolates, but I had gotten the piece of carrot cake and I knew he would like that so much better. Jake sat down in the lobby when we entered the hospital. He said he would come down to Tylar's room after he rested a while on the couch. I didn't ask him any questions; I walked straight to Tylar's room. He was sitting in a wheelchair waiting for me. I gave him the carrot cake and he put it in his lap.

"Thanks. I love carrot cake. I'll eat it outside. Can you help me with this thing?"

"I would love to. Is this the first time you've been outside?"

"It's the first time that I can remember that I've been anywhere besides this hallway. I think Dr. Jude had given me something to knock me out before we got to the hospital. I don't remember the ride here at all. I woke up and I had my leg in a cast and it wasn't hurting as bad anymore."

We rolled by Jake sleeping on the couch and out the door. Tylar wanted to wake him and tell him where we were going, but I though he might need the rest for the drive back. Mostly I didn't want Jake with us. He was in some kind of mood and I didn't want it to spoil our time. We went out on the grass under a big oak tree where there was a bench. It was a beautiful day, but we were the only ones outside. Probably because there was so much debris all around, but it was so easy to overlook it and escape into our own world. I sat on the edge of the bench and pulled Tylar right beside me. I started to unwrap his cake when he stopped me.

"Lacey, put that down for a minute."

I sat the cake down beside me on the bench, "What is it, Tylar?"

"Give me your hands." I placed my hands into his and turned my knees into the side of his chair. "I made another promise to myself while I was under that tree."

"What was that?"

"That if I ever saw you again I would not let the sun go down till I asked you if I could kiss you."

I reached up to the cut on his lip and asked, "Will it hurt?"

"I don't know, but I'm willing to take the chance if you say it's okay."

I never answered him. I guess he could see in my eyes that there was nothing at that moment that I wanted more. His kiss was soft and simple, so much like Tylar; the way I knew it would be.

Jake was still in a strange mood the drive back to my house. Mostly we listened to the radio and I watched the side of the road as far as the headlights would let me. Ray Noble was singing *The Very Thought Of You* and that was how I felt about Tylar and our first kiss. I would never forget the look in his eyes as he drew closer to my lips. When we pulled into our drive I told Jake that I really appreciated him taking me to see Tylar. He stopped the car at the front walk and turned the engine off.

"I know you do. I didn't know how much he meant to you till I saw you with him today. I'm glad you have someone that makes you're eyes sparkle with so much love. You deserve that. I pray he will love you more than you deserve. I'll always be close by if he ever hurts you. You tell me and I'll take care of him."

"Oh, Jake. He won't ever hurt me, but if he does, you will be the first to know it," and I reached over and hugged him. "Thanks again for taking me."

He got out of the car, opened my door and walked me to the porch. I gave him another hug.

"Do you still want to go into town tomorrow?"

"If Mother can do without me I do."

"I'll call you in the morning,"

I hadn't thought about the fact that I would not sleep most of the night thinking about Tylar. In fact I wouldn't sleep for many nights after that. All I wanted to do was get back to Tylar and soon.

chapter eleven

Shortly after I turned seventeen my life took a turn I was not prepared for. Even though Kimmy was younger than me, she was shy and didn't make friends outside of the family easily, so she spent her spare time at my house with us girls. I had grown to love her like a sister and I think she looked up to me. She had helped me on many occasions with my siblings and I had found her to be nothing like Aunt Penny or Theodore. She was more like Uncle Alvin if it were possible that he had an influence in her life. I was thankful for Kimmy's friendship and it was useful in keeping Aunt Penny calmed down. My Mother was the most grateful of mine and Kimmy's friendship, as she was the one who took the most abuse from Penny's insensitive behavior.

Mayree and her family had been visiting Johnny Kale's church. It was named *Wonders Of Love Fellowship* and pastored by Mitch Sternfield, Johnny Kale's best friend. My Pappy would have nothing to do with the church or either of these men, but he had heard of some wonderful things going on and said God was using the church to heal broken people in spite of who was running the show. Silas had been suffering from a strained back for the past four years from picking up some logs we had cut while clearing the yard after the big flood. He had gone to the church one night when a visiting evangelist had come to town to preach their Camp Meeting. He was healed of his backaches. The evangelist had drawn the interest of a lot of the migrants because they were still suffering the most financially and physically. It seemed most folks didn't believe you had to go where God was moving unless you were in need. They were comfortable staying in their church where God hadn't been in years. I could tell that Pappy wanted to go, but either his dislike of Johnny Kale kept him away or he knew something the rest of us did not. I knew Pappy had a close enough relationship with God, even though he didn't attend any church anymore, but God let him know what was best for him so I didn't ask him any questions.

Kimmy and I had gone to visit Mayree and Mayree was begging Kimmy and me to come to church with her and her family, "I can't describes what yous sees in there. It's like God is in da room and He's touchin everybody in da room. Sometimes, one at a time, sometimes, everybody's all at once. Some are weepin, some are singin, some are shoutin. Some are just sittin very quite and God's healing theys broke heart. Da man sometimes never preaches he just prays and weeps repentin fo us all. They's talks about the Holy Ghost and says, 'Here He come, here He come and people fall to they's knees and weeps or cries out ta heaven. Some start talkin and talkin and I's not know a word they's be sayin, but I knows it's good. I wants that, Lacey Kale. Oooh, how I's wants that."

"Me too, Mayree. I've wanted that for a very long time."

"You knows what I'ma talkin about?"

"My Pappy talks to God like that. I have wanted to talk to God like Pappy does since I was seven or eight. I want to know what to do and when to do it because I'm growing up and I won't always have Pappy to talk to God for me. I wish I could go with you, but I doubt my parents will let me. Pappy and Pa don't seem to like Johnny Kale very much. They don't think he has good character."

"Well, I don't thinks he does either, but wes gos cause my P-pa's says da river has shifted and we have ta be in dat river. It might shifts again, but if wes stays in da river wes be all right. Asks um if youins can come. Yous just gotta come," and she grasped my hands like a desperate woman.

Kimmy and I walked back to the house where Mother was asleep on the porch in the daybed. She had become so frail the past couple moths that I wanted her to go to the hospital and see if there was something she needed done that would help her. She seemed afraid of what they would tell her so she refused to waste everyone's time. Sally and Dr. Jude were doing what they could, but she had even refused to let Dr. Jude examine her thoroughly. I didn't wake her to ask permission. I went to the phone and called my Pappy at work. He was busy, but always put whatever he was doing on hold to take a call from me. I only called him when it was really important and a chance to see the hand of God was pretty important to me.

"Pappy, I know how you feel about this place, but I have been invited to go with Silas and Mayree's family to *Wonders Of Love Fellowship*. The way she describes the meeting it sounds like what happened at Azuza Street. I want a touch from God, Pappy. Like what you got. I want to be able to talk to Him like you do and talk back to Him in His language, but I know how you and Pa feel about this church so I guess I'm begging for you to let me go and ask my Pa to say it's okay for me?"

"Where's your Mother?"

"She's sleeping on the porch."

"She and I have already talked about the possibility that you would hear about the meetings and want to go. You and Willie are allowed to go. It took some convincing of your Pa, but we knew he was going to be a hard sell. I ask that you not spend any more time than necessary with the likes of Johnny Kale. His friend might be all right, but we are the company we keep so watch out for him."

"Can Kimmy come?"

"Does she want to?"

"I think so."

"I'll call Alvin and call you back. Wait for my call."

"I will, Pappy."

It was close to an hour before Pappy called back. Mayree had walked out to our house and was waiting with us for Uncle Alvin's answer. Mother had woken so we were sitting with her on the porch.

"Lacey, have you talked to Willie about going tonight?"

"No ma'am, but I know he will want to go. We've talked about talking to God and hearing what He has to say and even though sometimes I think Willie hears God better than anybody; he says he wishes he could say more to God that he knew was getting through."

"He's certainly capable of making up his own mind about things. I won't try to talk him out of it. He's growing up so fast; you all have grown up, *way* too fast. Mayree have you gotten a job in town now?"

"Yes Ma'am. I works fo Mr. Caffee at da accounting office. I loves it. He's real good ta me, too. Says now dat I's finished school he's gonna give me mo hours. 'Not too manys mo right yet,' I's tells him. I wants ta have some time withs my friends now dat schools out and not miss out on da summer fun!"

"What kind of plans do you have for college? I know you and you're parents have always dreamed of college for you."

"One things fo show, I's nots gettin married anytime soon. I's raised enough babies and seen enough babies till I's could scream right now. Maybes when I's twenty-fives or thirty. If'ins a man will have anything ta do withs me then. But, I's not lookin fo a man. More trouble dan theys worth most da time," and she laughed at her logic.

"Miss Kimmy, have you got a boyfriend?'

"No Aunt Abigail! I'm still too young. Besides I could never fine someone to love me like William loves you or Tylar loves Lacey so I'm not going to even try then I won't fail at that too."

"Why, Miss Kimmy, what in the world have you ever failed at?"

"I've failed my Mother somehow and my Father is always unpleased with me. I just don't seem to be able to do the right thing for either one of them. Guess that's why I like being here so much. You all treat me so kind. All but Uncle Marty, but I know he's not in his full mind so it doesn't hurt from him like it does from my parents."

"You know what? Sometimes people treat people cruelly because they are jealous. You can be jealous of your own child at times, but they love you. Don't ever think any way different. Your Mother is someone we all have failed at sometime or another. Failed her in her own mind that is. Just love her, Kimmy, and go on with your life. Don't let anything you have ever heard someone say to you or about you change your direction. That would be the biggest failure, to fail yourself because of something that never measured to a hill of beans that someone thought or said about you. You are a smart and a beautiful young girl with plenty to offer a man or this world for that matter.

You're whole life is ahead of *all* you girls. Don't ever let anything or anyone try to pull you down. It's not worth it."

My Mother always knew the right thing to say. She encouraged so many people to strive and pursue to make their life all it could be; even in her frail state she still had fire. That quality I admired most in my Mother along with her loyal and nurturing spirit. She was so different from my Nanny in that Nanny just expected everyone to be strong and she wouldn't understand anything different. She never accepted Uncle Marty's sickness. "He's just fine," would be her reply.

Uncle Marty had come home, but he was not able to do much work anymore. He spent his days in his room reading or staring out the window and visiting occasionally with Joan. She was coming by less and less. Jake said he saw her with a boy from Brevard, but they were keeping any relationship quiet, if there was one. She just seemed awfully sad to me, and Uncle Marty even sadder. It didn't make since to me why they didn't get married and be sad together. They might have been able to help Uncle Marty shake whatever was causing him to be so withdrawn. It was obvious to everyone that Joan truly loved Uncle Marty. Why he couldn't love her back was a mystery to everyone, I think even to Uncle Marty.

Jake and Tylar were living in Brevard attending college there. I saw them on the weekend. They both were determined to earn their bachelor's degree in less than three years by starting the day after they graduated from high school and attending every summer for the next two years. They were "football stars" so during the fall and winter Willie and I would drive down to watch them play. They hated to see us leave and I think Jake missed us and home the most. I realized how much Jake had dreaded leaving home to attend college and figured that was why he chose all those good-bye songs the day we ate lunch at Greenway's Café. I was proud of both of them and had learned to love the game of football. We usually made a full day of it and sometimes I would stay with the girls in their dorm room and Willie with the boys and we would stay till Sunday evening. But, we didn't get to do that till Mother met the dorm mother, of course.

It was spring, the best time of year. It was still chilly so we had to keep a sweater close by even during the day. I had poured a large canning jar full of vegetable soup, Mother and I had put up at the end of the summer the year before, into the stewing pot. It was ready to eat other than being warmed up again. The camp meeting at the church started at seven and I was so excited I forgot to cook the cornbread. We three girls were in the kitchen pulling out the ingredients when Pappy called back with Uncle Alvin's answer. It was a go for Kimmy, too. We were anticipating wonderful things and I was getting anxious to tell Willie. But, the cornbread had to come first.

Mayree and Kimmy stayed for supper. Then we walked to Silas' house and waited for everyone there to get ready and load up in the truck bound for the church. I had seen it from the road, but I had never been close to it before. It was about three hundred yards from Johnny Kale's house. It sort of reminded me of his house in that it was large, painted white, five brick steps leading to a porch on the front with two doors that opened from the middle, rocking chairs, lots of windows down the sides and two round stained glass windows peering out at the porch. The only differences were that Johnny Kale's house had four tall rectangle windows on the front with stained glass in the top sash, a porch all the way around and it was missing a steeple on the top. There was a small house behind the church were Reverend Mitch Sternfield lived.

Before the service, Reverend Sternfield met everyone at the door. Some people he asked their names, others he seemed to know. I simply said Lacey when he asked me and shook my hand. I didn't get the feeling he was paying too much attention to the younger people, but some people, he made over them as if they were celebrities. Silas said they were his supporters. When the service began, Reverend Sternfield welcomed everyone and especially those he had been so friendly with at the door. "You are so faithful to serve this church by being here every time the doors are open and you've come back night after night during this camp meeting and I know God is going to keep blessing you as you keep blessing us by being here. And all those who have not been here before I send out a special welcome to you and thank you so much for being here. Now that you have come through those doors, you too are family."

He talked about the meetings they had already had and how God had blessed each one that had attended, the number of people saved and baptized in the Holy Ghost and how gracious the giving had been, "If this is your first time here don't let them out give you. God will bless your gift and bless you and your family. How many of you need a blessing tonight? Amen? How many of you have been praying for a family member who needs to be saved? Amen? Give with your heart tonight and watch how God answer your prayers."

They passed the wooden offering plates from one side of the room down a row of pews and back across the next pew to the side where it started. The plates were filling up quickly and when it came to me, I had fifteen cents to deposit. I was expecting big things from God, but that wasn't why I contributed so much to the plate. I hoped the money would help the evangelist travel to more towns taking with him the move of God.

A beautiful woman stood up and sang a song during the offering collection and I noticed the smiles on Johnny Kale and Revered Sternfield's faces as they whispered to each other. I wasn't sure if they liked the song, the woman or the money being collected, but I told myself I had to stop hunting for things to be wrong and prepare myself for an encounter with God. Reverend Sternfield was so personable and charming. He made you feel like he was your best friend. I could see why this church had been growing.

Johnny Kale went to the podium and told about the evangelist, where he was from, how many camp meetings he had preached, and what God was doing in his life. It was strange seeing him in this role because Pappy had painted a picture of a man who spent his life chasing women, playing poker and drinking till the sun came up. To hear him talking about God and things God had done in the life of the evangelist was not in character with what I had visualized to be Johnny Kale Butler. People could change, I guess, that's what God could do, but I wondered if the man I had met out at the migrant camp was one to change. I saw him more as a type of politician. The type that could put on the charm and kiss babies in a crowd and later in the privacy of his own home beat his wife and children. But, Tylar had a lot of respect for him and he wanted to go back to work for him when he came home for good after college. Somehow, if I planned on being Tylar Lane's wife, I was going to have to find a way to respect my parent's feelings, but make a judgment about Johnny Kale that I could live with and help Tylar be all he desired within his career. I had plenty of time to figure that out though.

After Johnny Kale introduced the evangelist he walked over to a door where the evangelist was seated nearby. He reached out and shook the hand of the evangelist who was holding his Bible in the other hand when he stood from his seat. Johnny Kale departed through that door. The lady who had sung during the offering was seated toward the back of the room. She got up and left shortly after Johnny Kale did. The two never returned. The evangelist was slow getting to the pulpit. He seemed to be praying. Once he reached the podium there was a slight tremble and a heaviness filled the room. It would have been frightening, but this calmness came with the heaviness. I had sensed something like it while lying on my back in the river, but nowhere near this paralyzing. It was as if we were all unable to move, but we were shaking. The evangelist began to sing a beautiful hymn and through his words you could hear the sobbing of many who were sitting on the front row. Kimmy reached out and took my hand.

The evangelist began to pray out loud for the Spirit of God to fill the room and then he started speaking as if he was talking for God Himself. He said. "There is a young person, a young girl who has spent many years seeking God. He has used you many times to communicate His desires for others through you. You've prayed over and over for the filling of the Holy Spirit and to see the evidence of speaking in unknown tongues become real in your life. God wants you to step out and come to the front and let me pray with you."

No one moved. Then he called out for another person and told about how they had suffered with a hidden secret that had stopped them from doing anything for God out of shame and that He wanted to erase the memories that haunted them and that He loved them and had a plan for their life. A young girl about fifteen wept as she slowly walked to the evangelist. He prayed and she shook with a supernatural force that somehow kept her from falling until he stopped praying. Then she fell away from him into the arms of a man who had been sitting earlier by the door with the evangelist. He laid her down on the floor and there she shook and prayed and wept and I watched to see if she ever prayed in an unknown tongue, but I couldn't tell.

The evangelist prayed and swayed to the music now being played on the piano. He said, "God is still waiting for the young girl to come forward and there is a man whose wife is very sick and the doctor's have said there is nothing they can do, but God says He can and will heal her. If you are that husband come down to the front and let me pray with you."

I knew the young girl he was talking about was me, but fear or something had gripped me and I was not able to lift my arms or my legs. I started praying that God would come to where I was and either get me or touch me in my chair. Suddenly there was a wind that entered the room as if someone had opened both doors and the spring winds had come calling, but there was no door open. No papers blew off the podium, no curtains move in the baptistery, however, the air was stirring and you could feel it on your face, but your hair didn't move. The sound was like a train at top speed without the clucking of the wheels on the rail. As I looked around the room I saw flashes of fire above our heads. Mayree was holding tightly to Silas who was now cradling Kimmy who was bent over into her lap with her hands over her face sobbing. I was standing looking up, breathing in deeply, wanting to take in every moment and have it never end. I was filled with unexplainable peace. It was like being a bottle half full of every emotion known to man; joy, regret, calm, anxiety, encouragement, despair, and just a touch of hate for the evil one who had kept me and so many others from being able to see that God is real and you can be this close to Him. And then the bottle was filled when He poured in the love, His love and shook it all up together. I was sure I could float at that moment, but the heaviness that filled the room kept me on the ground. And during all of this the man whose wife was sick was trying to make his way to the front. The evangelist met him halfway. He was crying and trying to speak. The only words I could hear were, "I'm hot and burning, my skin is burning." Of course he wasn't, but I understood that God was doing something in that man that was between him and God and I was sure his wife was being healed. There was no doubting God in this moment. Oh, how I prayed it would never end.

The man was lying on the floor after the evangelist prayed with him and then the evangelist turned to make his way past me back to the podium. He stopped, turning slowly, scanning the congregation and then came back to where I was standing. Kimmy began to sob louder. He stood looking us over with a smile and then he reached out his hand to me.

"God is doing a powerful work in the lives of these two young ladies."

Looking down at Kimmy he placed his hand on her head, closed his eyes and said, "There are wounds, but you have never seen the scars that go so deep they have not surfaced. These wounds will heal, but the scars will remain so that I can be glorified. What this world says about you means nothing to Me. I know who you are. I knew you before I formed you and I placed you in this family for such a time as this. Today you have met your Father. I am the only Father, the only Mother you need. Remain in My arms. Lift your head. You have nothing to be ashamed of. Keep your eyes on Me. You will know joy because of Me," and he prayed for a while in tongue as Kimmy leaped to her feet, arms in the air, twirling on her toes, then collapsing to the floor sobbing with joy.

Then the evangelist turned back to me. "Your heart is willing, but the weight of the world has kept you silent. I put that weight on you so you can understand what My Son endured. Now you too must rise above it and I will show you how. Keep you eyes, heart and thoughts on Me daily and I will be lifted through your obedience. This road will not be easy. This road will be unstable, but I will hold you up until I bring you home. I have chosen you to carry a light into dark places. You must take My Word to those who hate Me, but if you keep your eyes, heart and thoughts on Me you will always feel My love greater than the sifting from those who will hate you because of Me. Because I am greater than he that is in this world, you will endure, you will prevail and the kingdom will grow because of your sacrifice. I have planted a small seed of hate within you. Watch that seed. Keep it trimmed back. It is planted so you will hate the sin, hate the devourer, but love the sinner and those he seeks to devour. Without it you would not recognize the urgency of this calling. My love will overflow out of you if you keep watch over that seed. I will give you words to speak, I will give you wisdom and knowledge of Me that others will not understand, and I will give you desires that will tear at your heart, but choose Me. Always choose Me. Follow Me along the road and when it ends I will be there waiting for you my good and faithful servant."

I was lying back in my seat and the evangelist was being held up by some of the men. A lady was praying in tongues cradling my head in the palms of her hands. Kimmy had her head in my lap still sobbing and Silas was praising God for the call He had placed on my life. I did not know where Mayree was so I began to pray for her to receive whatever God had for her. The lady behind me said, "Open your mouth to speak. The rivers of living water cannot flow from you if you keep your mouth shut. Let the prayer you desire to pray come forth," then she continued to speak in tongues.

I felt like there was a river deep inside of me wanting to burst out of every pour on my body. I opened my mouth and said, "God! Mayree. Don't forget Mayree. Sadamonecaya, Sadamonecaya."

I was taken back to a time when I was very young and I was being cheered on to take my first step, to take my first dose of cough medicine, dress for my first day of school. The excitement in the voices of those around me made me giggle. The sound of the new language coming out of my mouth made me laugh. I had felt this peace for a split second while floating in the river, but never so much inner joy. There was no doubt God had spoken to me. Only God knew about the emotions being poured into me when the wind was blowing and the fire was dancing. Only God knew that I felt the twinge of hate coated with all that love and that in my prayers I called my journey of life, the road He had placed me on. But more than any of these, I had told God that I wanted to sacrifice my life to know Him more and He was calling me out because of that prayer. I was excited about what had happened, but something in side of me was telling me that what was ahead was going to cost me greatly.

The meeting lasted several hours, but I was not concerned with the time. In that moment I wanted everyone I knew to experience what was happening to me and I was sad that Tylar wasn't there, but in the same moment I wanted this all for myself and I was more than ready to simply leave this earth and walk off with Jesus forever. If He hadn't placed that tiny bit of hate in me I wouldn't have felt a desire to help rescue others from a life empty and incomplete. I knew I had a job to do and I was honored to be working for the King of Kings and the Lord of Lords.

As the meeting came to a close we were all still very drunk in the

Spirit, but completely capable of doing what we needed to do. But, there was no sense of urgency to do anything. We just wanted to talk about what had happened to us even though the hour was quite late. When I got home my Mother was waiting up for me in the living room. She wanted to hear all about the meeting, but she was tired and I was more than eager to be alone in my room with God and my journal. I knew I needed to write down everything God had said to me because Pappy was going to ask and he loved details. Besides, these details were very important and I was hoping God would be waiting for me so He could help me remember what He had spoken to me at the church.

I kissed Mother goodnight and made my way up the stairs to my room. Willie was asleep in my bed. I had completely forgotten him. I went over to the bed and gently rocked Willie's shoulder. When he opened his eyes he said, "God showed up tonight!"

"He sure did, Willie. How did you get home?"

"Mrs. Silas brought me home. I could barely walk."

"Can you believe what happened tonight?"

"Yeah, I believe it. I knew God had it in Him all along, just glad I could be there when He showed everybody. What did He show you while you were lying in that chair?"

"Did you hear what the evangelist said? He was speaking for God, but did you hear what He said to me?"

"Yeah. I didn't understand a lot of it. Tell me again."

"Well, can you wait until morning? I need to write it all down and then I'll read it to you. What happened to you, Willie?"

"Well. I don't know. There was a wind and fire; did you see the fire, Lacey?"

"Yes I did. It was beautiful."

"And it didn't burn. I was watching it and wondering why it didn't burn when something just knocked me back. It was like a hard punch, but it hit all over and it didn't hurt like when Theodore socks me. And I fell back on the floor, but it didn't hurt me when I fell and I was shaking all over and I felt warm rushing all through my body and I heard in here that I was being healed. That I would understand things that confused me before and that those thoughts that come to me that aren't good would not come anymore."

"What thoughts are those, Willie?"

"Thoughts that come when I want to talk to God, but I can't because something just comes and keeps me from being able to do it. Like when my mind just jumbles up and I can't keep doing something because I think I have to do something else when I don't. Like when I can't learn my letters, or numbers or colors or how to crank the truck."

"You shouldn't be cranking the truck, Willie. You're not old enough."

"Yeah, but sometimes Pa asks me to warm it up and I forget how and something tells me I'm stupid and that I will never be able to do it."

"Willie! I didn't know you thought stuff like that."

"I don't think stuff like that. It's thoughts that come and tell me that."

"But, you don't believe them do you?"

"Not all the time. Something's I do."

"Like what?"

"Like that I won't ever find a girl to marry and have a job that will buy a house and raise a family."

"Willie, maybe you won't ever find someone to marry. Maybe I won't either. That doesn't change you. I would love to tell you that you will find a girl and have a home and a family, but that might not be what God wants for you. But, I can say that you will have a job, if that's what you want, because you are a bright young man with plenty of talent that will find a place to be of use. As for a house to live in, you will always have a home. Pa has made sure of that for all of us."

"Well, now that God is taking those thoughts away that make my mind all jumbled up, maybe I'll know what He wants for my life and if there is a girl in it."

"Is that really important to you, Willie?"

"I want someone to love me the way you love Tylar. And I have to be able to take care of myself. Mother is way too weak to have to keep taking care of me and you will have your own family, so yeah, I need to be able to do it myself."

"Why wouldn't you be able to? You have come so far in pulling that little person out who I knew was in there all along. You are a wonderful boy with so much to give and there is no reason why you won't find a place to give it. And as for girls? I don't know why God introduced me to Tylar so early in my life. You know what? I was your age when I met him. But, if I had not met him I would date all the boys and not have a special one! What's wrong with that? The most fun I've had has been with new people just getting to know them. I hope I can always do that even if I do get married, I just can't let them pay for supper!"

We laughed and hugged and I was so thankful that God had blessed me with Willie.

"Can you sing me a song, Lacey?"

"Sure. What song do you want to hear?"

"The one you were singing while you were laying back in the chair tonight."

"I was singing?"

"Yeah. It was beautiful, but I didn't understand a word of it here," and he pointed to his head, "but I knew what it meant here," and he laid his hand over his heart.

"And what did it say there?"

"It said God is to be praised. Love will bring you home. Give thanks to God, forever give thanks to God. And stuff like that."

"I'm sorry, I don't remember it."

"That's okay," and he pulled the covers up around his neck and lay back on my pillow, "I remember it. You better go write down what God told you before you forget that, too. I'll just rest right here while you do that. I feel closer to God in here," and he reached under my pillow and pulled out my paper journal with Tylar's note in it.

"Willie! Did you read that?"

"You know I can't read."

Pappy had given me a hardback book with blank pages in it to keep my thoughts. I kept it in my vanity drawer under the rose Jake had given me after the flood. Mother had ironed it between two pieces of waxed paper so I could keep it. I had slid the journal I had made out of notebook paper tied together under my pillow the night before after reading Tylar's note again. I missed him and Jake so much and I was looking forward to them coming home from school soon. Everything seemed changed for me. Clearer, if that was possible. I had a purpose. I didn't know how everyone would fit into the call God had given me, but I knew He had it all worked out. It would be fine whatever came. Together we would push through it and somehow in the end it would touch others because God had said it would.

I spent several hours writing and praying and hearing. I was sure I had gotten on paper what God had spoken to me and heard some more as I was writing. I wrote it all down. I wasn't tired at all, but I wanted to lie down and just soak in this overwhelming joy I was saturated in. I picked up the pages with Tylar's note and my journal and put them both in the vanity drawer under the rose. I left Willie sleeping in my bed and walked out into the hall to make my way to his room. As I passed Uncle Marty's room I heard something. It was dark, but I could see my way with the light from the moon shining in the window at the end of the hall. Uncle Marty's door was open slightly so I walked over to it. There was no light coming from his room. Uncle Marty had insisted on hanging the blackout shades back up over his windows to keep any light from entering his room at night. He said he had gotten used to sleeping in pitch black while in the hangers with his airplane. I had sensed he was trying to keep something else out, but I never asked him. I always felt like he was on the edge and anything could push him on over.

With my ear in the door opening I could hear a sound like a small child whimpering. I thought of Cole and wondered if he had gotten out of bed and wandered into Uncle Marty's room instead of coming to mine. I pushed the door open and walked into the darkness whispering Cole's name. I heard the tussling of Uncle Marty's bed covers and suddenly I was grabbed and thrown to the floor. Uncle Marty had his hand over my mouth and he said, "Shhhh. Be quiet. I hear them outside the house walking in the street. Not another word."

I didn't move. His weight was beginning to crush me, but I lay there for what seemed like hours, though it was just minutes. Uncle Marty had gone back to sleep and I was afraid to wake him. I didn't want him to be embarrassed by how he had acted in his sleep or feel like he had to explain anything to me. I knew he was troubled and I knew it was because of fear he had learned while fighting in the war. All I could do was pray that he would move off of me so I would be able to escape without him ever knowing I had been there, and since he was crushing me, I prayed that I would be able to endure.

God was gracious to us both. Uncle Marty shifted just enough that he was no longer on my chest, but he was still on my legs. I was still basking in the sweetness of the Holy Spirit and able to pray very quietly in my new prayer language. At times I would find myself singing and I wondered if that was what Willie had been talking about. There was no doubt that it was beautiful, though I did not know what the song was saying. Something rose up in me and let me know that the song and prayers were for Uncle Marty. I had tears of sheer joy rolling down the side of my face puddling up in my ears. I didn't care, God was doing something in Uncle Marty and I needed to be obedient. I was praising God in my heart for helping him and rivers of living water were bubbling out of my mouth healing Uncle Marty. My ears were just getting the over flow.

At some point I fell asleep. I woke up with my back to Uncle Marty's chest with his arm wrapped around me and his voice asking, "Lacey, what are you doing in here?"

"It's kind of a long story. Not really worth going into. I'll just go back to my room and you can get back in your bed and we'll just forget about this," and I tried to wiggle out from under his arm.

"I don't think so young lady. I love a long story. So, what are we doing in the floor? That seems like the logical place to start."

"This is where we ended up after we fell down," and I wiggled again.

"That isn't going to get it. You will not leave this room till you spill it, all of it."

"All of it?'

"Every moment of what took place from the time you crossed that threshold. The longer you stall, the longer we lie here in this floor."

"I can't even get up to tell the story? I do so much better when I can walk."

"You will tell more truth lying right here."

"Hey that was funny."

"It was, wasn't it? But, it wasn't meant to be. Look, you're a lot like Pappy and I've watched Pappy dance around an issue and turn it into a walk in the park while pacing the floor. You will not white wash this.

You will tell me what happened in this room and we will get through it, somehow."

Uncle Marty let me sit up and turn towards him. "It wasn't *that* bad. Willie fell asleep in my bed while I was up writing in my journal, *that I did not just tell you about*."

"Deal. Keep talking."

"So I decided not to wake him up and send him to his room. Instead I was going to stay in his bed. I heard a noise that I thought was coming from this room and I pushed the door open just a little, the squeak must have woken you, or scared you in your sleep and you jumped up, ran into me and we both went down and you landed on me and fell back asleep. So I went to sleep and here we are. Funny, huh?"

"Yea, funny. Funny that my door has suddenly developed a squeak. Try again."

"What? That's it."

"So what was the noise you heard?"

"I guess it was the way your face was on your pillow. It must have been making you snore funny. I thought it was Cole. That he had wondered into your room thinking he was in mine and with it being so dark got all confused. Why is your room so dark, Uncle Marty?"

"Why are you so hard headed, Lacey?"

"I'm not hard headed!"

"Then why don't you just tell me what happened?"

"I did."

"Let me rephrase that question. Why don't you tell me *all* that happened and tell it with truth this time?"

"Do you know how nice it is to talk to you, Uncle Marty?"

He didn't speak for a while and he never took his eyes off of mine. I could tell he was moved by what I had said, but I didn't know if it was in a good way or if I was going to witness something I didn't want to see. Finally he spoke, "Tell me."

"Hum. So I was wrong."

"About what?'

"I thought you were softening and were going to drop this."

"No such luck. All of it, *now*."

"*Ok*! Gees. Truth. You were having a bad dream and it must have made you sad because you were sort of whimpering like a child. I thought you were Cole so I came in to this dark as soot room and whispered Cole's name. You leaped, I guess 'cause I couldn't see you leap because it's so dark, but you grabbed me so fast you had to have leaped ..."

"Move on!"

"And you threw me, but I didn't get hurt or anything, down on the floor and held your hand over my mouth and said to be quiet. Then you fell asleep lying on top of me so I had no choice, but to fall asleep right here. Now how we got turned around and me out from under you? I don't know."

"That's all I said, be quiet?"

"No. You didn't say, 'Be quiet,' you said, 'Shhh.' Same thing."

"That's all?"

"You might have said something else, but I don't remember. It's not important."

"You remember that I said, 'Shhh' and not, 'Be quiet,' but you can't remember if I said anything else?"

"Uncle Marty! It doesn't matter."

"Tell me!"

"You said you could hear them walking outside of the house and to be quiet. That was it. Then you fell back asleep. It was just a dream and you were sleepwalking. I've heard about people doing that. It's not anything to worry about. I'm fine. I didn't get hurt except for this crick in my neck that will be gone before breakfast if I get to sleep a few hours in a bed with a pillow. Sound good?"

"Yeah."

The sun was starting to rise and there was a slight glow in the room from the window in the hall. Uncle Marty rolled over on his back and looked up at the ceiling. I just couldn't leave him lying in the floor after telling him he was dreaming about people walking around the house and being frightened by them. It would have been okay for Willie, but Uncle Marty was a grown man who had flown airplanes and fought the enemy with a vengeance. I couldn't leave him with questions like how could he have regressed to this?

"Uncle Marty? After you fell asleep God had me to pray for you.

See? Last night Willie and I went with Silas and Mayree to a church down the road a piece—"

"Yeah, I know. Johnny Kale's church."

"Yeah, that's right. Anyway, something really wonderful happened to me while I was there. Have you ever heard Pappy talk to God?"

"Yeah."

"In a language that you didn't understand?"

"Yeah, in tongue."

"You know about that? Do you speak to God like that?"

"I stopped speaking to God, but when I did I didn't know how to speak in tongues."

"You stopped speaking to God?" I had to shake that off or we would never get anywhere. "Okay I'll let that go for now. Last night I was filled with the Holy Ghost and spoke in tongues. God had me pray in tongues while you were squashing me and I began to sing in the Spirit and He told me I was praying and singing about you."

Uncle Marty turned his head and looked at me. He squinted his eyes and said, "What did it mean?"

The room filled with sweetness. I was as light as a feather and I wondered again why I wasn't floating. A calm peaceful flow of tears came from my eyes and I was not ashamed of them, nor did I try to stop them. It was as if I was crying the tears Uncle Marty had wanted to cry for years. Uncle Marty had turned his face from me, but I did not feel rejected. I put my hand on his shoulder and he began to weep.

"God has healed you, Uncle Marty. Your heart was broken, but He has mended it. Your bravery was challenged, but your inner courage remains. You have turned away from Him, but He has never left your side. The sights you have seen are images you cannot erase, but God can. You saw things and you did things that you don't see how God could ever love you again, but He never stopped loving you. He wants you to know that, Uncle Marty. You did what He needed you to do to advance the Kingdom of God. You saved those He wanted saved and you removed those He wanted removed. You cannot live in the past. The past is not life; living in the past is death. No one benefits from your death. God is calling you out of the past and into your future. Go with Him. Go with Him, Uncle Marty."

He was sobbing all curled up in the floor. I didn't know what to do for him. I just kept thinking that he was the first person God had placed in my path to minister to and having him healed would change my family. Maybe Mother would be next! My thoughts were going in all directions when I heard a tap at the door. I turned around and Willie was rubbing his eyes and yawning. I put my finger to my lips as Willie entered the room. I stood up and leaned over Uncle Marty putting my hands down on his arm.

"Uncle Marty? I'm going to leave you now to talk to God alone. He loves you so much."

He reached up and patted my hand. "You said God had mended my heart, but it doesn't feel mended."

I leaned down close to his ear, "You've been living with it broken for so long you've forgotten what it feels like mended. Don't go on feelings, they will lie to you. God said He mended it. Now live like you believe Him."

I took Willie by the hand and we left Uncle Marty's room.

"Go get in your bed, Willie and let me have mine now."

"Have you been up all night, Lacey?"

"Pretty much. Now go to bed. We'll talk about everything later. Hopefully everyone will sleep in a little bit later than usual."

Willie turned to go to his room and said, "I think Pappy's going to be over pretty soon. Said he wanted to talk to you."

"Oh great, guess we'll talk about it all sooner than later."

chapter twelve

I got to sleep about two hours before Pappy was in my room opening the curtains and lifting the windows. "Lacey, today is a day you will forever remember," and he threw his arms up and circled them around like he was dancing with Nanny. "I couldn't wait to get here to make sure you didn't get a glimpse of it before I got here. Come on. You have to come over to the window."

His enthusiasm was mimicking what I was feeling. It was a new day and I was so excited about starting it. I slowly sat up and stretched my arms out. Pappy ran to my bedside, hugged me and pulled me out of the bed, "Come see what God has made," and he stood me up by the window.

"Wow! Pappy, it's beautiful. I've never seen the sky so blue. Look at the trees, Pappy. They're . . . they're green. Oh my gosh! Look at the detail on the tree bark and the flowers, what color. It's perfect. I have to see the river. Let's get Willie up and take him with us. I have so much to tell you."

"Get dressed, I'll get Willie. I stopped at Katie's Kafe and picked up breakfast for us. Also, I got Willie and Cole a new fishing bobber. Think Cole might want to go?"

"I know he will. Try to be quiet, though. Uncle Marty might need to sleep in this morning. Willie and I kind of kept him up late last night."

I was putting my shoes on when Pappy and the boys came back by my room.

"Ready?"

"Just about, Pappy."

"Lacey!"

"Good morning, Cole, come give me a hug."

"I missed you last night. I wanted you to finish reading the story about the giant. Mommy said you went to church. Why didn't we all go to church like we always do?"

"I went to a different church for a special meeting."

"Just for grownups?"

"No, not just for grownups. You know that church is for everybody. Willie and I were invited by Mayree to go with her family and there wasn't any more room in the truck. Maybe you can go another time."

"I don't think I can. You were gone way past my bedtime."

"Oh, that's right. Well, when you get a little older and you have a later bedtime you can go then. But, for now let's go catch a fish!"

"If you two don't come on the fish are going to be taking their naps."

"Hang on, Pappy. I have to get something."

I went over to the vanity and took my journal out of the drawer, "Got it. Let's go."

The minute I stepped outside the brightness of the day overwhelmed me. It was not a glare or anything that would strain your eyes, but it was brighter than any day ever, and I knew it was supernatural. "Do you see it, Pappy?"

"Yes Lacey, I've seen it many times before, but none quite like the morning after I was baptized in the Holy Ghost. But, this morning I prayed that He would let me see what you were seeing and He has heard my prayer."

"Lacey! Can you see the water drops on the leaves in the trees sparkling like diamonds?"

"Yes, Willie. I see them. Willie! You see this?"

"It's the brightest, clearest day I have ever lived. What happened?"

"Well Little Man, I think of it as the blindfold being taken off. A veil being lifted, a kind of screen Satan must have put on every man back in the garden where Adam and Eve lived. Most people will live their life time looking through a veil and never know any better."

"Is that what happened to me last night when something socked me and pushed me to the floor. Is that when God took my veil?"

"Indeed He did."

"Pappy?"

"Yes, Cole?'

"I still have a veil 'cause I don't see water on the leaves in the trees."

"Hum. Let's keep walking down to the river and see what God has to say about that."

We had rebuilt the dock out over the river, but this time it was much bigger so that all my family could be sitting on the dock at the same time, though we never had everyone out there at the same time. But, if we all wanted to hang our feet over the side of the dock and fish we could. It didn't go out into the river as far as before and it lined the shore about four times longer than the old dock. We had to hang our rope in the tree across the river because the big ones that were along the shore on our side were all washed away during the flood. If we had made the dock go out over the river any farther it would have been in the way of our swinging on the rope. Pa had put a small platform under the tree for us to stand on and get the rope. It wasn't big enough for fishing with more than two people, but the dock on our side of the river was perfect for fishing.

The river looked like something from a fairy tale. The glistening of the sun's reflection off the water was like a shiny new piece of tin. "Oh Pappy, I bet even the fish will be bigger today. Have you ever seen it so beautiful?"

"I think you've asked me that at least ten times."

"Did you answer me, Pappy?"

"Yes, Punkin. But, you can keep asking me if you want to."

"Oh, Pappy. I never thought anything like this was what you were talking about all these years. I even smell it, whatever it is."

"Who it is. You smell the presence of God, His Holy Spirit. You are seeing through His eyes right now. He is graciously allowing you and Willie into His world."

"I could live in this world forever."

"That may be why it will soon fade back to what we are used to."

"Why, Pappy?"

"Because He doesn't want you to feel that way. He wants you to long to be with Him in the new earth and the new heaven that will be even better than this. But, if you are happy with this, you won't want to see something more. He's just giving a glimpse of what it will be like. I know you can't imagine it right now, but it will be even better than this."

"No way, Pappy. If it is, He is truly greater than anyone can fathom. Even the evangelist."

"Tell me about last night. Did you see Johnny Kale?"

"He was there for a little while. He introduced the evangelist and then he left. I think he might have had a date with the soloist, because she left right after he did."

"What was the evangelist's name?"

"I'm not sure. Somehow I missed that, or the presence of God shaking the room with wind and fire and, Oh Pappy! It was unbelievable!"

"Mr. Crocker. His name was Mr. Crocker. He prayed for fire and we got fire. He prayed for God to blow on us and He did. And one time he said to send the Hounds of Heaven on somebody, but they didn't come."

"He was praying for Mr. Jackson's son, Willie. You remember him? He ran away from home and they wanted Mr. Crocker to pray for him to come home. I thought that was just something he was saying like when we use hound dogs to hunt down rabbits and raccoons and Sheriff Cromwell's bloodhounds track down a criminal? Well, just think what a better job a hound dog from heaven could do tracking somebody down."

"And don't forget, Lacey and Willie, that those hounds are filled with the Spirit of God so they know exactly where Mr. Franklin's son is."

"Why haven't they brought him home already if they've always known where he is?"

"Well, Cole, God's hounds, God's angels, God's horses or His army or anything that's in heaven can't do a thing till God tells them to do it. And God is waiting for someone to ask Him before He just fixes something. That's why I keep telling you kids to pray. Every time you see something that needs fixing, tell God about it. He might not fix it the way you think it should be done, but when He gets finished with it, it will be the right way to fix it. That's how He makes sure that He gets the praise when the job is done. Most people just think they can fix things for themselves and they won't have to ask God to do anything, and they get away with that for a little while, but sooner or later if they want it to be fixed right and they want it to be permanent they will have to go to God."

"Well, old man. No truer words have been spoken in these poor sad ears in a long, long time."

"Uncle Marty!"

"Good morning, Son. I hope we didn't wake you."

"I haven't been asleep since I woke up lying in the floor with your granddaughter."

"Lacey?"

"Don't look at me. I don't know anything."

"Have ya'll noticed something different about today?"

"Not you too, Son!" and Pappy got up from the dock and walked over to Uncle Marty who was very calmly leaned against the dock rail looking up at the sky with a smile. Uncle Marty hadn't smiled in years and the word calm was never used to describe him. Maybe lethargic at times, but not calm.

"Are you okay, Uncle Marty?"

"I'm better than okay. Seriously, have you ever seen a more beautiful day?"

Pappy started laughing and slapping his legs and dancing and praying in the spirit. Willie and I caught that same spirit and pretty soon the three of us were laughing and dancing. Pappy lifted Cole up in his arms and prayed for him to be saturated in the Holy Spirit. God's presence was thick like a hot humid day, but you could breathe and laugh and dance and never get tired. Uncle Marty just watched us with a big smile on his face. Pretty soon baby Cole had his hands in the air and he was speaking to God in his own prayer language. I wanted my whole family to be on this dock with us, but the girls had spent the night with Ruthy, Pa had left early to plant with Silas and

Mother was resting. So Willie, Cole, Pappy, my Uncle Marty and I spent the morning and most of the day laying on our backs looking up at the heavens talking about what God had done and basking in His glory.

"Did God erase the images, Uncle Marty?'

"Not really, He just made them a lot dimmer and made today so much brighter. No doubt He wants me to focus on today."

"So do you think you will give Joan a call?"

"I think I would be a fool not to. I just hope she will forgive me."

"She already has, but I think you better go and see her instead of calling and you need to do it today."

Later that afternoon Uncle Marty took a bath, put on a dress shirt and slacks, and drove Pappy's truck out our drive and down the road in the direction of Joan Griffin's house. Pappy and I were praying that she was not in Brevard for a weekend visit with the man Jake had told me about. After supper we all went out on the front porch to have some peach ice cream Pappy, Willie and Cole had churned. When we heard the truck coming up the road we held our breath waiting to see if Uncle Marty was still wearing that smile. He pulled up close to the walk, jumped out of the driver's side, bounced around behind the truck to the passenger's side, watching all of us watching him with that big grin that usually meant, I'm up to no good, but I'm cute, then he opened the door. Joan stepped out and everyone sighed and cheered with excitement. Joan just blushed like a schoolgirl with a crush. That night Uncle Trell, Aunt Gail, along with their children, Sally, Jude, the twins, Marge, Bob, Ruthy and Pauley came over to eat ice cream with us. I just sat in that peaceful state that had carried me though the day watching everyone loving each other as only family and friends can do. It was a perfect spring evening except for the absence of Tylar and Jake. I was longing to see him. Even with a day like this he would have made it all complete.

chapter thirteen

Mayree and I graduated high school on a Wednesday; she in the afternoon from Lincoln High School, an all-colored school, and I in the evening from Valley Grove. I was glad it didn't happen at the same time because I was so proud of her that I would have missed mine to watch her receive her diploma. Mine didn't mean near as much to me as hers did to her and she was going to do great things with her education. I was going to follow God. My future sounded very important, but you didn't need an education to do it. God had all the brains, and besides that, he had employed donkeys before. No doubt I was qualified for the job.

We had our commencement in the school auditorium. There were 32 students who graduated. It was drawn out much longer than necessary, but the teachers seemed to have a need to lecture us one last time. I just wanted to go home and be with my family and friends knowing there would be no more homework in my life unless God chose to send me to college. It would have been nice to have somewhere to go after graduation like some of the other girls who had dates. I was all dressed up in a beautiful paper white linen dress with hand embroidery around the cuff on the puffed short sleeves. There were rows of pin-tucks down the front on either side of the button placket with embroidery between the rows. The waistband buttoned tightly around my waist with a full skirt. Mayree and Kimmy had helped me pick it out for just this occasion. I felt very pretty wearing this dress. Mayree had chosen a pale blue fitting dress with a jacket so that she could wear it to parties without the jacket and to work with the jacket. She was going to be a career woman if the prejudices of this world would allow it.

I found Mayree standing just outside of the auditorium talking with several friends from her school who had come to watch our graduation. She ran to me when she saw me coming down the steps, "Miss Lacey! We did it. But, I's always gets ta say I's graduated first! Ya Mamma and Daddy said they would meets us around behind the cafeteria. Mrs. Baker said there's plenty of refreshments left over and theys wanted everyone to come by and gets some ta take home. They had to park back there anyways so theys just goin to the car after they gots the refreshments. Somebody's showed up ta surprise you."

"Who?"

"He's waitin' by the tree. I's sees ya at the car."

There was a big oak tree in the front yard where everyone met before school and after and there was a boy squatted down by the tree with his back up against the trunk. I wasn't quite sure who it was from that distance so I walked out into the lawn that surrounded the tree. It was Jake. He saw me coming toward him and he stood up and walked to me, "Good job, Red. I didn't think you would ever be able to fake your way through it."

"Jake, it's always a pleasure getting an insult from you. I've missed you so much," and I jumped into his arms.

"I've missed you more, I'm sure."

"That's possible! Did you come home by yourself?'

"If you are wondering where Tylar is, he's in town. Johnny Kale needed him over at the station."

"Has he gone back to work already?"

"I don't know. Can I give you a ride home?"

"I'm supposed to meet my parents behind the cafeteria."

"I'll drive you around there."

"Are you coming by the house?"

"Do you want me too?"

"You know I do."

"Then I will. I need to check in with the folks first."

"They don't know your home?"

"No. You are the one I came home to see, so I came here first."

"Stop teasing me, Jake!"

"Who says I'm teasing? Today is a historical day. I wouldn't have missed this for anything."

"It's nice to have you home."

"It's nice to be home."

Pa and Mother had planned a party for me that was a total surprise. Tylar wasn't there, but he had called and spoken to his Mother to let her know that he was with Johnny Kale trying to fix something with one of the trains. I never understood a thing about the railroad. I had ridden a train once, but it frightened me a little and it was way too noisy and dirty at the train yard so I didn't go when Tylar was working there during the summers. I was a little sad that he hadn't asked to speak to me, but she assured me that he was only able to talk for a minute, "The longer he stayed on the phone the longer he would have to stay at the train yard. Wouldn't you rather him try to get finished so he can come by and see you later?"

"Did he think he would be able to come by tonight?"

"That was his plan."

I felt better knowing that he was thinking about me even if he had chosen to go help Johnny Kale rather than come see me graduate. After all, even I didn't want to go through *that*. I was glad that Jake had come. He always found a way to surprise me and even with his well thought out mean remarks he made me feel like I was the only one worthy to receive such an effort.

I was so surprised to see how much work everyone had gone through to plan a party in my honor and keep it a secret from me. Mother and Sally had made a carrot cake, my favorite, and several pies: one pecan, Pa's favorite, one banana cream, Willie and Cole's favorite and the rest were Double Chocolate Mud Pie, a favorite of everyone else's. Nanny made four-dozen sugar cookies, some plain, some with cranberries, and lime and orange Nehi punch with orange sherbet scooped into each cup. She added some other things to it like pineapple juice, but it was her secret recipe and she would never tell. She used to laugh and tell me that keeping it all a secret was her way of making sure she was always invited to the party. "Give out the recipe of a crowd pleaser and the next thing you know there will be parties all over town serving your recipe and you will be at home wondering why no one seems to get together anymore. Not this old woman! I'm gonna makem' invite me."

At least Nanny had a great punch recipe to offer. Aunt Penny had nothing, but she made my family invite her to every gathering anyway. Uncle Alvin had made some progress learning to walk with a cane. He still kept the wheel chair close by for when he got too tired to use the cane. He suddenly seemed so old to me. He was not that much older than my Mother or Uncle Marty, but he looked more like my Pappy's brother than his son. I didn't know if it was the war, his injuries or living with Aunt Penny that had aged him so quickly. In either case, I felt sorry for him. He had a son that was awful to him and a wife that used him and blamed him for her misery. Although, they had a wonderful daughter in Kimmy and Uncle Alvin treated her as kindly as he did any stranger, they both seemed to hold Kimmy responsible for all the unpleasantness in their lives. I made a mental note to pray for Uncle Alvin's veil to be removed before it was too late for him.

Uncle Marty looked ten years younger than just a few weeks ago. He was so happy and in love. He and Joan had been talking about getting married, but Uncle Marty wanted to save some more money and get settled in at his new job at one of Pappy's banks. He was dreaming once again about becoming a commercial airline pilot, but he wanted to make sure he and Joan were meant for each other before he married her and uprooted her from the only home she had ever known. She was ready to follow him to the ends of the earth without a second thought. "One thing I've learned," Uncle Marty said sitting on the railing of the front porch, "is that women think with their hearts and men think with there brains and I'm not so sure that us men aren't the ones who are wrong. But, I have to be sure that I do what's best for both of us. I would die if I ever hurt Joan again or made her sad," and he pulled blushing Joan in closer to him and kissed the side of her forehead.

"Oh, Uncle Marty, that was so sweet. You two are perfect together. I'm sure that any decision you make that is not the best for both of you could be re-decided. That's another thing us women do that you men could learn from: change our minds."

"I just don't want her to change her mind about me."

"Marty, I thought I had proven to you that no matter how hard you might try to run me off, I'm not going anywhere!"

"And I thank God, Joan, that you waited for me and now I'm going to make sure your wait was worth it. Just trust me on this."

"I do."

My Pa raised his punch cup, "Ah. We all heard that. Someone get the preacher. Let's get this thing over with. Sometime you can spend way too much time thinking things through when you could have been living and making memories. She's already said, 'I do,' and she's stood by you, young man, during the poorer and the sickness and she's forsaken everybody else so how about giving her the rest of it including a wedding band?"

We all raised our cups and shouted, "Yeah," and gave them our applause.

"Calm down, calm down. You all will be invited. Now go pick on somebody else. How about Lacey? She's graduated from high school and most girls already have their wedding plans in the works if they aren't going to college. So what are your plans, Lacey?"

"My plans are . . . to not have any plans."

"Ah. That's no answer."

"Yea, everybody has some kind of thought about what they want to do next."

"Hey! Where are you going?"

"It's my party and I don't have to answer questions tonight. I'm just going to eat and enjoy having nothing to do tomorrow of any great importance. Anyone want some more dessert?"

Jake stood up and walked over to the doorway, "I'll take some more punch and I am always ready to eat some more."

Uncle Alvin shouted out, "That a boy, Jake. Pass up the women and go for the food. It's healthier for you," and all the men laughed.

Jake and I walked into the dining room where the table was covered with dishes still quite full of sandwiches, cookies, cake, pie, mints and assorted nuts. We fixed a plate and Jake asked me if he could have some water in his punch cup. He needed something to quench his thirst and the sweet punch just wasn't doing it. We walked into the kitchen to get some water where I saw several gifts on the table. "Oh my, Jake. Do you think these are for me?"

"Who else?"

"Well, I don't see a name on any of them."

"That's because this is *your* kitchen, *your* party, *your* graduation day, so why would anyone have to put *your* name on the gifts. Oh brother."

"Some could be for Mayree. It's her party, too."

"If you say so. There are two gifts I know for sure are yours."

"Which ones and how do you know?"

He picked up a small pink paper wrapped square box with a white ribbon tied around the box into a bow on top. "This one's for you and I'll let you open it ... one day."

"Jake! Who's it from?" and he put the box behind his back. "Jake? Who's it from? You can't take my gift."

"It's from me and I haven't given it to you yet, so technically it's not yours it's mine."

"Ah. You exhaust me."

"And you love it. Go ahead, say you love it."

I charged him with my arms held out and pushed him against the kitchen cabinet reaching behind him for the package, but Jake was so tall now, all he had to do was hold his arm straight over his head and only a monkey could have climbed to get it.

"If I had known all this time that all I had to do was wrap up a box and dangle it in front of you to get you to want me this bad I would have done it a long time ago."

"How sad for you Jake Foresight to find yourself so desperate for a woman that you wouldn't care that she was wanting what was in the box over you. Now give it up."

"Maybe it is just a little fleshly pleasure that I'm receiving, but who is it that looks foolish here. Besides, how do you know there's even something in the box?"

"That would be more like you to get me to react this way just so you could be close to me and the joke being that there was just an empty box, but I'm willing to take the chance." I was able to wiggle my toe around the leg of the chair and pull it out from under the table and beside me. I stood on the chair and just as I reached the box Jake dropped his arm down and wrapped me in his arms pulling me off the chair and out the door to the mud room.

"These are for you, too." Jake stood me just inside the room spinning me around towards the backdoor. Sitting on the bench at the back door was a vase with two dozen or more beautiful roses of every color. "I was so surprised to find that my bushes had made such a beautiful display while in my absence. As soon as I turned into our drive and saw them I was reminded of you."

"And how is that, Jake? The red one made you think of my carrot head on a stem with thorns like the thorn that I am in your side?"

"Well, not exactly. I just thought that in my absence," and he touched the side of my face, "you too, have bloomed into a beautiful display."

"I don't think I will ever understand you, Jake Foresight," and I turned my head, picked up the vase, sitting it on the sink and placing my fingers into the vase to check for water, "but you do keep life interesting."

He reached out his hand towards me holding the box, "Here, you can open this now."

"Are you sure you want me to have it?'

"I do, now that we're out here, alone," and he looked over his shoulder back towards the kitchen.

I dried my hand off and took the pink box. It was heavy for such a small box and the wrapping had been put on the lid and the bottom separately so all I had to do was pull the end of the ribbon to untie the bow and lift the lid. Inside was a dark blue velvet box. "Jake? What have you done? Enticing me with a luscious velvet box inside of a beautifully wrapped pink package, and what will I find inside? Beautiful stones? Like river rock or gravel? How much more of your teasing will I have to endure?"

"You'll have to open it to find out how cruel I am."

"Okay. I'll bite. Nice one minute, insulting the next. Beautiful roses and now . . ." and I lifted back the lid on the velvet box. I had no words. I was expecting a spring to fly out and hit me in the nose, or a smelly old dead gold fish, but not this. Jake had given me a gold bracelet with three charms attached. I sat the open box on the counter and dropped my hand to my side. "You must have brought someone else's gift to me by mistake. Where's my smelly dried up dead gold fish?"

Jake lifted the bracelet from the box and said, "Well, Bright Eyes, if you just took a look at the charms you would know that this is for you." He let one dangle from his fingers and said, "This music note is because every time I hear Ray Noble singing *The Very Thought Of You*, I'm reminded of our drive to the hospital after the flood." He changed charms in his fingers and said, "This is a car. It speaks for it's self, but just incase you have forgotten how much I appreciated you riding with me to the hospital that day, let me say thank you again. Your company was greatly appreciated." Then he put the last charm in his fingers and said, "Look close to this one because it's hard to see, but it's a Café. I never pass by Greenway's Kitchen Café without wishing you were with me. Can I put it on you?"

Jake unhooked the clasp and attached the bracelet around my wrist. "I don't know where God is going to send you, Lacey, but now you can collect charms from every city, state or country where you go and put them on your own bracelet. The joke is that you will always have these three charms and the bracelet to remind you of me."

He placed his hands under my chin and tilted my head back to look into my eyes. "Congratulations, Sunset," and he pulled at the curls hanging over my shoulders, "I always knew you could do it and now the future is wide open for you to conquer," and he turned and left the mud room.

I stood still having no words, but I had to sit down on the bench to collect my thoughts. I was starring at the bracelet when I suddenly realized I hadn't thanked him. But, I had to figure out what all this was about before I did. I was sure there was a bigger joke than just being reminded of him for the rest of my life. I couldn't let him get to me yet. There was no way he gave these beautiful roses to me without expecting to see me prick my finger or sneeze my head off or something, but the bracelet had me baffled. It had to be something really bad. Could it be Tylar? Could Jake know that Tylar had found someone else while away at school and he was just trying to make me feel better before the blow? It was working, maybe it was working. The bracelet was beautiful, but no, it was not going to work. If Tylar

Lane had found someone else it would take more than this beautiful bracelet to make me forget about him.

Jake had left the party before I came out of the mud room. His mother said he had some studying to do for his final exam on Friday. He hadn't mentioned going back to school before his graduation. He and Tylar both were graduating this year with a Bachelor of Science degree, Jake for medical and Tylar for engineering. Jake wanted to be a doctor and Tylar wanted one day to run his own train yard. Part of me wanted to know what I was destined to do and who I was destined to be with, but I knew that these were the desires God said would tear at my heart.

The evening was very special having my friends and family with me and I hated to see everyone make their way to their cars and go home. I had hoped that Tylar would have come by before the party came to an end, but he was still very involved with his work according to Miss Marge. Mother, Nanny and Pappy were cleaning up and the girls, along with Willie, had taken Cole upstairs to get him ready for his bath. Pa and I were sitting on the front porch swing having a daughter/father talk about the events of the day. "Lacey, I know you have heard me tell you many times how proud I am of you and all you have accomplished, but today I saw for the first time that you have achieved something so much greater than graduating from school. You have become a beautiful young lady with the heart of God for a lost world. You carry yourself with dignity and grace. For now the world loves you, but there is coming a day when you will have something to tell them that they will not be ready to here. Instead, they will turn on you. But, just as you have seen people turn against your Pappy from time to time, do as he has done. Do not let them cause you to stumble. Keep focused on the path before you. The world is not ready for you and I don't know if they ever will be, but never give up. You will not change the whole world, but you can change one person at a time. No matter what comes before you never let it take you off the path God has worn for you. The scenery along the way may be ugly and difficult, but if you stay on His path the walk will be easy."

"Pa? When I was born did you know that God was going to use me in a special way?"

I saw tears come into my Pa's eyes, "The day I first saw you, your

Pappy told me that God had told him that he would have a grandchild who would have a greater gift than he did and he was sure that grandchild was you. I agreed. I knew that you were here for a purpose greater than any of us had imagined. Your Pappy's gift is knowing what to do in every aspect of his life and how his decisions will bless others or negatively affect them. This has been a gift that the town, as a whole, has benefited from, as well as our family. But, God has chosen to do something that will bless each person by speaking through you to each of us. In the past when we needed a school, God told Pappy how to achieve that goal. It blessed the community, but we were still sick and needing direction for our lives. Getting a school or a new post office didn't change our hearts. Now He has sent you to bring us His words. Just like the evangelist spoke to you, you will speak to others as God leads you."

"Do you really think that's what God has planned for me?"

"Yes, and even greater."

"I pray I will be able to please Him and carry out the job as he wants."

"You will, if you keep your eyes on Him. And now I'm going to take these tired eyes inside and spend a little time with your mother before I get ready for bed. You coming?"

"No. Not right yet. I just want to savor the wonders of the evening."

"It's getting cooler; you better get a throw to put around your shoulders if you stay out much longer."

"I will, Pa. If I need it." He kissed me good night, opened the screened door and walked in through the doorway.

"Hello, my beautiful Lace."

The voice I knew better than my own was coming from the azalea bush on the other side of the porch rail beside the swing. Out of the dark Tylar stepped into the light and walked up the front steps.

"Hello, Mr. Lane."

"Forgive me?"

"Can you make me understand?"

"Probably not."

"Then I will have to forgive you."

Tylar sat beside me on the swing and I curled up in his arms where

I was more content than anywhere else in this world. Several hours passed when I heard Uncle Marty drive back into the driveway after taking Joan to meet with some friends in town. We had fallen asleep on the swing and I hadn't noticed the chill that had settled in. Uncle Marty came up on the porch and said, "I have to tell someone before I bust and you are the best person I know to tell. After all without you this might not have happened. I asked Joan to marry me tonight and I gave her a ring *and* she said 'Yes.'"

"Oh, Uncle Marty!" and I jumped up and hugged him. Tylar stood up and shook his hand.

"Maybe you will get the bug, Ol' Boy," and Uncle Marty wrapped his arms around him and slapped him on the back.

"You've got a great gal, Marty. But, somehow I think you know that."

"You do too, Tylar. Hope you don't waste as much time finding that out as I did. Good night, kids. I have to tell the folks," and he walked into the house.

"I guess I need to let you get some rest, Lacey. I'm so sorry I wasn't here for you today. Johnny Kale had an engine stuck on the track and nothing could move till he got it off that track. The breaks had froze up and no one knew how to get it loose."

"You knew what to do?"

"Well, somehow I did. I didn't learn it in college, but I have a knack at understanding how these things work. I can fix just about anything that comes on a train. It's like I was born to understand them."

"I bet you were, Tylar. God needs someone to understand his trains, too. You have to come in the house and have some cake before you leave. I just haven't had enough time with you."

"You're not tired?"

"No. Are you?"

"No, not since I've had a nap. I have something for you. Can you go for a drive with me?" and he took me in his arms.

"I think so. Let me get a sweater and ask Mother and Pa. Would you like some desert before we go? There is so much left over."

"I'll come inside and say hello, but I'm too excited about being with you to eat right now."

I got my sweater, said good night to Pappy, Nanny, Mother and Pa and jumped in the front seat of Tylar's beautiful blue convertible Sportsman and slid over to the middle of the seat. He was very proud of his little hotrod. We drove down the road about a mile to a dirt road that turned toward the river. Once we reached the river Tylar stopped the car and left the lights on even though there was a bright moon.

"Would you like to get out and walk or just sit in the car looking at the river?"

"I don't know, Tylar. It's warmer in here, but it's a beautiful night and you know how I love the river.

"Well, grab your sweater and let's get out for a little while then," and he got out and pulled me through the driver's side and into his arms. "I've had a hard time working today. All I could think about was getting to you and holding you. Shall we dance?" and he made me giggle as he whirled me around. "My sweater, silly!"

Tylar helped me with my sweater. He had left the radio on in the car so we swayed to the sounds of Tommy Dorsey and his band. My heart would race every time he showed me any attention, but to be in his arms caused me to wilt. I just wanted to know what he thought of me. We had always been so close, but never made a commitment to a deeper relationship. I had dreamed that he would passionately kiss me and announce to the world that he was in love with me, that no one else could ever touch his soul like I did and then we would live happily ever after, but so far we were just very, very good friends. I tried to live in the moment and just be thankful for anytime he gave me, but it was getting harder to do. I had an array of emotions when I was with him, but most of the time I had a deep sadness and it seemed I was always on the edge of tears. I didn't want him to know that I hurt when I was with him because, I didn't. I was thrilled just to be with him, but I was longing for what we didn't have. It was so difficult for me to explain it to myself so I knew I could never talk to him about it without pushing him away if he didn't feel the same way. Most of the time I was sure he didn't, because I watched other relationships grow and it seemed so easy for them to share what they felt for each other openly and very early in their relationship. Maybe the problem was that Tylar and I had known each other so long that our relationship had already been determined years ago and he didn't know if I wanted it to change. Maybe *he* didn't want it to change. Somehow I had to simply love being what he needed me to be no matter how I longed for more.

"Can you see the river still, Lacey?"

"Yes."

"And if I turn you this way what do you see?"

"The river to the side of me, oh, and the river again. It's turning around this side. I didn't know it did that."

"Now what do you see?"

"The headlights."

"Hum. That could be prophetic. Look beyond the headlights."

"Now you have my interest. I see … beautiful old trees. Water oaks? A lovely moonlit sky. And a beautiful hillside that seems very happy basking in the moonlight. Oh my, the river is there on the right, too"

"Now what do you see?"

"Tylar! I've lived here my whole life and I've walked this riverbank for miles, but I never realized the river turned like this. It's going in the opposite direction on *that* side of the hill. Why didn't I see this from the road? I've never noticed that the river tree line had a break in it and started again."

"Well, that's because you really can't tell that the land we are standing on is almost an island. The road we came in on drops down beside that hill so you can't see how close the river comes to almost pinching the land off. From up on top of that hill you can see the river on all sides. It's a perfect place to build a house, but only if you are someone like you who loves the river. A farmer wouldn't like this land much because the hike from the top everyday to the barn and back would make you crazy. And these bottoms flooded during the flood season so anything you build or planted down here would be subject to a good washing. But, for a family where the father worked in town and the mother loved raising a family on the river, well, it's perfect. Don't you think?"

We stopped dancing and Tylar's eyes slowly scanned my face and down my neck across my shoulder to his hand holding mine as his thumb rubbed the back of my hand to the rhythm of my heart throbbing in my ears. At this moment God had stopped time just for me.

"The minute I discovered this little plot of land I knew I had to have it. I found it one day when you and I were swimming with your Pa's old tractor inner tube and we floated way down here and I saw this road and walked out to the big road to find out how far we were downstream. Do you remember that day?"

"Yeah, the sun was about an hour from setting and I was so cold. I learned that it takes a lot of energy to pull an inner tube up stream."

"What I remember about that day besides finding this little plot of heaven is that when I'm with you we can do anything. We got that tube back up the river and no one ever knew that we had floated so far away. What an adventure. Seems like when I'm with you everything becomes an adventure. I feel so alive and ready to take on whatever comes my way." He pulled my hand up to the side of his face, "I know that you love this river and that you will always want to live here near your family and, of course, your Pappy. I can't imagine ever being without you in my life so I bought this land from him."

"So . . . you can live near me?"

He took my hand into both of his and looked at the back of it and then the palm. "It's time for you to become a woman who is taken care of instead of the one who is always taking care of everyone else. I know that some of what you do you choose to do it, but you were born with so much even though you haven't lived like it. I don't want to ever see these hands work so hard again." He rubbed my arm and picked up one of the charms on the bracelet Jake had given me. "Where did you get this? I don't remember you having this before."

"It's a graduation gift."

"It's very nice. From your parents?"

"No. You probably won't believe this. I'm still having a hard time believing it. It's from Jake. I keep waiting for the joke. Like the jeweler driving up in my yard and taking it because he bought it on credit and stopped making payments."

"That sounds like Jake. But, it looks like his trying to move in on my girl."

"Since you brought it up I guess I can ask. Is that what I am, Tylar?"

"What?"

"Your girl?"

"You have to ask me that? Wow, I haven't been obvious?" He pulled me in close to him. "I don't kiss every woman I meet or hold her this close," and he captured my breath as he squeezed me. "It's all about you. Everything I do, every decision I make is because I have you in my life and I want you to always be here. I bought this land from your Pappy because I knew that you would always want to live here and because you deserve to be surrounded by the things that make your eyes shimmer like the river you love so. I want us to always be together. I love you more than there are stars. If you filled buckets with every ounce of sand on this earth my love for you would out weight them." He dropped down to one knee. "My beautiful Lacey, my answer to emptiness, I have always loved you." He reached in to his pocket and took my other hand. "Since you have Jake on that arm I will have to upstage him with this hand. Lacey," and he took a deep breath looking into my eyes then continued, "I bought this land for us. I want to build a house with you. Our house, where we can raise a family if God so chooses or we can simply love each other solely. I don't want to try and paint a picture for you that might not be and have you disappointed if it doesn't come out that way. So all I can truly offer you is myself. I feel like I will be able to provide for you where you are very comfortable, but if I couldn't, would you still love me? I know I can build a home for you, but maybe not with everything I want you to have right away, but maybe you could wait? Maybe this isn't the place where you would want to be forever. I am willing to do anything to have you with me. I can change anything you don't like or stop working for Johnny Kale if that's a problem? You can stop me anytime."

"Tylar, you talk all the time, but never about things like this. There is no way I want to stop you."

"Have I convinced you yet?"

"Do you have more?"

"Oh Lace. I have so much more. I've been holding back for so long afraid you wouldn't desire me unless I became something."

"Became something?! What are you now? What have you always been?" I fell to my knees where I could look him straight on, "You have been something since the day you picked up Rebecca's tray out of the cafeteria floor."

"You remember that?"

"Are you kidding? I still have that note you pinned to the tree by the river after the second time I saw you again. You held my heart from that day and I have never offered it to anyone else, even though I wasn't sure you wanted it."

"I want it. I want your heart, I want your love, I want ... I want you to be my wife."

"For-ev-er?"

"Forever! Always, all year round. Every day, every hour, ever moment. Night and day, day and night. Morning, noon and night, hour to hour, day to day, month to month, year to ..."

"Okay, okay. Stop, stop, stop."

"Incessantly. Lacey Kale Rutledge, will you incessantly be my wife?"

This was another one of those dreams. I did *not* just hear that. "Tylar, are you sure?"

"I'm only sure about what's right for me. I hope that you feel like this is right for you. Do I need to give you some time to think about this? Go ahead, take your time. Look around the land and make sure your getting a good deal?"

"Oh my dear, Mr. Lane, one thing I am is my Pappy's granddaughter and I know a deal when I see one and you have been the only deal for me. I've waited a lifetime to hear those words from you. And yes, Tylar Lane, I would be honored to be your wife. Now kiss your bride to be like you mean it."

He whisked me into his arms holding me so tight I felt like a doll in a papoose. We had never had such freedom to kiss each other before. He lifted me and carried me to the car. "There's more where that came from, but first we haven't finished with this yet." He sat me down on the hood of the car taking my hand again. "I wanted something bigger and brighter, but everything I looked at would have paled in you presence. I also wanted to buy this land and owe nothing so we could start our lives with no debt. After this summer I will be promoted and we will be able to start the house and I knew that would be more important than the size of the stone in your ring. But, now that I'm competing with Jake's bracelet this may look smaller than before," and he slid a beautiful antique white gold filigree setting with a single stone on the top onto my finger. "It's the ring my Father gave my Mother and my Father's Father gave his wife. When I told Mother I was going to ask you to marry me and that I needed a ring she took me to her jewelry box and said she would be honored if you would wear my Father's ring. I know he would be proud of the woman I found and want you to have it, too. It's platinum. My Grandfather bought it in England."

"It's the most beautiful ring I have ever seen and I am honored that you feel like I am worthy to wear a ring that signified your grandparent's marriage, but more importantly your own parent's marriage. I only hope that I never prove otherwise."

"We can get you something else later when we have some extra money or maybe for a special anniversary?"

"If it's okay with you, I love this one and I never want to replace it."

Everyone was in bed when Tylar and I returned to my house. I didn't want him to leave, but we both were a little tired from the day we had. The next morning I had fought a restless night, but I was feeling so content with my life. It had been hard to sleep and I was sure that I was up before anyone else, but Uncle Marty knocked on my door.

"Come in."

"I thought I heard someone up in here. Have a good night?"

"Oh, Uncle Marty! You shared your news first with me and now I get to share mine with you! I guess Tylar got that Ol' bug you were talking about last night 'cause he asked me to marry him! Look!"

"Wow! He did get the bug and I didn't think he could afford to get you a ring?"

"You knew!"

"He asked everybody if it was okay. He asked your Pa first, then your Pappy, then me and then as if that wasn't enough permission he asked your Ma, Nanny and then Trell and Gail. I think he even asked Willie."

"Not Willie? He can't keep secrets from me!"

"Well, maybe not Willie, but most everyone else. Oh and even Silas. That's why I said what I did to him last night. He knew what I was going to do also, but you were the first one I told that I actually did it."

"Did everyone else know you were thinking about it?"

"No. Just Tylar."

"I can't believe that everyone knew and that they were able to keep that from me *and* the party last night. I might not know my family as well as I thought I did! I wonder if Jake knew?"

"I don't know, but I can't imagine that he didn't with them at school together and all."

"Yeah, you're probably right. I never saw it coming and everybody knew."

This just seemed to make Jake's behavior even more confusing. Was he trying to move in on Tylar's girl like Tylar said? No way. Jake had shown me affection the night Tylar was hurt and then when we drove out to the hospital years ago, but nothing like that had happened again. Now that I had accepted Tylar's proposal I wondered if it was okay for me to accept Jake's gift.

"Are you headed down to breakfast?"

"Isn't it too early for everyone to be up?"

"I think they are all anxious to see you this morning. Pappy and Nanny stayed the night just so they could see you first thing. I heard the backdoor screen slam so I know someone has gone out for wood. I'm pretty sure I smell coffee."

"Yea me too ... I'll be right down."

Uncle Marty kissed my cheek and said, "Congratulations, Punkin, he's a fine man. You could have done a lot worse."

"Uncle Marty! You sound like Jake."

"But, if he had chosen the finest catch in three counties *he* would have done worse."

"Oh, that was sweet. Thank you." And he left my room.

I took the box out of my vanity drawer and removed the bracelet from my arm. I thought about the night in Jake's family's living room when he held me to comfort me when Tylar was hurt. I remembered how he seemed to be a little different on the way home from the hospital and I wondered if he had a crush on me. Jake would never just come right out a say so, because he was too tough for that. It wouldn't be right for me to keep the bracelet if he felt anything for me more than friends do. I placed the bracelet back in the box, closed the lid and placed it back in my drawer. "I will take it back to him today. God, I was sure you simply wanted to spare me from such confusing emotions when you sent Tylar to me. I was also sure if there was a man to love me for the rest of my life that it was Tylar. Even though I wasn't sure of his feelings until last night. Is it possible to go from no love at all to being loved by two all within one day? Oh, if I had only had several beaus during my childhood I might know how to ... what do I say to him? I would die before I would hurt his feelings, even if he has hurt mine since the day I met him. He had to know that Tylar was going to ask me to marry him. So if it hurts his feelings to watch us being happy about our engagement it is all of his own doing. I have never led him to believe that my intention was anything more than a deep friendship. I'm sure I'm making this more than it is. But, I can't keep his bracelet and I have to take care of it today."

When I got downstairs Nanny and Pappy were there just like Uncle Marty said. They were busy in the kitchen with Pa and Mother frying up bacon and ham, Pappy beating a bowl of eggs and the pot we used to cook a big bait of grits was on the stove. "Ah!" my Pappy said as I entered the room. "Look who's up this morning? It's our newly engaged graduate?" and he reached out for my hand. "Ah yes!" and he lifted my arm up over my head, "Look we have a bride to be among us."

"Pappy, leave her alone. You're making her blush."

"A blushing bride to be!" and he laughed his jovial laugh. "I can't wait to see that boy. I'll make him blush too."

"Pappy, don't be too hard on him. If he's like me this morning he hasn't had a lot of sleep," and I drug the chair out from under the table and sat down. "Is there anything I can do from here?"

"No my sweet angel. I'm sure you've had a hard night. All that pressure he must have put on you and I can just hear him, can't you hear him, Jo Rett, talk, talk, talk. Trying to sell himself to my granddaughter. I'm sure it was exhausting."

"Yeah, probably for both of them, but more for Lacey!"

"Stop making fun at my husband to be. I love to hear him talk. I will never get tired of it."

"Oh, honey. I hope you can still say that after sixty years of marriage."

Pappy put his hands on his hips and asked, "Jo, what are you trying to say?"

"Just that God is merciful. That is why we lose our hearing as we get older. Then we only hear the really loud stuff."

Pappy shouted, "Can you hear me now?!"

We all just laughed. "Last night was the night I had been dreaming about since I met Tylar Lane in the third grade. He has never said sweeter words to me or had my attention so completely as he did last night. I didn't want the night to end or for him to stop talking. I love him so much and I was beginning to think he was never going to love me back."

"But, I do and always have." Tylar was leaning against the door jam of the mud room door.

Uncle Marty came in behind him. "I found him wondering aimlessly out back. I think he's been out there all night."

"I didn't know you were coming for breakfast," and I ran over to him and held him tight. "Oh my gosh! I just got out of bed! I'm in my pajamas."

"And your hair is a mess, Punkin. I bet he takes back the ring now that he sees what he's really in for."

"Martin!" my Nanny was always acting shocked at what my Pappy and her boys would say, but you could see that she was laughing inside.

Pappy put his arm around Uncle Marty's shoulder. "Yea, son, the first time I saw your mother dressed in that ragged old house coat her old boyfriend bought her that she *wouldn't* throw away, I thought, good thing I've come around to help this woman. She's way to pretty to be saddled with a man who would keep her in curlers and rags. Maybe you can help Lacey like I helped her Mother and Grandmother, Tylar. You know when she was younger it was all we could do to get her to take a bath. She never wanted to wash or brush her hair. You know it's red because one summer tomatoes grew in there. Yeah, I say you got here just in time to save her, Tylar. Welcome to the family."

"And excuse me while I go upstairs and change and brush the dirt out of my tomato crop."

"I'll let you go, but only if you know that I think you're beautiful dressed in your pajamas or in that dress you had on last night, which was pretty by the way. A vision I will never forget. But, I remember a little girl in a green jumper with a soggy bow clipped in her hair, which was in an awful mess by the way, that I didn't think Miss Sally would ever get combed out. You were just as beautiful to me then as you are this morning. I've always loved you no matter what you were wearing or what your hair looked like."

"What green jumper? I don't remember you having a green jumper."

Pappy said, "It's her glory you know?"

"Her *green jumper*?"

"No, Abigail. Her hair. A woman's glory is her hair. That's why you women spend a lifetime trying to get it just right. But, Tylar even though I've spent hours waiting on Jo Rett to get it 'perfect' through the years I have learned that if you want a happy household, never rush a woman when she's working on her glory. And for heaven's sake always tell her it's just perfect no matter what you really think 'cause just when you least expect it to be true, that will be the very day she paid somebody a whole lot of money to fix it or spent an afternoon making it look just that way."

"Oh Daddy, what are you talking about?"

"It's in the Bible, Abigail."

"Where?"

"I'll show you," and Pappy picked up Mother's Bible lying on the kitchen table. "Right here in 1 Corinthians 11:15 *'But if a woman have long hair, it is a glory to her: for her hair is given for a covering.'* Now I translate that to mean that woman is so proud of the gift or ornament if you will, that God has given to her that she glories in that gift and wants it to always look its best. You know children are what a family glories in. You'll learn that one day and, Tylar, you know already that man glories in his woman. You've been down to Silas' cabin before when we've been ... you know just doing men stuff,"

"Playing cards, Jeremiah. I know what you're doing down there. So does God. Can't hide it from Him, why do you want to hide it from me?"

"I love you, Jo. Anyway, Tylar, you know how us men talk about how wonderful our wives are and how they've made us the men we are today?"

"Oh brother. You think that will make it alright with me that you are down there gambling if you're talking sweet about me? A man your age ought to be smarter than that, but it is nice to think that's possibly what's going on down there."

"It is, Jo. Trust me. We learned this behavior from God himself."

Nanny cut her eyes over towards Pappy and mumbled, "I guess they were playing a hand of cards at the last supper?" We all just snickered waiting to see how Pappy was going to get himself out of this one.

"He *did* teach us this, because He glories in His creation, which is man. So I look at it like this. Woman feels great when her hair looks good and if a woman feels good and looks good than her husband will be proud and glory in her. Your children will be blessed when the two of you are boasting on each other. That teaches love and that is what God is, love. And somehow through it all God will cause us men to love our wives as Jesus loved the church and gave himself for it. In other words, he was willing *and did* die for the church and in order to have the home God intended we have to love our wives enough to die for them. And when us guys are getting together we are just encouraging each other to be willing to do whatever we need to, even if it's die for our wives." Pappy walked up behind Nanny and wrapped his arms around her, "So girls, keep up the good work and see if you can help Lacey learn to be a little more creative with her scarlet tresses. Tylar, forever is a long time to look at the same woman. You'll be thankful if she learns to make it interesting."

Nanny turned her face towards Pappy and popped his hands, "Try not to run him off the first day, Jeremiah."

Pa stopped laughing at Pappy long enough to add his wisdom, "Don't run, Tylar. I've never gotten tired of looking at Abigail. Even if she never changed a thing about herself just looking into her eyes every morning I see new hope, desire, and more love. It's what makes me want to get up and start the day," and my Pa kissed my Mother.

Nanny cuddled into my Pappy's arms and sighed at the sweetness of my Pa's love for my Mother. No matter how sweet the moment

Mother had something else on her mind. "I still want to know about the green jumper."

"Well, Mrs. Rutledge, Lacey wore it the day of the cookout for my family just before we moved here."

"Oh, William. He remembers what she wore to that party. How did your bow get soggy and your hair messed up? I remember telling you not to get into that river."

Pappy said, "Abigail, they were kids. Things happen."

"Yea, well Daddy? What do you know about it?"

"Okay … I think I will *bow* out now. Don't let the bacon burn, Mother," and I turned to go up the stairs.

"I'll talk to you later, young lady, you're not married yet."

Our breakfast was the first of many that Tylar and I had with my family. The summer seemed to pass so quickly with house plans and clearing off the land to build our new home. I spent my mornings helping Mayree take eggs and butter to needy families in an area about 30 miles from us known as Little Africa. It wasn't a very safe place to venture if you didn't know the people, but Pappy and Silas had been taking us since we were small children to help build housing and roads for the colored families who were hit very hard during the depression because they later lost their jobs working on small farms when so many of the owners were drafted during WWI. Some had lived like the migrants after the farms were sold and they were removed from the only home they ever knew. They settled on some land given to the state when the owner died and had no will or heirs to receive it. They named it Little Africa and begin to police it themselves. Most everyone was making moonshine as their first occupation, though they denied it to the local sheriff. But, even if they told him what they were doing, he wasn't going to take his own life into his hands and try to stop them. We were treated like family when we came to visit them all.

Mayree and I had started a small summer school for the children and after we delivered eggs and butter we spent a few hours teaching the children to read. I loved these people as if they were my second family. God was giving me words of encouragement for them and I saw great leaders living among those who had given up on a better life. Most of them had settled with what they had and were perfectly happy, but the younger children had a gleam in their eyes and I knew that they would lose it too if they didn't ever hear someone tell them that there was more. We used the Bible as our reading book and it was hard for most to read so Mayree and I would rewrite the scriptures to make them easier to understand and read. If we came to one we couldn't change because we didn't understand we would ask Pappy. He seemed to always know just what God was thinking and saying. However, since the day we were filled with the Holy Spirit, the Word of God seemed to leap from the pages and into our hearts and we understood it as never before.

Tylar didn't like us going there everyday, but I had made him understand how important these people were to God and how He had given me the desire to love them as He did. I couldn't turn my back on them. Some of them were related to Silas and Mayree and if I didn't help them it would be like turning Silas and Mayree away. I could never do that to them so how could I do that to their people? Besides we had put our blood, sweet and tears into seeing them have food and shelter. How could I deny them an education? They had a school, but it didn't have enough books or teachers to teach them all they needed. The reading skills of the teachers were not much better than my brother Cole's so we were thrilled when one or more of those teaching would come to our summer schools. I simply felt like Abraham Lincoln did. All men were created equal in the eyes of God and all men, women and children deserved a chance. I had been born with all the chances offered in this world. How could I hoard them all for myself and close my eyes to those without? I had recognized that a teacher would never be able to teach to a student all that they knew and if they didn't even try by simply teaching enough to get by, then what would that student offer their students. The wisdom and knowledge lost to the next generation would be lost to the next and more. What would be left for the generation a hundred years from now? It was only a small part of the world, but I was determined to give as much as I could to offer hope for the next generations in my community. Tylar tried to understand, and I think he did, he just worried about my safety. "But, God goes with me and He will not let Satan kill me. Anything else that might happen we can live with."

chapter fourteen

At the end of the summer my eighteenth year the land had been cleared in preparation for our house to start. Tylar had hoped that there wouldn't be much rain during the fall so that the building wouldn't take so long. We hadn't settled on a date for the wedding because he wanted the house finished when we returned after the honeymoon. It would take months to build the house so we knew it would not be before next spring. Johnny Kale had given Tylar an all expenses paid trip out to the Grand Canyon by train for our wedding gift and we were both looking forward to seeing some of the world. I was a little afraid of taking a train so far away from home and I just didn't have the excitement in me that I thought I should. I couldn't even imagine us riding on the train, meeting new people or the beauty of the sleep car that was going to be just for us. Even the first night with my husband, alone for the first time with no reservations was not easily played out in my mind. I could see us in our own home together, but not in that train. It was like something telling me inside that it just wasn't going to happen like that at all, but I brushed it off as my own silly nerves about that train. One thing I had learned, a lot can change in a year.

Pa had taught me and Willie how to drive the tractor and we had borrowed it to clear the drive leading up to the house site. I was determined to help with our house as much as I could. Tylar was working full time for Johnny Kale so he was only available on the weekends. Willie and I were able to get quit a lot done for two amateur house builders, but we had been around building long enough and watched Pa and his workers to know what the end results should be. I noticed from time to time some of the workers coming behind us and fixing our mistakes. That was becoming a sport for Willie, but I didn't like making the mistakes.

Pa had drawn up our house plans one evening while Tylar and I sat and conversed about what we thought the perfect house should have and what our selfish wishes were. Such as three indoor bathrooms, one for him, one for me and one for anyone else who might stop by or desire to live with us.

"Put them in now before you finish the house. You know what a hard time I had adding this bathroom after someone came up with the bright idea of having such luxuries inside the house! Because I'm your Pa and I can make it happen for you; I want your house to be grander than any home in the south. Some of the plantations in Charleston have as many as five bathrooms. People put them right next to the bedrooms."

"Pa! We want a house full of children so we need several bedrooms."

"How many?"

"At least six, William."

"Oh no, Tylar. At least eight."

"Lacey, are you going to have seven children?"

"Well, maybe more. I thought if I had one a year that they could stay together for a few years and as they grew up they would need more privacy, like I had and then when Pappy and Nanny come to stay they will need a room and ..."

"And we will build the house where bedrooms can be added as they are needed, but for now let's settle on four large bedrooms, two of which have bathrooms and two bedrooms share a bath and then one on the main floor for your guests that's fairly large so you can divide it if and when you add more bedrooms to the ground floor. Remember you were wanting a large living room and dining room with a small kitchen for you and Tylar to use and a large one for the cooks."

"Oh Pa, that's just a dream. We need one large kitchen for all of us. I have learned to cook now so I don't need to hire cooks like Nanny has. I know I said I would when I was a little girl, but I want to do things like that for my family. Oh my, I did have some wonderful dreams though, didn't I? The only one that mattered was the one where I met my Prince Charming and lived happily ever after. And that one is coming true, the rest have faded from my memory."

"Ok then. Four baths, four bedrooms large enough for several cribs, bunk beds and wardrobes."

"Lot's of wardrobes," I added.

"Tylar, any objections?"

"I have none. If she wants eight bedrooms, a ballroom, two kitchens and a cook I have no objections."

So our house was drawn and we were building a four bedroom, four bath home with one very large kitchen with a mud room and pantry. We hoped to entertain many friends as my family always had, so in anticipation of a much larger family with time, we doubled the size of our dining and living rooms from what we were used to living with. Finding a table large enough to fill the dining room was Pa's job. He knew all the furniture builders. And my job was to be available for any job I could do. Mostly I made trips to the lumberyard and to the hardware store. I was much happier in this role than the one planning a wedding.

I had no idea what kind of wedding I wanted so that was left up to Aunt Gail, Marge, Nanny and Mother. They were also planning Uncle Marty and Joan's. All was decided on theirs except the date. Uncle Marty was waiting for an offer to come from Charlotte Municipal Airport to become one of their commercial pilots with United Airlines. He had been offered a job at Charleston, but because of the Korean War the US Air Force had joined with the Municipal Airport making a greater need for pilots to fly the Air Force planes than commercial, but Uncle Marty was not interested in flying so far way and being gone for such long periods of time. Also, he had his heart set on flying a Boeing B.377 Stratocruiser instead of the 307 Stratoliner they used in Charleston. Manassas, Virginia had offered him a job at a small airport there, as well, but he wanted to keep Joan as close to home as possible. So for now we were praying for a call from Charlotte so they could begin their lives together close to home.

Mother and Pa said Joan was welcome to move in with us till they were able to decide which job Uncle Marty would take, that way they could go ahead and get married. I think Mother was hoping to get Joan living with us and maybe Uncle Marty would never leave. She didn't want her brother to ever leave her again.

Mother had become very dependant on her brother. She was so weak at times during the day that it was difficult for her to lift herself from her chair or the bed. Uncle Marty would check in on her several times during the day to see if he could do anything and he always ate his lunch with her. They had a bond something like Willie's and mine, but Willie needed me when he was little and Mother needed Uncle Marty now that they were grown. I think they kind of needed each other.

By the time Thanksgiving arrived, Charlotte had called and Uncle Marty and Joan had found a house to rent very close to the airport. It seemed as though our lives were right in the middle of God's will. Our house had made great advancements because the rains had been held back and if all things continued we would have a finished home by April. Uncle Marty and Joan had scheduled their wedding for March and Tylar and I were scheduled for May fifteenth. That was to allow for the family to rest after Uncle Marty's wedding and to guarantee the completion of our new home.

Joan had asked me to be her maid of honor. Abbie, Retta and Kimmy were bridesmaids along with Joan's sister, her niece and two friends. Willie, Cole, Uncle Alvin, Theodore, Pa and Tylar were groomsmen and Uncle Trell was Uncle Marty's best man. Joan's Father had died when she was fourteen so Pappy was asked to be the one to walk her down the isle. He told me that he could never say that he was going to 'give Joan away' so he wanted the preacher to say, "Who will exalt God for the blessing of this woman?" I wanted him to do the same at my wedding, but he said that he was ready to give me away, besides that would be left up to my Pa.

"Well, it just might take both of you to get rid of me."

Everything was more than perfect in our backyard the day of Uncle Marty and Joan's wedding. Joan was one of those people who was obsessed with one color. Everything in her life was orange. There were so many shades of orange, but most of them did not make you think wedding. I was sure with my red hair and an orange dress I was going to look like an overripe pumpkin and live up to my nickname. But, this was the Bride's day so I was willing to do whatever I could to make her happy. Fortunately, for all of us Mrs. Marge had found a beautiful pale tangerine that was flattering on all of us girls. As you looked out into the yard the tables were covered with crisp white linen tablecloths. Tangerine colored napkins folded just right popped out around the rim of the tall stemmed glasses. The centerpieces were silver urns holding groundcover rosebushes with tiny orange colored blooms spreading their vines out over the table and between the place settings. White and tangerine mesh sheets were twisted and draped throughout the gazebo and the railing around the house and back steps. God had smiled on our backyard, because every bush had new full green foliage and the early bloomers were showing their spender. Sally and Jude were tying tangerine and white bows to the bushes when I walked out onto the back porch.

"Good morning you two."

"Oh, Jude. Isn't she beautiful. Oh Lacey you look like a picture in a Hollywood magazine. I love your hair fixed like that. And the white flowers in your hair. Oh honey, you are going to outshine the bride today," and she hugged me with tears in her eyes. "I don't see how you can top this for your own wedding day, but I know you will."

"Lacey, are you dressed early or are we running later than we thought?"

"I'm dressed early, but why are you running late?"

"Oh Lacey, Jude and I had a very important phone call this morning. Jake is coming home for the wedding today. It's been so long since he was home. We were talking this morning after he called. You know it's been since your graduation party since he's been home? But, he's getting so much studying done."

"It takes a lot of discipline if you want to be a doctor so he's done the best thing for himself. It's just been hard on us, especially his Mother," and Jude walked over to where we were standing and put his arm around his wife.

"I hadn't realized it had been quite that long. I guess I was just caught up in my own wedding plans and building the house. My, the time has flown by," and I picked up a bow and tied it to a bush. "Could ya'll use some help?"

"Guess we could use some, now that we are later than we thought."

"It's still a couple hours before the wedding. Joan just got here a few minutes ago. She's sampling the sandwiches."

About that time Joan came out on the porch, "Sally! I need your help," and she ran out to the yard. "How does this taste to you?"

"Um. What is that?"

"Here Jude, try this."

"Wow. That has a zing."

"It's something Lacey came up with. It's made with ... "

And they all said together, "Tangerines!"

"You should see all the things she and Marge have done with the tangerines! We even have punch."

"I hope we have other things or everyone will be walking around like this," and Dr. Jude made his lips look like a fish.

"Of course we have other things, beautiful pink salmon to go on crackers, vegetables, fruit ... "

"Besides tangerines?"

"Yes, Jude."

"Have you got some manly foods or is this all just that stuff that fits in the palm of you hand?"

The backdoor screen opened and Jake walked out chewing on a piece of fried chicken. "Got chicken Doc and it will fit in the palm of your hand."

"Jake! You're home! My baby boy." Sally ran up the steps grabbing Jake and kissing him all over his face.

"Mom! Save some of that for later. I'm not leaving just yet."

"Oh Jake. Tell me you don't have to get right back."

"Leave the boy alone, Sally. Don't make him feel guilty the minute he gets home. Hello, son," and Jude walked up the steps, hugged his son patting him across his back and then taking him by the shoulders. "Gosh it's *so* good to see you."

I slowly made my way around the yard tying the bows in the bushes hoping I could escape from the backyard without Jake noticing me. My mind was on the box that was up in my vanity drawer, buried under my journal with the rose in the wax paper. So much time had passed since Jake gave me that bracelet and I had not worn it since the morning after when I resolved to return it.

I made my way to the front porch and up the steps to the door. I heard Sally and Jude coming around the side saying something about me getting all the bows on and how they needed to hurry home to get dressed. I was sure Jake was with them so I sprinted into the house. Just as I reached the stairs leading to my room I heard Jake's voice behind me.

"Hey Bright Eyes. The chicken's real good."

I slowly turned and saw Jake kicked back in one of the kitchen chairs with what was left of his piece of chicken. "These orange sandwiches are good too. Kinda adds a pucker to your smile, but I like them. I heard they're your invention. You're gonna make Tylar a real good cook. So when is *your* happy day?"

"We decided on May fifteenth."

"That's when I would want to do it... in May. It's still cool enough for the coats not to make all the men sweat, yet warm enough most of the time to have it outside like today. This could have been a disaster. I've seen it snow three feet before as late as April. Guess this wedding was meant to be and God is blessing it with a beautiful day."

"That's what I was thinking this morning when I looked out and saw how beautiful it was."

"Did you see the sun rise?"

"Yeah, yeah I did." I sat across from him at the table. "Were you up that early?"

"I'm up before the sun comes up everyday. I like to get my classes as early as possible so I can study in the afternoons and get to bed after supper. I usually take my first break at the lab just as the sun is getting up. It amazes me what God does on that huge canvas. I know of no artist that can match it. And just think He erases it every day and we spend countless hours and money on a painting that never changes." Jake stretched his arms out across the table and took my hands in his. "How do you do it, Red?"

"What?"

"Each time I go away and come back you are more beautiful. I'm thinking I better stop doing that or you're just going to … be so beautiful I won't be able to talk to you anymore."

"Jake, do you love me?"

He slid back into his chair. "Wow, where did that come from? You're an engaged woman. Should you be asking me such things?"

"Maybe not, but I don't want to hurt you for anything."

"You could never hurt me. I thought you knew I was tougher than frozen cowhide. You're way too intense for a lovely day like today."

"I need to return your bracelet."

"What? I take that back. If you returned my gift you just might hurt me."

"Oh, Jake. I don't want to hurt you or return your gift if I know that you gave it to me because we are friends and that you … don't … want anything more?"

He stretched out across the table again. "Lacey, what if I did want something more? I know you love Tylar and you've promised him that you will be his wife. I can't change that even if I dropped to my knees and confessed my undying love for you and told you I would wait for you till the day I died. How silly that would be of me. I want what you want. And I must say that I will be very vigilant to get all that you will give me, but no more. I'll never want more from you than you are willing to give. Please keep the bracelet and do with it as I told you the day I gave it to you. Collect memories. Like that necklace you have on. Where did it come from?"

"Uncle Marty and Aunt Joan gave all the girls in the wedding necklaces. There's have lockets with their initials on the front and Marty's and Joan's initials and today's date inside. Joan wanted me to have a charm to put on my charm bracelet she saw me wearing at my graduation party."

"Well then, there you have it. You have to keep the bracelet. What's the charm?"

"It's a bridal bouquet and she had today's date and May fifteenth engraved on this separate gold disk that hangs in the back."

Jake had gotten up and come around to my side of the table and knelt down so he could look closer at the charm. He reached out his hand and took the charm letting the back of his hand ever so lightly touch my neck. Blood was racing through my body, but my heart was not beating. I was screaming inside, "Oh my gosh, drop it, Jake!" In my mind my feet were kicking and wanting to jump up from the chair, but I could not move. "Oh God, he's going to kiss me and, and I'm going to let him. Jesus, stop him!"

And then Jake stood up and said, "That's pretty. I need to go out to the house and get dressed. I'll see you at the wedding," and he left.

I found myself staring into the vacant room he left though and shortly afterwards having to talk myself out of slamming my head on the kitchen table. "Oh God, what was *that*?"

"Lacey?"

I lifted my head from the table. "Oh Mother. You look beautiful."

"You look ... flushed. Are you alright?"

"Yes. Jake was here. You know how crazy he makes me."

"Oh how nice. I'm so glad he was able to get away from school long enough to come share this day with us. I know Sally must be beside herself. She has missed him so much. How was he?"

"Jake."

"That's nice."

"I'm going upstairs to freshen up my makeup and hair. Do you need anything?"

"No. I don't think so. You said I was beautiful so I guess I'm good."

"How do you stay so cheery?"

"Why Lacey Kale Rutledge, what on earth is there that is unknown to God? Those are the only things that would cause me to feel any other way and since they don't exist ... "

"You're right Mother, there's certainly nothing that God doesn't know. I'll be in my room if anyone needs me."

I took my dress back off and hung it on the door of my wardrobe. I just needed to crawl in my bed and hug my pillow for a little while.

"So you know everything, but you keep letting this ... *whatever* ... keep happening between me and Jake? What are You trying to tell me? And what is this that rises up in me whenever he gets close to me? It's not Jake, it's me. He doesn't want anything more than friendship and I keep making it into something. What is *wrong* with me? He never said he just wanted to be friends, but he never said he loved me either." I balled my feather pillow up and punched it several times possibly wishing it was Jake. "Oh Jake, you drive me crazy. Just leave me alone. Go back to school and leave me alone!" and I buried my face in the pillow.

"Lacey?"

"Ah. What? Who ... Willie? What?"

"I thought you were with somebody. Jake?"

"No, oh ... Willie. You look so nice."

"I need some help with this bow tie and Pa gave me these cufflinks, but I can't seem to get them in the holes. I'll help fix your hair back like it was if you will help me."

"Sure, Willie."

"Have you been crying? Did Jake hurt your feelings again?"

"No. No, I'm fine. Jake always makes me mad, but he can't hurt my feelings. You know that. Silly boy. Now sit down right here and let me fix you up."

"I'm a teenager now, not a boy."

"You are no boy indeed. You're a silly goose, but I love you anyway. Do you know if Cole is dressed?"

"Yeah, he's with Pa getting his hair combed. His shoes need shining, but he wouldn't let me do it. Said Pappy put the best shine on a pair of shoes so he was waiting for him."

"Pappy just might not have time to fool with his shoes. Make him let you do it."

"Pa will see to it. You can't miss noticing that they need a shine. Speaking of shine, Miss Sunshine sent over a great big box of cookies. They have orange gumdrops in the middle. I'm going down to the kitchen to get one."

"Does Nanny know?"

"Not where they came from," and out the door he trotted.

"And God, what is up with that? Are Pappy and Sunshine like me and Jake? Hopefully they understand their relationship better than I understand ours. Maybe I just need to believe that we *are* just friends to Jake and never question that again. You do know I will need Your help to do that and to get me through this day. I need You to promise me on that, otherwise there is no need for me to fix my hair because it will look ten times worse by the end of the day."

The wedding went off without a hitch. The ceremony was beautiful and when the preacher said, "Who will exalt God for the blessing of this woman," there was not a dry eye in the house. Uncle Marty shouted, "Praise God" right after Pappy said, "Her Mother, and her family, and I, and our family." I was so honored to be chosen to stand with Joan on her special day and I wondered who I would want to stand here on my wedding day? If Jake had been a girl it would have been him, but since he wasn't, my next choice would be Mayree, but I was sure the society pages would have a hay day with that choice and I didn't want to cause my family any more pain. So that left Kimmy or Ruthy and I didn't think I could pick one over the other. Maybe we just needed to elope. But, when I looked at how handsome Tylar was standing in his tux I wanted to have our own special day and I wanted him to be wearing a tux, not a pair of overalls. I would figure something out about my bridesmaids because with God's will nothing was going to cause me grief on my wedding day.

chapter fifteen

Two weeks later Uncle Marty and Joan had finished packing the last of their things and left to start their new lives in Charlotte North Carolina. Mother was taking it much better than I had anticipated. She had been a little more active than usual cleaning out kitchen cabinets and getting the dust out of the canning jars. I was afraid she was overdoing just to keep busy, but Pa said he was sure it was good for her so we needed to let her be.

"Mother, I have breakfast ready. Can you stop dragging things out of Uncle Marty's closet long enough to eat?"

"I'll be right down."

"Why is she cleaning out Marty's closet? Didn't Marty just do that and didn't she just pack those blankets in there?"

"Yes, Pa, but she just keeps going in circles taking things from one closet to another and back again. I think she needs a good scolding myself."

"What do you mean?"

"I mean I have a wedding coming up and she could be focusing all that energy into that instead of these cabinets and closets. She never meets with us anymore to see what we've done or decided about the flowers or food. She doesn't even ask. I know she just misses Uncle Marty, but she has another family who needs her."

"I'll talk to her, but I won't hurt her feelings by telling her she has neglected you."

"I don't want you to do that, but she needs to see that her children need her. She hasn't given five minutes to the girls or to Cole. He's only eight Pa. He could use a hug from his Mother every once in a while. I bet you could use one, too."

Pa just lifted his eyebrows. "I'll talk to her."

Mother was breathing heavy when she reached the bottom of the stairs. "I've never seen so much dust inside a closet in all my life."

"Abigail, you can't keep doing this. I'll get someone in to clean those closets. You have got to stop pushing yourself. Your girls are wondering where their Mother is and Cole needs his Mother to sit with him and help with his homework. These have always been the things that were important to you, not a clean closet."

"Yeah Mother. Are you planning a tea in the closet?"

"Don't be absurd. We have lived in this house thirteen years and I have never cleaned out a closet. It's time they get cleaned. So what are your plans today, William?"

"I need to help Silas with the bottom field. We need to get in the watermelon. Lacey, what are your plans?"

"Mayree is coming to get me and we are going to try our dresses on again. Her's had to be taken in at the waist and mine needed hemming. Would you like to go, Mother?"

Pa chimed in, "I think that would be a nice outing for you girls."

"I have all those blankets in the floor upstairs. I need to get them put somewhere."

"Where did they come from, Mother?"

"Well, I don't know really. We've just collected them through the years."

"No, Mother. How did they get on the floor?"

"Oh! I'm a silly old woman! Well, I took them out of the closet to fold them better and it was just easier to get them all out and start over and that way I could sweep in the corners."

"So you're going to put them back in the same closet? I can help you do that and then you can go with us."

"Lacey, you don't need me. After I get those put back I'm going to clean out your Pa's wardrobe and my dresser drawers."

"Abigail, my wardrobe does not need cleaning out. I know where everything is and I like it just the way it is. Go with the girls and have a fun day with your daughter. She is only getting married once, God willing, and you will be sorry you missed these days with her later. 'Let the spider webs collect the dust balls,' is what my Mother always said and I'm one happy boy because she did."

"William, your Mother is a blessing, but she is *not* a housekeeper."

"Abigail. Go with the girls."

"William, if I get finished before they leave I will go with them. Lacey, this is a very good breakfast. I'm so thankful that you have had Marge to teach you to cook. Heaven knows we have eaten well as a result of her teaching. I could have never taught you to cook this well."

"Yes you could, Mother. You have always been a great cook and now that you are feeling better you can teach Abbie and Retta. I'll get them to come in and learn about cleaning closets, too."

"I sent them to Ruthy's with some of the clothes I cleaned out of their wardrobe that they can no longer wear. You know how they love to play. I don't expect them till after lunch. I should be finished by then, but I won't be if I don't get back to work" She leaned over and kissed Pa and said, "Have a wonderful day my Sweet William."

"You too, sweetheart. *Please* don't overdo." She turned and gave him a cold look. He dropped his eyes, "I'll be in for lunch."

"Thank you, William," and Mother disappeared into the stairwell and closed the door behind her.

"She'll be alright, Lacey. Maybe she will go with you girls next time. She just needs to deal with Marty's leaving in her own way. He's coming back for the weekend in two weeks. She will see that he's not so far away and get settled down."

"I'm just not as sure as you are, Pa. I don't feel good about this at all."

Knowing Mother was not going to come with us Mayree, Kimmy and I left for the bridal shop shortly after breakfast. We had a day of *glorious* girl fun trying on our dresses and I also chose a dress to wear on the train for our honeymoon. I spoiled myself by getting the coat and hat that matched the dress, shoes and a handbag. I would look good all day on May 15, 1953.

We went to the hardware store to see Aunt Gail and show her my going away outfit and the four of us went to *"The Garden Patch"* for lunch. It was a beautiful colonial home that was left abandoned after the Civil War because all the heirs had been killed except one of the sons of the slave foreman. As the will read if there were no family living to inherit the home, all the furnishings and any estate money, then it would be given to the slaves starting with the foreman and his family and so forth. Yankee soldiers had killed the family and all the slaves, but this one child survived. He was old enough to plant a crop and raise chickens to live on. As he grew up, and with help from neighbors, he sold his vegetables to make a living. He taught himself to cook and became an excellent chief and he sold his meals for extra money. Through the years he turned the house into a restaurant and restored it to as much like the original as possible. It was the place to eat in town if you were anyone of good breeding. However, some people were welcome who would not have been classified as good breeding in most homes in our town. Miss Sunshine was sitting at a table out on the side porch, alone, directly across the room from us and she was looking so beautiful compared to the last time I saw her. I just had to go and speak to her.

"I hate to interrupt our conversation, but I must go speak to someone. I'll be back in a little while. Order me the vegetable special."

"That's it, no chicken?"

"I'm watching my figure. I have a dress to fit into in a few weeks."

I made my way through the maze of tables and out the open doors leading to the porch. Miss Sunshine was reading the menu and unaware of my presence. She looked very well and the sun was causing a shimmer across the braid she had wrapped around her head and then twisted into a small bun at the back of her neck. She had pierced ears, something no one else I knew had, but Pappy told me what it was called. She had a comb with ruby and diamond stones pressed down into the top of her bun that matched the long earrings she had hanging from her ears. She was still quite beautiful for a lady her age and I wanted so badly to understand her story. All I knew about her I had to piece together from things people said, but I was sure she ran a brothel, but why? That I wanted to know.

"Miss Sunshine? May I sit with you for a few moments?"

"Lacey Kale. You may sit with me all day or as long as they will let us stay. How are you doing, child?"

"*Me*? I'm here to find out about you. I'm so thankful you pulled through."

"It's a miracle." And she patted my hands lying in my lap. "Nothing short of a miracle. Thanks to you and your Pappy's prayers."

"Are you completely healed?"

"The doctors say I am doing better than anyone they have ever treated and they, too, call it a miracle."

Mrs. Geraldine Waldrop walked toward our table glaring at me and then turned her head as she passed.

"Mrs. Waldrop." She had no response. "I'm sorry about that Miss. Sunshine."

"Oh don't you worry your pretty little head about that. She's just jealous that I have such a splendid young lady who cares enough about me to come and check on me."

"I'm sorry I haven't before now."

"Oh my, dear girl. You have been way too busy. You must tell me all about this young man who has stolen your heart and about your new home. I must confess I drove out there to it last week and your grandpappy was there looking things over. He was kind enough to show me around. It's a beautiful home and I do hope the doors wear off their hinges with the foot traffic of little feet. Your Pappy also told me you wanted to have a house filled with children, so many you have to add on. I hope that blessing is granted to you."

"Thank you Miss Sunshine. Did you ever want children?"

"Well, I had two children, but I lost them both."

"Oh Miss Sunshine, I'm so sorry. I didn't mean to bring up any sadness. All my memories of you are good ones, even when you were so sick. I felt such joy to be with you. I will change the subject so I don't spoil our time."

"It was a long time ago and they didn't die or anything. Their fathers took them from me, but I was not what a mother should be so I suppose it was for the best. They are grown now and I hear they are happy. That's really all a mother wants for her children so I see now that God had His reasons."

"You don't get to spend time with them?"

"I don't guess they even have a clue who I am."

"Do you want them to?"

"I would never want them to have any anger or bitterness in their lives and I'm afraid finding out that Miss Sunshine, the town ... ah ... Lady of the Evening, was their mother would bring them shame so I do not want them to know."

"I would not be ashamed to find out you were my mother, not that I would want to replace the one I have, mind you, but if I didn't have one you would be someone I would be proud to call my mother."

"You are too sweet to an old marked woman, but I won't ever turn your kindness away. I simply pray you won't suffer too much ridicule over being seen sitting at my table."

"These whispering busybodies don't move me. Besides, I am called to be ridiculed. I find it an honor."

"Bless you. And your marriage? I would love to meet your young man one day."

"His name is Tylar Lane and I know that he would love to meet you, as well. When can we get together again?"

"Anytime, dear. But, you have so much to do preparing for your wedding and finishing that house. I just know that you will find your greatest joy when you are in that house. And your Mother, is she still quit frail?"

"She is, but she has found new energy now that her brother Marty has moved to Charlotte, North Carolina. She misses him so much that she is busying herself with closet cleaning. I just hope she doesn't have a relapse and become bedridden." I suddenly felt very uncomfortable when I said those words to her.

"I heard that wonderful news that your Uncle Marty came to his senses and married that lovely girl, Joan Griffin? Your Mother has to be thrilled for them?"

"Oh, she is. It's just that she and Uncle Marty have always been so close, even as children and she has relied on him so much over these past years he has been living with us. I'm afraid this new found burst of energy is nerves and not her body truly getting stronger."

"I do hope that she will get stronger. You have spent most of your childhood taking care of your Mother and I know that you have never complained, but you should be able to start your new life with Mr. Lane feeling good about moving away from your Mother and your siblings. Maybe with you leaving home she will finally allow William to get her the help she should have had all these years."

"It will be hard for me to leave home because we are all so close, but I have wanted Tylar to be my husband from the day I met him."

"And how long ago was that?"

"I was in the third grade!"

"Oh my, you do have self control!"

"Not too much. I see the waiter bringing our lunch. It has been so nice talking to you and as soon as we get home from our honeymoon we will come to visit."

"I would love that, dear. When is the day?"

"May fifteenth."

"I'll be watching the paper for your picture and all the news about your trip." She leaned in closer to me and whispered, "Where are you going?"

"Tylar works for Johnny Kale Butler and he has given us a trip out west by train to the Grand Canyon."

She moved back away from me and I saw tears forming in her eyes.

"Did I say some . . . ?"

"I have always wanted to see the Grand Canyon. I'm sure you will have a lovely time. Now run along to your friends. Your lunch is getting cold."

"I will send you a postcard."

"Oh, please do. That will be, I'm sure, the highlight of my year."

I reached out and hugged her and said, "Oh Miss Sunshine. I love you."

"I love you too, dear. Now run along." And she waved her hands at me as if she was shooing a chicken out of a pea patch.

"Good bye. I'll see you soon."

"Good bye."

When I got back to our table Mayree said, "I thought Is gonna have ta eat your's too. Where ya been?"

"I had to speak to a friend who was very sick the last time I saw her, but Praise God, she is so much better now," and I looked across the room where Miss Sunshine was sitting just in time to catch a glimpse of her leaving some money on the table and walking out of my site. She never ate a bite.

"That is good news."

"Yes Aunt Gail, it is."

"That was Miss Sunshine wasn't it? I heard she had TB. Not many people get over that."

"She's a very strong lady. I happen to believe she could get over just about anything. I wish I knew her better. I would like to have her strength."

"Lacey, she runs a whore house."

"Yes I guess she does, Kimmy. You sure couldn't do that unless you were a very strong lady. I hate she's had to live that kind of life, but I admire the woman none the less."

Mayree reached over and took Kimmy's hand, "Don't look so shocked at Lacey, Kimmy. She's just livin out her prophesy. 'Hate the sin, love the sinner."

"And I do love that little lady, Mayree. There's just something about her."

"Well, I don't know much about her, but I can tell you that through my years of being in this family, my mother-in-law does not have feeling of love for that woman."

"No, Nanny Jo Rett does not."

"Hum, guess us better swear we ain't saying a word 'bout Miss Lacey havin a chat with the woman."

"No need to swear. I'm sure Mrs. Waldrop will spread it around town."

"Ooowee, Miss Lacey. Please don't tell us that woman saw you talking ta her?"

"Fraid so, Mayree. But, I have a little time to figure out the answers to all the questions she's going to have for me before I see Nanny again."

"That is if we hurry up our lunch. I wouldn't be a bit surprised if Jo Rett walked through those doors. You know how she loves to eat here and I think Trell told her we were coming here today."

"Oh my."

We did finish our lunch in record time and we tried to think of where I had met her before and why I would be talking to her. I hoped our plan would work, because we had sworn to that story and nothing else if Nanny ever asked them any question. I just hoped I wouldn't have to change anything in the middle of her interrogation.

Mayree dropped Kimmy off at her house before she took me to mine. We saw Pappy's truck park in front of the house as we turned into the drive.

"Good God, Jesus in heaven, how does word travel so fast?"

I took a deep breath and prayed in the spirit for help, so I hoped that was what I was praying for.

"You wants me to come in withs you?"

"It would seem more natural if you did. Can you handle it?"

"I'm ready if you lets me be quiet."

"You can."

We opened the trunk to get my 'going away' clothes when I saw Doctor Jude Foresight coming out of my house. I could see that something was wrong. Just as I started to walk towards him a car pulled quickly into the yard. It was Jake driving and Tylar was with him. "What's going on Doctor Jude?"

Tylar barely let the car stop before he jumped out and ran over to me with a forced half smile on his face, "Hey, babe." And he kissed my cheek and pulled me in close.

"Will someone please tell me what's going on?"

"Your Mother has taken a fall."

"How is she, Dad?"

"Jake, I can give you the medical terms later, but let me just say that for now her body has gone into a coma."

"A coma? Doctor Jude, what are you saying?"

"That's not necessarily a bad thing, Lacey, this early after her fall. Sometimes it's better that the brain get a little rest when there has been an injury this severe."

"Severe? What happened?"

Mayree was steady as always as she took a hold to my arm. "Tylar, let us take Miss Lacey to da porch where in she can sits down before her knees gives out." We started slowly walking to the porch as Doctor Jude continued to explain my Mother's condition.

"It looks like she was up on a chair in Marty's room. William said she was doing some cleaning up there so I think she must have been dusting the top of the wardrobe from the way she was laying on the floor. She hit her head on the footboard of that old iron bed. You know iron just doesn't give much so she has quite a knot on her head and there was a lot of bleeding. I got her sewed up and she's resting, but she hasn't woke up, as far as we know, after she fell."

"Is that a bad thing? I thought you said the coma wasn't a bad thing?"

"We have a lot of unanswered questions that may not have answers for sometime. It's all up to your Mother. We have to wait on her. I'm not sure I can answer anymore of your questions. For now I need to go back in and check on her vital signs and get in touch with the hospital. She may need to be there. I'll know more after I do some more tests and share those results with the neurologist."

"Where's my Pa?"

"He's with your Mother. Pappy and Nanny are with her too."

"And my brothers and sisters?"

"They're all with Margie at her house."

"Do they know anything?"

"I'm not sure. I'll tell your Pappy you're here."

"Thanks. Oh, when can I see her?"

"Anytime at all. I'm sure she would like to hear your voice, but let's not get too many in at one time for the next couple days," and he pushed open the screen door leading into our living room.

I sat on the swing with Mayree on one side of me holding my hand, Tylar on the other with his warm arms around me looking at the feet of Jake who was leaning on the porch railing. "Where are your shoes, Jake?"

"I didn't have classes today so I was studying in my room when Mom called asking me to pray. I ran out of the dorm and drove straight to the yard and got Tylar. Then we came here."

I reached my hand out to him still staring at his feet, "I'm glad you did." He took my hand and knelt down in front of me.

"Lace, I might be able to help you understand what is happening with your Mom right now."

"Do you know why she's in a coma?"

"Not without seeing her, but I can tell you that what Dad is most concerned with is why she fell."

"Because she was on a chair and she is too weak to even be up those stairs much less climbing in a chair."

"Lacey, she could have had a stroke or a seizure and that's why she fell. She may not have even gotten up on the chair. Or she could of started to get in the chair and her hip or leg broke. She's been frail a long time and bones can get weak without exercise just like muscles. There are so many unanswered questions, but once Mom and Dad get all her vitals stable they will know if she is in a coma from the fall or if something else happened."

"So which is worst?"

"Just my opinion, if something else happened, but if she had a stroke and it was a light one there wouldn't be much damaged."

"Then she would be awake by now."

"Not if the fall caused a concussion and then the coma."

"So what your saying here, Jake, is that she could have so many more things wrong than we can ever come up with."

"No, Tylar. I hope it's not coming out like that at all. I'm just saying that sometimes waiting is not a bad thing. It's better to know everything we're dealing with before we start administering drugs or therapy that would only cause further damage if we have jumped too quickly on a diagnoses ... What are you smiling at, Lacey."

I put my hand on the side of Jake's face. "You sound like a doctor already. I'm glad you're here. You're gonna be a fine doctor someday." And he took my hand in his. "I'm glad you all are here. My best friends. I can't think of anyone else I'd rather have here with me right now ... Willie. I have to go to Willie."

"Don't you want to see your Mother first?"

"Yeah, I guess I need to find out what they know before I go to your house, Tylar. I guess I need to talk to Pappy."

"Do you want me to go and get him?"

"No, Tylar. I'll find him when I go in to see Mother."

"Unless you just want me with you, I think you should go in with

Jake. He can tell you what they are doing for her and what is being said to the hospital. I can't help you with that. We also need to do as Jude says and not overcrowd her room."

"Yea, I guess you're right. Is that okay with you, Jake?"

"Sure, Lacey. I'll try to explain everything I understand. Just know that I won't have the answers for everything."

"That's okay, Jake. I need you, Tylar, and Mayree to pray. I know God can fix this," and we all got up and walked into the house.

Mother and Pa's room was at the back of the house through the living room and past the front staircase. There was a small sitting area at the end of the hallway with doors on every wall. The doors lead to another bedroom, a bathroom, Mother and Pa's bedroom and a door that lead to a back hall leading to the mud room and kitchen. Nanny, Pappy and Pa were sitting outside of Mother's room and Sally and Jude were with Mother. Tylar and Mayree had stayed in the living room.

Pappy stood to his feet when he saw us coming down the hall. "Lacey. Thank God you're here. You're Mother needs to hear your voice, Punkin," and he started to cry.

"Pappy! What are you doing? You need to be praying and believing God for a miracle, not crying as if there's no hope."

He reached around me and pulled me in close. "Oh my baby girl. You are so right. I knew you would know what to do. Good evening, Jake. Are you home for good from school?"

"No, sir. I came as soon as Mom called me. I had to be here for Lacey and all of you. She's like a second Mom to me."

"Of course she is, Son. She needs all her children praying for her."

"Jake will you please go in there and see what her condition is now."

"Yea sure, Bright Eyes. Excuse me."

Pappy and I sat down on the sofa, "Pappy, what do the children know?"

"Your brother, Willie, found her."

"Oh, God, no. Is he okay?"

"He is remarkably okay. He wrapped her head with a shirt and did it very gently, in case her neck was broken, he told me. He told Cole to sit with her and not touch her or try to wake her. Then he called Jude, then he called me and once Jude got here he went to get your Pa out of the field. Then he took Cole over to Marge and Bob's to be with the girls."

"Do you think he told the girls?"

"He wanted to wait for you, but I'm sure Cole was not able to keep quiet. Margie is there. She will take care of them."

"I want to see Mother and then I will go over there and be with them. How are you holding up, Nanny?"

She just lifted her hands and flipped them over as to say there was nothing she could do. Pappy got up and sat beside her comforting her and I went to the door of Mother's room. Pa got up and stood behind me.

"Has there been a change."

"Come in Lacey and William. Her pupils react to the light and there was a slight movement with her right hand."

"Is she waking up?"

"No, William, not yet. It might be days or weeks, possibly months before she wakes up, but I see no sign of a stroke and that is good news. There is just not much known about the neurophysiology of the brain as it moves through different levels of consciousness so I have no way of telling how deep her coma is and when she will come out of it. The sooner she wakes up of course the better her chances of having lost none of her senses."

"What does that mean?"

"I mean that with brain trauma you can have blindness, dizziness, loss of memory, loss of speech, fine motor skills, as well as, walking, sitting up, feeding yourself. She could even wake with a different personality. The longer she's asleep the greater the chances of a long rehab to gain back some of what is lost. But, for now this coma is her friend while the brain heals. Brain injuries this severe need a slow recovery period and if she's asleep there will be less frustration. We want some brain activity, but not stress. Of course we want the swelling to go down quickly and not return. I would like to see her out of the coma no more than two months, but I have heard of miracles where people were in comas for years and they woke up saying the names of their family members and with time learned to walk again and so forth.

I would like to see her wake up long before that so she doesn't have to learn all those things over again, but we can't give up hope if she doesn't react as I want her to. Everybody is different and her body knows what is best for itself. So, let's have some faith that what God created will heal itself if we see to the needs around her. I have a call into the hospital for a nurse to be assigned to her here. I don't know of a thing that the hospital can offer her there that we can't do here. Driving back and forth to the hospital will only wear all of you down and she would not like that at all. We also have no idea what coma patients can hear or sense so I have always felt like they heal better in their own homes. Does that sound good to all of you?"

"Of course, Jude. I want what is the best for Abigail and being right across the road from the best doctor I know and in her own home sounds like the best to me."

"I want you all to go about your day as you always have telling her where you are going and what you did during the day. Make it as routine as possible. William, if you think you can sleep with a nurse coming in a couple times a night to check on Abigail I would like for you to sleep right here beside her just like you always have. She has to know you are all still with her. That will help her more than anything I can do medically."

"Sure, Jude. I can do that. I would be in the floor if you had said I couldn't get in the bed with her."

Doctor Jude stood up and patted my Pa on the shoulder, "I'm going to call the hospital and check on the nurse. Does anyone stay in the room next door?"

"Just Pappy and Nanny when they stay the night with us."

"We're gonna need this room for the nurse."

"Absolutely."

Doctor Jude left the room and Pa turned to me, "We might need to freshen that room up a bit before the nurse moves in."

Sally stood up and took our hands in hers, "I'll take care of that. I'm sure Jo Rett needs something to do with herself about now. Lacey, you need to check on your siblings. Jake, drive her out there, will you."

"Sure, Mom, when she's ready to go," and Sally and Pa went out to the sitting room to get Nanny and start cleaning the guest room.

"I'll wait with Tylar and Mayree..." he saw the fear on my face and took me in his arms and pulled me to the back corner of the room. "Red, you can't let her see you like this. You're the strong one, remember? She's always leaned on you."

"I just need to cry for a moment, maybe a day."

"I'll hold you as long as you need, but these tears might be wasted. She could wake up any minute and you will be dehydrated for nothing. There's nothing sadder than a tomato with no juice."

"Oh Jake. Why do I love you so ... you're incorrigible."

"Look at me," and he wiped the tears from around my eyes. "Maybe I am, but you stopped crying and you have your fight back. And I got to hear that you love me."

"Oh Jake," and I stomped my foot. "You know what I mean."

"Yeah, sickness in a family always brings out the charity in a person."

"I must have been feeling charitable today before my Mother fell, because you're the second person I have blurted those words out to today."

"What was his name? I'm feeling rather jealous. Competition with one man is enough, now you tell me there's a third you've confessed your undying love."

"I had no idea you had such a wild imagination. It was a sweet old woman old enough to be my grandmother."

"Thank goodness. Who was she?"

"No one you know. Now scram. I want some time with my Mother before we have to leave."

"Okay, but I hate to go just when you're getting all feisty."

"Tell Mother goodbye, Jake. Your Dad said we needed to talk to her."

"Goodbye, Miss Abigail. I'll see you later tonight around suppertime. College food has made me appreciate Lacey's cooking even more, so I'll see you then," and he stepped to the door, turned back and winked at me.

"Oh Mother, Jake will never grow up no matter how long he goes to college. Mother, I wish you had listened to me and stopped worrying about the closets and just rested today, but now that you have fallen you can get some rest. Doctor Jude says you need to rest so you can heal, but we will all be right here for you when you feel like waking up. Look Mother, Pappy is here."

"Hey darling. I hope your head doesn't hurt too badly. You have a knot on there and some stitches, but nothing to worry about. Right now you just need to rest until we tell you it's time to wake up. I'm gonna be right here all day and Mama is here too."

"I'm right here, Abigail. Sally and William are straightening the guest room so a nurse can come and take care of you while you rest. You have that room so clean I don't see anything we can do to it to make it any better."

"Mother, I have to go to Marge's to get the girls and boys and bring them home. They've been over there playing long enough. I bet Marge could use some rest, too, about now. I will see you in a little while," and I kissed my Mother on her cheek."

"Bye, dear."

"I'll be back soon, Nanny. Will you and Pappy please stay with Mother? And Pappy, please pray?"

"I will, Punkin, we're not going anywhere."

"Thanks."

I took the back hall way to the kitchen to get a glass of water. Tylar was standing in there alone.

"Oh, come here, babe. How is she?"

"Oh I just thought of something."

"What?"

"Here I am thirsty and coming for a drink of water and I don't know if my Mother is thirsty and if I can even give her a drink."

"Jude and Sally know. They will do what has to be done. Don't worry about all this right now. Right now you need to be with Willie. I heard he was the one who found her."

"Yeah. Pappy said he was *incredible*. I have to tell him how proud I am of him and help him understand what is going on with her. He probably saved her life."

"I'm sure he did. Listen, Jake said he would drive you out to my house to get the kids. I need to check in at work. I didn't tell anyone why I had to go, I just ran out. I'm sure I'm not being looked at favorably right now. I will be back this evening."

"How will you get there?"

"Trell just brought Gail out here and he said he had to go back to the store and lock up so I asked him for a ride."

"Okay. Is he waiting?"

"I don't know. He wanted to speak to William before he left. Are you sure you will be alright if I leave you for a short time?"

"Yes, I will be fine. We need you to keep your job more than you need to be holding my hand."

"I like holding you hand," and he kissed me. "I will be back shortly to hold it some more. Will you be waiting for me?"

"I always have and I guess I always will," and he tenderly kissed my tears and held me for a while.

Three weeks had passed and there had been changes in Mother's condition, however, it was not what we had hoped for. She was awake; she could swallow and blink her eyes, but not make any communicable gestures. It was like she wasn't really there, but she had full use of her throat. Feeding her was much easier and we weren't as afraid that she would get choked on soft foods like we had been right after the accident when we tried to give her water. Nothing else seemed to move by Mother's own power, but we were hopeful that soon something would.

Pa and I had been taking turns plowing the upper ten acres getting it ready for our bean crop. Silas had a crew of men who were thinning out the apples and the small peach orchard Pa had planted for Mother. Most of the crop was ruined by frost, but enough made it through for us to have peach ice cream in the summer three or four times and put up a few cans for winter time cobblers. There was a lot to be done this time of year on a farm and Pa wanted to spend as much time as possible with Mother so he would plow in the morning, after lunch I would plow till I needed to come in and cook, then he would plow while I prepared supper. Retta and Abbie Lou spent the day reading to Mother and the boys were in charge of all the animals. Jake and Tylar came on Saturdays to relieve me and Pa of the plowing.

Tylar and I had postponed our wedding till Mother was well, or until we knew better what her condition was going to be. I didn't want to have it without her and then have her come back to us and know that she just missed being a part of it by a few days or weeks. He was a little anxious I could tell when I brought up the subject, but he said he knew it was the right thing to do for all of us. The house was still not finished, probably because Pa was not there everyday to keep the men busy, but I was in no hurry to leave my Mother anyway, so I just believed the men were doing a much better job now that they were not being rushed. The critical trim work around the doorframes, ceilings, baseboards and windows was what they had left to finish up. I wanted it to be special so it needed patience to make it look just right. My Pa was the man who had the steady hands to make the pieces fit without showing where they were pieced together, but I was sure he would not be able to help with this tedious work. He had been the one to draw the patterns for the decorative molding and saw to it that the best wood carvers inspected each piece. We had made plans to go out to the house together to see the beauty of his design once it was completed. I was looking forward to this time alone with my Pa as our summer had been spent passing each other by seeing to all the chores and my Mother's needs.

chapter sixteen

No one really knows what a day will bring them, but I had a kind of radar that told me when things were good and when things were bad. The bad usually caught me off guard because I had been quite blessed in that most days were good days so I didn't look very hard for the revelation of what degree radar would make a very good day. But, I did know when God was warning me without hearing words from Him and this day I woke with a strange oppression that seemed to hold me in the bed. The fields were full of tinder growth; Mother was well taken care of so I thought that maybe my body had finally relaxed. The sun was barely touching the horizon so I knew that I had woken much earlier than my normal time. It could have been that I heard someone climbing the back stairs because shortly after I woke I heard Pa lightly tapping at my bedroom door.

"Come in, good morning."

"Good morning."

I stretched my arms out and said, "Bear hug."

Pa sat on the edge of my bed and gave me my morning hug. "I have several things to do today and one is to go out to your house and see if the men are truly finished."

"I didn't know they were done."

"Frank told me that he was sure they would have things complete by the end of the day yesterday and wanted me to come out this morning and give him the okay to send the men over to the Harrison's so they can get started over there. I wanted to see if you would come with me?"

"Yeah sure. Has Hattie gotten up?"

"She got up about ten minutes ago. She put on a pot of coffee and said she would fix us some breakfast, but I told her just some cereal for now. We can eat something hot when everyone else eats."

"Okay, I would love to go with you, Pa" I sat up in the bed and hugged him again. "This will be fun. I'll be down in a minute. Hope Hattie doesn't mind cooking for all of us. She's only supposed to cook for Mother."

"She's fine with it. I told her I would put something extra in her check this week."

"Oh Pa. A check! Tylar and I have put the money we've been saving in the bank to start paying you back for what you have paid on our house. We're going to pay you every Friday after Tylar gets paid till we pay you back for every penny you have spent and your time too, Pa. Should I write this check out to the company or to Mr. Frank so he can pay the men today?"

"I took care of that already. You and Tylar can see Mayree for the total cost of the house. She'll collect the weekly payments."

"Okay, thanks, Pa," and I swung open the doors to my wardrobe and wondered what I should wear for my first time in our finished house being with my Pa looking at the beauty of his creation. I chose something a little dressier than a pair of shorts and a blouse. After all this was like going to a fine museum to see an artist's work, but this time it was the building that was the art work. So I choose my white and red striped blouse with the red tie that went under the collar and crossed at the first button and pinned, with a mother of pearl inlayed in gold broach, down to the placket. Nanny had gotten me a straight skirt that matched the red stripe in the blouse perfect. I had not worn it yet so I thought this was the perfect day. I wanted to wear my tennis shoes because of the mud that was still around the house in places, but I needed to look like the lady of the house and so I chose my best shoes. After pulling my hair up and twisting it to the side I pinned a small red and white hat to my hair on the top. It was made of velvet with white ribbon stitched across the ends of some wild turkey and pheasant feathers that hung past the edge of the hat and cupped around my head filling the space opposite my twisted bun. I looked older than I was, but I was soon to be a married woman so I thought I needed to look the part.

When Pa and I left the sun was just burning away the reds from the sky. Hattie had pack our coffee in a thermos bottle and sent us off with a basket full of cereal, cream, bowls, cups and saucers, spoons, napkins and anything else we could possible need so we could have our first father/daughter breakfast in my new home. She was very good to our family and she was a wonderful nurse to my Mother seeing to every need she had. There was such a relief for me and Pa to be able to visit with Mother and pray for her or just hold her hand when we were with her instead of being her care giver. The first week Mother had an IV in her hand giving her fluids. Pa and I had no idea how to change the bags and having Hattie there to do that was a blessing beyond words. Now Mother was able to swallow liquids and some soups. Hattie was the one determined to get Mother this far. I was sure she would still be on the IV if Pa and I had been left to see to her. I don't think that another nurse would have been so patient. Hattie told us that as much as she needed this job and as much as she loved all of us she wanted Mother to be well where she wasn't needed anymore. I wanted the same thing, although, Hattie was helping us with the housekeeping, as well. It was a lot to running a home, a hospital and a farm. And thinking I soon would be living in a different house with my own set of chores, made me appreciate Hattie all the more.

We pulled into the drive between two open iron gates that told me some of the men had already arrived. Everything was so pretty with the Mountain Laurel and Azaleas blooming that Tylar had planted on the sides of the drive. Just as you passed through the small area of land where you could see the river on both sides, the drive turned to the right and started the climb up the hill circling around the back of the house before looping in front through the three story high portico. The barn was positioned behind the house and it was completed several months earlier so we could store the doors and windows, bath fixtures and lighting and anything else that had to be ordered beforehand and kept out of the weather. Our barn was smaller than Pa's because we would not be keeping large farming equipment or large amounts of hay. We were not going to be farmers so we only needed a place to keep the car, a buggy and a couple horses. I was going to raise children and Tylar was going to run a train yard.

Pa pulled up under the portico and I sat in the car studying the beauty of my new home. The bricks were handmade in Georgia brought to us by train. They were a pale yellow with small amounts of that red Georgia clay running through them. A circular garden pool was made from the same bricks and sat out in front of the house beyond the stone pillars holding the extended roof that made the portico. The same red brick that was used to make the drive made a walk out to the garden pool directly across from the front door. My gardens would have to be in the front of the house because that's where the sun was. Tylar had surprised me one day by asking the brick mason to build the pool as a focal point for the garden. Pappy had brought a statue of a lion sitting on his back legs with both paws off the ground, one paw raised higher than his head with his mouth open. You could almost hear him growl. It had belonged to Pappy's grandmother and it was sitting out in their barn for years. I always loved sitting on that lion's back pretending to be the King of Judah coming to save the world. The mason had built a pedestal in the middle of the pool for the lion to sit. He was very much at home sitting in front of our house so we named our small estate *Lion's Hill*.

The house had two wings that branched off both sides of the three-story center. The third floor was an attic and only had small round windows at each end, one looking to the back, one looking to the front. There were two steps to get to the half circle shaped brick stoop at the front door. I didn't want the house up high off the ground and having the house built up on this hill kept it from being necessary. Steps were just too difficult for toddlers to master and I didn't want to spend my day watching so closely. The ground was within one step of being level with the back of the house, however a storm cellar had been dug before the foundation was laid and you accessed the cellar through a door in the floor of the pantry.

As you entered the front door, the center portion of the house was about fifteen feet wide. It was open all the way to the back door that mimicked the front door. The open staircase started in the middle of the hall on the right side and turned back to the left creating half of an arch as it met with the landing on the second floor. This made a grand entry hallway that would be used for buffets, china cabinets and linen closets as well as room for guest to spill out of the living and dining rooms. There was no door or divider from the hall to the living room on the right as you entered the front door. There was an opening about ten feet wide leading into the dining room to the left. The dining room was connected to the dish pantry that backed up to the guest bathroom that you could only enter into from the center hallway. The dish pantry led into the kitchen. There was a food pantry in the far corner of the kitchen on the left and the mud room was to the right. It was open to the center hallway close to the back door. Directly across from the mud room behind the staircase was the master suite. This side of the house was larger than the left wing. As you entered the suite from this door you entered a small sitting room for me to use as a nursery when needed. The master bedroom was in the far corner with a bath. Between the bedroom and bath was a small library for Tylar that also had a door leading into the living room.

What made the house so special was the trim work around the doors and windows. Pa had designed a grape vine motif that was carved in the six-inch boards that trimmed the openings. A cluster of grapes were carved on the rosettes instead of a circular design like most blocks of wood that sat in each corner of the windows and doors. The ceilings were fourteen feet high and each window had a half moon shaped window above it. The windows were large and went from the floor to the ceiling in every room except the kitchen. Tylar had insisted that I be able to see the river from every room in the house and Pa had made that happen.

The dining room was the most beautiful with the grape vine motif being carried out in the barreled ceiling. A plaster artist had created the look of lattice behind a flourishing vine loaded heavy with ripe grapes. Two gold leafed chandeliers had the design of grape vines with leaves holding the lights and globes and rounded crystals hung like grape clusters under the lamps. My Pa had spent many hours thinking of me and I was humbled standing in the grandness of it all.

"Pa, there's so much I can't take it all in. You have exceeded way past my greatest desire and I'm afraid that I am not worthy of such exquisite artistry. You truly are an artist and I don't know how I missed recognizing that in you."

"I must confess that I have done my best work right here. I guess you inspired me. But, as I look back on it, God was the one who brought all this together for you. As you know I have not been able to work here as much as I wanted to. It's like He wanted to show me that I did my best work when I had to rely totally on Him. And that's what I had to do with this house. I would spend my days plowing praying for things to come together here and He would give me visions of what this place should look like when I was listening to you and Tylar and while I was working the fields. Then I would call Frank and he would get to work. He was the one who made it all happen. He and Trell. They spent nights calling craftsmen and manufactures trying to find just the right fixtures. Come see the guest bathroom. The spigots are gold with grape leaves and a potter in South Carolina made the sink bowl. Who ever thought there was a potter in South Carolina?"

The sink looked like a bowl lined with grape leaves and a vine twisted along the top edge. There was a cluster of grapes that popped out from under the leaves on one side. The glaze was a mixture of green with purplish blue running through out. The handles for the hot and cold were small grape leaves. The spigot was tall and reminded me of the water pump at the well. The same was on the claw-footed tub. I had never seen anything like it, not even in a magazine.

"Pa, my guests will feel very special using this room. Anyone who knows you will be able to see your hand in it."

"The whole house is like this. It has a little bit of all of us in it."

"Ah, William. I see you've brought Lacey with you this morning. I hope everything meets your approval Miss Rutledge."

"Oh it does. So far. I haven't seen the whole house, but if the rest is like what I have seen then I am more than approving. Your work here is unprecedented. I am honored to be the owner of this one of a kind mansion. And it is a mansion. I never pictured myself living in a mansion and certainly not something so grand."

"Well, it's yours and Tylar's now. I hope you will always be happy here."

"Thanks, Pa. I just feel so undeserving."

"Let's go into the kitchen and have some coffee and cereal before we venture upstairs. You'll join us won't you, Frank?"

"I would love some coffee, William. I've already eaten a big breakfast this morning so just some coffee."

I was too busy looking at the cabinets in the dish pantry, the food pantry, and the kitchen to have an appetite, but I did join them for some coffee.

"Pa, has Tylar seen the house finished?"

"No. He told me he would stop by on his way to work this morning and meet us. I thought he would be here by now."

"He doesn't have to be at work for another hour and a half. He still has time if he got up early enough. I would love for him to be here so we could see the children's rooms together."

"I had the walls painted in bright colors. I didn't think you would want wallpaper in their rooms, yet. Let each child decide if they want wallpaper and they can pick out something they like. The painted walls will be easier to keep clean while they are small."

"I love the paper you put in the living room and this paper is very nice."

"Tylar, he picked out both."

"You are kidding me?"

"No. He did. I think Margie helped him."

"She did not!"

"Tylar. You came!"

"Good morning my angel. Can you believe how beautiful it turned out?"

"No I can't. It's truly a miracle and you! Here I thought that you were avoiding me because I've been so preoccupied with Mother and here you were picking out wallpaper!"

I walked over to Tylar and kissed him. He hugged me and said, "Uhm, you smell wonderful. Excuse us for a minute." And he pushed the swinging door open to the dish pantry as Pa and Frank laughed.

"Hey, hey! She's not your wife yet, Mr. Lane."

Tylar called back, "We're just going to check out the master suite."

My Pa said, "I'm coming with you."

Tylar took my hand and pulled me through the dining room and up the stairs to the second floor. "This is my favorite view." He stopped at the top of the stairs and pointed out the window directly over the front door. "Do you know what that is?"

"Mother and Pa's house. Oh my gosh. It's a long way over there, but it's there. And why is this your favorite view?"

He stood behind me and wrapped his arms around me. "Because that's the place where I found you again and that's the place where I fell in love with you. And that's the place I will find you if ever you're not here."

My Pa and Frank came around the corner of the dining room. When Pa saw us he said, "I built this house. There's nowhere you can take her that I can't find you."

"Maybe not, William, but you are too old to track us down before I have time to steal more kisses from her," and he pulled me up the step and into a bedroom over the dining room. "I can hear him if he comes up the stairs so I can have my way with you before he finds us," and he pushed me against the wall kissing my neck while I giggled at his playfulness. "But, I know I can't have my way with you until we are married, but I can hold you and kiss you passionately before he finds us."

"And what has you so frisky this morning Mr. Lane?"

"I have missed you and you are so beautiful in red. If you don't want me frisky you should not look so good especially when we haven't seen each other in a while. It's all your fault, Miss Rutledge. You drove me to this madness."

"Well, once we are married I won't have to worry about you being this frisky in the mornings 'cause I look like a scarecrow before I've combed my hair and splashed water in my face."

"No matter what kind of night you've had, you, my Dear, are no scarecrow. But, let me stretch your arms out like this and see what you look like." He pushed my arms out holding my wrist against the wall then leaned back looking me over when my Pa came into the room.

"Ah William, I know that if I hold a rail up to the end of my nose that it will measure three feet to the tip of my middle finger. Is that for everyone or is everybody different. I was showing Lacey how wide this wall is and that there is plenty of wall space for a dresser and a twin size bed before the bathroom door."

"She's not tall enough to have arms that span out six feet. How tall are you?"

"Six two."

"The only way to know right this minute is for you to lay on the floor and she can lay beside you with her arms stretches out and I will tell you if she reaches from the top of your head to your feet. But, she won't. Or I can just tell you that this wall is twelve feet. Wide enough for two scarecrows to stretch out." And he walked into the bathroom. Tylar and I were surprised that Pa had heard our conversation, but we found it funny and snickered quietly. "I painted this one a pale blue thinking this could be the boys' bath." And he popped his head back into the room and said, "This would be a boy's bedroom of course. And if you go through this door it will take you into another bedroom for a boy. Nice closets in here. I know you like wardrobes, Lacey, but for the children, closets are better so they can put their toys in here too. See how big this is?"

Tylar and I walked through the bathroom into the other bedroom. "Good heavens, Pa. You can put a bicycle and a toy box in here and have room to walk around it all."

"I thought it might be nice to have shelves along this wall for books and board games and things like that, maybe shoes, hats or gloves. It's a wardrobe that's big enough to walk inside of."

"I love the color in this room. It reminds me of the next day after the first warm day at the end of winter when all the leaves pop past that brown bark that's been protecting them from the cold?"

"How do you do that, Lacey? When I looked at it, it was a pale lime green, but now I know better."

"I guess my Pa the artist taught me how to see color, Tylar. It's so much more than lime green."

Tylar had to get to work so I walked him out to his car while Pa and Frank finished discussing what would be taking place at the Harrison house that day. Their home would be so different from mine in that they wanted a very modern home like what Frank Lloyd Wright was building up north. Mine was modern in that there were several bathrooms inside the house and electricity was throughout, but the only place I knew for sure it would be used was in the kitchen and for heating the water. I was still very comfortable using gas lanterns and heating the house with wood stoves and fireplaces. Every room had a chimney and every chimney had a fireplace with coal baskets and andirons. Tylar had access to all the coal we could use so we planed on using coal to heat the house, although wood stoves could be hooked up to any fireplace. My home was a combination of Greek Revival and Beaux Art style like that which Richard Morris Hunt designed with a touch of Queen Anne's Victorian Style, especially in the roof lines. The Harrison's would be similar to the Hagan House in Kentucky Knob, Pennsylvania. This was known as the Usonion style. It would have been nice having Mr. Wright build our furniture to match the style of our home as he had done for some of the homes he had built, but I didn't think he made anything in a Victorian or Greek Style.

Pa and I left when Mr. Frank did so we could get back to the house for breakfast with the family. As I did every time I was returning home, I was anticipating someone coming out to meet us with news that Mother had started talking and demanding that we all stop fussing over her. No one was out side when we arrived, but I could smell bacon cooking so I knew we weren't too late.

After breakfast Pa sat with Mother for a while reading scripture from the Bible before he went out to start the tractor, but the radiator had a leak and water had soaked the ground. He had run over a limb the day before and assumed it had punctured the radiator. It would take a week to get a new one so he hitched up Old Plow.

"Pa, don't you think you should wait for Silas to get back with the other tractor? It's been a while since Old Plow has done any plowing."

"I'm almost finished and the ground is nice and soft. I just have to pull it back into place before we plant the late crops tomorrow. It will set us back a whole day if I wait," and he looked toward the southwest, "and it feels like rain in a couple days. God's sending the rain so I better sow while I can. Now run inside and get my pistol. I saw two copperheads stretched out on that warm dirt yesterday. No need to let them get any bigger or hatch out a load of babies to go swimming in the river with you or your brothers or sisters this summer."

I went back in the house and got Pa's pistol and four bullets. "You better not miss cause I only brought you four bullets."

"What if I see five?"

"Kill what you can and high tail it back home. That's entirely too many snakes."

"I'll be in for lunch."

"It's almost that time now."

"I told you there wasn't that much left to do. Call Trell and tell him to order me a radiator and give me ninety days to pay for it. I have a daughter getting married soon and I'm over extended." He had a happy laugh that morning, one I hadn't heard in some time.

"Pa! Did I tell you how much I appreciate all you have done for Tylar and me? The house is truly the most beautiful home I have ever seen. It's a shame that more people can't have something like that, but I'm the only girl blessed with the love of a Pa like you. Except for Retta and Abbie, but I know you love me more."

"You do?"

"Yes I do! I really mean it, Pa. Thank you. I'm so proud that you are my Pa."

"Bear hug," and I jumped into my Pa's arms like I always did feeling as safe as when I was in Pappy's. "I love you, baby girl."

"I love you too, Pa."

I called Trell and ordered the radiator and took the clothes Hattie had washed that morning out on the porch to hang them out on the clothesline. I hadn't had a chance to change my clothes and my feet were crying to come out of my good shoes so I sat down on the porch to put on my tennis shoes. I heard Old Plow's bells ringing so I looked out toward the field Pa was plowing, but I didn't see Pa. Old Plow was standing in the middle of the field shaking his head and stomping his feet. "Where are you Pa?" Old Plow danced around some more and shook his head and I thought I heard Pa tell him to whoa, but I didn't see him. I started walking out to the field and as I got closer I was sure I saw Pa lying on the ground a few feet in front of Old Plow. I ran to Old Plow and saw the bees swarming his head and knew if he was to run he would run that plow right over Pa. I grabbed the reigns and turned Old Plow around and gave him a swat then I ran over to Pa.

"That was a close one, Lacey girl. But you need to go catch Old Plow and put him in the barn."

"Where are you hurt, Pa? Is it your back?"

"Those darned yellow jackets spooked Old Plow and he lunged

forward and I guess he pulled me down. My back is fine but you need to go get Old Plow."

"I need to get you out of this sun and then I'll go and get some help." I stood up and put my hands under my Pa shoulders and pulled to get him up out of the dirt and over to the shade.

Pa's face tightened and with cinched teeth he said, "Lacey don't." Pa's legs and boots didn't come with him, only a stream of blood from the lower half of his body. "Better leave me right here, Punkin. I like the sun."

I pulled my skirt off and tried to wrap it around what was left of his legs packing dirt up against the skirt hoping to stop the bleeding. I was screaming "Help me" to anyone who could hear me and praying in tongues.

"Stop screaming, Lacey. I don't want Cole to see me like this and he is down by the river.

"Pa, Doctor Jude is in the house. If he can hear me he will come, Pa. Are you in pain?"

"Take care of your Mother, Lacey. And when she's fully awake tell her that I love her with all my heart."

"I can't do it without you, Pa."

He grabbed my face hard and said, "Never say that again. You are the strongest woman I know, more than your Mother and Nanny put together. You can do all things through Christ who strengthens you. Now go. I hear Cole coming up from the river. Stop him, Lacey. Don't let him see me like this."

"I love you, Pa. I'll be right back, Pa."

I jumped up and started running in the direction of the river, but I didn't see anybody only the crows as they flew up from the field when my Pa pulled the trigger on his gun.

I guess Doctor Jude heard my screaming then or maybe it was the gunshot that brought him to the field, in either case he held me sitting in the dirt of that freshly plowed ground wearing my red and white striped blouse over my blood soaked white slip until Jake came and relieved him.

The rain did come the day of my Pa's funeral, but the late seed was not in the ground. The preacher said that my Pa was a brave man and although some had taught that to take one's life was a sin that would send you to hell, he knew that there was only one sin that would send you to hell and William Rutledge had not blasphemed the Holy Ghost, he had indeed accepted Jesus and been washed by the blood of the Lamb.

"William was either given over to Satan for a short moment to cause him to go mad so he could put himself out of the pain and suffering that had suddenly come upon him or he was a very courageous men. He quoted scripture to Lacey moments before he pulled the trigger so I believe God guided his hands. I have never heard of a madman quoting scripture."

I was feeling quite empty. I had lost the support I desperately needed from my Mother and the strength my Pa gave me in just a few short weeks. My Pappy was my rod, but his heart was battered. My siblings needed me to be strong and I needed to be quiet. That's all I wanted to do was be in my room, quiet. As I turned to leave the church I was amazed at the people who had come to say their goodbyes to my father and encourage my family or simply give me a hug. The children from Little Africa who came to our school were there and the people who had been in the migrant camp. All those men with their families who helped my Pa build our house and people who banked with my Pappy where paying their respects. It was a sea of people inside the church and out on the grounds. I even witnessed my Pappy take a hug from Johnny Kale Butler and my Nanny shook the hand of Miss Sunshine.

"When a baby is born a few people send you a card. When someone's life is taken the whole town shows up and miraculously old hatreds are buried, at least for a day. I will never understand that, Tylar."

Tylar stood beside me during every moment of that day, although I had very little to say to him. Jake had been the one who saw what I saw. He took his shirt off and wrapped my father's head before he took me from the arms of Doctor Jude. He was the one who brought me into the house and gave me a sedative and stayed with me till I fell asleep and then with his father lifted my father's body out of the field and carried what was left of him across the road to their home and waited for the coroner to come and get him. I felt as much hurt for Jake as I did any of us because he had gone through the most. I watched him fall apart several times with no one to comfort him. He loved my father as much as we did and for many years before Willie came out of his shell Jake was the son Pa didn't have. They had a special bond that I didn't realize how deep it went till this day.

As the day turned to evening most of the mourners had gone home. We were in the kitchen, Tylar, Margie, Bob, Sally, Doctor Jude, Pappy, Nanny and all the kids. I noticed Jake was not with us. "Does anyone know where Jake is?"

"I saw him on the porch a few minutes ago. Why?"

"I just wondered. I need to check on him."

"I'll go check on him. You can stay here with your family."

"Tylar. I need to go," and I walked out of the room.

"I'll come with you."

I heard Doctor Jude said, "No Tylar, let her go; they should talk. It was hard what they went through. He needs her right now."

Jake was standing on the porch looking out at the dark yard when I saw him through the window. I knew that I had nothing to say to him, but I wanted to be there for him if he needed me like I needed him in that field. I went out and stood beside him, but he didn't look at me or speak. He was so much taller and bigger than Tylar and I certainly didn't feel like the stronger one, so I just stood there with him staring out at nothing for a long time. I walked over to the steps that led out into the yard and sat down on the top one. I looked back at Jake and said, "I'll be right here if you need me."

Shortly he came and sat beside me. He slowly rocked back and forth as he sat and his tears began to flow more rapidly. "How could things happen to a man so vital, so full of life, so gifted and giving? How could God take him when we all need him and love him so much? He was my father when my father was so far away, but just because Dad came home didn't mean I didn't need William anymore. He taught me how to use my hands. I might not have wanted to be a surgeon if he hadn't showed me that I was good with my hands. He taught me how to love and how to be a man about certain things no matter what comes your way. He told me I could be anything I wanted to be when others said I was just a class clown and I wouldn't amount to anything."

"I think I was the one who said that."

He let out a slight chuckle, "You always make me smile, Lacey Kale, just like you did him. How are we going to get along without him? What kind of surgeon will I be if I couldn't even save the man who encouraged me ... "

"Jake Forsyth! He never gave you the chance. Stop that. Don't you ever doubt what you can do or who you are no matter what happens? Come here." Jake laid his head into my arms, then wrapped his arms around my legs putting his head in my lap and cried silently while I questioned how my life had suddenly turned upside down and what was I going to do about Mother, my siblings and Tylar.

I spent the next few days hiding in my room except when Jake came by, talking to no one, not even God. One day I heard my Aunt Penny telling someone to go home in my front yard so I went to the window to see what she was saying. Miss Sunshine was in the yard holding a cookie-can just a few feet from the porch. Aunt Penny was telling her to get back in her car, that she was not welcome here.

"The last thing I heard was that the Master of this house was in heaven, the Misses is unable to speak or communicate so that would leave their oldest daughter, who is the person I came to see, *in charge*, not you. I want to see Lacey. I have brought her a gift. Just tell me if she available?"

"Not to you, but I will give her the gift. Goodbye." And she took the cookies and walked into the house leaving Miss Sunshine out in the yard. She stood for a moment and then she got in her car and drove away. I wrote her note thanking her for the cookies and for coming to the funeral.

A week or so had passed and Aunt Penny was at my house bossing our help around while Kimmy and Theodore were sitting on the porch. I stood by the window watching Kimmy swinging on the swing.

"It's all so hard for me to believe. William's in heaven and Abigail is suffering from something that makes her unable to talk to anybody. Lacey has lost both her parents in just a matter of moments really. How will she go on with her plans to wed Tylar and leave these other children with no parent?"

"And what makes you think William is in heaven, Kimmy?

Preacher Burton says if you take your life it's same as murder and there'll be no murderers in heaven."

Pappy was on the porch, too, though I could not see him. "Theodore! Preacher Burton is a buffoon! Did William kill anybody else?"

"No, Sir"

"I might let you get away with saying he committed a murder when he took his own life, but I will not let you call him a murderer. A murderer is just like a liar, in that they tell lies over and over and over and do not know the truth. A murderer kills over and over like Bonnie and Clyde with no thought to another person's life. If that person never accepts Jesus as their Lord and Savior they are doomed. Even if they murder over and over they can still be forgiven as long as the Holy Ghost is still coming around calling them into change. There is a day when He stops coming to that person, so no one needs to wait too long once He starts asking for them to accept Jesus as their Savior. I know William was thinking of everyone else when he took his life. He had a cousin who worked as a logger. There was an accident one day when a tree snapped prematurely in two while they were sawing it down. The saw came back on him and was shoved into his thigh by the trunk of the tree cutting into the bone. He lay in the bed for two weeks suffering with gangrene and eventually died from lock jaw because of the rusty blade. This is a death no one is likely to ever forget. It was as torturous for the family as it was for the cousin and I know that William was thinking about that when he pulled that trigger. No where in the Bible does it say that a person who takes there own life will have their name removed from the Lamb's Book of Life and I know that William's name is there."

"Well, so was Judas' and we all know where he is."

"Yeah, well, only God knows for sure about that. I don't believe God will remove your name from the book once it's written in there no matter what you do. No one here can tell me that Judas had a fruitful life, so I tend to believe he isn't in heaven either, but it's not because he took his own life! I believe that Judas is in hell today because he did the only unpardonable sin. He never had a born again experience. He never received the cross, he never trusted in Jesus. He was always looking for man or money to give him what he needed and Jesus didn't stand for personal gain. Jesus taught to give it away."

Kimmy said, "But, Pappy. Judas did ask for forgiveness don't you think?"

"When?"

"Well, the Bible said he was so sorry about betraying Jesus that he was over come with grief and that's why he killed himself. He even threw the money back at those men."

"He was remorseful, yes, but even a heathen can be remorseful. If he wanted to change he had the opportunity when Jesus made it clear to him, at the table that night, that He knew what Judas was going to do and then He told him to go on and get to it. Judas could have fallen to his knees then and begged for forgiveness and asked Him to keep him from doing this, but he left. His heart was evil and there was no stopping him. If he recognized Jesus as Lord and that's why he threw the money away, he would have gone to the feet of Jesus, to the cross and asked for forgiveness, but he took his life, possibly out of fear. Fear that the others would kill him. A starving child can be remorseful for stealing bread while he's eating it, but when he gets hungry again he will steal again and have a perfectly good explanation for it. But, until he relies on Jesus to give him what he needs he will have to steal every meal. Judas never relied on Jesus.

"William was not anything like either one of these people. He put his trust totally in God and God did not say, 'Part from me you evil doer.' No, God said, 'Welcome William, thy good and faithful servant.' We'll never know if the pain was what drove him to do it, or the thoughts of the agonizing death, or his thoughts of his family being spared from the lingering days watching him suffer, but one thing I do know, William *is* in heaven."

"But, Pappy, he didn't get to ask for forgiveness after he did it."

"Kimmy, if an airplane fell out of the sky right now and killed all three of us, where would we be?"

"You and I would be in heaven. I don't know about Theodore."

"You worry about yourself you little snot . . ."

"Okay, that's enough. Let's just use you and me. Is there anything that you haven't asked God to forgive you for? A thought, a word, a judgment like you just made about your brother?"

Kimmy hung her head and said, "I'm sorry, Theodore, but you know that you don't act like a person who has Jesus in their heart. Yes, Pappy, I guess there are things."

"Well, did Jesus die for your sin?"

"Yeah."

"He died for your sin before you were even born to commit a sin and His blood was powerful enough to do that, don't you think it's powerful enough to cover your sin once you die?"

"Yeah, I guess it is."

"Who knows, William may have said, 'God forgive me' right before he pulled the trigger."

"Then that doesn't count, Pappy. He asked for forgiveness for a sin before he did it and that would mean he knew it was wrong."

"I've asked God to forgive me before I did something that I knew I had to do and God was not showing me a 'for sure' escape. I took the escape that was before me and it turned out to be what God wanted. Maybe that was the escape God sent to William. After all he planted it in his mind to take the gun to the field in the first place."

"What escape are you talking about, Pappy?"

"The one in I Corinthians 10:13, *'There has no temptation taken you but such as is common to man: but God is faithful, who will not suffer you to be tempted above that ye are able; but will with the temptation also make a way to escape, that ye may be able to bear it.'*"

Theodore said, "Would you call getting your legs cut off a temptation? I thought a temptation was a sin."

"The Bible is clear. Sin is called sin, temptation is temptation and in this case in the Greek it refers to trial and I believe William was faced with a trial. Only God knows what could have happened to William if he lay in the bed for days suffering such a death. He may have become bitter towards God and caused a greater tragedy for his family to watch their Father turn bitter towards God. Then we really would be confused and have no peace in his death. God knew what was going to happen on that day and He made an escape. I refuse to believe anything else. There is no sin that is greater than the blood of Jesus. None, except never allowing Him to cover you with His blood in the first place, by never accepting what He did on the cross for your sin. That, and *only* that, is what sends a man to hell."

I knew in my heart that what Pappy had said was true; my Pa was in heaven and no one could convince me other wise. It didn't make the pain go away; it didn't make it easier to live without him. At the time I simply had no relief or comfort in knowing that God had my Pa. I was lost without him and my life was taking turns I never anticipated.

About six months later Johnny Kale had offered Tylar a promotion and he was more than anxious to accept. He came to the house and asked me to go with him out to our house so we could talk alone. I had sent Hattie to the store with Tula so I couldn't leave with him right then, but I told him I would drive out to the house and meet him in an hour. I had hired Tula to help with the household chores so that Hattie could be with Mother constantly. With Pa gone and me and Silas doing all the farming Mother didn't have anyone to sit with her now that the kids had gone back to school. Aunt Penny had offered, but I knew that Penny was the last person Mother would want to wake up and find hovering over her bed. It didn't stop her from calling me everyday to tell me what I should do about this and that. Mostly she was telling me how to raise Cole. I had raised three children before Cole, and I didn't need her help in raising the last one. But, Aunt Penny was Aunt Penny and nothing would stop her from making our business hers.

I went out to the house to meet Tylar, a place I had not been since the day my Pa and I had seen it together; the same day he died. Looking through the windows I noticed that some of the furniture and the dining room table had been delivered. Seeing the beautiful trim around the opening from the dining room into the foyer, I was reminded of the red skirt I had to wrap his legs in and the terror I felt that day. Leaving was my desire when Tylar pulled in behind me and jumped out of the car. He seemed so excited to be at the house, to see me and tell me his good news.

"Johnny Kale has offered me a job running my own train yard. In two years I would own it outright. It's a bigger yard than this one and it has three times the traffic. Northern, Atlantic, Pacific and Southern trains all converge at this yard. I could own the largest train yard in the country. We could live like a Vanderbilt!"

I was listening to him, but I was walking around the house my Pa had finished building just a day before his death and I was remembering our day together and admiring the wood trim throughout the house. "So what's the catch?"

"We move to Chicago."

"What?"

"Chicago. I know it sounds crazy at first, but think about it. Your Pa is gone. He has left enough money to take care of your Mother and the kids till they finish school. Silas can cut the farm work in half and still make plenty of money to live on and give the rest to your Mother. Frank is running the building business and Hattie and Tula are seeing to your Mother and the house and when she wakes up they will call you. And we will be making trips monthly to see her and my folks. I'm so ready for you to become my wife and I know you don't want to have a wedding yet without your mother so we can go to the justice of the peace and get married without a big wedding and party and catch the next train out of town. We can still go on the trip Johnny Kale has promised us or wait till we get settled. Let's just do something wild and crazy for a change. You need that."

"And who is going to see to this house?"

"We will sell it. I need the money as a down payment on the train yard and we can use some of it to get a small apartment in the city till we find a house we like once we're on our feet."

"Sell my Pa's masterpiece? It doesn't sound crazy, it is crazy. My whole world has gone mad!"

"It's just a house, Lacey. He built many houses. It's not him, it's just a house."

"I can't think about this right now."

"When can you think about it?"

"I don't know. I may not ever be able to think about it!"

"How can you say this to me? I have been patient, Lacey. I want you to be my wife. We have to move on. This offer is once in a lifetime. Everything I've ever wanted is right before me. You, my own train yard, the big city, it's all right here, but I can't make it work without you."

"And yet you can give up what we have right here, right now for something you have never seen."

"Isn't that what faith is?"

"It is when God has said to do it. Did God tell you to do it?"

"He gave me the desires of my heart."

"He gave you the desire to want to move to Chicago and run a train yard?"

"I believe he gave me the desire and then provided the fulfillment."

"Then He will give me the same thing if I'm supposed to go with you."

"Of course you're supposed to go with me. It's been you and me forever, Lacey. Who else would I go with? Who else could I ever love?"

"Then you will have to wait till God speaks to me and if there is a time limit He will speak quickly."

Tylar threw his arms around me and said, "Has He said anything yet?"

"No." Then he kissed me all over my face.

"Has He said anything yet?"

"No." More kissing.

"Yet?"

"No!"

"Tell me when He says something."

"You are so crazy!"

"Crazy about you and ready to have you be my wife. Lacey, I want you so much," and he put his hands up inside my shirt rubbing the skin on my back. I wanted him too, but not with things so unsettled. He had just told me he wanted to move to Chicago. I had never heard God say that I would be leaving. But, I did know God to do things spontaneously, but not with me. He always slowly chiseled out the path He wanted for me. Could I stop Tylar from taking me right here, right now? I wanted him so badly, like I had never wanted him before, but I had to wonder if it was my emptiness that I was wanting filled or did I know that he and I were destined to be together forever and we were already sealed as one by God? He had my blouse unbuttoned and he was laying me down in the floor of this vast living room and I was wanting this moment to stop so I could think, but at the same time I wanted it to go too far, quickly, so I couldn't change my mind.

"Oh God! Tylar, what are we doing?'

"Has He told you yet? Can't you feel that we need each other? I love you, Lacey. I've always loved you. I have never even kissed another girl. I've waited my whole life for you. I've always wanted you to be my first; I couldn't imagine making love to anyone else. When other guys at school were with several girls I saved myself for you, but I can't wait anymore. You drive me crazy."

He was holding me like I had never been held and I was caught up in the moment not wanting him to ever let me go.

"Shouldn't we wait, Tylar? We have to wait since we've waited this long. Our honeymoon. Don't we want our honeymoon to be special?"

He stopped and looked at me with a hunger I had never seen, "Every time with you will be special. We can have our honeymoon here in this house right now and then we will leave here and go into town and get married, if that's what you want?"

"But, I don't see us in Chicago. I've never seen us on a train. I have seen us in this house and I feel wonderful when I'm *here*!"

"What are you talking about . . . seeing us here and not there?"

"When conversation is going on around me I see what people are saying, if it's going to happen as they say or as I say, but if I don't see it, it doesn't happen. I've never seen us on the train going to the Grand Canyon and I've certainly never seen us in Chicago."

"Have you ever seen us making love?"

"I've never seen us making love, but I've wonder if it's because . . ." I started to say because I don't know what it's like to make love to another person, but then I remembered that I had seen Jake and I doing something that I had to close my mind to the day he held the charm on my necklace, but I could never be sure that we were going to make love because I wouldn't let my mind go there.

"Because what? You wondered if it was because of what?" I could tell he was getting frustrated with me so I pulled out from under Tylar and sat up leaning against the wall. "Lacey? Talk to me. Why haven't you ever seen us making love?"

"I don't know, Tylar. I don't know," and I started buttoning up my blouse.

"What are you doing?"

"I'm going home." I stood up and started towards the door.

"You're just going to leave? You string me along. We build this house. We make these plans. You buy the dress. I buy the tux. We order the flowers. I wait and wait and wait, for *you,* Lacey! I've waited for you and you're just going to *leave?*"

"You already left, Tylar." And I picked up my purse from the floor and walked to the door. "You've already left."

chapter seventeen

Several days passed and I heard rumors that he had taken Johnny Kale's offer, but he had not come to me to ask for permission to sell the house. I hoped he wasn't so mad at me that he wouldn't come by and tell me in person what he had decided to do. I didn't want to lose this beautiful house that my Pa had put so much of himself into, but I couldn't keep up two houses and how greedy it would be to keep a wonderful home that could be a safe place for a family to raise their children. It would slowly fall apart if someone didn't live in it, love it and take care of it. The truth was I had already fallen apart. I was still resigned to my room far removed from my family and friends and even more from God. I didn't talk to Him; He didn't talk to me. All I could do was think and nothing made any sense at all. I had lost my Mother, my Father and the man that God had created for me. There was hope that my Mother would wake up and come back to me, but my Father was gone and it seemed that Tylar had easily made his choice to make a new life without me.

"So God, why have you decided to leave me, too?"

I walked out to the field where my Father had died and I wondered if I had done something there that would have caused God to turn away from me. All I could think of was being so caught up in the fear of that moment when Pa asked me to leave him and I did and he took his life. Was that why God was away from me now? Is that when

I let Him down? If I had stayed with Pa, I would have kept him from shooting himself and maybe he could have been spared? "But, maybe God, he would have suffered in pain and days gone by while the gangrene ate away his flesh before he died days, maybe weeks, later like Pappy said. How will I ever know if you don't talk to me? How can you just leave me when you know I haven't ever wanted to disappoint you? How can You be so cruel? How can Tylar be so cruel?"

I dropped down on to the warm dirt and looked at all the tender new grass sprouting in the field. Life had no right to pop up in this field of death. It was like another slap in my face and I was so angry. Pappy had not shared this side of God with me before, but I had witnessed His creation move on when disaster struck and I realized that it would not hold still and wait for me.

A voice so strong and vibrating within my soul said, "Neither will I. I have moved on and you have sat down in judgment of Me. I will not address your case against Me. You may sit or follow Me."

The sun was climbing higher into the sky and I had to find out where God had gone. I was directed to the house. Of all places that was where I was the last time I felt His hands on me. I walked around in the house for over an hour feeling so close to my Pa. The dining room table was another work of art. The craftsman's name and the city in which it had come from, Hickory, North Carolina, were on a brass plate under the table on the side of the trim. I was going to look him up and ask him what my father had commissioned him to do. Did Pa draw up plans or just tell him what kind of table would complete this room? I had so many questions for my Pa now that he was gone. Somehow the craftsman knew about the grapes because there were small grape clusters on the four corners near the top of the table and about every twelve inches down the sides. There were ten legs with scrolled beams that connected five legs on one end and five legs on the other making two Xs. In the middle of both Xs sat hand carved fruit bowls on top of the fifth leg. The grapes were the most prominent fruit hanging out of the bowls with large leaves protruding away from the other fruit. The table pulled apart leaving a gap between the Xs exposing a storage space that housed six extra leaves when they were not needed. This table sat twenty comfortably, but I was sure with the added leaves as many as thirty could sit easily. I missed my Pa and the fact that he and I would never have a meal together at this beautiful table, but I thanked God we had coffee sitting on some buckets in the kitchen.

As I rubbed my hand over the smooth finish of the table I saw in my mind lots of children sitting at this table. Enough children to fill every seat. "God, how funny these thoughts that go through my head are. I may not even have a husband and I see babies filling this room." I bent over the table top putting my face down on its cool surface seeing my reflection in the shiny glass-like finish. Just like I did without warning these days I began to quietly cry. "How can everything feel so hopeless when I know that nothing is hopeless?"

I heard footsteps coming into the front door, but I didn't lift up to see who had entered my home. Some one started rubbing my shoulders and brushed my hair away from my face. "I have news, Lacey."

"Oh great, more news." I suddenly thought of Mother and lifted my head. "Oh, Pappy, is it Mother?"

"Shhh, no little one. She's still the same. I have news of Tylar."

"Oh," and I climbed up on the table and laid my whole body on this marvelous work of art. "Did he send you?"

"No. I ran into Johnny Kale today. Tylar must have sent him to me. I was supposed to meet with him this morning, but he has left for Chicago."

I waited for my soul to react, "And without seeing me. Why did I expect anything else? How did we fall so far apart? I guess it's a good thing we found out that we weren't as devoted to each other as we thought. You know the funny thing about it all is it doesn't hurt. I guess I just didn't have any hurt left when it was Tylar's turn to leave. I don't feel anything anymore, not unless I'm in this house." I sat up on my elbow and looked at Pappy. "Why is that? This is as Tylar said 'just a house.' And a house that I have never lived in or made a memory," I had a flash of Tylar and I laying in the living room floor, "well, a memory worth remembering, except for breakfast with Pa and Mr. Frank the day Pa died. Is that it, Pappy? I do feel closer to Pa when I'm here and I know it's because the beauty that takes your breath is a result of Pa's own imagination. But, every stick nailed in that house where my Mother is lying I watched my Pa put in there. There's so much more of Pa there. But, I don't feel this, whatever *this* is, there."

"But, he built that house for your Mother and the family they would raise together, this house he built for you. That's what makes it special, just knowing he was thinking of you with so much love. It really is a grand place," and Pappy walked to the window. "And the lion is at home here. My grandmother is smiling knowing he has a home. Could you ever see yourself living here?"

"I don't know what I see anymore."

"Well, do you think you could ever forget that it was built for you and Tylar?"

"You know what Pappy, I can say it now, I was afraid to say it before, but I never thought of this house as Tylar's. He and I never came here together to work on the house and we only met with Pa once to tell him what we wanted the house to have. I was shocked when Pa said Tylar picked out the wallpaper and even though he denied it, I'm sure Marge was the one who picked it out." I climbed off of the table and walked around the hallway looking at the dentil molding that bordered the hall ceiling. "All this wood work," and I rubbed the trim on the blunt end of the living room wall just before stepping up onto the bottom step of the staircase. I reached out for the railing and noticed that Pa had inlaid a carved grape leaf with the words, *Built with love for my daughter, Lacey Rutledge* 1954, on the top of the flat spiral newel.

"I've never seen this before, Pappy. Did you know it was here? It's like Pa is making it impossible for me to ever sell this place."

"I wrote Tylar a check this morning for his part in the house. I'm willing to offer you the same if you want out of it."

"You did what?"

"I want you to think about something. The orphanage at Willow Creek is closing. There are twelve children there right now. Some will be placed at the State Hospital. You know that children who are well do not need to be there. I thought we could give them a home here, until something else could be provided for them if you wanted to ever live here. Or if you wanted out I could buy your part and make it a full time orphanage. I've been looking over William's plans he drew up for you if you ever needed to add bedrooms and I thought I would flip his idea and have the dormitory come off of the dining room instead of the living room, mostly because the living room would have to be used as a reception area and possibly offices. We wouldn't want the children to have to cross through that area to come in for breakfast and to leave supper that way again. I also thought that maybe the house should be all classrooms and we could build a dormitory beside the barn. Some more trees would have to be cleared and it might be difficult for the children when it's raining or there's snow on the ground."

"My goodness, Pappy. You have put a lot of thinking into this. You're serious."

"Very serious. I would love to have your input no matter what you decide to do with your part."

"I'm in no need of the money." I walked around the house looking at it differently. "Is it too grand for an orphanage?"

"Think hard about that question."

"I just mean are the gold leafed spigots practical for thirty children?"

"Thirty? Grand sakes alive, girl! I said there were only twelve."

"Twelve or thirty, it doesn't matter. Once you've past the number one you might as well have thirty because there's no difference when you're counting children."

"If you thought it was a bit extravagant to have the gold spigots we could change them, but the children might finally feel like someone thought they were special if we were to leave them. Of course just having a place like this to grow up in could give them the conformation that all children need."

"We could open the school up to the children at Little Africa and those living in the government project."

"Yes, we could. Does that mean you're on board?"

"And you're sure Tylar isn't coming back to want to sell this house?"

"It isn't his to sell anymore."

"You have that in writing?"

Pappy reached in his pocket, "Right here."

I shook my head. "I don't want to see it. It was all far too easy for him to walk way. We really didn't know each other, did we Pappy?"

"Don't be so hard on him or yourself. He had to go. He doesn't know why, he just had to go. I know he loved you more than he ever loved anyone else."

"I just wasn't enough."

"His loss, Punkin."

"Oh, Pappy. I don't want to talk about it. I don't want to think about it or talk about it ever again. I want to talk about your vision. Just a little while ago when I put my hands on this table I saw in my spirit children, lots of children filling up the chairs around this table. Oh Pappy, where are the chairs?"

"Trell said they were almost finished and would be shipped out at the end of the week."

"Are they coming from Hickory?"

"Yep, same place."

"How many?"

"Twenty."

"Well first thing, we need to order more. I want them all to match and even though we don't need that many now, we will at some point."

"So how many more?"

"Fourteen. I feel strongly that thirty-four chairs can line up along the walls. Thirty will fit at the table when it's pulled out and that will leave four for the workers to sit in while they feed the babies in high chairs. We will need high chairs, too."

"Do you want them to match?"

"Oh Pappy! Of course. And the dormitory must attach to this side of the house. It can be three stories if it needs be and we can put in another staircase if we can't figure out how to get the children back into this section of the house so they can use these stairs. They need a living room where they can visit their parents, those who have parents or visit with people who want to interview them. Offices should be under the dormitory. The master suite can be for the head mistress, the rooms upstairs for classrooms. I think this will work out perfect. I'm so glad you were listening to God when He told you why He had Pa build this place. I must confess I haven't talked to him, until today, in weeks, maybe months much less listened to Him. If I'm honest, I haven't talked to Him since Pa's death. But, today when I went out to the field I told Him some of my thoughts and He said He had moved on and I was wondering where to and now I know."

"And He spoke to you when you got here."

"When?"

"When He showed you the children. He was preparing you to hear what He told me."

"You're right. You know that's what I was trying to tell Tylar. If God had wanted me to go to Chicago with him, He would have prepared me to hear what Tylar was saying to me." I walked around the living room holding to the placket of my shirt looking at the wooden floor where we came so close to becoming one. For the first time I felt the lost of Tylar come over me. "Why couldn't it have been me? What's so wrong with me?"

"Hello, anyone home?"

"In here Mr. Frank."

"I got your message, Jeremiah. I came straight here. Is there something we missed?" He took off his cap and nodded in my direction, "Good morning, Miss Rutledge."

"No Frank, the house is perfect; it's just not big enough." Mr. Frank looked like he was on an episode of Candid Camera. "We need a place big enough for thirty children so we need to ask you about adding another wing to this side of the house and possibly needing another staircase. Lacey can fill you in on the details of what we want. I have the overall vision, she has the details. She's like her Pa that way."

"Is this a joke, Jeremiah?"

"I assure you, this is no joke. I have to go and make the arrangements for the children. You two get started; they'll be here in two weeks. We can make do with what we have for now, but pencil us in right away to get this started. You can work around children, can't you Mr. Frank?"

"I . . . I, sure."

Pappy came to me and kissed my hands. "Praise God for you, my little breath of sunshine. Thank you, from the children and me. Be thinking of a headmistress. For now think about taking the job."

"What about the person who's doing it now?"

"It's forty miles or more to Willow Creek. They may not want to relocate. Oh my, doesn't *Lion's Hill* sound lighter and braver, or something, than Willow Creek?"

"It sounds like hope, something I know we can offer these children."

Mr. Frank and I stayed at the house for nearly five hours drawing and re-drawing plans for the addition. We had settled on two floors in keeping with the wing that was already there, but it protruded about twenty feet farther out on the back side of the house. This gave a place for a playground protected by the house on two sides and access to this wing from outside close to the back entrance into the main hallway. The playground could be watched by the new classrooms on the bottom floor as we thought it was better to keep all the bedrooms upstairs and all parts of the school downstairs. Especially if we had children from town come to our school. If the teachers wanted to live at the school they could use the bedrooms upstairs located in the main part of the house. The longer we worked on the plan the more excited I was to be a part of it. I was amazed at how God had turned something so devastating around to something so positive, but then I also had to wonder if He had this in mind from the beginning, even back when he let me meet Tylar. It was hard to think that a loving God would cause me to fall in love, build this beautiful home and then dash my hopes just to get His will accomplished, but the God I knew had sent His Son to die on a cross to save the world, so why wouldn't He turn my world upside down to save a few orphaned children?

Knowing what God was doing and that I was connected to it all was at times not enough to keep me from feeling empty and alone. I tried to stay as busy as possible, but Hattie and Tula had the household things in order, Mayree was watching the expenses, Mr. Frank had the building company working over time, thanks to Pappy and I, and Silas, with Willie's help, had the farm in working order. He didn't have time to work on the equipment and the new radiator had been sitting in the barn for months. Silas couldn't drive two tractors and it hadn't been needed during the fall months, but I decided that I would change it out and have Willie a tractor to drive by spring. No one was ever going to use Old Plow again. He had been turned out into the pasture to sleep under the moon in the fresh air with the other horses.

I had gotten Uncle Trell to order me a service manual for the tractor so I could read up on how I was going to do this job. Uncle

Trell thought it would be way too difficult for me to do which made it all the more desirable. I spent what seemed like three days figuring out how to start disconnecting the hoses and removing the brackets. I had to label each bolt one at a time with a drawing as to where it came from so I would know where it went back. Willie helped me for a couple hours after school.

"Today is the day, Willie, when the old comes out and the new goes in. I should have it ready for bolts to go back in by the time you get home."

"I can't wait to hear it crank up again."

"I will save that job for you."

It was way after lunch by the time I had the hoses connected to the new radiator. I was getting used to my new attire, overalls and Pa's old work boots. I didn't feel much like a woman anymore anyway so why try looking like one. I hadn't cared at all about keeping dirt or the grease off my hands. It was just me and my siblings now and they certainly didn't care what I looked like.

"Can you use some help?"

I pulled my head out from under the engine and saw Jake standing at the end of the barn. "I've got it now. Besides a surgeon doesn't need to get his hands dirty like this," and I held out my greasy black hands holding a wrench. "When did you get home?"

"About fifteen minutes ago."

"Was no one there to meet you?"

"Yeah, the folks are there."

"And you came over here to see me so soon after just getting home?"

"I wanted to see you and your Mother. How has she been?"

"Hattie seems to think there's an improvement, but I can't tell it. She just stares. It's like she knows about Pa, so I think the change Hattie sees might be a woman morning her husband."

"How would she know he's ... gone? Did someone tell her?"

"He's dead, Jake. He's not just gone. Tylar is gone, Pa is dead. And Mother knows that only death would keep Pa from her this long."

"And you? What are you?"

"I'm fine. How about you, Jake? How have you been? How's school?"

"Well, I'm good. I would love to tell you all about school and what's going on there if you really care. Maybe you can take some time away from the tractor, clean up, just a little. Maybe just wash your hands, cause you look fine other wise, and I thought maybe we could go into town and have supper?"

"I do care, Jake. I'm sorry. Are you talking like a date?"

"Is that so hard for you to see someone, other than Tylar Lane, as a date?"

"Hattie has soup already made. I wouldn't want to disappoint her."

"She might understand if I talk to her and tell how much I would like to spend some time with my friend and catch up on things."

"I'm trying to keep things as normal as possible around here. I make sure the four of us sit down to supper together. It's important to Cole to have some structure and know that none of us are going to leave him."

"Wouldn't it be better for him to learn that people do leave and come back rather than always having a fear that if someone doesn't make it to supper they aren't going to ever come home again?"

"I thought you were studying to be a surgeon, not a psychiatrist. You don't understand what we all have been through here. It's not easy learning to live without a dream, but it's safer."

"Is that what ya'll are doing here?"

"We're just trying to cope. I personally have been living in a fairytale from the day I met Tylar Lane and what did I get from that? A lesson that there's no such thing."

"You haven't been living at all."

"What does that mean?"

"It means that Lacey died the day she met Tylar Lane. She lived his life, his dream and tried to make it fit hers. You just couldn't see what everyone else saw because you were too wrapped up in that fairytale to see that God never wanted you to be Tylar's wife. You wanted that and He had to stop you before it went too far."

"Don't you think building that house, buying the dress, planning every moment of the ceremony, is going too far?"

"No. I think marrying the wrong man is going too far."

"Well, He stopped me. It's over. But, Tylar isn't the wrong man, I'm the wrong woman."

"You think everyone is wrong if they're not Tylar."

"You don't know what you're talking about."

"You measure everyone by some imaginary ruler that carries the name 'The Tylar Lane Scale' and everyone falls somewhere beneath the lowest digit. And the sad thing is the great Tylar Lane himself doesn't measure up, but still you make excuses for him. You are doing the very thing you claim to detest, judging everyone by some standard that is worthless. And now that you have been rejected by Mr. Wonderful even you have fallen beneath the scales. So now you're on some crusade to destroy yourself thinking there's nothing in you that could possible be worthy of breath itself because you have been rejected by the one who you have lived to be worthy of? I'm not minimizing the tragedies that have fallen on you and this family, but destroying yourself is not going to make everything better. And waiting for him to reconsider his choice and come back for you is what will destroy you if you ever let him back into your life. You have a chance to be truly happy now that he's gone and I'm not going to sit by anymore and let you fight the person God made you so you can become an empty shell. A house divided against itself can not stand and, Lacey, you are crumbling."

I was trying to shake off what he was saying so I could run him out of my barn and back to wherever, just away from me. But, something kept my mouth shut. I turned away from him and prayed silently, "God, God! What is he saying? Make him leave. I can't think." Then I blurted out, "I don't want to talk about it anymore."

"Well, I do," and he pulled me around to look at him. "I came over here because I want to talk about it."

"Stop it, Jake. I don't!"

"Then you're gonna listen. I'm sorry more than I have words that Tylar didn't turn out to be your prince charming; okay, I'm lying about that. I love Tylar like a brother, but he was always wrong for you. But, I am deeply sorry about your Father losing his life and even more so that he died as he did. It haunts me, but I have to leave it in God's hands cause I don't understand. And your Mother lying in that bed day after day with no communication with anyone is enough to peel away all flesh from your heart, but I'm more grieved about not holding you. Not being with you. The woman I know you are. Not having your love, Lacey, more than any of it all put together." He had grabbed my arms and pulled me up close to him and that feeling was back.

"Jake, I'm dirty. Stop it."

"You asked me once if I was in love with you. You knew the answer then and you know it now. Nothing has changed for me and if you are honest with yourself nothing has changed for you. I'm not going to let another day go by without letting you know what you have always wanted," and he kissed me in a way that Tylar never had. The way a man should kiss a woman. When he stopped, he looked deep into my eyes, dropped his hands and left the barn walking across our yard in the direction of his parent's home.

"How dare you, Jake Foresight."

"Lacey?"

"Oh shoot, Willie. How long have you been standing there?"

"Long enough. Do you want me to crank up the tractor now?"

I mumbled under my breath, "Yea, and run that man over."

"What did you say, Sissy?"

"No, Willie. That's gonna have to wait."

"Where are you going?"

"I don't know."

I went into the mud room and threw my cap on the counter of the sink and washed my hands and splashed cold water on my face. I had to stop for just a moment and rest against the sink to gather my thoughts. It was hard to do because they kept taking me back to Jake in the barn. "Mother. I need you now, Mother," and I dried off and went to her room.

"Hattie, I need to be with Mother. Alone."

"Sure, Honey. You lookin' a little flush, yous okay?"

"Yeah, I just have to talk to Mother."

"If'ins I can help, Is here fo ya."

"Thanks, but I need my Mother."

"Ok baby girl. You so pretty like yo Mother. Now doncha upsets her."

"I won't."

Hattie left the room and I pulled the door almost closing it. "Hey,

Mother. How are you today?" I picked up the hand towel lying on the bedside table and submersed it into the water in the bowl on the wash stand then I patted her face and mouth with the towel. She seemed to like that. "Mother, I have to talk to you. I'm afraid I don't have anyone else who will listen to me anymore. You probably know this because Tylar hasn't been around in months, but the wedding is off, for now, oh Mother, probably for good, and even though I tell myself it doesn't matter I find myself looking out the window thinking he will drive up and dash in here frantically looking for me, desperate to beg me to forgive him for leaving without me. Mother, he didn't even try to get me to go with him. He just said I'm taking a job in Chicago and that was that. It just took me by surprise. So Pappy has bought Tylar's part of the house and he's going to bring orphans from Willow Creek here because it's closing and the children have nowhere to go, but if God wanted an orphanage built on that property rather than our home then okay, He can have it. And maybe it would be okay for me to go with Tylar because you have plenty here to take care of you and, but, there's this other problem, Mother, and I don't have any idea what to do about it. It's Jake. Mother, he has all but declared it from the rooftop that he's in love with me. Mother, he just kissed me!" She didn't seem to respond to anything I was saying so I began to pace the room wondering how to describe what Jake did to me when I was near him. "Mother, you never told me how Pa made you feel. Sure you said he was the most wonderful man who ever graced your parlor and that your life was hopeless until he brought love into it, but you never told me what happened to you inside when you touched him or how his kisses gave you goose bumps. Or if he ever put his hands on the sides of your face and then ran his hand to the back of your neck as he kissed you. I'm full of so much joy when I'm with Tylar and we go together and until that day when he told me all about his plans to buy that stupid train yard from Johnny Kale in Chicago we had never spoken harsh words to each other."

    I almost saw a change in my Mother's expression, but I wasn't sure. "Mother, are you trying to tell me something? What is it? Do you need something to drink?" I got a sponge from the water glass and pressed it against her lips letting the water run into her mouth. Somehow she was able to swallow even though she seemed to be asleep. "Mother, I have thought of no other man but Tylar Lane. Even when I first had these ... these whatever it is that I feel for Jake, I wouldn't even consider that they might mean something. I kept my mind solely on Tylar and us as a couple even when I didn't know if he loved me like I loved him. Now I have to wonder if he ever loved me like I love him. I guess you can never really know how much someone loves you. All I know for sure is the love I have in me and I'm afraid I've measured everyone else's love by my own. I don't need to go around expecting that anymore. But, Jake said today that he was in love with me and then he said that if I was honest about my feelings that I would see that I was in love with him, too. But, he doesn't really know *that* either, cause *I* don't even know that. Jake said a lot of things. He accused me of being prejudice toward everyone, not just other men, but everyone who didn't measure up to some false standard I had created for Tylar. Agh! It's so frustrating to have no idea what to do. It's not like Jake is asking me to marry him or anything, he just asked me to get something to eat with him in town tonight. I told him I needed to be here with the family. But, something in me wants to go. I'm not engaged anymore. I am a free woman. But, what if Tylar came back?"

"Would you really want him back?"

"Pappy!" He pushed opened the door. "How long have you been standing there?"

"Long enough to know that you need to get cleaned up and call Jake. Go with him. It can't hurt anymore than sitting right here going on and on about it. Forgive me, Abigail, but I have to suggest this to her. Lacey, I know someone who faced just what you're going through who has a lot of wisdom. You need to go and talk to her. She would find it a privilege to listen and to give you some advice. She asks me every time I see her if there is anything she can do for you. Now there is. In the morning go and see Sunshine. She will be able to shine great light on your dilemma. In the meantime, go call Jake."

"Pappy I couldn't do that. How embarrassing to call him and tell him that I've changed my mind. It would be like me asking him out on a date."

"Sometimes you women are just too silly for your own good. I don't see a problem with a young girl returning a man's phone call."

"He didn't call me, Pappy. He asked me in person and I told him I needed to be with the family."

"I heard all that. And the reason I did is because Jake called here asking to speak to you and Hattie said you were in here talking with your Mother and that she would have you call him when you were finished. I came looking for you to give you the message and the rest, as they say, went in these tired old ears and gave me new hope for romance. I just might turn on the old jukebox when I get home and twirl Mrs. Hawthorne around the kitchen floor. By golly, I think love is in the air. Now, go call him and let me visit with your Mother while you get cleaned up. You look a sight. He must have it bad for you, Punkin, to leap out and kiss a woman in overalls with a wrench in her pocket."

"I had it in my hand!"

"I call that brave."

I was nervous about calling Jake, but I was curious about these feeling I had for him so I dialed the number. Sally answered the phone. "Lacey! Any change with your Mother?"

"You know what, Ms. Sally, I think I did notice her have a reaction about something I was telling her, but I can't remember what it was that I was saying at that time. But, she may have just needed some water."

"Well, just keep talking to her."

"Ms. Sally, is Jake there? Pappy said he called and I wanted to return his call."

"Yes. Hold on while I get him to the phone. It was nice talking to you. Call me if you need us for anything."

"Yes, ma'am, I will. Thank you."

It seemed like forever before Jake came to the phone. "Hello?"

"Hi, Jake. It's me, Lacey."

"Hello beautiful. Have you changed your mind about supper tonight?"

"Maybe."

"I'll be over in five minutes to convince you."

"No, Jake. I have to clean up and put on some clean clothes."

"That means you've changed your mind."

"Okay, yes. I've changed my mind."

"And you would love to have supper with me?"

"Yes. I said I changed my mind."

"No, no. Tell me you would love to have supper with me or I will be over there in two minutes to get you to say it."

"Jake! What are you doing? What difference does it make if I say I've changed my mind I will go to supper with you . . ."

"You would *love* to go to supper with me."

"Jake!"

"Because if you say you would love to go to supper with me and you bring that Tylar guy up I will be able to remind you that it is I whom you said you would love to be with tonight, not him."

"I would argue that it was the supper part that I was loving."

"And you would be lying, cause I'm taking you to the worst place in town to eat."

"Jake! Please don't do that. I would never forgive you if you made me suffer through a meal inferior to Hattie's soup. But, if I'm honest, it wouldn't matter where we ate 'cause I would love to just be with you tonight."

"And no mention of Tylar. I'll be there in an hour?"

"I'll be ready."

chapter eighteen

I took a bath and scrubbed my hands trying to get the black grease off the skin. I had most of it, but the nails revealed what I had been doing with my time. I stood in front of my wardrobe looking for something to wear that did not remind me of Tylar. There wasn't anything. Everything in there was bought because Tylar would have approved. I wanted to pull the overalls back on so I could be that little girl I was before I ever met him. I thought about calling Jake and telling him I just wasn't ready for this and maybe I would be in a few days once I had time to go shopping. Then I thought of borrowing something from my Mother, so I put on my robe and went to her room again. She wore simple designs with earth-toned colors and I welcomed the simplicity. Tylar had always liked me in bright colors and expensive lace. I chose a forest green skirt with a simple tan blouse. My tan and brown saddle oxfords finished off the outfit.

I was ready a little bit early so I spent the time going over what Jake had said while we were in the barn and I reached for his rose in my drawer and saw the box that housed the bracelet he had given me. "I can move on, too, God." I pulled the box out and opened it looking at the bracelet and marveling at the thought Jake had put into the gift. "I could at least show him some respect by wearing it tonight and try and make up for how I've treated him." I put it on and sat looking at myself in the mirror, at my auburn hair and green eyes and wondered why anyone would want to be with such a creature. Thank God the freckles had faded now that I kept a hat on when I was out working in the sun. A spotted leopard was what Jake had called me once. Oh, how I miss those days.

I heard his car pull into the yard. "Am I ready for this? I don't think I've ever been on a real date before. God, help me have fun tonight and not think about Tylar at all. I need to have this if I'm ever going to be able to forgive myself."

"I hadn't really noticed the time when you said you would be for me in an hour. We have left quite early for supper."

"Well, Lacey, I thought I would take you into Brevard. I know a lot more about where to eat there than I do here since I spend so much time there. Also, I wanted to have you all to myself and way too many people know you here. I don't want to share you with anyone."

I reached over and took Jake's hand. "Do you already have a place picked out?"

"I do," and he smiled at me. "Somewhere that we can have some privacy, but the owners know me well. I called them earlier and told them to be expecting us. They're excited to meet you."

"Me, or just your date?"

"No," and he shook his head. "You. They know all about you."

We pulled up to what I would have called a cabin with a sign that said *Mancini's*. Jake said the people who own it had migrated from Italy and they built it in a style to remind them of home.

"Is this what a chateau looks like?"

Jake laughed, "Hardly, Beautiful. It's more like the barn that those with a chateau would keep their animals in. This is not a wealthy family at all, if you measure wealth by money. They are very wealthy in love and charm. This is where they lived when they first came here fifty years ago or so. Back then the restaurant was in the front of the house and the living quarters in the back. They had small children and as their family grew, they built up there and made this whole place the restaurant." Jake pointed to a hill behind the restaurant where a home was built behind some trees.

"How do you know so much about these people?"

"I work here on the weekends to help pay for my food during the week at school. They love me like family, so don't be surprised if they hug you and kiss you all over, it's the Italian way."

"Are they even open yet?"

"No, but I have a key if I need to use it to get in. They're all in the back cooking, I can promise you that. Concetta is baking bread and Giovanni is making some type of antipasto special just for you."

I had never heard of antipasto or names quite like these and when Jake opened the door, I stepped into a new world. It was chilly inside, but not cold. It was far from cold. There was a warmth so welcoming that you didn't notice the chill for long. The lighting was dim even though they used electric fixtures and the dark wood walls gave a red glow throughout the room. A woman of years came from a closed door at the back wearing a red apron that she was untying as she entered the room. "Giovanni, come quickly. Our boy Jake has arrived with his beautiful Lacey." She walked towards us as a small dark haired man came from the same door.

"Ah, my Jake has finally brought you to see us. You are more lovely than he had expressed. You must come to me," and he took my hands and kissed me on both sides of my face as the woman did the same to Jake.

Then the woman stepped between us and said, "Let me have a look at her. You are right, Giovanni," and she took my face by my jaws and squeezed, "she is more lovely than I expected. Although, my boy Jake is too handsome to settle for just any, so your heart better be three times your looks."

The man spoke in Italian I supposed and then said, "Concetta, let the girl in the door before you judge her. We have been anticipating your arrival with fresh bead and cheese, antipasto and a fine Bistecca Floentima for your main course."

"Are your ready to eat something now, Jake? Of course you are; a growing boy is always ready to eat. Come sit down, I will get you some bread."

"Concetta, give the boy a moment to come in and take his coat off. Take his hat and I will show Lacey around. You can pick out the table where you would like to sit. This, my son, will tell you what a woman has in mind."

I smiled at Jake and said, "We haven't seen each other in some time so I guess somewhere out of the way would be nice."

Giovanni winked at Jake and said, "I have the perfect table for you. Please, this way." He moved to the side with his arm extended pointing around the fireplace towards a room in the far corner. He mumbled to Jake, "She is wise. We already prepared this room for you two. It is Concetta's room for lovers."

"We are far from that, Gio."

"Yea, but maybe it will bring a fresh desire for you both."

"I'm afraid I have *too* much desire and she has very little. Maybe we can just find quiet and ..."

"Of course, Jake. We will see to it that you have lots of privacy. I will have to keep Concetta busy with the baking."

The room was filled with landscape paintings of what I assumed was Italy. They were framed in massive wooded carved frames painted or gold leafed. The art work was beautiful and it gave you a feel of where these people were from. The paintings in the other room were religious; all representations of Jesus and his life on earth.

"These paintings are quite beautiful, Mr.... ."

"You call me Giovanni, my Father is Mr. Mancini and I make those who I don't like call me Mr. Mancini. Those I do business with call me Mr. Giovanni and beautiful ladies like yourself call me Giovanni or just Gio, like your man, Jake."

"I call him ... " and she spouted off something in Italian holding her empty hand up in the air with her fingers pressed together.

"Ah, ah," Giovanni said and kissed his wife just before she placed the tray with a loaf of bread, a dish with something red and asparagus wrapped in some type of meat on our table.

"For you, my son, and your lovely young lady. Antipasto."

"This looks wonderful, Mrs. Mancini, Jake told me ... "

"Ah ya ya, you cut me, Miss Lacey. My mother-in-law is Mrs. Mancini. We have only known who each of us are for a short moment, but surely I have made you welcome, eh?"

"Of course you have."

"Then call me Concetta."

"Yes ma'am, Concetta. Thank you for the antipasto. Which is the antipasto?"

"You tell her, Jake, I have to check the Florentina. Come Giovanni, we leave them now. Enjoy."

Jake pulled a chair out for me to sit down just as someone in the other room started playing a violin. "Oh my, this is so special. I can see why you would want to be here on the weekends."

"I would rather be with you and my family, but this is the next best place. That's Luciano playing the violin. He is married to Eleno. He is the youngest child of Gio and Concetta. They have three children who all work here. Sergio is the best cook out of Gio, Giovanna, Sergio's wife, and himself. He comes up with the recipes. Catari bakes with her mother. Eleno helps me serve and seat everyone, and Luciano plays the violin and takes the money when people are leaving. I've wanted to bring you here for a long time. I knew you would like it."

"I love it, Jake. I just wish I knew something about Italy so I would feel some kind of connection. Like this food. I feel so silly not knowing which is the antipasto."

"They all are! Antipasto means 'before the meal' in Italian. It's like our appetizers. Concetta says you must have something that will wake up the taste buds so you will have a good appetite for the main course. This is a sun-dried tomato spread to put on the bread and these are asparagus rolls. Usually you just get one antipasto so you don't over eat before the main part of the meal, but Concetta knows I can eat a lot and she wants to spoil you a little."

"What's around the asparagus?"

"There is some type of cheese. Italians love cheese and pesto, I don't know all that's in this one, but I promise there is olive oil, rosemary and sage with some other things and this is prosciutto."

"It looks like dried beef."

"It could be. Taste it. It's very good."

Jake sliced the bread and spread some of the sun-dried tomato spread on the bread while I tasted the asparagus. "Oh my heavens. If this is any indication of the meal, my taste buds are awake. This is fabulous."

"Here, open up." I took a bite of the bread Jake was holding out to me. "Um, that's good too, but this is wonderful. They're quite good together. Most of the time when things have so much flavor I don't like them mixed, but this is good."

Jake was sitting with his arms resting on the table watching me eat. "Why aren't you eating?"

"I'm enjoying this moment watching you."

"Well, get over it and eat or I will go and get Concetta."

"Yes ma'am. I wouldn't want you to do that just yet."

"I should because I want to ask her about these paintings."

"She will tell you they are of her beautiful homeland in the Tuscany valley. And that she is not a descendant of the Etruscans that some say lived there during the Roman Empire or some time way back when."

"And why is that significant?"

"I'm not sure, but she seems to think they were backward people and Sergio says no one would think she was an Etruscan because there are none living today, but she seems to think it would be a disgrace to be a descendant of these people. She says they had too many gods and that there is only one God and He was jealous so even though they were thought to be brilliant people they have suffered greatly because they did not know the true God. Probably some truth to that if it's so that they don't even exist today. Kind of like the Babylonians. You never hear of any of those guys walking around."

"No, I guess not. I haven't really thought about that before. Oh my, Jake. Just think of all the people who believe in all kinds of gods and don't worship the God of this universe. They could slowly disappear, too, if God turns His back on them. Sometimes the thought of how many lost people there are in the world takes my breath away. I'm so glad I know where I will be if I wake up dead. Just think what it would be like to try and sleep at night without that."

"I heard your Pappy had purchased part of your house to help the children at Willow Creek."

"He did. Mr. Frank is going to add a dormitory to the right wing of the house. He's building two stories with bedrooms upstairs and the school downstairs. It will be a few months before they can start on that." It got quiet and I was thinking about Tylar in the living room.

Jake reached out and opened his hand in front of my plate. I put my hand in his and he said, "It was my rule, so I guess I can break it..."

"What rule was that, Jake?"

"The one where we don't mention Tylar. Well, I can, but you can't."

"And why would you want to bring him up?"

"I have no idea, but I'm sure he's bound to come up if only in your mind, and if he does I can plead my case and tell you again why he's all wrong for you."

"Tonight I went to get dressed and I noticed that everything in my wardrobe I bought because he would like it. Bright colors and frilly lace that I have never been comfortable with. I thought about what you said and there might be some truth in it. I had to go borrow something from Mother to wear."

"There's a lot of truth to what I said, but I will leave it at that for now. I must say that you look more beautiful tonight than I have ever seen you. This color blouse compliments your hair and brings out your eyes. Those bright colors seemed to overpower the parts of you that make you stand out in a crowd."

"You mean like hide my carrot top and my leopard spots?"

"A small boy so enamored by your beauty he was driven to cruelty so he could cover his lust."

"You have always done that for me."

"What?"

"Made me laugh away my imperfections."

"One man's imperfections are another's perfections. You could laugh because you've always known that I was crazy in love with you."

"No, I just think you're funny."

"Ah, speaking of perfect, perfect timing, Eleno. I would like for you to meet Lacey Rutledge. This is Eleno Mancini."

"Oh Miss Lacey, Jake has told us so much about you, but he did not describe you well enough. You are more beautiful than he said. We are so glad you could come and be with us."

"Thank you, El . . . le."

"E'-lee-no. Jake calls me Leenie. It's easier. You may too."

"Thank you, Leenie. I am so glad Jake brought me here to meet all of you. The food is wonderful, the music, the ambience, I love it all."

"Well, now you have to try the Bistecca Florentina. I will tell you what it is so you will know. Jake cannot remember all this yet. It is the best meat on the T-bone steak grilled lightly, but a little more than we usually do it because Jake likes his more done than Italians. Then we cut it and serve it on arugula with course ground pepper, sea salt and dribble the olive oil on the meat. These are saltare vegetables, artichoke, and the green beans with roasted hazel nuts. Mother has some carrots cooked in Marsala wine if you would like some of those too, Jake."

"Um, I would love some."

"I told her you would. I will bring them to you, is there anything else I can get you?"

"Some more bread."

"I'll be right back."

"Thank you."

"Now *she* is charming. And if she wasn't married I might be jealous."

"Hmm, I should have left that part out of my story."

Jake thanked God for our meal and for our time together and then for me. That was nice. The steak was like nothing I had ever fixed for dinner. I was sure I would never want to prepare a meal again after being so enlightened as to what food could taste like. Leenie brought more bread and the carrots. Pappy would have loved the carrots.

"We could bring him sometime."

"Nanny would think it was way too extravagant and pick at the food. She's changing a lot these days. Probably no more than all of us, it's just very noticeable in her. She just doesn't have that determination that was so evident in her eyes before. Maybe tonight Pappy can make her feel better. He was going home to sweep her off her feet and dance the night away, so he said."

"That sounds like fun. Have you ever gone dancing?"

"You know Tylar never took me dancing. Oops. Sorry."

"You owe me a dance for that."

"Don't be silly, I don't know how to dance well enough. Although, I have a dress, had a dress, that I always though would be perfect for someone who did know how to dance."

"So are you never going to wear those clothes again?"

"Maybe to feed the chickens. I had never thought about my wardrobe being affected by my thoughts of . . . you know."

"It's okay, say his name. I'll get two dances. Lacey, everything about you has been affected because of him. I remember a girl who would have died before putting on a dress. And I know girls become ladies and ladies become women and they put on a dress, but the dresses you wear are not who you are, they were who he is. But, that didn't really matter because you were still more beautiful than the dress. When's the last time you went fishing? Until today when was the last time you got your hands dirty? You had become exactly what Tylar told *all* of us his wife was going to be. A woman who would never have to work again, living with a nanny raising her children so she would have time for the deeds of high society. You were headed to that place you loath, dangling that silver spoon you said you didn't like the taste of. All to please a man who couldn't see that you didn't need to be anybody different than you are."

"I may have come too far away from that girl, but I would have never let someone else raise my children. And I must admit that I do enjoy the luxuries I was born with even if I don't take advantage of them all. I don't think I can go back or find her again. It all seems so childish or something. I can't put my finger on it."

"Unless you become like one of these children you'll not see the Kingdom of God. I think it took you so long getting filled with the Holy Ghost because you wanted God to fill you in a dignified manner. Or maybe deep down inside you thought that Tylar wouldn't approve. Unfortunately, I have not received the Spirit, *yet*! But, I have prayed and prayed. I think something is blocking it from happening or maybe something else. Maybe it's just not God's time for me. But for you, I think that until you went to a place where other people seeking the same thing were, who were not the crazies that the 'dignified' are so ashamed of, you couldn't let go enough to let God have His way with you. Can you see any of this that I'm saying to you?"

"I can. I'm ashamed that I can, but I can."

"You don't have to be ashamed, be thankful that you have seen the truth. You are a girl with passion and fire and a desire to help others. You have been sitting at home waiting on Tylar Lane to give you a scrap of his time. When's the last time you visited the government project? Tylar tried over and over to stop you from going out to Little Africa. I think he built this home to have a place to house his little bird and show it off when it was an asset to him; it looks like God wants to use it to glorify Himself. Homeless, parentless children. Do you see a pattern at all with what God does in your life? Pappy told me he asked you to think about taking the position of headmistress at the orphanage. I hope you are considering it. Those children could use your wisdom and those boys need to know how to put a radiator in a tractor. I'm afraid I don't even know how to do that."

"Yes you do. You just haven't done it, but you know how. Anyone who can study what you study and make straight A's doing it can change out a radiator."

"So far that's just book knowledge. I haven't removed someone's spleen or anything like that."

"But you know how."

"Well, I guess I do at that. Would you be willing to be my first try?"

"I like my spleen very much thank you."

Leenie popped her head into the room. "Do you need anything else right now, Jake?"

"Is the dining room full tonight?"

"Not at all. We have only four tables right now."

"I thought I would cash in on a dance Miss Rutledge owes me and I wondered if there was room near the fireplace for me to cut a rug with her."

"I not know about cutting rugs, but there is room for dancing, but it might be better for you right in here. I will have Luciano come to this side of the room closer to your door so you can have privacy in here."

"Oh, Leenie, if he convinces me to dance it will be in here, because I'm afraid I am not a dancer."

"Jake is good dancer, he will show you how. His friend is a very good dancer, but he is a playboy. Jake is not like that. He is very nice and patient. You will see."

"What is his playboy friend's name?"

"He is that boy who went to school with you, Jake. What was his name? I not remember."

Jake hesitated looking directly at me.

"I'll help you out, Jake. I bet his name was Tylar Lane. Is that right, Leenie?"

"Yes, that is the name. Do you know him, too?"

"I thought I did. Jake was just talking about him, but turns out I was thinking of someone else."

"I will get Luciano and then Mother has Pecorino Tuscano with honey for after your dancing," and she left the room.

Jake and I sat looking at each other for several minutes. There wasn't anything to say and I just wanted Luciano to come closer so he could drown out what I was feeling and I could dance.

"It wasn't my place to tell you, Lacey."

"I don't suppose it was. I guess that makes two lies he's told me. The first that I know about is that he would never leave me and the second he told me just before he left me, after he tried to convince me to . . . give him what our relationship had been missing. He said that unlike the other guys at school he saved himself for me."

"I don't know that he didn't. But, he gave himself opportunities to be unfaithful. He would have never shared that with me if he was. He knew how I felt about you."

"You told him?"

"Oh yes. He knew. But, he also knew that I wouldn't hurt you and as long as you were in love with him anything against him would have hurt you." It was silent again as we simply stared at each other. "And we weren't going to talk about him."

"And why are we, Jake? I hear music. I don't think we should let it go to waste, but you will have to help me."

"I will be glad to." He reached out his hand to mine and squeezed. Then he stood and walked to the side of my chair and pulled it out as I stood and met him.

"We will do a simple box step first. You know that don't you?"

"It's been a while. Pappy taught me."

"Just follow me. Put your left hand here," and I placed my hand on his shoulder, "and hold this hand." He lifted his left hand up and I placed my right hand in his. "When I step back you step forward with the leg in front of the one I use. And then over and down and back and down and over and down. That's it, you remember."

We danced to the song Luciano played and Jake turned me twice before it didn't feel awkward any more. We laughed and I enjoyed his attention. The song was over and I was a little winded and started to the chair when Jake said, "I'm not ready to let you go just yet. I know I said one dance, but I meant to say a night of dancing."

"I can't dance like that again right yet. I need a rest."

"And so do I. Play something slow, Luciano. Come here, Lacey. We can move slow so you can rest, but we will keep our heart rate up so we don't get sleepy. If I don't do something after I eat a big meal like we just had I get sleepy if I sit down."

There was no way I could fall asleep even if I had eaten the whole cow because my heart had been racing since he kissed me in the barn. "Even with my company?"

"I can't imagine, but I don't want to take the chance." He pulled me to him close looking over my shoulder with his chin very close to my ear. "I'm so glad to see the bracelet make its way out of the box. Thanks for wearing it."

"You're welcome. Thank you for giving it. I wish I hadn't taken it off after the day you put it on."

He pulled my hand up to his face and kissed my wrist then laid my hand around his neck running his finger tips down the back of my arm and resting his hand at my waist. "Pretty soon the news will be out that you are no longer engaged and that Tylar has left town. Your porch will be filled with possible suitors looking to steal a moment with you. I know that you will want to explore the possibilities and I certainly can't fault you for that. I would just like to ask that you remember this night and if there is anything that I could do to make it better, will you tell me?"

"And let you become me?"

"How's that?"

"Wanting to change so that you win my love? First of all, not wanting to let it out that you are a rarity in that there are no other boys, *men*, who have ever shown me the slightest interest so there is nothing for you to worry about there. And second, this night has been perfect. I wouldn't change one minute of it, and you have been a perfect gentleman."

"I happen to know of seven or eight fellows who have told me personally that if you weren't so frighteningly beautiful they would have asked you on a date years ago. Now that they have grown some and are much braver, I'm sure you will get a call or a visit. Tylar just happened to be at the right time at the right place when he met you and you helped him out a lot by talking to him."

"I talked to you."

"Yeah, but I was stupid. I was sure that you were just wanting to be my friend and I didn't want anyone to think I was weak in the knees so I teased you shamelessly thinking I would get over whatever feelings I was having for you. But, they have only grown stronger and deeper. At times it's impossible to study. I just want to go home. Right now I feel like I am at home and it's just because you are with me. Working here will be easier now that you have been here, but I don't know if I will be able to work for days dreaming about tonight."

"Then I will have to come more often so there will be too many memories for you to focus on one."

We had almost stopped moving when Jake turned his head, looking at me. I kept my eyes on my fingers looking back at me from the top of Jake's shoulder. He moved in closer to my ear and said, "I want you to be mine, my girl," and he leaned his face against mine, "I have no right to ask and I know you have so much to deal with right now, but I have to let you know how serious I am about you, about us. Can you think about us at all?"

I closed my eyes trying to hold steady in spite of the numbness that came over me the moment his face touched mine. I nodded my head and laid my forehead against his neck. He held me tighter in his arms and our dancing turned into embracing. "I love you, Bright Eyes, and I will wait till the day you can say the same thing to me. There is no pressure, I just want you to know what I'm thinking," and he kissed the side of my face.

The rest of the evening was better than the beginning in that we didn't talk about Tylar again and I didn't think about him either. Leenie, Catari, Gio and Concetta came into our room and danced with us while Luciano played, as I called it, Italian folk music for nearly an hour. By then it was getting late and Jake needed to get me back home. I wondered to myself why, because there was no one there to make me adhere to a curfew, but I had a sense of responsibility that had been taught to me from early on and I had to set an example for my siblings by coming home at a decent hour. How easy it would have been to have stayed out with Jake till dawn, but I had enough respect for both of us not to get caught up in the moment.

We said our goodbyes to the Mancinis and I told Catari that I had a younger brother named Willie who I was sure she would enjoy meeting sometime even though she was a year older than he, but she seem very shy about meeting boys. Willie needed someone who would do most of the talking. Jake said she would once she got to know you. We drove back to the house and Jake pulled the car over to the shoulder of the road a ways from our drive and stopped.

"Lacey, I can't take you back quite yet, I hope you don't mind, I just wanted a few more minutes to say goodnight, alone. I bet Pappy and Nanny are waiting at the window for your arrival."

"Oh, I bet not. Pappy had plans with Nanny tonight, I hope."

Jake bent his knee and pulled his leg up onto the seat turning to look at me as he put his arm on the back of the seat and around my shoulders. "I've wanted to thank you for the night of your Father's funeral when you let me lie in your lap and cry like a baby. Thank you for not paying me back for all the cruel things I said to you through the years. You could have told the world what a mess I was."

"No more than I was. You were too genuine in your grief for me to make fun of you."

"Well, nevertheless, you could have and I would have been served right, but that's what makes you different," and he placed his hand to my face rubbing my cheek with his thumb. Slowly he leaned toward me, watching me, as if he was making sure I wouldn't stop him. My eyes darted from his eyes to his lips as I waited his arrival. At that moment he was more handsome than anyone I had ever laid eyes on and he was within an inch from my face. The air was getting warmer around us and I had to reach up and touch his face to let him know that I wanted him to kiss me. His lips were soft and moist as his lightly touched mine, something I hadn't noticed earlier that day as I was so caught up in the unexpected moment. But, this time I had been anticipating his kiss and I was determined to remember every move he made, how we touched and then pressed our mouths together, how he smelled and the warmth of the air he breathed out his nose onto my skin. He was far from forceful, far from demanding, and far from Tylar. He was, however, dangerous. I could crawl in his arms and let him take me as far as he wanted to go and be depleted of any strength to resist him. Praise God, he had the strength for both of us.

He kept his hands on my face and around my neck till he finished kissing me then he got back under the steering wheel and drove to my house. I fell back onto my seat. As I had told him, Pappy's truck was gone and my sisters and brothers had not even thought to turn the porch light on for me as Mother and Pa would have. Their lights were on in their rooms and the first floor was dark except for a light in the hall outside of mother's and Hattie's bedrooms.

We walked up on the porch and Jake kissed me again. "Thank you for going tonight. I know it wasn't easy for you. I also know that all of this is a bit soon for you, but I can't take the chance that you will get away again."

"Jake, I'm going to tell you something, but don't tease me or this might be our last date."

"Then you know I will promise not to tease you. But, I'm sure at some point I will, years from now of course."

"Jake!"

"Just being honest. I'll stop, tell me."

"For a long time now there's been something going on inside of me whenever we're together."

"Like what? Describe it to me."

"I don't know like what. I've never felt it before with anyone, but even as far back as the night I ran into the goat fence in your back yard, but the strongest times were in the mud room when you gave me this bracelet and even that day out in front of the school by the tree, but other than tonight the time it was the strongest was when you held the charm on the necklace that Uncle Marty and Joan gave me? The back of your hand was barely touching my neck and I had electricity, but I've never felt electricity, but something so jolting I was shaking all inside, but I was frozen, and I wanted to scream out for you to stop it and go away."

"Is that how you felt tonight like you wanted me to stop, stop holding you, not kiss you?"

"No, no, Jake. Not like that. No, I just hadn't ever felt that way and it was frightening like when you're about to step on a roller-coaster that you've never been on. You can't wait to ride, but you are having anxiety because it's the unknown. Plus, there was him. Tonight I never thought I wanted you to stop because you kissed me already in the barn and even though the feeling was definitely there, I didn't die or something so I wanted you to do it again. I wanted to kiss you without the fear so I could remember everything about it. I've never felt anything like this with Tylar. Maybe because he was so familiar to me being with me all the time from such an early age, I don't know, it's just different with you and I wanted you to know that I couldn't think about seeing someone else when you make this happen to me. Now, if a young man comes up on my porch and he makes me have goose bumps and lightning, I might have ... "

"No you won't." He took me by the waist and pulled me in looking so deep into my eyes he made mine water up. "I won't ever let you forget this if I have to drive back and forth to school everyday just so I can remind you. Do you feel it now?"

I nodded.

"Good. Thank you for letting me know. That's just what I need to keep you wanting more."

He took advantage of the fact that we were alone, and no one had turned on the light, and kissed me again. "I'll be by in the morning before I go back to class to give you another one of those. Now be ready."

"What time?"

"I told you I get up before the sun so I can be at the early classes."

"So what time is that?"

"I'll be by here at five thirty."

"That doesn't give me much time for beauty sleep."

"You don't even have to dress or get woke up. Just meet me out here at five thirty in your house coat and then you can go back to bed."

"Okay." He started walking down the steps still holding my hand.

"Good night."

"Good night."

Then he popped back up the steps and kissed me again. "I didn't even make sure the door was open for you," and he turned the knob of the door and it opened. "Okay. I would have worried about you being stuck out here trying to get one of them to come let you in if I hadn't made sure you could get in. Now, back to where we were." He took my hands and kissed each of them, then kissed me softly and hugged me before telling me good night again.

I watched him drive out of the yard and down the road till I saw his break lights come on once he reached his drive way. "I might just as well stay up all night. I know I will never get any sleep after this."

chapter nineteen

I met Jake on the porch with coffee and biscuits at five fifteen. Neither of us had slept because of the anticipation of our rendezvous. I knew he wouldn't be able to study well with no sleep, but he told me he wouldn't study well anyway because all he could think about was me. He laid out his plans for the day: a lab that morning and then another after luch, then he would be back to see me. The Mancinis were not expecting him to work that weekend. It seemed they knew a lot more about me than I thought, because Jake told me he had shared with them that he felt like he needed to be home for the weekend to spend some time seeing about our relationship. He would be leaving for Charleston, South Carolina, to study four more years right after Christmas, but I didn't want to let that fact sway me in one direction or another. I needed God to be my only motivator now. Tuesday and Thursday consisted of only one class first thing in the morning and he would be able to come home and see me then just like he had done the day before. Fridays had tests or labs so on lab days he would be a little later getting home than on test days. That day was a lab, so it would be about 4:30 before he would be home.

"That's perfect. I'll wait till Willie gets home from school to crank the tractor and you will be here just in time to see my handy work in motion. I'll fix supper for us."

"No, I'm taking you out. I have to be alone with you again."

"Okay. Where to this time?"

"Another surprise."

Jake left for school at about six o'clock. I missed him already, but I had just enough time to make sure that tractor was going to crank, go to town, buy a new outfit and see if Miss Sunshine had a little time to see me. I told Hattie where I would be and went to the barn to finish attaching the radiator. It was ready to crank when my brothers and sisters came out to tell me they were ready for school. "Hop on the tractor, Willie, and let see if she will crank."

"She? Everyone knows a tractor's a boy."

"Well, that makes sense, only a man could be so much trouble."

Retta said, "And take a woman to fix."

"You are so right, Retta. How did you find that out already?"

"Shoot, I learned that in kindergarten!"

I knew I had learned it early in my life, too, but I hadn't understood the full truth of that till Pa's death. I often wondered if mother had been awake if Pa would have had the desire to live for her even if he had been without his legs. Willie cranked up the tractor and Cole and I looked for any possible leaks around the hoses. Everything looked like it was working correctly. Retta and Abbie Lou were applauding me and telling me they knew I could do it while Cole and Willie were begging to take it for a ride.

"No, not now. You have to go to school and I have to go into town."

"Take us to school, Lacey?"

"What time is it?"

"Seven twenty."

"Oh please, Lacey? We haven't had much time with you lately."

"Ok, Abbie. Let me get cleaned up. You need to call Tula and let her know so she can have a little extra time at home this morning. She might like that."

They all ran into the house and I took some gasoline and tried to get the grease off my hands. Then I got dressed in another one of Mother's outfits, grabbed my old dresses off the chair in my room and met them out at the truck.

"Lacey, I think we need to have a car now that we are getting bigger. There's not enough room in here for all of us anymore."

"I think you're right, Willie. I'll talk to Pappy about that. Maybe he knows someone who has a car they are selling or a place to get a good deal. We need to watch our spending closer than ever right now."

"Are we broke, Lacey?"

"No, Retta. Why would you think that?"

"Well, Rebecca Hall's Pa was killed at the saw mill and she and her family had to sell their house and move in with their grandparents."

"That was a little different circumstance, Retta. Her Pa's business couldn't run without him. They didn't have any sons to work it and his saws weren't worth a lot of money because they were old and no one wanted to start a business with old saws. They were fine for him, but the men who worked there just got hired on somewhere else. Her Mother didn't know how to keep it running either. They are doing okay. Her Mother didn't have to go into town and get a job. They can make it with the money they got from the sell of the house for a long time if they invest it wisely and watch what they spend. That's what we are doing. Praise God Mr. Frank was willing to stay and run Pa's business. We aren't going to get near what Pa was bringing home, but Mayree is watching our interest. And Silas and Willie are doing a great job with the farm."

"But, once you and Tylar get married and move away will Mayree still look out for us?"

"Mayree will always look out for *all* of us, Abbie. God only knows what kind of mess our finances would be in if we didn't have Mayree. But, I won't be leaving home for a while."

"Why not? The house is finished."

"Cole, Tylar has moved to Chicago and I'm not going there. I'm staying right here with you."

"I'm glad. I will miss Tylar, though. Did you know he was moving to Chicago?"

"No. He didn't know till he left. It was sudden, but he needed to go."

"I knew we hadn't seen him in a long time. Is that why you've been so sad, Lacey?"

"Have I been sad? I didn't mean to be sad, but I guess . . ."

"I've been sad, but I'm feeling better."

"Hey, I think we all have had plenty of reason to be sad lately, but God's going to help us. We just need to stick together."

"Are you mad at Tylar for leaving?"

"Yeah, if I'm honest about it, I am a little. But I understand. No one needs to stop someone else from doing what they feel is best for them. Chicago is best for Tylar, and ya'll are what's best for me."

"In a few years I'm gonna work with Mr. Frank and build houses. Are you going to get a job, Lacey?"

"Maybe. We'll see what God says. I am still needed around here, aren't I?"

"You sure did fix that tractor."

"Well, look-a-there, I am worth my keep."

I dropped my siblings off at school and drove over to Pappy and Nanny's to see if I could catch him before he left for the bank. He and Nanny were eating breakfast when I went in through the back door.

"Good morning!"

"Come in, come in, come in! How nice to see you this morning. Were we expecting you?" Nanny looked at Pappy as if he had forgotten to tell her I was coming.

"No, Nanny. The children wanted me to take them to school today and I have some errands I need to run, but it's still early so I had some time and wanted to see my favorite Nanny. What did you two do last night?"

"Well, your Pappy came home with some notion that love was in the air after talking to you and he convinced me to go with him to that new restaurant in town where they have a big jukebox. Have you seen it?"

"No."

"Looks like a place where all the kids are going to end up hanging out, but last night there were several couples our age there. And we ate supper and danced a little."

Nanny seemed giddy and I teased her about the rosy color she had in her cheeks. Pappy just chuckled.

"They're having a dance tonight with a live band. They asked us to come back and tell everyone. They want a crowd for tonight I'm sure to encourage the band."

"That sounds like fun, Nanny. You should go."

"We might. I heard you had an interesting date last night."

"How did you hear that?"

"Your Pappy told me that Jake had called?"

"Oh, yeah, he did and we went all the way to Brevard for supper."

"Brevard? You would think that boy gets enough of that place and would want to stay around here."

"This place is where Jake works on the weekends. That's why we haven't seen him much lately."

"I bet we will now."

"Pappy! Not on the weekends I don't think. This restaurant is *so wonderful* and very special to Jake and the people who own it are like a second family to him. It's a really neat place. They are Italian and everything inside takes you to a foreign land. The food is like nothing I have ever tasted. I guess Italians are known for their cooking. Luciano plays the violin and we did some dancing of our own."

"I'm so happy for you, dear. You needed a night out with someone who would make you feel special."

"He did make me feel special, Nanny. And the Mancinis were expecting us and they fixed Jake's favorite dishes and some antipastos just for me. It was a night I will always remember."

"Does this mean you will be seeing Jake again?"

"Well, I will be seeing him tonight, but I have to talk to someone I think can help me with some decisions. I hope to talk to her today. So, we'll see."

"What does your heart tell you?"

"Oh Nanny, my heart is telling me way too much. That's why I'm going to talk to someone who has been where I am right now and may have some advice that will shine some light on what is best for me."

"What does God say?"

"Funny you ask that, Nanny. He hasn't told me one way or the other about Jake or Tylar, but He has told me to go and have a talk, so I'm going to do that."

"Can you tell us who you are going to talk to?"

"Well, no. I don't think too many people know that she's been through what I have and maybe she doesn't want them to know. She might not even want to talk to me about it, but I'm going to ask her anyway."

"Okay. That's alright, I understand."

"Can I use your phone to call her?" Nanny sort of looked at me as if she was hurt that I wouldn't tell her and then wanted to use her phone to call my misery friend.

"Yea, Punkin. Go into the hall and use that phone. There's more privacy."

"Thanks, Pappy."

I called Miss Sunshine and she was more than willing to spend some time with me, but she didn't think I should come to her house so we decided to meet out at *Lion's Hill* around twelve o'clock and I could show her the place and tell her about Pappy's plans. I told Nanny and Pappy about Willie suggesting we buy a car and asked them to help me pray about that. Then I drove into town to Irene's Dress Shop. This was the shop Penny had been purchasing her dresses from so I decided to drop off the dresses I didn't want anymore for her to sell for me.

"Lacey, your dresses are beautiful and they are of the finest workmanship. I'm afraid I don't have the clientele that can afford these. Why, these are Dior and Chanel."

"Ms. Irene, I need to change the direction I've been heading in and these dresses are reminders of that old direction. If I don't bring them here they will be taken apart and used for doilies, table clothes, rags or some other purpose. I would much rather know that someone else is getting some use out of them. Price them where they will sell to your clientele. God will bless me anyway, and we can bless someone else's day who may have never had the chance to wear something like this."

"Are you sure?"

"Very sure. I'll drop by next week and see if they are selling. I may have some other things, too. Pa has a closet full of beautiful suits and dress overcoats," and I saw the coat I had purchased that matched the going away outfit I had bought, " ... that I'm sure someone could use." I threw another dress on top of it trying to stay on task. "And Mother is so thin now when she wakes up she won't be able to wear them anyway."

"Do you want me to call you when something sells so you can come by and pick up your money?"

"No, I can wait till the end of next week. Thank you for being so considerate, though."

"Oh, no ma'am. Thank you, Miss Rutledge."

"Lacey, just call me Lacey."

Okay, thank you, Lacey."

I went to Montgomery Wards to shop for some simple tops and skirts. I decided to buy some pants, too. I was much more comfortable in a pair of pants, but Tylar had asked me not to wear them so much and it had been years since I had bought a new pair. I bought a pair of denim jeans to wear around the house. All the girls were wearing them rolled up around the bottom and they wore them everywhere. I just wasn't sure I was ready for that big of a change. I bought three pairs of pedal pushers, two in pastel and a gold pair with blouses that matched. One blouse was white with baby blue polka dots, one striped with white, pink, green and yellow, a cardigan sweater in white that had the same strip as the blouse bordering the placket, and a scoop neck, three-quarter length sleeved, white sweater to wear with the gold ones. I bought a poodle skirt that would match the white sweater because all the girls my age were wearing them, and Tylar would have hated that, and a scarf to tie at my neck that matched the color of the poodle. I picked out an evening dress that was simply black. Most all the evening dresses had full skirts with net petticoats, but this one had a straight fitted skirt and the top was strapless with bone suspension. It had a white velvet swing coat that was paired with it in the window so I got that too. If Jake took me back to Mancinis, I wanted to have something special to wear. I found a couple simple dresses that would be perfect for dancing and the lady at the store told me they enhanced the beauty of my hair color and made my eyes stand out so I knew Jake would like them, too. No hats, no beaded purses, but I did get a pair of black high heeled pumps to go with the evening dress and another pair in cream to wear with the pedal pushers and dresses. What I liked the best was a neatly pleated skirt that went with a cashmere sweater, but mostly I just liked the fact that I made choices that suited me.

I loaded the truck with the boxes the clerk had packed my clothes in and drove to "The Garden Patch" to pick up some lunch for Miss

Sunshine and me. When I came in the door I gave my order to the host who then told me to sit on a bench near the coat and hat racks and she would bring it to me. As I started to the bench I noticed Aunt Penny sitting just outside the open door to the porch with the four town busybodies: Mrs. Waldrop, Mrs Black, Mrs. Burton and Ms. Franklin. I knew this was not good. What would they have to talk about unless it was about me and Tylar and what if Ms. Franklin told Aunt Penny about seeing me with Miss Sunshine. Nanny was having such a good day I didn't want her to get a call from Aunt Penny stirring up trouble for Pappy. And he would be blamed for it as always, I was sure of it. I stepped around the tables staying close to the wall of the room till I got to the door opening where I could hear their conversation.

"Well, Penny, we heard he had found another girl, the daughter of a wealthy car manufacturer that Johnny Kale had introduced him to and he took Johnny's offer so he could be close to her."

"I assure you my niece knows nothing of that. He told her about buying the train yard in Chicago, but she is just too simple minded to see the opportunity before her. Serves her right to lose him to an heiress. I'm happy for Mr. Lane. He is too fine a man to be pulled down by a spoiled 'Grandpappy's Girl.' They would have never been happy. Do you know what those two are doing now?"

"Which two, Penny?'

"Jeremiah and Lacey, Dotty. They are turning that *grand* new home into an orphanage."

"That beautiful place that Mr. Lane built for Lacey?"

"*Yes!*"

"How on earth did Jeremiah get *his* hands on it?"

"He bought it from Tylar. That poor boy will be devastated when he comes back to visit and finds *bastard* children inhabiting that mansion. It's almost a slap in his face."

Mrs. Burton said, "And a slap in William's face, too, Penny. He was such a charming man. It broke my heart to lose such a wonderful asset to our community. How could his family have such a lack of consideration for him and his memory?"

"The same way they have no consideration for Alvin and I.

Letting his own son live in a house built for hired hands. You would think we were not family at all."

"But, Penny, my *dear*. You have a lovely home. It looks like it's a lot bigger than Jeremiah and Jo Rett's now that you've had all those rooms added on."

"Maybe in space it is, but it looks like a migrants' house with added rooms, there's no style to it at all and it's certainly no mansion. They never asked me, but they should have, I would have been glad to relocate to *Lion's Hill* and let the orphans have my house. That's exactly what it looks like, a house where orphans should live."

"What possesses Jeremiah, with all the money he has, to associate with the likes of bastard children?"

Ms. Franklin said, "Good breading is everything, Dotty, he may have been able to make some money in his life time, but if you look back into his past he did not come from good breading. The rain falls on the just and the unjust. It's just a shame that even with God doing all he can for that man he just can't get the love of the slums out of him."

I walked around the door and stood behind Aunt Penny smiling at the ladies, mostly Ms. Franklin. "Oh, my. Well, hello Lacey. How nice to see you."

Aunt Penny turned her head and looked at me. "What brings you into town?"

"I had some dresses I no longer wanted so I took them by Ms. Irene's so she could sell them for me. I decided to wear some of Mother's things now that she is so thin. Isn't the food here wonderful? I'm having a guest out at *Lion's Hill* today for lunch so I wanted to make it special by picking up some sandwiches."

"We were just wondering when you would be moving in."

"Well, Ms. Franklin, maybe you haven't heard the latest gossip, but I will fill you in on the truth. Tylar and I are no longer engaged. He has moved to Chicago. He's been given an opportunity he never thought he would have, but he's dreamed about it since his own Father was killed many years ago. He is purchasing a train yard in Chicago. I could not leave my Mother who, you may not have heard, is in a type of coma and has been since before the death of her husband, and might I add, the love of her life. I just couldn't take the chance that she would wake up and someone besides me tell her that her husband was dead. After all, his dying words to *me* were 'take care of your Mother and be with her when she wakes up.' So I know that, you being a caring woman yourself, Mrs. Burton, I know you understand that I couldn't bring myself to disrespect him by leaving my Mother after he had asked me to do this for him. So, as you can see it would not be wise for me to move into the house at *Lion's Hill* either, not right now. Tylar, without my knowledge, sold his part of our house to my grandfather because he needed the money to make a down payment on the train yard. I was torn not having any idea as to what Tylar would want to do, because even though I can't live there I didn't want to let go of this gift my Father had created for me. Now I don't have to let it go so I guess Tylar had my interest at heart. My Pappy has heard from our Lord as to what to do with the house. He has offered it to the children at Willow Creek orphanage, because they are closing that facility. It seems so like God, don't you think Ms. Franklin, that His heart would be set on little orphaned children. After all His own Son, Jesus, was looked upon by those who found that judging others was a righteous behavior as being nothing but a bastard raised by a carpenter in a slum town. Oh my, how wrong they were. Mighty things can come from bastard children and I intend to be right beside my grandfather offering them the very best that life has to offer. I hope that you will discuss this opportunity with the Reverend Burton. We will be taking donations of clothing and food and any other gifts God lays on the hearts of the churches of our community that will help make these children feel welcome. I'm excited about being a part of what God is doing, aren't you Aunt Penny? I know you have to feel as I do, thankful to be a member of a family that has God's blessings, and pure pride in a man so unselfish as our Pappy. Oh, I hate to run, but I see the waitress looking for me with my bag of sandwiches. I was supposed to wait over by the coats and hats, but when I saw you all having lunch I just had to come and stand by the door and listen to what you were talking about. I was hoping I would here something new and enlightening to share with The One I spend my day talking with, but seems like you had nothing to offer and there's nothing that you say that God doesn't already know anyhow, so He doesn't need me to report any of this back to Him. Besides, your information was

the road

all wrong. I hope that what I've shared with you will shine some light on your confusion. Good Day ladies." And I left for my lunch with Miss Sunshine wondering what they would do if they had *that* little bit of information.

Miss Sunshine was already there once I reached the house. I was thankful that it looked like we would be able to have our lunch and discussion alone. I thought after we had made our plans that there was a possibility that some of the workers might be at the house marking off the foundation for the new wing, but no one else was there. Miss Sunshine was sitting by the garden pool with her hat off, skirt pulled up and her face pointed in the direction of the sun.

"It's a lovely day, isn't Miss Sunshine? I have sandwiches, shall we eat out here or inside at the table?"

"How about right here. I was just enjoying the sun. It's been so long since I got my legs out in it. Hasn't the weather been odd this fall? It seems more like a spring day."

"Have you been here long? I ran into those old busybodies when I stopped to get the sandwiches. Ugh. They sure get my blood boiling, but I didn't let them see it."

"Who? That group that clings to Ms. Franklin and her gossip?"

"Those are the ones and it seems my Aunt Penny has joined them or maybe they invited her to their pow-wow just to get some juicy tidbits about me, Tylar and Pappy."

"I was sorry to hear about you and your Mr. Lane. Are you alright, dear?"

"I'm working on that. I have some other things going on besides all that stuff with Tylar and that's kind of what I wanted to talk to you about, I think? Pappy just said that you were the one I needed to talk to so that's why I invited you to meet with me. I can't thank you enough for coming all the way out here to listen to my problems."

"Oh my, child. I find it an honor and I wouldn't want to be anywhere else. So hand me that bag and I'll get our lunch ready and you talk. And don't be afraid to tell me anything. There's nothing that you can say that I haven't already heard or done and you don't have to worry about me, I don't belong to the town busybody's club."

"Thank God for that, and not because what I have to say is all that juicy, but because being a member of that group would not make you a good friend to me."

"Well, no matter what group I might be a member of, I hope that you will always see me as a friend to you, because you can trust that."

"Thank you."

"Now, get started, and pull your socks off and get some sun on those legs and feet."

As I was taking my shoes and socks off I began to tell Miss Sunshine all about Tylar, how we met, how I had wanted him from the first day I saw him and that Jake had always been in my life, too, even before Tylar, but nothing was between us except childhood. I told her how I felt when I was with Tylar and how I felt something so different, but stronger for Jake. I also told her that Jake had told me he was in love with me and always had been. I told her everything I could think was important and then I said, "Pappy overheard me talking to my Mother about some of this and he said I should see you, that you would have some wisdom to share so I called you."

"Are you thinking about going to Chicago?"

"That's what I'm confused about. I don't want to miss God if he wants me with Tylar, and He did put him with me for all these years and let our friendship develope into love and then go so far as to being engaged."

"Did you sleep with him?" I know I looked at Miss Sunshine sort of stunned, because I was. She must have felt she had to rephrase her question so she asked, "Make love with Mr. Lane?"

"No."

"But, you did get intimate with him?"

"We kissed and one time just as he was telling me he was moving to Chicago he was very passionate with me. Well, more passionate with me than usual, but I stopped him from ... from *violating* me or anything like that."

"Why was that?"

"Because, because that's just wrong."

"But, you were engaged to him. He was going to be your husband where he would have, *violated* you, as you put it once you were married."

"But, he was talking about moving and I couldn't go."

"And why is that?"

"Because my Mother needs me here and I promised my Pa I would be here when Mother woke up and I need to be the one to tell her about his death."

"Okay, let's move on to Jake. What is your relationship with him?"

"What do you mean?"

"Have you slept with him?"

I snickered and said, "No!"

"So why did you look so horrified when I asked about Tylar and with Jake you laugh?"

"I don't know?"

"Is it because you can't see yourself having that kind of relationship with Tylar, but you can with Jake and the question makes you blush, a sort of uncomfortable giddy?"

I had to think about that for a moment, but I seemed more confused so I just rubbed my head. "Maybe I'm just uncomfortable with this whole mess. I should hope that I would never succume to something God wouldn't want me to do. I guess I laugh because Jake makes me nervous. He makes me forget about what I know is right and wrong. It's like he sweeps me out of this world and nothing else matters but him. But, just for that moment. Oh! I don't know!"

"Could it be that with Jake you want something more to happen and that somewhat embarrasses you and all these years with Tylar you never wanted things to be any more than they were? Lacey, let me tell you a story, while you eat your sandwich, that might help you see clearer what is best for you." She handed me a sandwich and I sat across from Sunshine by the garden pool with my legs stretched out under the sun with my back leaned up against the concrete flower urn where I could see her face as she talked to me.

"When I was a small girl my family lived down on Brierwood Lane. Do you know where that is?"

I shook my head.

"Well, you shouldn't. No woman should live anywhere near that neighborhood, much less a child. It's not a nice place at all. There was a young boy, a few years older than me who I later found out was very much in love with me, but just smitten I guess when we were kids.

He was like a guardian angel sent just for me. I was raped three times before I was nine and once I felt safe enough to tell my friend he watched over me and kept it from happening again, until I was fifteen. That's the time his family found out that they had a wealthy Aunt who had died and left some money to them and they wanted more than anything else, even more than getting out of that neighborhood, to send their boy to college. So my friend left me with great distress, but I convinced him that I would be alright and if I had the chance to get out of there I would take it, too, so he should go for both of us. I thought that I was going to be fine because I was older and could stop anyone from raping me again, but I was wrong. His father, led by an old dog, found me beaten and left for dead in the woods out behind their house. That's where the man who did this to me caught me after I broke away and ran towards the only safe place I knew. I didn't make it.

"I didn't have any idea who it was, because he put a gunny sack over my head when I went outside to see why my cat was screaming. Although she died, my cat had enough in her to jump on his back after he put the bag over my head, which made him let go of me, but then he killed her. I probably hated him more for that than raping me.

"Enough of that. My best friend found out what had happened and after the first year of school he came back home to keep me safe. I was mortified that he was giving up everything for me. It wasn't right and it wasn't anything I had ever wanted someone to do for me. We just weren't taught how to give or how to receive. No one did either of those things in our neighborhood. Except my friend.

"A few years passed, he went to work in town earning lots of money because he was so smart and pretty soon he had moved his parents out of the neighborhood, hired me to help in his business and put the down payment on that house I still have today. I could have never done that without his help. Maybe I could have rented something for a few years and hopefully saved enough, but that would have left my parents back on Brierwood and there was no way I could leave them there."

Somehow I just couldn't see Miss Sunshine running a brothel

with her parents living with her so I asked, "How long did your parents live with you?"

"Almost two years. They both got sick with Typhoid Fever and died three days apart."

"I can almost say I know what you were feeling, but I don't."

"No, dear girl. You still have hope that your Mother has not left you. You hold on to that. You also have more family to support you and encourage you. Let them."

"Yes ma'am."

"So let me get back to my story before you think I'm one of those old ladies who goes on about nothing just reminiscing about hard times. Trust me, I am going to get to your problem."

"Wait. Can you tell me who this friend was?"

"Well, just a boy. I don't have permission from him to tell you his name."

"Because his name is Jeremiah Hawthorne?"

"Maybe."

"Well, how about we pretend his name is Jeremiah Hawthorne so you don't have to keep stumbling through looking for just the right words so as to not give it away."

"Lacey, please don't tell him you figured that out or go to him with a bunch of questions."

"Well, it might answer more than just a couple questions that I've had for a long time if you tell me it was my Pappy who was your friend, like why my Nanny has been less than friendly to you."

"She just doesn't understand our relationship. We are all afraid of what we don't understand. She doesn't mean any harm in it and I hold no grudge."

"Oh! I'm so glad you said that cause it's bothered me. So go ahead with the story."

"After my parents' death, Jeremiah was the president at the bank. I was his secretary and the owner wanted to sell the bank and your Pappy bought it. He and I were close."

"How close?"

"No. I never slept with him, but I loved him more than words could say, but I was stupid. I felt used, dirty, unworthy of such a wonderful man so I kept him at bay. I think he just knew too much about me, who I really was, and I was ashamed and I wanted to forget it. Jeremiah wanted to go back to the neighborhood and help others who wanted out of that life and I never wanted to talk about it or be associated with it again. One day a very handsome wealthy entrepreneur came into the bank with a proposition for Jeremiah to invest in his business and Jeremiah became his partner. We sort of wined and dined the man and I saw my chance to get out of town and away from all the misery that plagued me here. He would come in on the weekend and go back up north during the week. It wasn't long till he and I were meeting under the sheets and I was working on getting a ring on my finger, but what I hadn't bargained for was a pregnancy. He accused me of trying to trap him into marriage and he would have nothing to do with me or my child. But, he lied. He had lied about a lot of things. Turned out he was married and once my son was born he and a team of lawyers came with threats to ruin me and take my son. I was advised that he probably could. So because I had always been motivated by what I didn't have when he offered me eighty thousand dollars to keep quiet as to whose baby I had given birth to and to hand the child over to his father and his wife to raise; I took the money. The hardest part was that I loved this man. I had passion with him. He was forceful and dynamic and I felt wild when I was with him. I even thought that he would come back one day and get me and we would be a family. I was wrong.

"Your Pappy was so angry with me and I felt like the useless piece of trash that my Father had always said I was. I paid your Pappy back and paid off my house, bought beautiful new furniture and invested the rest in your Pappy's bank. Then I opened my own business by soliciting young girls from Brierwood Lane and bringing them into my home where they could get paid for what they were suffering from every night for nothing. I offered them a safe place to work, and room and board. They had never had anything like this before and not one has ever left angry with me for what I did for them, but if I could go back.

"After a couple years, your Pappy met a young girl that I think he truly loved and they married. I honestly can say that I died inside. Your Pappy has remained my friend after I started my own business and although he didn't approve at all, he didn't judge me or the girls.

He spent lots of nights hanging out in my kitchen playing cards with us girls and being a friend to all of us. Those days were going to end once he married.

"He begged me several times to reconsider the business and marry him and even though every time he touched me I melted, I couldn't forget where I had come from and the things that had happened to me. I loved him too much to be the wife of such a great man who would bring him nothing, but shame. I was also holding out hope that the father of my child would come back for me."

"You said you had two children. What happened to the second child and who was its Father?"

"This is supposed to be about loving the wrong man and letting the right man get away, not my history."

"Did you have a child with my Pappy?"

"No, honey. I already told you, nothing like that ever happened between me and your grandfather. I had a child by a customer. A man I met after your Pappy married his first wife. I didn't work the men, I just collected the money and made sure everyone was safe, but I was weak once your Pappy was gone and I started a friendship with one of the customers and soon it was more and then there was a child. A baby girl. He was married, and his wife had lost a child. The doctors said she would not live if she tried to have another. So that's what drove him out to my place, but I knew he was married when we started our affair. I couldn't have my daughter raised in the environment in which I lived, so her father and his wife adopted her. I don't know if his wife ever knew the truth of where the baby came from, although, she has been extremely kind to me. Jeremiah's first wife had died and he started coming around the house again. Just to see me, mind you. Jeremiah has never been a customer, let me make that clear. Well, I told him I had a baby girl who was living with her father and he acted like I had stabbed him in the heart. It just seemed like all I did was hurt the one person who ever truly loved me and I didn't know how to make it stop. So I told him I never wanted to see him again, that I could never love him and he needed to move on, but I was dying inside because that was the farthest from the truth. But, I was successful. He didn't come around anymore. I never got under the sheets with another man because every time I was with someone I wanted them to be Jeremiah and in my mind they were. But, then the morning would come and he wasn't there.

"I guess what I want you to see is some times someone is there for you that you don't think is what you want so you go seeking, without even knowing it, a thing you think is what you want, what will fulfill you, make you special. But, it won't. If you pass up stability, contentment, security, real honest love for passion and abundance you will never have anything. Passion fades, abundance gets depleted, but true love will rise above it all and be there at the finish line ahead of the rest.

"Someone once told me, 'It's just as easy to fall in love with a rich man as it is a poor man' and there is some truth to that. If you really want it bad enough you can make any relationship work. But, if there is a man who puts you before himself and everyone and everything else, and he loves who you are and never tries to change you into someone you aren't, you have found riches beyond any this world can offer. Don't let him get away. Don't chase after the riches of this world when you have something far greater in the palms of your hands. Even if you're not sure if you love him, it won't matter, you will. When you were born you didn't love your mother or your father, but because they loved you more than anything else, you couldn't help but love them back and want to be your best for them. All relationships are like that. If you grab hold to someone who doesn't put you first, but they have other things to offer, you will find your time spent with the things wishing you could make them love you. That's a life of heartache and way too much work."

We sat in quiet for some time, her basking in the sun and I thinking about Jake and Tylar. Jake was going to be a doctor, a humble profession, and Tylar was going to be a millionaire. Had I sought after him because I knew that? Cause I did know that. Anyone who was around him for even a minute knew that he had the personality and the determination to take him farther than anyone else had ever dreamed of going. But, that was what attracted me to him, his drive, his passion and Jake was more like Pa, more like Pappy in that he had compassion. He was tender and he had a vision to save lives and souls that was planted in his heart before he was born. I know Tylar said he asked Jesus into his heart, but he didn't seem to totally trust God like

Jake did. Jake and I had a spiritual connection that I never had with Tylar. I had to be very honest, Tylar wanted money and fine things and a wife to sport on his arm like a prize hunting dog on a chain. I could see that now, and I was ashamed of how wrong I had been and that I was willing to give up living to be a trinket. Thank you, God, for not letting me do something that would have brought me the shame that drove Miss Sunshine to push my Pappy away. I would never want to have to tell Jake, or any man that God might want me to marry, that I had not waited for him. Jake deserved a wife who shared those kinds of moments with just him.

I looked at Miss Sunshine and said, "So when did my Pappy forgive you for pushing him away and become your friend again?"

"Well, he stayed my friend; he just didn't come around the house. After all I was one of his best customers at the bank. But, years later we had some things come up that brought us close again. It should have always been that way for us and we knew it. He's my best friend, always has been and he always will be. Your Nanny knows that and she might not like it, but she's okay with it. She and I have talked and she knows how I feel and how your Pappy feels. He loves her very much and I could never get in the way of that. And I wouldn't want to. We have a different relationship now and it works nicely for all of us."

"Thank you for sharing with me."

"Thank you for calling me," and she put out her hand and I took it turning around putting my head on her lap. We laid in the sun just enjoying the quite whisper of the river in the distance and the warmth of the sun. I felt a connection to my Pappy's best friend and because I was in such great need of a woman in my life that I could talk to about such personal things and totally trust, I thanked God for sending her to me.

We must have fallen asleep lying stretched out on the ground next to the garden pool, because I was suddenly startled by the sound of a car driving into the drive. I popped my head up and saw Pappy's car making the turn up the hill.

"Who is it?"

I laid back down. "Just Pappy."

"Oh good, he can join us."

"Did you take a nap?"

"Yes, I think I did."

"Wonder what time it is?"

"I have no idea, but I bet that's what your Pappy has come to tell you."

I heard the car door slam on Pappy's car and I hope it was just him. Nanny would not like this. "Well, my, my. I don't think I have seen that much leg ... well, not in a public place."

"It was private till you got here. Good afternoon Jeremiah. Pull your britches up and get a little sun."

"I'm not sure I have the time girls. I just came out to tell Lacey what time it is. Don't you have a date with a certain Mr. Willie who wants to crank that tractor?"

"Oh, shoot. What time is it?"

"He's going to be home in about fifteen minutes. And then don't you have a date with Jake? Ya'll did get that worked out didn't you?"

"I told her all about my past sins and regrets, Jeremiah. If she chooses the wrong man it's not because I held anything back."

"Yes, Pappy, I have a date with Jake tonight and any other night he might find it in his heart to ask me. I just lost my way for a little while. I thank God that He will leave the ninety-nine to come after the one who has gone astray. Thank you for spending the day with me. I know why my Pappy calls you friend."

"You are so welcome. Any time and I do hope that we can spend some more time just sitting in the sun if nothing else."

"Me too. And we will. But, right now I have to go. Pappy I didn't even get to tell her about our plans for the house. You'll have to do that."

"She already knows. She's pledged to be our first supporter."

"Oh, Miss Sunshine, thank you for that."

"Lacey, will you please just call me Shine? You do know Sunshine is a nickname your Pappy gave me back when we were little kids. My real name is Joanie, but through the years the girls shortened my nickname to Shine. So can you call me Joanie or Shine? The Miss just doesn't seem to suit our relationship anymore. I think we are better friends than that."

"If you don't mind, I would like to call you Sunshine, because you have brought me sunshine today in more ways than one."

"I would like that."

I left the garden with Pappy sitting on the concrete bench and Sunshine still lying on the ground. I was happy that she had shared her story with me and that I had a clearer idea of what was best for me, but I was sad for her. Sad for my Pappy. If someone had asked me earlier that day if I could ever admire my grandfather more I would have said, no way. But I would have been wrong. As I got to my car I turned back to see my Pappy sharing something with the woman he had loved for years, but could not have. He was untying his shoes and pulling off his socks and by the time I cranked the car he had his pant legs rolled up and was seated down by the pool's edge. He seemed content just being her friend.

Tylar Lane was not like my Pappy or my Pa. He had left town without a word to me. I don't think those were the actions of a true friend. But, maybe he was like Sunshine and he had lost his way. I would have to be like my Pappy and not hold a grudge and let him know I could be a friend if I ever saw him again. For my life I needed the stability of Jake or someone like him. It was way too soon to make a lifetime commitment to anyone right now and Jake had lots more school ahead of him. It was just going to be nice having a very close friend to love and date and grow stronger with.

He and Willie were sitting on the porch when I got home. "Where have you been, Lace. I want to drive that tractor. Let's go."

"Hold on, little man. I got here first." Jake came out to meet me at the truck and hugged me. "You sure feel good to these tired old arms."

"You shouldn't stay out so late and then get up so early, Mr. Foresight. How are you going to take me out dancing tonight if you're all worn out from staying out late the night before?" I walked over to the other side of the truck to get the boxes out. "You two come help me. I have a new wardrobe that needs to find its way up to my room."

"Did you bring anything for me?"

"Yes, Willie."

"Not clothes?"

"No. In the bag. There's candy for you and the others. Now share." Willie grabbed the bag and ran off into the house with one of my boxes. "Take the box to my room."

"I will."

"Wow, Lacey. You did make some purchases."

"I took my dresses to Ms. Irene's today. She's going to sell them for me. I hope I get at least half what these cost me."

"Are you sure Irene's was the best place to take them? I could have taken them to Brevard and maybe gotten a little more?"

"Irene's is fine. God will bless me if someone who has never had anything so nice as those dresses are is able to buy one of them. We're doing okay and I shopped at Montgomery Wards so it's not like I spent a huge amount. Not like what I was spending on dresses. I got some simple things and some things Tylar Lane would hate, just because he would I'm ashamed to admit. But, I like them and that's what matters."

"You're absolutely right and I'm proud of you."

We put the boxes on the kitchen table and I fixed a glass of water for both of us. "So where else did you go today?"

"I went out to *Lion's Hill* and had lunch with, and if you tell a soul I'll never trust you again."

"Who would I tell? And why would it be so awful?"

"Well, it wouldn't be awful, just something for this stupid old gossipy town to talk about. I've given them way too much lately and I would just rather be off their list for a while."

"That's not going to happen. You are the most interesting person living here. Who else is there to talk about?"

"My heavens, this town is boring. I don't want them to know about my relationship with her. She's had enough hard times from the likes of that Ms. Franklin and her crowd. Oh Jake, if you haven't already made some other plans for tonight, let's give them something they can really talk about."

"Now you have my attention. What have you got in mind?"

"You beat all."

"What?"

"Nanny told me about a new restaurant in town that she and

Pappy went to last night. They're having a live band tonight. Let's go dance the night away."

"Sounds like your Nanny has spoiled my surprise, but I'm glad you are so willing. I was afraid you wouldn't like it since you don't dance."

"You bring that wild side out in me."

"So what did the bad news committee do today to get you all riled up? And who did you have lunch with?"

"Oh, they have their version of what happened between me and Tylar and they as much as said, with the aid of my own Aunt Penny, that Pappy and I were idiots for housing *bastard* children out at *Lion's Hill*!"

"And you told them?"

"You don't want to know what I wanted to tell them, especially when they said my Pappy was not of good breeding, but that was when my blood was boiling. I'll spare you all that I did tell them, but I addressed Ms. Franklin specifically when I told her that it was just like God to care about orphaned children, after all the world viewed Jesus as a bastard."

"No you didn't."

"Yes I did and then I let them know I had been standing on the other side of the wall listening to all the judgmental remarks they had been saying and I let my aunt know I saw her as a traitor in so many very nicely put words."

"You do have a gift when it comes to that. So what did happen between you and Tylar and what was their reason for him leaving town?"

"It seems that he met a young heiress to an automobile mogul who he's fallen in love with and after I turned him down because I'm too spoiled to know a good man when I meet one, which could be true, but let's skip that part. He has gone off to be with her and serves me right. They are all happy for him now that he's rid of the spoiled brat and that he will be marring this rich woman, blah, blah, blah. I'm tired of them. It's bad enough that they sit around wasting the day that God blessed them with but, I let them wasted my time, too."

"So where did you see them?"

"At The Garden Patch. I picked up sandwiches for us out there and then went to the house."

Willie popped his head in through the back door screen and yelled, "Lacey! Come on. We're all waiting to go for a ride on the tractor."

Hattie stepped into the kitchen. "Pipe down, Young man. Yo Mother does not need da stress."

"How is Mother, Hattie?"

"She ett a good lunch today and Is gonna gets her some water with a little fruit juice."

"She eats?"

"Not really, Jake. She drinks her meals."

"She had some baby cereal today and ett it all.

"*Lacey?*"

"Willie, I'm coming right now." I got up from the table and started to the barn. "You coming Jake or are you going to sit there and daydream?"

"I was wondering what was in these boxes and who did you have lunch with and how does your Mother eat?"

"Well, you can just sit there and wonder, but we'll be in the barn."

"You cans open those boxes and find outs, Mr. Jake. Then yous can takesem' up stairs and puts them away. That'll keep me from havin to do it."

"I think I'll go out side with the rest of um. But, I promise I'll make Lacey take these up stairs as soon as we get back in."

"Thanks, Mr. Jake. She's an awful handful, but you cans do it ifs anyone can."

The tractor ran great and I was feeling quite proud of myself. Jake and I went dancing at the newest restaurant in town, a great place to hang out with friends, and I had made the decision to put everything within me into pushing forward. However, I slowed things down with Jake because I was not strong enough to stop us. He agreed to cool things and we dated as many times as he came home from school and Willie and I drove down a few times to see him in Brevard before he left for Charleston. He needed to finish school and by then I had a house full of children that needed everything I could give them. I had such a desire to stay in the Word of God and to become more like Him everyday. How else would I ever get to that place where the Bad News Crowd could trash me and accuse me and I would smile saying nothing in response. I had always had a hard time with that.

chapter twenty

In 1953, our new president, Dwight D. Eisenhower, signed a truce that brought peace to the borders of South Korea. In 1954, Joseph McCarthy got the country all riled up when he alleged that communist had snuck into our State Department and other government agencies at a time when no one in this country liked a communist. Our boys were home, some bruised and beaten, but many never made it home from World War II. The Korean War was one about communist rule, too, so no one was going to sit still and let anyone with that way of thinking get into our government. The hearings were broadcast on TV and most everyone who could was watching closely. Mr. McCarthy picked a fight with our Army and they hired a lawyer to represent them at the hearings. He accused one of the lawyers on the team of being a communist and he was shot down pretty quick with a, "You have done enough. Have you no decency?" People lost interest, because it seemed so foolish and he died a few years after that. It was all very sad, but I had my hands filled with orphans.

It seemed like there were more than just me and Pappy who didn't much like the way people judged others before they knew them because racial segregation was ruled unconstitutional by our countries Supreme Court. I never have understood how we came to the conclusion that mankind has different races. I only know of one, the human race. Animals have different races, birds can't hatch eggs from a crocodile, but Moses, a Jew, married an Ethiopian and King Ahasuerus, ruler of India and even as far as Ethiopia, made Esther the Jew his Queen. Now that just never sounded like God intended a person to be ostracized because of their nationality. In 1955, Rosa Parks refused to stand up on her ride home from work and give her seat to a white man because she was just too tired to do it. Everybody got all riled up over that. I've often wondered what kind of man wouldn't show a woman enough respect by *refusing* to let her give up her seat for him no matter what our laws were. Maybe I was just too naive. I could see Mrs. Geraldine Waldrop pitching a fit over a Negro woman sitting in a seat and her not having one, but I didn't see that kind of haughtiness from the men who lived around me. Maybe they were that way with the other Negro men at work or something, but I didn't see it. I had heard about lynching taking place in other parts of our country and I prayed nothing like that would ever come to our town, but everyday I could see the bigotry rising to a new level. One night at Pappy and Nanny's we were having a family supper and Silas and all his family were there. About half way through the meal a brick came through the dining room window and a car full of men pulled through the drive shouting, "Nigger lover!" We hoped it wasn't true, but the Spirit within Pappy and Me was saying that this was going to become a common occurrence and we needed to suit up for the battle.

My favorite TV shows were *The Adventures of Ozzie and Harriet, I love Lucy, Toast of The Town* and a new show *Father Knows Best*. Seemed like all young girls wanted to be TV stars and all the boys wanted to be Marlon Brando or James Dean, you know, rebels without a cause. I was being mother to twenty-four children, finding placement for as many as I could and reading the Bible daily along with some help from Norman Vincent Peale. I loved reading the Guidepost Magazine and I used his book named *The Power of Positive Thinking* to keep me from sliding into despair when my house was over flowing with children. We had over the years found ourselves with more children than we could house and I had to take them home with me in the evenings so they would have a bed to sleep in. Things ran smoother when everyone had a bed and I could go home in the evenings and rest.

Willie and I had been taking turns sleeping with Mother so she wouldn't be alone, but I had gotten used to it more and I liked being close to the phone in case someone at *Lion's Hill* needed me, so I moved most of my things into Mother's room. Dr. Jude wasn't nearly as optimistic about Mother's recovery as he had been and I could see that every day she was withdrawing more. I didn't like thinking that she could be suffering, but I didn't think I couldn't take on another change, not yet, in my life. Even though she never responded it was a comfort to talk to Mother and know that she was there. Pappy tried to help me let go by telling me over and over, "She would rather be where William is than anywhere else. Maybe she's just trying to get there. I would hate to be holding on to one world because my children who were grown people were telling me they needed me when my heart wanted to go home." My prayers seemed like they never got past the edge of my lips and most of the time I didn't know what to pray. I had stopped asking her to wake up or telling her I needed her. I wouldn't allow anyone else to tell her that either. It was hardest for Cole, but he was the one who kept my faith in the possibility that God would raise my Mother up.

Cole was ten, Retta was thirteen, Abbie Lou was fourteen, Willie was fifteen and ready for dating. He seemed a little sweet on Aunt Joan's niece, Albie, short for Alberta. She was a cute girl who seemed a little shy, but pulled out the best in Willie. They had met when Uncle Marty and Joan got married and he had not forgotten her. He had his permit to drive and we had been blessed with a car a couple years back, so he and Cole along with some of the boys from *Lion's Hill* worked on it to make it their own by fixing it to look as much like a hot rod as possible. Willie had become quite the mechanic so he was teaching the boys at the orphanage how to fix machinery. Tylar would have been proud of him.

I saw Johnny Kale every Sunday. As it turned out, only one church in town was interested in these children at *Lion's Hill*. Even Pappy and Nanny were coming with us to worship at *Wonders of Love Fellowship*. The people who God had joined together there were from all different backgrounds, financial groups from poverty to the elite, widows and widowers, broken homes, abused women and children, and me with my family and our orphaned children. We were able to help each other and the children were feeling a sense of family. Everyone had something to offer: a talent, a gift or a Word from God. There was so much love brought into that building each time we met. We were all family.

God had given me words of encouragement to so many and in our ladies Bible Study. He had used me to bring prophetic words to those who were hurting and in need of direction. There were times when He filled them with the Spirit as we prayed over certain ones. There was no doubt that God was blessing this congregation and word of that was spreading. By some the church was mocked and by others it was praised. Even though I was very pleased with the body of believers I knew that it wouldn't last. It was just something God had planted in my spirit. I knew that it would come to and end, but I did not know when or how.

My Pappy said that Johnny Kale had changed a little, but not a lot. But, Johnny Kale had never tried to convince anyone that he was not far from perfect. He was still carousing with women, as Pappy called it, and he spent most every Saturday night over at the Indian Reservation playing cards with some of the Indians. Some said he had a few Indian babies that he had fathered living on the reservation, but he never talked about any of that with me. He and I were simply cordiale; he and Pappy seemed to be working on a friendship. I guess something in me kept him at a distance because he had been the one who helped take Tylar away from me. With Jake so far away, even with the children, I had way to much time to feel lonely and I missed my friend. Both of them.

Preacher Sternfield, that's what I called him behind his back because he was adamant that everyone call him Reverend and I found titles so unnecessary. I realize he went to school and earned this title, but if he was really worthy, his life would have to show me. So far he was anything but reverent. He was always flirting with me and several other ladies in the church. I didn't like it even though he wasn't married, but he was way too old for me and he knew I had someone else in my life even if he was many miles away. I suspected that he was going with Johnny Kale to the reservation for more than ministry, but I didn't know that for sure. I had to give him the benefit of the doubt seeing that he was a preacher of God's Word and he truly seemed to know the Word and what the meaning of each scripture was. He brought the scriptures out in a way I had never heard another do and he made them relevant to our lives. He was refreshing to listen to and he taught me so much about the Word, but I was not interested in him in any other way.

It was the winter of fifty-six when Jake came home after graduating from the medical school in Charleston. He was practicing medicine with his father in a clinic Dr. Jude had built in town not far from Pappy's bank. Pappy had retired from going into work everyday, although he and Nanny were on the board of trustees and Pappy was still the bank's president; they helped raise money and worked with the children at *Lion's Hill*. Jake was involved with the children in that he became their doctor and they loved him taking Doctor Jude's place because he wasn't much older than them in so many ways. He brought joy to us all.

Doctor Jude had prepared my sisters, brothers and me for my Mother's impending death. He didn't think she would live till Christmas, but she was still with us as Christmas came and went with a new year as well. I had prayed that if God was going to take her and not raise her up that he wait till Jake came home so I would have someone, but I didn't expect that prayer to be answered because God had been teaching me to lean on Him solely for all my needs. There were just times that I needed the arms of someone to hold me and I hoped that He would give me that.

I was in my office in early January praising God for yet another large deposit into the account for *Lion's Hill* when Willie stepped into the door opening, somewhat out of breath. I looked up to see his dark silhouette holding the door frame with his hands on both sides of the opening. The light was coming in from behind him so I could not see his expression, but I could see that the side of his face was wet from tears. The moment was frozen, but I knew why he had come. He turned away and ran back down the hall and out the front door.

I didn't have an urgent desire to rush out of the office and run to my Mother's side. I knew she was not at home in her bed anymore. She was with Jesus. She was with Pa. What a beautiful completed love story. I spent the next few minutes reliving flashes of their lives. The births of their children, the weddings in their home. The parties, the friends, the family. Oh how he loved her. God had blessed their time on earth with so much. There was nothing to be sad about anymore and I wept with joy and envy.

A little time later Jake came into the room and walked over to the chair facing my desk where I was sitting. He sat very quiet waiting for me to need him. He and I had not been more than friends since he came home. He was busy getting moved into the clinic, as well as learning about the children at *Lion's Hill*. It had been nice knowing he was close by if I needed him, but I had surprised myself at that moment because I was comfortable just sitting where I was looking at him.

"I just saw Willie sitting on the front step. He didn't say anything to me, but did he say anything to you?"

I shook my head. "He didn't have to. I know."

"Can I drive you two out to the house?"

"Not right yet. Can we walk out to the river?"

"Sure. We can go where ever you want to go."

"Thanks. We have to take Willie, too. Do you know where the others are?"

"No. I think he came alone."

We went out to the river and prayed. Willie cried out to God to see everything like we did the day we were filled with the Holy Spirit so he could see something close to what Mother was seeing. Jake didn't know what we were talking about because he still had not been baptized in the Holy Spirit so we prayed for Jake to have that gift and be able to see what our Pa was showing our Mother. It was so cold standing on the side of that river, but there was just something about being near that water that gave me peace so I didn't want to leave. We stood side by side looking across the river praying in the spirit as I kept thinking of the song about crossing the Jordan River and how I would love to take that step and be with my family and Jesus. Suddenly it became very warm as if it was late spring and Willie shouted, "I see it! Lacey, I see it."

He grabbed hold to Jake praying in tongues and then in English for Jake to be filled. Jake dropped to his knees with tears in his eyes and began to chatter something and shake all over. There was nothing to do, but join Jake on the ground and pray in the spirit with him. He opened his eyes and the Spirit enveloped the three of us with His presence. We all were seeing a new day. The detail of the new sprouts just hidden beneath the covering of the old bark. The warmth of the sun was beating down on us and the sky was that blue that only came from heaven's throne. This was Jake's new day. His new life and we were sharing in it. It was also Mother's new day, her new life and we were seeing a glimpse of heaven and rejoicing in it. For that moment my Mother was more alive than she had ever been to me and we were fellowshipping with her and my Pa through the power of the Holy Spirit. No one could ever make me believe that heaven and earth were two places that never mingled together, because on that day they did.

Pastor Burton and Mitch Sternfield conducted their first funeral together in all the years they had ministered in the same town. The man who once received the Spirit and now denied the need for the gifts of the Spirit, and the man who woke those who were hungry to the truth, had found a way to make peace long enough to speak about heaven and the need to know Jesus as your personal Savior and Lord over your life. One was solemn and almost apologetic and the other was joyful and praising God for giving us all hope for a better place. But, neither seemed to know God like I did, they simply went through the motions.

Our house was full again with mourners, friends and family. I wanted those who mourned to leave, but they could not do what they did not understand. My family was there for them. We all knew where my Mother was and she was not somewhere that anyone needed to mourn for her. My Nanny was a mourner, but I had never had a child so I couldn't feel her pain. She had missed my Mother for so long I think the emotional dam broke for her when they put Mother's body in the grave. She probably needed to cry.

Jake was there for me. He had been away for so long, too, and our relationship was no more than what it had been the day we decided to cool things down between each other, but he was there beside me day and night just in case I needed him. I leaned on him, not because of Mother's death, but because I was ready to see if there was something still between us. His letters from school were loving, but he never mentioned what he wanted to happen between us. I didn't know if he was still in love with me or not, but he had stirred something in me that no other had and I needed to find out why.

"Lacey? Most of the people who have dropped by to see you have left. The family is in the kitchen fixing something to eat. Do you want something?"

"No thank you, Marge. I just need to take a walk and catch my breath."

"Honey, it's too cold outside for a walk. Let me fix you a hot drink."

"Lacey? How about if you and I go for a drive?"

"Yea, that's what I want to do. I just need to get out for a little while, Marge. You understand, don't you?"

"Yes, honey. Everyone will understand. You and Jake go ahead and take a drive. I'll be here when you get back and there will be plenty left over for you both to eat when you come back."

"Thanks."

We got our coats, got into Jake's car and drove into town to the drive-in diner and ordered a cup of coffee when Debbie Dunn skated up to the window and placed the tray on the side of the car.

"Why, Jake Foresight! I heard you were home. It's just like you to order coffee so you can watch me get burned while I try to bring it out to you on these skates. I've just had this job a week and I'm not real good at this. Hi Lacey. I was sorry to hear about your Mother. We all were praying she would come out of that coma and be alright."

"Thank you, Debbie. She's just gone home."

"Amen to that sister. So how do you like being a doctor? Pretty important now aren't ya? But how 'bout giving me a call sometime? I'm not busy this Saturday."

"Hmm. Well, I would, but I think I have plans Saturday."

"Well, do you or don't ya?" She kept chewing her gum and staring at Jake. He sort of fidgeted while he scanned his brain for what it was he had to do on Saturday. "Well, can you date during the week? I have Tuesdays off so we could do something Monday night or during the day on Tuesday?"

"No. I'm pretty busy during the week."

"Well, you have my number. Let me get that coffee for you." She winked then skated off to the order window.

Jake watched her skate away and said, "Cute girl."

"If you like that kind."

"What kind? She's a nice girl. Of course everything seems so much more beautiful than it ever has to me."

"Yea, I know what you're seeing and feeling right now. But, do you want a girl who is so forward? I don't think I could ask a man to take me out on a date."

"Maybe you should think about it. Sometimes a guy doesn't know a girl is interested and he needs a little push."

"So why can't you go with her?"

"I might can."

Debbie skated back over to the car and put our coffee on the tray. Jake paid her and gave her a tip for her service then he passed my cup over to me and got his off the tray. "Thanks Jake. For a man too busy to take me out, you sure did give me a nice tip. Seriously, give me a call. It's been way too long. We have a lot of catching up to do."

She took the tray and skated off to the next car. Jake rolled the window up and tried to get comfortable by leaning against the door looking my direction. I reached down and turned on the radio.

"So, you're going to ignore me or drown me out?"

"Oh, did you want to talk to me? I thought maybe you wanted to think about Debbie Dunn for a little while."

"Maybe I need to look at her again? Yeah, she's pretty cute. I bet she would love having a doctor for a boyfriend. You know how parents want their girls to marry doctors. I bet they would love me. Maybe I'm not busy Saturday night." He started rolling down his window and shouted, "Hey, Deb . . ."

"Jake!"

"What?"

"Stop it. Take me home if you just want to pick up young girls to flaunt around in my face. I'm not interested in your dating life."

"You used to be."

"It was more limited. Guess things have changed over the years."

"Nope. It's been very limited. I've been studying, but now I'm ready to start dating again. Just checking out the possibilities. Can't fault me for that."

"No, guess I can't, but I can ask you to do your picking up when I'm not in the car."

"I could do that. But, I'm hoping I won't have that opportunity."

We drove out to *Lion's Hill* so I could make sure all the children were fed and finished with their homework. We had two babies under a year old and they needed me. I liked being there to see them fed, bathed and dressed in their night clothes. There is something so refreshing about a just washed baby all cuddled up under your chin. I took Eliza and Jake took baby Ben after they ate their supper and we bathed them in the nursery. Then we sat side by side and rocked them till they fell asleep. There was something prophetic about that moment, but it could have been wishful thinking.

We put the babies in their cribs and said goodnight to the other children then drove back to my house. As we got out of the car and started toward the porch Jake asked, "So, can I pick you up Saturday night?"

"Don't you have plans?"

"I was hoping you would say you would go out with me."

I had mixed feelings and didn't know if there was anything between us anymore. "I don't think so, Jake. Maybe we just need to be friends. I'm not sure I'm ready for a relationship and I don't want to keep you from dating. I'm sorry, but I think that's best for both of us."

I turned and reached for the front door knob when Jake reached out and stopped my hand. It was still there. How could just a touch grip all my organs and change my blood flow?

"Apparently I went too far teasing you tonight. I thought you knew that there was no one else and never will be and if you won't date me then I won't date. If you only care for me as a friend I will somehow live with that, but you won't ever get rid of me. I hope you can handle a friend who sticks closer than a brother."

I couldn't say anything. He zapped my energy completely. Then he pulled me around to look towards him. "You will let me hug my friend good night won't you? I haven't been gone so long that you've forgotten what it feels like to be in my arms, have I? Do you remember what it feels like to hold me and dance with me?" He slowly came closer and wrapped his arms around me. I felt so safe, so complete, so scared. He whispered into my ear, "How can you say you want no more than friendship? I know you can feel it. It's still there isn't it?"

I knew that I had more than friendship in my heart for Jake, but I didn't want to make any mistakes with where God was leading me.

But, why would God let me feel this way for Jake if he was all wrong? He had let me fall for Tylar and that was all wrong. But, God had used that situation to do great things for these children. Was He going to do something wonderful because of us, too? I didn't know if I could stand it again if we were drawn together only to be apart for the good of His Kingdom. I remembered the evangelist saying that He would give me desires that would tear at my heart and to choose Him, always choose Him. If I chose Jake would I be choosing God? "So what were you thinking about doing Saturday?"

"More of this."

"I have to be honest with you, Jake, I don't want to put my love out there again only to have it trashed. I know that's not what happened, but it's how I feel. You've been here for me for so long, even when I didn't recognize your friendship, and I don't want to have you stripped from me. We can always be friends, but if we step over that line it will never be the same."

"And I don't want it to be the same."

"I mean if it doesn't work out for us. If God doesn't want us together."

"Do you think I am exactly like Tylar?"

"No! This isn't about Tylar and you are nothing like Tylar."

"I'm going to take that as a complement."

"Well, you are as handsome, maybe more handsome, but it was a complement. You know what? I was thinking about the day Mother died and how wonderful it was to be with you out on the river, with Willie, and watching you soak in the Spirit and receive. I know you have to want Him in order to receive; God doesn't just slam you with Himself. Tylar never showed a desire even when I told him what happened to me. We never shared scripture like you and I do. I always felt like I was teaching him. You are always teaching me, but I feel like we grow when you share with me. I love that about you. I know that you are close to God and that means the world to me. I would have been unequally yoked with Tylar and the sad thing is I knew that. But, I wanted him to be the one for me so badly. How can I trust myself to ..."

"You are being tossed to and fro. You just answered that question before you asked it. Let me share a scripture I read the other day that made me think about Tylar. I've heard preachers teach it in a different way than how I interpret it, but it's First John 2:19 and basically what it says is that they came out from us so we would see that they were not part of us, or joined to us. If they were meant to be with us they would have stayed. He left you because he was not joined to you and how are we joined to each other? By the Spirit of God. He has a deeper walk designed for you and Tylar was not ready for it. He probably knew that, but for sure he knew he had a different walk."

"So how have you heard it preached?"

"That members of a church that left, and went to another church or stopped going to church, were not really saved. But, I don't think that's what is being said. If a church splits or someone leaves who, most of the time, was trying to show the leadership where they were falling into some type of deception, and Heaven knows no leader wants someone who hasn't gone to all the colleges and schools that they have, to tell them they are in error! So they pretty much trash that person or people, and then out of a bad seed planted, people shy away from them not sure what is right. That's just what Satan loves and here's why. God is forever moving and He has to move us. We might learn something in one congregation or they may learn what they need from us, but we have to take that message to the next place and gather the pieces that they have that fit into the puzzle God is unfolding in our lives. That's the mystery that Paul talks about in First Corinthians the second and third chapters. *'Eye hath not seen, nor ear heard, neither have entered into the heart of man the things which God hath prepared for them that love Him. But, God hath revealed them to us by His Spirit; for the Spirit searches all things even the deep things of God.'* Most preachers leave out the part about God revealing them to us through the Spirit. They just want us all to believe no one knows what God is doing or what He's up to so they can explain away their own ignorance."

"Now *that* sounds like truth to me."

"I believe that everything we go through is so He can open up another mystery about Himself to us. He wants to show us who He is as He reveals the depths of His workings. Someone out there has gone through just what you have gone through, just what I've gone through and they have the answer. I hope they don't stay where they are for long because I need them to move with God so they can cross my path and reveal the answers to me, don't you?"

"Of course. Miss Sunshine does that for me and she doesn't even know God is using her. Pappy has the deeper things, I guess, because he's been walking with God a long time."

"I want to be available to Him just like your Pappy is if there is someone needing that little bit of revelation that I've gotten."

"I don't think it's so little. I think you are very in tuned with what God is saying and doing. I think you have a great knowledge of who God is. I can see Him in you."

"I think Paul was also saying that if people, mostly the religious leaders, had been allowing His Spirit to teach them instead of a man they would have seen who He was and not crucified His Son. But, they were determined to be in control and rejected anyone who was teaching the people who was not one of the elite so called Bible scholars. That kind of thinking gets under my skin. God is not choosy as to who He speaks to. That choice is up to us. So I don't fault people who are moving and gathering. If you stay under one man and his teachings you only become part of who he is. What good is that? God would have made us all alike if that was His goal. He wants us to become like Jesus, not our preacher. I can't be angry with Tylar and who knows, he may have had to go to Chicago to find the place that would feed him with the truth that would set him free. I hope you can find a way to be thankful that he opened the door for you and me!"

He had given me so much to think about. "I'll be ready by five. Don't be late."

"I think that's too late, I'll never be able to wait till then. I was thinking I would be here by eight for breakfast and we would pack a lunch and then have supper out and go dancing and come home sometime Sunday morning."

"Whoa, whoa! Hold on, Jake. Picnic? Not a bad idea, but I'm sleeping late Saturday morning because we will be out late Friday night."

"Okay, I like *that* so far."

"Well, then supper some where nice with dancing."

"Got that picked out already. Then what?"

"Then home by midnight. I have to get the children to church Sunday morning and we would love for you to be with us?"

"I will be glad to be with you. So what time can I get you Friday?"

"Hmm. I need to get everything taken care of in the office Friday and I don't know right now how many people I have meetings with or who will need me to help them with something so I can't say for sure."

"Guess at it."

"About six-thirty?"

"How many hours is that from now?"

"Jake, you are so sweet. You sure know how to make a girl feel special. But I have to tell you that while you have been gone I have made it my quest to do the will of God and only what He wills. I don't know if you and I together are what He wants for us, but if He does I don't want to miss it. But, we can't push this just because it feels good to us. It has to be right, it has to be the best or we will miss His best. Do you understand any of that?"

"I'm in complete agreement with you, but I also believe that God blesses what we build if our hearts are pure. That includes family. I would love to be able to say that I lived my whole life with no regrets, but I have found that I can say that no matter what choices I make, I don't have to look on anything that may seem like a wrong move as a regret. I can see them as stepping stones. Places for God's forgiveness to be exalted and for me to learn more about Him and what He wants for me. I can't just sit down and wait till I know Him completely before I do something. If I did that I would never date, never marry, never offer advice to a patient out of fear that I might make the wrong choice. I can't stop living out of fear of missing God. I have to pray everyday for Him to guide me, speak to me, let me know what I need to do in everything I face. And He always brings me back to you. He kept me all these years while I've been away from you. I've had opportunities to date girls, girls with a lot more to offer than Debbie Dunn, but I couldn't. He wouldn't let me stop longing for you. If it wasn't right for us I would have been able to move on. There are a lot of single women in Charleston. If I wanted to play the field and chase after the things of this world I would not have come back here."

He ran his hands under my hair, pulling it out to the sides and then smoothed it down my back. "I don't want to be wrong again, Jake."

"You cannot stop living out of fear. I'm not going anywhere. I'm not Tylar. I would die before I would hurt you. Trust me. Did you have any beau's coming around seeking your attention while I've been gone?"

"A few. They didn't come back once I told them I wasn't interested. Except one, but he's kind of strange."

"What do you mean?"

"He's too old for me. I'm not interested in him at all, not even a little. He's not someone I would ever be attracted to. He has lots of other women, even goes after the married ones who are young and attractive. I really don't think he's a nice man, but I keep taking my children to his church every Sunday."

"Johnny Kale?"

"No."

"The preacher?!"

"Yeah. He has more to offer than any other preacher in town from the pulpit, but he just doesn't seem to live a pure life. But, I don't know that for sure. I just see him flirt and is that a sin?"

"If a man thinks it, he has done it in the eyes of God so if he is thinking impure things about these women he's as good as done it, to God. He says it's about our heart now, not the law."

"Explain that to me."

"Well, before Jesus came on this earth, in other words before the New Testament, God gave his laws, and you were expected to keep them. You could not physically have a relationship with a married person without it being called adultery, and people were stoned to death for such behavior. Knowing you would be faced with that type of punishment made it easier not to do that! But, there were other laws that were much easier to break, like having other gods. They did a lot of that. But Jesus said, 'I have come to fulfill the law.' What He meant was He was here on this earth to do what man could not, and he didn't have to fall under His fleshly desires and break the laws. He didn't even *desire* to break the laws! He didn't sleep with someone else's wife, He didn't lie, steal, cheat, He honored His Mother and

Father because He wanted to, not because of the law, but out of love. He kept the law because it was in His heart to obey His Father. And that's what He wants us to do. Obey these laws because we love Him and want to do what He asks of us. It's so much harder to live under this new command than it was for the people who lived in the Old Testament. They just had to look good on the outside and their sacrifices took care of the messes. Now Jesus has come and sacrificed for all our sin, way back then, before we were ever born, so He expects us to love Him enough for doing that, that we will keep our thoughts pure. He says if we just look at a woman and imagine sinning with her then we have as good as done it. If we just have a fleeting moment where we think about taking something that's not ours, we have sin in our hearts that we need to deal with. Because of His great love for us we must strive to keep pure hearts and obey Him. I have never held anyone else in my heart, but you. I don't think it's a sin right now for me to want you this badly. If you were married it would be a sin. Probably some of the things I dream about happening between you and me are sins. But, I also know that if I entertain a thought long enough, whether it's a sin or a desire, I will act on it. "

"Jake!"

"Just being honest. I'm planning in my thoughts a place for you in my life. Preacher Sternfield needs to be told that you are taken, if you are, and then if he doesn't stop his pursuit I'll have to have a talk with him. Now that I've been filled with the Holy Ghost I have a lot of fight in me. He better watch out."

"I'm sure it's harmless. It may just be his personality because why else would he be flirting with me. I'm way too young for him."

"Beauty is beauty, men don't care what age it is. I will definitely be with you Sunday morning. He needs to know that you aren't interested in him once and for all, even if you haven't chosen me. We'll let him think you have."

"That sounds good to me. I'll even let *you* think I have!"

"Hey! I don't like the sound of that, Lacey Kale Rutledge, but that's alright. I'm going to win you over, you just wait and see."

"I'm going to love being courted by you. Now be sure and do a good job. If there's one thing I don't like it's sloppy courting."

Jake walked up close to me and put his hands on both sides of my face, "There's one thing I don't like."

"What's that?"

"Waiting one more minute to kiss you. I've studied for four years and driven hundreds of miles to get back to this very spot where I kissed you goodbye so that I could kiss you hello. Please don't make me wait any longer?"

"Can you promise me you didn't think about jumping out of the car and kissing that Debbie Dunn?"

"Never crossed my mind, ever."

"Then you can, wait, did you ever think about kissing any of those girls in Charleston?"

He moved in closer to me, "Not one."

"Luciano?"

"What?" He moved closer. "She's married."

"Kimmy?"

He moved closer almost touching my lips. "You're stalling. I've never wanted to kiss anyone other than you and I never have. I love you," and he softly kissed me while I held on to his arms desperate for more.

"Do you think preacher Sternfield or any other man could make you feel like this?"

"Right this minute I have no desire to find out."

He pulled away and looked surprised at me. "Have you ever?"

"All I can say is you leave a girl wanting more so you better not leave me for long."

"I should have never teased you as a child."

"You reap what you sow, Mr. Foresight."

"So if I sow great kisses and lots of love I can expect it to be returned to me?"

"Hey! That's what Sunshine promised me would happen. It's going to be wonderful being courted by you."

chapter twenty-one

Jake and I drove out to the church together, seven children with us. The others followed in Nanny and Pappy's car, Willie's car and Miss Margaret and Mr. Jenis drove a car. Miss Barbara stayed with the babies and the cook, Mr. Yen. He was not a believer and would never leave his kitchen unattended.

When we arrived the children piled out of the car running in all directions meeting up with their church friends and Jake came around to open my door. Once I was out of the car, he took my hands and said, "Today we let everyone know that you and I are jacketed so hold my hand."

"You didn't ask me to go steady with you."

"Well, that's because I thought that was understood."

"I need to be asked."

"I'm twenty-six years old! I feel quite silly asking you to go steady with me."

"Too bad. Ask me."

"Lacey, will you go steady with me, just me and no one else, but me?"

"Nope."

"No?!"

"You made a joke of it."

"Lacey?" and he gritted his teeth and looked to either side of him and whispered sternly, "I love you and I want you to be my girl and no one else's. Is that so hard?"

"It was for you, but I would love to go steady with you, Jake."

"Then hold my hand and after church I'll try to find my letter jacket and bring it over to you."

"You know what? I've always wanted to wear someone's jacket. That would be great."

"If this preacher makes a pass at you I may go home and get it so you can wear it now."

"It wouldn't really look that great with my dress. I think if you just stay right beside me and hold my hand he will get the picture. Did you get a letter jacket from Charleston? Cause you know a letter jacket from a medical school would really be neat. Why do you roll your eyes at me?"

We walked up to the door and Mitch Sternfield was standing in the door way as always on Sunday morning shaking everyone's hands and patting his closer friends on the back making some kind of joke about how they spent their weekend or the cute girl on the roller skates that fell out at the drive-in. His remarks always seemed out of place, but those he was talking to seemed to enjoy his attention.

When we were the next in line to shake his hand, he had a broad smile on his face and his eyes lit up until he saw Jake and my hand holding on to his. "Miss Lacey, you look lovely as always. Who have you brought with you this morning?"

Jake extended his hand past me and said, "Jake Foresight. I'm Lacey's boyfriend. I've been away in medical school and I've just finished up and gotten settled back home. You may have heard I'm working in the clinic in town with my dad, Doctor Jude Foresight?"

"Yes. I do remember hearing that you were home and working with your father. So where have you been hiding him all these weeks, Lacey?"

"I've been with her Mother. You do know her Mother just recently passed on, oh yes, you resided over the funeral. I was there; you must have just missed me."

"Jake has also been quite busy getting settled in at the clinic. It's hard to do that when you are seeing patients. He has so many books and they all needed to find their place in his office. Also, building shelves and things. He's just been too busy to come with us on Sunday mornings, but he's here now and I'm so glad he will be sitting with me and the children finally so we can all worship together."

"Well, it's nice to have you, Mr. Foresight."

Jake said, "Doctor, Doctor Foresight, Reverend."

"Yes, yes of course. Welcome. I hope you will enjoy the service."

It was the first time I had ever seen Mitch Sternfield look at me with a scowl. Until that day I had convinced myself that he was just a flirty kind of guy, but after the service I was sure he had enjoyed my being single more than I thought. I had been given freedom to pray with people as the Spirit of God moved about the room when Preacher Sternfield asked if anyone needed prayer to come down to the front. Sometimes people were moved by the sermon, but they didn't want to go down to the front for prayer because it was just something small to them, but nothing is small to God so He would press me to speak to them or just walk over and sit with them and pray quietly. I only wanted to be a comfort to them, but sometimes God would speak through me to them and I would see people get on fire for God after those encounters. I loved being able to flow with the Spirit so freely, but on that day I didn't feel free to do anything.

I felt his anger or something so strongly I wasn't able to feel God's unction. There was just something that wasn't right about Preacher Sternfield, but I couldn't put my finger on it. It wasn't just that day, it was all the time. There seemed to be a jealousy of people's gifts, but if he liked you it was okay for you to use them in the service. He liked me and let me move about praying and prophesying to those who were in need. Sometimes the Spirit would be moving through the congregation and he would quench the Spirit by rebuking someone or something someone was doing and we all knew it was because he had a grievance with them. It was embarrassing for them, but more embarrassing for all of us who had to watch it. Pappy said he was just a young whipper-snapper who couldn't stand for the attention to be removed from him even if his sermon had led us to put it on Jesus. But, it just seemed deeper than that to me. Jake later asked me how I could think he was okay to let my spirit listen to while he was behind the pulpit if he was not someone I felt safe with when he was not behind the pulpit? I didn't have an answer for him, but I had to really pray about it, because I was taking my children there as well. I would die if they somehow got hurt by him or anyone while they were under my care.

Several weeks passed and Preacher Sternfield dropped by my house twice asking if there was anything he or the church could do for me or my family. He also had a check from the fund some of the ladies had started for the orphanage. They sold baked goods and sold their sewing to make money for different missions and one they had chosen was our children. I was more than thankful that they were so good to the children and that they wanted to be a part of their lives. It was still hard finding support from the other churches in the area. One person, Pappy said, was far away who made a deposit into our account each month. It was enough to keep *Lion's Hill* running if no one donated another dime, but having people in our community involved was a blessing for us all and I never wanted them to think they were not needed or wanted.

Pappy and I had taken the money left over each month and invested it so that if we had a child come to us who did not get adopted and they wanted to go to college we would have the money to fulfill that dream for them. It looked like we were going to have more children than we had thought in the beginning because most of our children over seven were not what people were looking for when they came to visit the orphanage. Everyone wanted babies unless they were in need of farm hands and I had removed from those farms seven of the eight who were adopted for that reason. Good hard work never hurt anyone, but labor from sun up till sun down for children was just plain abusive and I would not have these children used as slaves. I wanted to build families. Everyone deserves that and these children had suffered so much already, they didn't need to be abused again.

Both times Preacher Sternfield dropped by Jake was there. I was so thankful because it reinforced our relationship. I was sure I was being silly, but nonetheless, I didn't want to be caught alone with him for fear he might ask questions about Jake and me and I wouldn't have the answers that would prove without a shadow of a doubt that I was *not* interested in him.

I got a call from Jake one afternoon and I was alarmed because Jake never called me while he was at the clinic seeing patients. "I won't be by till late tonight and maybe not at all. Preacher Sternfield has fallen doing some work on the church and it seems he's broken his leg and may even need surgery. Dad thinks there's some internal bleeding. We're leaving right now to take him to the hospital. Pray for him and I'll call you when I get him stable."

"No matter what time."

"No matter what time. I promise. I love you."

"Please be careful and I will be praying for you to know what is wrong with him."

"Thanks. Bye."

"Jake ... ?" He hung up. I wanted to tell him I loved him too, something I had not told him yet. I didn't know why because I did love him so much, but it just never seemed like the right time. I just wasn't use to telling someone who was not my Mother, Pa, Pappy, Nanny or the rest of my family that I loved them. But, I always wondered that if something happened to Jake and I didn't tell him, would I be able to live with myself? I thought he knew, but still he wanted to hear me say it I was sure. I know I loved hearing him tell me.

I called some of the ladies in the church who I prayed with, who truly prayed because they cared and had a direct line to the throne of God, unlike some of the other ladies who wanted to be in our prayer group so they could know what was going on in everyone's life. None of them were as open about their gossip as the town busybodies, but the spirit was the same.

I called Kimmy and Mayree to ask them to pray for Jake. I didn't know if he had thought about it or not, he seemed so calm on the phone as if this was a routine day, but he had not done any surgery since he moved back home. Surgery was what he studied so he had performed many while in his residency, but not at home, not without his instructors and not with the pressure of his own Father being there to watch. Dr Jude didn't do many surgeries that weren't considered routine anymore. He had left that up to the surgeons at the hospital and referred his patients to them. Having Jake in his clinic was an answer to prayer for Dr. Jude. I was praying that Jake would be an answer to prayer for Preacher Sternfield and if anything was wrong, more than he understood, that Jake would find the right doctor to help him.

After supper, Kimmy and Mayree came over to the house and we made plans to call different ladies to fix a dish to take to preacher Sternfield after he was released from the hospital. Everyone was more than willing to do whatever we needed done for him even if he was not well enough to fix for himself for sometime after he came home. Even though we were all busy with our own families and some with our jobs as well, we were eager to help a neighbor. That's what made those days special.

Once everything was set up with the other ladies we took some more time to pray for Jake and Preacher Sternfield. Kimmy and Mayree had gone home when Jake called me somewhere around nine o'clock. He was still at the hospital and the surgery was over. Preacher Sternfield had broken his leg and caused his appendix to rupture when he fell from the roof against the step railing. He was patching the roof above the porch and was stepping back onto the ladder when it moved sideways and he fell.

"Is he going to be alright?"

"Yeah, he'll live."

"Jake!"

"Well, he will. I patched him up, took out his appendix and he will need about a week to ten days here and then he can go home."

"How long will he need the cast on his leg?"

"It's broke, so that's good. If it was cracked it could take longer to heal up and be sensitive to walk on and we would want him walking on it. With it broken he can get up and walk and the cast will let him put pressure on that leg without it hurting. We'll take the cast off... when it's ready! You ladies won't have to take care of him forever."

"Well, that's a relief! But, I bet he will want some of the ladies to try."

"Well, it ain't gonna be you."

"Kimmy and Mayree came over and we called some of the ladies in the church, all married ones, the ones who have been married forever, and they are going to fix different dishes and get them to him once he gets home. I'm sure he will hate that!"

"Ha! He *will* hate that!"

"It won't stop his healing will it?"

"No. It should help it. He will be ready to get back to his normal life of chasing women."

"We shouldn't be talking like this, Jake. We don't know that he does that for sure and you know how the operators enjoy listening in. We don't need to get a rumor started on a man who won't be able to defend himself for weeks."

"Yeah. You're right. I'm just tired and I was enjoying the comic relief."

"Come home."

"I need to check on him again and make sure he's not in too much pain. I have to talk to the night nurse and let her know what he needs and how often, then I'll be headed home."

"Will you call me once you get home?"

"You should be in the bed."

"I can't sleep till I know you are home, safe."

"You really *do* care about me. You know if we lived in the same house you would know . . ."

"Just call me when you get home. I'll be up."

"Of course we would have to be married to live . . ."

"Jake, call me when you get home."

"We can talk about this then."

"Don't be too long. You and I need to get some sleep before we have to do it all over again tomorrow, so don't keep me up all night waiting to hear from you."

"Okay. I should be home in an hour or less."

I spent the rest of the evening thinking about Jake and his desire to live with me permanently. I was flattered, but getting married was a big step. I tossed the thoughts back and forth in my head and one part of me wanted to have a husband and a family, but part of me was desperately afraid that God would want me to be available to Him and Jake would hold me back. God had said to choose Him, always choose Him. How could I do that and be Jake's wife? What if God had plans for me that moved me to another country? Would he be willing to go? Jake was someone who was so close to God just like I wanted my husband to be and I knew he would talk everything out with me, but could I be the one responsible for him having to leave his family, the clinic, his patients?

As I fixed hot water for some tea I started praying in the spirit for an answer. After getting my cup and tea bag down from the cupboard I heard His voice.

"Jake gave his life to me. I am in control of his goings and comings. I will send him, I will send you. I send them two by two."

A few minutes later Jake called. "I'm home. It was all I could do to make myself drive by your house and come here instead of pulling into your yard."

"Are you tired?"

"Maybe a little, but never too tired for you."

There was silence for a while as I ran through so many things to respond with, none of them were right.

"Are you still there, Lacey?"

"Yeah. I love you, Jake."

"I know, but I'm glad you know it, too. Now I really wish I had come by cause what I want to say to you I can't say on here. Too many ears. I've been waiting a long time to hear you say that. I never thought you would tell me and the town at the same time and you know they are listening being this late and all."

"I don't care anymore. If I'm the only thing exciting in their lives I'm glad I was able to give them a thrill."

"Well, you've given me a thrill and I could show you how much if you would let me come over?"

"Go to bed, Jake!"

"Why? I'll never sleep."

"Me either."

"See you in a minute," and he hung up the phone.

chapter twenty-two

A little over a week passed and Preacher Sternfield was home from the hospital. He didn't want anyone to stay with him, but Johnny Kale had spent the first few nights he was home with him just in case he needed help getting up during the night. Several of the ladies brought their dishes to my house so I needed to take them over to Preacher Sternfield's but I was not looking forward to doing it alone. I hoped that Johnny Kale would still be there so I wouldn't have to even go inside. I called Kimmy for back up support and she told me she had made some cookies that she was planning on taking by there so she would meet me. I was so relieved.

Just as I was heading out the door the phone rang and it was one of the boys at *Lion's Hill*. He was very upset about a rejection letter he had gotten from a college he had applied to so I spent sometime talking with him trying to help him feel better. Before I knew it I was forty-five minutes late meeting Kimmy, but hopefully Johnny Kale would still be there.

I got to Preacher Sternfield's house to find Kimmy sitting out on the steps. I jumped out of the car and opened the back door reaching in for the different dishes.

"I'm sorry I'm so late. Bailey didn't get into North Carolina State and he was upset. Before I knew it we had talked forty-five minutes." Kimmy just sat on the steps. "Are you okay, Kimmy? I kind of thought you would have gone back home by now. Aren't you a little cold to be sitting out here on the steps?" I picked up one of the dishes I had laid on the trunk of my car and walked over to the steps. "If you were gonna wait for me you should have gotten in your car." I put my arm around her and rubbed up and down hers. "Where's your coat? Kimmy, what's wrong?"

"I just don't feel good. I guess I'm coming down with something. I need to go home."

"Honey, you should have gone on home and not waited for me. Both the girls have that nasty winter cold. I'm so sorry I was late. Did you see Johnny Kale?"

"Yeah. He was here when I got here."

"And . . . so. Where is he now?"

"He left to go to work, I guess. He let me in. I put my cookies on the counter in the kitchen."

"Is Preacher Sternfield still in the bed?"

"Right now?"

"Was he in the bed when you went in the house?"

"I feel really bad. I have to go home."

"Do you want me to take you?"

"No. I can make it home."

"Are you going to be sick?"

"No, I don't think so. I just feel bad."

"Well, let me help you to the car."

"Okay. Are you going to stay?"

"I'm going to take the dishes inside and then leave."

"Do you want me to wait?"

"If you feel this bad I don't want you to. I'm so sorry you're sick. I don't like you driving if you are this sick."

"It's okay. I can drive; I just want to go home."

I put Kimmy in her car and told her to be careful and that I would call her as soon as I got to *Lion's Hill*. She backed out of the drive and I walked out a piece into Preacher Sternfield's yard to try and see Johnny Kale's house. I hadn't noticed his car being there when I pulled in, but I was hopping it was an oversight. It wasn't there. I took the last two dishes out of the car and took them to the porch where I had placed the other one. Then I opened the screened door and checked the door and it was unlocked so I picked up two dishes and went into the house. I had never been there before so I wasn't sure where the kitchen was, but like most homes I though it would be towards the back of the house. I walked down a center hallway and passed a bathroom on my right and continued to the back. At the end of the hall was a door way to the right and one to the left. The kitchen was to the left and Preacher Sternfield was to the right sitting up in the bed with his eyes closed.

I stepped lightly into the kitchen and sat the dishes on the table where some others were sitting. Then I went back out to the porch and got the last one and did the same. Some of the dishes needed to be in the icebox so I quietly opened the icebox and placed them on the wire shelves. As I came back out of the kitchen I looked towards Preacher Sternfield's room and saw his eyes open. I stopped walking hoping he would close his eyes back and I could get out of the house without him seeing me. "Who's there? I need some water to take my pill. I'm starting to have pain again."

"Hi Reverend Sternfield. It's just me, Lacey. I put some food in the kitchen some of the ladies at church sent to you. They will come by and pick up their dishes later this week."

"Lacey, beautiful, Lacey. Can you bring me some water and help me take my pills?"

"Yeah ... sure. I'll be right back."

I got a tall glass from the cupboard and filled it with tap water and took it into Preacher Sternfield's bedroom where he was sitting even straighter in the bed.

"Thanks, Lacey."

"How are you feeling?"

"I'm better now that you are here. My pills are on the dresser."

I got the bottle and read the directions and asked, "When's the last time you took one of these?"

"I don't remember, but I need one."

"This says every four to six hours as needed. Did Johnny Kale give you a pill before he left?"

"No, I don't think so, but it's needed now. He was in a hurry this morning. Someone came to the door and he answered it and left. I don't remember even talking to him this morning."

"Maybe I should call Jake and ask him what your schedule is?"

"He doesn't know anything about when I take my pills."

I thought for a minute about how long Johnny Kale could have been gone and tried to figure out if giving him the pill would cause him a problem this soon. Then I thought about how badly I wanted out of there and that Jake would tell me to get out. "Reverend Sternfield, I'm not comfortable giving you this without knowing if you took one already. I'll go and call Johnny Kale to make sure it's okay."

"Johnny doesn't know about my pain! And call me Mitch. We are better friends than that aren't we, Lacey?"

"But, you are my preacher. Even if we are friends it would be disrespectful for me to call you anything else."

"Not if I ask you to call me Mitch."

"I'm going to call Johnny Kale, I'll be right back."

"Well, at least give me that water. I've been sitting here forever needing some water. I need someone to stay here with me all the time and help me with things. Do you know anyone?"

I walked over to his bedside and handed him the glass. "Well, Miss Hattie who took such good care of my Mother is staying with someone else now. How about Tula? Have you thought about her?"

"I want you to stay with me," and he reached out and took a hold on to my wrist.

"Well, I have to work and I have my own family that needs me so I can't be here, too. Tula might be available. I'll ask her if you want me to, or maybe some of the other ladies know someone."

"Can you just sit a while with me? I hate being here by myself all day."

"Can you get up at all?"

"I can make it over to the chamber pot and back, but after that I'm worn out and usually in a lot of pain."

"You need someone right away. I'll go and call Tula."

"Please don't leave me yet. Just sit and talk to me."

There was no where to sit so I just stood by his bed still connected to him by his grip. "Do you want something to eat?"

"No. I just want you. So how are things going out at the orphanage?"

"Fine. We have too many children that need families, but I love them all so I don't mind being their family for now."

"Are you going to have a family of your own one day?"

"Maybe. Sure. If that's what God wills for me."

"You and your boyfriend haven't talked about that?" and he sank down into the bed some and closed his eyes.

"We have the same thoughts about God so we are ready to do whatever he wants of us."

He seemed to be going to sleep so I lifted the glass out of his hand and reached across him to set it on the only bedside table. Just as I sat it down he through his arms around me and pulled me down on top of him kissing me. The glass crashed to the floor and I pushed with all my might to get away from him, but he didn't let go of his grip. "Stay with me. No one has to know. I won't tell your boyfriend. I know you want me, too. I've seen it in your eyes. This can be our little secret. You can come here as often . . ."

And he tried kissing me again. I couldn't believe he had that much strength and that I wasn't hurting his surgery incision.

"Reverend Sternfield! I think you've had way too much medication. I'm glad I didn't give you anymore. Now, in the name of Jesus, let me go. I'm not interested in you in that way. If you will let me go I will forget all about this and just look at it as a man who has no idea what he's doing."

I wasn't sure what made him let me go, but I thought maybe he was beginning to feel pain from the incision. I got up from the bed and walked to the door. "Aren't you going to clean up the water in the floor?"

"No. I think you have enough strength to do that yourself."

"I can't bend over and clean that up."

"Use a mop."

I was more angry than scared. I hoped he was just drugged to the point he didn't know what he was doing, but the fact that he was concerned about the water in the floor made me think other wise. When I got to *Lion's Hill* I called Johnny Kale and told him that Reverend Sternfield needed a full time nurse to take care of him.

"Lacey, he's fine. He can get around like a jack rabbit. I think his stitches come out in a day or so. I don't think he's even taking his pain medicines anymore. I told him this morning I wasn't coming back tonight because he was doing so well. I hope he hasn't had a relapse and he isn't going to tell me. I'll go by and check on him at lunch time. Thanks for calling me and send my thanks to all you girls who have sent over food. I ate there last night and it was great. Maybe I'll have lunch there today! He'll need help eating up all those dishes so maybe I'll stop back by for supper," and he laughed. "We sure have some good cooks in town. Seems like sickness and funerals brings out the best dishes. I hope if I ever have to have surgery you will bring me some food and care about me like you have Mitch. I know he appreciates it."

"Of course you know I would see to it that you were fed and had a nurse if you needed one."

"Hope the next time you cook for me it's not for my funeral," and he laughed again.

"Well, if you're going where my Mother and Father are she will fix you a meal that's out of this world and you will feel sorry for everyone stuck here eating my cooking."

There was no response from Johnny Kale. I held the phone in silence for about a minute and then he said, "You're a sweet girl. Thanks again for helping us out. I'll see you Sunday if not before."

"Okay, see you then," and we hung up.

I wanted to ask him about Tylar and if he ever heard from him, but I knew he did and I really didn't want to know what he was doing or how he was. For all I knew he was married and had a couple kids. He sent flowers when Mother died, but nothing personal in the card. It just said, "She was a beautiful woman and she will be missed. I love you all, Tylar." No one else's name was signed, but if he was married I wouldn't expect her name to be on there. I could ask Marge anytime I wanted to know something, but I didn't want her to know I ever thought about him. She was so hurt by our break up and worried so much about me and all I had faced these past few years. If she knew I ever thought about him she would pity me and I never wanted that from anyone.

My mind went back to the disturbing moment in Preacher Sternfield's bedroom and I wondered what I was going to do about it. It didn't sound like he was on any medication so that meant that he knew exactly what he was doing, but I told him if he let me go I wouldn't say anything about it. Do I have to keep my word to a scoundrel? Then I remembered Kimmy and grabbed the phone and called her.

"How are you? Do you feel any better?"

"No, not really."

"So what is wrong? Do you need me to come over?"

"No, Mom and Dad are here. I just want to sleep."

"Kimmy, did Preacher Sternfield ask you to give him some of his medication."

She was quiet for a moment. "Did ... he say ... I did something wrong?"

"No! I just wanted to know if anyone helped him get his medication today. Johnny Kale said he didn't and he asked me to give him one of his pills, but I didn't because I didn't know if he had taken one already. I was just feeling bad for him if he needed one and I didn't give it to him."

"He asked me for one, but ... I told him ... I didn't need to be the one to do that ... he would have to wait and that I was supposed to meet you out front."

"You told him I was coming over there?"

"Yeah. Why?"

"No reason I guess. He just didn't seem like he was expecting me. Kimmy, are you sure you don't need me to come over there?"

"I'll just be in bed. I'm fine, Lacey. Nothing that a little time won't cure."

"Okay. Can I pray for you?"

"Yeah, but make it a short one cause I want to get into bed."

"Well, if you won't hurry God you may not have to get back in bed. How about if you believe He will heal you?"

"Okay. I'll try."

I prayed for God to give Kimmy peaceful rest and for her body to line up with the Word of God and function as God had made it. "I love you. Get some rest and be well soon."

"Okay, thanks. I love you, too."

As the day continued I seem to get madder and madder at what had happened with Preacher Sternfield. I was convinced that he knew what he was doing and he thought I would go along with his advancements either out of sympathy for him and his condition or fear. Maybe even thought I was the kind of woman who would find a secret little game exciting passion. But, somehow I was convinced it was fear he was counting on. He just didn't know me very well. If he thought he would use a threat of trashing me and my reputation to get me to submit to his sick games he really was living in the dark. As far as this town was concerned, I didn't have one to trash. In my opinion, I had been accused of much worse than having an affair with someone. To say that I was abusing the gifts of the Holy Spirit was so much worse to me. Besides, I wasn't married, he wasn't married and, although people didn't talk about such behavior, it was going on and no one was all that shocked about it. He was so much older than me he would look like the fool.

I called Jake at the clinic, something I never did, but I had to talk to him.

"Boy, this must be good for you to call me during the day like this. Not that I'm complaining. I would stop in the middle of a delivery to take a call from you."

"I won't ever do it again. That could be one of my sisters or my friends about to deliver. I would never forgive myself if you left them to answer the phone. Please tell me you aren't in the middle of something like that."

"I'm not in the middle of anything. I would like to be in the middle of something with you."

"Good, because I need you. Can you get away for lunch?"

"Yeah. I'm leaving right now. Meet you where?"

"In my office."

Jake came in to the office bringing me a rose. "I stopped by the house and cut this for you. I saw it this morning."

"Oh, Jake, it's beautiful. You are so gifted with your hands in surgery *and* gardening!"

"And with dancing and holding you and . . ."

"Yes all those too. But, I didn't call you over here to talk about that. Well, kind of. I want to talk to you about one of your patients."

"Who?"

"Preacher Sternfield."

"He's not one of my patients anymore. I released him yesterday. He's Dad's again. He will see him to have the stitches removed."

"When will that happen?"

"Maybe tomorrow. I don't know. Why?"

"I saw him today and I was just wondering how sick he still was?"

"You saw him where?"

I didn't want to tell him, but I had to. I knew he was going to be so mad at me for going over there. "At his house."

"*His* house?" He walked over to the chair and sat down. "Okay. So let's hear all about how you thought it was a good idea to go to *his house* for ... what now?"

"Some of the ladies thought they were supposed to bring their dishes to my house, or they didn't want to go over there ..."

"Wonder why?'

"Jake, I called Kimmy and she said she had made some cookies and she would meet me over there. I didn't plan on going alone."

"But Kimmy never made it?"

"No. She was there, but she wasn't feeling good and wanted to go as soon as I got there so she did."

"What's wrong with Kimmy?"

"I don't know. It's weird. She was just sitting out on the steps of his house when I got there and she looked bad. Like she had been crying maybe. So I thought she was hurting, but she didn't act like it. I called her when I got back here and she said she was okay she just wanted to sleep. I thought I would go by and check on her later."

"I'll go with you. So why are you asking about Preacher Sternfield?"

"Well, Jake, please keep a cool head about this, okay?"

He dropped his head back on the head rest of the wing-backed chair. "I'm not going to like what I'm about to hear, am I?"

"I wouldn't call you at work if it wasn't something ... "

"Awful, disgusting? Jesus, *No!*" He jumped up and ran to me. "He didn't."

"No! Calm down. Sit down!"

He took my hand and pulled me over to the couch and sat me down. Then he sat beside me looking straight into my face. "This is not what I had in mind when I said I wanted to be in the middle of something with you, but tell me everything. About the moment Kimmy left until the moment you left. And don't leave out one second of it."

"Okay. But calm down."

"I *am* calm! This is calm?" Jake sat back against the couch. "I can do calm. How's this?"

"Better. I need your help as my friend right now, not as my ... protector."

"I can do that. I think."

"I took the dishes into his house. I have never been there before so I didn't know where the kitchen was or his bedroom, but I figured the kitchen would be in the back of the house so I walked down the hall to the end of it and the kitchen is on the left and his bedroom is on the right. When I first went in he seemed to be asleep so I was quiet then I went out for the last dish I had left on the porch. This time when I came out of the kitchen he had his eyes open and he asked who was there. The strange thing is Kimmy said she told him I was coming so you think he would have said, 'Is that you, Lacey?' and not 'Who's there?' but, anyway he asked me for a glass of water to take his pain pill because he was starting to hurt and I went and got him some water. I gave him the glass of water and went to get his pills and saw that he was supposed to have them four hours apart. I asked him some questions about when he had the last one and so on, but he acted like he didn't know when he had the last one and that he was in pain and needed them. So I told him I was going to ask Johnny Kale, because he had been there that morning, according to Kimmy, and I didn't know if Johnny Kale had given him one already. Anyway, he didn't want me to call him, he just wanted the pill. We talked about him needing someone to help him."

"What? He told you he needed help?"

"Well, maybe I just said he did. He said he only had enough energy to get to the chamber pot and back in the bed so ... "

"Seriously?"

"Yeah, why?"

"If he's like that I need to check on him. Something's not right.

He walked from the hospital door to the car with no problem at all. He was driving the nurses crazy wanting to get out of there."

"Well, here's the rest of the story. He wouldn't let me call you and he just kept saying things like he wanted me to take care of him and that he needed help, but he wanted me. I told him I was way too busy and I would call Tula and see if she could help him. Then he kind of quieted down and lay back on his pillow and he had my wrist in his hand about the whole time we were talking. So he asked me to sit down and stay with him for a little while. I asked him if I could fix him something to eat, but he said no. Well, there wasn't a chair in the room so I just stood there. He said a few more things and seemed to drift off to sleep. He was holding the glass in his hand so I took it from him and he only has one bedside table and it was on the other side of him so I reached over him to set it down on the table. He grabbed me and held me so tight there was no way he was as sick as he led me to believe. He wouldn't let go of me until I said, 'In the Name of Jesus, let me go. I'll forget all about this if you will just let me go,' and he did. Well the glass of water had fallen to the floor and he said, 'Aren't you going to clean that up?' Well, when he said that I knew he wasn't under the influence of medication, cause you wouldn't care about that, would you?"

"Probably not. Did he do anything else besides grab you?"

I closed my eyes and sighed, "He kissed me. I couldn't stop him. It happened so fast and he had his arm under my arm and he was pushing on the back of my head and the other arm was pulling me down on top of him. All I could think was no way I wasn't hurting him where he had been cut open, even though I don't know where that is I knew it had to be there somewhere under me. Jake, what am I going to tell the kids? I can't face this man again."

"Why not? You didn't do anything wrong, he did. Maybe, if you didn't want him to grab you?"

"Jake! What are you saying?"

"I just mean that you're a single woman, he's a single man. People kiss all the time. It's not like he would raise eyebrows with information like that, except that he would look like a pervert chasing after someone so much younger than he is. I don't think you ever have to worry about him saying anything to anyone. Hopefully he was taking the medication, even though he shouldn't need it and he will be a bit embarrassed and never say or do another thing in regards to you."

"That's not the impression I got."

"Why not?"

"He said things to me when he was holding me. Sick things."

"Like what?"

"Like he wanted me to sleep with him right then and there, and we would keep it a secret from you and everyone else. It would be our secret, as if he wanted me to sleep with him then and often behind everyone's back. He didn't even have the decency to ask me to marry him!"

"And if he had you might have considered the offer?"

"Jake! No! I just mean ... "

He put his arms around me, "I know what you mean, baby girl. I'm teasing you."

"You are teasing me and I'm really mad about this."

"I'll go out and check on him and I'll know for sure if he was high as a kite or if he is a sick dirty old man. If he turns out to be a dirty old man, you know I don't want you anywhere near him without me. Not with Kimmy, Johnny Kale, Pappy, Mayree, nobody except me. I have to be there. So if some Sunday I can't go to church with you, you aren't going. Willie and the rest can take the children, but you aren't going."

"Even if it turns out that he was doped up, I'm not going anywhere around him without you."

"I like that. It will be hard for you two to have an affair with me there."

I slapped Jake on the leg. "Stop it! It's not funny. I think he's a nut and he scared me ... " Jake looked at me with disbelief. "Well, okay. He didn't scare me he made me madder than a swatted hornet. I haven't been able to trust him at all and now I don't like him."

"But, you have to love him."

"Not if he turns out to work for the other side! I only have to love my brothers."

"He's a preacher! Surely you don't think he's unsaved?"

"The behavior I saw today is not that of a man who has the fruit of the Spirit. 'You shall know them by their fruit'!"

"Good point."

"Do you need to get back to work?"

"No, I told Dad you sounded like you had a big problem and I might not make it back in. He didn't have anymore appointments and I only had two so he said he would take them for me. Let's go out and check on Kimmy and then drop by Preacher Sternfield's."

"Okay on seeing Kimmy, but you can just leave me at her house if you're going over there."

"No I'm not. You're going with me."

"No I'm not. I have no reason to go back over there."

"How about if you give me some news to share with the preacher?"

"Like what?"

"I would love to tell him you're having my baby, but that . . ."

"You are so silly sometimes."

Jake walked over to the rose I had laid down on my desk and brought it over to where I was standing. "Maybe I could tell him that you are going to let me plant some of my roses in your yard."

"Why would he care if you planted roses in my yard? Are you *really* going to plant some in my yard?"

"I would like to."

"I've always wanted roses, but I can't seem to make them grow. Of course you would put me to shame so that's the real reason I don't have any. But, they are so beautiful in your yard. How nice it must be for your mother to walk out into that beautiful garden and smell their fragrance and cut some to bring inside. But, you would have to take care of them because I would just kill them. But, again I don't think you planting roses in my yard is enough to keep the preacher from thinking he and I might be able to get together. You know he even said he saw it in my eyes that I wanted him. He's crazy. Crazy people don't care who planted your roses."

"There's something really special about this rose. It comes with its own gardener, who has no life unless he's planted next to you. Sometimes the outside looks a little bruised and worn and has been known to be a bit prickly at times, but with a lot of tender love and coaxing it always brings forth something quite beautiful. And if you look deep inside there's always a surprise that you never expected God to put there." He held the rose up close to my face and slipped his fingers between the pedals. "Do you see anything in there?"

"Just your fingers."

"Lacey, will you let me plant a garden in your backyard and work it and keep it and make it grow for you? And will you let me love you and work together, to keep each other, to make our love grow stronger and stronger, forsaking all others, as if I haven't already? And would you marry me and be my wife and raise a family together?" And he pulled the pedals down and exposed a ring with a thin setting holding a small diamond set between two emeralds.

"Oh my gosh, Jake. I wasn't expecting this at all. It has my birth stone. Did you know that?"

He smiled and nodded. "That's me in the middle."

"You've really caught me off guard."

"You don't need to be on guard with me. I love you. I would never hurt you."

"I know that, Jake. I just didn't expect this, I didn't expect you."

"You didn't expect me? What do you mean by that?"

"I didn't expect you to know my birth stone and get a ring so pretty and simple and just perfect. I don't know what to say."

He took my hands in his and pleaded, "Say yes. I can't stand another night without you. Do you ever wish I was lying beside you?"

"Every night."

He stood back with a look of surprise, "You know? That's something you've never told me. What are we waiting for? Everyday apart is a day lost to me. I have a hard time concentrating during the day because I've spent the night looking at the ceiling wishing you were with me. Every time the phone rings I hope you're having a problem and it's you calling. Now that's just not right! But, I know you won't call me unless you're having a problem. I want to call you every minute of the day, but I'm afraid you will think I'm a nut and want me to go away. I couldn't bare that, but I promise to give you the space you need, the time you need to teach the children, visit those God has placed in your heart. I will never stand between you and Him, ever. I won't hold you back. I want you to be all God wants you to be, but I want to have a small piece of you. I promise not to take too much or more than you are willing to give me."

"But Jake, I would want to give you all of me."

"Yeah, well I know you would, but ... you would?"

"Of course. I want to have a marriage where two people are one, just like the Bible teaches. I can't imagine being married to someone who was doing one thing, going in a different direction than me. I want us to be together in our thinking, our playing, our relationship to God. All that has to work together."

"Is that 'us' you and me, or do you mean whoever you marry?"

"That 'us' is *us*, you and me. I've just been waiting for ... I have to have a husband who wants to do the will of God no matter what that will might be or how much it will cost us. And it will cost us to follow God."

"I know, and I want that, too, but I just guess I want you more than I want to tell you no or stand in your way or ... I don't know. I don't know what I'm saying."

"I do. I know too well. You've been listening to me way to closely and I've caused you to compromise because you think that's what you have to do to have me. But, you don't. I want to be your wife. I want to be one with you and go where God sends us and be what God wants each one of us to be. We can be ourselves and love each other. I see that now. I would never want you to give up who you are so that you could be my husband under my selfish rules. I want to be happy. I want to be complete and if I set out a bunch of rules we will never be at peace as a couple. I know now that the only way to be successful in a marriage is to do as the Bible teaches. I want to be your helpmate. I want to lift you up and hold you when you need me and encourage you as you lead our family. I know that you love me as Jesus loved the church and was willing to die for it. And there shouldn't be a but to this sentence, but I'm not going to ask you to die to who God has made you just so you can have me. I'm sure that's a physical death that Paul is talking about; I hope you would never have to do that! Jake, do you know, really know deep down inside that I love you? I've never loved anyone like I love you and I didn't think it was possible to love another human being like I love you. I'm not on the rebound; I've waited long enough to prove that to myself. These past years that you have been in Charleston I've thought of you. I wanted you to come home to me. I'm not just lonely, reaching out to whoever will show me a desire. If that were true I would be in the bed with Preacher Sternfield. Oh, that's not a good vision, but you get my point. I have such a peace when I'm with you. I never feel like I have to pretend to be someone else with you. You are who I need to spend the rest of my life with cause we just ... fit. I love you Jake and I do want to be your wife."

"But?"

"I don't have a but, really. If I did it would be that even though I read about marriage in the Bible I don't know how to do it. It would be something we both would have to work at and be completely honest and open with each other about. I don't think you ever would, but I would need you to be so patient with me and not get hurt or angry if I wasn't doing something right. We would need to pray about it and seek His Word to know what will make our marriage work. You will be perfect, I will make mistakes. Can you put up with that?"

"Silly girl, of course I can. That's what will make it a beautiful relationship. Growing together. Learning together. I can promise you one thing for sure, I will make mistakes. I will disappoint you, but I will always try harder. What other reservations do you have?"

"I just always thought my parents would be there. I don't want to have a big wedding and maybe not a wedding at all because I miss them and I would be a mess. That's not really fair to you or your family. Your parents would want a wedding for you."

"Your Nanny would be the one who would have a problem. But, I know you. You will regret it later when our own daughter is getting married and she asks about your wedding and wants to see pictures. We can think about that later, for now will you put this ring on your finger and kiss me like you really do mean 'yes'?"

He put the rose down on the desk and took my hand. "Lacey, tell me again. Will you marry me?"

"Yes, Jake. As long as you don't get cold feet and run out on me, I will marry you."

"Maybe we should just seal it right here so that neither one of us has a chance to change our minds," and he slid the ring onto my finger.

"What do you mean by that? It would take a day or so to get a license?"

"I don't remember God teaching us anything about getting a license by the state to become man and wife. Jacob worked for seven years to make Rachel his wife. Sure Laban threw a party right before he sent his first daughter Leah into the tent for Jacob to make his wife, but it wasn't a wedding. It was years later when man came up with that tradition. Before that a man and a woman gave themselves to each other and God recognized their union once they consummated the relationship. Like Adam and Eve, they didn't have a wedding. Eve came from Adam's rib and God said that because woman came from man, from now on man would leave his parents and unite with his wife and become one flesh. How intimate is that? I know some guys at school united with several girls and I wonder if God sees them married to them all or just the first one. I hear God saying that the uniting part is what made them man and wife. The only decree I read about was a divorce decree, and the guys at school didn't write one out for those ladies they were with. I guess in God's eyes they are polygamists or adulterers?"

"Or forgiven."

"That, I prayed for years to see happen for them. They're good boys, just lost."

"But, if they do have a born again experience and receive Jesus as their Lord and Savior they will be forgiven for all that stuff and be the husband of one wife?"

"Oh, absolutely. If they stop doing it. But, their carousing is not God's best."

"I've never though about this before, but you're right I don't know anywhere in the scriptures that says we have to have a wedding and a piece of paper. I want the paper, but that's not what makes you my husband or me your wife."

"No. Documents can be torn up or destroyed, but a covenant is forever. I want to covenant with you, Lacey, to always love you and keep myself pure in mind, body and spirit. I want to make that covenant today, right now. Do you?"

"Yes, Jake. You know I do. I don't want or need all the traditions of this world. I want what God wants and I want to ask Him to give us to each other. No one else has the right to do it. Tomorrow I will get you a ring, because I want my husband to wear a ring."

"I will be honored to wear a ring pronouncing to the world that you are my wife and I am completely yours. Come sit with me in front of the window."

Jake and I sat on the floor looking out the full length window towards the back courtyard where the children played when they were not in class. We spent some time in prayer asking God to bless our union and to watch over us as a family. Mostly we prayed about being in His service in all that we did from that day forward. Jake asked that our families be behind us and not try to tear apart what the three of us had joined together. Then we said our vows to each other.

"I, Lacey Kale Rutledge, take you, Jacob Harrison Foresight, to be my best friend, my lover and my husband from this moment until the day we are parted by death. I promise to love you with all that is in me, to comfort you when you are needing comfort, to hold you up when you are falling down, to create a home that you long to get back to. I promise to keep my thoughts and motives pure. And I promise to never shame your reputation, but to cherish you, honor you, and reverence your leadership in our home. You are a gift from God and even though I'm sure there will be days I won't think so, you are the most perfect gift that God has ever or ever will give to me. Even more precious that our children will be. I promise to never lose sight of that. I can never thank you enough for what you have been to me during these really hard days I have faced. Your friendship is what kept me breathing. Your love is what brought me out of that field when my Father died. Your's and your families compassion and devotion to my Mother's care is what helped me let her go when she died, because I knew that she had been given the best care possible and it was indeed God's plan to take her home. You are a part of every piece of me. I am so honored to be loved by you and blessed to have you as my husband."

"I have no words to express my love for you, but I will try." Jake took a deep breath and began his vow, "I, Jacob Harrison Foresight, take you, Lacey Kale Rutledge, to be my wife. You are the only woman I have ever loved, except my Mom, but she doesn't count. I promise to keep it that way, too. I will never love another even if you leave me by death. May God see to it that I go first because I could not bear to live without you. I promise to love you, honor you, protect you, let you cry on my shoulder, and never question your efforts because I know you hear from God. I will always trust you. You will have to give me a shocking reason to do otherwise. I watched you grow into a woman of complete integrity. That is your greatest attribute, besides your beautiful green eyes and blazing locks. I could spend the rest of the day telling you how beautiful you are and what I see in you, but I need to tell you what I'm willing to covenant with you and I can only say that you have all of me. There's nothing that I do now that I don't think about how it will affect you and I don't ever see that changing. You are my world and I promise to shelter your world from the rain, from raging storms, from whirlwinds, from cold. I promise to always be that safe place you can come to. I never want to stop being your friend to be your husband. I can be both and I promise to do so. Thank you for seeing me." And he lowered his head, "Thank you for seeing past the frightened Jake," he took a deep breath and looked back at me, "the Jake who is so awkward and thought he would never get the girl of his dreams. Thank you for looking deeper and finding the man who's always loved you and always will. I promise, if you will let me, I will be your everything, just like you are mine. I will make you happy, Lacey. After today there's no going back to that girl that lives across the road. Are you willing to honor me by being my wife forever?"

"I am."

After some time of quiet just basking in the Glory of the Lord we went out the back of the house and walked down to the river taking a blanket to sit on once we got there.

It was still warm, although the sun was behind the trees making its way to the horizon. I was blissfully happy to be in Jake's arms feeling no shame for being so close and tangled around him. It was passion one minute and joy the next. I didn't know how I would ever pull away from him long enough to walk back to the house once the sun was gone.

We were laying on our sides looking into each other's eyes when Jake said, "How sick do you think Kimmy is?"

"Oh my gosh. We have to go and check on her, but I don't want to ever leave here."

"We have to pretty soon or we'll never find our way back up that hill when the sun sets. So ... where am I sleeping tonight?"

"With me, in our home. Hope you don't mind that we have a full house."

"Are you sure?"

"You are my husband, Jake Foresight, and my husband lives with me. I just need to talk to Pappy."

"Do we need to do that together?"

"We can. I think he would like to hear you tell him how you've whisked his granddaughter away and now you want to sleep with her without a piece of paper."

"That doesn't sound good."

"I'm just trying to make you nervous! My Pappy will be completely behind us. He knows more than anyone how God builds a family and how the traditions of this world clutter up the simplicity and beauty of God. That was a beautiful ceremony we three shared in that home built for His children by the hands of my Father. How beautiful and special is that? I praise God He showed you what He wanted for us. That is the kind of wedding I *want* to tell my children about."

We walked back up to the house and saw Pappy coming out of the front door.

"Aha. There you are. Jake! I sure didn't expect you to be out here this time of day. Kind of slow at the clinic?"

"Pappy, Jake and I want to share something with you."

He looked down at my hand immediately and saw the engagement ring. "It's about time, little Lady. I thought you were going to run this poor boy around in circles for the rest of his life. Ya-ho-oo!" and he picked me up and spun me around. "This family has something to smile and laugh about again. Your Nanny will be crazy with wedding plans. I'm gonna give you the biggest and the most extravagant wedding any woman has had in these parts, in any parts! I don't care what it cost, it's yours. You just do . . ."

"Pappy, Pappy. Whoa. You're really going to like what Jake and I have to tell you better than your plan. You just don't know it yet. We aren't going to have a wedding. We're already married."

"Hold on Jeremiah, all but the consummating part."

"What are you taking about, Jake? Lacey, you eloped?'

"Pappy. We got married a few hours ago, in my office. We made a covenant with each other and God gave me to Jake and Jake to me and it was beautiful. It was just like God wanted it, not like what man has made out of getting married. I love Jake, Pappy, and I want him to be my husband forever and there's just no reason to keep putting it off."

"I would have asked you, Sir ..."

"Why would you have to ask me? You asked the person you should have asked, Lacey. She's the one who has to put up with you for the rest of your life. As for me and Nanny, we couldn't be happier for both of you and you have more than my blessings if that's what you are seeking."

"Well, yes and also, I'm taking Jake home with me tonight and I guess I'm hoping you are okay with that seeing how we don't have a license."

"You apply for it tomorrow. Who cares about it anyway. Your Nanny and I didn't have our license for three weeks after we set up housekeeping together. We had a honeymoon period of about two weeks and then drove to my Mother's house and picked up Alvin. While we were there we applied for our license, because there wasn't a town hall here at that time, and it arrived about a week later. No one knew the difference. You *will* let us have a party for you?"

"Lacey doesn't want ..."

"Pappy, Mother loved parties; I miss her and Pa so much."

"But, your brothers and sisters will want to have a party for you and if you don't let them this family will start skipping chances to get together. We don't ever want to do that. If there is one thing God loves its families coming together and sharing with each other so they can remain close. 'Don't forsake the fellowship of the brethren,' or the brothers and sisters, or aunts and uncles."

"Maybe a family reunion party, but nothing big and out there. I know how you and Nanny can make something so much more than it has to be. I would rather save the money and use it for Abbie Lou or Retta's wedding or send one of my kids to college. You know that Bailey has applied at several schools already. I really want that for him. Let's wait a few weeks, too, before we have the party. What I would like more than a party is some time with my husband, alone, so once he can get away I want to be able to take a few days and spend them with him, not planning a party."

"Where are you thinking about going?"

"Oh, I don't know if we can go anywhere. I just mean it would be nice to be at home with Jake alone. The kids would be at school during the day and we would have time then. If Dr. Jude will let him have some time? We don't need a vacation, just a little time to break Jake into his new family life."

"Did I tell you how thrilled I am that Jake's the man you chose to spend your life with?" Pappy reached his hand out to Jake and he said, "Congratulations, Son. You finally did it. You wanted this one a long time didn't you?"

"Yes, sir. I was ready to walk to the ends of the earth if that's what it took."

"William would be so proud and later today I suppose Jesus will sit down and tell him and Abigail all about it. I know you have their blessings, as well." Pappy hugged Jake and hugged me again. "I have to make a call before I leave. Where are you two headed?"

"Kimmy wasn't feeling good this morning so we want to check on her and then Jake may need to see one of his patients and then we will be headed home to tell the kids our news."

"Before we do that we have to tell my parents I won't be home tonight."

Pappy yelled back, "Or any other night. That ought to break Sally's heart. Her baby boy leaving the nest for good this time."

"She's gotten used to me living away from home. She complains every day about my stuff being in her way. I think she will have me all packed up and ready to move out by morning." Jake wrapped me in his arms. "I can hardly believe this. I keep thinking it's a dream and we're going to wake up, you in your bed and me in mine, and ..."

"Jake, let's go see your parents, get whatever you need for tonight, go see Kimmy and then come back to my house before we wake up. I'm so looking forward to the honeymoon and I don't want to wake up before that. Skip Preacher Sternfield, please? Johnny Kale is there by now and if he's having a problem your Dad has been available. I don't want to waste another minute."

"It's started already. I'll never be able to say 'no' to you."

"Jake!"

"I'm just kidding. Sounds good to me. Get your sweater and purse; I'll pull the car around to the back. We'll get your car tomorrow."

"Okay. See ya at the back door."

Just as I was going in to get my things Pappy came out. "Jake, hang on a minute. Lacey, where are you going?"

"To get my purse and sweater. I'm going out the back door, are the kids at supper?"

"Yeah. Your baby girl was asking for you."

"I will miss her tonight. Hopefully they will let me leave."

"When are you going to tell them?"

"Right now, I guess. They need to understand why I'm not going to be here to tuck them in."

Pappy went out to Jake and I went in to tell my children that I was married to Jake Foresight. They wanted to know what to call me and I told them to call me what they had always called me, Lacey. That was not going to change. I did hate not being there to bathe my babies and rock them to sleep, but I would be able to the next night. There would be plenty of nights to rock babies and I praised God for each one of my children and my best friend, and now husband.

chapter twenty-three

We drove out to Jake's house, but Jude and Sally were not there. Jake got a change of clothes and left a note saying he was going to be out all night and he would explain in the morning. He also said that if he was needed for an emergency that they could call my house; that I knew where he would be. Mollie was home, but Millie had gone with Willie into town to get a soda. That was the first we had heard of the two of them going off together. "I think they're just friends," Mollie said. "But who knows, things change so fast these days. That sure is a pretty rock you have there, Lacey."

"Thank you. Your brother gave that to me."

"That reminds me," and Jake left the room and went back down the hall.

"Does that mean that you are . . . "

"Crazy about each other, that's what that means."

"I'm so glad. I hoped Jake wouldn't marry a mean old girl that wouldn't let him come home and see his family anymore."

"Now, who do you know that does that? There's not a man out there who doesn't do just what he wants to do. My Pa's Mother always thought my Mother kept him from driving all the way up to their house to see them, but my Mother begged him to go and see his parents. He was just too busy in his own mind or something. Who knows, but it wasn't because my Mother didn't try to get him to go.

I guess it has something to do with what the Bible says about a man leaving his mother and father and cleaving to his wife. God just gives them a desire to stay at home with their wives and family, but you live right across the street and you will see your brother Jake all the time. Besides he works with your parents every day. No one is going to take your brother away from you."

"Jake came back into the room. "Are you girls finished man bashing?"

"We were not man bashing. I was just telling the truth."

"Tell Mom and Dad everything's fine and give them the note. Talk to you tomorrow, we've got to aggravate the gravel."

"*Agitate* the gravel. You are so far from cool, Jake."

"I'm working on it. Besides who says it's agitate? I'm so cool I know what it really is and you and your greaser friends are just nerd wannabe's."

"Keep telling yourself that, Big Daddy."

We walked to the door and Jake said, "We've got to split, our chariot awaits."

Mollie laughed and said, "Ya'll be cool."

Kimmy was in her room when we arrived and Aunt Penny was being her usual angry insulting self. Jake and I went into her room and found her lying on her bed curled up with her back to the door.

"Kimmy? Are you awake?"

She slowly turned her head and looked at us. "Yeah, I'm awake," and she rolled back over.

"Do you mind if Jake and I come in and check on you?"

"No. Come on in."

She slowly turned on to her back and pulled herself up in the bed. I went around to the far side and sat on the bed near the foot. I could tell she had been crying. Jake pulled a chair up beside her where he could check her out easily.

"Kimmy, I told Jake that you weren't feeling well so he offered to ride out here with me so he could ease my mind."

"Where do you feel bad?" Jake asked her as he took his stethoscope and thermometer out of his bag.

"Nowhere really, just everywhere."

"Do you hurt somewhere?"

"No. I'm really okay. I just need to rest. Maybe my body is just running down."

"Have you had a fever?"

"I don't think so."

"You don't feel like you do right now, but let's take your temp just to make sure," and he put the thermometer in her mouth.

"Have you been sleeping good at night?"

Kimmy nodded, then she shook her head, then she put her hands up as to say she didn't know.

"How long have you felt like this?"

"Jake, just this morning. Right Kimmy? She sounded fine when I talked to her this morning."

Kimmy nodded at me.

"Let's wait another minute and get her temp and then she can answer the questions. I bet you haven't had anything to eat or drink all day have you?"

She shook her head.

"Lacey, will you get her some water. If she has had a temperature her body would have used up all her water and I wouldn't feel a temp on her skin anymore. Let's not get dehydrated on top of what else is wrong. You have to drink water to keep that from happening."

I got up and left the room. I had a feeling Jake wanted me out so he could talk to Kimmy alone so I took my time getting the water. Uncle Alvin was sitting at the kitchen table reading the paper.

"Have you had something to eat?"

"No, not yet. Jake and I are going to get something on the way home."

"Aren't you usually at the orphanage this time of day?"

"Yeah, but today is a special day for Jake and I so we are doing things different."

He dropped the paper and looked at me. "What makes it so special?"

"Well, Jake and I got married today and we're going to go by the drive-in and pick up a sandwich and take it home and have our first meal together as husband and wife."

"A sandwich from the drive-in? That doesn't sound very romantic." He put the paper back in front of him and said, "Maybe starting out simple is just what will make it last. Congratulations. I like that boy. There ain't many like him or his Daddy. You sure did better than I thought you were . . . you got a good man. Take care of him."

Aunt Penny walked in the door.

"What are you two talking about?"

"Who said we were talking? I'm reading the paper and she's listening. Help her find the glasses or offer her a drink."

"I came in to get Kimmy some water."

Aunt Penny glared at me, "She can get her own water. She's done nothing all day to help me, just sat in her room and now she wants everyone to wait on her. She can forget it if she thinks I'm going to stop what I'm doing and wait on her. You go tell her to com get her own water."

"Penny! You didn't tell me Kimmy hadn't come out of her room. What's wrong with her?"

"Uncle Alvin we don't know. That's why I had Jake come with me. He's taking her temperature now and he told me to get her some water."

"I never have understood you. What did you have children for if you weren't going to be their Mother?" Uncle Alvin harshly folded the paper and pressed it down on the table as he slid back his chair. Then he rolled out of the kitchen and down the hall.

"Why can't you just leave people alone? No one asked you to come over here. I hope you don't think I'm going to wait on her, too. My life has been ruined taking care of a crippled husband, I'm not about to take care of a grown woman who's just spoiled. She looked fine to me. She's always looking for someone to wait on her. She needs a man, a real man, someone with an education and a desire to aspire to something other than a farmer or a country doctor. I sure wish she had met that Tylar Lane before you did. I would have never let her allow him to get away. But, I guess you spoiled girls don't know how important it is to find a rich man and hold on to him no matter what it cost you. If I had a son-in-law like him I could get out of this hell hole."

"Aunt Penny, you don't know your own daughter. She is far from spoiled and she is one of the most giving people I know. It's a shame you can't see that. Is this where the glasses are kept?"

She reached into the cabinet next to the sink. "Here. I'm sure you've never seen glasses like these, but this is what we have to drink out of because Alvin has a stingy Father. There's cold water in the ice box."

The glass she handed me was a beautiful cut crystal glass. "Aunt Penny, my Nanny and Pappy have plastic cups they got from the drive-in and jelly jars for everyday glasses. I have jelly jars and each one is special to me because they remind me of breakfasts with my Mother and Pa and Nanny and Pappy. I wouldn't trade them for a dozen of these so I guess you're right. You should ask Pappy nicely to come over for breakfast. He will bring the jelly every time and you can keep the jars after the jelly's gone, too. These are pretty, but your right I've never seen anything like them and I'm really glad I haven't. Excuse me, Kimmy needs this water."

I took the water into Kimmy's room where Jake was standing by her bed and Uncle Alvin had pulled his chair up on the side where I had been standing. He was holding Kimmy's hand and saying, "You can tell me when you don't feel good. I think there's some stew left. Your Mother told me you and Theodore where eating in town so I kind of overate, but if there's no more I will fry you an egg or something. What would you like?"

"I really don't want anything."

"The doctor says you have to eat, here's Lacey with your water."

Jake took the water from my hand, "Drink every bit of this and Alvin, she needs two more, full, before she sleeps for the night."

"I can do that. Kimmy, did they tell you their news?"

Kimmy looked over at Jake and I and said, "What?"

Jake smiled at me and said, "So you've been in the kitchen sharing?"

Uncle Alvin said, "Just with me. Penny and her busybody friends need to be kept in the dark for a while. I just love seeing how long it takes for them to find something out. They think they are the first with the scoop, but most of the time their news is old news," and he chuckled.

"So what's your news?"

"Well, Jake and I got married today."

"Oh, Lacey. You guys are perfect for each other and I know how long you've wanted this, Jake. I'm so glad you finally realized that this is what God has wanted all along, Lacey."

"I've know for a while now. He told me one day while I was praying about what to do with my life and how I could serve Him," and I looked up at Jake who had wrapped his arm around me and pulled me in close to his side.

"You never told me that. What did He say?"

"That I could love you and serve Him at the same time."

"You guys are going to have beautiful babies."

"Kimmy!"

"Well, you are. And I can't wait to baby-sit."

"I have a house full right now that you can baby-sit anytime you want."

"I like baby babies, like Eliza and baby Ben."

"Well, you could go and rock them to sleep tonight for me if you weren't feeling bad. Doc, what's wrong with Kimmy?"

"I didn't find anything other than she needs some fluids and some rest. Hopefully that's all it is and not the start of something else that hasn't shown up yet. If you start to run a fever or get sick to your stomach call me immediately."

"So where will you be tonight, Doc? Are you sure you want us calling you?" and Uncle Alvin laughed again.

"Call my Dad. He will be here in a minute, and if you get really sick, so will I. He'll know where to find me."

Kimmy reached her arms up and hugged my neck tighter than she ever had. She started to cry again as she said into my ear, "I'm so happy for you. You got one of the good guys."

"God has one for you, too. Just hold on, he's coming."

She whispered, "Not now."

I lift up away from her and looked at her face. "What are you talking about? You are still very young. My heavens, you are five years younger than me and look how long it took me and God to get this thing settled. And Jake didn't go anywhere while I was trying to figure it all out. You will have someone, silly girl. Just because I'm married I'm not leaving you. And you will still go places with me, with us, and meet people who will introduce you to boys and you will meet the one God wants for you, you will. Just pray about it and tell Him what you want and He will send Him. Now drink some of this water and dry those tears. You've got to get to feeling better and then you won't be so sad."

She drank over half the water and I gave her a tissue to dry her eyes. Uncle Alvin said he would sit with her for a little while and make sure she drank the water Jake had prescribed.

"I'll call you in the morning, Alvin, to see how she is if you don't call for me during the night."

"She'll be fine. I won't bother you tonight, but I will call your Dad if she was to get worst. Now you kids go on and have a good night. Hey, where'd you get marr ..."

The door opened and Aunt Penny came into the room. "Well, is she dying?"

"I'll check back with you in the morning, Alvin," and we walked out of the room.

"You sure know how to clear a room, Penny."

"Well, is somebody going to tell me what's wrong with her?"

We closed the door behind us as we left the house and all I could think was how I hated to leave Kimmy there to take the abuse her Mother dished out to her daily. When we got in the car I could tell that Jake was deep in thought about something, but when I ask he just said he felt the same way I did about leaving Kimmy there and he was feeling sorry for her.

We drove to the drive-in dinner where Debbie Dunn was waiting for us. She skated out to the car and said, "Jake Foresight, I wait here night after night for you to come see me. Where have you been?"

"Well, Debbie today I was off ..."

I pinched his leg so he wouldn't tell her that we were married. I didn't want that getting around just yet. I needed to talk to Retta, Abbie, Willie and Cole. I was sure Nanny knew by now, but Willie would probably be hurt if someone besides me told him. I didn't know where he and Millie had gone and I didn't want to take a chance that they might come by the drive-in.

"I've been off with Lacey. She and I are jacketed you know?"

"No I did not know that. Hey, Lacey. If you ever get tired of him send him my way."

"I'll do that, Debbie."

She flipped open her order pad, "So what will you have?"

"We need two chili burgers to go."

"Fries with that?"

"Yea, make um' a plates."

"What do you want on the burgers?"

"All the way."

"Drinks?"

"Na. We got something at home, don't we babe?"

"Yeah, I made some tea."

"Okay. It will be about ten minutes on the burgers. Anything else? We've got a good apple pie today."

"Have you got any cake?"

"I'll check, but I think we're out. I know we have pie."

"Two pieces of cake if you have it. If not we'll take the pie."

"Okay, it will be right up."

Jake looked over at me and said, "Now that we're married don't you think you could come over here and sit closer to me. Maybe all these girls will stop hitting on me."

I slid over in the seat beside Jake and laid my head on his shoulder putting my arm around his waist. "Is that better?"

"Much better."

We got our supper and pulled out of the dinner headed in the wrong direction. "Are you going to Preacher Sternfield's!"

"I though he should be the next person we told about our marriage."

"He won't believe you and I'm not going in."

"Oh come on. Don't you think it will be fun to see his face when I tell him how I don't appreciate him grabbing at my wife?"

"No. I really don't care if I ever see his face again, but I know that I will have to sometime or another, just not tonight."

Jake turned the car down the road leading to Nanny and Pappy's house.

"You're messing with me again. Now where are we going?"

"You'll see."

He turned into Nanny and Pappy's drive, "Why didn't you tell me I was coming here? You know Pappy told Nanny by now."

We drove around to the back of the house and Jake got out of the car. He went to the flower pot on the back porch and lifted it up and got something from under it. Then he went to the door and opened it and back to the flower pot. I looked around the backyard and over at the garage and saw that Pappy's truck was there, but Nanny's car was gone. Jake came to my door and opened it saying, "Well, here we are. Your honeymoon awaits."

I got the boxes with our dinner from the floorboard and stepped out of the car and walked with Jake to the back door. "Where is everybody and why are we going to the back door and what's under that flower pot? And my honeymoon awaits at my house!"

Jake lifted me up in his arms and pushed the door open with his foot as we went through the door way and into the back hall. "I've always wanted to do that and I will do it again when I take you into the house we will be living in, wherever that is?"

"What's wrong with my house?"

"We'll have to talk about that later, but to answer your other questions, Pappy put the key under the flower pot and Nanny and Pappy are staying at your house tonight so we can have the place to ourselves."

He carried me into the kitchen and I reached out for the light switch. Nanny and Pappy had set the table with a white table cloth and their good china with a large silver candle arbor in the center of the table. "Oh Jake, did you know about this?"

"No. He just said for me to bring you here and they would stay at your house for the night."

On the table by the candle arbor was a box of matches and a small round cake with white icing and a blue and pink ribbon tied in a bow stuck off to the side with a toothpick. Someone had written, *We Love You, Lacey & Jake* on the top. "Guess we'll have the pie for breakfast," Jake said as we stood by the table looking at all my grandparents had done to make our wedding night even more special. "Guess I should have gone to the Garden Patch and picked up steaks?"

"Does seem a little overdone for chili burgers, but it will seem like the finest cuisine in this setting with my husband. I'm so happy, Jake," and I held him like I had always dreamed of holding him.

He kissed my neck and said, "I'm not hungry, but I'm going to sit at this lovely table and savor every minute. I don't want to rush this night. I've waited too long for everything to be perfect and I'm asking you to keep me from getting in a hurry."

"You think I can do that? I want you to carry me off from this room to any room and . . ."

He pulled away from me and said, "I can see that I'm on my own here. You're not going to be any help. Okay, the french fries are getting cold. We may have to invite some people over to keep you from throwing yourself at me and having your way with me right here . . ."

"Now you better stop it or you will get cold french fries for breakfast with pie and cake and burgers. And you will have to eat them all because Nanny will have a hundred questions as to why we didn't eat anything."

He just sighed and opened the boxes with our supper in them and placed the paper plates on top of the china plates. "No need to have to wash the plates when we have perfectly good plates with the food already on them. Now, let's see what we have to drink."

He went to the ice box and pulled out a pitcher of iced tea and filled the glasses on the table. "Guess we'll have to wash them."

"Not till the morning."

"Okay, my beautiful wife, dinner is served."

He pulled the chair out for me to sit and as I did he took my hand in his and kissed me from my finger tips to my shoulders and across to my neck. "Hmm, I better sit down. But, before I do . . ." He struck a match and lit four of the eight candles before he had to strike another match. Then he walked over to the light switch and turned the overhead light off. The candles were just enough light to see our food and each other, but low enough to make the room enticing. I was nervous and surprisingly calm at the thoughts of exposing myself completely to another person. I sensed that Jake was feeling the same way.

He picked up his plate that was at the end of the table and brought it to the side so he could sit closer to me. "I don't ever want to be that far away from you again. Even when we have children, at Sunday dinners you are going to sit beside me not at the other end of the table, okay?"

"I like that, too," and I held out my hand for him to take. "If we can work it out I don't want you farther than this from me, ever."

"What about when I have to go to work?"

"I've decided you can never do that again."

"Wouldn't that be wonderful? But, how about this?" And he reached into his pocket. "I got a little something for you so you will always remember this night and have a piece of me close to you always."

"When? When did you have time to get me something?"

"Oh, my Lady. I have a bedroom full of gifts for you for every occasion. I've been planning for this day since, since before you and Tylar ever met it seems like."

"No you have not."

"No, I haven't been buying you gifts that long cause I was just a kid, but I've wanted you to be my wife since I met you and I heard the preacher say one day that if you wanted something you should start preparing for it. If you just sit around wishing, it would not come true, but if you showed God that you were serious and if you kept speaking it you and He together would bring it to life. So I planned for our engagement, I planned for our wedding day and I've planned for our future, but right now I'm going to give you what I bought for your wedding night," and he handed me something small wrapped in tissue paper.

"Jake, I'm ashamed to say that I have nothing for you."

"Never be ashamed and never say that to me. You have everything and you are everything for me. Without you this is just stuff."

I pealed open the paper and inside was a gold charm with two hearts overlapping each other with an F engraved where they met at the top hanging on a gold chain. "The F is for Foresight, but it's also for forever. I will love you forever."

"I love it, Jake. And I love you," then I kissed him. "Put it on me?"

"I got it to go on your bracelet, but the other day I saw this necklace and though you might like to wear it on a chain for a little while, till I give you another one."

"You cannot spoil me."

"You can not tell me that now. What will I do with all my surprises?"

"I guess you have no more gifts to buy for me. You can give me one for my birthday, one for Christmas and so on."

"But, I have one more to give you now."
"No. I'll feel bad."
"You won't."
"No, eat your supper. No more gifts."
"I'll give it to you after supper."
"No."
"Do not tell your husband no. A wife needs to learn that first off."
"Behave yourself and she won't have to."

When we finished our meal we cut our cake and Jake fed me and I fed him just like we had always seen people do when they got married. Then we covered it with the cake tin and set it in the ice box to keep it fresh. Jake turned on the light while I cleaned off the table and then he took the candle arbor down the hall. "Hey, where are you going with that?"

"You'll see," and he turned into the living room and disappeared.

Shortly he came back and asked if I was finished, and I was, so he lifted me up again into his arms and carried me down the hall, through the living room, up the stairs and walked toward one of the upstairs bedrooms. "You are going to be surprised when you see what your grandparents have left in here for you."

As we turned into the doorway of the room I could see the light from the candles glowing. The bed was made and turned down with a dark blue robe laying next to a white negligee and matching robe. Jake stood me on the floor and said, "Do you want to change?"

I walked over and picked up the gown. It was made of thin material that my Nanny had smocked across the straps of the v-necked front. There were roses embroidered down the neck-line and around the bottom at the hem. The robe was full with puffy three-quarter length sleeves that Nanny had embroidered the same rose pattern around the cuffs and down the placket in the front. She had smocked on both sides of the placket on the front and across the back. There was a tag sewn in the neck that said, *Made with love by Nanny.* "She's been planning this night for me for a while, too. I think I would like to put it on if that's okay with you?"

"I'll be right here waiting."

I went to the bathroom down the hall and put the gown and

robe on and brushed out my hair. For the first time in my life I felt beautiful. When I walked back to the bedroom Jake was wearing the blue robe Nanny had left for him on the bed. He hung his pants on the latter back chair sitting beside a small table near the window. "I'm amazed every moment at the blessing God sent to me. No man in my family ever hung his clothes up. Usually I have to pick them up out of the floor."

Jake hung his shirt across the back of the chair and turned around to look at me. "This is a special day, it might not happen again. Wow. You couldn't be more beautiful to me if you were wearing a thousand dollar wedding dress fresh off the runway in Paris. Of course it's not the gown that makes you beautiful; it's you that makes the gown beautiful. She really did go to a lot of trouble for you, for us. I'll never be able to repay them for this night."

"You make their granddaughter feel special, that's payment enough."

Jake walked over to me and took my hands, "You're not just special, you're priceless and God has blessed me beyond words." He opened his hand and said, "I had these made for us by a jeweler in Charleston. I know how much you love grapevines so I asked him to make our rings look like grape vines."

Jake was holding two gold wedding bands; the smaller with a high relief grape vine and leaf design coiling around the band and the large one had the same design, but it was set down in the middle of the band and was protected by a higher trim around the outside edges.

"I can't believe I didn't have these in my pocket today. I've been carrying them around for a month hoping everyday that it would be the day you would decide to marry me. When I went to work this morning I had no idea this was going to be the day. I had the scripture reference John 15:4 - 5 engraved inside both of them."

"Jake, they are beautiful."

"Hey, is that a tear I see? Baby, don't cry," and he kissed my tears, "this is your wedding night. You're supposed to be happy."

"I am happy. I'm past happy. There's no word for what I'm feeling. I just can't believe that you were right there, always right there and I just overlooked you. How foolish I've been. I had no idea that you even loved me, much less that you *truly* loved me, and so much. It is true what they say that love breeds love. An hour ago I didn't think it was possible to love someone as much as I was loving you, but I love you even more. You are my heaven on earth and each time you reveal another piece of yourself to me, I feel like the angels at the throne of God who can't say anything else, but Holy, Holy. I'm in awe of you, Jake Foresight, and I have no idea what I ever did to deserve a thought from you much less your love. Thank you."

He kissed me ever so softly and slid the ring on my finger. I picked his ring up out of his hand and put the ring on his finger. "Soon God can pronounce us husband and wife." He reached behind me to push the door closed, lifted me in his arms and carried me to our marriage bed.

chapter twenty-four

Lying in the arms of my sleeping husband, morning came as I watched out the window across from the foot of the bed; a sky turning bright red as the sun began to rise. I wanted to wake him to watch our first sunrise together, but I had woken him several times during the night and I knew we needed to get some sleep; however, sleep was not what my mind would allow. I was overwhelmed with how quickly everything had happened for us and yet how long it had taken me to allow us to get to this place. I guess I wanted to stay awake to make sure this was all real and he wasn't going to disappear.

Once the sun had climbed high enough to stretch a beam of light across the ceiling, I decided to get up and close the curtain so that Jake could sleep a few more hours. I wiggled lose from Jake's arms and put my new gown and robe on so I could make my way downstairs to put a pot of coffee on the stove. Nanny and Pappy had oatmeal in the pantry and a loaf of bread. Toast and oatmeal seemed like a more valuable breakfast than cake and pie. While I waited for the coffee to perk and oatmeal to cook, I went into Pappy and Nanny's room to find a Bible so I could have some quiet time with the Lord. Nanny had left her Bible lying on her bed open to *Song Of Solomon* so I sat in the kitchen and began to read.

As I read the scriptures I knew my Nanny had left this just for me to find and I wanted to share it with my husband. I fixed a tray with the toast, oatmeal, two cups of coffee and Nanny's Bible and went back upstairs to see if Jake was interested in something to eat. He was still asleep when I entered the room so I cleared off the bedside table and placed the tray there. I wanted to sit and watch him sleep, but I knew he wouldn't like cold oatmeal so I sat down on the edge of the bed and opened the Bible to the verses again. I began to read softly to him hoping to wake him with wonderful words from the scripture that had excited me.

"'*Let him kiss me with the kisses of his mouth: for thy love is better than wine. Because of thy good ointments thy name is as ointment poured forth, therefore do the virgins love thee.*' But, not any more my sweet angel. '*Draw me, we will run after thee: the king hath brought me into his chambers: we will be glad and rejoice in thee, we will remember thy love more than wine: the upright love thee.*'" I skipped down to the second chapter. "*As the apple tree among the trees of the wood, so is my beloved among the sons. I sat down under his shadow with great delight, and his fruit was sweet to my taste. He brought me to the banquet house, and his banner over me was love. Stay with me flagons, comfort me with apples: for I am sick of love. His left hand is under my head, and his right hand doth embrace me.*'"

Jake never moved or opened his eyes he just smiled and said, "Now you're talking. Come here and let me show you what that looks like."

I skipped down a little and continued reading, "Ah! '*The voice of my beloved! behold, he cometh leaping upon the hills. My beloved is like a roe or a young hart: behold, he standeth behind our wall, he looketh forth at the windows, shewing himself through the lattice. My beloved spake, and said unto me, Rise up, my love, my fair one, and come away. For lo, the winter is past, the rain is over and gone; The flowers appear on the earth; the time of the singing of birds is come, and the voice of the turtle is heard in our land; The fig tree . . .*'"

"Let's skip down to the good part."

"It's all *good part*. How bout here, '*By night on my bed I sought him whom my soul loveth; I sought him, but I found him not.*'"

"No, no, no. I'm right here. Skip down to my part, the fourth chapter, '*Behold, thou art fair, my love; behold thou art fair; thou hast doves' eyes within thy locks: thy hair is as a flock of goats, that appear from the mounts of Gilead.*'"

"Oohh!"

"It's a good thing!"

"To have eyes like a bird and smell like a goat?"

"Well the next part says your teeth are like sheep's."

"Oh my gosh, it does and that she will bear twins."

"Yea, twins. I could live with twins."

"I guess you could, seeing how you have."

"Oh yeah, they run in my family."

"So how can smelling like a goat be a good thing?"

"Remember when that was written. Men loved their herds and all they knew was how beautiful their animals were. Some goats really have beautiful hair."

"Smelly, they're all smelly. There's nothing beautiful about a goat to me so don't think you can use these words on me to get me in the mood."

"Here's the best part ... "

"You amaze me."

"I just did my best, you're amazing, too, but I thought we were talking about this scripture!"

"Jake! I mean because you know this by heart."

"I've read this so many times even though it's a picture of Jesus and His bride, I think of you. Hey, I have a new nickname for you."

"Oh, this better be nice."

"Oh it is."

"You're crazy, what is it?"

"Flame."

"I have no feeling one way or the other about that one, but I'm sure I will when you tell me what it means."

"It means this, *'Thy lips are like a thread of scarlet, and thy speech is comely.'* That means it draws me in. *'Thy temples are like a piece of pomegranate within they locks. Thy neck is like the tower of David; ... Thy two breasts are like two young roes that are twins, which feed among the lilies. Until the day break and the shadows flee away, I will get me to the mountain of myrrh and to the hill of frankincense. Thou art all fair, my love; there is no spot in thee.'* Now put that down and get over here and let me check you over in the light to see if there are any spots on you."

"But, I brought you hot oatmeal and coffee."

"You're the only hot thing I want right now my little flame who becomes a wild fire."

"I should have brought you some water to quench your thirst."

"Just get back in here with me."

"Don't you need to call your parents?"

"I figure they called your house last night and Pappy announced our news and they are happy for us and all is well."

"What makes you think that?"

"Because my Dad didn't come beating on the door in the middle of the night to drag me out of here."

"That would have been scary. If I had known that was possible I would have sent you home."

"That's why I didn't tell you."

"Am I going to have to wonder if you're keeping things from me?"

"Not any more. Well, some things, like what other gifts I have for you and stuff like that. But, get back in here."

"Your bride has fixed your breakfast and brought it to you in bed. You will sit up and let her feed you, cause it will probably be your last chance to have her spoil you this way. Or you can hurt her feelings and let it get cold."

"Hmm, I think I will," and he grabbed me and threw me to the bed, "hurt your feelings and make it up to you later." And he pulled the covers over our heads. The phone began to ring down the hall and we froze not knowing if it was someone for Nanny or if it was important for one of us. It stopped ringing, but started again and I knew it was someone wanting one of us so I went to the phone.

Jake got his robe on and followed me to the phone table in the hall. "Hey Nanny."

"Good morning. I want to ask how your evening was, but I don't want to know. I called to let you know that Jake's parents called here last night and they are anxious to speak with Jake this morning. I don't want to rush you and have your honeymoon end too soon, but Jake needs to call them."

"Did you tell them?"

"I didn't talk to them. Your Pappy talked to Jude and he told him, but Jude was not going to tell Sally that you were married. He was going to let you two do that. He said he would tell her that Jake was needed over here and that he would be over in the morning to let them know what was going on."

"Okay." There was no need to ask to speak to Pappy and get details from him, because he never said much over the phone. Guess he spent so much time talking to customers on the phone and family he liked to talk to in person. "We'll get ready and go over there. Thanks Nanny for everything. The cake was delicious and the table was so perfect, but the best two things are my gown and robe, well that's one, and finding your Bible this morning is the very best. You are so good to me, Nanny, you and Pappy. Thank you."

"I wanted to try and think like your Mother. That's what she would have done for you."

"You did just what she would have done and even more. I love you."

"We love you too, sweetheart. Oh, will you let us take you and Jake out for lunch today?"

"I don't know. We'll have to see if Jake can have lunch off. He has some patients to see today. We'll call you from Jude and Sally's. Did the kids get off to school yet?"

"They are leaving in a minute. Willie is dropping them off and then taking the car to Trell's and walking back to school."

"I hate that he has to do that. Do they know?"

"No. Just that you had to spend the night away from home and that you will be back tonight. They think it's about a new child."

"Okay, I'll call you soon. Will you still be at my house or are you coming home?"

"Your pappy and I will be here for a few more hours. He's out with Silas right now."

"Okay. Love you."

"I love you and Jake. Bye"

"Bye, Nanny. Oohh, Jake." He had gone back into the bedroom and was eating breakfast. "Nanny says she loves you too."

"I know."

"You are so sure of yourself all of a sudden."

"Yes I am, thanks to you. Now that I have your love I know that I must be pretty wonderful. Who could resist me?"

"I've created a monster."

He pulled me by my arm back onto the bed, "You've ignited an eternal flame in me. How long do we have?"

"Maybe a couple hours?"

"Oohh, let's make the most of every second."

"You have to go tell your parents and go to work and . . ."

"You're what is important to me. All that other can wait."

"Those words are going to come back to haunt you."

After spending as much time as we could enjoying our time alone we dressed and drove out to Jude and Sally's, my new in-laws. I was a little afraid that Sally would not be pleased, but she and I had been so close, maybe she would forgive us for not telling her before and not having a wedding ceremony. Jake told me not to worry about anything, that Sally was well aware of his feeling for me and she had helped him make a decision on the bracelet so many years ago even when I was with Tylar. "She has known that I was going to do whatever I had to do to make you mine."

"I understand that. But, will she understand that I truly love you more than anyone and that I am not still pining over Tylar? I don't want her to ever think that you are not my first choice."

"I'm not!"

"Yes you are, Jake Foresight. You are the first and only man I have ever known in my soul, body and mind was perfect for me. Tylar was what I wanted in my head, but I never felt anything close to this for him. I am completely at peace about this decision and I don't know of another decision I ever made that I've felt this right about."

"Well, tell Mom just what you told me, if she seems to have some doubt. You just convinced me. She'll see your heart."

When we pulled into the drive it was about ten till nine; Jude was in the car backing out and Sally was standing in the drive still in her robe.

"Jake, you had me a little worried. Is everything okay at your house, Lacey? Come on in. It's a little nippy still this morning."

We went into the house and followed her to the kitchen.

"You want some coffee?"

"Sally, I don't want to keep you. I know you probably need to get ready for work."

"Actually, Jake, *you* need to get ready for work, but first, where have you been?"

Jake put his arm around me and said, "Mom, we've been over at the Hawthorne's, all night."

"Oh my, please tell me your grandparents are okay?"

"Oh, yes ma'am. Jake, don't scare her like that."

"Okay. Let me try this. Mom, Lacey and I got married yesterday and Nanny and Pappy let us stay at their house last night and they stayed with the kids at Lacey's."

She sat down at the table with the cups of coffee she had poured and looked up at us.

"Sally," and I reached out for her hand and sat down across from her at the small table. "It just happened so fast and we neither one wanted a big wedding."

"I couldn't take the chance that she would get away from me once she said yes."

"You make it sound like you asked me several times before. He asked me once yesterday, and I love Jake so much of course I was going to say yes. Part of me wonders why he waited so long, but I'm glad he did so that he knows that I said yes because I love him not because I'm just wanting to fill a void. I've never loved anyone like I love Jake and every moment of the day he makes me fall more in love with him. I'm sorry we didn't come and tell you yesterday, but I wanted to be with my husband as soon as possible and I was very selfish and I'm sorry. Can you forgive me?"

"Lacey. Stop, honey. You don't have to explain love to me. I always knew you two would be together. Sooner or later you would see what a wonderful man he is. I just thought you would want a wedding and all the fluff? Where did you get married?"

"Mom, she agreed with me about how God marries two people so we sat down in her office and made our vows to each other just a few minutes after I asked her."

"Oh. So you aren't married in the eyes of the law?"

"Mom, we're married in the eyes of God and He's the only one that matters. I'll get the license today so we will be legal, too."

"And what are her grandparents going to say about that,

Jake? They are going to see you as a boy taking advantage of their granddaughter."

"Oh no, Sally. Not at all. My Pappy completely agrees with what we did. He and Nanny fixed us a beautiful honeymoon setting with a cake and a table set for royalty. Nanny smocked me a gown and robe and ..."

"And she made me a robe, too."

"Jake? Nanny made *your* robe too?"

"Yeah, I noticed that when you were on the phone with her this morning. She put the tag inside the pocket. She made mine with love, too."

"You're so silly."

"I told you, I'm wonderful and no one can resist me."

"Except your Mother who knows better."

Jake put his arms around his Mother from behind her and hugged her neck. "And what do you know, Mom?"

"How did you snow all these people into believing your ideas?"

"It's not my ideas, they are God's. You've been caught up in the protocols of the world and medicine so long you can't move with the Spirit of God."

"Oh Sally, it was the most beautiful wedding I've ever been a part of, and it was mine," Jake sat beside me and I looked into his eyes, "and Jake's, and that made it even more special of course. I think everyone should get married like that. It was so personal and simple and beautiful." Jake had his arm around me on the back of my chair and he took my hand in his and kissed it. I put my other hand on his face and wished we were back at Nanny's in the upstairs bedroom that will always be our special place.

"Welcome to the family, Lacey. You will let us have a party for you both, won't you?"

"Of course, but ..."

"Mom, first we need a honeymoon. What's the chance I can have a few days off?"

"We'll need to talk to your Father. He's going to be so surprised and so are the girls, but pleased as I am, really, Lacey, I have never wanted anyone else for Jake. He's been in love with you since you were just kids. I know you've made him the happiest man on earth, today anyway."

"Thank you, Sally," and I hugged her, "thank you for not being angry with us."

"I couldn't be angry with you. But, I know someone who's going to be really hurt by this and you may want to talk to her yourself."

"Who?"

"Margie. She wanted you to be her daughter-in-law so badly. I think she was still holding out hope that you and Tylar would get back together."

"Sally, Tylar and I were never together. We were just living in some kind of lie we created that we thought was what God wanted and everyone around us, but it was never right for us and we knew that. It just seemed natural to everyone else and we were trying to deliver. I can't begin to tell you what a mistake that would have been. We would have ended up hating each other and hurting our families in the process. I'm so grateful to Johnny Kale for offering him that train yard; otherwise, we might have gone through with it."

"Not if I had found out before you did it."

"I'm so glad God had you watching out for me. You are my guardian angel."

"Nah, you have a real one of those. I'm just a love warrior who would have charged in and taken you away where no one could find us until you submitted to me."

"Okay! I'm going to get ready for work now. Are you two going to break it up long enough for you to come in today?"

"I may have to bring her with me."

"No you won't. I have to see Willie at sometime today and check on Kimmy."

"What's wrong with Kimmy?"

"I'm not sure, Mom. She's just not feeling good, but I think something else is going on."

He caused me to be concerned more than I had been. "What do you mean, Jake? Did she tell you something?"

"I'm going to get dressed while you talk about this."

"Okay, Mom."

"Tell me, Jake. What did she say?"

"Nothing. I just think something's going on. I want you to go and see her and see if you can get her to talk to you."

"About what?"

"Maybe start with yesterday morning and what happened from the time she left her house and when you saw her on the steps at Preacher Sternfield's house."

"Okay. I'll try. But, maybe you can tell me what you're thinking is wrong?"

"I don't want to guess. I'm a doctor and I deal with facts and then I come up with a diagnosis not the other way around. Get me some facts and I'll give you a diagnosis if you don't figure it out on your own."

We couldn't go to lunch with Nanny and Pappy so we made plans to go with them on Saturday. I needed to see Kimmy and Jake was too busy with patients. We did go into town and apply for a wedding license before he dropped me off at *Lion's Hill* to see the children and get my car. Kimmy was still in her room when I got to her house. Uncle Alvin said she had drank plenty of water, but she wasn't eating. She wasn't talking either. I finally got her to come outside with me for some fresh air, but she didn't give me any more information than I already had about her morning before I saw her at Preacher Sternfield's.

I almost told her what happened to me when I went into the house with the covered dishes, but Aunt Penny came out of the house and into the yard and there was no way I wanted to take a chance that she would over hear me.

Kimmy assured me that she would be better in a day or two so I left her sitting in the yard swing by the apple trees. Aunt Penny yelled across the yard at Kimmy, "Maybe now that you're well enough to get out of bed you will get up and help me hang these wet clothes up on the line?"

Kimmy walked over to the basket at Aunt Penny's feet and pulled a dress out of the basket and pinned it to the line. She seemed like she was fine to me, but something was wrong. I was thinking it would be a long time before I would know what had caused Kimmy to be this sad. I just hoped it wasn't anything life changing.

Willie was a happy boy when I told him what Jake and I had done and that Jake would be living with us. He couldn't wait to tell the others so I let him pick them up from school like he had planned and I went home to start supper and wait for them. There was no doubt what they all were feeling when they entered the house. It sounded like twenty excited children instead of four almost grown youth.

"Lacey!! We love Jake! Where is he?" Abbie Lou ran to me and hugged me so hard I thought she was going to knock me over on the kitchen floor. Cole came right behind her and Retta brought up the rear.

"This place has been missing a man..."

"Hey! I'm a man!" Willie shouted as he came through the door.

"We need a real man, Willie. A man that will make our Lacey smile again."

"Retta, I've been smiling haven't I?"

"Not like you did when Pa was here."

"I miss him, too, Retta."

"I know you do, Cole, and maybe Jake will help you smile again, too"

"I love Jake, Lacey. I'm glad he will be with us all the time. I didn't like it when he went away to school for so long."

"Well, he's never going away from us again."

"When will he be here, Lacey?"

"I don't know, Willie. He missed half a day yesterday and it was late this morning before he got to the clinic so he may be late tonight, but I wanted to get supper finished so when he gets here it will be ready and we can sit down and eat and then have all evening to enjoy him before we have to get to bed. Then Saturday we're all going to the Garden Patch for lunch as a family with Nanny and Pappy. Sound good?"

"Where did you spend last night?"

"We stayed at Nanny and Pappy's, Retta. Why?"

"I just missed you last night. I don't want you to go anywhere else again either."

"Well, we might get a few days off from work so we can have a honeymoon, but we'll stay right here most likely. I don't think Jake can be out of town right now. He's trying to lighten the load off of

Doctor Jude and if someone needed surgery Jake would hate that he was gone."

"He's here! Come on you guys! Jake's here!"

They all ran to the door and out into the yard to welcome Jake as if he had been away at war for ten years. My family was happy for me and Jake's family was happy for him and I couldn't wait to have my husband in our room alone, but for now there were four people who wanted his attention so I blew him a kiss from the front door and went back to the kitchen to finish my cooking.

chapter twenty-five

Being married was very different from being single. It wasn't a bad thing, just different. I had to remember that what I did in every area of my life had to include my husband, and I wanted it that way, it was just different. Willie had been my sidekick, but he didn't know everything I did and with Jake I wanted us to be one, thinking and feeling the same things as much as possible. I was a businesswoman, although I hadn't seen my life with the orphans as a business, I had a board of directors and I had investors and all this needed to be revealed to Jake. It wasn't so much that it was all some kind of big corporate secret; it was just something I wanted him to know all about. He and I spent hours talking about our lives and what we had done while he was in medical school, repairs I had made to the house and the simple things of life because I wanted him to be in every aspect of my life and feel welcome. I never wanted him to feel like he was just visiting and I knew that because he had moved in with us that he could easily feel like this was not his home and have a desire to move us out and away from my siblings. That day was going to come, but I was hoping it would be later than sooner.

My parents had left the house to Willie and the property around the house to both my brothers with provisions for Cole to be able to build a home for himself and his family whenever Willie married or Cole wanted to move out of the family home. If Willie and Cole both wanted to farm they would do it together. If one did and the other did not all the land would be used for farming with a fourth of the profits going to the one who did not want to farm as lease money for the property. Pappy and Pa had bought some land together closer into town and Pa's half was seventy-five acres. That was split between Abbie Lou, Retta and me. The architecture firm was left to us by giving us a lifetime seat on the board receiving a small income for that, as well as a small share of the profits. Willie and I were the only ones old enough to have a vote, but Willie had given his vote to me. I didn't understand why Mr. Frank didn't just close Pa's business and open one with his own name and be done with all of us, but he said that Pa's name was what made the business and it was Pa's name that kept people coming back making us a small expense for a lucrative business.

My parents had a large amount of savings. More than I realized they were worth, because we had been taught to save, scrimp and be frugal so you could be a blessing to someone else. Those habits were hard to break. Even though I was not born during the depression I understood the effects of it and had been taught to never live in a style you couldn't afford to lose. That money was split between us down at the bank and Pappy had set up each one of us an account to use when we needed the money. He kept the account Pa and Mother had used for household expenses to deposit any income the farm or the architecture firm made while we were all still under the same roof. This was the account we used to buy our groceries and pay the household and farming expenses. Jake wanted to contribute to this account, but the others said no. They just wanted him to feel welcome enough that he wouldn't take me away from them, but he wanted to feel like part of the family and he didn't when he didn't contribute. So Jake was responsible for maintaining the house and barns and he did such a great job at it we appointed him to be the grounds keeper and maintenance man for us at *Lion's Hill*. Because his time was limited with the clinic hours he hired two of the boys who lived at the orphanage to be his helpers. They did most of the work and Jake just checked behind them and showed them how to do a few things.

Abe and Benjamin had been at *Lion's Hill* since the doors opened. Bennie, as we called him, was sixteen and Abe was seventeen. They were very mature boys with sweet sensitive hearts. They had both been physically abused by family members and they were broken spirits when they arrived at *Lion's Hill*. Over the years they had grown to love the Lord and find forgiveness for their family members. But, more impressively, they had become confidant, bold, and self assured that what they had been through was what God would use to reach the lost world. They both wanted to preach somewhere, although they didn't think God would use them in a church. Bennie saw the world before him and Abe thought evangelizing in the poor areas of big cities was his calling.

Abe had been raised in Brooklyn, New York, after his family migrated from England to New York at the end of the nineteenth century. His father worked in textiles and his Mother took in sewing to help buy food. Abe ran a paper rout at age six for *The Daily Eagle*. His father was an alcoholic, although Abe referred to him as drunk, who spent his pay before he made it home and left his family to starve. Out of guilt he beat Abe and his siblings because of the hunger in their eyes. Abe's oldest brother was killed by their father one night when he fought his father back. Abe and his family moved to North Carolina where his aunt and uncle lived. There he found more abuse from an uncle who did not want the extra burden of his wife's family. Abe and his siblings ran away and were found by Miss Margaret. She took them back to the aunt's home where Abe's mother signed for the children to go to the orphanage. After several years his mother purchased a home of her own and she came to *Lion's Hill* to get her family, but Abe refused to go with her citing that we were his family now, however, the other children left with their mother and she brought the family every weekend to see Abe.

Bennie had a different life in that he never knew his father. His mother was the abuser. Through much prayer and counseling we surmised that she hated being without a husband and hated the man who fathered this child she was saddled with so she took her anger out on Bennie. Mostly we tried to help Bennie understand that it was not Bennie she hated, it was herself. She had spent a lifetime seeking the approval of men believing they were who declared her worth and because they used her and basically rejected her she felt of no value. Bennie was a daily reminder of how she had been rejected and how, in her own eyes, she had become a failure. He was not the problem, he was the solution God had sent to her, but she couldn't see it so God sent Bennie to us. His love for the other children and for me and Pappy was a blessing that everyone at *Lion's Hill* desperately needed and received openly. If she could have only seen through her pain that it's what we give to someone else that measures our worth and not what we get, maybe she could have found that Bennie was more than enough to define her worth. She never came back for him or contacted him in anyway, but Bennie wasn't bitter. He saw the world as an open wound in need of a place to ooze. He wanted to infect others with the love of Jesus and introduce them to the Healer of all wounds.

Abe, Bennie and Bailey were our oldest boys. Bailey was the only one out of these three who showed a great desire to go to college, although Abe and Bennie would be spending one year at the small two year college in town so they could see if there was any way that they might want to continue. I required that of everyone who was at *Lion's Hill* when they finished their high school studies. We were so blessed with the donations that helped to keep the orphanage running and with so many children being older and wanting to have after school jobs, our college fund was growing to the place that all the children would have an opportunity to attend that first year of college at the expense of *Lion's Hill*.

I sat Jake down and told him about the silent investors who deposited money into the orphanage's account each month and who our board members were and who our silent board members were.

"You have no idea who gives money to the orphanage?"

"I do not, Pappy does I'm sure. Someone has to know so that they receive credit at the end of the year. The sum of money we are talking about for two of the investors is more than we earn on the farm in a year. I'm sure they are doing it because they have so much money they need a place to give it."

"And who are your silent board members and why are they silent?"

"Well, one is A.P. Cromwell and he keeps everything *wonderful* that he does from his family. They just don't think anyone should help out people who can't do for themselves. They've been very vocal in county meeting trying to keep me from using money donated to *Lion's*

Hill to send these children to college. They say there are children who are more worthy, because they have married parents, I guess, who can't afford to send their children to school and that money should be used for them first. Of course everyone has a right to donate their money where they want it used so their arguments just interrupt the meetings and make the council crazy. The fact that A.P. loves my Pappy is their greatest objection, but there's no committee that will listen to that. If they knew he was giving money or time to this place they would drive him crazy. When that man dies they will probably try to sue everyone he ever gave a dime to for the money back. But, Pappy's willing to take the flack if it ever happens just to have A.P.'s wisdom on the board."

"Who else?"

"Miss Sunshine."

"You're kidding?"

"No. Pappy is her best friend and she is one of my closest friends and she needs this place as much as we need her. Nanny knows nothing about her involvement, so I've been told, although I doubt she would be upset. She does know about three or four times that Sunshine and I had lunch and she's never said a word to me about it. Sunshine had two children that she lost to the fathers of those children and by being on the board and by giving her money to these children she feels like she's righting that wrong. I would never deprive her of the blessing and neither would Pappy, even if it caused Nanny to fuss at him. But, we aren't going to say anything about it to anyone so that won't happen."

"You aren't going to keep stuff from me, are you?"

"That's why we're having this meeting. You aren't going to be all jealous over silly things like Nanny is, are you?"

"You don't think Nanny has a reason to be jealous?"

"No. Pappy chose Nanny and that should be the end of it."

"How do you just stop loving the woman you feel sure is the one God birthed just for you?"

"You just do. God sent Nanny to take her place. He knew Sunshine was going to make the choices she did, but He wasn't going to make Pappy suffer for her choices. He gave him the ability to love Nanny completely, supernaturally."

"If you had married Tylar I would have never stopped loving you."

"You would have been able to move on."

"Never."

"Well, Praise God, you won't ever have to find out." I walked around and sat in Jake's lap. "Can we make a deal?"

"Maybe. What will it cost me?"

"Can we stop bringing Tylar up? I never think about him like that anymore. Not even when I drive into this drive and walk up to this house. It's the house built for these children, not for Tylar and me. I have my heart so full with love for you and no one else, in that way of course, that I don't even think about him romantically. Sometimes I miss my friend, but that's it. God did that supernaturally so I know all to well how Pappy loves Nanny. I've told you before you never have to think of yourself as my second choice. There was only one choice for me; I was just a little slow at seeing it. So, forget about Tylar. He might even come back here one day. If he does we will be glad to see him because he is our friend, but that's it. You are my husband, so let's not bring him up anymore in regards to what almost happened, okay?"

"Okay, but it will be hard for me if he ever comes back."

"Jake! Don't you believe me?"

"Yeah, I guess I just need God to do a supernatural work in me."

"He will, if you pray for that and I will pray with you. I feel like He did a work in Nanny, too."

"Why do you say that? She's not friends with Sunshine."

"Well, she doesn't have to be her *best* friend, but she is kind to her. I saw them at Pa's funeral and at Mother's, too. They spoke to each other at both and held hands at Pa's and they hugged each other at Mother's. I think Pappy has told Nanny everything, but he wants us to believe she doesn't know so we don't talk about Sunshine in front of Nanny. I don't know all that took place way back then and I don't guess I ever will. It's between them and how they want to handle it is their business. I just want to respect both of them by handling it the way Pappy tells me."

"Then I will follow you when it comes to Pappy, Nanny and Sunshine. I don't need my new grandparents upset with me."

"Or your new wife."

The boys came into the office looking for Jake. They were always in need of him when he was at *Lion's Hill*. Jake was so good with them it made me very aware that Jake would want his own children some day soon, even though we hadn't ever discussed that. I had help raise my family and been there for these children, but the thoughts of having my own child was frightening to me. I wasn't sure why, it just seemed like I was spread so thin and I never wanted to neglect my own child. I had seen far too well what hurt that caused in these orphans and in Kimmy. She was still depressed, as Jake called it, and there seemed to be no reason that I could tell for her to be depressed. Jake thought maybe all the negative things her Mother had told her all her life were catching up with her. I just knew she needed me right then and I was doing all I could to get her out of the house when she wasn't at school.

"You boys go and get your work done. I need to pick Kimmy up now anyway. We'll talk some more about the ins and outs of running *Lion's Hill* later. I love you."

The boys snickered, "We love you, too, *Mrs. Foresight*," and Jake hugged me before they left the office.

I drove out to the school and picked Kimmy up. I had given her a job helping me with the filing and other paperwork that had to be filled out. Some of the teachers used her to help grade papers and design bulletin boards in their rooms. Kimmy had an artistic ability that was a gift from God. I was hoping she would pursue that as she got older. She loved to paint and always kept a sketch pad in her purse. Some days she would sit on the bench in the garden and sketch the children playing or the boys building something. She could capture the expressions on the faces of the children and the mood of an event. She seemed to like to use watercolor more than any other medium and sometimes she would add color to the sketches she did out at *Lion's Hill*. Jake was fixing a bulletin board on the wall going up the staircase for Kimmy to pin up her drawings so the children could see themselves in her work.

"So what have you got for me to do today, Lacey?"

"Oh, I don't know. There are a few records that need filing after they have been updated. Sherry had her eye exam yesterday."

"Does she need glasses?"

"Oh, yeah. The doctor said it's a wonder she can walk. No wonder she hasn't been able to keep up with her class, she can't see. How could someone have missed that all these years?"

"Some people just don't care what others are going through or at least they don't care enough."

"Well, someone cares now. She will have her glasses soon and be able to read the board like the other children. So that needs to be documented on her chart and put with her record. And several others had eye exams at the same time. None with her problems, but they will get glasses, too. Then we'll just see what else we can get done. Maybe we will get to spend a little time talking about you and how you are doing?"

"If we aren't too busy I would like to finish my sketch of Bennie and Abe, if they aren't busy with something else."

"They're working with Jake on something. What were they doing when you started the sketch?"

"They were fixing a rope swing down at the river and finishing the railing on the dock. Pappy was there too."

"Is he in the sketch?"

"No. Just Bennie and Abe."

"Well, maybe you can watch them doing whatever they are doing with Jake today and be able to finish that sketch?"

"Yeah, maybe. And maybe I can start another one?"

She seemed to have a small smile on her face, something I hadn't seen in a few weeks and I was pleased that maybe she had found a friend in Bennie or Abe even though they were a little bit younger than her. Abe, by a few months, and Bennie was almost a year younger. Maybe she would find someone who could help break this spirit of depression and help her see that she needed to fight against this attack. Sometimes just being told that you are suffering from the enemies fiery darts and that you have to stand against them to overcome is not enough. Sometime we need Jesus in the flesh to comfort us and bring the way of escape. It's not true that God doesn't allow us to face things that we can't handle, but it is true that in every adversity He shows us the way of escape. I didn't know right then what God was showing her, but I knew if we kept praying and seeking His face in this matter that He would show Kimmy her way of escape.

"Have you developed any friendships with the kids?"

"A few. Mostly I just draw them."

"Have you talked to Bailey? He's a little bit older than you, but he's not at all full of himself like the boys who were older than me when I was your age."

"Yea, I've talked to him, but he's so focused on his school work that he doesn't get out and play as much as the other boys like Abe and Bennie. They are always outside doing something. I don't want to bother Bailey."

"So you've gotten to know Abe and Bennie?"

"Yeah. Abe more so than Bennie just because he takes an interest in my drawings and stops what he's doing sometimes and sits and watches me. He's nice."

There was silence as we pulled into the drive at *Lion's Hill*, but I could see Kimmy looking around toward the river and back behind the barn. The three boys, including Jake, came out the back door as we pulled up.

"Hey. We were looking for you."

"I told you I was going to get Kimmy."

"I guess I thought you would be back by now. Hey Kimmy."

"Hey, Jake."

"The boys were looking for you. They said you might want to go with us down to the river."

"I would love to, but Lacey needs me in the office for a while."

I saw how Kimmy looked at Abe and there was no way I was going to keep her from spending time with him if he could bring her out of the shell she had crawled into. "Kimmy, go on with them. The files can wait."

"Can you join us, Lacey?"

"Maybe in a little while. I have a few phone calls to make and I need to check with Cook and see if there is anything we need to get before tomorrow's delivery."

"Okay. We'll be at the river."

"What are you doing down there?"

"Getting the ladder finished before summer. We'll need it when everybody's down there swimming. I told Pastor Rick that we could have baptisms down there this summer. Need to be able to get them out once we dunk'um in."

Pastor Rick was the greatest blessing sent to *Wonders of Love Fellowship*. He came the next Sunday after Preacher Sternfield fell from the roof. Johnny Kale had met him years earlier traveling through Greensboro. He never had a church of his own to preach in because he said God moved him too quickly filling in for pastors who were sick or taking a vacation. I was hoping that God would never send him away from us, because he was a breath of fresh air.

He played the guitar, the harmonica and the mandolin. His music welcomed the Spirit like none I had ever heard before. After he played just two or three bars you were so ready to enter into worship you were sure you were sitting at the feet of Jesus. When he taught the Word, you could almost hear the sounds of Jerusalem and smell the dust. Unlike Kimmy who brought a picture into being with her hand and a pencil, Pastor Rick painted the life of Jesus and the struggles of His disciples with his words. They became real people with real problems and he showed us how their lives paralleled with ours. The most important thing I learned from Pastor Rick was that we all have sinned, but even if we asked Jesus to become Lord over our lives and forgive us of those things we did against Him, chances were that we would sin again at some point in our lives, but He would not throw us away because of that. We are not sinners any more in His eyes. Not at all! He calls us saints, joint heirs to His throne. What a joy it was for me to know that.

There was no telling how much longer Preacher Sternfield would be unable to walk the floor and preach, but I was hoping it would be a lot longer. I was not ready for Preacher Rick to leave our congregation. He had seen the gift God had put in me and he was using me during the service to speak to the congregation as God gave me understanding. He said I was another Catherine Coolman except God had not used me in seeing people healed right before our eyes. I did pray for them to receive healing and some were healed, but I didn't see a miracle healing while Pastor Rick was pastoring our church. God had opened my eyes up to a person's ailment through His Spirit many times and I prayed for them; however, He told me more about the conditions of their hearts and how He wanted to bring them into the fullness of the Kingdom than use me as a healing minister. I just wanted to do what God wanted me to do and have the freedom to do it and Pastor Rick gave me that platform.

Because of this like Spirit that Pastor Rick and I shared, he and his wife had become great friends of mine and Jake's. He had caused Johnny Kale and me to become better friends and Pappy wasn't too upset about that fact. It seemed that Pastor Rick and Halley Walters, along with their two children, Ashlynn, who was four and Dutch, who was sixteen months, had brought a harmony that we all needed at *Wonders of Love Fellowship*. Halley was licensed to teach kindergarten through third grade and she wanted to teach at our school so badly, but they stayed on the move too much for her to be able to get a job. Pastor Rick said that one day God would plant them long enough for her to do that, but he didn't know when that would happen so for the time that she and Rick were in town due to Preacher Sternfield's recovery she came to the orphanage and read stories to the children and helped with some of the children, like Sherry, catch up on their reading skills.

While Jake and the boys with Kimmy were down at the river, I finished my phone calls and had some quiet time reading and praying. I had asked God to accept my praise for sending Pastor Rick and Halley to our church family, and to ours, and I asked Him, "God, why does Pastor Rick see this gift You have given me and welcome it and Preacher Sternfield keeps me hidden or uses me in silence? God, I don't know what Your plan is for our church and maybe it's just my flesh talking, but how I wish Preacher Sternfield could be recovering for a long time so we could keep learning what Pastor Rick has to share."

I sat down with my journal on the sofa to write down my prayers and what I had read when I had the unction to read from Matthew. "Where God? Where in Matthew?" I got my Bible and sat very quite waiting for God to show me where to read. 7:15 were the numbers that I saw scroll across my mind like a ticker-tape.

Beware of false prophets, which come to you in sheep's clothing, but inwardly they are ravening wolves. Ye shall know them by their fruits. Do men gather grapes of thorns, or figs of thistles? Even so every good tree bringeth forth good fruit; but a corrupt tree bringeth forth evil fruit. A good tree cannot bring forth evil fruit, neither can a corrupt tree bring forth good fruit. Every tree that bringeth forth not good fruit is hewn down, and cast into the fire. Wherefore by their fruit ye shall know them. Not every one that saith unto me. Lord, Lord, shall enter into the kingdom of heaven; but he that doeth the will of my Father which is in heaven. Many will say to me in that day, Lord, Lord, have we not prophesied in thy name? And in thy name have cast out devils? And in thy name done many wonderful works? And then will I profess unto them, I never knew you: depart from me, ye that work iniquity.

I prayed that God would show me what He was warning me about and wrote down every thought that came to me including my love for Pastor Rick and his wife. I was writing down how I felt about them staying as long as possible and instead of writing out the words *Wonders of Love Fellowship* I wrote the initials. It was the first time I had ever abbreviated the name of our church and in doing so, in capital letters, I saw in bold print the word WOLF. It was as if God had struck me on the top of the head with a bolt of lightning. I knew exactly what God was saying and exactly who the wolf in this story was, but in my heart I did not want to believe it.

I picked up the phone to call Pappy when I heard him talking outside the door to one of the children. "Pappy!" I ran to the door and pulled him inside closing the door behind me.

"Punkin! He was asking me a question."

"Did you answer it?"

"Yeah, sort of."

"Why isn't he in class?"

"He went to the bathroom and his class went outside. I was waiting for him to come out to tell him where they went."

"He'll find them. I need to talk to you right now."

Pappy took a deep breath and said, "He's been here again."

"Yes, He has, and He had something interesting to tell me, look," and I held out my journal.

"Wow, I get to read this?"

"The page I have it open to. After you read that I have something else to tell you."

Pappy sat down on the sofa. "This can't be in reference to Pastor

Rick, cause he just got here. He didn't name the church. Johnny Kale? Well, no cause we know where he's coming from."

"Oh, Pappy. Johnny Kale's really trying to make a change, I think. I don't know what he's doing late at night, but he seems like he's wanting to make a better way of life for himself."

"Is he still going to the reservation?"

"Probably. I think he has children there so I hope he goes to see them and take care of them."

"If he wanted to take care of them he would get them off that reservation."

"That sounds like a great thing to do, but Pappy they would be ostracized and belittled by the snobs in this town. Besides their mothers and grandparents are there and they should be with the people who truly love them and can teach them about their Indian heritage. What heritage does Johnny Kale have to offer them?"

"That's true. So you must be talking about Sternfield. Guess I've been right about him."

"What? What have you been right about when it come to him?"

"That he is a political preacher. Loves his title. Just out for the bucks. Tells you what you want to hear so you feel good about all that mess you're into on Saturday night and you keep paying him to make you feel even better. You know, tell you you're okay. If the Spirit could be found anywhere else I would be there. It makes me burn inside when he looks out on that congregation of hard working people who make a modest salary and tells them to go out and bring in rich people to the church that God is interested in wealthy, professional people, too. And then tries to build some kind of dream of how the church could grow and have nice things and meet all our needs if we had more people, people with more money."

"I've never heard him say it quite like that, but that is what he's saying. Geez, I guess he's had me blinded, too, from his real motivation."

"His real motivation is a bigger congregation equals a bigger pay check. The church pays his mortgage, all of his expenses and gas for that fine ride the church bought him. I've really never seen a church run quite like this one, but then again it got started like I've never seen one get started before, too. That should tell us all something. If it's new, it's not God. He's the same yesterday, today and forever."

"But, what about where it says, 'I'm doing a new thing'?"

"That new thing was an old thing He had done it before; it was just that it was new to them. Yeah, I knew I didn't trust him, but I thought surely he was on our side."

"Well, we are both very foolish, don't you think. Doesn't all of what we just said sound foolish? How could we have trusted him with our minds, much less or spirits?"

"It was for a season. Look at the good that did come of it and how wonderful things are now that Pastor Rick is there."

"Yeah, but for how long? Then what will we do?"

"What God tells us to do. Now what else did you have to tell me?"

I told Pappy about the day I took the food over to Preacher Sternfield's house and, just as I expected him to be, he was horrified and thankful that he didn't know when it happened. "He would have two broken legs and a broken head if I had known! I'm sure you told Jake?"

"The day it happened, it was the same day we got married."

"Well, it's his battle now."

"It's no ones' battle. I don't even know if my suspicions are right. He may have been over medicated and doesn't remember any of it." Pappy shot his squinting eyes at me. "Well, it's possible."

"When wolves in sheep's clothing fly! I'm going to talk to Johnny Kale."

"About what? Not that!"

"Ah, no... but I will let him know that he needs to re-think who the pastor of the church should be and possibly offer the job to Rick."

"Pappy, that doesn't make sense. He wouldn't do it just because you said that! He would want more and I'm not sure trashing a man that I'm not sure was in his right mind at the time is a good idea. Besides I don't know Johnny Kale well enough to trust him with something so personal. I don't want to start a big snowball on the top of the mountain headed straight at my house and this place. What if people believed I was starting trouble because I liked Rick and Halley and I just wanted Preacher Sternfield out to make room for them? Then they would be involved. It's just not worth it. We need to wait on God. He will show us what to do. If He closes that door on us, He will open another one. Maybe He wants us to go to another church?"

"Move all these children out? I'm not sure, but He might. I see your point in most of what you said, and even though I've seemed to distrust Johnny Kale, we can trust him on this issue. But, we'll wait for now and see what God brings out in all this."

"I hope not a scandal. I hate scandals. And I know I will hate one that I'm smack in the middle of."

"Do you think he hurt Kimmy?"

"Who? What do you mean?"

"Isn't this the same day Kimmy got in this mood she's in?"

"Yeah ... "

"Well, were you late enough that he could have pulled the same stunt on her?"

"Surely not, Pappy. She's a baby compared to him."

"Wolves don't care how old their victims are."

"Pappy! Please tell me you don't really think that he would have ... Pappy, she's just a kid."

"I'll kill him if he touched her."

"No you won't!" I grabbed Pappy's arms and looked straight into his face. "Don't ever say something like that again, Pappy. She's okay. If he did anything to her she will be okay. God will see to that. *He* will make him pay; it's not your fight. Do you hear me?"

"I want to talk to Jake." And he pulled away from me and started to the door.

"Pappy. Stop." I grabbed his arm. "Kimmy is at the river with him and the boys. Don't go down there like this. You will upset her."

"I'll flat out ask her."

"No you won't. We'll never be able to help her if you put her on the spot like that, especially in front of the boys. Just wait till you calm down. You may be all worked up for nothing. Please, Pappy. I'll get you some tea and we'll walk down to the river together and you and Jake can walk back up here and you can ask him all the questions you want to, but you cannot do your talking anywhere near Kimmy. Okay?"

Pappy sat back down on the sofa and I went to get some hot water to make tea. As I reached the kitchen I was so thankful that Cook was the only one in there. He never paid me any attention; he just kept preparing his meals. I walked over to the tea kettle and put it on the stove. Then I held onto the counter to keep my body steady. I knew that Pappy was right. I knew Preacher Sternfield had violated Kimmy in some way. I knew because God told me, while Pappy was speaking the words, that what I was hearing was the truth. How would I keep Pappy from beating this man to a pulp? How would I restrain *myself*? "Oh Dear Sweet Jesus, help us find Your strength in us and make it stronger than ever. God, please help us be strong for Kimmy's sake."

chapter twenty-six

"So Pappy, what are we going to do? Don't we need to go to Preacher Sternfield?"

"So he can deny that he assaulted you and anything more than that, that he might have done to Kimmy?"

"The Bible says if you have aught against your bro—"

"He's not my brother. He's not your brother either. He's a child of Satan himself."

"Pappy, I'm so angry, too, but maybe he didn't know what he was doing and maybe he has this one thing in his life that he can't get free of. Doesn't he deserve a chance to get help?"

"He does. And if he was trying to overcome, if he was saved in the first place, he would be looking for you and Kimmy to make this right and own up to what he's done. There's no doubt in my mind that he knew full well what he was doing so I don't buy the over-drugged scenario. And if he was he would have some sense that something was wrong. I've been medicated before, heavily medicated and I would have remembered if I was kissing some woman."

"But, maybe he just thinks it's a dream?"

"Maybe. But, something tells me he knows it was real and he's just too full of the devil to care."

"So, if he's not one of us then don't we need to ask someone else, someone who knows God and is not so close to the situation?"

"We could talk to Rick about it, but he's just passing through. He won't want to be involved and I'm not sure it's fair to get him involved."

"He took the job! Just being with us makes him involved. I wish we could ask Kimmy if we are even right in what we are thinking. It doesn't seem right to assume something so vile and not know for sure."

"We know for sure what he did to you. And how did Jake keep from killing him?"

"Jake thinks before he reacts."

"So do I and I think I want to kill him."

"Stop it and I mean it. I won't have you saying such foolishness especially when I'm one of the reasons you are thinking this. I'm fine! Kimmy will be, too. He didn't do anything that we cannot find the way of escape, right? I know that it is not our escape to have you kill Preacher Sternfield. How absurd that sounds, don't you think?"

"I may need to see Rick just for spiritual guidance."

"That sounds like a plan."

We waited for Jake and the others to come up from the river. Pappy told Jake his suspicions while Kimmy and I helped set the table for the children's supper. Kimmy fed baby Ben and Eliza while I helped serve the others. After supper Jake told me he was going with Pappy to Rick and Halley's and he wanted me to join them after I took Kimmy home. On our drive to her house Kimmy asked me where Jake and Pappy went and why they didn't eat with us.

"They needed to see Pastor Rick about something God had shown me today."

"What was that?"

"God showed me that there was a wolf among us at the church."

Kimmy's head jerked quickly in my direction. "Who? Who's a wolf and what does that mean?"

"It means someone who is pretending to be a Christian, someone who says they love the sheep, but they are there only to devour them."

"What does devour mean?"

"Eat them, but in this case it means to harm them, use them for their own gain."

"So … who is that?"

I thought hard about whether to tell her it was Preacher Sternfield and tell her what he had done to me, but I kept thinking that if she knew she might tell me what had happened to her. So I prayed in silence waiting for God to tell me what to do.

"Lacey? Who is it? I want to know."

"Do you know something?"

"No! I don't know. It's your word from God, not mine. How would I know?" and she turned looking back out the front glass of the car.

"Do you remember that day I met you at Preacher Sternfield's house to take those dishes to him?"

She didn't move, "Yeah."

"Well, he acted strange that day and he tried to … well he did. He kissed me and he grabbed me." She turned her head and stared at me. "I wasn't sure if he was over-medicated and didn't know what he was doing, but I didn't take a chance. He seemed to be a little weak, although he had the strength to grab me and pull me down onto him. Maybe it was the soreness of his surgery that made him have to loosen his grip, I don't know, but I got away from him. That's just not what a Christian should do even though he's not married and at that time I was not married, it still didn't make it right. He scared me and he violated me and my trust. He's supposed to care for us as Jesus cared for the sheep, not frighten me or make me feel like common trash. I'm not common trash, you know. I'm a child of the Most High God! He should have respected me. If he was not a wolf pretending to be a sheep he would not have done that to me even if he was medicated."

She turned her face back towards the front glass saying nothing.

"Hey Kimmy, you were there before I was and you had taken your dish inside, did he say anything to you?"

She seemed to fidget a bit, turning her face to the side window. "Yeah, but I don't remember what."

"So he was awake?"

"Yeah, I guess, yeah."

"Kimmy, you can tell me."

"What? Tell you what?!"

"It's okay. You can tell me what he said. Tell me what he acted like. Was he medicated? Did you give him any pain medicine cause when I got there he wanted me to give him pain medicine, but I didn't know if he already had some that morning. That was when he asked for water and got me close to him so he could grab me. That's how wolves do. They wait till you least expect them to strike and then they have you. In his case we didn't know he was a wolf so how could we have known not to get too close? Did he ask you to get him some water? You know it was a long time before I got to his house that morning. Bailey distracted me and it had to have been at least forty-five minutes before I left the house to go over to Preacher Sternfield's. A lot can happen in forty-five minutes. I'm so sorry I left you there waiting for me for that long."

"It's not your fault, Lacey. You didn't do anything wrong," and she began to cry.

I pulled the car over to the side of the road. "I know I didn't do anything wrong. You didn't do anything wrong either. Why are you crying?" I reached over and took her hands trying to pull her around so I could look her in the eyes.

"Because I left you. If I hadn't been sick I would have stayed and kept that from happening to you. I'm so sorry, Lacey," and she began to sob.

"It's okay, Kimmy. I didn't tell you so you would feel guilty. You have nothing to feel guilty about. I'm a grown woman! I can take care of myself against a foolish, even evil man, with a broken leg."

"He can do a lot with a broken leg, he's strong."

"How do you know that?"

She looked up at me with such fear, "I just mean I saw him lift his self up from the bed and move across the floor with no trouble at all, that's all. I should have stayed till you got those dishes in the house and we could have left together. I was so scared and just wasn't thinking. I'm so, so sorry."

"Kimmy there's nothing to be sorry about. But, why were you scared?"

"I want to go home now, Lacey. I'm tired."

"Are you sure?"

She rubbed her face to dry the tears and sat up straight looking out the front glass, "Yes, I know when I'm tired and I'm tired. I want to go home now."

I took Kimmy home and left her knowing that Preacher Sternfield had indeed done something to her, but what and how bad I didn't know. I was anxious to get to Pastor Rick and Halley's to hear what was being said between the men and how it was going to affect me and Kimmy. Mostly I didn't want her hurt anymore. I was sure that things were not going to get any easier as the days passed, but I wanted to protect her with all I had. I would deny the whole ugly truth if it looked like Kimmy would be damaged for life by the fall out.

"I just got a call from John Butler saying Pastor Sternfield was ready to resume his place at the church. He said it would be a few more weeks before he took over completely, but he was going to be able to sit behind the pulpit this weekend. Jake, didn't you tell him he would get a smaller cast this week?"

"No, Rick. My dad is his physician; I just put him back together when he fell. We hadn't discussed his progress. Dad must have told him that. It would be about time to shorten the cast and he should have healed from the surgery by now. Oh, hey, my flaming beauty." Jake saw me standing in the doorway and walked over to me. "We were just getting the news that Sternfield will be back in church Sunday."

"That doesn't give me much time."

Rick spoke from across the room, "For what?"

"Hello everyone." Jake and I walked into the room, "To prepare my children for their departure."

Halley came into the room from behind me. "Where are they going?"

"I can't subject them to a place where the leadership is corrupt. They will have to find another church. *We* will have to find another church. But where? I don't know."

Halley placed a tray with glasses of iced tea on the coffee table. "Everyone help yourself to a drink and let's take some time thinking about what God would have each one of us do. We don't need to rush any decision. These children have been in this church and the corruption has been in there with them all this time. God has protected them and He will continue to protect them until we do as He wants us to."

Rick walked over to the glasses and sat down on the couch as he took one. "Halley's right. Let's talk this all out and seek God as to what is the best for all of us. What did you find out from Kimmy?"

We all sat down around the coffee table and pick out a glass of tea. "I found out nothing concrete, but he did do something to her."

"How do you know?"

"It was the way she acted when I told her what had happened to me. And then she cried saying she was feeling guilty for leaving me there, but she was scared. She also said he had plenty of strength and was able to get around on his broke leg with no trouble at all. There's no doubt something happened that has caused her to withdraw, but how bad he hurt her is something she's not going to share with me. I don't know if she will tell anyone. And if she did I have no idea who she trusts that much. So I want to leave her out of this for now."

Jake laid his head back on the couch and looked up at the ceiling. "Maybe we don't need to say anything. Maybe we just need to do what is right for us and the children at *Lion's Hill*."

"What is that?"

"Well, we have to leave the church. I cannot stay where there is this spirit of divided loyalties first of all and I can't stay where the leadership has a spirit of lust. I love those children as if they were mine and I won't let them be infected by those demons. I've seen them at work far too many times at school and I don't want that for these kids."

"And I feel this so strong in my heart that those who do not get away from him and stop sitting under his covering will be victims, worst than I was, now that this has been exposed to us."

Pastor Rick interrupted, "Just for those who have been told?"

"Didn't you say I was a watchman on the hill?"

"So what are you saying, Lacey? We have to tell the congregation?"

"It *has* to be told, Jake. It happened to *me* so *I* would know. God told me that he was a wolf, no one else. Rick prophesied over me and because of that prophesy, Rick said God was showing him that I was the one who would bring His Words to this congregation. Are you thinking He would tell me to sit on this information? I don't think so. He will hold me accountable if I keep this hidden from the very people He sent me to. I have to expose him somehow, but how I do not know. It will be a mess if it's not handled just as God tell us. And for now, Kimmy has to be kept out of it. He will have to show me how telling something about her or insinuating in any way that he did something to her is going to save the lives of hundreds, well okay, just one, but He will have to show me why she has to be laid out for the world to persecute before I will do that to her."

We sat in quiet, each one of us praying or thinking about what should be done. Then Pappy said, "Rick? Do you and Halley like it here?"

"Sure." He looked over at Halley.

"Why, yes, Mr. Jeremiah. We love being here. Everyone is so sweet and helpful and hungry. That's the best part. These people are hungry for what God has for them and they are the ones who bring His presence into the church each week. It's not anything that Rick or I do."

"Do you sense God wanting you to settle down here?"

"We've talked about it, but we aren't sure."

"What makes you unsure, Rick?"

"Well, we don't have a home or a church that's calling us and the little bit that I make doesn't give us any money to put into savings so I would have to give up preaching and find a job to save enough to get a home and there's not enough time especially now that Pastor Sternfield will be returning so soon. Even if Halley went to work full time we couldn't swing it. I'm afraid we have gotten ourselves into this life style and we couldn't get out of it without a miracle."

Pappy said, "Well, I know who works in those and if He's the one who planted this thought in my head, which I know He did, then He will grant the miracle."

"What miracle is that, Pappy?"

"Well, we need a church with a pastor that has a heart after God and I know that man is Rick. Rick and Halley need a home. Halley already has a full time job if she wants it out at the school . . ."

"And Pappy has three houses right now that no one is living in."

"You're getting my picture."

"But, Jeremiah, I need a job and Pastor Sternfield is about to take that from me. I'm afraid I don't have any other skills. Not any that someone would pay me to do. It would take months of apprenticeship to get me to a place where I would be hirable."

"We need a place to meet, that's all. You can keep doing what you do, just in a different place. What about meeting in the school for now?"

"It's probably big enough in the gym room for the small number of people we will have at first. Even when we expose the truth about Preacher Sternfield, not everyone will leave."

"That's hard to believe."

"No, she speaks the truth, Jake. We've seen that happen many times throughout our travels to churches. There's some kind of false sense of loyalty to these men who are living double lives. It's like the congregation feels like they are judging themselves if they walk away from their leaders. Almost like they can't judge him because they also have sin. I hate to say this in a heavily male gathering, but the husbands in the churches where we saw Pastors having affairs or behaving like Pastor Sternfield, they find it comforting that their preacher acts like they do or how they want to. The wives would never speak out against their husbands, much less the Pastor so the double standard continues and the church ultimately suffers. But, these pastors will be judged more harshly for their sins than those they pastor."

"What Halley is saying is I took a long look at the awesome responsibility when I answered the call of God. I didn't have a choice, of course, but God told me He called me because He had planted the ability to walk the walk of righteousness within me before I was born. If I cause one, just one, to stumble I would be better off tying a concrete mill stone to a rope connected to my neck and jumping in the deepest part of the ocean pulling it in with me. I do not want to face judgment that is of that kind or worse, do you Lacey?"

"Lacey? What does she have to do with this?"

"Because, Jake, I have been called by God to teach and preach His Word and I'm subject to the same if I do not tell the people what God revealed to me. I don't care what they say about me or how bad this gets, I only care that I do what God wants done."

"I don't care what people say about me either, but I do care what is said about you, Lacey."

"Oh, Jake, honey. You can't fight that battle. I count it joy when

I am persecuted because of the name of Jesus. Those who love Him will know the truth. Those who love themselves or fear for their own reputations will stay with Sternfield and spread his lies. They don't frighten me. I've lived with that my whole life. Maybe I should have told you that before I let you sign on. I thought I had told you everything. What can I say, your wife is someone who just stirs up trouble in the spiritual world. The devil hates me and he always will because He hates Jesus and Jesus loves me."

"He loves me, too, but I don't get into as much trouble as you do because of it. Can't you do more like me?" Pappy and Rick started laughing. "And what do you two find so funny about that?"

"Well, first of all you've only been married," Pappy looked at his watch.

"What's your point, Pappy?"

"Well, you will never get your wife to act like you."

Rick chimed in, "And second, you will never understand the hate between a woman and the devil. It's so powerful that no man can match it. Tell him about it, Lacey."

"Well, all I can do is go to scripture. God put enmity between that age old serpent and the woman and her seed. He would strike at her heel, but she would stomp on his head. That's what I feel whenever I see the devil doing things to hurt someone else. I want to stomp on his head, but I know that I have to be as humble as a dove with the cunningness of that evil snake. Satan hates me, he hates women because we produce children that grow up to evangelize the world and bring others into the Kingdom. It was a woman who brought Jesus into the world to destroyed Satan's wicked world. He knows he's been done in and now he wants to break Jesus' heart by bringing turmoil into the lives of the very people He died for. All he's doing is pouring more fuel on that fire in hell that's waiting for him. I personally can't wait for the day when he is shoved off into it."

"I've never heard you talk like that before."

Pappy and Rick started laughing again. Rick said, "Just wait till she has children. You'll really see her fangs then."

"Children? We may have to postpone that for now. I need to see how she gets through this!"

"Hey! You said you wouldn't question my decisions because you know God speaks to me. I'll have you know He appreciates my hatred for His number one enemy. And right now his number one enemy has a nymph working overtime that God wants out of office. I have to be obedient and tell the congregation."

"I think we need to go to him and let him resign without it being exposed to everyone. That way he has a chance to get right with God. It just seems like it would be wrong to just blow him out of the water with no place to go for safety."

"I see your point, Jake. Every man deserves the chance to make things right. So what do the rest of you think?"

"Well, Jeremiah, Jake may have a point. I guess you would want me to be the one to do it?"

"Pastor Rick, I don't know about this. I think I just need to stand before the congregation and tell them everything that happened. I don't have to be judgmental, just tell what happened and go at it at the angle that I need to get it off my chest."

"Lacey, you know as well as I do that if you do that it could backfire. I don't think you need to be involved at all."

"I am *so* involved."

"I just mean you don't need to be the one who talks to him. Let me go, I'll take ... Dan Mitter. I won't say any names or talk about the incident at all. I will simply let Mitch know I know what happened and that he needs to repent and repent to everyone involved or I will be forced to go before the church. The ball will be in his court and we will have our answer as to whether or not he's willing to make it right. Dan will never be told the details. He will be there simply as a witness to the conversation. I trust him completely. Does everyone else?"

"I like it, Rick."

"Well, I don't, Jake, and I want it on record that I don't think this is the way it should happen, but I'm going along because Rick is my covering right now and my husband has agreed with him and because I'm not able to come up with anything better, which is very frustrating right now. But, to answer your question, Dan Mitter is a fine man and I do trust him."

"Lacey, if this doesn't cause a change, a real change in him or cause him to resign then you can tell the church."

"Why do I feel like it might be too late?"

Jake put his arms around me. "No one will hurt you, I will see to it."

"For the last time, I don't care about me. It's the people in that congregation that I feel responsible for. If he has a chance to deceive them, he will. I don't want him to get that chance."

Suddenly someone was knocking on the door loud and anxiously so Pastor Rick walked quickly to the door. "Mayree. Come in."

"Is Lacey here?"

"We're all in the living room."

I jumped up and met Mayree in the middle of the room. "What's wrong? Is everything okay at *Lion's Hill*?"

"Yeah, yeah. They're fine. I needed to show ya'll sumpin. I's glad you're here, Pappy. You will understands more than anyone else. Lacey, I knows you took Kimmy home. Was she okay when ya left her?"

"Not really, why?"

"I's went to *Lion's Hill* to find you, they says you took Kimmy home, sos I went there and she was all red eyed like she's been a cryin all day. She told me you's here. Did you know she's been a cryin?"

"Yeah. But, that's not why you came here. What's up?"

"Well, okay. That ain't none of my business and neither is this, but I's making it my business and telling ya'll. I's ran across sompin when I's working today. My boss asked me to file some financial statements for some of our clients and when I's putting this in the drawer it had the bank statement with it. I knows that the client would want this so I pulled it out and the check stubs was with it. They fells all in the floor. Look here, Pappy. It's from the church. I saw all these checks was made out to Preacher Sternfield and I knew that wutten right. So I looked at the financial statement and these checks is marked as donations to different missions. Most of um I's never heard of, but white churches give to different ones than us, but they don't cash the checks, Preacher Sternfield does. I can'ts think of any reason why he needs to cash them checks and give them the cash, can you, Pappy? Even if they was overseas?"

Pappy looked perplexed and angry at the same time.

"What are you thinking, Pappy?"

"That Sternfield is embezzling from the church."

"But, that would mean that there's more than one person that knows about that."

"Like who, Pastor Rick?"

"Well like Gloria Simpleton, for one, Lacey. Let me see one of those." Mayree handed a check to Pastor Rick. "Well, she didn't sign this one, Sternfield did, but she would still have to know about it."

"Looks like the only one she's signed are for the power bill, his and her payroll, here's one for the groundskeeper, oh and the flower shop. He signed the rest of them. Why would she know about these others?"

"Well, Jeremiah, she's the secretary. She would see the checks missing and see the ... "

"Yeah, but if he takes the check and writes on the stub that it's for these missions, she wouldn't know any thing different."

"He's right, Pastor Rick. I works with this kinda thing every day and rarely do I's look at the actual check, unless the bank says it's for something different than what the stub says. Most our clients just puts the bank statement right in with the paperwork for that month never openin' the envelope."

"So you're saying that she probably doesn't know and your boss doesn't know either?"

"Might not."

"What are you thinking, Pappy?"

"I'm thinking about putting his sorry as ... putting him in jail."

"Oh Pappy, I might lose my job."

"Hold on, Jeremiah. You can't prove anything."

"Like hell I can't, Rick! Please ... excuse me, Ladies."

"He'll just weasel out of it. It will take years to research these names to find out if they are legit. If they do exist they will say he gave them the money to keep any one from investigating them. What lawyer would take a case against him? What police department would press charges against a man of the clergy? You'll never get anyone to listen to you."

"The IRS will."

"No they won't. They might slap him on the wrist and make him pay a penalty, but this is small change to them. They have too many thugs to chase after. The illegal stills, mobsters and gangsters, people like that who have serious money. They won't prosecute a preacher from a two horse town. We need to handle this the same way. It's just something else I can use to scare him. Let's stick to the plan and watch him and see what he does. He stole from God and God's people. God will punish him and His punishment is far better than whatever the government, or you, or I can come up with."

"Amen to that, Rick. But, I still say we need to tell the people."

"We've heard you, Lacey. It ain't gonna happen that way. We're sticking to Rick's plan."

"Okay, Jake. I promise not to hold it against any of you when this blows up in our face."

"Lacey? What is all this about? What kinda plan and how come yous in the middle of it?"

"I'll tell you all about it later, Mayree. Just keep Pastor Rick in your prayers and everyone who attends *Wonders Of Love Fellowship*."

"So Halley? Which house would you like living in? I have a real nice old Victorian home in town that's big enough for you to grow your family in. Do you and Rick want to come by the bank tomorrow so I can drive you out to it?"

"Maybe Rick and I need to talk about this some more and maybe we better wait and see what happens after he talks to Reverend Sternfield."

We were making our way to the door to leave when Pappy asked, "And when will you talk to him, Rick?"

"I was thinking tonight after supper if Dan is free to go with me."

"You will call me and Jake and let us know how things went?"

"Of course I will. It's going to be fine. Ya'll have a nice evening with your families and don't worry about any of this again."

Why was my spirit not comforted by his words?

chapter twenty-seven

The next morning I was sitting in my office when a call came in from Preacher Sternfield. "Good Morning, Ms. Foresight, this is Mitch Sternfield. Let me congratulate you on your marriage. Jake is a very blessed man."

"Thank you, but I'm sure you didn't call me to congratulate me on our marriage?"

"No, I didn't. I wanted to tell you that I need to see you today if you have time. I would like to explain a few things and I would rather do it in person."

"Well, Jake is very busy today and I'm not sure when he will be able to come with me. He had a surgery in Asheville today so I will have to get back with you on that."

"Well, I'm over here at the church and several of the deacons are present and Rick will be by soon. I want them all to hear what I tell you so that everything is brought out in the open. There can't be any healing unless it gets air, my Mother used to always say, and I hope we can both find some healing. Even Dr. Jake would agree to us finding healing, don't you think and the quicker the better? I think things have gone unsaid long enough. I know that you have a right to feel concern, but you don't have to be concerned because these others will be here."

"Well, let me call you back. You will be at the church all day?"

"I will, but these men are only here for an hour or so. They can't stay all day; they do have other things they need to tend, as well. It would be so helpful if you would come now and we can get on with our day with a fresh start."

"Let me see if I have any appointments this morning that I can't change."

"I'll just hold the line while you check. This is too important to me that we get this straightened out as quickly as possible."

"Preacher Sternfield, I don't have anything to get straight ... "

"Lacey, I would rather talk about this in private with just those I can trust, who *we* can trust, rather than on the phone where there are ears that don't need to know our personal lives. That needs to be kept between God and us and of course these trustworthy men who are here now."

Something about him just creeped me out, but if he was sincere I wanted to give him a chance to make things right with God. I looked at my planner and I had a meeting in a hour and forty-five minutes with a young woman who needed counseling because of an unwanted pregnancy, but I had nothing else pressing at that moment. "I need to be back in my office in a hour and a half. Will that give us enough time?"

"I think that would be plenty of time. How long does it take to apologize?"

"I will see you shortly."

I called Pappy's office, but he was out of the office with a client. No one knew where he was. I called Mayree, but all she could do for me was pray. I called Sally just to make sure Jake was gone and he was. My last hope was Halley. I thought at least I would have a woman on my side, but no one answered the phone. I had to go by myself or not go at all. I went.

When I got to the church I was pleasantly surprised to find several cars parked in the lot beside the church. As I walked inside I heard men talking and laughing in the sanctuary so I poked my head around the corner to see who was in there. Just as Preacher Sternfield said three of the deacons were sitting in the first pew looking at Preacher Sternfield who was sitting in a chair faced towards the men and me.

Suddenly he stood to his feet and started sprinting across the front of the church. "Ah! Lacey, we're all waiting for you. Come right in. I have a chair for you."

He sat me down in the chair and walked around to the pew behind the other men. Mr. Clarke spoke first as he reached out and took my hand. "We are so glad to see you this morning. I know you are busy so we will get started. First I just want you to know that Mitch has told us everything and we completely understand the necessity for discreetness. No one wants to blow this out of proportion and hurt anyone. We have talked among us and we are very willing to stand up before the congregation in your place so that you will not feel ashamed or be left open for wounds from people who think they can help you, but only end up hurting you. You know how busybodies think they know how you feel and want to tell you more about themselves than help you with your own problem. You don't need to be subjected to that."

"Thank you, I think?"

They looked across at each other and then back to me. "For the time being we would like to offer you a position helping with the nursery or with the children. We are aware that these are mostly the very children that you see on a daily basis and that you may not want to spend your Sunday worship hour with the children, but I think it will be uncomfortable for you and Mitch if you are in the sanctuary in the leadership position you now operate in, under Pastor Rick's leadership."

"Where *is* Pastor Rick? Reverend Sternfield said he would be here and I called his house . . ."

"Why would we want to subject you to more people knowing this ugly secret?"

"What are you talking about?" Suddenly I felt like I was on a witness stand and the lawyers were trying to pin the murder on me. "Rick knows all about Preacher Sternfield's secret. And why are you doing all the talking? I came here to hear an apology from him not all this . . . this. What is this?"

"He said you might not be willing to come clean with us here. We know you have had a very bad year, Your Father's death, your Mother's passing, your longtime boyfriend leaving you practically at the alter and when Mitch didn't return your advances you had some kind of mock wedding, without a preacher of course because you couldn't involve the very man who had rejected you? And to a young man who had barely unpacked his bags after returning from medical school."

"Oh my gosh! He did it. I knew he would. This is unbelievable. You are something else Sternfield."

I stood up to leave when Preacher Sternfield said, "Sit back down. I told them this would be your reaction. You can't leave here until we get this all talked out. You have to own up to what you did or you will never have forgiveness. Your so-called marriage will never have a chance if you leave us no choice but to open this up for the whole church body to judge your sin."

"First of all you know nothing about my marriage, none of you do. And second, I wanted to go straight to the church body and let them hear all about the man we have as a leader. And if you men are so foolish as to believe his lies the curse that will befall you, you deserve."

"And you think you are so mighty that you can now curse people? Why Rick ever let you speak into the lives of my congregation while I was at home recovering is a sign of his lack of good judgment. No doubt that's why God has never given him a church."

"I'm done here. Mr. Sternfield, you and I both know what you did and I was willing to give you the benefit of the doubt, but I can promise you one thing. Because you have brought false witness on one of God's prophetesses you will lose everything and these men who have chosen to judge me before hearing the truth and seeing the proof of who you really are, they too will suffer. I will be praying for the welfare of your families, but you, I will leave in the hands of God."

"I told you she was crazy."

"Ms. Foresight, one more question before you leave."

"And what on earth could that be, Mr. Jonas?"

"Well, you prophesied something one day in this very room and after the service my daughter asked you what it meant and I was standing there so I heard this from you, not her."

"What?"

"You said in the service that it was not the Pastor's job to go after the lost and that God doesn't see lost people; that he is focused on His children."

"That's just crazy. See she's crazy."

I glared at Sternfield and said, "In The Name of Jesus may your mouth be shut as the lion in Daniel's den. What's your point, Mr. Jonas?"

"Well, when my daughter asked you about that, you said again that God doesn't care about the lost and that a pastor shouldn't either. I just think that's blasphemous."

"That's because you walk in the flesh, Mr. Jonas. If you walked in the spirit you would see the truth."

"Ms. Foresight, I plead with you, there is no truth to that. How could anyone get saved if God did not seek out lost people?"

"If you read the scripture you will see that it is not God who seeks out the lost it's the Holy Spirit that moves in the hearts of man, but all of this is way over your head and the point God was trying to make that day was that it's not for the pastor to go out and look for people to bring into the church, and in Sternfield's case, just so there is more money for his greasy pockets. If you have been listening to his sermons you would have heard Sternfield's cry for all of us to seek out the rich because 'they need God too.' Isn't that what you said? But, you and I and God know that you were saying that you needed a bigger paycheck and then some."

"I don't appreciate you disrespecting him by calling him Sternfield."

"And I have no respect for him, but I see that you are not at all bothered by the fact that he has disrespected me and my family and who knows how many others, but I will find out, you can place bets on that!"

"Well, speaking of scripture . . . "

"And I had so hoped you wouldn't speak again."

"Even Jesus went out looking for the one lost sheep. Can you men see how crazy her thinking is."

"Sheep! Mr. Sternfield! Sheep! Not lost people, not wolves!! Sheep!"

"Now what are you talking about?"

"Jesus was the Shepard, something pastors are supposed to be, Shepard of *sheep*! Saved people who come into the fold, into the church. Sometimes they lose their way and a pastor's heart should be as the Shepard's and hunt down that one that has lost their way and bring them back into the fold, back into fellowship with God. They are not unsaved! Only a sheep can bring in other animals, if you will, because they talk the language of the other animals. They were lost souls too at one time needing a Shepard and they are the ones who will go out and tell others about Jesus and bring them in so they can hear the Word and get nurturing from the Shepard. If the Shepard is doing his job, checking out the sheep, seeing who's been cut, seeing who needs brushing, grooming and so on he won't have time to be out there trying to steal other sheep or casing the woods for some benefit to his own need, leaving his own sheep vulnerable to the wolves that seek to devour them. We have not had a Shepard to lead our church body, we have had a hireling and he will flee when the truth of who he really is ... is exposed.

"God cannot look at sin therefore He did not see me when I was living in sin away from Him. He didn't hesitate to wipe out everyone who was lost in the flood of Noah's day. He did it again in Sodom and Gomorrah and He was ready to do it again when Jesus said, 'Wait. I want to go and try to help them see the light. I will take their place. Let me die instead.' Jesus is the one who cares for the lost and you and I are to be like Jesus and lay our lives down just as a sheep would be doing if that sheep went out and drew a fox or a wolf in close to the fold. They are taking a chance with their very lives by doing that. Look at the missionaries around the world who put their lives on the line everyday going into places where people don't understand them; some are killed and some are able to reach their hearts. But, the Kingdom is advanced either way. Great revivals have taken place at the death of one saintly sheep willing to do whatever was necessary to see just one person escape hell. Once we do make friends with the lost, then we can bring them to the Shepard who will show them the love that comes from the Father and reveal to them why they need a Savior. When they receive in their hearts Jesus and what He has done in their place, the blood that flowed from the Sacrificial Lamb, who we all know is Jesus, will cover them. Even you know that, don't you Mr. Sternfield. His blood covers us and now when God looks down He is able to see us, because even if we sin, Jesus' blood is able to withstand and cover any sin we can come up with. Even attacking innocent women, Mr. Sternfield. But, you have to be born again before you have the ability to recognize how wrong that is and repent of such behavior. I do hope that the Spirit of God will have mercy on you and come back around offering you that opportunity.

"Do any of you men love my children?"

"I don't know your children."

"She doesn't have any children, Clarke."

"I have a house full of children, Mr. Sternfield, and a few in heaven that I haven't had the pleasure of meeting yet. But, my point is that none of you love my children because you don't know them and they are mine. You love your children and God loves His children. If you aren't one of His children do you think He loves you? Jesus loves you. His heart is crying out for the lost, so much so, that He came to earth and gave His life. He is before the Father day and night praying for each one of us, but God does not know the sinner."

They were all staring at me perplexed so I silently prayed, "God give me the words to help them understand." I took a deep breath and began, "Mr. Jonas, you recently started a football team for your Son's school and you coach that team, don't you?"

"Yes, but what does that—"

"Just give me a few minutes of your time and I'll tell you. You had a vision of a team of boys who would learn the rules, be able to mesh together and win games, didn't you?" He nodded. "Well, God had a vision too. His vision was a Kingdom full of people who would love and respect Him, learn the rules, make the team, and learn to love each other as He led them. There is only one of you, Mr. Jonas, so you have been the one recruiting players, setting up the ball field, teaching the game, and doing all that has to be done to make this team a success. That's how God was in the beginning. Jesus and the Holy Spirit have always been with Him, but in the Old Testament you only heard about Jesus as He was prophesied to come later. Think about it like this. God created man so He would have someone to fellowship with, a team of people, a family, but these people allowed doubt into the kingdom, their faith was jeopardized and sin was the next step. The team was divided and some of the players chose not to be a part of the team at all. However, with time there were more players and the team got better and better and moved into the big leagues. There were also those who had the potential to play on the team one day even though they hadn't chosen to do so yet. So God divided Himself up, like you will have to do one day hopefully, and He created within Himself three parts. Having fellowship with man has always been the heart of God; to love His children unconditionally. Once man fell back in the garden God wasn't going to spend His time begging those who rebelled to come and spend time with Him. He wanted to focus on those who were close to Him and spend His time loving on them. By dividing Himself up into three departments He found the capacity to fulfill all the needs of man and then God was able to focus on what He loves the most; His children. 'Where your heart is, there your treasure will be also.' God's treasure is His children, the saved, the redeemed. Therefore, God is the one who sees over the needs of the team. Jesus is the one who was sent to coach, and the Holy Spirit is who does the recruiting.

"You could use some help couldn't you, Mr. Jonas? Wouldn't it be great to have someone *just like* you, who thinks *just like* you schedule the games, get the sponsors, make sure all the boys have uniforms and a ball to play with? Then you would be free to focus on the special needs of your players and coach them to greatness! Someone else could spend time recruiting. That's all God was trying to make clear that day.

"Businesses are set up the same way. Think of the Kingdom of God as a corporation. God is the CEO. He's not concerned with the competition. Never has been. No worthy opponent, not even Satan. He knows the competition is out there, but He doesn't know them personally or worry Himself over them. He *is*, however, concerned with someone getting hired on who is not, shall we say, a corporate man? Someone who is *stealing* from the business and sewing evil into the other employees, Mr. Sternfield? But there's a reward for them, so again He doesn't spend a lot of effort concerning Himself with that. Mostly what the CEO is concerned with is seeing those who work for Him be healthy, prosperous, joyful and do the best job they can that will bring a profit to everyone. Someone else is in charge of the competition; that would be the Holy Spirit. Jesus is the boss. The one all the workers answer to and go to when they have a need. He talks it over with the CEO because He's His right hand man.

"Each one of us works in the same manner. We just aren't quite like God in that we cannot actually send part of ourselves to another place.

Wouldn't that be great! I'm a wife when I'm at home and when I'm in that role I don't think about the children at *Lion's Hill*. I have people who I have all confidence in to take care of things in my absence. I'm a sister, but when I'm at *Lion's Hill* I'm not thinking about my siblings and my husband, well, maybe my husband just because I miss him, but I have all confidence that God has Jake in the palm of His hand and the same with my siblings. I focus on the job that is before me. I don't get involved in anything that I'm not qualified to do like the curriculum at *Lion's Hill*, that job is being performed by the state first and then the teachers review it and I trust their judgment. They know what I expect these children to learn and not learn. In other words, I don't spread myself thin doing everyone's job. I focus on mine and what I'm anointed to do, the place where my heart is. You men do the same thing. You just may not have ever thought about it quite like this before. God set it up a long time ago and every corporation, ball team, marriage, or church that has found a way to make it work thinks it's because of hard work and some bright idea that they came up with. If it's working it's because they are doing it God's way. If it isn't it's because they are trying to find a new way and we all know that there is nothing that we can come up with that will outdo God's way. A kingdom built on the principals of God's will stand; build on man's it will crumble, Mr. Sternfield.

"I hope I was able to answer your questions, gentlemen. My heart is aching for your souls so the extra time I've spent explaining the deep things of God to you I feel will be worth it. He is a big God and there is so much about Him to learn."

Preacher Sternfield stood and clapped his hands, "That was truly amazing. What an imagination you have."

"I have things that matter to do today so I have to leave now. I don't care what you do with whatever lie you decide to believe. God is on my side and therefore no weapon any of you come up with will harm me. Good day."

I started walking toward the door when Mr. Clarke said, "We need to finish this now. We need you to . . . "

"You don't need me, Mr. Clarke. Seek God for truth. But, if you still can't find it you know my number."

"You will not be allowed to lead in any capacity this Sunday."

I stopped and turned looking at the four manned freak show, "Whose church is this? Your's, Sternfield's? Johnny Kale's? Or is this God's church? Don't tell me how God will use me this Sunday or any other Sunday."

As I reached the door I heard Preacher Sternfield say, "Women shouldn't speak in church anyway. I told you she had a Jezebel Spirit. We have to put a lid on these women before they get out of hand."

As I reached the car I heard the voice of the Lord, "Those I sent you here to minister to, bring them out. They will come to the top like cream. Dust your feet off and go. Release your protection from these men and others and let me have them."

I sat down on the seat of my car and wept for those who would receive His judgment, but I did as He told me and removed each shoe and clapped them together removing the partials of sand from their soles.

I went back to the orphanage and God blessed me greatly by sending a young woman who had seen a world of anger, abuse and broken heart. She had been raped by a farmhand who lived year round on a peach farm that she and her family had migrated to for the summer. She was beaten by her Father when he found out she was pregnant and raped by him as a punishment in hopes the baby would die. She was on the run from her Father who told her he would kill her if the baby didn't die. The farmer's wife told her she knew of a place that would take women like her and sent her to Miss Sunshine. Sunshine brought her to me.

What blessed me the most, besides being given the opportunity to save her life, was being given the chance to save her soul. She had heard of God, but was sure He hated her. I told her, "God has a Son who loves you and wants to be everything you need. The Father to your baby, your husband . . . "

"What's his name?"

"Jesus."

"That's a pretty name. Does he live here?"

I guess that was the first time I felt an urgency to win souls. Right here, in America, in my neighborhood a young girl had lived eighteen years of her life with no one telling her that God sent His Son, Jesus, to die on a cross for her sin. That was possible, I supposed, but

Christmas? Everyone in America knew there was a baby in a manger named Jesus! Not Amelia Pinkerton, with Scottish-Irish parents who traveled the foothills in search of a peach orchard to make enough money to keep them through the winter in the back of a stationwagon and a cheep hotel.

"Amelia, we don't take children in who have reached the age of eighteen, but I have several here that are your age; however, they came to us when they were younger and this is their home. They are going to start collage this fall or next so I would never make them leave. They work, as do all the children over the age of fourteen, and I have the room for them to stay. You are a special circumstance. You are over eighteen and because of your condition you can't go out and work like the others, but you could help me. Sunshine has made some changes in her home atmosphere and I know the girls would love to have you there..."

"Lacey, we don't have any more rooms available and I couldn't ask one of the other girls to let her and a newborn room with them."

"I understand, Sunshine. Crying babies are common around here."

"But, I don't want to keep this baby."

"Well, right now, that's too bad. You have it. You are too far along to do anything to rid yourself and I wouldn't let you if you weren't."

"He raped me! I could never love this baby."

"If you can't you don't have to, but you have to let someone else have the opportunity."

Sunshine came over to Amelia. "You don't think you can now, but once you see that baby's face and see how much it loves you, you will change your mind."

"No I won't. I hate him!"

"But, you won't hate your own child. You'll forget all about how it came to be. That's the blessing of God. That baby is the band-aid so to speak for the hurt you've endured."

"You don't have to make any decisions now. We will be here for you if you don't want to keep your baby and we will be here for you if you do. But, if you stay here you will have to work like everyone else once the baby is born and you've had some resting time. Let me ask Miss Margaret to prepare you a room. You can help her if you would like?" I pressed the buzzer that rang in the main part of the house to let Miss Margaret know I needed her in the office.

"Yeah, okay. But, what kind of job will I have before the baby is born?"

"There's plenty to do here. When you need to sit down, Cook needs someone to help him cut up vegetables, snap the beans things like that. After supper dishes need washing, the tables and chairs cleaned off. When you need to sit again, babies need rocking, can you sing?"

"Yeah, sort of."

"Oh good. The children love for someone to sing to them or with them. They love books, too. Can you read?"

"Not as well as I sing, but I think I can read children's books."

"Okay then. Just make yourself available; that would be the greatest blessing for all of us." Miss Margaret entered the office. "Margaret, this is Amelia Pinkerton. She will be staying with us for a while. As you can see she will be delivering a new life very soon, so she will need a room big enough for her bed and a crib. Let her go with you to the attic to find the perfect little bed for her baby."

"Hi Amelia, I'm Miss Margaret. You have lovely eyes. They are almost as green as Ms. Foresight's."

"And her beautiful black silky hair sure has mine beat. Miss Margaret, Amelia will be working here, doing as much as she can, of whatever we need her to do while she is waiting the birth of her child. Then, if she decides to stay with us, she will continue in the same manner, but longer hours of course."

Miss Margaret started picking up Amelia's coat and sweater and taking her suitcase and a hat box. "I'm sure we will get along just fine while you are here and you won't want to go anywhere else. Cook is a grouchy old man that all of us women just love to spoil. You will, too. He always needs help pealing a potato or something. There's a nice rocker in the kitchen I like to sit in when I'm waiting for the cupcakes to come out of the oven. He hates that. Come on, follow me."

"Can't I get something?"

"No dear, you don't need to carry anything up these stairs except you and that baby. Now be careful."

The two of them went to the door. "Thank you Margaret."

Amelia poked her head back in the doorway. "Thank you, Miss Sunshine."

"You are so welcome, honey."

"And you, too, Ms. Foresight."

"Your welcome, Amelia, but you can call me Lacey. Now run along. Oh, and tonight after supper I'll tell you about Jesus." She sort of blushed as she walked away from the door. "Can you believe that Sunshine? I would have never thought there was a child past the age of two who hadn't heard about a baby named Jesus being born in a manger."

"I don't think her parents, well, her Father spent much time talking to her about anything. Her Mother died when she was just a toddler and he abused his next wife so badly that Amelia said she has never heard the woman speak."

"Is she his only child?"

"No, the only girl. She has brothers, but I didn't ask how many."

"How did you find her?"

"She just showed up on my doorstep, dirty and looking like a child from the wild. If I hadn't seen something like it before I would have been too afraid to let her in. The girls fixed her a bath and even had to wash her hair and show her how to bathe. She's had nothing and that suitcase and hat box came from my girls. They gave her that coat and sweater and several dresses she will be able to wear after the baby is born. She has a few nightgowns too in that suitcase, but no maternity dresses. The one she has on is one of mine. It just barely made it around her."

"I noticed that. I guess I need to take her into town to get her a couple things."

"She won't need much. That baby will be here any day."

"Is that what she told you?"

"No, but she looks like she's about to pop and I know it was over eight months ago that she was raped."

"Did she tell you that?"

"No, she told me her last period was at the end of August."

"Well, let's change the subject. Come over here and sit with me. Tell me how you've been doing and how are the girl adjusting to the changes you've made?"

Sunshine and I sat on the couch in my office talking about the things we were passionate about until Miss Margaret brought Amelia back to my office. Then Sunshine, Amelia and I went into town to find some things for her to wear for the next few weeks. There was something very special about this new girl and something very special about spending time with Sunshine. I never spoiled the day by sharing how my morning had started, because God had chosen to bless me with so much more than I had hoped for.

When we returned to *Lion's Hill* the three of us went in through the back door and met Margaret just inside. "Miss Lacey, Johnny Kale Butler is waiting for you out in the garden. He says he needs to speak to you."

"No he doesn't. Send him away."

"Sunshine, he's been very kind to me. What does he want, Margaret?"

"He didn't say, just that he needs to speak to you."

Johnny Kale entered the front door dressed in a tailored suit holding a matching cap in his hand. He nodded when he saw me and the others standing in the hallway. "Good afternoon, Ms. Lacey. Could I have a minute of your time?"

Sunshine started toward Johnny Kale, "No you may not. She is a very busy woman and you have no business with her."

"Sunshine, what is the matter? I have ... "

"Your right ma'am, she has no business with me, I have something I need to talk to her about."

"No you don't."

"Sunshine, stop this. Johnny Kale has been a friend to me. I have no reason to snub him."

"My dear child, he is a man of no good. You are too much of a lady to even grace him with your presence."

"She's right, Ms. Lacey. I just need to ask you a question."

"Well, ask her and go on about your business."

"I think she might want me to ask it in private?"

"This is as private as it's going to get."

"It's about a meeting she had this morning."

"What meeting. She met with us this morning. She doesn't ... "

"Margaret, take Amelia up to her room and help her get her new things put away. Sunshine, we have had a wonderful time together today and this matter that Johnny Kale wants to discuss would only ruin your day so may I please ask you to let me talk with him? If you want to stay you can. I'm sure Amelia would love to show you her room, wouldn't you, Amelia?"

"Oh yes! I have never had a room that was just mine before or one so beautiful. Well, I couldn't even imagine it. Please come up with me."

"Mr. Butler, you can follow me to my office where we will have some privacy."

When Johnny Kale passed by Sunshine she whispered, "You better not hurt that girl."

"I just want to ask her a question."

We walked into my office and I closed the doors behind him. "I hope this won't get ugly like this morning."

"I'm here to listen, not judge you."

"What is your question?"

"What did Mitch do to you?"

"I'm not so sure that's nearly as important as what he has done to the whole church."

"Then what is that?"

"It has been discovered that he has been stealing money from the church's bank account, but I can't positively prove that. I have seen the checks written out to him, but put in the ledger as missions. He doesn't know I'm suspicious. And I'm not sure why I'm telling you."

"I've suspected that, but I'm not sure I'm one to pass judgment on that kind of behavior."

"You have stolen God's money?"

"I'm guilty of making transactions within my business that favored me, but now that it's become so profitable I'm watched very closely. Seems like the larger the amount the more the IRS comes calling and they have their own set of bookkeepers who like to audit my business transactions."

"Yeah, that's the way greed acts. They know the more you have the more likely you are to steal really big and they are watching out, for you of course, by making sure they get all they can."

"Boy, ain't that the truth. I do all the work, take all the risks and get rewarded for it and then the government comes along and claims it their's. Leaves me scratching my head saying, 'Now what was it they contributed to my blood, sweet and tears?"

"Freedom. It's your cost for freedom."

"I don't have a problem paying for our men to fight for our freedoms, but what about when we aren't at war? Why do I have to pay the salaries of a bunch of men sitting in high back chairs somewhere writing down laws that have been written for years? Why do we have to make everything so complicated when God made it so simple?"

I laughed and Johnny Kale smiled at me, "That wasn't meant to be funny."

"Oh Mr. Butler, God's been asking that question for centuries. 'Have no other God before Me,' I always like to say love the Lord God with all your heart soul and mind for the first one because it means the same thing and the children understand it easier. Don't carve out an idol, don't be flippant with God's Name, keep the Sabbath Holy, do right by your parents, don't seek out to murder, don't commit adultery, don't steal, don't lie or bring false witness about anyone or anything, and don't lust after another's belongings or their wife. Now how complicated is that?"

"And our own Mitch Sternfield has broken these laws?"

"And we were having such a nice chat. Let's see, the one that hurts the most is stealing from God, then bringing false witness against me, and even though I was not married to Jake at the time I was his in my heart and I never showed any interest in Mr. Sternfield so I guess you could say he lusted and tried to violate another man's wife because God had chosen me for Jake and him for me since before we were born, but that's just a technicality."

Johnny Kale held his head down looking at his fingers as they rubbed the thumbs. "Tell me what happened the morning you went by Mitch's."

"Kimmy, my cousin Kimmy."

"Yeah, I know her."

"She was going to meet me there because truthfully I didn't want to go there alone. He had been sort of flirting with me or something. He just made me uncomfortable. I had asked the ladies to take their dishes to him, but some of them brought the dishes to my house.

Makes me wonder if there aren't several ladies who are uncomfortable around him. Anyway, I told Kimmy I was on my way; she left her house and one of the boys here called me as I was going out the door. He was excited and perplexed about some things and before I knew it we had been talking forty-five minutes or more. I hurried over to his house and found Kimmy sitting out on his steps. She said you had been there that morning."

"Yeah, I saw her and I let her in and left pretty much at the same time. I had a meeting early that morning and I had to pick up my guests at the depot. She told me you were coming by and she would just wait outside, but I told her to take the dish on in and lock up when you two left."

"Well, she was on the steps and she was very upset. Told me she was sick and needed to go home. I felt bad cause I thought she had stayed there waiting for me and here she was sick, but she wasn't sick when I talked to her earlier. Anyway, she left, I went in, put my dishes on the table in the kitchen, some had to go in the ice box and then he spoke to me asking for medication. I wasn't sure when someone had given him medication before and the bottle of pills was over on his chest of drawers so I though maybe you had given him something before you left and put them over there so he couldn't get them. I wanted to call you, but he said to just get him some water. So I did. I handed it to him and he acted all drowsy and I was afraid he was going to spill the water so I took it from his hand. Well, I wanted to leave it close to him and the bedside table is on the other side so I leaned across him to set it down and he grabbed me and pulled me down onto him and kissed me. He was so strong. Not like a man who was over medicated at all. I think I was hurting his incision squirming around trying to get free because he loosened his grip and I was able to pull away. The water spilled in the floor and he had the nerve to ask me to clean it up. I told him to get a mop. Then I left."

Johnny Kale dropped his head again. He swallowed hard and rubbed his hand across his mouth several times, then fiddled with his hat. "Ms. Foresight, Mitch had been medicating himself for days. His pills were on his bedside table that was on the left side of the bed where you would not have had to reach across him when I left that morning. He also had a pitcher of water because he went into the kitchen that morning and filled it up. I carried it in for him. I think Mitch was up to his old tricks and you fell into his illusion."

"Well, you're the only one who can verify my story or make me out to be a bigger liar than some of the deacons believe I am."

"Tell me about the meeting."

"Well, I was led there by Preacher Sternfield's phone call where he said he wanted to apologize, so I thought that's what he meant. You know he's quite the double-tongued fellow."

"Oh yes. That's what intrigued me about him when we were kids. He could convince you you needed a dog even if the dog was dead, sell you a motor for your bicycle, tell you he would install it, and it would turn out to be a simple cloths pin and a playing card. But, some how he made you feel like you had not been taken, it was worth every dime he charged you. He's really a likable guy, but it's like I want him to grow up now."

"Well, he hasn't and he's not going to. He sold those men a pack of lies and they believe every word he said. They even questioned my gift and told me I would not be allowed to take my leadership place in the church anymore. In other words after questioning some things God said through me in the services, they were saying I would not be allowed to prophesy to the people anymore. I told them they didn't have that authority, only God did." I sat against the front edge of my desk looking at Johnny Kale sitting in the chair across from me. "Nothing they said really hurt me, not even when they brought up all that's happened in my life this past year, until I was walking out the door and I heard Sternfield say I had a Jezebel spirit. That got to me for some reason. But, it doesn't matter. He'll sell that to some, but God assured me he won't be able to sell his lies to those in the church He sent me to."

"He brought up your mother?"

"Yes. Her, my pa, and Tylar. All the cause of me losing my senses and desperately throwing myself at Preacher Sternfield. And once he rejected me, my quick marriage to Jake."

"I can't believe he brought up Abigail. Her accident and then death has broken ... well, he knows how the whole church prayed for her."

"Did you know my mother?"

"We went to school together. Abigail Hawthorne was the classiest lady, well she was loved by everyone; your Father was a lucky man."

"Luck had nothing to do with it; they were a blessing to each other."

Johnny Kale kept his head down most of the time while we talked. I felt kind of sorry for him because Mitch Sternfield had been his friend for a long time and I was sure this was breaking his heart to hear how greedy he had become.

After a long time of silence Johnny Kale said, "I've known Mitch a long time. There's nothing he's done in the past that I was not right there in the middle of it with him. But, I guess these past few weeks having Rick at the church I've had a chance to hear a man who truly believes what he's saying and I've actually stayed in the service long enough to hear God speaking directly to me. And I've listened." Tears welled up in his eyes, "I've changed. Not completely, but I've changed. The man I used to be would have flown out of here, slinging the door off its hinges and beat him to a pulp. He knows there are limits, there are places he shouldn't go and he has violated our friendship, as well as you. What did he do to your cousin?"

"She won't talk about it."

He dropped his head, "I hate him. Please excuse me."

"You're excused. Hate the one who has him bound and blinded, the sin not the sinner. I almost feel sorry for him, but right now because the meeting is so fresh to me I'm just angry. But, God told me to dust my feet off and go on, so I did. Whatever happens there God will deal with it."

"And he will use me to do the dealing."

"What do you mean?"

"Well, all of this is my fault and I need to ask you to forgive me."

"Of course I forgive you, but how is this your fault?"

"I brought him here. I gave him a job, a church, a house; he had access to my whole town! But, it wasn't enough. He wanted what wasn't his. He had to cross that line and now he has to pay for that."

"Pay? How?"

"I just mean he has to ... he has to go."

"Well, I agree to that, but all the people in that church aren't going to agree."

"In all realistic terms that church belongs to me, the house he lives in and his car. It sounds like anything else he has belongs to the church so that makes it mine, too. Well, not mine, but certainly not *his*. I know it all belongs to God, but I'm new at this. He's going to have twenty-four hours to pack the clothes in his drawers and get out of my house. One thing I learned while hanging out with him is how to sell dead dogs, too. But, in this case the truth will speak for itself. We need your Pappy to be at church Sunday. Think he can make it?"

"He usually does."

"Good. And bring Jake along with you and the children of course? Things need to be normal."

"Let me see what you're going to do first before I commit to anything."

"I brought him in and I can take him out. I won't allow you to be hurt anymore."

"But, years of friendship? He's your friend. It's not going to be easy for you to just end it and boot him out of town all at the same time? What if he won't go? He doesn't have to, you know?"

"He has to get out of my house and off my property. I need some new friends. The old ones are dragging me down. God has something planned for me and I'm not able to play with Mitch and his games and walk with God, too. Isn't that how a drunk does it? Throws the bottle away and that's it, cold turkey? Well, I've done that before and if I can kick that habit, I can kick Mitch Sternfield, too."

"Can I ask you a favor?"

"You can ask me anything."

"Will you call me and let me know how it goes?"

"Yes ma'am. And I'll even let you know if Kimmy accepts my apology."

"Are you going to see her? Maybe that's not . . ."

"Because she hasn't told you if he did anything to her?"

"Yeah, if you go over there and say something to her she's liable to think we're all talking about her or *worse*, that *he's* talking about her. She's so fragile right now. She doesn't need your apology; *she needs* to be able to talk about it. An apology from him is too much to ask for and heaven knows she doesn't want him anywhere near her."

Johnny Kale stood up and reached out to shake my hand. As I

extended it to him he looked me in the eyes and said, "You've grown into a very wise woman. I see Abigail when I look at you." His eyes filled with tears again as he smiled at me. "I can't take away the fear you must have felt or remove the humiliation, but I can make this right and I will do everything within me to make this right." He took a deep breath and almost whispered, "I dread passing by that old woman out side that door more than dealing with Mitch."

"What woman is that?"

"Miss Sunshine. That woman has hated me since I can remember. She even turned me away back in the day when I was wildcatting, if you know what I mean."

"I'm afraid I do. But, Sunshine doesn't hate you. She doesn't hate anyone. She might have been looking out for you. Guess after she turned you away the next stop was the reservation?"

"My wife and children live at the reservation. Guess I should thank Miss Sunshine, I would have never met Ama unole."

"Oh my gosh. I just assumed . . . why don't they live with you?"

"One day they will. For now my Father won't acknowledge my family. I'm not surprised, he barely acknowledges me. They are better off out there where they have plenty of family to love on them. That's really all that matters. It's not important who your parents are if they don't know how to love you. You're better off with . . . with a place like this than learning how to hate. I sure haven't been a father to my children, but I have seen to it that they were living in a loving environment. I think that's the best gift I could give them. And who knows, with Pastor Rick and God teaching me everyday, maybe I can be a good friend to all of them one day."

"I'm sure you can. You're on the right road, anyway. I'll be praying for you and your family. I hope you can find a way to bring them to live with you. I for one would welcome them as members of our community. And think about this. Your children will have so many friends in their lives. What they need and what they want is a father. Don't let your shame keep them from that."

He lifted our hands and kissed the back of mine. Then he walked over to the mirror and adjusted his cap on his head. He looked back at me reaching for the door knob opening it quickly allowing Miss Sunshine to stumble into the room.

"Good day, ladies. I will call you when I have some news."

"Thank you, Johnny Kale," and he left us standing in my office.

"I had no idea you would still be waiting, however, I didn't mean for that to take so long."

"What did he want?"

"Why, weren't you listening at the door?" I walked around to my desk chair and sat down.

She leaned onto my desk top. "Your Pappy would never forgive me if I didn't watch out for you."

"And why would you have to watch out for me? And why does Johnny Kale bring such anger from you?"

She shifted back to a standing position and paced like a cat looking for the right spot to sit. "It's not anger. I'm just concerned. I'm not sure I can trust him, and neither does your Pappy. What did he want?"

"He just wanted to tell me he was going to answer my prayer, but how he's going to do that, I'm not sure."

Just then Amelia came to the door. "Jake's calling you, line one."

"Thank you." I picked up the receiver and twisted the knob to switch to line one. "Are you back in town?"

"I miss you so much."

"I miss you more."

"How has your day been?"

"Eventful. I'm in my office now with Sunshine. We did some shopping for a new girl who arrived today. I'll tell you all about it when I see you. Are you home?"

"No, I'm still at the hospital. I just checked on my patient in post-op. They're doing great so I'm gonna grab something to eat in the cafeteria and then check one last time and come home."

"I'll see you about?"

"It may be as late as nine. Is she with you right now?"

"Yes."

"Well I'll tell you what I'm going to do to you when I get my arms around you later then."

"That will be fine. I'll wait up."

"You may want to get a nap, cause I really miss you and I may keep us up all night."

"Oh, I'm so glad. Be careful coming home. Don't get into to big a hurry. I promise I'll wait up."

"I wish you were here."

"Oh, Jake. Me too."

"I love you."

"I love you, more."

"Bye." I always hated saying good-bye to Jake even when I knew I would see him shortly.

"I need to get home, Lacey. It will be dark soon and the girls will be worried."

"Are you sure, Sunshine? I could drive you home. Jake's going to be late."

"No, I need to go. I love you, dear," and she kissed me on my cheek. "I had a wonderful time today. Thank you so much for taking in Amelia. I think she will find greater comfort here with all of you."

She seemed to hurry out the door and down the hall to the front door. This day just got stranger and stranger, but I was thankful that Johnny Kale had found out everything and that he was going to be the one to take care of Mitch Sternfield. It was nice to know that for once my family was not going to have to be in the middle of some kind of breach of peace or cat and dog fight. In this case it would have been more like a wolf and sheep fight. But, in any case, if Johnny Kale was able to maintain control of the situation I was sure he would keep my involvement out of it. I was anticipating his call, but first I needed to find Pappy. I called his office.

"Hello?"

"Pappy, I think we have a solution to our problem. It seems that Johnny Kale has found out about it and he finds the leader we now have has blessed him greatly so he's going to deal with the other one."

"Are you going to be at the orphanage for a while?"

"Yes. Jake is in Asheville and won't be home till nine. We have a new girl who's asking about Jesus. I promised I would share with her tonight after supper. You and Nanny could come for supper?"

"She's at Alvin's spending some time with Kimmy. I'll call her and see what her plans are, but I'll be right over."

"Okay, bye."

We never discussed anything of great importance on the phone. In our little town there weren't that many calls taking place and staring at a switchboard waiting for someone to want a connection didn't offer much hope that you were having a two way connection.

I told Pappy all about the day; however, Sunshine had stopped by the bank to tell him Johnny Kale had been to visit with me. If everything went smoothly with Preacher Sternfield, Rick and Halley could continue to reside over the church. But, I wasn't sure what God wanted me to do. He had told me to brush the dirt off my shoes and go on. And what about the deacons, how much fuss would they make. I was sure there was a can of worms still waiting to pop open and all I could think about was Kimmy.

Nanny stayed at Uncle Alvin's for supper, something she and Pappy did more often now that Mother was gone. Uncle Marty had always been Nanny's favorite and even though Alvin was not her son, I think she had a connection to Marty through him because they both had served our country in the military; something Uncle Trell had not done. Whatever the reason, Nanny was not close to Trell and Gail and their family like she had become to Uncle Alvin and his. I missed our relationship, but I was thankful to still have my Pappy so close. Pappy and I spent our evening with Amelia helping her understand who God is and why He sent Jesus to the earth. She was very bright and eager to listen. There was no doubt that she would make it, she and her baby.

When Jake got home I filled him in on the events of my day and before we finish our breakfast the next morning there was someone at our front door. Willie answered the door and brought Johnny Kale into the kitchen.

"Oh, good morning, Mr. Butler. Come in. We are just finishing up, but there's plenty. Have a seat. Abbie Lou, pour Mr. Butler some coffee."

"Thank you, Jake. But, I didn't mean to interrupt; I just wanted to get here early enough to catch you both before you left for work."

"Don't be silly, Johnny Kale. You are not interrupting us. Our home used to be fuller at breakfast. Having you this morning is a treat. Cole, pass Mr. Butler some eggs. Do you want some grits?"

"Well, if I'm going to stay and eat, then I have to have some grits."

"Biscuit? I made them."

"Of course then. Thank you Miss Retta."

"Mr. Butler, Lacey told me all about yesterday. I appreciate your kindness to her. Sounded like she needed some of that yesterday. I hated I was away. I had a patient who needed surgery and we had to go to Asheville. So, do you have some news for us?"

I had to add, "Some *good* news?"

"Well, yes and no, and please, Jake, call me Johnny. On the good news part, Lacey. Mitch is gone out of my house, but he isn't gone far. He checked in at the boarding house. Said he wasn't going to be run out of town."

"Did he admit anything to you?"

"Not really. He avoided my questions which gave me the ammo to remove him from the church. I don't think this is over. I think he's going to spread lies from one end of town to the other. We need to be prepared, but I don't know how."

"Prayer. That's the only way to fight against the unknown. I don't care what he says against me. I hope he doesn't have things that he could use against you?"

Johnny Kale laughed, "Sure he does, but I'm a big boy. There's nothing he can say about me that he can't say about himself, but I'm not wanting to get into a 'let's see who can out sin the other' war."

"I don't want to see that either. Mostly because of your children and wife."

"It wouldn't ever reach them."

"It will when they come here to live, and they will, cause I've been praying for that. And that is privileged information, too, kids."

"Thank you. I talked to Rick and Halley and they are willing to stay on if the congregation wants that. I was hoping to present them as full-time Sunday stating that Mitch was not sure when he would be well enough to come back and didn't want to leave us without a full-time pastor. But, I don't think that's going to be the path. We may have to just lay it all out there."

"I wanted that from the beginning so I have no problem with that."

"I do."

"Jake, why?"

"I just don't want my wife put out there for any more abuse. Those men had no right to accuse you yesterday and by the time Sunday gets here the lies will have spread and they will be ready to crucify you. I couldn't bear it."

"I can make them see the truth."

"No Lacey, *I* will help them see the truth. You and Jake need to stay out of the limelight, for now. I'm sure people will have things to say to you after I explain why Mitch had to go. I can only hope that what they say will be heartfelt concern for you, but you and I both know there will be some."

"Oh yeah. I understand that, God had already told me there would be some who would believe him. There's something else you need to talk to them about and that's changing the name of the church. This time the people need to name the church, not one person."

"Do I have to address that Sunday? Can't it wait for a few weeks?"

"No. Well, it could, maybe, but I can't be a part of it till the name changes. It can't be the same place God had me dust my shoes off, too. He said to bring those He sent me to, out. But, He didn't say to dust my shoes off so He could bring judgment on the church, He just said do it so I could release these men to Him. I have to know where He wants me before I jump threw those doors again. I don't think Jake and I will be there Sunday, unless I'm going to tell them what happened to me. If you're going to do that then I will stay away and let everyone say and ask what they want. If I'm there I will cause an atmosphere of suppression."

"I agree with her on that, Johnny Kale. You can tell more and they can ask more if we aren't there. Pappy too."

"And the children?"

"We'll need to think about that."

"I need to ... *we need to* talk to the children, Jake. Some of them work in town and it would kill them to be faced with lies and accusations about me. They've had to live their whole lives facing hurtful things at every turn. They don't need to think that's going to start back up again."

Sunday came, the children didn't want to go to the church till everything was worked out, but things were not as peaceful as we had hoped. Johnny Kale was sharing with the congregation the ugliness of all that had happened and took with him the canceled checks that were returned to the church secretary so he could present them as well. Mitch Sternfield showed up in the middle of it to tell his tawdry lies. His story went something like this: My Pappy had decided that he preferred Pastor Rick over him and because Johnny Kale was tied to Pappy's bank through loans to his business, so to keep things running smooth there, Johnny Kale was forced to do whatever my Pappy wanted. It hadn't helped that Pappy's own grandchild had made advances toward him that were not reciprocated. This whole thing was because I was a Jezebel. And most likely a witch casting curses on people who didn't agree with me.

Suddenly, while he was telling his lies, Abe burst into the room and charged at Preacher Sternfield shouting that he would kill him. Sheriff Cromwell and others pulled Abe off of Mitch and tried to get him to calm down. Abe kept shouting at Preacher Sternfield that he would kill him for what he had done to Kimmy. Of course Preacher Sternfield denied that he even knew who he was talking about and demanded that Sheriff Cromwell have him arrested and removed from the church property. Johnny Kale told him he didn't have jurisdiction over the church anymore and certainly didn't have any over the property and Abe could stay, but he would need to calm down so everyone could hear what he wanted to say.

After some time of demanding calmness, Sheriff Cromwell told Preacher Sternfield he had to sit on one side of the room being watched by two of the biggest men in the congregation and Abe was seated in one of the chairs down front by the alter. Abe was given time to talk and tell what he was so upset about while Johnny Kale and A.P. kept him in his seat.

Abe told everyone about the day when the new girl Amelia shared her story with him and Kimmy when they were working out at *Lion's Hill*. He had noticed something had been bothering Kimmy for a while so when Amelia started telling Kimmy about some things that happened to her at the hands of her own Father, Kimmy seemed upset. "I recognized the look, because I saw that same look on my sisters' faces after they were raped by my uncle. It took a while to get it out of her, but she finally told us that," and he shouted, "That man!" and he tried to lunge over to Preacher Sternfield again, but he was held back by Johnny Kale and A.P. "That man raped her in his home when she delivered food to him. She was doing something nice for him and he ... he threatened to tell her parents that she was a whore and had been paid well for sleeping with him on a weekly bases, if she didn't keep quiet."

"Liar! She's a liar and so are you. God will bring damnation down on both of you, on all of you who believe these lies!"

Two ladies in the congregation ran to the alter sobbing and dropped to their knees weeping and praying and crying out for forgiveness. The whole place was in turmoil and Pastor Rick was at a loss as to what to do.

"I'll kill him for what he's done!"

Preacher Sternfield shouted, "Have him arrested for threatening my life. My lawyer will hang him for slander."

Pastor Rick called for order again and sat down in front of the two ladies who had come to the front. "Is there something you two would like to share with the rest of us?"

Patty Broom shook her head, but Lindy Logan dried her tears and stood up slowly and turned to face the congregation. "I made a mistake so I am being punished."

Pastor Rick said, "God doesn't punish mistakes, we punish ourselves. He does punish things we do over and over. Was this a mistake or something you did several times?"

She hung her head, "No, I only did it once."

"What was your mistake?"

"My parents were out of town and I snuck out of the house after my siblings fell asleep. There was a boy I liked who I knew was going down to Fred Wheeler's club and I wanted to go and meet him. A bunch of other kids were going. I took my Dad's truck and drove down there and met with my friends, but the boy I wanted to see wasn't there so I left earlier than the rest of them did. Preacher Sternfield was down there in the back room playing cards and we all had seen him, but we kind of hid from him over in one of the corners."

"She's a liar!" Preacher Sternfield shouted.

"We will have order in this room, in the Name of Jesus. Now, be quiet." Pastor Rick said.

"This is no courtroom and you are no judge. None of you are!"

Pastor Rick said, "You are absolutely correct, Reverend Sternfield. You are free to go at any time, but if you plan to stay you will keep quiet when someone else has the floor. Now, continue with your story, Lindy."

"Well, like I said, I left before my friends so when I got out to the truck and got into the seat Reverend Sternfield opened the passenger's door and asked me to give him a ride home. I was feeling scared that he was going to tell my parents, but he promised he wouldn't tell if I didn't tell. I thought he was being really cool about it so we were just talking and laughing and he was telling me I was a pretty girl and I needed to be careful because there's a lot of things that could happen to a pretty girl in the middle of the night. He said he would keep me safe, but he didn't keep me safe. He didn't. He hurt me and after that he said I was blessed because He had chosen me, but I'm not the only one he chose. He also chose Patty. He violated her and he violated me. Made me feel dirty and disgusting and trashy and..." Then she fell to the floor in tears. "I hate him. I hate him."

While she was telling her story Patty Broom openly wept. It seemed that there had been others, a lot more than we would ever find out about, but none of them willing to press charges against him after they spoke to a lawyer. There wasn't enough evidence to put them on the witness stand and I was the only one willing to testify and what I had wasn't enough to put him in jail. The church wanted to let the money issue go and believe that God would be paid back another way. I agreed that vengeance does belong to God, but I wanted him stopped and I was sure he would go on to do this to others in another town, in another church.

Mitch Sternfield lived in town for a few weeks, after he was removed from Johnny Kale's house, calling my house wanting desperately to tell me something, but Pappy insisted that I refuse his calls and so I did. "Whatever he wants to say to you is not an apology, I can assure you, Punkin. If it was he could use the newspaper, or better yet apologize to everyone by calling Rick and then Rick could convey his apology before the whole church. Instead, he's held up in his room at the boarding house making calls in a drunken state. We just need to ride it out. He will get tired and go away."

Apparently he did get tired because he left town and headed to Chicago looking for Tylar to give him a job. Ms. Marge didn't want to talk about it which made me think Tylar had given him a job and she was hurt by it. I didn't care. He didn't owe me anything and as long as he was aware of what Mitch Sternfield was capable of doing, he was as safe as any man would have been having him working for them. My hope was that Tylar would not be his only friend in town because Tylar wasn't spiritually strong enough to resist the wiles of this man alone. And my prayers were that Tylar would not be influenced in anyway by the thinking of a refined madman, but I knew that sometimes prayers aren't answered as we would like.

chapter twenty-eight

Founders Street Fellowship was greatly blessed with the presence of the Holy Spirit for the next four or five years. We met in the gym of *Lion's Hill* for a year while Johnny Kale and Pappy saw over the building of a new church just past our house going into town. There was no doubt after much prayer by everyone that God did not intend on us returning to that building ever again. The old church had been sold to a Baptist congregation in Ohio. They sent a preacher along with a few members to help get the church growing, but they really didn't have to because there were six or seven families that believed Mitch Sternfield and they didn't want to come to the church at *Lion's Hill*. Our country had gone through quite a change, but those who remained at the heals of Mitch Sternfield had suffered changes that shattered not just there lives, but the lives of those who they touched. The most incredible fact was they didn't recognize their lives were shattered. They had hated the migrants and judged the beatniks and swingers and become another version of the very same thing, only they added a proud version of denial.

Kimmy, Patty and Lindy along with Amelia and the other children who had similar experiences became very good friends and had found a bond that no one on the outside looking in could understand. It wasn't something any of us would have said at that time, but looking back the outcome had brought a freedom to Kimmy that she had needed for years. Aunt Penny was more concerned with how the whole mess reflected on the family, mostly her, and she feared her delusional standing in the elite society was going to be marred if she didn't disassociate herself from her own daughter. In all reality, she had done that years ago when questions arose as to who Kimmy's father was. For Kimmy, having the other girls to relate to, not only in the physical abuse, but the emotional abuse they all had suffered at the hands of their own family members is what caused Kimmy to find her place, her reason, her uniqueness. Those things and Abe.

Abe was who Kimmy had prayed for, but never thought in her wildest dreams would come for her. All possibility of such a dream was quenched the day Mitch Sternfield was waiting behind the broom closet door for me to enter the kitchen. Kimmy found herself bent over the back of a kitchen chair with her head in the seat and the edge of the table top pressing down against her back. There was no escape as long as he kept pushing her against the table top. Maggy Jordan told me that she had called Preacher Sternfield just to check on how he was recovering and told him that I would be bringing food by that morning. No doubt his plan was to inflict this torture on me. God had another plan, but why? That's one of those questions I have on a list waiting to ask Him when we are face to face if I don't know the answer the moment I see Him.

I do know that good had come out of it all for Kimmy and other people were healed through her testimony. She lost any relationship she had with her mother and her dignity had been turned into humility as the grapevine found the story fascinating dinner conversation. She and the other ladies had become the butt of jokes and often had to endure tasteless chants and innuendos from vile men as they walked through town. But, Kimmy became stronger and stronger with every passing day.

Things at *Lion's Hill* had changed some. God sent children who had suffered from unimaginable things instead of babies born to mothers without husbands or couples who believed they weren't ready for a family. I wouldn't have understood any of them if I had not been a small part of what had happened to Kimmy and so many others. I praised God that Kimmy, Amelia, Abe, and Bailey had chosen to stay at *Lion's Hill* and work with these children, though I never will understand why it is necessary to offer a place like *Lion's Hill* in a country so full of every blessing available to man. However, it is so apparent that the absence of God in the hearts of man will yield evil no matter how blessed we are.

Over the next few years Kimmy and Abe became engaged. Bailey married Amelia and took her son as his own. They moved into a house just a mile from *Lion's Hill*. Patty and Lindy were considered an embarrassment to their families and were thrown out of their family homes. Pappy, along with some of those silent investors, paid for their college where they studied psychology. They both wanted to understand the human mind so they could help others overcome the horrors of abuse.

Jake and I lived at *Lion's Hill* with our children waiting for God to give us one of our own, but content with whatever He decided. Our baby Ben and Eliza had been adopted by Uncle Marty and Aunt Joan. I was filled with mixed emotions in that I loved these two so much and never wanted them to leave. But, they deserved a family and there couldn't have been a better home for them. The greatest blessing was that they would stay in my family, but the heart break was having them live so far away. And my heart did break the moment they drove out of our drive.

The day Kimmy turned eighteen she and Abe married in the place they met, the garden at *Lion's Hill*. Abe was invaluable to me at the orphanage. Because the number of children who wanted to attend our school had increased, we built another wing on to *Lion's Hill*. I needed the help in administration so I put Abe in that position giving me freedom to spend more time with the children.

Willie found that he was adored by many young ladies in town even with his learning problems, but Mollie was the one who had stolen his heart. Jake and I were thrilled for him and excited to one day become double in-laws. They weren't ready for that yet, even though Willie had turned nineteen at the end of the summer. He still clung to me and I was more than thankful to have my brother at my side. Mayree was still my closest girlfriend. I would have been lost without her. Jake was quite a surgeon and a very loved doctor so he traveled often to the hospital in Asheville leaving me alone several nights a week. Mayree would come and stay at *Lion's Hill* with me and kept me company or we would go into town and have supper. She lived at the boarding house in town within walking distance to the accounting firm where she had been promoted after earning her CPA license. When we were together everything was funny. We could be our silly selves and never care what anyone else was thinking. We had been through so much together through the years so we had our own language and inside jokes. Joyous release was what I felt each time I knew we would have girl time.

It was mid spring and the weather had turned hot overnight. Jake was in Asheville for a doctor's seminar so Mayree and I had three glorious days of girl stuff planned. The first being a trip to Montgomery Wards to pick out new bathing suits for the summer. After we picked out our bathing suits it was time for lunch so we started down the sidewalk towards Mr. Gregory's drug store for sandwiches and a soda pop. As we were passing Miller's Market the screen door opened in our path. His eyes met mine and for what seemed like minutes my heart stopped beating. Tylar was holding the door open for a young lady to come out, but his eyes never left mine.

"Tylar." The lady passed me as I went to him and hugged him with all my strength. "When did you get home?"

"Last night. I went by the school and ... Abe? I think that was his name. Nice boy. Married Kimmy! I must have missed that when Mother was telling me all the news about home through the years. Anyway, he said we would find you in town shopping."

"We?"

"Let me introduce you." He held out his hand past me and as I turned I saw the lady who had come out of the market standing behind me.

She held out her hand and said, "Lacey, you are as beautiful as Tylar told me you were. I'm so glad to finally meet you."

"Lacey, this is my wife, Marianne."

She was beautiful with her long brown hair twisted up and clipped at the back with bangs and long strands falling around her face. Her eyes were so dark and big they drew you in with their mystery. She was just what I knew Tylar would be attracted to. She didn't need extravagant clothing to make her any more interesting.

"Tylar calls me Annie. My family calls me Anna."

"I think Marianne is beautiful, but she's my Annie."

"What would you like me to call you?"

"Lacey, you seem like family to me because you mean so much to Tylar, call me Anna."

"Nice to finally meet Tylar's wife. I would like you to meet my best friend, Mayree."

"Hello."

Tylar reached out and hugged Mayree. "It's been so long! You have grown up, girl! Wow I would have thought you were your Mother, you look so much like I remember her looking. Are you married yet?"

"You know better 'in that."

"Never did want to be saddled with a man. Bet there are several miserable men wishing that wasn't true."

"Huh. A few. Better they be miserable where they is than anywhere near me. How about we takes our conversation into da drug store. Have ya two eaten yet?"

Anna spoke up. "We had hoped we could find you before you had lunch so we could eat with you. Is that alright?"

"That's wonderful. I would like that very much. I've waited a long time to get to meet Tylar's wife ... since I was a little girl. Even though I didn't know you existed yet!"

"Margie didn't tell you?"

I put my arm around Anna's shoulder and started walking to the drug store. "She and I haven't seen each other in quite a while. I've been busy with work and she's been ... busy. How long have you been married?"

"We recently had our forth anniversary."

"Wow." I looked over my shoulder at Tylar letting him know I wasn't happy that Margie had kept this bit of news from me. "Has it been that long since she and I have had a heart to heart talk? Guess I need to fix that."

We sat at a small table near the counter. Several people were just as happy as me to see Tylar again and kept coming to the table to welcome him and his wife home. It was hard getting to talk to Tylar so Mayree and I spent our time talking to Anna while he reminisced with old friends. She told us how they had met and things about their lives and she kept mentioning someone named Garry. Mayree finally asked, "Who's this Garry you keep talking about? A friend of Tylar's?"

Tylar heard the question and turned to look at me. Anna said, "Oh, I'm sorry. I wasn't thinking that because you didn't know anything about me that you might not know about Garry! Garry's our son. He'll be four years old in a few months. He's the joy of our lives."

I don't know why her words caused my eyes to well up, especially after all these years, but they did. I was suddenly whirling in a tunnel looking straight into Tylar's eyes. He never took his eyes off of mine. I smiled at him and said, "That's your brother's name. He would be so proud."

It was quiet for a few minutes, saved by Mayree's declaration as to what she was going to order. I was thankful for that. We all looked at the menu and Tylar went to the counter to place our order. "Anna, do you have pictures of Garry?"

She went for her purse and said, "What kind of mother would I be if I didn't. I grabbed the ones I thought people might want to see before we left. He's staying with my parents in Charleston for a few days. We'll go down to get him before we head back to Chicago. We'll just take the train from there. Marge and Bob are going to drive us down and stay a few days so they can visit with their grandson."

"Have they ever met him?"

"Sadly they have not. Tylar has been so busy with the yard and I must confess that I was blackmailing him by saying I would not bring Garry by myself to meet his grandparents, people he had not even introduced *me* to! It didn't work. It's my fault. I should have brought him anyway, out of respect for Marge and Bob. I just didn't know that they were such lovely people and that they would make me feel so welcome. I guess I thought they were ogres or something because he didn't want to drop everything and come home once in a while."

"What made him come now?"

"I told him I was going to Charleston and taking Garry with me and I wasn't coming back till he came for us. Then I was going to come up here while he was on his way down there to get us and wait for him to get here! I hated the thought, but I meant it. Every child deserves to know their grandparents no matter how awful they *might* be! Praise God, that isn't the case. Tylar's just too busy, but my son and his welfare come first. Tylar's learning that I will do whatever is right by that boy."

Mayree said, "And ya'll all wonder why I leaves the mens alone."

"Aww. It's not as bad as it sounds, is it Lacey? You just have to make a believer out of them. They have to know that you mean what you say."

Tylar sat back at the table, "Make a believer out of who?"

"Men! They have to believe that when a woman sets her mind to something there's no changing her mind. I was telling them about my determination to bring Garry to meet his grandparents."

Tylar looked at me, "I learned a long time ago that when a woman has her convictions there's no amount of charm that will change her mind. I do hope you explained that the business was at a place where I couldn't just up and leave for longer than a day?"

"I told them that you felt like that, but ..."

"So tell us about the business. Is it as successful as we all thought you would make it?"

Anna spoke first. "We have so much. Too much. The business is very successful. Tylar works way too hard so we can have way too much."

"The business is quite successful, but Anna, you know that things can change overnight. That's why I hate to leave it for very long."

"Why? How could it change?"

"We're losing our travel to airplanes. People would rather fly somewhere and be there in less than an hour, to some places, than take the train and see the country. I can be in California in half a day by plane where it would take two days by train. The competition for services is growing, too. Businesses don't want their products sitting in a train yard for a day waiting for the train to pick them up that's going the way they want their products to go. Someone has to be there to make sure there's not a car sitting for days with the food rotting while we wait for a train. It's hard to find people who really care anymore and take their jobs seriously. Gives us a bad name and the next thing you know companies are sending their cars to someone else's yard. You know what I'm talking about, Lacey, being in farming all these years. You wouldn't like it if you spent blood, sweat and tears not to mention prayers for a good crop, and you sent the produce out on a train car expecting delivery overnight and your apples were sitting in the hot sun for an extra day before they arrived at the grocer's. You would do business with another train company, wouldn't you?"

Mayree spoke up, "She don't deal with farmin anymore, but I does. And you bet I'd be on the phone letting every body know I's dissatisfied if we was treated that way."

"Well, I rest my case then. Mayree, the smartest of us all, has spoken the truth. Truth I have to face every day."

"I just miss my husband and I think he could spend a little more time with his family."

"But, I do it for both of you."

"And I give it away as fast as he makes it."

"Boy, that's the truth."

"You taught me how."

"Anna is very involved with missions and missionaries throughout the world."

"I'm very moved by people who give up everything they have to go to a people who have nothing and live with them so they can help to enrich their lives with the Word of God."

"She's like you in that she loves the hurt and broken."

Mayree said, "She's like Lacey in a lot of other ways, too."

Anna said, "What ways are those, Mayree?"

"Determined."

Tylar laughed, "You are right about that."

We spent about two hours at lunch talking about their lives and what Tylar had been doing while he was away. I kept wanting to ask how they met and how she got to Chicago from Charleston, but I waited for someone else to ask. We told them our plan was to go to the river and swim till dark and Anna wanted desperately to see the river that Tylar talked so much about. There was this little twinge of jealousy that flared up in me and I didn't want to take her to the part of the river where Tylar and I had played as children. It was our spot so we told them we would meet them out at *Lion's Hill* so Anna could see the school. It was Saturday so there wouldn't be any classes going on so she could take a tour throughout if she wanted to, and she did. She was much more interested in the school than I thought she would be. I understood her interest in me, but I didn't understand her interest in the school. I assumed that her interest was because it had been at one time the house Tylar and I planned to live in. Maybe she just wanted to see what expense he was willing to pay for our house. Of course it had changed so much since those days.

The road leading to *Lion's Hill* was cluttered with automobiles lining the side of the road. It was like that when the baptist came to the river to baptize. They had picked a perfect day to do it. Tylar and Anna were following us to *Lion's Hill* and we had to squeeze past the cars to turn into the drive. We pulled up to the front portico and parked there. When Tylar and Anna got out of the car, Anna said, "Tylar, it's beautiful. Not at all like you described it."

"It's changed a lot since I saw it last." He walked up to me looking up at the ceiling of the portico and put his arm around my shoulder. "I'm proud of what you've done with the place."

"Pappy's vision, not mine, but I've been blessed by it."

We went inside and I took Tylar and Anna around to the classrooms and dormitories. Kimmy and Abe joined us. Anna took to the nursery and held every baby and sat down to read to some of the smaller children. Tylar looked at me, "She's more at home right now that any place else. She would have ten or twelve children if it was left up to her."

"And it's not?"

"I guess not. Garry's almost four and ..."

"Don't give up and don't speak anything other than positive words over her, if you want more children."

"So, what about you and Jake? Do you have children?"

Tylar and I walked out of the nursery leaving the others behind. "We have a house full! A very big house full."

"Do you two live here?"

"We do. And every child that lives here with us is like our own. We couldn't love them more."

"Do you not want your own?"

"We want whatever God wants. Sure, there are days that I wonder why we haven't had any yet, but it's all in His timing. Maybe He has something else planned, something better."

"I can't imagine anything or anyone better than Garry."

"That's what makes Him God."

"Are you happy?"

I kind of chuckled and shook my head. "I didn't think it was possible to be so completely content. Jake is a wonderful husband and a beautiful soul. I can't understand what I did to deserve him, but I'm so thankful that he waited for me."

I didn't mean it like I saw Tylar take it, but I didn't try to change my words. Some of the children were running around our feet being a distraction, a welcomed distraction. Then Tylar rubbed the molding around the doorway and said, "He was quite an artist. You've kept the place up nicely."

"It has been a haven for me. I see my Pa every time I walk through these doors. I couldn't imagine this place not being in my life. Thank you for selling your part to Pappy. You certainly could have done something else."

"I never would have sold it to anyone else. I knew it meant too much to you, or that it would one day. It never really was mine. It was always yours."

Everyone came out of the nursery, Mayree leading the pack. "Lacey, we's ready to go to da r-i-v-e-r now."

"Why is she spelling?"

"Do you want to take all these kids with us?"

"Oh."

"Then watch what you say."

Tylar and Anna went out to their car and got their suits while Mayree and I went to my room to change. "Oh my gosh, Lacey! Did you wana to die?"

"For a split second I thought I did! Man was that a shock!"

"And then he says, 'Here's my wife.' I couldn't believe it! Why didn't Marge ever tell ya?"

"I have no idea. Surely she doesn't think I still carry a torch."

"You don't, do ya?"

"Mayree Porter! You know I don't."

"Well, I saws that look on ya face and those watery eyes when she says she had his baby."

"Yeah, that did get me, but just because Jake and I want one so bad. Of course I didn't tell him when he asked if we had children."

"What'd ya say?"

"Oh, something like that's not what God has planned for us right now and we want what He wants."

"Oh, brother."

"What? We do!"

"If it includes a baby of ya own!"

"Yeah, well. He doesn't have to know that. And what if I don't ever have a baby? I better be fine with it or it will tear us apart wishing for what might have been."

"Ya not doing *that*, are ya?"

I threw a towel at Mayree and said, "Stop it! If I had married him I wouldn't have you as my best friend. No man is worth giving that up!"

Kimmy came with the four of us down to the river. We had to walk up stream a little piece so we wouldn't interfere with the baptismal going on in the river closer to the dock at *Lion's Hill*.

"What church is that?" Anna asked.

"It's a congregation closer into town. They are of the baptist faith. Tylar they're the ones that sent a pastor down from Ohio after they bought the church from Johnny Kale. Most of those folks are the ones who chose to believe Mitch over me."

"Oh yeah, I heard about all that. You know Mitch Sternfield came to see me. Mama had told me what had happened here and what ..." he looked at Kimmy who was sitting with her back to us taking off her shoes. "What kind of preacher he turned out to be."

"Yeah, well. Praise God he's gone now. Did you give him a job?"

"No way. Johnny Kale had called, too. I couldn't do that out of respect for him and all of you. No. Interesting what's happened to him. He joined the Jesus People in the north side of Chicago. Mitch Sternfield has rebelled against everything he went to college to become. He no longer uses the name Reverend. He's got some beatnik name now, I guess, unless he's changed it again."

Kimmy turned around and asked, "Who are they?"

"Who?"

"The Jesus People."

"I don't know a lot about them, but they kind of pulled out of the mainstream church and started a church that is founded on simplicity and a Holy poverty."

Anna said, "We could never join."

Mayree laughed and said, "I wouldn't want to. I's been poor and now I's gots. It ain't much, but I'll take the gots."

Tylar continued, "Well, they found out that he got a whole lot more than he told them about and while they were living without he was secretly living with all his needs met, leaning on God for nothing so they threw him out. The funny thing is how they found out about it. He was sleeping with the leader's daughter and she told her Father what she saw when she was snooping around his place after he fell asleep one night."

"So Sampson falls again."

"Oh, Kimmy. That hurt Sampson, I'm sure."

"Sorry about that, Sampson. So where is he now? Not headed here I hope."

"Last I heard he was in Indianapolis with some preacher named Jim Jones."

Anna and I laid a blanket out on the bank to put our clothes and shoes on and joined the others who were already in the river. From the middle where there was a rock jetting up out of the water you could look downstream and see the folks being baptized. Some of the children were in the water along the shore playing with rocks and looking for fish or crawdads. It was a beautiful picture seeing these people baptized into the faith of Jesus Christ and I was sure it was much like the day Jesus had come to the shore where John was baptizing and walked out in that water asking to be baptized and then sent to the desert to be tested. Tylar, Anna and I sat on the rock watching while Kimmy and Mayree floated in the river.

"So, where's Jake? I want to meet him."

"He's in Asheville at a seminar. He will be back Monday afternoon. The seminar is today and tomorrow, but he's staying because he has some patients to see on Monday."

"Does he work in Asheville now?"

"No. He still has his practice here, but he does lots of surgeries in Asheville. The hospital is better equipped; well the one in Brevard is catching up, but he knows all the doctors and the staff in Asheville so he likes being there for now. Will you still be here Monday?"

"Yeah. We leave Wednesday."

the road

"Oh, good. Not that you're leaving, but that you will be here when Jake gets home. He would hate it if he missed seeing you again. And if he missed meeting you, Anna. I wasn't the only one who lost a friend when you left."

One of the Mothers was screaming at her child to get out of the water. She had everyone's attention as the child hollered back to his mother, "Why, Mommy?"

"Don't ask me questions. When I tell you to do something, do it!" The little boy went to his mother and she turned him around to look at us and she said, "You see that nigger in the water! We don't swim in water with a nigger!"

Everyone else that was in the water stood still looking in our direction as if the water had frozen. I guess we were all sort of shocked, even though we had heard stuff like this all our lives, but this was churched people! Mayree slowly stood up staring them down and then she spit in the water and watched them all run to the shore. She turned and looked at me and said, "You see any niggers around here?"

"Not me."

"Maybe they won't come back and we can have this place to ourselves again. If I had known it be that simple."

"One things for sure, Mayree, that's the last time I give up my own dock so that I don't interrupt their service."

"Now that was fun. Do you girls always have this much fun?"

"We try, Anna. So what are ya'll doing for supper?"

"Haven't made those plans yet. Eating with Mom and Bob I guess. What have you got in mind?"

"Oh, I don't know. Just having some more fun, I guess. Ya'll are welcome to join us. There's a great place in town with a jukebox and a dance floor. The foods not bad, but we usually eat somewhere else and have a shake or a float at Mac's."

"Is that the name of it?"

"Na, it's name is the *Do Drop In Dinner*, but we call it Mac's. The name's too long and Mac Davis owns it."

"Well, is that alright with you, Anna? Maybe we need to talk about it and check in with Mom and Bob? She's probably wondering where we are."

Tylar put his arm around his wife who looked up at him with so much love, "I'm fine with it. Maybe Margie and Bob would like to join us? I like your friends and I wouldn't mind getting to spend some more time with them?"

"Maybe I need to let you girls have the night alone and I'll eat with Mom and Bob?"

We all spoke up and said, "No, Tylar! You are welcome to come with us."

"We'll say whatever we wants whether yous there are not. Even if we says it about you."

Miss Marge and Bob did join us for supper and dancing at Mac's. It was nice seeing my old friend again and sharing stories with Anna. She was a true southern lady. Her Charleston breeding was obvious in the words she spoke and the way she carried herself. I was happy for Tylar and thankful that he had come back to town to visit. It was just as it should have been.

When Jake got home it was hard for me to keep our commitment to spend the evening with Tylar and Anna. I didn't realize how badly I had missed him till I saw him get out of the car once he pulled in the drive. I wanted the night to be the two of us shut up in our room with no interruptions, but Jake wanted to see Tylar and Anna wanted to meet Jake because I had told her so much about him. I wished I hadn't made him out to be so wonderful!

It was just the four of us and we drove all the way to Brevard to eat at Gio's. They all made over Tylar and Jake as if they were their own sons coming home after being away for years. Anna loved meeting them and seeing this special place as much as I did the first time Jake took me there. It was nice reliving that through her eyes. I knew I would miss my old friend all over again and maybe even more this time when he left.

When we got back to *Lion's Hill* Jake took Anna into the kitchen to help convince Cook to let him cut one of the lemon pies he had made for the next day's desert. Tylar and I sat down in the parlor looking out over the front garden and the statue of the lion he and Pappy had put in the pond. "Lacey?"

"Yeah?"

"I'm sorry."

"For?"

"I haven't been able to come home because . . . it was so hard for me to face you."

"You kept your son from his grandparents because of *me*!? I'm not sure I believe that."

"I knew Jake loved you more than I did."

"Did you ever stop to think about how I felt?"

"That was the problem. I never gave you a chance to think. If I had you would have been able to see that Jake was the better man. I couldn't keep being selfish. I wanted to so badly; I wanted you to show me that I was truly the one you wanted, right over there on the floor. I'm sure you remember that. But, you showed me just what I had suspected. It wasn't the move to Chicago that stopped you. We could have worked all that out. It was the move with me. You could love me and be happy as long as you were here with everyone else you loved around you, but with them out of the picture and just us? I think our relationship was more of an obligation to them than something you truly wanted. I'm just sorry I ran out on you at such a hard time for you. But, I knew Jake would be here for you and that's how it should have been. What I wanted for my life was not what you wanted. It's not what anyone wants, really. But you would have hated being in Chicago entertaining dignitaries and CEOs. I knew you would have done it for me, but you would have been home sick and . . . I don't know."

"And Anna? Does she love this life?"

"Anna? I met Anna at one of these functions. She was the hostess. Her mother and father own cotton and lots of it. They ship cotton to the north using one of our rails. She loves being in charge and she's dang good at it, too. Something she learned in Charleston, I guess. They have lots of parties in Charleston. She loves me more than she loves her position and she would give it up to have more time with me. She will soon enough."

"It's never soon enough to spend time with your family. Ask my mother and father. My pa would have given up all his money, the farmland and his business all together to have been at home with mother and kept her off that chair or out of that cleaning mode she was in. And if he had he would not have been out in the field with 'Ol

Plow. Never take today for granted with a dream of tomorrow. Think about what it will cost you."

"I will think about what you've said. But, only if you will forgive me."

"I see where Anna learned her blackmailing schemes. I forgive you and I will think about what you have said, too. But, promise me you won't ever stay away from home this long again. And you will bring that son of yours to see me. I bet he is very handsome."

"He is. He looks like his mother."

Jake and I were like two kids with a secret to tell once Anna and Tylar drove down the drive. We ran to our room with one thing in mind, being alone.

chapter twenty-nine

Two things that stand out in my mind as emotionally life changing for most all Americans during those years was the assassination of a loved president and the beginning of the draft into the Vietnam War. Two of our boys had gone to Laos with our U.S. troops to help in the stability of that country after the royal Laos Government collapsed in 1959. Laos was in a civil war for a couple years during which time our boys went to help bring stability to the new government, but it collapsed as well, and the civil war resumed. However, right next door in Vietnam a war had been going on since the mid forties and it was growing so much that Laos was pulled into the efforts to fight against the Vietcong of North Vietnam. US troops trained those they recruited from Laos into a secret army that helped us in the war. Our boys were helping to train this army. How we prayed they would return home soon.

Jake loved being a doctor and being the doctor at *Lion's Hill* gave him the greatest joy. I don't see how he could have loved these children more if they had been his own. He literally paced the floor at night when one of them had a fever and needed antibiotics every four hours. He wouldn't let anyone other than himself or me be in charge of administering their medication. When babies arrived and they were colicky for lack of their own mother's milk, he would milk Sally's goat and mix a concoction that would sooth their cramps. I couldn't stand to hear them cry, but he could listen to a baby cry for hours as long as he had seen to their needs and had the magic potion. He would try and calm me by explaining that once they were fed, changed and healthy, any more crying they did was their way of growing.

Jake was a blessing to every child who came there in one way or another. If one came to us that was seriously ill and he couldn't figure out what was wrong, Jake would exhaust himself trying to find the cure. When he reached the point of exhaustion he was even more of a blessing to these children, because he had to rely completely on the power of God to heal them and stop searching through his medical books. I often had to remind him to pray first before seeking the advice of his books, but his drive to be the hands that God used to bring healing sometimes kept him from listening to me. So I prayed. Other orphanages suffered a very high mortality rate. However, through prayer and Jake's anointed hands, we had suffered the loss of only one child.

Aunt Joan was on a foreign mission board that helped children in war torn nations be placed in orphanages in other countries that would allow these children to come. She had been introduced to Dr. Verent Mills who had touched her heart because of his testimony of saving 142 starving Chinese orphans by walking 300 miles from Toishan, China, to Ku Kong fleeing from the Japanese army in 1942. He then went to Korea and helped place children on Cheju Island after the Korean War. He and Dr. Calvitt Clarke had teamed up and were working with the Christian Children's Fund now in many countries, as well as Korea. That's how Aunt Joan heard about him. She had told us his story and it moved us so much that we sent money towards their efforts. It was a place the children at *Lion's Hill* sowed their offerings, too. Being orphaned gave you a heart for others in the same position no matter what the circumstance.

It was the middle of the summer of 1960 when Uncle Marty and Aunt Joan arrived at *Lion's Hill* with Jake pulling into the drive right behind them. I had no idea they were coming and I was running in all directions making plans with Cook to have the whole family over for supper.

"Lacey, we need to talk to you and settle something before Nanny and Pappy get here. Can you come and sit with us in the parlor?"

"Well, of course, Jake. What in the world can be more urgent than preparing a family dinner? Nanny will be so thrilled to see her baby boy and I want to get all this done so I can spend some time with the kids. Oh Jake, isn't Eliza just the prettiest little thing you've ever seen and our baby Ben is growing up so fast. You could help me here. I want everything to be perfect."

"It's not that it's all that urgent, well maybe it is, but it's just that we need to talk about something and we need you to be paying attention. When the whole family is here we won't be able to talk."

I walk into the parlor with Aunt Joan, Uncle Marty and Jake being ready to get it over with so I could see to the needs of the children and finish the supper menu with Cook. Uncle Marty stood in the middle of the room and held out his hands and said, "Let's make a circle and pray before we begin."

If I had not seen the excitement on their faces I would have been nervous. But, I could tell this was a meeting that needed me to push aside my desire to get everyone organized and focus on the subject at hand. "You are all smiling, but I feel like there's something ... something I need to be concerned about."

"No, not at all. We have a mission and we need to pray and ask God's will to be on us and we want to see if you hear anything that we need to know."

We prayed for the children in Korea and for the right people for the mission to come forward and take their place. Mostly we prayed that God would be with all those who He had called out to go. Then we sat down around the coffee table as Uncle Marty opened a map of countries I didn't recognize.

"This is Korea, Lacey. This is where Dr. Mills is living. He and Dr. Clarke have been having a hard time with parents abandoning their children in the streets so they will get picked up and taken to the orphanages."

"Why on earth would they do that?"

"Because the orphanages offer the children better education and health care. It's so hard on these people to keep their families alive, much less educate then. They see it as a way out for their children. But, there are not enough funds, or workers, or orphanages to keep allowing them to do this."

"So what are they going to do?"

"They've already started a program called *Family Helper Projects* that sends missionaries right into the homes with food, money, medicines, tools to better educate, whatever that family needs the most, so that they can take care of their own children and the missionaries are teaching the parents how to do these things. They have teachers, but they are low on resources and doctors."

Jake interrupted Uncle Marty, "Several doctors in Asheville have been approached to consider going to help show the doctors in Korea how to cure the things that are killing the children and some adults in the country. We have medication that can stop the spread of so many of the diseases that are not even heard of here anymore, but they are killing the Korean people."

"How many are going?"

"Only three are willing to go right now, and me."

"*You?*"

"I'll be flying the team down so you don't have to worry about him, Lacey. We'll be home in two weeks, three at the most."

"What are you saying? Jake, you're going?"

"I have to. I know this is what God wants me to do. Some are suffering from wounds they received during the war that have never been treated. I might as well go, you know I won't sleep till Marty gets back and tells me they are all healed and doing fine. But, you know they will need for their doctors to be educated in the best medical treatments available in order to keep them healthy. I love to teach people how to take care of themselves and I love—"

"You love children."

"Yeah. I'm not comfortable just sending a check once a month anymore. It's just something burning in me. God has put the desire in me and He has opened the door. I have to go."

"How soon?"

"This Friday."

"That's three days away! I can't get away that soon."

"You can't go. You have to stay here. I will miss you more than words can say, but *Lion's Hill* is where you have to be. I will be home before you know it."

Joan said, "I can't go either, Lacey."

"Girls, don't think we don't want you to go, but with Jake and the other three doctors I can't take anymore passengers on my small plane. We have to have room for their luggage, supplies, medications, the books, and anything else they ask us to bring."

"I understand. But no longer than three weeks. I couldn't do without you for any longer."

Jake wrapped me up in his arms and said, "You are the strongest woman I know and you could do without me for a lifetime, but I made a promise to you that you would be stuck with me forever. Even in the new Millennium I'm building my house right next to you," and he laughed as if that would not make me happy. But, little did he know that I had already spoken to God about this very thing and I had asked that Jake's house be the same house as mine so I would never ever have to be without him if that was something I would desire in the next world.

"Even if there isn't marriage in heaven, I will never forget you and I know I will always long to be with you."

Jake kissed me and held me whispering, "Thank you. Thank you for loving me and thank you for letting me go."

"I'm not letting you go. God is taking you and He's not letting me have a say in it."

Uncle Marty showed me and Joan on the map right where they were going and the stops they would make to fuel up his plane. I was excited for Jake and the others who were going to Korea to bring a better life to these children and their families. This was what God had always used us to do even though we didn't see families reunited very often at *Lion's Hill*. I wanted to go, but I also knew that God had placed me in the lives of these children and I also knew that He had something else waiting for me.

Jake had been gone about a week when Mayree called with a mission of my own. She was at Silas and Tula's house listening to screams coming out of Madam Farley's house.

"What does it sound like?"

"It sounds like she's beatin' Mr. Williams to a pulp."

"Oh my heavens! What is *he* doing over there? I've told that man a hundred times not to think he could go into that house and save that woman's soul *without* the Holy Ghost. Why does he insist that he can make her see the light? The only light she has ever seen is the light in that crystal ball of hers. What on earth is he thinking?"

"Lacey! Will ya get over here?"

"I guess. Though, I ought to leave him there and teach him a lesson."

"If ya waits much longer I'm gonna have to call da undertaker. It sounds really bad."

"Oh, I'm sure it sounds worst than it is. I'll be there in a minute."

On a normal day I walked down to Silas and Tula's, but for old Mr. William's sake I drove the car so I could get there as quick as possible. Silas wasn't home, but Tula and Mayree were standing on the porch when I pulled up.

"Are ya goin' in there, or just holler from da porch?"

"If I was just going to holler from the porch, you could have done that and I could have stayed home."

"And miss all this fun?"

"Doesn't sound like Mr. Williams is having too much fun in there." I walked to the front door of Madam Farley's house just as something was turned over and crashed against the door. For a split second I was reminded of those nights long ago when my Pa would throw things in a rage at my Mother. "Oh God, how I wish I had known that You were always with me back then." Things got very quiet inside and I no longer heard Mr. Williams asking Madam Farley to settle down and think about asking Jesus into her heart. "I refuse to believe that we are too late. God, You are always right on time so I know You will let Mr. Williams get out of there before it gets any worse."

I slowly opened the door hearing broken things scrape the wooden floor. "Madam Farley, may I come in?"

I didn't hear a reply so I continued to open the door. Mayree was now on the porch with me, but standing at a safe distance. She whispered, "Be careful, Lacey. That woman knows the devil like he's her brother. For all we knows he could be in there, too."

"Oh I expect to see him. I'll be surprised if he *not* in there."

I pushed the door open wider and looked around the door's edge. Madam Farley had Mr. William's in a headlock with a butcher's knife at his throat and she was speaking in a high pitched voice softly into Mr. Williams' ear. "I told you not to come back here. Other's warned you. You wouldn't listen. Now I'm going to have to kill you for being so stupid."

"Mr. Williams, why can't you listen to the warnings of other people? And don't you people travel in groups when you come calling with your *Watch Tower* magazine? Lot of good that's going to do you now."

"I can take care of this. I just need some more time to tell her . . ."

"Go ahead, Mr. Williams. Make her madder. That sounds like a plan. I've always wondered if the Jehovah's Witnesses had a martial arts back up plan for the times they come face to face with the devil."

Madam Farley scraped the knife up and down Mr. Williams' neck putting greater fear in his eyes.

"In the Name of Jesus, put the knife down."

Madam Farley darted her eyes in my direction. In the spirit I could see that there was someone else holding that knife with her. "What do you want? I've left you alone. What business do you have with me? Get out."

"In the Name of Jesus, put the knife down."

Madam Farley's voice changed. "I'm just playing with him. Let him stay."

Mr. Williams managed to plead, "Lacey, do something."

"I did, months ago when I told you to stay out from here. Now look what you've got, a mess! Now pray with me, Mr. Williams. Father God, cover us with the blood of Jesus. Now Madam Farley, I'm not talking to you, I'm talking to the one you serve." I spoke in a loud voice, "In the name of the most High, Son of God, Jesus Christ, *let, her,* GO!"

Madam Farley looked down at the knife and Mr. Williams and lifted the knife from his neck. "In the Name of Jesus, put it down, Madam Farley, and let Mr. Williams go." She took her arm away from his neck and Mr. Williams quickly pulled from her and ran to the door pushing past me as he made his way to his car.

"Why are you here?"

"Madam Farley, we didn't mean to disturb you, but while I'm here let me tell you about the Man who sent me."

I talked with her for a few minutes, but she was not going to let go of her bondage or Satan was not going to let her go. I feel like it was her decision, because Satan has no power over the will of God, but she could choose not to yield to the Truth. I guess she had lived denying the Son of God for too long.

Mr. Williams was shaking like a scared rabbit when I got out to his car. Tula had given him a glass of iced tea that only seemed to make him more jittery. "Why do you insist on coming here when I've told you over and over, until you come to the understanding that you can do nothing to overcome the devil and his ways without being baptized in the Holy Spirit you don't need to be here! You might just have well been spitting into the wind. If you want to be Jehovah's Witness at least take His power with you when you go!"

"I's have Jehovah with me!"

"I know, I know! I've heard it all before, but you better stop trying to evangelize the world into believing that God is jealous because us Christians talk to His Son and the Holy Spirit more than we do Him. When will you ever get it in your thick head that He is all three just working in different ways. I haven't found anywhere in the Bible that says in the Name of God demon's will flee, *or*, dear sweet Mr. Williams, just show up and they will bow down to you. Next time you come here, you better have the power and use the Name that will chase away the very things that drive that woman or we will find your head lying in her lap again and next time it will be detached.

Mr. Williams cranked his car and backed out of Madam Farley's drive as Mayree, Tula and I watched with Madam Farley standing in her door way holding her butcher's knife. "Stay for supper, Lacey?"

"She's already accepted our invitation, Madam Farley," and Mayree looped her arm through mine and started to pull me down the road to her grandparents' home.

"Thank you, Madam Farley. Maybe some other time."

"Okay then. I really need to do some cleaning before I have guests."

The three of us walked back to Tula's, Mayree looking back every other step. Made me wonder why on earth did she call me to come over when she had the same Spirit living in her as I have in me. But, as I learned years later, people like Mayree and her family are so sensitive to the evils that plague the spiritual world and the effects there of it, that they have seen things that most of us haven't and you sure can't talk them out of what they've seen. Mayree and Tula saw things that day that I didn't, but what I did see could have caused a less dedicated person to rethink spiritual battles. But, no one could ever talk me out of what I had seen God do. Even though I knew the devil would be after me with all he had after this, I had no fear. God had been, and always would be, with me.

The next day Joan came to *Lion's Hill* alone. I knew that something was not right for her to drive so far to visit so soon after she and Uncle Marty had just been there the week before.

"The plane went down, Lacey. Marty's in a hospital somewhere. I don't even know where," and she began to cry.

"Where's Jake?"

She shook her head.

"You don't know? He's not with him? What? Joan! Where's *Jake?*"

"They don't know. They found the plane with Marty and two of the doctors all cut up and some broken bones, but Jake and the other doctor weren't there. I'm so sorry, Lacey," and she sobbed some more.

"Stop it! What are you crying about? Marty's in a hospital. Is he going to die?"

She shook her head. "No, I've talked to him. He said someone had dressed their wounds and given them something for pain when they set the broken bones before they were found so . . ."

"So Jake is fine and they went for help. That's good! Everybody's okay. It's going to be fine, Joan. So stop crying."

"Lacey. The plane went down in a country that's at war. If he went walking he probably got captured!"

"Hush your mouth, Joan Hawthorne! We don't talk like that. We don't lose hope! We don't assume the worst." I went over to the window and looked out at the Lion in the garden pool remembering the day I sat with Sunshine talking about Jake and when I realized I loved him, but I never loved him more than I did at that moment. I placed my hands on my stomach and held the news I had to tell him and knew in my heart that it wasn't over. Looking at the strength in the face of that Lion I felt his courage and whispered to God, "It's just *begun*. I know it's not over yet, *not yet.*"